KU-749-476

The Master and Margarita

"One of the great writers of the twentieth century."
A.S. Byatt

"A lasting fable about the human need for truth and the
mysterious power of love."
Elaine Feinstein

"One of the greatest modern Russian novels."
The Independent

"A gloriously ironic gothic masterpiece."
Patrick McGrath

"Bulgakov's *The Master and Margarita* is a soaring, dazzling
novel; an extraordinary fusion of wildly disparate elements. It
is a concerto played simultaneously on the organ, the
bagpipes, and a pennywhistle, while someone sets
off fireworks between the players' feet."
The New York Times

"A wild surrealistic romp... Brilliantly
flamboyant and outrageous."
Joyce Carol Oates

"What I find most extraordinary about *The Master and
Margarita* is its scale, its daring, its sheer imaginative reach. Part
satire, part love story, part mystical experience, it refuses to be
pigeonholed. It's a book that makes other books look safe."
Rupert Thomson

15 343 707 5

ALMA CLASSICS

Other books by MIKHAIL BULGAKOV

published by Alma Classics

Black Snow

Diaboliad and Other Stories

Diaries and Selected Letters

A Dog's Heart

The Fatal Eggs

The Life of Monsieur de Molière

Notes on a Cuff

The White Guard

A Young Doctor's Notebook

The Master and Margarita

Mikhail Bulgakov

Translated by Hugh Aplin

ALMA CLASSICS

ALMA CLASSICS LTD
3 Castle Yard
Richmond
Surrey TW10 6TF
United Kingdom
www.almaclassics.com

The Master and Margarita first published in Russian in 1966–67
First published by Alma Classics Ltd (previously Oneworld Classics Ltd)
in 2008
This new edition first published by Alma Classics Ltd in 2012
Reprinted 2013, 2014, 2015, 2016
The Master and Margarita © the Estate of Mikhail Bulgakov
English translation and notes © Hugh Aplin
Background material © Alma Classics Ltd

Printed in Great Britain by CPI Group (UK) Ltd, Croydon CR0 4YY

ISBN: 978-1-84749-242-5

All the pictures in this volume are reprinted with permission or presumed
to be in the public domain. Every effort has been made to ascertain and
acknowledge their copyright status, but should there have been any unwitting
oversight on our part, we would be happy to rectify the error in subsequent
printings.

All rights reserved. No part of this publication may be reproduced, stored
in or introduced into a retrieval system, or transmitted, in any form or by
any means (electronic, mechanical, photocopying, recording or otherwise),
without the prior written permission of the publisher. This book is sold
subject to the condition that it shall not be resold, lent, hired out or otherwise
circulated without the express prior consent of the publisher.

Contents

Mikhail Bulgakov (1891–1940)

Afanasy Ivanovich Bulgakov,
Bulgakov's father

Varvara Mikhailovna Bulgakova,
Bulgakov's mother

Lyubov Belozerskaya,
Bulgakov's second wife

Yelena Shilovskaya,
Bulgakov's third wife

Bulgakov's residences on Bolshaya Sadovaya St. (above) and Nashchokinsky
Pereulok (bottom left); an unfinished letter to Stalin (bottom right)

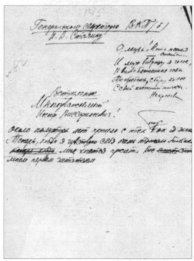

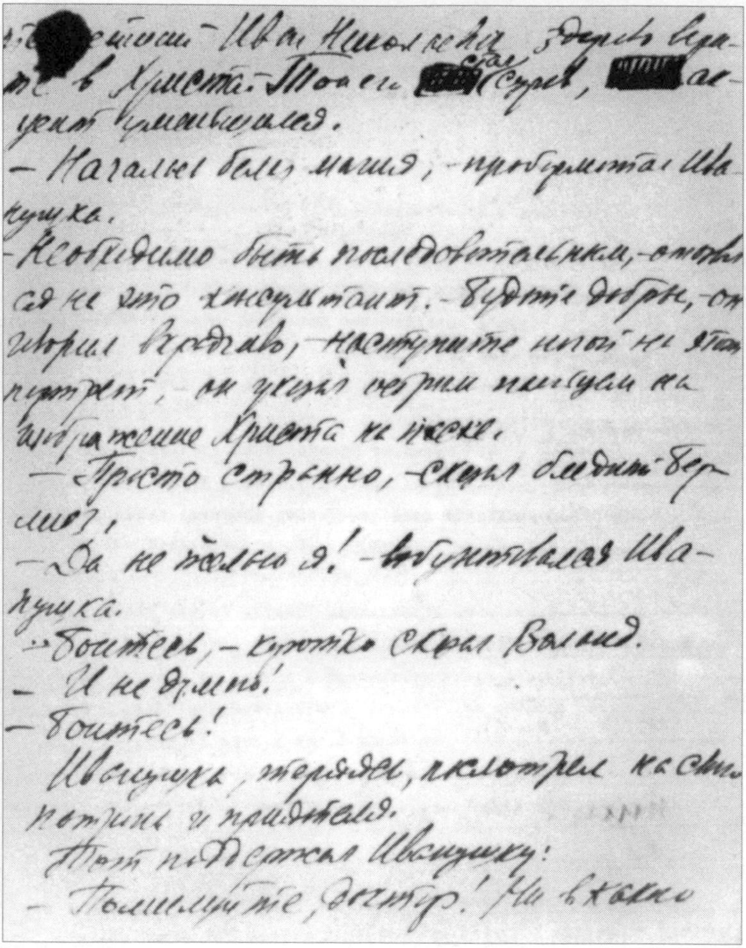

An autograph page from *The Master and Margarita*

The Master and Margarita

"...so who are you in the end?"
"I am a part of that power which eternally
desires evil and eternally does good."

Goethe, *Faust**

Part One

1

Never Talk to Strangers

A T THE HOUR OF THE HOT SPRING SUNSET at Patriarch's Ponds two citizens appeared. The first of them – some forty years old and dressed in a nice grey summer suit – was short, well fed and bald, he carried his respectable pork-pie hat in his hand, and had a neatly shaved face adorned by spectacles of supernatural proportions in black horn frames. The second – a broad-shouldered, gingery, shock-headed young man with a checked cloth cap cocked towards the back of his head – was wearing a cowboy shirt, crumpled white trousers and black soft shoes.

The first was none other than Mikhail Alexandrovich Berlioz, the editor of a thick literary journal and chairman of the board of one of Moscow's biggest literary associations, known in abbreviation as MASSOLIT,* while his young companion was the poet Ivan Nikolayevich Ponyrev, who wrote under the pseudonym Bezdomny.*

Entering the shade of the lime trees that were just becoming green, the writers first and foremost hurried towards a colourfully painted little booth with the inscription "Beer and Minerals".

Yes, the first strange thing about that terrible May evening should be noted. Not just by the booth, but along the entire tree-lined avenue running parallel to Malaya Bronnaya Street, not a single person was about. At that hour, when people no longer even seemed to have the strength to breathe, when the sun, having heated Moscow up to an unbearable degree, was toppling in a dry mist somewhere down beyond the Garden Ring Road, nobody had come along here under the lime trees, nobody had sat down on a bench, the avenue was empty.

"Narzan,* please," requested Berlioz.

"There's no Narzan," replied the woman in the booth, and for some reason took umbrage.

"Is there beer?" enquired Bezdomny in a hoarse voice.

"They'll be bringing beer towards evening," the woman replied.

"What is there, then?" asked Berlioz.

"Apricot squash, only it's warm," said the woman.

"Well, come on, come on, come on!"

The apricot squash produced an abundant yellow foam, and there was a sudden smell of the hairdresser's in the air. Having quenched their thirst, the writers immediately started hiccuping; they settled up, and seated themselves on a bench with their faces to the pond and their backs to Bronnaya.

At this point the second strange thing occurred, concerning Berlioz alone. He suddenly stopped hiccuping, his heart gave a thump and disappeared somewhere for a moment, then returned, but with a blunt needle lodged in it. Moreover, Berlioz was seized by terror, groundless, but so powerful that he felt the urge to flee from Patriarch's Ponds at once without a backward glance.

Berlioz glanced back in anguish, unable to understand what had frightened him. He turned pale, mopped his brow with his handkerchief and thought: "What is the matter with me? This has never happened before... my heart's playing up... I'm overtired... Maybe it's time to let everything go to the devil and be off to Kislovodsk..."

And then the sultry air thickened before him, and out of this air was woven a transparent citizen of very strange appearance. On his little head a jockey's peaked cap, a little checked jacket, tight, and airy too... A citizen almost seven feet tall, but narrow in the shoulders, unbelievably thin, and a physiognomy, I beg you to note, that was mocking.

Berlioz's life had been shaped in such a way that he was not used to extraordinary phenomena. Turning still paler, he opened his eyes wide and thought in confusion: "It can't be!..."

But, alas, it could, and the lanky citizen you could see through swayed to both left and right in front of him without touching the ground.

At this point Berlioz was horror-stricken to such a degree that he closed his eyes. And when he opened them, he saw that everything was over, the mirage had dissolved, the one in checks had vanished, and at the same time the blunt needle had dropped out of his heart.

"Well I'll be damned!" exclaimed the editor. "You know, Ivan, I almost had a seizure just now because of the heat! There was even something like a hallucination..." he tried to grin, but alarm was still dancing in his eyes and his hands were trembling. However, he gradually calmed down, fanned himself with his handkerchief and, saying quite brightly, "Well, and so..." he renewed the speech that had been interrupted by the drinking of the apricot squash.

This speech, as was learnt subsequently, was about Jesus Christ. The thing was, the editor had commissioned a long anti-religious poem from the poet for the next issue of his journal. Ivan Nikolayevich had written this poem, in a very short time too, but unfortunately had not satisfied the editor with it at all. Bezdomny had outlined the main character of his poem, that is, Jesus, in very dark colours, yet nonetheless, in the editor's opinion, the whole poem needed to be written all over again. And so now the editor was giving the poet something in the way of a lecture on Jesus, with the aim of underlining the poet's basic error.

It is hard to say what precisely had let Ivan Nikolayevich down – whether it had been the graphic power of his talent, or his utter unfamiliarity with the question on which he was writing – but his Jesus had come out as just a living Jesus who had once existed: only, true, a Jesus furnished with all the negative features possible.

And Berlioz wanted to demonstrate to the poet that the main thing was not what Jesus was like, whether he was good or bad, but that this Jesus, as a person, had not existed in the world at all, and that all the stories about him were simply inventions, the most commonplace myth.

It must be noted that the editor was a well-read man, and pointed very skilfully in his speech to the ancient historians, for example, to the celebrated Philo of Alexandria* and to the brilliantly educated Josephus Flavius,* who had never said a word about the existence of Jesus. Displaying sound erudition, Mikhail Alexandrovich also informed the poet, incidentally, that the passage in book fifteen, chapter forty-four of the celebrated *Annales* of Tacitus,* where the execution of Jesus is spoken of, is nothing other than a later forged insertion.

The poet, to whom everything being imparted by the editor was news, listened to Mikhail Alexandrovich attentively with his lively green eyes fixed upon him, and only hiccuping occasionally, cursing in a whisper the apricot squash.

"There isn't a single eastern religion," said Berlioz, "in which, as a rule, a chaste virgin doesn't give birth to a god. And without inventing anything new, in exactly the same way, the Christians created their Jesus, who in reality never actually lived. And it's on that the main emphasis needs to be put..."

Berlioz's high tenor resounded in the deserted avenue, and the deeper Mikhail Alexandrovich clambered into the thickets into which only a very educated man can clamber without the risk of coming a cropper, the more and more interesting and useful were the things the poet learnt about the Egyptian Osiris, the most merciful god and son of heaven and earth,* and about the Phoenician god Tammuz,* and about Marduk,* and even about the lesser-known stern god Huitzilopochtli, who was at one time much revered by the Aztecs in Mexico.*

And it was at precisely the moment when Mikhail Alexandrovich was telling the poet about how the Aztecs used to make a figurine of Huitzilopochtli from dough that the first person appeared in the avenue.

Subsequently – when, frankly speaking, it was already too late – various organizations presented their reports with a description of this person. A comparison of the reports cannot help but cause amazement. Thus in the first of them it is said that this person was small in stature, had gold teeth and limped on his right leg. In the second the person was enormous in stature, had platinum crowns and limped on his left leg. The third states laconically that the person had no distinguishing features.

It has to be acknowledged that not one of those reports is of any use at all.

First of all: the person described did not limp on either leg, and was neither small nor enormous in stature, but simply tall. As far as his teeth are concerned, on the left side he had platinum crowns, and on the right gold ones. He wore an expensive grey suit and foreign shoes the same colour as the suit. He had his grey beret cocked jauntily over one ear, and under his arm he carried a walking stick with a black handle in the shape of a poodle's head. To look at, he was about forty plus. Mouth a bit crooked. Clean-shaven. Dark-haired. The right eye black, the left for some reason green. Eyebrows black, but one higher than the other. In short – a foreigner.

After passing the bench on which the editor and the poet were located, the foreigner cast a sidelong glance at them, stopped, and suddenly sat down on the next bench, two steps away from the friends.

"German…" thought Berlioz.

"English…" thought Bezdomny. "And look at that, he's not too hot to be wearing gloves."

But the foreigner cast his eye over the square of tall buildings bordering the pond, and it became apparent that he was seeing this place for the first time, and that it had grabbed his interest.

He arrested his gaze on the top storeys, where there were dazzling reflections in the window panes of the broken sunlight that was leaving Mikhail Alexandrovich for ever, then he moved it down to where the window panes had started darkening, as they do towards evening, he grinned condescendingly about something, screwed up his eyes, put his hands on the handle of the walking stick, and placed his chin on his hands.

"Ivan," said Berlioz, "your depiction of, for example, the birth of Jesus, the Son of God, was very good and satirical, but the real point is that a whole series of sons of god had already been born before Jesus, like, let's say, the Phoenician Adonis, the Phrygian Attis, the Persian Mithras. To put it briefly, not one of them was ever born and none of them existed, including Jesus too, and it's essential that, instead of depicting the birth or, let's suppose, the visit of the Magi, you should depict the absurd rumours about that visit. Otherwise, according to your narrative, it turns out that he actually was born!"

At this point Bezdomny made an attempt to stop the hiccups that had him in agony, and held his breath, and as a result he emitted a louder and more agonizing hiccup, and at that same moment Berlioz interrupted his speech, because the foreigner suddenly rose and headed towards the writers.

They looked at him in surprise.

"Excuse me, please," he began on coming up, with a foreign accent, but without garbling the words, "if I permit myself, without being acquainted… but the topic of your learned conversation is so interesting that…"

Here he politely removed his beret, and nothing remained for the friends but to half-stand and exchange bows.

"No, more likely French…" thought Berlioz.

"Polish?…" thought Bezdomny.

It is essential to add that from his very first words the foreigner made an abominable impression on the poet, yet was found by Berlioz rather

9

to be pleasant, that is, not exactly pleasant, but... how can one put it... interesting, perhaps.

"May I take a seat?" asked the foreigner politely, and the friends, involuntarily somehow, moved apart; the foreigner settled in neatly between them and immediately entered the conversation.

"If I heard correctly, you were so good as to say there was never any Jesus on earth?" asked the foreigner, turning his green left eye towards Berlioz.

"Yes, you heard correctly," replied Berlioz courteously, "that is precisely what I was saying."

"Ah, how interesting!" exclaimed the foreigner.

"But what the devil does he want?" thought Bezdomny, and frowned.

"And were you in agreement with your companion?" enquired the stranger, turning to the right towards Bezdomny.

"The full hundred per cent!" confirmed the latter, who loved to express himself in a mannered and ornate fashion.

"Astonishing!" exclaimed the uninvited interlocutor and, looking around furtively for some reason and lowering his deep voice, he said: "Forgive my persistence, but my understanding was that, apart from anything else, you don't believe in God either?" He made frightened eyes and added: "I swear I won't tell anyone."

"No, we don't believe in God," replied Berlioz, with a faint smile at the fright of the foreign tourist, "but it can be spoken about completely freely."

The foreigner reclined against the back of the bench and asked, even emitting a little squeal of curiosity:

"Are you atheists?"

"Yes, we're atheists," replied Berlioz, smiling, while Bezdomny thought angrily: "This foreign goose is being a real nuisance!"

"Oh, how charming!" the amazing foreigner cried, and he began twisting his head, looking first at one, then at the other man of letters.

"In our country atheism surprises no one," said Berlioz with diplomatic politeness, "the majority of our population consciously and long ago ceased to believe in fairy tales about God."

At this point the foreigner wheeled out the following trick: he stood up and shook the astonished editor's hand, at the same time pronouncing these words:

"Permit me to thank you from the bottom of my heart!"

"And what is it you're thanking him for?" enquired Bezdomny, blinking.

"For a very important piece of information, which is extremely interesting to me as a traveller," the eccentric foreigner elucidated, raising a finger most meaningfully.

Evidently the important piece of information really had made a powerful impression on the traveller, because he looked round in fright at the buildings, as though afraid of seeing an atheist at every window.

"No, he's not English…" thought Berlioz, while Bezdomny thought: "Wherever did he get so good at speaking Russian, that's what's I wonder!" and frowned again.

"But permit me to ask you," began the foreign guest after an anxious hesitation, "what's to be done about the proofs of God's existence, of which there are, as is well known, exactly five?"

"Alas!" replied Berlioz with regret. "Not one of those proofs is worth a thing, and mankind gave them up as a bad job long ago. You must agree, after all, that in the sphere of reason there can be no proof of the existence of God."

"Bravo!" exclaimed the foreigner. "Bravo! You've repeated in its entirety that restless old man Immanuel's idea on that score. But here's a curious thing: he completely demolished all five proofs, and then, as though in mockery of himself, constructed his own sixth proof!"

"Kant's proof," objected the educated editor with a thin smile, "is also unconvincing.* And not for nothing did Schiller* say that the Kantian arguments on the question could satisfy only slaves, while Strauss* simply laughed at that proof."

Berlioz spoke, yet at the same time he was thinking: "But all the same, who on earth is he? And why does he speak Russian so well?"

"This Kant should be taken and sent to Solovki* for two or three years for such proofs!" Ivan Nikolayevich blurted out quite unexpectedly.

"Ivan!" whispered Berlioz, embarrassed.

But not only did the proposal to send Kant to Solovki not shock the foreigner, it even sent him into raptures.

"Precisely, precisely," he shouted, and a twinkle appeared in his green left eye, which was turned towards Berlioz, "that's the very place for him! I said to him then over breakfast, you know: 'As you please,

11

Professor, but you've come up with something incoherent! It may indeed be clever, but it's dreadfully unintelligible. They're going to make fun of you.'"

Berlioz opened his eyes wide. "Over breakfast... to Kant?... What nonsense is this he's talking?" he thought.

"But," the foreigner continued, with no embarrassment at Berlioz's astonishment and turning to the poet, "sending him to Solovki is impossible for the reason that he's already been in parts considerably more distant than Solovki for over a hundred years, and there's no possible way of extracting him from there, I can assure you!"

"That's a pity!" responded the quarrelsome poet.

"I think it's a pity too," confirmed the stranger, with a twinkle in his eye, and continued: "But this is the question that's troubling me: if there's no God, then who, one wonders, is directing human life and all order on earth in general?"

"Man himself is directing it," Bezdomny hastened to reply angrily to this, to be honest, not very clear question.

"I'm sorry," responded the stranger mildly, "in order to be directing things, it is necessary, for all that, to have a definite plan for a certain, at least reasonably respectable period of time. Permit me to ask you then, how can man be directing things, if he not only lacks the capacity to draw up any sort of plan even for a laughably short period of time – well, let's say, for a thousand years or so – but cannot even vouch for his own tomorrow? And indeed," here the stranger turned to Berlioz, "imagine that you, for example, start directing things, managing both other people and yourself, generally, so to speak, getting a taste for it, and suddenly you have... heh... heh... a lung sarcoma..." the foreigner smiled sweetly, as if the idea of a lung sarcoma gave him pleasure, "yes, a sarcoma," narrowing his eyes like a cat, he repeated the sonorous word, "and there's an end to your directing! No one's fate, apart from your own, interests you any more. Your family begin lying to you. Sensing something wrong, you rush to learned doctors, then to charlatans, and sometimes to fortune-tellers too. Like the first and the second, so the third too is completely pointless, you realize it yourself. And it all ends tragically: the man who just recently supposed he was directing something turns out suddenly to be lying motionless in a wooden box, and those around him, realizing there's no more use whatsoever in the man lying there, burn him up in a stove.

But it could be even worse: a man will have just decided to take a trip to Kislovodsk," here the foreigner screwed his eyes up at Berlioz, "a trifling matter, it would have seemed, but he can't accomplish even that, since for some unknown reason he'll suddenly go and slip and fall under a tram! Surely you won't say it was he that directed himself that way? Isn't it more correct to think that someone else completely dealt with him directly?" here the stranger laughed a strange little laugh.

Berlioz had listened with great attention to the unpleasant story of the sarcoma and the tram, and some alarming ideas had started to torment him. "He isn't a foreigner... he isn't a foreigner..." he thought, "he's an extremely strange type... but permit me, who on earth is he?..."

"You want to smoke, I see?" the stranger unexpectedly addressed Bezdomny. "What kind do you prefer?"

"You have various kinds, do you?" the poet, who was out of cigarettes, asked gloomily.

"Which do you prefer?" the stranger repeated.

"Well, *Our Brand*," Bezdomny replied bad-temperedly.

The stranger immediately took a cigarette case out of his pocket and offered it to Bezdomny.

"*Our Brand*."

Both the editor and the poet were shocked not so much by the fact that it was specifically *Our Brand* that were in the cigarette case, as by the cigarette case itself. It was of huge proportions, of pure gold, and, as it was being opened, a diamond triangle on its lid flashed blue and white fire.

At this point the writers had differing thoughts. Berlioz: "No, a foreigner!" and Bezdomny: "Well, the devil take it, eh!..."

The poet and the owner of the cigarette case lit up, while the non-smoking Berlioz refused.

"I shall have to counter him thus," decided Berlioz, "yes, man is mortal, and nobody is arguing against that. But the point is that..."

However, he had not had time to voice these words before the foreigner began:

"Yes, man is mortal, but that would still be just a minor problem. The bad thing is that he's sometimes suddenly mortal, and that's the whole point! And he can't possibly say what he's going to be doing the same evening."

"An absurd sort of formulation of the question," considered Berlioz, and retorted:

"Well, there really is some exaggeration here. This evening is known to me more or less exactly. It goes without saying that, if on Bronnaya a brick should fall on my head…"

"Without rhyme or reason, a brick," the stranger interrupted edifyingly, "will never fall on anybody's head. And in particular, I can assure you, a brick doesn't threaten you, not under any circumstances. You'll die a different death."

"Perhaps you know what one precisely?" enquired Berlioz with completely natural irony, getting drawn into a really absurd sort of conversation. "And you'll tell me?"

"Willingly," responded the stranger. He sized Berlioz up, as though intending to make him a suit, muttered under his breath something like: "One, two… Mercury's in the second house… the Moon's gone… six – misfortune… the evening – seven…" and announced loudly and joyfully: "You'll have your head cut off!"

Bezdomny goggled with wild, angry eyes at the free-and-easy stranger, while Berlioz asked with a crooked grin:

"By whom, precisely? Enemies? Interventionists?"

"No," replied his interlocutor, "by a Russian woman in the Communist League of Youth."

"Hm…" mumbled Berlioz, irritated by the stranger's little joke, "well, excuse me, but that's hardly likely."

"I beg you to excuse me too," replied the foreigner, "but it's so. Yes, I'd like to ask you what you're going to be doing this evening, if it's not a secret?"

"There's no secret. In a moment I'll pop into my apartment on Sadovaya, and then at ten o'clock in the evening a meeting will be taking place at MASSOLIT, and I'm going to chair it."

"No, that can't possibly be," objected the foreigner firmly.

"And why's that?"

"Because," the foreigner replied, and looked with narrowed eyes into the sky, where, with a presentiment of the cool of the evening, black birds were flying in noiseless lines, "Annushka has already bought the sunflower oil, and not only bought it, but even spilt it too. So the meeting won't take place."

At this point, quite understandably, silence fell beneath the lime trees.

"Forgive me," began Berlioz after a pause, casting glances at the foreigner who was talking such rubbish, "what has sunflower oil got to do with it... and who's this Annushka?"

"This is what sunflower oil has got to do with it," began Bezdomny suddenly, evidently having decided to declare war on their uninvited interlocutor, "have you, Citizen, ever happened to be in a clinic for the mentally ill?"

"Ivan!" exclaimed Mikhail Alexandrovich quietly.

But the foreigner was not in the least offended, and gave an extremely cheerful laugh.

"I have, I have, and more than once!" he exclaimed, laughing, but without taking his unlaughing eye off the poet. "Where haven't I been! It's just a pity I didn't find the time to ask the professor what schizophrenia was. So do find it out from him for yourself, Ivan Nikolayevich!"

"How do you know my name?"

"Come, come, Ivan Nikolayevich, who doesn't know you?" Here the foreigner pulled the previous day's issue of *The Literary Gazette* from his pocket, and Ivan Nikolayevich saw his own image right on the front page, and beneath it his very own verse. But the proof of his fame and popularity, that just the day before had gladdened the poet, on this occasion did not gladden him in the least.

"Excuse me," he said, and his face darkened, "can you wait for just a moment? I want to have a quick word with my comrade."

"Oh, with pleasure!" exclaimed the stranger. "It's so nice here under the lime trees, and, happily, I'm not hurrying off anywhere."

"You know what, Misha," began the poet in a whisper, pulling Berlioz aside, "he's no foreign tourist, but a spy. He's a Russian émigré who's made his way back over here. Ask for his papers, otherwise he'll be off..."

"Do you think so?" Berlioz whispered anxiously, while thinking to himself: "he's right, of course..."

"Believe you me," the poet's voice became hoarse in his ear, "he's pretending to be a bit of an idiot so as to pump us about something. You hear the way he speaks Russian," the poet was casting sidelong glances as he talked, looking to see that the stranger did not make a run for it, "come on, we'll detain him, or else he'll be off..."

And the poet drew Berlioz back by the arm towards the bench.

The stranger was not sitting, but standing beside it, holding in his hands some sort of booklet with a dark-grey binding, a thick envelope made of good-quality paper and a visiting card.

"Excuse me for forgetting in the heat of our argument to introduce myself to you. Here's my card, my passport and my invitation to come to Moscow for a consultation," said the stranger weightily, giving both men of letters a piercing look.

They became embarrassed. "The devil, he heard it all..." thought Berlioz, and indicated with a polite gesture that there was no need for papers to be shown. While the foreigner was thrusting them at the editor, the poet managed to make out on the card, printed in foreign letters, the word "Professor" and the initial letter of the surname – "W".

"Pleased to meet you," the editor was meanwhile mumbling in embarrassment, and the foreigner put the papers away into his pocket.

Relations thus restored, all three sat down once more on the bench.

"You've been invited here in the capacity of a consultant, Professor?" asked Berlioz.

"Yes, as a consultant."

"Are you German?" enquired Bezdomny.

"Me?" the Professor queried, and suddenly became pensive. "Yes, if you like, I'm German..." he said.

"Your Russian's brilliant," remarked Bezdomny.

"Oh, I'm a polyglot in general and know a very large number of languages," replied the Professor.

"And what do you specialize in?" enquired Berlioz.

"I'm a specialist in black magic."

"Well there you are!" Mikhail Alexandrovich had a sudden thought. "And..." he faltered, "and you were invited here to use that specialization?" he asked.

"Yes, that's what I was invited for," confirmed the Professor, and elucidated: "Here in the State Library they found some original manuscripts of a tenth-century practitioner of black magic, Gerbert of Aurillac.* And so I'm required to decipher them. I'm the only specialist in the world."

"Aha! You're a historian?" asked Berlioz with respect and great relief.

"I am a historian," the scholar confirmed, and added without reference

16

to anything in particular: "There'll be an interesting bit of history at Patriarch's Ponds this evening!"

And again both the editor and the poet were extremely surprised, but the Professor beckoned both of them close to him and, when they had leant towards him, he whispered:

"Bear it in mind that Jesus did exist."

"You see, Professor," responded Berlioz with a forced smile, "we respect your great knowledge, but on that question we ourselves adhere to a different point of view."

"But you don't need any points of view," replied the strange Professor, "simply he existed, and that's all there is to it."

"But some sort of proof is required," began Berlioz.

"And no proofs are required," replied the Professor, and he began to speak in a low voice, his accent for some reason disappearing: "Everything's quite simple: in a white cloak with a blood-red lining, with the shuffling gait of a cavalryman, early in the morning of the fourteenth day of the spring month of Nisan…"*

2

Pontius Pilate

I N A WHITE CLOAK with a blood-red lining, with the shuffling gait of a cavalryman, early in the morning of the fourteenth day of the spring month of Nisan, there emerged into the covered colonnade between the two wings of the palace of Herod the Great* the Procurator of Judaea, Pontius Pilate.*

More than anything else on earth the Procurator hated the smell of attar of roses, and everything now betokened a bad day ahead, for that smell had been haunting the Procurator since dawn. It seemed to the Procurator that the smell of roses was being emitted by the cypresses and palms in the garden, and that mingling with the smell of his escort's leather accoutrements and sweat was an accursed waft of roses. From the wings at the rear of the palace that quartered the Twelfth Lightning Legion's First Cohort, which had come to Yershalaim* with the Procurator, a puff of smoke carried across the upper court of the garden into the colonnade, and with this rather acrid smoke, which testified to the fact that the cooks in the centuries had started preparing dinner, was mingling still that same heavy odour of roses.

"O gods, gods, why do you punish me?... No, there's no doubt, this is it, it again, the invincible, terrible sickness... hemicrania, when half my head is aching... there are no remedies for it, no salvation whatsoever... I'll try keeping my head still..."

On the mosaic floor by the fountain an armchair had already been prepared, and the Procurator sat down in it without looking at anyone and reached a hand out to one side. Into that hand his secretary deferentially placed a piece of parchment. Unable to refrain from a grimace of pain, the Procurator took a cursory sidelong look through what was written, returned the parchment to the secretary and said with difficulty:

"The man under investigation is from Galilee, is he? Was the case sent to the Tetrarch?"

"Yes, Procurator," replied the secretary.

"And he did what?"

"He refused to give a decision on the case and sent the Sanhedrin's death sentence for your ratification," explained the secretary.

The procurator pulled at his cheek and said quietly:

"Bring the accused here."

And immediately two legionaries led a man of about twenty-seven from the garden court and onto the balcony under the columns, and stood him in front of the Procurator's armchair. This man was dressed in an old and ragged light-blue chiton. His head was partly covered by a white cloth with a band around the forehead, and his hands were bound behind his back. Under his left eye the man had a large bruise, and in the corner of his mouth there was the dried blood of a cut. The new arrival looked with uneasy curiosity at the Procurator.

The latter was silent for a while, then asked quietly in Aramaic:

"So it was you inciting the people to demolish the Temple of Yershalaim?"

While speaking, the Procurator sat like stone, and only his lips moved a tiny bit as he pronounced the words. The Procurator was like stone because he was afraid of shaking his head, which was on fire with hellish pain.

The man with his hands bound edged forward a little and began to speak:

"Good man! Believe me…"

But the Procurator, immobile as before and without raising his voice in the least, interrupted him right away:

"Is it me you're calling a good man? You're mistaken. Everyone in Yershalaim whispers that I'm a savage monster, and it's absolutely true." And in the same monotone he added: "Centurion Rat-catcher to me."

It seemed to everyone that the balcony grew darker when the centurion of the first century, Marcus, nicknamed the Rat-catcher, appeared before the Procurator. The Rat-catcher was a head taller than the tallest of the legion's rank and file soldiers, and so broad in the shoulders that he completely blotted out the still low sun.

The Procurator addressed the centurion in Latin:

"The criminal calls me 'good man'. Take him away for a minute, explain to him how I should be spoken to. But don't mutilate him."

And all except for the motionless Procurator let their eyes follow Marcus the Rat-catcher, who had waved his arm at the man under arrest, indicating that the latter should follow him.

The eyes of all generally followed the Rat-catcher wherever he appeared because of his height, and also, for those who were seeing him for the first time, because of the fact that the centurion's face was disfigured: his nose had once been broken by a blow from a Germanic cudgel.

Marcus's heavy boots pounded across the mosaic, the bound man followed him noiselessly, complete silence fell in the colonnade, and the doves in the garden court by the balcony could be heard cooing, while the water too sang an intricate, pleasant song in the fountain.

The Procurator felt like getting up, putting his temple under the jet of water and freezing like that. But he knew that would not help him either.

Leading the prisoner out from under the columns into the garden, the Rat-catcher took the whip from the hands of a legionary who was standing by the pedestal of a bronze statue, and, with a gentle swing, struck the prisoner across the shoulders. The centurion's movement was insouciant and easy, but the bound man instantly collapsed to the ground as though his legs had been chopped from under him, he choked on the air, the colour drained from his face, and his eyes became senseless.

Easily, with just his left hand, Marcus tugged the fallen man up into the air like an empty sack, set him on his feet and began in a nasal voice, mispronouncing the Aramaean words:

"Call the Roman Procurator 'Hegemon'.* No other words. Stand to attention. Do you understand me, or do I hit you?"

The prisoner staggered, but controlled himself, the colour returned, he took breath and answered hoarsely:

"I understand you. Don't beat me."

A minute later he was standing before the Procurator once more.

There was the sound of a flat, sick voice.

"Name?"

"Mine?" the prisoner responded hastily, his entire being expressing his readiness to answer sensibly and not provoke any more anger.

In a low voice the Procurator said:

"I know mine. Don't pretend to be more stupid than you are. Yours."

"Yeshua,"* the prisoner replied hurriedly.

"Do you have another name?"

"Ha-Nozri."*

"Your place of birth?"

"The town of Gamala," replied the prisoner, indicating with his head that over there, somewhere far away to his right, in the north, lay the town of Gamala.

"What are you by blood?"

"I don't know exactly," replied the prisoner animatedly, "I don't remember my parents. I was told my father was a Syrian..."

"Where is your permanent home?"

"I don't have any permanent place to live," replied the prisoner shyly, "I travel from town to town."

"That can be expressed more briefly, in a word – a vagrant," said the Procurator, and asked: "Do you have relatives?"

"There's no one. I'm alone in the world."

"Are you literate?"

"Yes."

"Do you know any language other than Aramaic?"

"I do. Greek."

A swollen eyelid was raised, an eye clouded with suffering stared at the prisoner. The other eye remained closed.

Pilate began speaking in Greek:

"So it was you meaning to demolish the building of the Temple and calling on the people to do it."

At this point the prisoner again became animated, his eyes ceased to express fright, and he began speaking in Greek:

"I, goo…" at this point there was a flash of horror in the prisoner's eyes at having almost said the wrong thing, "I, Hegemon, have never in my life meant to demolish the building of the Temple and have not incited anyone to commit this senseless act."

Surprise expressed itself on the face of the secretary, who was hunched over a low table and recording the testimony. He raised his head, but immediately bent it down again towards the parchment.

"A host of people of various kinds throngs to this city for the feast. Among them there may be magi, astrologers, soothsayers and murderers," said the Procurator in a monotone, "and liars may be found too. You, for example, are a liar. It's clearly recorded: inciting to demolish the Temple. Such is people's testimony."

"These good people," the prisoner began, hastily added "Hegemon" and continued: "learnt nothing and muddled up all I said. In general, I'm beginning to worry that this muddle will continue for a very long time. And all because he records what I say incorrectly."

Silence fell. By now both painful eyes were looking hard at the prisoner.

"I repeat to you, but for the last time, stop pretending to be mad, you villain," pronounced Pilate in a gentle monotone, "not a lot of what you've said is recorded, but what is recorded is enough to hang you."

"No, no, Hegemon," said the prisoner, his whole body tensing up in his desire to convince, "he goes around, there's this one that goes around with goatskin parchment and writes incessantly. But once I took a glance at the parchment and I was horrified. I'd said absolutely nothing of what was recorded there. I begged him: for God's sake, won't you burn your parchment! But he tore it out of my hands and ran away."

"Who is this?" Pilate asked with distaste, and put his hand up to his temple.

"Levi Matthew," explained the prisoner willingly, "he was a tax-collector, and I first met him in the street in Bethphage, where the corner of the fig orchard sticks out, and I got into conversation with

21

him. His initial attitude towards me was hostile, and he even insulted me, that is, he thought he was insulting me by calling me a dog." Here the prisoner grinned, "I personally see nothing bad about the animal to make me take offence at the word..."

The secretary stopped recording and cast a surreptitious look of surprise, not at the prisoner, but at the Procurator.

"...however, after listening to me he began to soften," continued Yeshua, "finally threw the money down on the road and said he would come travelling with me..."

Pilate grinned with one cheek, baring his yellow teeth, and said, turning the whole of his trunk towards the secretary:

"Oh, city of Yershalaim! The things you hear in it! A tax-collector, do you hear, throwing the money onto the road!"

Not knowing how to reply to this, the secretary deemed it necessary to duplicate Pilate's smile.

"And he said that henceforth money was hateful to him," Yeshua said, explaining Levi Matthew's strange actions, and added: "And since then he's become my travelling companion."

With his teeth still bared, the Procurator glanced at the prisoner, then at the sun, which was rising steadily over the equestrian statues of the hippodrome lying far below to the right, and suddenly, in a nauseating sort of anguish, he thought of how it would be simplest of all to banish this strange villain from the balcony by pronouncing just the two words: "Hang him". To banish the escort too, leave the colonnade for the interior of the palace, order the room to be darkened, drop onto a couch, demand some cold water, summon the dog, Banga, in a plaintive voice and complain to him about the hemicrania. And a sudden thought about poison flashed seductively through the Procurator's aching head.

He looked at the prisoner with lacklustre eyes and was silent for a while, agonizing as he tried to remember why, in the full blaze of Yershalaim's pitiless morning sun, a prisoner with a face disfigured by blows was standing before him, and what other totally unnecessary questions he would have to ask.

"Levi Matthew?" the sick man asked in a hoarse voice, and closed his eyes.

"Yes, Levi Matthew," came the high-pitched, tormenting voice.

"But what were you saying, after all, to the crowd at the bazaar about the Temple?"

The voice of the man answering seemed to stab into Pilate's brow, it was inexpressibly agonizing, and that voice said:

"I was saying, Hegemon, that the temple of the old faith would collapse and a new temple of truth would be created. I put it like that so it would be clearer."

"And why were you, you vagrant, stirring up the people at the bazaar, telling them about truth, of which you have no conception. What is truth?"

And at this point the Procurator thought: "O my gods! I'm asking him about something unnecessary during the trial... My mind isn't serving me any more..." And again he had a vision of a goblet of dark liquid. "Give me poison, poison..."

And once more he heard the voice:

"The truth first and foremost is that your head aches, and aches so badly that you're faint-heartedly contemplating death. Not only do you not have the strength to talk to me, you find it hard even to look at me. And now I'm your involuntary torturer, which grieves me. You can't even think about anything, and you dream only of the arrival of your dog, evidently the only creature you feel affection for. But your torment will come to an end in a moment, your headache will go."

The secretary stared goggle-eyed at the prisoner and stopped in mid-word.

Pilate raised his martyr's eyes to the prisoner and saw that the sun was already quite high above the hippodrome, that a ray had stolen into the colonnade and was creeping towards Yeshua's worn-down sandals, and that he was trying to stay out of the sun.

At this point the Procurator rose from his armchair, gripped his head in his hands, and on his yellowish clean-shaven face an expression of horror appeared. But he immediately suppressed it by will-power and lowered himself back into the armchair.

The prisoner, meanwhile, was continuing with his speech, yet the secretary was recording nothing more, and merely stretching his neck out like a goose, trying not to let slip a single word.

"There you are, it's all over," said the prisoner, casting benevolent glances at Pilate, "and I'm extremely pleased about that. I'd advise you, Hegemon, to leave the palace for a time and take a walk somewhere in the surrounding area, well, perhaps in the gardens on the Mount of Olives. The storm will begin..." the prisoner turned around and narrowed his eyes at the sun, "...later on, towards evening. The walk would do you a lot of good, and I'd accompany you with pleasure. Certain new ideas have occurred to me that you might, I think, find interesting, and I'd willingly share them with you, particularly as you give the impression of being a very intelligent man."

The secretary turned a deathly pale and dropped his scroll on the floor.

"The trouble is," continued the bound man, whom nobody was stopping, "you're too self-contained, and you've utterly lost your faith in people. I mean, you must agree, you really shouldn't make a dog the sole object of your affection. Your life is a poor one, Hegemon," and at this point the speaker permitted himself a smile.

The secretary was thinking about only one thing now, should he believe his own ears or not. He had to believe them. Then he tried to imagine in precisely what whimsical form the anger of the hot-tempered Procurator would express itself at this unheard-of impertinence from the prisoner. And this the secretary was unable to imagine, although he knew the Procurator well.

At that moment there rang out the cracked, rather hoarse voice of the Procurator, who said in Latin:

"Untie his hands."

One of the legionaries in the escort struck his spear on the ground, handed it to another one, went forward and took the ropes off the prisoner. The secretary picked up the scroll and decided not to record anything for the time being, nor to be surprised at anything.

"Confess, are you a great doctor?" Pilate asked quietly in Greek.

"No, Procurator, I'm not a doctor," replied the prisoner, rubbing a twisted and swollen purple wrist in delight.

From under his brows Pilate's eyes bored sternly into the prisoner, and those eyes were no longer lacklustre; the sparks that everyone knew had appeared in them.

"I didn't ask you," said Pilate, "perhaps you know Latin too?"

"Yes, I do," replied the prisoner.

Colour appeared in Pilate's yellowish cheeks, and he asked in Latin:

"How did you happen to know I wanted to call my dog?"

"It's very simple," the prisoner replied in Latin, "you were moving your hand through the air," and the prisoner repeated Pilate's gesture, "as though you wanted to stroke something, and your lips..."

"Yes," said Pilate.

They were silent for a moment. Pilate asked a question in Greek: "And so are you a doctor?"

"No, no," replied the prisoner animatedly, "believe me, I'm not a doctor."

"Well, all right. If you want to keep it a secret, do so. It has no direct bearing on the case. So you claim you didn't call on anyone to demolish... or set fire to, or in any other way destroy the Temple?"

"I repeat, I haven't called upon anyone, Hegemon, to perform such acts. What, do I seem feeble-minded?"

"Oh no, you don't seem at all feeble-minded," the Procurator replied quietly, and smiled a fearsome sort of smile, "so swear, then, that it didn't happen."

"What do you want me to swear on?" asked the unbound man, who was now very animated.

"Well, on your life, perhaps," replied the Procurator, "it's the very time to swear on it, since it hangs by a thread, be aware of that."

"And do you think it was you that hung it up, Hegemon?" asked the prisoner. "If so, you're very much mistaken."

Pilate started and replied through his teeth:

"I can cut the thread."

"And you're mistaken about that too," retorted the prisoner, smiling brightly and using his hand to shield himself from the sun, "you must agree that it's quite certain the thread can be cut only by the one who hung it up?"

"Right, right," said Pilate, smiling, "now I have no doubt that the idle layabouts in Yershalaim followed on your heels. I don't know who hung your tongue in place, but they certainly hung a quick one. Incidentally, tell me: is it true you entered Yershalaim through the Susim Gate, riding on an ass and accompanied by a crowd of plebs, who were shouting out greetings to you as though to some kind of prophet?" – here the Procurator indicated the scroll of parchment.

The prisoner looked at the Procurator in bewilderment.

"I don't even have an ass, Hegemon," he said, "I did, indeed, come into Yershalaim through the Susim Gate, but on foot, accompanied by Levi Matthew alone, and nobody shouted anything at me, since nobody in Yershalaim knew me then."

"Do you know these people," Pilate continued, without taking his eyes off the prisoner, "a certain Dismas, a second man – Gestas, and a third – Bar-rabban?"*

"I don't know these good people," replied the prisoner.

"Truly?"

"Truly."

"And now tell me why it is you use the words 'good people' all the time? You call everyone that, do you?"

"Everyone," replied the prisoner, "there are no evil people in the world."

"First I've heard of it," said Pilate with a grin, "but perhaps I don't know enough about life!... No need to record any further," he addressed the secretary, although the latter had been recording nothing anyway, then continued saying to the prisoner: "Did you read about it in some Greek book or other?"

"No, I came to this conclusion with my own mind."

"And is that what you preach?"

"Yes."

"And so, for example, centurion Marcus, he's nicknamed the Rat-catcher, is he good?"

"Yes," replied the prisoner, "he's an unhappy man, it's true. Since good people disfigured him, he's become cruel and callous. I wonder who it was that mutilated him?"

"I can readily tell you that," responded Pilate, "for I was a witness to it. Good people were falling upon him like dogs on a bear. Teutons had hold of his neck, his arms, his legs. An infantry maniple had walked into a trap, and if the cavalry turm which I was commanding hadn't hacked its way in from the flank – then you, philosopher, would not have had occasion to converse with the Rat-catcher. It was at the Battle of Idistavizo,* in the Valley of the Virgins."

"If I could have a talk with him," said the prisoner dreamily all of a sudden, "I'm sure he'd change dramatically."

"I imagine," responded Pilate, "you'd bring the legate of the legion little joy if you took it into your head to talk with any of his officers or soldiers. It won't happen, however, luckily for everyone, and I'll be the first to see to that."

At that moment a swallow flew speedily into the colonnade, circled beneath the gold ceiling, descended, almost caught its sharp wing on the face of a bronze statue in a niche, and disappeared behind the capital of a column. Perhaps it was thinking of making a nest there.

In the duration of its flight, a formula had taken shape in the now lucid and lightened head of the Procurator. It was this: the Hegemon has heard the case of the vagrant philosopher Yeshua, also known as Ha-Nozri, and failed to find *corpus delicti*. In particular, he has failed to find the slightest link between the actions of Yeshua and the disturbances that have recently taken place in Yershalaim. The vagrant philosopher has turned out to be mentally ill. Consequently, the Procurator does not confirm the death sentence pronounced on Ha-Nozri by the Lesser Sanhedrin. But in view of the fact that Ha-Nozri's mad utopian speeches could be the cause of unrest in Yershalaim, the Procurator is removing Yeshua from Yershalaim and will subject him to imprisonment in Caesarea Strato on the Mediterranean Sea, that is, in the very place where the Procurator's residence is.

It only remained to dictate this to the secretary.

The swallow's wings crackled just above the Hegemon's head, the bird sped towards the bowl of the fountain and flew out to freedom. The Procurator raised his eyes to the prisoner and saw that a column of dust was suddenly ablaze beside him.

"Is that all there is about him?" Pilate asked the secretary.

"Unfortunately not," the secretary unexpectedly replied, and handed Pilate another piece of parchment.

"What else is there?" asked Pilate, and frowned.

After reading what had been handed him, he changed countenance still more. It may have been that dark blood had flooded into his neck and face, or something else may have happened, only his skin lost its yellow tinge, grew brown, and his eyes seemed to sink.

And again it was probably the fault of his blood, which had flooded into his temples and begun pounding inside them, only something happened to the Procurator's vision. And so it seemed to him that the prisoner's head had floated off somewhere, and another had appeared in its place. On this bald head sat a sparsely toothed golden crown. On the forehead was a round sore that was eating away at the skin and was smeared with ointment. A sunken, toothless mouth with a wilful, drooping lower lip. It seemed to Pilate that the pink columns of the balcony and the roofs of Yershalaim down below in the distance, beyond the garden, had disappeared, and everything around them was submerged in the dense, dense verdure of the gardens of Capreae. Something strange had happened to his hearing too – trumpets seemed to sound, low and threatening, in the distance, and a nasal voice was heard very distinctly, haughtily drawling out the words: "The law of lese-majesty…"

His thoughts raced, brief, incoherent and extraordinary. "He's done for!" then: "We're done for!" And among them was one utterly absurd one about some sort of immortality, and immortality for some reason provoked unbearable anguish.

Pilate tensed, drove the vision out, returned his gaze to the balcony, and before him again were the eyes of the prisoner.

"Listen, Ha-Nozri," the Procurator began, giving Yeshua a strange sort of look: the Procurator's face was threatening, but the eyes were alarmed. "Have you ever said anything about the Great Caesar? Answer! Have you? Or… have you… not?" Pilate drew out the word "not" rather more than one ought to at a trial, and sent to Yeshua in his gaze a particular thought which he seemed to want to suggest to the prisoner.

"Telling the truth is easy and pleasant," remarked the prisoner.

"I don't need to know," responded Pilate in a choked, angry voice, "if you find telling the truth pleasant or unpleasant. But you will have to tell it. But, when speaking, weigh every word, if you don't want not only inevitable, but also agonizing death."

No one knows what happened to the Procurator of Judaea, but he allowed himself to raise a hand, as though shielding himself from a ray of sunlight, and behind that hand, as behind a shield, to send the prisoner a look with some sort of hint in it.

"And so," he said, "answer, do you know a certain Judas from Kiriath, and what precisely did you say to him, if you did say anything, about Caesar?"

"It was like this," the prisoner willingly began recounting, "in the evening the day before yesterday I met a young man outside the Temple who gave his name as Judas from the town of Kiriath. He invited me to his home in the Lower Town and gave me hospitality…"

"A good man?" asked Pilate, and a devilish light glinted in his eyes.

"A very good and inquisitive man," the prisoner confirmed, "he showed the greatest interest in my ideas, received me most cordially…"

"Lit the lamps…"* said Pilate through gritted teeth in the same tone as the prisoner, and his eyes were glimmering as he did so.

28

"Yes," continued Yeshua, a little surprised at how well-informed the Procurator was, "he asked me to set out my opinion on the power of the state. He was extremely interested in that question."

"And so what did you say?" asked Pilate. "Or will you reply that you've forgotten what you said?" But there was already a hopelessness in Pilate's tone.

"Among other things," the prisoner recounted, "I said that any sort of power is coercion of the people, and that the time will come when there will be no power, neither of the caesars, nor of any other sort of authority. Man will move on to the kingdom of truth and justice where no kind of power will be needed at all."

"And after that?"

"There was nothing after that," said the prisoner, "at that point people ran in, started tying me up and led me off to prison."

The secretary, trying not to miss a single word, was rapidly scribbling the words down on the parchment.

"There has never been in all the world, is not and never shall be a greater and finer power for the people than the power of the Emperor Tiberius!"* waxed Pilate's cracked and sick voice.

For some reason, the Procurator was looking with hatred at the secretary and the escort.

"And it is not for you, you mad criminal, to deliberate about it!" At this point Pilate exclaimed: "Dismiss the escort from the balcony!" and, turning to the secretary, added: "Leave me alone with the criminal, it's a matter of state here."

The escort lifted their spears and, with their metal-shod *caligae** pounding rhythmically, they went from the balcony into the garden, and the secretary followed them too.

The silence on the balcony was for some time broken only by the song of the water in the fountain. Pilate could see the disc of water swelling at the top of the pipe, its edges breaking off and dropping down in little streams.

The prisoner was the first to speak:

"I can see that something bad has happened because of my talking with that young man from Kiriath. I have a premonition, Hegemon, that he will suffer some misfortune, and I feel very sorry for him."

"I think," replied the Procurator with a strange grin, "there is someone else in the world you ought to feel more sorry for than Judas from

Kiriath, and who will have a much worse time of it than Judas! And so, Marcus the Rat-catcher, a cold and confirmed butcher; the people who, as I can see," the Procurator indicated Yeshua's disfigured face, "beat you for your sermons; the villains Dismas and Gestas, who, with their gang, killed four soldiers; and finally the filthy traitor Judas – they're all good people?"

"Yes," replied the prisoner.

"And the kingdom of truth will come?"

"It will, Hegemon," replied Yeshua with conviction.

"It will never come!" Pilate suddenly shouted in such a terrible voice that Yeshua staggered backwards. Thus, many years before in the Valley of the Virgins, Pilate had shouted to his horsemen the words: "Cut them down! Cut them down. Rat-catcher the giant's been caught!" Once more he raised his voice, cracked by commands, yelling out the words so they were heard in the garden: "Criminal! Criminal! Criminal!"

And then, lowering his voice, he asked:

"Yeshua Ha-Nozri, do you believe in any gods?"

"There is one God," replied Yeshua, "I believe in Him."

"Then pray to him! Pray as hard as you can! Still…" at this point Pilate's voice sank, "it won't help. You have no wife?" asked Pilate, mournfully somehow, and not understanding what was happening to him.

"No, I'm alone."

"Hateful city…" the Procurator suddenly muttered for some reason, and flexed his shoulders as if he were cold, and rubbed his hands as though washing them, "if you'd been murdered before your meeting with Judas from Kiriath, truly, it would have been better."

"You could release me, though, Hegemon," the prisoner unexpectedly requested, and his voice became uneasy, "I can see they want to kill me."

A spasm distorted Pilate's face, he turned the inflamed, red-veined whites of his eyes to Yeshua and said:

"Do you suppose, you unfortunate man, that the Roman Procurator will release someone who has said what you have said! O gods, gods! Or do you think I'm prepared to take your place? I don't share your ideas! And listen to me: if from this moment on you utter so much as a word, start talking to anyone, beware of me! I repeat to you: beware!"

"Hegemon..."

"Silence!" exclaimed Pilate, and his furious gaze followed the swallow that had again fluttered onto the balcony. "To me!" shouted Pilate.

And when the secretary and the escort had returned to their places, Pilate announced that he was ratifying the death sentence pronounced at the meeting of the Lesser Sanhedrin on the criminal Yeshua Ha-Nozri, and the secretary recorded what Pilate said.

A minute later Marcus the Rat-catcher stood before the Procurator. The Procurator ordered him to hand the criminal over to the Chief of the Secret Service, and at the same time to convey to him the Procurator's order that Yeshua Ha-Nozri be kept apart from the other condemned men, and also that the Secret Service detachment be forbidden, on pain of severe punishment, to converse with Yeshua about anything whatsoever, or to reply to any of his questions.

At a sign from Marcus, the escort closed up around Yeshua and led him off the balcony.

Next in front of the Procurator appeared a handsome man with a blond beard and eagle's feathers in the crest of his helmet, with gold lions' faces glittering on his chest and gold studs on his sword-belt, wearing triple-soled boots, laced to the knees, and with a crimson cloak thrown over his left shoulder. This was the legate in command of the legion.

The Procurator asked where the Sebastian Cohort was now. The legate reported that its men were forming a cordon on the square in front of the hippodrome where the criminals' sentences would be announced to the people.

Then the Procurator gave orders for the legate to detail two centuries from the Roman Cohort. One of them, under the command of the Rat-catcher, was to escort the criminals, the carts with the instruments of execution and the executioners when they departed for Bald Mountain,* and when they arrived there, was to form the upper cordon. The other one was to be sent to Bald Mountain straight away, and was to begin cordoning it off immediately. To this same end, that is, to guard the mount, the Procurator asked the legate to send an auxiliary cavalry regiment – the Syrian *ala*.*

When the legate had left the balcony, the Procurator ordered the secretary to invite the President of the Sanhedrin, two of its members and the chief of Yershalaim's Temple guard to the palace, but added as he did so that he would like things arranged in such a way that he could speak with the President in advance and in private before the conference with all of these people.

The Procurator's order was carried out quickly and precisely, and the sun, which was burning Yershalaim with an extraordinary sort of frenzy during these days, had not yet had time to approach its highest point, when, on the upper terrace of the garden by the two white marble lions guarding the steps, the Procurator and the Acting President of the Sanhedrin, the High Priest of Judaea, Joseph Caipha, met.

It was quiet in the garden. But, having emerged from under the colonnade into the garden's sun-drenched upper courtyard with its palm trees on monstrous elephantine legs, whence there opened up before the Procurator the whole of the Yershalaim he hated, with its suspension bridges, forts and, most importantly, the block of marble that beggared all description with the golden dragon's scales instead of a roof – the Temple of Yershalaim – the Procurator detected with his sharp hearing, far off and down below, where a stone wall separated the lower terraces of the palace garden from the city square, a low rumbling, above which at times there would soar up, faint and shrill, what could have been either groans or cries.

The Procurator realized that there in the square an innumerable crowd of Yershalaim's inhabitants had already gathered, stirred up by the recent disturbances, and that this crowd was awaiting with impatience the pronouncement of sentence, and that shouting among it were restless water-sellers.

The Procurator began by inviting the High Priest onto the balcony to take shelter from the pitiless heat, but Caipha apologized politely and explained that he could not do that on the eve of the feast. Pilate threw a hood over his slightly balding head and began a conversation. This conversation was conducted in Greek.

Pilate said that he had heard the case of Yeshua Ha-Nozri and had ratified the death sentence.

Thus, sentenced to execution, which was to be carried out that day, were three villains: Dismas, Gestas and Bar-rabban, and in addition, this Yeshua Ha-Nozri. The first two, who had taken it into their heads to incite the people to revolt against Caesar, had been taken by force by the Roman authorities and were in the domain of the Procurator, and consequently they would not be under discussion here. But the latter two, Bar-rabban and Ha-Nozri, had been seized by the local authorities and condemned by the Sanhedrin. In accordance with the law and in accordance with custom, one of these two criminals would have to be set free in honour of the great Feast of the Passover that was starting that day.

And so the Procurator wished to know which of the two criminals the Sanhedrin intended to free: Bar-rabban or Ha-Nozri?

Caipha inclined his head to indicate that the question was clear to him and replied:

"The Sanhedrin requests the release of Bar-rabban."

The Procurator knew very well the High Priest would reply to him in precisely this way, but his task was to show that such a reply elicited his astonishment.

Pilate did just that with great artistry. The brows on his haughty face rose, and the Procurator looked in surprise straight into the High Priest's eyes.

"I confess, that reply has amazed me," began the Procurator gently, "I'm afraid there may be a misunderstanding here."

Pilate explained himself. The Roman authorities were not encroaching in any way on the rights of the local spiritual authorities, the High Priest was well aware of that, but in this instance an obvious mistake was being made. And the Roman authorities did, of course, have an interest in the correction of that mistake.

In truth: the crimes of Bar-rabban and Ha-Nozri were quite incomparable in gravity. If the latter, an obvious madman, was guilty of the utterance of absurd speeches which had stirred up the people in Yershalaim and several other places, the former was much more significantly burdened. Not only had he permitted himself direct calls to revolt, he had also killed a guard during attempts to capture him. Bar-rabban was incomparably more dangerous than Ha-Nozri.

On the strength of all he had set out, the Procurator requested that the High Priest review the decision and leave at liberty the less harmful of the two condemned men, and that, without doubt, was Ha-Nozri. And so?...

Caipha said in a quiet but firm voice that the Sanhedrin had familiarized itself carefully with the case and was reporting for the second time that it intended to free Bar-rabban.

"What? Even after my pleading? The pleading of the man in whose person speaks the power of Rome? High Priest, repeat it a third time."

"And for the third time I report that we are freeing Bar-rabban," said Caipha quietly.

It was all over, and there was nothing more to talk about. Ha-Nozri was going away for ever, and there was no one to cure the Procurator's terrible, vicious pains; there was no remedy for them but death. But this was not the thought that struck Pilate now. It was still that same incomprehensible anguish which had already visited him on the balcony that was permeating his entire being. He immediately tried to explain it, and the explanation was a strange one: the Procurator had the vague feeling there was something he had not finished saying to the condemned man, something he had not finished hearing.

Pilate banished this thought, and it flew away in an instant, just as it had come. It flew away, but the anguish remained unexplained, for it could not possibly be explained by the other brief thought that came in a flash, like lightning, but that was extinguished straight away: "Immortality... immortality has come..." Whose immortality had come? That the Procurator did not understand, but the thought of this mysterious immortality made him turn cold in the full blaze of the sun.

"Very well," said Pilate, "so be it."

At this point he looked around, took in at a glance the world that was visible to him, and was amazed at the change that had taken place. The bush laden with roses had vanished, the cypresses that fringed the upper terrace had vanished, as had the pomegranate tree, and the white statue in the verdure, and the verdure itself. In place of it all, some sort of dense crimson mush began floating around, seaweed began to sway about in it and then moved off somewhere, and Pilate himself moved off with it too. Now he was being borne away, smothered and scorched by the most terrible rage – the rage of impotence.

"I feel stifled," said Pilate, "I feel stifled!"

With a cold, moist hand he ripped the clasp from the neckband of his cloak, and the clasp fell onto the sand.

"It's close today, there's a thunderstorm somewhere," responded Caipha, not taking his eyes from the flushed face of the Procurator and foreseeing all the trials and tribulations yet to come. "Oh, what a terrible month Nisan is this year!"

"No," said Pilate, "it's not because it's close, I've started feeling stifled with you, Caipha." And, narrowing his eyes, Pilate smiled and added: "Take care of yourself, High Priest."

The High Priest's dark eyes flashed, and he expressed surprise on his face no worse than the Procurator had done earlier.

"What am I hearing, Procurator?" replied Caipha proudly and calmly. "Are you threatening me after a judgement that has been pronounced and ratified by you yourself? Is this possible? We are accustomed to the Roman Procurator choosing his words before saying anything. Could anyone have heard us, Hegemon?"

Pilate looked at the High Priest with lifeless eyes and, baring his teeth, imitated a smile.

"Come, come, High Priest! Who can possibly hear us now, here? Do you think I'm like the wandering young simpleton who's being executed today? Am I a boy, Caipha? I know what I'm saying, and where I'm saying it. The garden is cordoned off, the palace is cordoned off, so that a mouse couldn't get through a single crack! Not just a mouse, either, even that – what's his name... from the town of Kiriath couldn't get through. Incidentally, do you know such a man, High Priest? Yes... if such a man got in here, he'd feel bitterly sorry for himself, you'll believe me on that score, of course? So be aware then, that you, High Priest, will get no peace from now on! Neither you, nor your people," and Pilate pointed into the distance to the right, to where the Temple was glowing on high. "It's I that am telling you this – Pontius Pilate, the horseman of the Golden Lance!"*

"I know, I know!" black-bearded Caipha replied fearlessly, and his eyes flashed. He raised his arm up towards the sky and continued: "The Judaic people know you hate them with a fierce hatred and will cause them many sufferings, but you will not destroy them completely! God will protect them! And all-powerful Caesar will hear, he will hear and will shield us from Pilate the destroyer!"

"Oh no!" exclaimed Pilate, and with every word he was finding things easier and easier: there was no need to pretend any more, there was no need to pick his words. "You've complained about me to Caesar too much, and now my hour has come, Caipha! Now word will fly from me, and not to the Governor in Antioch, and not to Rome, but direct to Capreae, to the Emperor himself, word of how you shelter notorious rebels from death in Yershalaim! And it won't be water from Solomon's

Pond, as I wanted, for your benefit, that I'll be treating Yershalaim to then! No, not water! Remember how, because of you, I had to remove the shields with the Emperor's monograms from the walls, relocate the troops, I had to come here myself, you see, to take a look at what was going on! Remember my word: you'll see not just one cohort here in Yershalaim, High Priest, no! – the entire Fulminata legion will advance right up to the walls of the city, the Arab cavalry will come up, and then you'll hear bitter crying and moaning. Then you'll remember this Bar-rabban that was saved and you'll regret you sent the philosopher with his message of peace to his death!"

The High Priest's face was covered in blotches, his eyes were burning. He, like the Procurator, bared his teeth in a smile and replied:

"Do you yourself believe what you're saying now, Procurator? No, you don't! It wasn't peace, not peace that this seducer of the people brought to us here in Yershalaim, and you, horseman, understand that very well. You wanted to release him so he would stir up the people, ridicule the faith and deliver the people up to Roman swords! But I, the High Priest of Judaea, while I yet live, will not yield the faith up to profanation and will protect the people! Do you hear, Pilate?" and here Caipha raised his hand menacingly: "Listen carefully, Procurator!"

Caipha fell silent, and again the Procurator heard what sounded like the roar of the sea, rolling up to the very walls of Herod the Great's garden. This roar rose up from below to the feet and into the face of the Procurator. And behind his back, there, beyond the wings of the palace, could be heard disquieting trumpet signals, the heavy crunch of hundreds of feet, the clanking of iron – here the Procurator realized that the Roman infantry was already setting out in accordance with his order, hastening to the final parade before the deaths of the terrified rebels and villains.

"Do you hear, Procurator?" the High Priest repeated quietly. "Will you really try and tell me that all that…" the High Priest raised both arms, and the dark hood fell from his head, "…was provoked by the pitiful villain Bar-rabban?"

The Procurator wiped his damp, cold forehead with the back of his wrist, looked down at the ground, then, screwing his eyes up at the sky, saw that the burning hot sphere was almost directly above his head and that Caipha's shadow had shrunk away completely by the lion's tail, and quietly and indifferently he said:

"It's getting towards midday. We got carried away with our conversation, but in the meantime we do need to carry on."

Having apologized to the High Priest in refined phrases, he asked him to take a seat on a bench in the shade of a magnolia and wait while he summoned the remaining people required for a final brief conference and gave one more order concerning the execution.

Caipha bowed politely, placing his hand upon his heart, and remained in the garden while Pilate returned to the balcony. There he ordered the waiting secretary to invite into the garden the legate of the legion, the tribune of the cohort, and also the two members of the Sanhedrin and the commander of the Temple guard, who were awaiting a summons on the lower terrace of the garden in a circular pavilion with a fountain. To this Pilate added that he would himself be coming out into the garden straight away too, then he withdrew into the interior of the palace.

While the secretary was convening the conference, the Procurator had a meeting in a room obscured from the sun by dark blinds with some sort of man whose face was half-covered by a hood, though the rays of the sun could not possibly have troubled him inside the room. This meeting was extremely brief. The Procurator said a few quiet words to the man, after which the latter withdrew, while Pilate went through the colonnade into the garden.

There, in the presence of all those he had wished to see, the Procurator solemnly and drily confirmed that he was ratifying Yeshua Ha-Nozri's death sentence, and he enquired officially of the members of the Sanhedrin as to which of the prisoners they would like to let live. On receiving the reply that it was Bar-rabban, the Procurator said:

"Very well," and ordered the secretary to enter it in the minutes straight away, squeezed in his hand the clasp that the secretary had picked up from the sand, and said solemnly: "It's time!"

At this point all those present moved off down the broad marble steps between walls of roses giving off a heavy scent, descending lower and lower towards the palace wall, towards the gates leading out into a large, smoothly paved square, at the end of which were visible the columns and statues of Yershalaim's stadium.

As soon as the group had emerged from the garden into the square and gone up onto an extensive stone platform that dominated it, Pilate, looking around through narrowed eyelids, assessed the situation. The space he had just crossed, that is, the space between the palace wall and the platform, was empty, whereas in front of him Pilate could no longer see the square – it had been devoured by the crowd, which would have flooded both onto the platform itself, and into the cleared space, if a triple row of Sebastian's soldiers to Pilate's left hand and soldiers of the Ituraean Auxiliary Cohort to the right had not held it back.

And so Pilate went up onto the platform, squeezing the unnecessary clasp mechanically in his fist and squinting. The Procurator was squinting not because the sun was stinging his eyes, no! For some reason he did not want to see the group of condemned men who, as he knew very well, would be led up after him onto the platform in just a moment.

As soon as the white cloak with the crimson lining rose up on high on the stone cliff at the edge of the human sea, a wave of sound struck the unseeing Pilate's ears: "Ha-a-a..." It began softly, rising somewhere in the distance near the hippodrome, then became thunderous and, after being sustained for several seconds, began to abate. "They've seen me," thought the Procurator. Before the wave reached its lowest point it unexpectedly began to develop again, and as it rolled, it rose higher than the first one, and on the second wave, just as the foam rages on a roller at sea, there raged a whistling and the individual moans of women, discernible through the thunder. "They've led them onto the platform..." thought Pilate, "and the moans are because a number of women were crushed when the crowd surged forward."

He waited for a time, aware that no power could make the crowd fall quiet until it had exhaled all that had accumulated within it and fallen silent itself.

And when that moment came, the Procurator threw up his right arm, and the last sounds were expelled from the crowd.

Then Pilate gathered as much of the hot air as he could into his chest and shouted, and his cracked voice carried over thousands of heads:

"In the name of the Emperor Caesar!"

At this point his ears were struck several times by an abrupt iron cry – in the cohorts, tossing up their spears and insignia, the soldiers cried out fearsomely:

"Hail, Caesar!"

Pilate threw back his head and turned it straight towards the sun. Green fire flared up beneath his eyelids, which made his brain ignite, and above the crowd flew hoarse Aramaean words:

"Four criminals, arrested in Yershalaim for murders, incitement to revolt and assault on the laws and faith, are sentenced to a shameful punishment – hanging on posts! And this punishment will now be carried out on Bald Mountain! The names of the criminals are Dismas, Gestas, Bar-rabban and Ha-Nozri. Here they are before you!"

Pilate pointed to the right, not seeing any criminals, but knowing they were there, in the place they were required to be.

The crowd answered with a long hum, as though of surprise or relief. And when it had died away, Pilate continued:

"But only three of them will be executed, for, in accordance with the law and custom, in honour of the Feast of the Passover, one of the condemned men, chosen by the Lesser Sanhedrin and with the ratification of the Roman authorities, is to have his contemptible life restored to him by the magnanimous Emperor Caesar!"

Pilate shouted out the words, and at the same time listened to the way the humming was replaced by a great silence. Now not a sigh, not a rustling reached his ears, and there even came a moment when it seemed to Pilate that absolutely everything around him had vanished. The city he hated had died, and just he alone stood, scorched by the vertical rays, his face digging into the sky. Pilate continued to hold the silence, and then began shouting out:

"The name of the man who will now be released to freedom before you is..."

He paused once again, delaying the name, checking that he had said everything, because he knew the dead city would rise again after the lucky man's name had been uttered, and no further words would be able to be heard.

"Is that all?" Pilate whispered to himself soundlessly. "It is. The name!"

And, rolling the letter "r" over the silent city, he cried:

"Bar-rabban!"

At this point it seemed to him that the sun, with a ringing sound, burst above him and flooded his ears with fire. In that fire raged a roaring, screams, moans, chuckling and whistling.

Pilate turned and set off back along the platform towards the steps, looking at nothing but the multicoloured blocks of the flooring beneath his feet, so as not to stumble. He knew that now, behind his back, bronze coins and dates were falling like hail onto the platform, people in the howling crowd were climbing onto shoulders, crushing one another, to see a miracle with their own eyes – a man who had already been in the hands of death tearing free of those hands! To see the legionaries taking the ropes off him, involuntarily causing him burning pain in arms dislocated during interrogation, to see him frowning and gasping, but all the same smiling a senseless, mad smile.

He knew that at this very same time the escort was already leading the three with their hands bound towards the side steps to take them out onto the road leading to the west, out of the city towards Bald Mountain. Only when he found himself behind the platform, in its rear, did Pilate open his eyes, knowing that now he was out of danger – no longer could he see the condemned men.

With the moaning of the crowd, which was beginning to fall quiet, were mingled the readily discernible, piercing cries of the public criers, repeating, some in Aramaic, others in Greek, everything the Procurator had shouted from the platform. The staccato clatter of approaching horses' hoofs reached his ears too, and a trumpet trumpeting something briefly and merrily. In reply to these sounds, from the roofs of the houses on the street leading out from the bazaar into the square of the hippodrome came the piercing whistling of little boys and cries of "look out!"

The solitary soldier standing in the cleared space of the square with a standard in his hand waved it in alarm, and then the Procurator, the legate of the legion, the secretary and the escort stopped.

The cavalry *ala*, working up ever more of a canter, flew out into the square to cut across one side of it, passing the throng of people by, and to gallop by the shortest route, down a lane beside a stone wall with a vine creeping over it, to Bald Mountain.

On drawing level with Pilate, the fast-trotting commander of the *ala*, a Syrian as small as a boy and as dark as a mulatto, shouted something shrilly and drew his sword out from its scabbard. The wild, black, lathered horse shied and reared up on its hind legs. Thrusting the sword into its scabbard, the commander struck the horse across the neck with a lash, straightened it up, and rode into the lane, moving into a gallop. After him in a cloud of dust flew the horsemen in rows of three, the ends of their light bamboo lances began to bounce, and past the Procurator sped faces that seemed especially swarthy under their white turbans, and with cheerfully bared, gleaming teeth.

Raising the dust to the sky, the *ala* burst into the lane, and last to ride past Pilate was a soldier with a trumpet that burned in the sun behind his back.

Shielding himself from the dust with his hand, and with a discontented frown on his face, Pilate moved onwards, heading for the gates of the palace garden, and the legate, the secretary and the escort moved off after him.

It was about ten o'clock in the morning.

3

The Seventh Proof

"YES, IT WAS ABOUT TEN O'CLOCK IN THE MORNING, illustrious Ivan Nikolayevich," said the Professor.

The poet passed his hand across his face like a man who has just come to, and saw that it was evening at Patriarch's.

The water in the pond had blackened, and a light skiff was already sliding across it, and the splashing of an oar and the giggles of some citizeness in the skiff could be heard. People had appeared on the benches in the avenues, but again, on each of the three sides of the square apart from the one where our interlocutors were.

It was as if the sky above Moscow had faded, and the full moon could be seen on high perfectly distinctly, not yet golden, but white. Breathing had become much easier, and the voices beneath the lime trees now sounded softer, suited to the evening.

"How on earth did I fail to notice he'd managed to spin an entire story?" thought Bezdomny in amazement. "I mean, it's already evening now! Yet perhaps it wasn't even him telling it, simply I fell asleep and dreamt it all?"

But it must be supposed that it was, after all, the Professor who had been telling it, otherwise it would have to be allowed that Berlioz had had the same dream too, because the latter, peering attentively into the foreigner's face, said:

"Your story is extremely interesting, Professor, although it doesn't coincide at all with the stories in the Gospels."

"Pardon me," responded the Professor with a condescending smile, "but you of all people ought to know that absolutely nothing of what is written in the Gospels ever actually happened, and if we start referring to the Gospels as a historical source..." again he smiled, and Berlioz was taken aback, because he had been saying word for word the same thing to Bezdomny while walking along Bronnaya towards Patriarch's Ponds.

"That is so," replied Berlioz, "but I'm afraid no one can confirm that what you've told us actually happened either."

"Oh no! One can confirm it!" responded the Professor extremely confidently, beginning to speak in broken Russian, and in an unexpectedly mysterious way he beckoned the two friends a little closer towards him.

They leant in towards him from both sides, and he said, but now without any accent (which, the devil knows why, was forever coming and going):

"The fact is..." here the Professor looked around fearfully and began speaking in a whisper, "I was personally present during it all. I was on Pontius Pilate's balcony, and in the garden when he was talking with Caipha, and on the platform – only secretly, incognito, so to speak, so I beg you – not a word to anyone, and the most absolute secret!... Ssh!"

Silence fell, and Berlioz turned pale.

"How... how long have you been in Moscow?" he asked in a faltering voice.

"I've only just this moment arrived in Moscow," replied the Professor, perplexed, and only at this point did the friends think to look properly into his eyes, and they satisfied themselves that the left, the green one, was completely mad, while the right one was empty, black and dead.

"And there's everything explained for you!" thought Berlioz in confusion. "An insane German's come here, or else he's just gone barmy at Patriarch's. There's a thing!"

Yes, everything was, indeed, explained: the very strange breakfast with the late philosopher, Kant, and the ridiculous talk about sunflower oil and Annushka, and the predictions about his head being chopped off, and all the rest – the Professor was insane.

Berlioz immediately grasped what was to be done. Reclining against the back of the bench, he started winking at Bezdomny behind the Professor's back – as if to say, don't contradict him – but the bewildered poet failed to understand these signals.

"Yes, yes, yes," said Berlioz excitedly, "actually, it's all possible!... Perfectly possible, even – Pontius Pilate, the balcony and so forth... And are you here alone or with your wife?"

"Alone, alone, I'm always alone," replied the Professor bitterly.

"But where are your things, Professor?" asked Berlioz, fishing. "At The Metropole? Where have you put up?"

"Me? Nowhere," replied the crazy German, with his green eye wandering mournfully and wildly over Patriarch's Ponds.

"How's that? But... where are you going to be staying?"

"In your apartment," the madman suddenly replied in an overfamiliar tone, and gave a wink.

"I... I'm delighted," mumbled Berlioz, "but truly, you'll find my place inconvenient... And there are wonderful rooms at The Metropole, it's a first-class hotel..."

"And is there no Devil either?" the sick man cheerfully enquired all of a sudden of Ivan Nikolayevich.

"The Devil too..."

"Don't contradict him!" Berlioz whispered with his lips alone as he slumped down behind the Professor's back, grimacing.

"There is no Devil!" Ivan Nikolayevich exclaimed what he should not have done, bewildered by all this nonsense. "What a pain! Just stop behaving like a madman!"

At this point the madman burst into such laughter that a sparrow flitted out from the lime tree above the heads of the seated men.

"Well, now that is positively interesting," said the Professor, shaking with laughter, "what is it with you? Whatever you try, nothing exists!" He suddenly stopped chuckling and, as is quite understandable in a case of mental illness, after the laughter he went to the other extreme – became irritated and cried out sternly: "So, there really isn't one then?"

"Relax, relax, relax, Professor," muttered Berlioz, fearful of agitating the sick man, "you sit here for a minute with Comrade Bezdomny, and I'll just run down to the corner, make a telephone call, and then we'll see you to wherever you like. After all, you don't know the city..."

Berlioz's plan has to be acknowledged as the correct one: he needed to run to the nearest public telephone and inform the Foreigners' Bureau of the fact that there was a visiting consultant from abroad sitting at Patriarch's Ponds in an obvious state of madness. So it was essential to take measures, or else the result would be some kind of unpleasant nonsense.

"Make a telephone call? Well, all right, make a call," the sick man consented sadly, then suddenly made a passionate request: "But I implore you in farewell, do at least believe that the Devil exists! I really don't ask anything greater of you. Bear in mind that for this there exists the seventh proof, and the most reliable one, too! And it will now be put before you."

"Very well, very well," said Berlioz in a tone of feigned friendliness; and, with a wink to the disconcerted poet, who did not at all fancy the idea of guarding the mad German, he headed for the exit from Patriarch's that is on the corner of Bronnaya and Yermolayevsky Lane.

But the Professor immediately seemed to feel better and brighten up.

"Mikhail Alexandrovich!" he cried in Berlioz's wake.

The latter gave a start, turned, but calmed himself with the thought that his name and patronymic were also known to the Professor from some newspaper or other. But the Professor called out, cupping his hands into a megaphone:

"Would you like me to give instructions for a telegram to be sent to your uncle in Kiev now?"

And again Berlioz was flabbergasted. How on earth does the madman know about the existence of my uncle in Kiev? After all, there's nothing said about that in any newspapers, that's for sure. Aha, perhaps Bezdomny's right? And what if those documents are false? Oh, what a queer sort... Phone, phone! Phone at once! He'll soon be sorted out!

And, listening to nothing more, Berlioz ran on.

Here, at the very exit to Bronnaya, rising from a bench to meet the editor, was that exact same citizen who, back then in the sunlight, had issued from the heavy, sultry air. Only now he was no longer airy, but ordinary, fleshly, and in the beginnings of the twilight Berlioz distinctly made out that his little moustache was like chicken feathers, his eyes were small, ironic and half-drunk, and his trousers were checked, and pulled up to such an extent that his dirty white socks could be seen.

Mikhail Alexandrovich was simply staggered, but comforted himself with the thought that this was a silly coincidence, and that anyway there was no time to reflect upon it now.

"Looking for the turnstile, Citizen?" enquired the character in checks in a cracked tenor. "Right this way! You'll come out just where you need to be. How about the price of a quarter of a litre for the directions... for an ex-precentor... to set himself to rights!" Bending low, the fellow swept off his jockey's cap.

Berlioz did not bother listening to the cadging pseudo-precentor, but ran up to the turnstile and took hold of it with his hand. Having turned it, he was already about to take a step onto the rails when red and white lights sprayed into his face: in the glass box the inscription "Beware of the tram!" lit up.

And the tram did come rushing up straight away, turning on the newly laid line from Yermolayevsky into Bronnaya. Having rounded the bend and come out onto the straight, it suddenly lit up with electricity inside, howled and picked up speed.

The cautious Berlioz, although he was safe where he was standing, decided to go back behind the turnpike; he changed the position of his hand on the revolving part and took a step backwards. And immediately his hand abruptly slipped and came away, his foot, as though on ice, travelled uncontrollably across the cobbles sloping down towards the rails, the other foot flew up into the air, and Berlioz was thrown out onto the rails.

Trying to catch hold of something, Berlioz fell onto his back, striking his head a light blow on the cobbles, and he had time to see, high up, but whether to the right or the left he could no longer comprehend, the gilt moon. He had time to turn onto his side, at the same instant drawing his legs up with a violent movement towards his stomach, and, having turned, he made out the face of the female tram-driver – completely white with horror and hurtling towards him with unstoppable power – and her scarlet armband. Berlioz did not cry out, but around him the entire street began screaming in despairing women's voices. The driver tugged at the electric brake, the nose of the carriage went down onto the ground, then, an instant afterwards, bounced up, and with a crashing and a ringing the panes flew out of the windows. At this point someone in Berlioz's brain cried out despairingly: "Surely not?" One more time, and for the last time, there was a glimpse of the moon, but already it was falling to pieces, and then it became dark.

The tram covered Berlioz, and a round, dark object was thrown out under the railings of Patriarch's avenue onto the cobbled, sloping verge.

Rolling down off the slope, it started bouncing along the cobblestones of Bronnaya.

It was Berlioz's severed head.

4

The Pursuit

T HE WOMEN'S HYSTERICAL CRIES had died away, police whistles had finished their drilling, one ambulance had taken the headless body and the severed head to the morgue, another had taken away the beautiful driver, wounded by splinters of glass; yardmen in white aprons had cleared up the splinters of glass and scattered sand on the puddles of blood; but Ivan Nikolayevich remained there on a bench, just as he had fallen onto it without ever having reached the turnstile.

He had tried to get up several times, but his legs would not obey – Bezdomny had suffered something in the nature of paralysis.

The poet had rushed off towards the turnstile as soon as he had heard the first shriek, and had seen the head bouncing on the roadway. This had made him lose his senses to such a degree that, falling onto a bench, he had bitten his hand and drawn blood. He had, of course, forgotten about the mad German and was trying to understand just one thing: how it could possibly be that there he had just been, talking with Berlioz, and a minute later – the head...

Agitated people were running along the avenue past the poet, exclaiming something, but Ivan Nikolayevich did not take their words in.

However, two women unexpectedly bumped into each other beside him, and one of them, sharp-nosed and bare-headed, shouted to the other woman right in the poet's ear:

"Annushka, our Annushka! From Sadovaya! It's her doing! She bought some sunflower oil at the grocer's, and she went and smashed a litre bottle on the revolving bit of the turnstile! Made a mess all over her skirt... She was really cursing, she was! And he must have slipped, poor thing, and gone over onto the rails..."

Out of everything that the woman shouted out, one word took a hold on Ivan Nikolayevich's deranged mind: "Annushka..."

"Annushka... Annushka?" mumbled the poet, gazing around uneasily. "Permit me, permit me..."

To the word "Annushka" became attached the words "sunflower oil", and then for some reason "Pontius Pilate". The poet rejected Pilate and began linking together a chain, beginning with the word "Annushka". And that chain linked up very quickly, and led at once to the mad Professor.

I'm sorry! I mean, he said the meeting wouldn't take place because Annushka had spilt the oil. And, be so kind, it would not take place! And that's not all: didn't he say straight out that a woman would cut off Berlioz's head?! Yes, yes, yes! And the driver was, after all, a woman! What on earth is all this? Eh?

Not even a grain of doubt remained that the mysterious consultant had definitely known in advance the whole picture of Berlioz's terrible death. At this point two thoughts penetrated the poet's brain. The first: "He's far from mad! That's all stupid!" And the second: "Did he perhaps arrange it all himself?!"

But permit me to ask how?!

"Oh no! That we'll find out!"

Making a great effort with himself, Ivan Nikolayevich rose from the bench and rushed back to where he had been talking with the Professor. And it turned out that, fortunately, the latter had not yet left.

On Bronnaya the street lamps had already lit up, and above Patriarch's the golden moon was shining, and in the always deceptive moonlight it seemed to Ivan Nikolayevich that the man was standing there holding not a cane under his arm, but a rapier.

The retired precentor-cum-trickster was sitting in the very spot where Ivan Nikolayevich had himself just recently been sitting. Now the precentor fastened onto his nose an obviously unnecessary pince-nez, which had one lens missing completely and the other cracked. This made the citizen in checks even more repulsive than he had been when showing Berlioz the way to the rails.

With his heart turning cold, Ivan approached the Professor and, looking into his face, satisfied himself that there were not, and had not been, any signs of madness at all in that face.

"Confess, who are you?" asked Ivan in a muffled voice.

The foreigner knitted his brows, gave a look as if he were seeing the poet for the first time, and replied with hostility:

"No understand... no speak Russian..."

"The gentleman doesn't understand!" the precentor chimed in from the bench, though nobody had actually asked him to explain the foreigner's words.

"Stop pretending!" Ivan said sternly, and felt a chill in the pit of his stomach. "You were speaking excellent Russian just now. You're not a German or a professor! You're a murderer and a spy! Your papers!" cried Ivan fiercely.

The enigmatic Professor twisted in disgust a mouth that was twisted enough already, and shrugged his shoulders.

"Citizen!" the loathsome precentor butted in again. "What are you doing, disturbing a foreign tourist? You'll be called to account most severely for this!" And the suspicious Professor pulled a haughty face, turned and started walking away from Ivan.

Ivan sensed he was losing his self-control. Gasping for breath, he turned to the precentor:

"Hey, Citizen, help me detain a criminal! It's your duty to do it!"

The precentor became extremely animated, leapt up and started yelling:

"What criminal? Where is he? A foreign criminal?" The precentor's little eyes began to sparkle. "This one? If he's a criminal, then one's first duty should be to shout 'Help!' Otherwise he'll get away. Come on, let's do it together! Both at once!" And here the precentor spread his jaws wide open.

The bewildered Ivan obeyed the joker of a precentor and shouted "Help!" but the precentor had duped him and did not shout anything.

Ivan's lone, hoarse cry brought no good results. Two young women of some sort shied away from him, and he heard the word "Drunk!"

"Ah, so you're in league with him?" shouted Ivan, flying into a rage. "What are you doing, making fun of me? Let me pass!"

Ivan threw himself to the right, and the precentor – went to the right as well! Ivan – to the left, and that swine went the same way too!

"Are you getting under my feet deliberately?" cried Ivan, going wild. "I'll put you in the hands of the police too!"

Ivan made an attempt to grab the good-for-nothing by the sleeve, but missed and caught precisely nothing. The precentor had vanished into thin air.

Ivan gasped, looked into the distance and caught sight of the hateful stranger. He was already at the exit into Patriarch's Lane – and, moreover, was not alone. The more than dubious precentor had managed to join him. But there was more: the third figure in the group turned out to be a tomcat that had appeared from out of the blue, huge as a hog, black as soot or as a rook, and with the dashing whiskers of a cavalryman. The trio moved out into Patriarch's Lane with the cat setting off on its hind legs.

Ivan hurried after the villains and immediately realized it would be very hard to catch up with them.

In an instant the trio had slipped down the lane and come out on Spiridonovka. However much Ivan increased his pace, the distance between him and his quarry did not decrease in the slightest. And the poet had not managed to collect himself before, after quiet Spiridonovka, he found himself at the Nikitskiye Gates, where his position worsened. Now there was already a crush. Ivan hurtled into one of the passers-by and was sworn at. And what is more, here the gang of villains decided to employ that favourite trick of bandits – going off in different directions.

With great agility, while on the move, the precentor darted into a bus speeding towards Arbat Square and slipped away. Having lost one of his quarry, Ivan concentrated his attention on the cat, and saw this strange cat go up to the footboard of an "A" tram that was standing at a stop, impertinently move a woman aside – she let out a yelp – catch hold of the handrail, and even make an attempt to force a ten-copeck piece on the conductress through the window, which was open on account of the heat.

Ivan was so struck by the behaviour of the cat that he froze in immobility by a grocer's shop on a corner, and here he was struck for a second time, but much more forcefully, by the behaviour of the conductress. As soon as she caught sight of the cat clambering onto the tram, she shouted with an anger that even made her shake:

"No cats! Cats aren't allowed! Shoo! Get off, or I'll call the police!"

Neither the conductress nor the passengers were struck by the real essence of the matter: not the fact that a cat was clambering onto a tram, which would not have been so bad, but the fact that he was intending to pay!

The cat turned out to be not only a solvent but also a disciplined beast. At the very first cry from the conductress he ceased his advance, took himself off the footboard and alighted at a stop, rubbing his whiskers with the ten-copeck piece. But no sooner had the conductress tugged at the cord and the tram moved off than the cat behaved like anyone who is expelled from a tram, but who does after all need to get somewhere. Letting all three cars go past him, the cat leapt up onto the rear bumper of the last one, latched his paw onto some kind of hose that was protruding from the side, and rode off, thus saving his ten-copeck piece.

In concerning himself with the vile cat, Ivan had almost lost the most important of the three – the Professor. But fortunately, the latter had not managed to slip away. Ivan caught sight of a grey beret in the dense mass at the top of Bolshaya Nikitskaya or Herzen Street. In the twinkling of an eye Ivan was there himself. However, he had no success. The poet increased his pace, and was even beginning to jog, bumping into passers-by, but not by a centimetre did he get closer to the Professor.

However upset Ivan might have been, still he was struck by the supernatural speed at which the pursuit was taking place. Not twenty seconds had passed after leaving the Nikitskiye Gates before Ivan Nikolayevich was already blinded by the lights on Arbat Square. A few seconds more, and here was some dark lane with sloping pavements where Ivan Nikolayevich went crashing down and injured his knee. Again a well-lit main road – Kropotkin Street – then a side street, then Ostozhenka and another side street, cheerless, ugly and poorly lit. And it was here that Ivan Nikolayevich finally lost the man he so needed. The Professor had vanished.

Ivan Nikolayevich grew troubled, but not for long, because he suddenly realized the Professor was absolutely certain to be found in house number 13 and in apartment 47 for sure.

Bursting in through the doorway, Ivan Nikolayevich flew up to the first floor, found the apartment straight away and impatiently rang the bell. He did not have long to wait: some little girl of about five opened the door to Ivan and, without asking the caller anything, immediately went off somewhere.

In the huge hallway, neglected in the extreme and weakly lit by a tiny little carbon lamp beneath a high ceiling, black with dirt, there was a bicycle without tyres hanging on the wall, a huge iron-bound coffer, and on the shelf above the coat rack there lay a winter hat with its long earflaps hanging down over the edge. Behind one of the doors a booming male voice in a radio set was shouting something angrily in verse.

Ivan Nikolayevich was not in the least disconcerted in the unfamiliar setting and headed straight into the corridor, reasoning thus: "He's hiding in the bathroom, of course." The corridor was dark. After banging against the walls for a bit, Ivan saw a weak little strip of light below a door, groped for the handle and tugged on it gently. The catch came away, and Ivan did indeed find himself in the bathroom, and he thought how lucky he had been.

However, he had not been quite as lucky as he might have wished! Ivan was hit by a wave of moist warmth, and, by the light of the coals, smouldering in the geyser, he made out the large washtubs hanging on the wall and the bath, covered in ugly black spots because of the chipped enamel. And so, in this bath stood a naked citizeness, covered in soap and with a loofah in her hands. She squinted myopically at Ivan bursting in and, evidently mistaking him for another in the hellish light, said quietly and cheerily:

"Kiryushka! Stop messing around! What are you doing, are you out of your mind?... Fyodor Ivanovich will be back at any moment. Get out of here this minute!" and she waved the loofah at Ivan.

There was an evident misunderstanding, and Ivan Nikolayevich was, of course, to blame for it. But he did not mean to acknowledge it, and, with the reproachful exclamation: "You wanton woman!" he for some reason found himself straight away in the kitchen. There was nobody in it, and mute on the cooker in the semi-darkness stood about a dozen extinguished Primus stoves. The one moonbeam that had filtered through the dusty window, a window unwiped for years, threw a meagre light on the corner where, cobwebbed and covered in dust, there hung a forgotten icon; poking out from behind its case were the ends of two wedding candles.* Beneath the large icon hung a small paper one, stuck up with a pin.

Nobody knows what idea took possession of Ivan at this point, but before running out to the back entrance, he appropriated one of those candles, and also the little paper icon. Together with these objects he abandoned the unknown apartment, muttering something and embarrassed at the thought of what he had just gone through in

51

the bathroom, involuntarily trying to guess who this brazen Kiryushka might be, and whether the offensive hat with the earflaps belonged to him.

In the deserted, cheerless lane the poet gazed around, looking for the fugitive, but he was nowhere about. Then Ivan said firmly to himself: "But of course, he's on the Moscow River! Onwards!"

It would quite likely have been the right thing to ask Ivan Nikolayevich why he specifically supposed the Professor was on the Moscow River, and not in some other place elsewhere. But the trouble is that there was no one to ask him. The loathsome lane was completely empty.

In the very shortest time Ivan Nikolayevich could be seen on the granite steps of the amphitheatre of the Moscow River.

Having removed his clothes, Ivan entrusted them to some pleasant bearded man who was smoking a roll-up beside a torn white *tolstovka** and unlaced worn-down ankle boots. After waving his arms around to cool down, Ivan did a swallow dive into the water. The water was so cold it took his breath away, and it even flashed through his mind that he would quite likely not succeed in coming to the surface. However, he did succeed in doing so, and, blowing and snorting, with eyes round from horror, Ivan Nikolayevich began to swim about in the black water, smelling of oil, between the broken zigzags of the street lights on the banks.

When the wet Ivan danced up the steps to the spot where his clothing had remained under the protection of the bearded man, it transpired that not only had the former been carried off, but the latter had too, that is, the bearded man himself. On the precise spot where there had been a heap of clothing, there remained a pair of striped long johns, a torn *tolstovka*, a candle, an icon and a box of matches. Shaking his fist in impotent fury at someone in the distance, Ivan robed himself in what had been left.

At this point he began to be troubled by two considerations: the first was that the MASSOLIT identity card with which he never parted had disappeared, and the second – would he succeed in getting across Moscow unhindered looking like this? Wearing long johns, after all... True, it was nobody's business, but all the same, he hoped there would be no kind of gripe or hold-up.

Ivan tore the buttons off the long johns where they fastened at the ankle, reckoning that, looking like that, they would perhaps pass for summer trousers and, gathering up the icon, candle and matches, he moved off, saying to himself:

"To Griboyedov! Beyond all doubt, he's there."

The city was already living the life of the evening. Trucks flew by in clouds of dust with their chains clanking, and on their open platforms, sprawling on sacks with their stomachs uppermost, lay some men or other. All the windows were open. In each of those windows burned a light beneath an orange lampshade, and, bursting out from all the windows, from all the doors, from all the gateways, from the roofs and attics, from the basements and courtyards, was the hoarse roar of the polonaise from the opera *Eugene Onegin*.*

Ivan Nikolayevich's misgivings fully justified themselves: passers-by took notice of him and laughed and turned their heads. As a consequence of this, he took the decision to forsake the major streets and steal along little side streets, where people were not so importunate, where there was less chance they would pester a barefooted man, vexing him with questions about his long johns, which stubbornly declined to resemble trousers.

Ivan did just that, and plunged into the secretive network of the Arbat's lanes, and began stealing along by the sides of walls, casting fearful sidelong glances, constantly looking around, hiding at times in doorways and avoiding crossroads with traffic lights and the magnificent doors of embassy mansions.

And during the whole of his difficult journey he was for some reason inexpressibly tormented by the ubiquitous orchestra, to the accompaniment of which a ponderous bass sang of his love for Tatyana.*

5

There Were Goings-on at Griboyedov

THE OLD CREAM-COLOURED TWO-STOREY HOUSE was situated on the Boulevard Ring in the depths of a sorry-looking garden, separated from the pavement of the ring by fretted cast-iron railings. The small open area in front of the house was asphalted, and there, in the wintertime, a snowdrift with a spade in it towered up, while in the summertime it turned into the most magnificent section of a summer restaurant beneath a canvas awning.

The house was called The Griboyedov House on the grounds that at one time it had ostensibly been owned by the writer's auntie, Alexandra Sergeyevna Griboyedova.* Well, did she or didn't she own it? – we don't know for sure. If memory serves, Griboyedov never even seems to have had any such house-owning auntie... However, that is what the house was called. And what is more, one mendacious Muscovite used to tell how, allegedly, there on the first floor, in the circular columned hall, the renowned writer used to read extracts from *The Misfortune of Wit** to that same auntie as she lounged on a sofa. But then the devil knows, perhaps he did, it's not important!

But what is important is that this house was owned at the present time by that same MASSOLIT, at the head of which stood the unfortunate Mikhail Alexandrovich Berlioz, until his appearance at Patriarch's Ponds.

Following the example of the members of MASSOLIT, nobody called the house "The Griboyedov House", everyone simply said "Griboyedov": "I was hanging about for two hours at Griboyedov yesterday." – "Well, and?" – "I got myself a month in Yalta." – "Good for you!" Or: "Go and talk to Berlioz, he's seeing people between four and five today at Griboyedov..." and so on.

MASSOLIT had settled into Griboyedov so well that nothing better or cosier could be imagined. Anyone going into Griboyedov involuntarily became acquainted first of all with the notices of various sports clubs, and with group and also individual photographs of members of MASSOLIT, hanging (the photographs) all over the walls of the staircase leading to the first floor.

On the doors of the very first room on that upper floor could be seen the large inscription: "Fishing and Dacha Section", and there too was a picture of a crucian caught on the end of a rod.

On the doors of room No. 2 was written something not entirely comprehensible: "One-day writing trip. Apply to M.V. Podlozhnaya".

The next door bore the brief but this time completely incomprehensible inscription "Perelygino".* Then Griboyedov's chance visitor would start to be dazzled by the inscriptions abounding on the auntie's walnut doors: "Registration for Waiting List for Paper at Poklyovkina's", "Cashier's Office. Sketch-writers' Personal Accounts"...

Cutting through the longest queue, which had already started downstairs in the doorman's room, one could see the inscription on the door people were trying to force their way into at every moment: "Housing Question".

Beyond the housing question there opened up a splendid poster on which was depicted a crag, and along its crest rode a horseman in a Caucasian cloak with a rifle over his shoulders. A little lower down were palm trees and a balcony, and on the balcony sat a young man with a little tuft of hair, gazing upwards with ever such lively eyes, and holding a fountain pen in his hand. The caption: "Fully inclusive writing holidays from two weeks (short story-novella) to one year (novel, trilogy). Yalta, Suuk-Su, Borovoye, Tsikhidziry, Makhindzhaury, Leningrad (Winter Palace)". At this door there was also a queue, but not an excessive one, of about a hundred and fifty people.

Further on there followed, obeying the fanciful twists and ups and downs of The Griboyedov House, "MASSOLIT Board", "Cashiers' Offices Nos. 2, 3, 4 and 5", "Editorial Board", "MASSOLIT Chairman", "Billiards Room", various ancillary organizations, and finally that very hall with the colonnade where the auntie had enjoyed her brilliant nephew's comedy.

Any visitor who got into Griboyedov – if, of course, he wasn't a complete dimwit – grasped at once how good a life those lucky members of MASSOLIT enjoyed, and sullen envy would immediately begin to torture him. And immediately he would address words of bitter reproach to the heavens for their having failed to endow him at birth with literary talent, without which, naturally, there was no point even dreaming of winning possession of a MASSOLIT membership card – brown, smelling of expensive leather, and with a broad gold border – a card known to the whole of Moscow.

Who will say anything in defence of envy? It is a rotten category of feeling, but all the same, one must put oneself in the visitor's shoes too. After all, what he saw on the upper floor was not everything, was still far from everything. The entire lower floor of auntie's house was occupied by the restaurant, and what a restaurant! It was rightly considered the best in Moscow. And not only because it was accommodated in two large halls with vaulted ceilings, decorated with lilac horses with Assyrian manes, not only because on each table there stood a lamp covered with a shawl, not only because it could not be penetrated by the first person you came across in the street, but also because Griboyedov could beat any restaurant in Moscow at will with the quality of its provisions, and because those provisions were served at the most reasonable, by no means burdensome prices.

Thus there is nothing surprising in a conversation such as this, for example, which was once heard by the author of these most truthful lines beside the cast-iron railings of Griboyedov:

"Where are you dining today, Amvrosy?"

"What a question! Here of course, dear Foka! Archibald Archibaldovich whispered to me today that there's going to be portions of pikeperch *au naturel*. The work of a virtuoso!"

"You really know how to live, Amvrosy!" sighed Foka, emaciated, run-down and with a carbuncle on his neck, in reply to the rosy-lipped giant, the golden-haired, plump-cheeked poet Amvrosy.

"I don't have any particular know-how," Amvrosy objected, "just an ordinary desire to live like a human being. What you mean to say, Foka, is that you can come across pikeperch at The Coliseum too. But at The Coliseum a portion of pikeperch costs thirteen roubles fifteen copecks, whereas here it's five fifty! Apart from that, at The Coliseum the pikeperch is three days old, and apart from that, you have no guarantee either that at The Coliseum you won't get a bunch of grapes in the face from the first young man that comes bursting in from Teatralny Passage. No, I'm categorically against The Coliseum!" the gourmet Amvrosy thundered for the whole boulevard to hear. "Don't try and persuade me, Foka!"

"I'm not trying to persuade you, Amvrosy," squealed Foka. "We can have dinner at home."

"Your humble servant," trumpeted Amvrosy, "I can imagine your wife attempting to construct portions of pikeperch *au naturel* in a little saucepan in the communal kitchen at home. Tee-hee-hee!... *Au revoir*, Foka!" And, humming away, Amvrosy headed towards the veranda beneath the awning.

Oh-ho-ho... Yes, it was so, it was so! Long-time residents of Moscow remember the renowned Griboyedov! Never mind boiled portions of pikeperch! That's cheap stuff, dear Amvrosy! What about the sterlet, sterlet in a silver saucepan, pieces of sterlet interlaid with crayfish necks and fresh caviar? What about eggs *en cocotte* with champignon purée in little bowls? And did you like the little fillets of thrush? With truffles? The quail Genoese style? Nine roubles fifty! And the jazz band, and the polite service! And in July, when the whole family is at the dacha and urgent literary matters are keeping you in town – on the veranda, in the shade of the climbing vine, in a patch of gold on the cleanest of tablecloths a bowl of soup *printanier*? Remember, Amvrosy? But why ask! I can see by your lips you remember. Never mind your white salmon, your pikeperch! What about the snipe, the great snipe, the common snipe, the woodcock according to season, the quail, the sandpipers? The Narzan that fizzed in your throat?! But that's enough, you're being distracted, Reader! Follow me!...

At half-past ten on the evening when Berlioz was killed at Patriarch's, only one upstairs room was lit in Griboyedov, and in it languished the twelve writers who had gathered for their meeting and were waiting for Mikhail Alexandrovich.

Those sitting on the chairs, and on the tables, and even on the two window sills in MASSOLIT's boardroom were suffering dreadfully from the stifling heat. Not a single breath of fresh air was penetrating through the open windows. Moscow was emitting the heat accumulated in the asphalt during the course of the day, and it was clear that the night would bring no relief. There was a smell of onions from the basement of auntie's house where the restaurant's kitchen was at work, and everyone wanted a drink, everyone was on edge and getting angry.

The belletrist Beskudnikov – a quiet, respectably dressed man with attentive and at the same time elusive eyes – took out his watch. The hand was crawling towards eleven. Beskudnikov tapped the face with his finger and showed it to his neighbour, the poet Dvubratsky, who was sitting on a table, and out of boredom swinging his feet, shod in yellow, rubber-soled shoes.

"Really," grumbled Dvubratsky.

"The guy's probably got stuck on the Klyazma," responded the rich voice of Nastasya Lukinishna Nepremenova, a Moscow merchant's orphan who had become a writer composing maritime battle stories under the pseudonym "Navigator George".

"Forgive me!" the author of popular sketches Zagrivov began boldly. "I'd be happy to drink some tea on a balcony myself just now, instead of stewing in here. The meeting was arranged for ten, wasn't it?"

"It's nice on the Klyazma now," Navigator George was winding the company up, knowing that the literary dacha village of Perelygino on the River Klyazma was a shared sore point. "The nightingales are probably already singing. My work always goes better out of town somehow, especially in the spring."

"I'm in my third year of paying in money to send my wife and her Basedow's disease* to that paradise, but there doesn't seem to be anything visible on the horizon," said the novelist Ieronym Poprikhin with venom and bitterness.

"It's just a matter of who gets lucky," droned the critic Ababkov from the window sill.

Navigator George's little eyes lit up with joy, and, softening her contralto, she said:

"You mustn't be envious, Comrades. There are only twenty-two dachas, and there are only seven more being built, and there are three thousand of us in MASSOLIT."

"Three thousand one hundred and eleven," someone put in from the corner.

"Well, you see," continued the Navigator, "what's to be done? It's natural that the dachas were given to the most talented among us..."

"The generals!" the scriptwriter Glukharev butted into the squabble bluntly.

Beskudnikov left the room with an artificial yawn.

"Alone in five rooms in Perelygino," said Glukharev in his wake.

"Lavrovich is alone in six," cried Deniskin, "and the dining room's panelled in oak."

"Oh, that isn't the point at the moment," droned Ababkov, "the point is that it's half-past eleven."

A din started up, something akin to a revolt was brewing. They began ringing the hateful Perelygino, got through to the wrong dacha, to Lavrovich, learnt that Lavrovich had gone off to the river, and were thoroughly put out by that. Off the tops of their heads they rang the Commission for Belles-Lettres plus the extension 930, and, of course, found nobody there.

"He could have telephoned!" cried Deniskin, Glukharev and Kvant.

Ah, they cried unjustly: Mikhail Alexandrovich could not have telephoned anywhere. Far, far from Griboyedov, in a huge hall lit by thousand-candle bulbs, on three zinc tables there lay what had until only recently been Mikhail Alexandrovich.

On the first was his naked body, covered in dried blood, with a broken arm and a crushed ribcage, on the second was his head, with the front teeth knocked out and with dulled, open eyes, unperturbed by the extremely harsh light, and on the third was a heap of stiffened rags.

Alongside the decapitated man stood a professor of forensic medicine, a pathological anatomist and his prosector, representatives of the investigation team, and Mikhail Alexandrovich Berlioz's deputy at MASSOLIT, the writer Zheldybin, summoned by telephone away from his sick wife.

A car had called for Zheldybin and, as a first priority, he had been taken, along with the investigators (this was around midnight) to the dead man's apartment, where the sealing of his papers had been carried out, and only then did they all go to the morgue.

And now the men standing beside the remains of the deceased were conferring as to what would be better: to sew the severed head back onto the neck, or to display the body in the Griboyedov hall with the dead man simply covered right up to the chin with a black cloth?

No, Mikhail Alexandrovich could not have telephoned anywhere, and Deniskin, Glukharev, Kvant and Beskudnikov were quite wrong to be shouting and indignant. At exactly midnight all twelve writers left the upper floor and went down to the restaurant. Here again they spoke ill of Mikhail Alexandrovich to themselves: all the tables on the veranda turned out, naturally, to be already occupied, and they had to stay and have dinner in those beautiful but stuffy halls.

And at exactly midnight in the first of those halls something crashed, rang out, rained down, began jumping. And straight away a thin male voice shouted out recklessly to the music: "Hallelujah!"* It was the renowned Griboyedov jazz band striking up. Faces covered in perspiration seemed to light up, the horses drawn on the ceiling appeared to come to life, there seemed to be added light in the lamps, and suddenly, as though they had broken loose, both halls began to dance, and after them the veranda began to dance as well.

Glukharev began to dance with the poetess Tamara Polumesyats, Kvant began to dance, Zhukopov the novelist began to dance with some film actress in a yellow dress. Dragoonsky and Cherdakchy were dancing, and little Deniskin was dancing with the gigantic Navigator George, the beautiful architect Semyeikina-Gall was dancing in the tight grasp of an unknown man in white canvas trousers. The regulars and invited guests were dancing, Muscovites and visitors, the writer

Johann from Kronstadt, some Vitya Kuftik or other from Rostov, a director, apparently, with a purple rash completely covering his cheek, the most eminent representatives of the poetry subsection of MASSOLIT were dancing, that is, Pavianov, Bogokhulsky, Sladky, Shpichkin and Adelphina Buzdyak, young men of unknown profession with crew cuts and padded shoulders were dancing, some very elderly man with a beard in which a little bit of spring onion had become lodged was dancing, and dancing with him was a sickly young girl, being eaten up by anaemia, in a crumpled little orange silk dress.

Bathed in sweat, waiters carried misted mugs of beer above their heads, shouting hoarsely and with hatred: "Sorry, Citizen!" Somewhere through a megaphone a voice commanded: "Karsky kebab, one! Venison, two! Imperial chitterlings!" The thin voice was no longer singing, but howling "Hallelujah!" The crashing of the golden cymbals in the jazz band at times drowned out the crashing of the crockery which the dishwashers slid down a sloping surface into the kitchen. In a word, hell.

And at midnight there was a vision in hell. Onto the veranda emerged a handsome black-eyed man in tails with a dagger of a beard who cast a regal gaze over his domains. It was said, it was said by mystics, that there was a time when the handsome man had not worn tails, but had been girdled with a broad leather belt, from which had protruded the butts of pistols, and his hair, black as a raven's wing, had been tied with scarlet silk, and under his command a brig had sailed the Caribbean beneath a funereal black flag bearing a skull.

But no, no! The seductive mystics lie, there are no Caribbean Seas on earth, and desperate filibusters do not sail them, and a corvette does not give chase, and cannon smoke does not spread above the waves. There is nothing, and never was there anything either! There is, look, a sorry lime tree, there is a cast-iron railing, and beyond it the boulevard... And the ice is melting in a bowl, and at the next table someone's bloodshot, bull-like eyes can be seen, and it's terrible, terrible... O gods, my gods, give me poison, poison!...

And suddenly at a table a word flew up: "Berlioz!!" Suddenly the jazz band went to pieces and fell quiet, as though somebody had bashed it with their fist. "What, what, what, what?!!" – "Berlioz!!!" And people started leaping up, started crying out...

Yes, a wave of grief surged up at the fearful news about Mikhail Alexandrovich. Someone was making a fuss, shouting that it was essential, at once, here and now, right on the spot, to compose some collective telegram and send it off immediately.

But what telegram, we'll ask, and where to? And why should it be sent? Indeed, where to? And what good is any sort of telegram at all to the man whose flattened-out occiput is now squeezed in the prosector's rubber hands, whose neck is now being pricked by the curved needles of the professor? He's dead, and no telegram is any good to him. It's all over, we won't burden the telegraph office any more.

Yes, he's dead, dead... But us, we're alive, you know!*

Yes, a wave of grief surged up, but it held, held and started to abate, and someone had already returned to his table, and – at first stealthily, but then quite openly – had drunk some vodka and had taken a bite to eat. Indeed, chicken cutlets *de volaille* weren't to go to waste, were they? How can we help Mikhail Alexandrovich? By staying hungry? But us, you know, we're alive!

Naturally, the piano was locked, the jazz band dispersed, a number of journalists left for their offices to write obituaries. It became known that Zheldybin had arrived from the morgue. He settled himself in the dead man's office upstairs, and straight away the rumour spread that it would be him replacing Berlioz. Zheldybin summoned all twelve members of the board from the restaurant, and, at a meeting begun urgently in Berlioz's office, they got down to a discussion of the pressing questions of the decoration of Griboyedov's columned hall, of the transportation of the body from the morgue to that hall, of the opening of access to it and of other things connected with the regrettable event.

But the restaurant began living its usual nocturnal life, and would have lived it until closing time, that is, until four o'clock in the morning, had there not occurred something really completely out of the ordinary that startled the restaurant's guests much more than the news of Berlioz's death.

The first to become agitated were the cab drivers in attendance at the gates of The Griboyedov House. One of them was heard to shout out, half-rising on his box:

"Cor! Just look at that!"

Following which, from out of the blue, a little light flared up by the cast-iron railings and began approaching the veranda. Those sitting at the tables began half-rising and peering, and saw that proceeding towards the restaurant together with the little light was a white apparition. When it got right up to the trellis, it was as if everyone became ossified at the tables, with pieces of sterlet on their forks and their eyes popping out. The doorman, who had come out through the doors of the restaurant's cloakroom into the yard at that moment for a smoke, stamped out his cigarette and made to move towards the apparition with the obvious aim of barring its access to the restaurant, but for some reason failed to do so and stopped, smiling rather foolishly.

And the apparition, passing through an opening in the trellis, stepped unimpeded onto the veranda. At that point everyone saw it was no apparition at all, but Ivan Nikolayevich Bezdomny, the very well-known poet.

He was barefooted, in a ripped, off-white *tolstovka*, fastened onto the breast of which with a safety pin was a paper icon with a faded image of an unknown saint, and wearing striped white long johns. In his hand Ivan Nikolayevich was carrying a lighted wedding candle. Ivan Nikolayevich's right cheek was covered in fresh scratches. It is difficult even to measure the depth of the silence that had come over the veranda. One of the waiters was seen to have beer flowing onto the floor from a mug that had tipped sideways.

The poet raised the candle above his head and said loudly:

"Hi, mates!" after which he glanced underneath the nearest table and exclaimed despondently: "No, he's not here!"

Two voices were heard. A bass said pitilessly:

"A clear-cut case. Delirium tremens."

And the second, female and frightened, uttered the words:

"How on earth did the police let him walk the streets looking like that?"

Ivan Nikolayevich heard this and responded:

"Twice they wanted to detain me, in Skatertny and here on Bronnaya, but I hopped over a fence and, see, scratched my cheek!" At this point Ivan Nikolayevich raised the candle and exclaimed: "Brothers in literature!" (His hoarsened voice strengthened and became fervent.) "Listen to me, everyone! He has appeared! You must catch him straight away, or else he will bring about indescribable calamities!"

"What? What? What did he say? Who's appeared?" came a rush of voices from all sides.

"A consultant!" replied Ivan. "And this consultant has just killed Misha Berlioz at Patriarch's."

Here the people from the hall indoors poured onto the veranda. The crowd moved closer around Ivan's light.

"I'm sorry, I'm sorry, be more precise," a quiet and polite voice was heard right by Ivan Nikolayevich's ear, "say what it is you mean, killed? Who killed him?"

"A foreign consultant, a professor and spy," responded Ivan, looking round.

"And what is his name?" came the quiet question in his ear.

"That's just it, the name!" cried Ivan in anguish. "If only I knew the name! I didn't see the name on the visiting card properly... I can only remember the first letter, W, the name begins with a W! Whatever is that name beginning with a W?" Ivan asked of himself, clutching his forehead with his hand, and suddenly began muttering: "W, w, w... Wa... Wo... Washner? Wagner? Weiner? Wegner? Winter?" The hair on Ivan's head started shifting with the effort.

"Wulf?" some woman shouted out compassionately.

Ivan got angry.

"Idiot!" he shouted, his eyes searching for the woman. "What's Wulf got to do with it? Wulf's not to blame for anything! Wo, what... No! I won't remember like this! But I'll tell you what, Citizens, ring the police straight away so they send out five motorcycles with machine guns to catch the Professor. And don't forget to say there are two others with him: some lanky one in checks... a cracked pince-nez... and a fat black cat! And in the meantime I'll search Griboyedov... I sense he's here!"

Ivan lapsed into agitation, pushed those surrounding him away, began waving the candle about, spilling the wax over himself, and looking under the tables. At this point the words: "Get a doctor!" were heard, and somebody's kindly, fleshy face, clean-shaven and well-fed, wearing horn-rimmed spectacles, appeared before Ivan.

"Comrade Bezdomny," this face began in a gala voice, "calm down! You're upset by the death of our beloved Mikhail Alexandrovich... no, simply Misha Berlioz. We all understand it perfectly. You need a rest. Some comrades will see you to bed now, and you'll doze off..."

"Do you understand," Ivan interrupted, baring his teeth, "that the Professor must be caught? And you come pestering me with your stupid remarks! Cretin!"

"Comrade Bezdomny, pardon me," the face replied, flushing, backing away, and already repenting getting mixed up in this business.

"No, someone else, maybe, but you I won't pardon," said Ivan Nikolayevich with quiet hatred.

A spasm distorted his face, he quickly moved the candle from his right hand to his left, swung his arm out wide and struck the sympathetic face on the ear.

At this point it occurred to people to throw themselves upon Ivan – and they did. The candle went out, and a pair of spectacles, flying off a face, were instantly trampled upon. Ivan emitted a terrifying war whoop, audible, to the excitement of all, even on the boulevard, and started to defend himself. The crockery falling from the tables began ringing, women began shouting.

While the waiters were tying the poet up with towels, a conversation was going on in the cloakroom between the commander of the brig and the doorman.

"Did you see he was in his underpants?" the pirate asked coldly.

"But after all, Archibald Archibaldovich," replied the doorman in cowardly fashion, "how on earth can I not let them in if they're members of MASSOLIT?"

"Did you see he was in his underpants?" repeated the pirate.

"For pity's sake, Archibald Archibaldovich," said the doorman, turning purple, "whatever can I do? I understand for myself there are ladies sitting on the veranda…"

"The ladies have nothing to do with it, it's all one to the ladies," replied the pirate, his eyes absolutely scorching the doorman, "but it's not all one to the police! A man in his underwear can proceed through the streets of Moscow only in one instance, if he's going under police escort, and only to one place – the police station! And you, if you're a doorman, ought to know that when you see such a man, you ought to begin whistling without a moment's delay. Can you hear? Can you hear what's happening on the veranda?"

At this point the doorman, beside himself, caught the sounds of some sort of rumbling, the crashing of crockery and women's cries coming from the veranda.

"Well, and what am I to do with you for this?" the filibuster asked.

The skin on the doorman's face assumed a typhoid hue, and his eyes were benumbed. He imagined that the black hair, now combed into a parting, had been covered in fiery silk. The dicky and tails had disappeared, and, tucked into a belt, the handle of a pistol had appeared. The doorman pictured himself hanged from the foretop yardarm. With his own eyes he saw his own tongue poking out and his lifeless head fallen onto his shoulder, and he even heard the splashing of the waves over the ship's side. The doorman's knees sagged. But here the filibuster took pity on him and extinguished his sharp gaze.

"Watch out, Nikolai! This is the last time. We don't need such doormen in the restaurant at any price. Go and get a job as a watchman in a church." Having said this, the commander gave precise, clear, rapid commands: "Pantelei from the pantry. Policeman. Charge sheet. Vehicle. Psychiatric hospital." And added: "Whistle!"

A quarter of an hour later an extremely astonished audience, not only in the restaurant, but on the boulevard itself as well, and in the windows of the houses looking out onto the garden of the restaurant, saw Pantelei, the doorman, a policeman, a waiter and the poet Ryukhin carrying out of Griboyedov's gates a young man swaddled like a doll who, in floods of tears, was spitting, attempting to hit specifically Ryukhin, and shouting for the entire boulevard to hear:

"Bastard!... Bastard!"

The driver of a goods vehicle with an angry face was starting up his engine. Alongside, a cab driver was getting his horse excited, hitting it across the crupper with his lilac reins and shouting:

"Come and use the racehorse! I've taken people to the mental hospital before!"

All around the crowd was buzzing, discussing the unprecedented occurrence. In short, there was a vile, foul, seductive, swinish, scandalous scene, which ended only when the truck carried off from the gates of Griboyedov the unfortunate Ivan Nikolayevich, the policeman, Pantelei and Ryukhin.

6

Schizophrenia, Just As Had Been Said

WHEN A MAN WITH A LITTLE POINTED BEARD, robed in a white coat, came out into the waiting room of the renowned psychiatric clinic recently completed on a river bank outside Moscow, it was half-past one in the morning. Three hospital orderlies had their eyes glued to Ivan

Nikolayevich, who was sitting on a couch. Here too was the extremely agitated poet Ryukhin. The towels with which Ivan Nikolayevich had been bound lay in a heap on the same couch. Ivan Nikolayevich's hands and feet were free.

On seeing the man who had come in, Ryukhin paled, gave a cough and said timidly:

"Hello, Doctor."

The doctor bowed to Ryukhin, yet, while bowing, looked not at him, but at Ivan Nikolayevich. The latter sat completely motionless with an angry face, with knitted brows, and did not even stir at the entrance of the doctor.

"Here, Doctor," began Ryukhin, for some reason in a mysterious whisper, glancing round fearfully at Ivan Nikolayevich, "is the well-known poet Ivan Bezdomny... and you see... we're afraid it might be delirium tremens..."

"Has he been drinking heavily?" asked the doctor through his teeth.

"No, he used to have a drink, but not so much that..."

"Has he been trying to catch cockroaches, rats, little devils or scurrying dogs?"

"No," replied Ryukhin with a start, "I saw him yesterday and this morning. He was perfectly well..."

"And why is he wearing long johns? Did you take him from his bed?"

"He came to the restaurant looking like that, Doctor..."

"Aha, aha," said the doctor, highly satisfied, "and why the cuts? Has he been fighting with anyone?"

"He fell off a fence, and then in the restaurant he hit someone... and then someone else too..."

"Right, right, right," said the doctor and, turning to Ivan, added: "Hello!"

"Hi there, wrecker!" replied Ivan, maliciously and loudly.

Ryukhin was so embarrassed that he did not dare raise his eyes to the polite doctor. But the latter was not in the least offended, and with his customary deft gesture he took off his spectacles; lifting the tail of his coat, he put them away in the back pocket of his trousers, and then he asked Ivan:

"How old are you?"

"Honestly, you can all leave me alone and go to the devil!" Ivan cried rudely, and turned away.

"Why ever are you getting angry? Have I said anything unpleasant to you?"

"I'm twenty-three," began Ivan excitedly, "and I shall be putting in a complaint about you all. And about you especially, you worm!" he addressed himself to Ryukhin individually.

"And what is it you want to complain about?"

"The fact that I, a healthy man, was seized and dragged here to the madhouse by force!" replied Ivan in fury.

Here Ryukhin peered closely at Ivan and turned cold: there was definitely no madness in the latter's eyes. From being lacklustre, as they had been at Griboyedov, they had turned into the former clear ones.

"Good gracious!" thought Ryukhin in fright. "Is he actually sane? What nonsense this is! Why ever, indeed, did we drag him here? He's sane, sane, only his face is all scratched..."

"You are not," began the doctor calmly, sitting down on a white stool with a shiny leg, "in the madhouse, but in a clinic, where nobody will think of detaining you if there is no need for it."

Ivan Nikolayevich gave him a mistrustful sidelong look, but muttered nevertheless:

"The Lord be praised! One sane man has at last come to light among the idiots, the foremost of whom is that talentless dunderhead Sashka!"

"Who's this talentless Sashka?" enquired the doctor.

"There he is, Ryukhin!" Ivan replied, and jabbed a dirty finger in Ryukhin's direction.

The latter flared up in indignation.

"That's what he gives me instead of a thank you!" he thought bitterly. "For my having shown some concern for him! He really is a scumbag!"

"A typical petty kulak in his psychology," began Ivan Nikolayevich, who was evidently impatient to denounce Ryukhin, "and a petty kulak, what's more, carefully disguising himself as a proletarian. Look at his dreary physiognomy and compare it with that sonorous verse he composed for the first of the month! Hee-hee-hee... 'Soar up!' and 'Soar forth!'... but you take a look inside him – what's he thinking there... it'll make you gasp!" And Ivan Nikolayevich broke into sinister laughter.

Ryukhin was breathing heavily, was red, and was thinking of only one thing – that he had warmed a snake at his breast, that he had shown concern for someone who had turned out to be, when tested, a spiteful enemy. And the main thing was, nothing could be done about it either: you couldn't trade insults with a madman, could you?!

"And why precisely have you been delivered to us?" asked the doctor, after attentively hearing out Bezdomny's denunciations.

"The devil take them, the stupid oafs! Seized me, tied me up with rags of some sort and dragged me out here in a truck!"

"Permit me to ask you why you arrived at the restaurant in just your underwear?"

"There's nothing surprising in that," replied Ivan, "I went to the Moscow River to bathe, and well, I had my clobber nicked, and this trash was left! I couldn't go around Moscow naked, could I? I put on what there was, because I was hurrying to Griboyedov's restaurant."

The doctor looked enquiringly at Ryukhin, and the latter mumbled sullenly:

"That's what the restaurant's called."

"Aha," said the doctor, "and why were you hurrying so? Some business meeting or other?"

"I'm trying to catch a consultant," Ivan Nikolayevich replied, and looked around anxiously.

"What consultant?"

"Do you know Berlioz?" asked Ivan meaningfully.

"That's… the composer?"*

Ivan became upset.

"What composer? Ah yes… Of course not! The composer just shares Misha Berlioz's name."

Ryukhin did not want to say anything, but he had to explain:

"Berlioz, the secretary of MASSOLIT, was run over by a tram this evening at Patriarch's."

"Don't make things up, you don't know anything!" Ivan grew angry with Ryukhin. "It was me, not you, that was there when it happened! He deliberately set him up to go under the tram!"

"Pushed him?"

"What's 'pushed' got to do with it?" exclaimed Ivan, getting angry at the general slow-wittedness. "Someone like that doesn't even need to push! He can get up to such tricks, just you watch out! He knew in advance that Berlioz would go under the tram!"

"And did anyone see this consultant other than you?"

"That's precisely the trouble, it was only Berlioz and me."

"Right. And what measures did you take to catch this murderer?" Here the doctor turned and threw a glance at a woman in a white coat sitting to one side at a desk. She pulled out a sheet of paper and began filling in the empty spaces in its columns.

"Here's what measures. I picked up a candle in the kitchen…"

"This one here?" asked the doctor, indicating the broken candle lying beside an icon on the desk in front of the woman.

"That very one, and…"

"And why the icon?"

"Well, yes, the icon…" Ivan blushed, "it was the icon that frightened them more than anything," and he again jabbed his finger in Ryukhin's direction, "but the thing is that he, the consultant, he… let's talk plainly… he's in cahoots with unclean spirits… and it won't be so simple to catch him."

The orderlies stood to attention for some reason and did not take their eyes off Ivan.

"Yes," continued Ivan, "he's in cahoots! That's an incontrovertible fact. He's spoken personally with Pontius Pilate. And there's no reason to look at me like that! I'm telling the truth! He saw everything – the balcony, the palms. In short, he was with Pontius Pilate, I can vouch for it."

"Well then, well then…"

"Well, and so I pinned the icon on my chest and ran off…"

Suddenly at this point a clock struck twice.

"Oho-ho!" exclaimed Ivan, and rose from the couch. "Two o'clock, and I'm wasting time with you! I'm sorry, where's the telephone?"

"Let him get to the telephone," the doctor commanded the orderlies.

Ivan grasped the receiver, and at the same time the woman asked Ryukhin quietly:

"Is he married?"

"Single," replied Ryukhin fearfully.

"A union member?"

"Yes."

"Is that the police?" Ivan shouted into the receiver. "Is that the police? Comrade duty officer, make arrangements immediately for five motorcycles with machine guns to be sent out to capture a foreign consultant. What? Come and pick me up, I'll go with you myself... It's the poet Bezdomny speaking from the madhouse... What's your address?" Bezdomny asked the doctor in a whisper, covering the receiver with his palm, and then he again shouted into the receiver: "Are you listening? Hello!... Disgraceful!" Ivan suddenly wailed, and he flung the receiver against the wall. Then he turned to the doctor, reached out his hand to him, said drily, "Goodbye," and prepared to leave.

"Pardon me, and where is it you mean to go?" began the doctor, peering into Ivan's eyes. "In the middle of the night, in your underwear... You don't feel well, stay here with us!"

"Now let me pass," said Ivan to the orderlies, who had closed ranks by the doors. "Will you let me go, or not?" cried the poet in a terrible voice.

Ryukhin started trembling, but the woman pressed a button in the desk, and a shiny little box and a sealed ampoule sprang out onto its glass surface.

"So that's the way it is?!" pronounced Ivan, looking around with a wild, trapped air. "Well, all right then! Farewell!!" and he flung himself head first into the curtain over the window.

There was quite a heavy crash, but the glass behind the curtain did not so much as crack, and a moment later Ivan Nikolayevich began struggling in the arms of the orderlies. He wheezed, tried to bite them, shouted:

"So that's the sort of glass you've got yourselves!... Let me go!... Let me go!"

A syringe gleamed in the doctor's hands; with a single yank the woman ripped the tattered sleeve of the *tolstovka* apart and seized hold of the arm with unfeminine strength. There was a sudden smell of ether, Ivan weakened in the arms of four people, and the dextrous doctor made use of that moment to sink the needle into Ivan's arm. They held on to Ivan for a few more seconds and then lowered him onto the couch.

"Bandits!" Ivan cried, and leapt up from the couch, but he was set upon again. As soon as he was released, he was on the point of leaping up again, but this time he sat back down by himself. He was silent for a while, looking around in a wild sort of way, then unexpectedly yawned, then smiled maliciously.

"Locked me up after all," he said, yawned once more, unexpectedly lay down, put his head on a cushion and his fist under his cheek, like a child, and began mumbling in a now sleepy voice, without malice: "Well, jolly good too... and you'll pay for everything yourselves. I've warned you, now it's up to you!... What I'm most interested in now is Pontius Pilate... Pilate..." – here he closed his eyes.

"Bath, private room 117, and set a guard on him," the doctor ordered, putting on his spectacles. At this point Ryukhin again gave a start: the white doors opened noiselessly, into sight beyond them came a corridor lit by blue night lights. A bed on rubber wheels rolled in from the corridor, the now quiet Ivan was transferred onto it, he rode into the corridor, and the doors closed up behind him.

"Doctor," asked the shaken Ryukhin in a whisper, "he really is ill, then?"

"Oh yes," replied the doctor.

"And what is it that's wrong with him?" asked Ryukhin timidly.

The tired doctor looked at Ryukhin and answered limply:

"Motive and vocal excitement... delirious interpretations... evidently a complex case... Schizophrenia, one must assume. And add to that alcoholism..."

Ryukhin understood nothing of the doctor's words, except that Ivan Nikolayevich was clearly in quite a bad way; he sighed and asked:

"And what was that he kept on saying about some consultant?"

"He probably saw somebody his disturbed imagination found striking. Or perhaps he's been hallucinating..."

A few minutes later the truck was carrying Ryukhin away to Moscow. It was getting light, and the light of the street lamps that had not yet been extinguished on the highway was unnecessary now and unpleasant. The driver was angry about the night having been lost, he sped the vehicle on for all he was worth, and it skidded on the bends.

And now the forest had fallen away, been left somewhere behind, and the river had gone off to the side somewhere, and all kinds of everything came hurrying along to meet the truck: fences of some kind with sentry boxes and palettes of firewood, great high poles and masts of some sort with threaded coils on the masts, piles of ballast, earth covered with the lines of channels – in short, there was the sense that here it was at any moment, Moscow, right here, around this bend, and in a minute it would be upon you and envelop you.

Ryukhin was shaken and tossed about, the stump of some sort on which he was sitting was continually trying to slide out from under him. The restaurant's towels, thrown in by the policeman and Pantelei, who had left earlier by trolleybus, shifted all over the truck. Ryukhin started to try and gather them together, but for some reason maliciously hissing: "Oh, they can go to the devil! Really, what am I fiddling around for like an idiot?" – he kicked them away and stopped looking at them.

The mood of the man as he travelled was terrible. It was becoming clear that the visit to the mental asylum had left the most painful mark upon him. Ryukhin tried to understand what was tormenting him. The corridor with the blue lights that had stuck in his mind? The thought that there was no worse misfortune in the world than the loss of one's reason? Yes, yes, that too, of course. Yet that was just a general thought, after all. But there was something else. Whatever was it? The insult, that's what. Yes, yes, the insulting words thrown right in his face by Bezdomny. And the trouble was not that they were insulting, but that there was truth in them.

The poet no longer looked from side to side, but, staring at the dirty, shaking floor, began muttering something, whining, gnawing away at himself.

Yes, the poetry... He was thirty-two. What, indeed, lay in the future? In the future too he would compose a few poems a year. Into old age? Yes, into old age. And what would those poems bring him? Fame? "What nonsense! Don't deceive yourself, at least. Fame will never come to someone who composes bad poetry. Why is it bad? It was true, true, what he said!" Ryukhin addressed himself pitilessly. "I don't believe in a thing of what I write!"

Poisoned by the explosion of neurasthenia, the poet lurched, and the floor beneath him stopped shaking. Ryukhin raised his head and saw that he had already been in Moscow for a long time and, in addition, that the dawn was over Moscow, that the cloud was lit up from beneath with gold, that his truck was at a standstill, held up in a column of other vehicles at the turn onto the boulevard, and that ever so close to him stood a metal man on a pedestal,* his head slightly inclined, looking dispassionately at the boulevard.

Some strange thoughts surged into the head of the sick poet. "There's an example of real luckiness..." At this point Ryukhin stood up straight on the back of the truck and raised his hand, for some reason attacking the cast-iron man who was harming no one. "Whatever step he took in life, whatever happened to him, everything was to his advantage, everything worked towards his fame! But what did he do? I don't get it... Is there something special about those words: 'Stormy darkness'?* I don't understand! He was lucky, lucky!" Ryukhin suddenly concluded venomously, and felt that the truck beneath him had stirred. "That White Guard, he shot, he shot at him, smashed his hip to pieces and guaranteed his immortality..."*

The column moved off. In no more than two minutes the poet, who was quite unwell and had even aged, was stepping onto Griboyedov's veranda. It had already emptied. A party of some sort was finishing its drinks in a corner, and in its midst the familiar master of ceremonies was bustling about in his embroidered Asian skullcap and with a glass of Abrau* in his hand.

Ryukhin, laden with towels, was greeted cordially by Archibald Archibaldovich and immediately relieved of the accursed rags. Had Ryukhin not been so tormented at the clinic and on the truck, he would probably have taken pleasure in recounting how everything had been at the hospital and in embellishing the account with invented details. But now he had other things on his mind, and no matter how unobservant Ryukhin was, now, after the torture in the truck, he scrutinized the pirate acutely for the first time and realized that, though he might ask questions about Bezdomny and even exclaim "oh dear me!" he was in actual fact completely indifferent to Bezdomny's fate and did not pity him in the least. "Good for him too! Quite right too!" thought Ryukhin with cynical, self-destructive malice, and, cutting his account of schizophrenia short, he asked:

"Archibald Archibaldovich, could I have a drop of vodka?"

The pirate pulled a sympathetic face and whispered:

"I understand... this very minute..." and waved to a waiter.

A quarter of an hour later, Ryukhin was sitting in total solitude, hunched over some fish and drinking one glass after another, understanding and admitting that it was no longer possible to rectify anything in his life, it was possible only to forget.

The poet had used up his night while others had feasted, and now he understood that it could not be returned to him. He only had to raise his head from the lamp up to the sky to realize that the night was irrevocably lost. The waiters were hurrying, tearing the tablecloths from the tables. The tomcats darting up and down beside the veranda had the look of morning. The day was falling inexorably upon the poet.

7

A Bad Apartment

IF NEXT MORNING SOMEONE had said this to Styopa Likhodeyev: "Styopa! You'll be shot if you don't get up this very minute!" – Styopa would have replied in a languid, scarcely audible voice: "Shoot me, do with me what you will, but I shan't get up."

It seemed to him that he couldn't open his eyes, let alone get up, because he only had to do that for lightning to flash and his head to be smashed to pieces at once. Inside that head a heavy bell was booming, brown spots with fiery green rims were swimming by between his eyeballs and his closed eyelids, and to crown it all, he felt nauseous, and it seemed, moreover, that this nausea was linked with the sounds of some importunate gramophone.

Styopa tried to call something to mind, but only one thing would come to mind – that yesterday, there was no knowing where, he had apparently been standing with a napkin in his hand and trying to kiss some lady or other, while promising her that next day, and precisely at noon, he would pay her a visit. The lady had been declining this, saying: "No, no, I won't be at home!" – but Styopa had stubbornly insisted on having it his way: "Well, I shall just go and turn up!"

Styopa had absolutely no idea what lady it had been, or what time it was now, or what day of what month – and worst of all, he could not understand where he was. He attempted to elucidate this last point at least, and to do so he unstuck the glued-up lids of his left eye. In the semi-darkness something was dimly shining. Styopa finally recognized a cheval glass, and realized he was lying on his back on his bed, that is, on the former jeweller's wife's bed, in his bedroom. At this point he received such a blow on the head that he closed his eye and began groaning.

Let us explain ourselves: Styopa Likhodeyev, the Director of The Variety Theatre, had come round in the morning at home, in the very apartment he had shared with the late Berlioz, in a large six-storey building shaped like the letter *pokoi** on Sadovaya Street.

It should be said that this apartment – No. 50 – had already long enjoyed if not a bad, then in any event a strange reputation. Just two years before, its owner had been the widow of the jeweller De Fougeré. Anna Franzevna de Fougeré, a fifty-year-old, respectable and very businesslike lady, had rented out three of her five rooms to lodgers: one whose name seems to have been Belomut, and another with a name that has been lost.

And then, two years before, inexplicable things had started happening in the apartment: people had begun disappearing from the apartment without trace.

One day, on a holiday, a policeman appeared at the apartment, summoned the second lodger (whose name has been lost) into the entrance hall, and said that the latter was requested to drop into the police station for a moment to sign for something. The lodger asked Anfisa, Anna Franzevna's devoted and long-time maid, to say, in the event of anybody phoning him, that he would be back in ten minutes, and off he went with the correctly behaved policeman in white gloves. But not only did he not come back in ten minutes, he never came back at all. Most surprising of all is the fact that the policeman evidently disappeared along with him as well.

The pious, or to put it more candidly, the superstitious Anfisa came straight out and declared to Anna Franzevna, who was most upset, that it was witchcraft, and that she knew very well who had stolen away both the lodger and the policeman, only with night approaching she did not want to say.

Well, and witchcraft, as is well-known, only has to start, and then you simply can't stop it with anything. That second lodger disappeared, if memory serves, on the Monday, and on the Wednesday Belomut vanished into thin air, but under different circumstances, it is true. A car stopped by for him in the morning as usual, to take him to work, and it took him away, but it brought nobody back, and it itself came back no more.

The grief and horror of Madame Belomut beggar description. But, alas, both the one and the other were short-lived. That same night, returning with Anfisa from the dacha, to which she had for some reason hurriedly gone away, Anna Franzevna found Citizeness Belomut no longer at the apartment. But that is not all: the doors of both the rooms which had been occupied by the Belomut spouses proved to have been sealed!

Somehow two days passed. And on the third day, Anna Franzevna, who had been suffering from insomnia all this time, went off to the dacha hurriedly once again… Does it need to be said that she did not come back?!

Anfisa, remaining on her own, cried and cried to her heart's content and went to bed after one o'clock in the morning. What happened to her afterwards is unknown, but the tenants in other apartments told how some sort of knocking was allegedly to be heard all through the night in No. 50, and the electric light was allegedly burning in the windows till morning. In the morning it became clear that Anfisa was not there either!

For a long time all sorts of legends were told in the building about those who had disappeared and about the apartment with a curse on it, such as, for example, that the dried-up and pious Anfisa had allegedly carried twenty-five large diamonds belonging to Anna Franzevna in a little chamois-leather pouch on her withered breast. And that there allegedly came to light of their own accord, in the firewood shed at that same dacha to which Anna Franzevna had been hurriedly going, some incalculable treasures in the form of those same diamonds, and also gold currency of tsarist coinage. And more of the same sort of thing. Well, what we don't know, we can't vouch for.

Whatever the case, the apartment stood empty and sealed for only a week, and then it was moved into by the late Berlioz and his wife and that same Styopa, also with his wife. It is perfectly natural that no sooner did they find themselves in the accursed apartment than the-devil-knows-what began happening to them too. Namely, in the course of a single month both wives disappeared – but these two not without trace. Of Berlioz's wife it was said she had allegedly been seen in Kharkov with some ballet-master, while Styopa's wife is supposed to have come to light on Bozhedomka, where, as gossip had it, the Director of The Variety, exploiting his innumerable acquaintances, had contrived to procure a room for her, on the one condition that she should not show her face on Sadovaya Street…

And so Styopa began groaning. He wanted to call the maid, Grunya, and demand some pyramidon of her, but managed to grasp, after all, that this was stupid, that Grunya, of course, did not have any pyramidon.* He tried to call Berlioz to his assistance, twice groaned out: "Misha... Misha..." but, as you can understand for yourselves, received no reply. The most complete silence reigned in the apartment.

Upon moving his toes, Styopa guessed he was lying in his socks, and he passed a shaky hand over his hip to decide whether or not he was wearing trousers, but could not decide. Finally, seeing that he was abandoned and alone, that there was no one to help him, he decided to get up, whatever the inhuman effort it cost.

Styopa unstuck his gummed-up eyelids and saw he was reflected in the cheval glass in the guise of a man with his hair poking out in all directions, with a swollen physiognomy covered in black stubble, with puffy eyes, and wearing a dirty shirt with a collar and a tie, long johns and socks.

That was how he saw himself in the cheval glass, but beside the mirror he saw an unknown man, dressed in black and in a black beret.

Styopa sat up on the bed and, as best he could, opened his bloodshot eyes wide at the unknown man.

The silence was broken by this unknown man pronouncing in a low, heavy voice and with a foreign accent the following words:

"Good day, dearest Stepan Bogdanovich!"

There was a pause, after which, having made the most terrible effort with himself, Styopa said:

"What do you want?" and was himself amazed, not recognizing his own voice. The word "what" he had pronounced in a treble, "do you" in a bass, while "want" had not come out at all.

The stranger grinned amicably, took out a big gold watch with a diamond triangle on the case, let it ring eleven times and said:

"Eleven! And exactly an hour that I've been awaiting your awakening, for you gave me an appointment to be at your home at ten. And here I am!"

Styopa fumbled for his trousers on the chair beside the bed and whispered:

"Excuse me..." he put them on and asked hoarsely: "Tell me, please, your name?"

Talking was difficult for him. At every word someone was sticking a needle into his brain, causing hellish pain.

"What? You've forgotten my name as well?" here the unknown man smiled.

"Forgive me," wheezed Styopa, feeling that his hangover was favouring him with a new symptom: it seemed to him that the floor beside the bed had gone away somewhere and that this very minute he would fly head first to the Devil in the netherworld.

"Dear Stepan Bogdanovich," began the visitor, smiling shrewdly, "no pyramidon is going to help you. Follow the wise old rule – take the hair of the dog. The only thing that will return you to life is two shots of vodka with something hot and spicy to eat."

Styopa was a cunning man and, however ill he might have been, he grasped that, seeing as he had been caught like this, he had to admit everything.

"To be frank," he began, scarcely in control of his tongue, "yesterday I had a little…"

"Not a word more!" replied the caller, and moved aside on the armchair.

With his eyes popping out, Styopa saw that on a little table a tray had been prepared, on which there were slices of white bread, a dish of pressed caviar, a plate of pickled boletuses, something in a little saucepan and, finally, vodka in the jeweller's wife's voluminous carafe. Styopa was particularly struck by the fact that the carafe was covered in condensation from the cold. That was understandable, though – it was standing in a slop basin packed with ice. It had all been laid out, in short, neatly and capably.

The stranger did not let Styopa's astonishment develop to an unhealthy degree, and deftly poured him a half-shot of vodka.

"What about you?" squeaked Styopa.

"With pleasure!"

Styopa brought the glass up to his lips with a jerky hand, while the stranger swallowed the contents of his glass in a single breath. Munching a bit of caviar, Styopa squeezed out of himself the words:

"But what about you… something to eat with it?"

"My thanks, I never have anything to eat with it," the stranger replied, and poured a second glass each. The saucepan was uncovered – it proved to hold sausages in tomato sauce.

And now the damned greenery in front of the eyes melted away, words began to be properly pronounced, and, most importantly, Styopa remembered one or two things. Namely, that yesterday's doings had been at Skhodnya, at the dacha of Khustov, the sketch-writer, where this Khustov had taken Styopa in a taxicab. Even the way they had hired this taxicab near The Metropole came to mind, there had been some actor or something of the kind there too at the time... with a gramophone in a little suitcase. Yes, yes, yes, it had been at the dacha! And also, he seemed to recall, that gramophone had made the dogs howl. It was just the lady Styopa had wanted to kiss that remained unclarified... the devil knew who she was... she worked in radio, he thought, but maybe not.

The previous day was thus gradually being cleared up, but Styopa was now much more interested in the present day, and in particular, in the unknown man's appearance in his bedroom, and with vodka and food to go with it, what's more. It wouldn't be a bad thing to clarify that.

"Well then, I hope you've remembered my name now?"

But Styopa only smiled bashfully and spread his hands.

"Well really! I sense you were drinking port after the vodka! For pity's sake, how can you possibly do that!"

"I'd like to request that this should remain just between us," said Styopa in an ingratiating tone.

"Oh, of course, of course! But it goes without saying that I can't vouch for Khustov."

"So you know Khustov then?"

"I caught a glimpse of that individual in your office yesterday, but one cursory glance at his face is sufficient to realize that he's a bastard, a troublemaker, a time-server and a toady."

"Quite correct!" thought Styopa, amazed at such a true, accurate and concise definition of Khustov.

Yes, the previous day was being pieced together, but even so, uneasiness was not abandoning the Director of The Variety. The thing was that in that previous day there yawned an absolutely enormous black hole. Now this here stranger in the beret, say whatever you like, Styopa had definitely not seen him in his office yesterday.

"Woland,* Professor of Black Magic," the caller said weightily, seeing Styopa's difficulties, and he recounted everything in order.

Yesterday afternoon he had arrived in Moscow from abroad, and had immediately presented himself to Styopa and proposed his temporary engagement at The Variety. Styopa had rung the Moscow District Spectacles Commission and submitted the question for approval (Styopa blenched and began blinking), had signed a contract with Professor Woland for seven shows (Styopa opened his mouth), had arranged that Woland should call on him to define the details further at ten o'clock in the morning today... And so here Woland was. On arrival he had been met by the maid, Grunya, who had explained that she had only just arrived herself, that she was non-resident, that Berlioz was not at home, and that if the caller wished to see Stepan Bogdanovich, then he should go through into the bedroom himself. Stepan Bogdanovich was sleeping so soundly, she would not take it upon herself to wake him. Seeing the condition Stepan Bogdanovich was in, the artiste had sent Grunya to the nearest grocer's for the vodka and the food, to the chemist's for the ice, and...

"Allow me to settle up with you," the crushed Styopa whimpered, and began searching for his wallet.

"Oh, what nonsense!" exclaimed the touring artiste, and would hear no more of it.

And so the vodka and the food became clear, but all the same Styopa was a sad sight to see; he certainly could not remember anything about a contract, and had not seen this Woland on the previous day for the life of him. Yes, Khustov there had been, but Woland there had not.

"Permit me to take a look at the contract," Styopa requested quietly.

"Certainly, certainly..."

Styopa glanced at the document and went numb. Everything was in place. Firstly, Styopa's devil-may-care signature in his own writing! A slanting inscription to the side in the hand of the Financial Director, Rimsky, with permission to pay out ten thousand roubles to the artiste Woland against the thirty-five thousand roubles due to him for seven performances. What is more, here too was Woland's signature to the effect that he had already received the ten thousand!

"What on earth is this?" thought the unhappy Styopa, and his head began to spin. Is this the start of ominous memory lapses?! But it goes without saying that after the contract had been produced, further expressions of surprise would have been simply improper. Styopa asked permission of his guest to absent himself for a moment, and just as he was, in his socks, he ran to the telephone in the hall. On the way he shouted in the direction of the kitchen:

"Grunya!"

But no one responded. At this point he glanced at the door of Berlioz's study, which was next to the hall, and at this point he became, as they say, rooted to the spot. On the door handle he could make out the most enormous wax seal on a string.* "Hello!" somebody roared inside Styopa's head. "That's all I need!" And at this point Styopa's thoughts started running along what was now a double track, but, as is always the way during a catastrophe, in just the one direction and, all in all, the devil knows where. It is difficult even to convey the muddle inside Styopa's head. There was this devilish business with the black beret, the cold vodka and the incredible contract – and now, to add to all that, if you please, a seal on the door! That is to say, tell anyone you like that Berlioz had done something wrong, and he wouldn't believe it, honest to God, he would not believe it! And yet the seal, there it is! Yes, sir... Yes indeed...

And at this point there began to stir in Styopa's brain some most unpleasant little thoughts about an article which, as ill luck would have it, he had recently forced upon Mikhail Alexandrovich to be printed in his journal. An idiotic article too, between ourselves! Pointless, and the money wasn't much...

Following immediately upon the recollection of the article, the recollection came flying in of some dubious conversation that had taken place, as he recalled, on the twenty-fourth of April, in the evening, right here, in the dining room, while Styopa had been having dinner with Mikhail Alexandrovich. That is to say, of course, in the full sense of the word this conversation could not have been called dubious (Styopa would not have entered into such a conversation), but it had been a conversation on some needless subject. They could perfectly freely not have embarked upon it at all, Citizens. Before the seal, there is no doubt, that conversation could have been considered utterly trifling, but now, after the seal...

"Oh, Berlioz, Berlioz!" it came boiling up in Styopa's head. "I just can't believe it!"

But this was not the occasion to spend a long time grieving, and Styopa dialled the office number of The Variety's Financial Director, Rimsky. Styopa's position was a ticklish one: firstly, the foreigner might be offended by Styopa checking up on him after the contract had been shown, and talking to the Financial Director was extremely difficult too. After all, you really wouldn't just ask him like this: "Tell me, did I draw up a contract with a Professor of Black Magic for thirty-five thousand roubles yesterday?" It wouldn't do to ask like that!

"Yes!" Rimsky's abrupt, unpleasant voice was heard in the receiver.

"Hello, Grigory Danilovich," Styopa began quietly, "it's Likhodeyev. Why I'm ringing is... hm... hm... I've got this... er... artiste Woland here with me... The thing is... I wanted to ask how things were with regard to this evening?"

"Ah, the black magician?" Rimsky responded in the receiver. "The playbills will be here at any moment."

"Aha," said Styopa in a weak voice, "see you, then..."

"Will you be here soon?" asked Rimsky.

"In half an hour," replied Styopa and, hanging up, squeezed his hot head in his hands. Oh, what a nasty business this was developing into! Whatever was the matter with his memory, Citizens? Eh?

However, it was awkward to delay in the hall any longer, and Styopa drew up a plan on the spot: use all possible means to conceal his unbelievable forgetfulness, and now, first and foremost, slyly enquire of the foreigner what he was actually intending to do in his show at The Variety, the theatre entrusted to Styopa.

At this point Styopa turned away from the telephone, and in the mirror located in the hall, which the lazy Grunya had not wiped for a long time, he distinctly saw a strange sort of character – lanky as a lath and wearing a pince-nez (ah, if only Ivan Nikolayevich had been there! He would have recognized this character straight away!) But his reflection was there, and then immediately vanished. In alarm, Styopa looked a little deeper into the hall, and he was rocked for a second time, for there in the mirror the most strapping black cat passed by, then vanished too.

Styopa's heart missed a beat, he reeled.

"What on earth is going on?" he thought. "I'm not losing my mind, am I? Where are these reflections coming from?" He looked into the hall and cried out in fright:

"Grunya! What's this cat we've got wandering around? Where's it from? And someone else too?!"

"Don't worry, Stepan Bogdanovich," answered a voice, only not Grunya's, but the guest's from the bedroom. "The cat is mine. Don't fret. And Grunya's not here, I sent her off to Voronezh. She was complaining that you'd not given her any leave for a long time now."

These words were so unexpected and absurd that Styopa decided he had misheard. In utter confusion he trotted to the bedroom and froze on the threshold. His hair stirred, and on his forehead there appeared a sprinkling of tiny drops of sweat.

The guest was no longer alone in the bedroom, but in company. In the second armchair sat that same fellow who had been seen dimly in the hall. Now he was clearly visible: a feathery moustache, one lens of the pince-nez gleaming, and the other lens missing. But there proved to be even worse in the bedroom: on the jeweller's wife's pouffe there lounged in a free-and-easy pose a third someone – namely, a black cat of awesome dimensions with a shot glass of vodka in one paw and a fork, on which he had managed to spear a pickled mushroom, in the other.

The light, weak in the bedroom as it was, began to fade completely in Styopa's eyes. "So it turns out that this is how you go mad!" he thought, and grabbed hold of the doorpost.

"I see you're a little surprised, dearest Stepan Bogdanovich?" enquired Woland of Styopa, whose teeth were chattering. "And yet there's nothing to be surprised about. This is my suite."

At this point the cat drank the vodka, and Styopa's hand slipped down the doorpost.

"And the suite needs room," continued Woland, "so there's one too many of us here in the apartment. And it seems to me that the one too many... is specifically you!"

"Them, them!" the lanky one in checks began bleating like a goat, talking about Styopa in the plural. "Generally they've been acting like dreadful pigs of late. Drinking heavily, using their position to form liaisons with women, doing damn all – well, they can't actually do anything, because they don't understand a thing about what they're charged to do. Pulling the wool over their superiors' eyes!"

"He misuses an official car!" the cat snitched on him, chewing a mushroom.

And at this point a fourth and final coming took place in the apartment, while Styopa, who had by now slipped down completely onto the floor, was scratching at the doorpost with a weakened hand.

Straight from the mirror of the cheval glass there emerged a small but unusually broad-shouldered man with a bowler hat on his head and, sticking out of his mouth, a fang, which disfigured a physiognomy that was already of unprecedented loathsomeness. And with fiery red hair besides.

"I," this newcomer entered into the conversation, "don't understand at all how he came to be a director," the red-headed man's voice became more and more nasal, "he's as much a director as I'm an archbishop!"

"You're nothing like an archbishop, Azazello," remarked the cat, putting some sausages on his plate.

"That's what I'm saying," said the red-headed man nasally, and, turning to Woland, added deferentially: "Will you allow us, Messire,* to damn well chuck him out of Moscow?"

"Shoo!" the cat suddenly roared, with his fur standing on end.

And then the bedroom began spinning around Styopa, and he struck his head on the doorpost, and, as he lost consciousness, he thought: "I'm dying..."

But he did not die. Opening his eyes a little, he saw himself sitting on something made of stone. There was something making a noise all around him. When he opened his eyes up properly, he realized it was the sea making the noise and, even more than that – the waves were rising and falling right at his feet; in short, he was sitting at the very end of a mole, above him was the glittering blue sky, and behind, a white town in the mountains.

Not knowing how people behave in such situations, Styopa rose on shaky legs and set off down the mole towards the shore.

On the mole stood some man or other, smoking and spitting into the sea. He looked at Styopa wild-eyed, and stopped spitting.

Then Styopa came out with the following trick: he knelt down before the unknown smoker and uttered:

"Tell me, I beg you, what is this town?"

"Well, really!" said the heartless smoker.

"I'm not drunk," replied Styopa hoarsely, "something's happened to me... I'm ill... Where am I? What town is it?"

"Well, it's Yalta..."

Styopa sighed quietly, toppled onto his side and struck his head on the warm stone of the mole. Consciousness left him.

8

The Duel between Professor and Poet

JUST AT THE TIME WHEN CONSCIOUSNESS left Styopa in Yalta, that is, at about eleven thirty in the morning, it returned to Ivan Nikolayevich Bezdomny, who woke after a deep and prolonged sleep. It took him some time to grasp how it was he had ended up in an unknown room with white walls, with an astonishing bedside table made of some sort of bright metal, and with a white blind, behind which he could sense the sun.

Ivan gave his head a shake, satisfied himself it did not ache, and remembered he was in a clinic. This thought pulled along with it the memory of Berlioz's death, but today it did not elicit any great shock in Ivan. After a good night's sleep, Ivan Nikolayevich had become a little calmer and begun thinking more clearly. Having lain motionless for some time in the cleanest of soft and comfortable sprung beds, Ivan saw a call button next to him. Out of a habit of touching objects needlessly, he pressed it. He expected some sort of ringing to follow the pressing of the button, or someone to arrive, but what happened was something else entirely.

At the foot of Ivan's bed, a matt cylinder on which was written "Drink" lit up. After standing still for some time, the cylinder began to turn until the inscription "Nurse" appeared. It goes without saying that the ingenious cylinder amazed Ivan. The inscription "Nurse" was replaced by the inscription "Call doctor".

"Hm," said Ivan, not knowing what to do next with this cylinder. But at this point by chance he had some luck: Ivan pressed the button a second time on the words "Medical attendant". The cylinder gave a quiet ring in response, it stopped, the light went out, and into the room came a plump, nice-looking woman in a clean white coat who said to Ivan:

"Good morning!"

Ivan did not reply, for he considered this greeting inappropriate in the circumstances. Indeed, they had confined a healthy man in a clinic, and were pretending, what's more, that that was the way things ought to be!

But in the meantime, without losing her good-humoured expression, the woman, with the aid of a single touch of a button, had drawn up the blind, and sunlight poured into the room through a light and wide-meshed grille that reached right down to the floor. Beyond the grille was revealed a balcony, beyond that was the bank of a winding river, and on its other bank – a cheerful pine wood.

"Come and take a bath," the woman invited him, and under her hands an inner wall opened up, behind which there proved to be a bathing area and a splendidly equipped lavatory.

Although he had decided not to talk to the woman, Ivan could not restrain himself and, seeing a broad stream of water gushing from a shining tap into a bath, he said with irony:

"Just look at that! Like in The Metropole!"

"Oh no," replied the woman with pride, "much better. Such equipment isn't to be found anywhere, not even abroad. Scientists and doctors come here specially to see our clinic. We have foreign tourists here every day."

At the words "foreign tourists" the consultant of the previous day immediately came to Ivan's mind. Ivan became gloomy, and looking out from under his brows he said:

"Foreign tourists... How you all adore foreign tourists! Yet you come across all sorts among them, you know. I met just such a one yesterday, for example, and it was really something to see!"

And he was on the point of telling her about Pontius Pilate, but he contained himself, realizing these stories were nothing to this woman, and she could not help him anyway.

The washed Ivan Nikolayevich was straight away given absolutely everything a man requires after a bath: an ironed vest, long johns, socks. But that was not the end of it; opening the door of a little cupboard, the woman pointed inside it and asked:

"What would you like to put on – a dressing gown or pyjamas?"

Assigned to his new quarters by force, Ivan all but wrung his hands at the woman's familiarity, and jabbed a finger in silence at the crimson flannelette pyjamas.

After this, Ivan Nikolayevich was led along an empty and soundless corridor and brought into a consulting room of the most enormous dimensions. Having decided to treat everything there was in this wonderfully equipped building with irony, there and then Ivan mentally christened the consulting room "the factory-kitchen".

And with good reason. Here stood cupboards and glass cabinets with shining nickel-plated instruments. There were chairs of extraordinarily complex construction, bulbous lamps with radiant shades, a multitude of phials and gas burners, and electric wires, and appliances that were completely unknown to anyone.

Three people set to work on Ivan in the consulting room – two women and one man, all wearing white. First and foremost they led Ivan away into a corner behind a table, with the clear aim of finding something out from him.

Ivan started thinking the situation over. Before him were three paths. The first was extremely tempting: to launch himself at these lamps and intricate bits and pieces and smash up the damn lot of them, and thus express his protest at being detained for nothing. But today's Ivan already differed significantly from the Ivan of the day before, and the first path seemed to him dubious: who knows, they might be confirmed in the notion that he was a violent madman. The first path Ivan therefore renounced. There was a second: to begin at once the narrative about the consultant and Pontius Pilate. However, the experience of the previous day showed that this tale was not believed, or was somehow understood in a distorted way. Ivan therefore rejected that path too, deciding to choose the third: to retreat into proud silence.

He did not manage to realize this completely, being obliged to reply, like it or not, albeit both sparingly and gloomily, to a whole series of questions. And Ivan was asked about absolutely everything regarding his past life, right down to when and how he had been ill with scarlet fever some fifteen years before. When a whole page had been covered in writing down what Ivan had said, it was turned over, and a woman in white moved on to questions about Ivan's relatives. A long drawn-out sort of procedure began: who had died, when and of what, did they drink, did they have venereal disease, and everything of that kind. In conclusion they asked him to tell them about the occurrence of the previous day at Patriarch's Ponds, but they were very unexacting, and were not surprised by the information about Pontius Pilate.

At this point the woman gave Ivan up to the man, and the latter set about him in a different way, no longer asking questions about anything. He took Ivan's body temperature, measured his pulse, and looked into Ivan's eyes while shining some sort of lamp into them. Then the second woman came to help the man, and they pricked something, but not painfully, into Ivan's back, they drew signs of some sort on the skin of his chest with the handle of a hammer, they hit him on the knees with hammers, which made Ivan's legs jerk, they pricked his finger and took blood from it, they pricked him in the bend of his elbow, they put rubber bracelets of some kind on his arms...

Ivan merely grinned bitterly to himself and reflected on how stupidly and strangely it had all turned out. Just think! He had wanted to warn everyone of the danger threatened by the unknown consultant, had meant to catch him, but all he had achieved was ending up in some mysterious consulting room for the purpose of recounting all sorts of rubbish about Uncle Fyodor in Vologda being a binge-drinker. Insufferably stupid!

Finally they let Ivan go. He was accompanied back to his room, where he was given a cup of coffee, two soft-boiled eggs and some white bread and butter.

Having eaten and drunk all he had been offered, Ivan decided to wait for someone of seniority in this establishment, and then to secure from this person of seniority both some attention for himself, and justice.

And his wait for this person came to an end, very soon after his breakfast too. The door of Ivan's room opened unexpectedly, and into it came a host of people in white coats. Ahead of them all walked a man of about forty-five, carefully shaved like an actor, with pleasant, but very piercing eyes and polite manners. His entire suite was rendering him signs of attention and respect, and his entrance therefore had a very ceremonial effect. "Like Pontius Pilate!" it occurred to Ivan.

Yes, this was undoubtedly the senior man. He sat down on a stool, while everyone else remained standing.

"Dr Stravinsky," the man who had sat down introduced himself to Ivan, and gave him an amicable look.

"Here, Alexander Nikolayevich," said someone with a neat little beard in a low voice, and handed the senior man Ivan's sheet of paper, completely covered in writing.

"They've cobbled together a whole case!" thought Ivan. And the senior man ran his practised eyes over the sheet, muttered: "Aha, aha..." and exchanged a few phrases in a little-known language with his entourage.

"And he speaks in Latin, like Pilate..." thought Ivan sadly. Just then one word made him start, and it was the word "schizophrenia", already uttered, alas, on the previous day by the accursed foreigner at Patriarch's Ponds, and repeated here today by Professor Stravinsky.

"And he knew that too!" thought Ivan in alarm.

The senior man had evidently made it a rule to agree with everything and be pleased at everything his entourage might say to him, and to express this with the words "super, super..."

"Super!" said Stravinsky, returning the sheet to somebody, and he turned to Ivan: "You're a poet?"

"I am," Ivan replied gloomily, and for the first time suddenly felt an inexplicable kind of revulsion for poetry, and what came to mind straight away of his own verse seemed for some reason unpleasant.

Wrinkling up his face, he in his turn asked Stravinsky:

"Are you a professor?"

To this Stravinsky inclined his head with obliging courtesy.

"And are you the senior man here?" continued Ivan.

Stravinsky bowed to this too.

"I need to talk to you," said Ivan Nikolayevich meaningfully.

"That's what I'm here for," responded Stravinsky.

"The thing is this," began Ivan, sensing that his moment had come, "they've dressed me up as a madman and no one wants to listen to me!"

"Oh no, we'll hear you out very attentively," said Stravinsky seriously and reassuringly, "and on no account will we allow you to be dressed up as a madman."

"Well, listen then: yesterday evening at Patriarch's Ponds I met a mysterious person, possibly a foreigner, who knew in advance about Berlioz's death and had personally seen Pontius Pilate."

The suite listened to the poet in silence and without stirring.

"Pilate? Pilate, that's the one who was alive at the time of Jesus Christ?" asked Stravinsky, squinting at Ivan.

"The very same."

"Aha," said Stravinsky, "and this Berlioz died under a tram?"

"And he was the very one that was killed by a tram in front of me yesterday at Patriarch's, what's more, this same enigmatic citizen..."

"Pontius Pilate's acquaintance?" asked Stravinsky, who was evidently notable for his great insight.

"Precisely," Ivan confirmed, studying Stravinsky, "so he'd said in advance that Annushka had spilt the sunflower oil... And he did slip on exactly that spot! How do you like that?" enquired Ivan meaningfully, hoping to create a great effect with his words.

But that effect did not ensue, and Stravinsky very simply asked the next question:

"And who's this Annushka, then?"

This question rather upset Ivan and he pulled a face.

"Annushka is utterly unimportant here," he said fretfully, "the devil knows who she is. Simply some idiot from Sadovaya. The important thing is that he knew in advance – do you understand – in advance, about the sunflower oil! Do you understand me?"

"I understand perfectly," replied Stravinsky seriously and, touching the poet's knee, he added: "Don't get agitated, carry on."

"I shall," said Ivan, trying to hit the same note as Stravinsky, and already aware from bitter experience that calmness alone would help him, "and so this terrible character, and he's lying about being a consultant, possesses some sort of extraordinary power... For example, you chase after him, but there's no chance of catching up with him. And there's another pair with him, and they're fine ones too, but in their own ways: some lanky man in broken glasses and, on top of that, a tomcat of unbelievable size that can ride on a tram all by itself. On top of that," uninterrupted, Ivan spoke with ever greater ardour and conviction, "he personally was on Pontius Pilate's balcony, there's no doubt whatsoever of that. I mean, what on earth is going on? Eh? He needs to be arrested immediately, otherwise he'll bring about indescribable calamities."

"And so what you're doing is trying to have him arrested? Have I understood you correctly?" asked Stravinsky.

"He's clever," thought Ivan, "you've got to admit that uncommonly clever people do turn up among intellectuals too. It can't be denied," and he replied:

"Quite correctly! And how could you fail to try, just think for yourself! And in the meantime they've detained me here by force, they poke a lamp in my eye, give me a bath, ask me lots of things about Uncle Fedya!... And he's long gone from the world! I demand to be released immediately!"

"Well then, super, super!" Stravinsky responded. "So everything's been cleared up. Indeed, what point is there in detaining a healthy man in the clinic? Very well. I'll discharge you from here straight away if you'll tell me you're sane. Not prove it, but just tell me. And so, are you sane?"

At this point complete silence fell, and the fat woman who had looked after Ivan in the morning gazed reverentially at the Professor, while Ivan thought once again: "Positively clever."

He liked the Professor's proposition very much, but before answering, he thought long and hard, wrinkling his brow, and finally said firmly:

"I am sane."

"Well, that's super then," exclaimed Stravinsky in relief, "and if that's the case, let's do some logical reasoning. Let's take the day you spent yesterday," here he turned and was immediately handed Ivan's sheet of paper. "In the search for the unknown man who introduced himself to you as an acquaintance of Pontius Pilate you yesterday performed the following actions," here Stravinsky began unfolding his long fingers, looking now at the paper, now at Ivan, "you hung an icon on your chest. Yes?"

"Yes," Ivan agreed gloomily.

"You fell off a fence, injured your face. Right? Turned up at a restaurant with a lighted candle in your hand in nothing but your underwear, and in the restaurant you hit someone. You were brought here tied up. Finding yourself here, you telephoned the police and asked them to send machine guns. Then you made an attempt to throw yourself out of a window. Right? Is it possible, one asks, acting in this way, to catch or arrest anyone? And if you are a sane person, you will yourself reply: certainly not. You wish to leave here? Please do. But permit me to ask you where you will head for?"

"A police station, of course," replied Ivan, no longer so firmly, and becoming a little confused under the Professor's gaze.

"Directly from here?"

"Aha."

"And you won't drop by your apartment?" Stravinsky asked quickly.

"There's no time to drop by now! While I'm going round apartments, he'll slip away!"

"Right. And what will you say first of all at the police station?"

"About Pontius Pilate," replied Ivan Nikolayevich, and a murky haze clouded his eyes.

"Well, that's super then!" exclaimed Stravinsky, quite won over, and, turning to the man with the little beard, he ordered: "Fyodor Vasily-evich, please discharge Citizen Bezdomny into town. But keep this room unoccupied, and there's no need to change the bedclothes. Citizen Bez-domny will be back here in two hours' time. Well, then," he addressed the poet, "I shan't wish you success, because I don't believe in that success one iota. See you soon!" And he got up, and his suite stirred.

"On what grounds will I be back here?" asked Ivan in alarm.

As if he had been expecting the question, Stravinsky sat down immediately and began:

"On the grounds that as soon as you appear at a police station in your long johns and say you've met a man who personally knew Pontius Pilate, you'll be brought here instantly, and again you'll find yourself in this very same room."

"What have long johns got to do with it?" asked Ivan, looking around in dismay.

"It's mainly Pontius Pilate. But it's the long johns too. After all, we'll take the institution's linen off you and issue you with your own attire. And you were delivered to us wearing long johns. And in the meantime you weren't intending to stop by at your apartment at all, although I even dropped you a hint about it. Next will come Pilate... and that's your lot!"

At this point something strange happened to Ivan Nikolayevich. It was as if his will had broken, and he felt that he was weak, that he needed advice.

"So what's to be done?" he asked, only this time timidly.

"Well, that's super then!" responded Stravinsky. "That's a most reasonable question. Now I'll tell you what's actually happened to you. Yesterday somebody very much frightened and upset you with a story about Pontius Pilate and with some other things. And then, over-fretful and overstrained, you went around town talking about Pontius Pilate. It's perfectly natural that you're taken for a madman. Your salvation now lies in one thing alone – complete peace. And it's absolutely essential you remain here."

"But he must be caught!" exclaimed Ivan, now imploringly.

"Very well, but why run around yourself? Set out on paper all your suspicions and accusations against this man. Nothing could be simpler than to send your statement on to where it needs to go, and if, as you suppose, we're dealing with a criminal, it will all be cleared up very soon. But just one condition: don't strain your head, and try not to think about Pontius Pilate too much. People can go around telling all sorts of stories! But you don't have to believe everything!"

"Got it!" declared Ivan decisively. "Please issue me with a pen and paper."

"Issue paper and a short pencil," Stravinsky ordered the fat woman, but to Ivan he said: "Only I don't advise you to write today."

"No, no, today, it's got to be today," Ivan cried anxiously.

"Well, all right. Only don't strain your brain. If it doesn't come out right today, it will tomorrow."

"He'll get away!"

"Oh no," retorted Stravinsky confidently, "he won't get away anywhere, I guarantee it. And remember that here you'll be helped by every means, but without that help nothing will come out right for you. Do you hear me?" Stravinsky asked meaningfully all of a sudden, and seized both of Ivan Nikolayevich's hands. Taking them in his own and staring straight into Ivan's eyes, for a long time he repeated: "You'll be helped here... do you hear me?... You'll be helped here... You'll get relief. It's quiet here, everything's peaceful... You'll be helped here..."

Ivan Nikolayevich unexpectedly yawned, his facial expression softened.

"Yes, yes," he said quietly.

"Well, that's super then!" Stravinsky concluded the conversation in his customary way and rose. "Goodbye!" he shook Ivan's hand and, already on his way out, turned to the man with the little beard and said: "Yes, and try oxygen... and baths."

A few moments later neither Stravinsky nor his suite was in front of Ivan. Beyond the grille at the window, in the midday sun, the joyous and vernal wood stood out vividly on the far bank, while a little closer the river was glistening.

9

Korovyev's Tricks

NIKANOR IVANOVICH BOSOI, Chairman of the Housing Association of No. 302 *bis* on Sadovaya Street in Moscow, where the late Berlioz had been resident, had been having the most dreadfully busy time, starting from the previous night, Wednesday to Thursday.

At midnight, as we already know, the commission of which Zheldybin was a part came to the building, summoned Nikanor Ivanovich, informed him of Berlioz's death, and set off with him for apartment No. 50.

There the sealing of the dead man's manuscripts and property was carried out. Neither Grunya, the maid, who lived out, nor the frivolous Stepan Bogdanovich was in the apartment at that time. The commission announced to Nikanor Ivanovich that it would take the dead man's manuscripts away for sorting, that his living space, that is, three rooms (the jeweller's wife's former study, living room and dining room), was to pass into the hands of the Housing Association, and that his property was subject to storage in the space referred to pending the announcement of the heirs.

The news of Berlioz's death spread throughout the entire building with a sort of supernatural speed, and from seven o'clock in the morning of the Thursday, people began ringing Bosoi on the telephone and then also appearing in person with statements containing claims to the dead man's living space. And in the course of two hours Nikanor Ivanovich received thirty-two such statements.

In them were included entreaties, threats, slanders, denunciations, promises to carry out refurbishment at people's own expense, references to unbearably crowded conditions and the impossibility of living in the same apartment as villains. Among other things there was a description, stunning in its artistic power, of the theft of some ravioli, which had been stuffed directly into a jacket pocket, in apartment No. 31, two vows to commit suicide and one confession to a secret pregnancy.

People called Nikanor Ivanovich out into the hallway of his apartment, took him by the sleeve, whispered things to him, winked and promised not to remain indebted to him.

This torment continued until just after midday, when Nikanor Ivanovich simply fled from his apartment to the House Committee's office by the gates, but when he saw they were lying in wait for him there too, he ran away from there as well. Having somehow beaten off those who followed on his heels across the asphalted courtyard, Nikanor Ivanovich gave them the slip in entrance No. 6 and went up to the fourth floor, which was where this damned apartment No. 50 was located.

After recovering his breath on the landing, the corpulent Nikanor Ivanovich rang the bell, but nobody opened the door to him. He rang again and then again, and started grumbling and quietly cursing. But even then nobody opened up. Nikanor Ivanovich's patience cracked, and, taking from his pocket a bunch of duplicate keys that belonged to the House Committee, he opened the door with his masterful hand and went in.

"Hey, housemaid!" shouted Nikanor Ivanovich in the semi-darkness of the hallway. "What's your name? Grunya, is it? Are you here?"

No one responded.

Then Nikanor Ivanovich got a folding measuring rod from his briefcase, after that, freed the study door from its seal, and took a stride into the study. Take a stride he certainly did, but he stopped in astonishment in the doorway and even gave a start.

At the dead man's desk sat an unknown man, a skinny, lanky citizen in a little checked jacket, a jockey's cap and a pince-nez... well, in short, him.

"Who would you be, Citizen?" asked Nikanor Ivanovich in fright.

"Well I never! Nikanor Ivanovich!" yelled the unexpected citizen in a jangling tenor, and, leaping up, he greeted the Chairman with a forcible and sudden handshake. This greeting did not gladden Nikanor Ivanovich in the slightest.

"I'm sorry," he began suspiciously, "who would you be? Are you someone official?"

"Oh dear, Nikanor Ivanovich!" exclaimed the unknown man earnestly. "What is someone official or someone unofficial? It all depends on the point of view you look at the matter from. It's all variable and conditional, Nikanor Ivanovich. Today I'm someone unofficial, but tomorrow, lo and behold, I'm official! And sometimes it's the other way around, and how!"

This disquisition did not satisfy the Chairman of the House Committee in the slightest. Being by nature a suspicious man generally, he concluded that the citizen expatiating before him was actually someone unofficial, and quite likely had no business being there.

"Just who would you be? What's your name?" asked the Chairman more and more sternly, and he even began advancing on the unknown man.

"My name," responded the citizen, quite undismayed by the sternness, "is, well, let's say Korovyev. Would you like a bite to eat, Nikanor Ivanovich? No standing on ceremony! Eh?"

"I'm sorry," began the now indignant Nikanor Ivanovich, "what talk can there be of food!" (It must be admitted, unpleasant as it might be, that Nikanor Ivanovich was by nature somewhat on the rude side.)

"Sitting in a dead man's rooms isn't allowed! What are you doing here?"

"Won't you take a seat, Nikanor Ivanovich," yelled the citizen, completely unabashed, and began fussing around, offering the Chairman an armchair.

In an absolute fury, Nikanor Ivanovich refused the armchair and shrieked:

"Just who are you?"

"I am acting, don't you know, as interpreter to a foreign personage who has his residence in this apartment," the man who had called himself Korovyev introduced himself, and he clicked the heel of his unpolished, ginger-coloured boot.

Nikanor Ivanovich let his jaw drop. The presence in this apartment of some sort of foreigner, with an interpreter besides, was the most complete surprise for him, and he demanded explanations.

The interpreter explained willingly. The foreign artiste, Mr Woland, had been kindly invited by the Director of The Variety, Stepan Bogdanovich Likhodeyev, to spend the period of his engagement, approximately a week, in his apartment, about which he had already written to Nikanor Ivanovich the day before, with a request to arrange temporary registration for the foreigner while Likhodeyev himself went away to Yalta.

"He hasn't written anything to me," said the Chairman in amazement.

"You have a rummage around in your briefcase, Nikanor Ivanovich," suggested Korovyev sweetly.

Shrugging his shoulders, Nikanor Ivanovich opened his briefcase and inside it discovered Likhodeyev's letter.

"How can I possibly have forgotten about it?" mumbled Nikanor Ivanovich, gazing obtusely at the opened envelope.

"These things happen, these things happen, Nikanor Ivanovich!" Korovyev began jabbering. "Absent-mindedness, absent-mindedness, and exhaustion, and high blood pressure, Nikanor Ivanovich, dear friend of ours! I'm dreadfully absent-minded myself. I'll tell you a few facts from my biography over a glass sometime, you'll die laughing!"

"And when is Likhodeyev going to Yalta?"

"He's already gone, he's gone!" cried the interpreter. "He's already on his way, you know! He's already the devil knows where!" and here the interpreter began waving his arms about like the sails of a wind-mill.

Nikanor Ivanovich declared it was essential for him to see the foreigner in person, but to this he got a refusal from the interpreter: quite impossible. Busy. Training the cat.

"The cat I can show you, if you wish," offered Korovyev.

Nikanor Ivanovich refused this in his turn, but the interpreter immediately put to the Chairman an unexpected, yet extremely interesting proposal.

In view of the fact that Mr Woland did not wish to stay in a hotel at any price, and was accustomed to expansive living, would the House Committee not let to him for a week, for the duration of Woland's engagement in Moscow, the whole of the apartment — that is, the rooms of the dead man too?

"After all, it doesn't matter to him, the dead man," whispered Korovyev hoarsely, "this apartment, you must agree, Nikanor Ivanovich, is no use to him now."

Nikanor Ivanovich objected, in something of a quandary, that, well, foreigners were supposed to stay at The Metropole, and certainly not in private apartments...

"I'm telling you, he's as capricious as the devil knows what!" began Korovyev in a whisper. "He just doesn't want to! He doesn't like hotels! I've had them up to here, these foreign tourists!" Korovyev complained intimately, jabbing a finger at his sinewy neck. "Can you believe it, they've worn me out! They come here... and they'll either do a load of spying, like the worst sons of bitches, or else they'll get you down with their caprices: this isn't right, and that isn't right! But for your Association, Nikanor Ivanovich, it'll be entirely beneficial and obviously profitable. And the money won't hold him back." Korovyev looked around, and then whispered in the Chairman's ear: "A millionaire!"

There was clear, practical sense in the interpreter's proposal, the proposal was very sound, but there was something amazingly unsound both in the way the interpreter spoke, and in his clothes, and in that loathsome, utterly useless pince-nez. As a consequence of this there was some vague thing tormenting the Chairman's soul, yet nonetheless he decided to accept the proposal. The fact of the matter is that the Housing Association was, alas, very much in deficit. Oil for the central heating needed to be laid in before the autumn, and where the money was to come from was unclear. But with the foreign tourist's money they could quite likely manage. Still, the businesslike and cautious Nikanor Ivanovich declared that first of all he would have to tie things up with the Foreign Tourist Office.

"I understand!" exclaimed Korovyev. "It's got to be tied up! Without fail! Here's the telephone, Nikanor Ivanovich, you tie things up straight away! And regarding the money, don't be shy," he added in a whisper, drawing the Chairman towards the telephone in the hall, "who on earth are you to take from, if not him? If you could see what a villa he has in Nice! When you go abroad next summer, make a special trip to take a look – you'll be amazed!"

The business with the Foreign Tourist Office was settled over the telephone with an extraordinary speed that staggered the Chairman. It turned out that they already knew there of Mr Woland's intention to stay in Likhodeyev's private apartment, and had not the slightest objection to it.

"Well, marvellous!" yelled Korovyev.

Somewhat battered by his jabbering, the Chairman declared that the Housing Association agreed to let apartment No. 50 to the artiste Woland for a week for a payment of... Nikanor Ivanovich stumbled a little and said:

"For five hundred roubles a day."

At this point Korovyev stunned the Chairman conclusively. With a furtive wink in the direction of the bedroom, from where the soft jumping of a heavy cat could be heard, he croaked:

"So, over a week, that works out as three and a half thousand?"

Nikanor Ivanovich thought he would add on: "Well, that's quite an appetite you have there, Nikanor Ivanovich!" but Korovyev said something else entirely:

"What sort of sum is that? Ask for five, he'll give it."

Smirking in bewilderment, Nikanor Ivanovich himself failed to notice how he came to be at the dead man's desk, where Korovyev, with the greatest speed and dexterity, drew up two copies of a contract. After that he flew into the bedroom with it and returned, whereupon both copies proved already to have been signed with a flourish by the foreigner. The Chairman too signed the contract. Here Korovyev asked for a receipt for five...

"In full, in full, Nikanor Ivanovich!... Thousand roubles..." and with the words, unsuitable somehow for a serious matter, "*Eins, zwei, drei!*"* he laid out five wads of nice new banknotes for the Chairman.

Counting took place, interspersed with Korovyev's little jokes and silly remarks, such as "cash loves to be counted", "your own eye's the best spy", and others of a similar kind.

When he had finished counting the money, the Chairman received the foreigner's passport from Korovyev for the temporary registration, put it, and the contract, and the money away in his briefcase, and, unable to restrain himself somehow, he asked bashfully for a complimentary pass...

"Why of course!" roared Korovyev. "How many tickets do you want, Nikanor Ivanovich, twelve, fifteen?"

The stunned Chairman explained that he only needed a couple of tickets, for himself and Pelageya Antonovna, his wife.

Korovyev immediately whipped out a notepad and dashed off a complimentary pass for two persons in the front row for Nikanor Ivanovich. And with his left hand the interpreter deftly thrust this pass upon Nikanor Ivanovich, while with his right he placed in the Chairman's other hand a thick wad that made a crackling noise. Casting a look at it, Nikanor Ivanovich blushed deeply and began pushing it away.

"That isn't done..." he mumbled.

"I don't even want to hear it," Korovyev started whispering right in his ear, "it's not done here, but it is among foreigners. You'll offend him, Nikanor Ivanovich, and that's awkward. You took the trouble..."

"It's strictly prohibited," whispered the Chairman very, very quietly, and he looked behind him.

"And where are the witnesses?" Korovyev whispered in the other ear. "I'm asking you, where are they? What's the matter?"

It was then, as the Chairman subsequently maintained, that a miracle took place: the wad crawled into his briefcase all by itself. And next, somehow weak and even worn out, the Chairman found himself on the stairs. A whirlwind of thoughts was raging in his head. There, spinning around, were that villa in Nice, and the trained cat, and the thought that there had indeed been no witnesses, and that Pelageya Antonovna would be pleased about the complimentary tickets. They were incoherent thoughts, but, all in all, pleasant ones. And nevertheless, somewhere in the very depths of his soul some sort of needle would prick the Chairman from time to time. This was the needle of disquiet. Apart from that, right there on the stairs the Chairman was struck, as if by a seizure, by the thought: "But how on earth did the interpreter get into the study if there was a seal on the doors?! And how had he, Nikanor Ivanovich, not asked about it?" For some time the Chairman gazed like a lost sheep at the steps of the staircase, but then he decided to give it up as a bad job and not torment himself with such a complicated question...

As soon as the Chairman had left the apartment, a low voice was heard from the bedroom:

"I didn't like that Nikanor Ivanovich. He's a rogue and a cheat. Can something be done so he doesn't come here again?"

"Messire, you only have to give the order!" Korovyev responded from somewhere, only not in a jangling, but in a very clear and sonorous voice.

And straight away the accursed interpreter turned up in the hall, dialled a number there and began speaking for some reason very piteously into the receiver:

"Hello! I consider it my duty to inform you that the Chairman of our Housing Association at No. 302 *bis* on Sadovaya, Nikanor Ivanovich Bosoi, is speculating in foreign currency.* At the present moment in his apartment, No. 35, there's four hundred dollars wrapped in newspaper in the ventilation pipe in the lavatory. This is Timofei Kvastsov speaking, a tenant from apartment No. 11 of the aforesaid building. But I conjure you to keep my name a secret. I fear the revenge of the aforementioned Chairman."

And he hung up, the villain!

What happened thereafter in apartment No. 50 is unknown, but what happened at Nikanor Ivanovich's is known. Locking himself in his lavatory, he pulled the wad thrust upon him by the interpreter from his briefcase and checked that there were four hundred roubles in it. Nikanor Ivanovich wrapped this wad in a scrap of newspaper and stuck it into the ventilation passage.

Five minutes later the Chairman was sitting at the table in his little dining room. His wife brought in from the kitchen a neatly sliced herring, liberally sprinkled with spring onion. Nikanor Ivanovich poured out a wineglassful of vodka, drank it, poured out a second, drank it, caught up three pieces of herring on his fork... and just then there was a ring. But Pelageya Antonovna brought in a steaming saucepan, from a single glance at which it could immediately be guessed that inside it, at the heart of the fiery borscht, was to be found the thing than which there is nothing more delicious in the world – a marrowbone.

Swallowing his saliva, Nikanor Ivanovich started growling like a dog:

"The devil take you! They don't let you have a bite to eat. Don't let anyone in, I'm out, out. Regarding the apartment, tell them to stop hanging around. There'll be a meeting in a week..."

His wife ran into the hall, while Nikanor Ivanovich, with a serving spoon, dragged *it*, the bone, now cracked along its length, out of the fire-spitting lake. And at that moment into the dining room came two citizens, and with them Pelageya Antonovna, for some reason very pale. One glance at the citizens, and Nikanor Ivanovich turned white as well and stood up.

"Where's the loo?" asked the first man, preoccupied, and wearing a traditional white Russian shirt.

Something made a bang on the dining table (Nikanor Ivanovich had dropped the spoon on the oilcloth).

"Here, here," replied Pelageya Antonovna rapidly.

And the callers immediately headed for the corridor.

"But what's the matter?" Nikanor Ivanovich asked quietly, following after the callers. "There can't be anything untoward in our apartment... And your documents... I'm sorry..."

Without stopping, the first man showed Nikanor Ivanovich his document, while at that same moment the second proved to be standing on a stool in the lavatory with his arm stuck into the ventilation passage. Nikanor Ivanovich's eyes grew dim. The newspaper was removed, but in the wad there turned out to be not roubles, but some unknown money, maybe blue, maybe green, and with pictures of some old man. Nikanor Ivanovich made it all out only vaguely, however, as he had spots of some sort swimming before his eyes.

"Dollars in the ventilation," the first man said pensively, and asked Nikanor Ivanovich gently and politely: "Your little package?"

"No!" replied Nikanor Ivanovich in a terrible voice. "Planted by enemies!"

"It happens," he, the first one, agreed, and, once again gently, he added: "Well then, you must hand in the rest."

"I haven't got any! I haven't, I swear to God, I've never had them in my hands!" exclaimed the Chairman despairingly.

He rushed to the chest of drawers, pulled out a drawer with a crash, and from it his briefcase, exclaiming incoherently as he did so:

"Here's the contract… that snake of an interpreter planted them… Korovyev… in the pince-nez!"

He opened the briefcase, looked into it, stuck his hand into it, turned blue in the face and dropped the briefcase into the borscht. There was nothing in the briefcase: neither Styopa's letter, nor the contract, nor the foreigner's passport, nor the money, nor the complimentary pass. In short, nothing except a folding measuring rod.

"Comrades!" cried the Chairman in a frenzy. "Arrest them! We've got unclean spirits in our building!"

And then at that point Pelageya Antonovna imagined who knows what, only she clasped her hands together and exclaimed:

"Confess, Ivanych! You'll get a reduction!"

With bloodshot eyes, Nikanor Ivanovich brought his fists up above his wife's head, wheezing:

"Ooh, you damned fool!"

At this point he grew weak and dropped onto a chair, evidently deciding to submit to the inevitable.

At the same time, on the staircase landing, Timofei Kondratyevich Kvastsov was pressing first his ear, then his eye to the keyhole of the door of the Chairman's apartment, wracked with curiosity.

Five minutes later, the residents of the building who were in the courtyard saw the Chairman, accompanied by two other persons, proceeding straight towards the gates of the building. They said Nikanor Ivanovich looked awful, that he was staggering like a drunken man as he passed by, and was muttering something.

And another hour later, an unknown citizen came to apartment No. 11, at the very time when Timofei Kondratyevich was panting with pleasure as he told some other residents how the Chairman had been swept away; he beckoned with his finger for Timofei Kondratyevich to come out of the kitchen into the hall, said something to him, and together they disappeared.

10

News from Yalta

AT THE TIME MISFORTUNE OVERTOOK Nikanor Ivanovich, in the office of the Financial Director of The Variety, Rimsky, not far from No. 302 *bis* and on that same Sadovaya Street, there were two men: Rimsky himself, and The Variety's manager, Varenukha.

The large office on the first floor of the theatre looked out onto Sadovaya from two windows, and from another, right behind the back of the Financial Director, who was sitting at the desk, into The Variety's summer garden, where there were refreshment bars, a shooting gallery and an open-air stage. The office's furnishing, besides the desk, consisted of a bundle of old playbills hanging on the wall, a small table with a carafe of water, four armchairs, and a stand in a corner on which there stood an ancient dust-covered model of some revue. Well, and it goes without saying that apart from all that, there was in the office a battered, peeling, fireproof safe of small size, to Rimsky's left-hand side, next to the desk.

Rimsky, sitting at the desk, had been in a bad frame of mind since first thing in the morning, while Varenukha, in contrast, had been very animated and active in a somehow especially restless way. Yet at the same time there had been no outlet for his energy.

Varenukha was now hiding in the Financial Director's office from the holders of complimentary passes who poisoned his life, particularly on days when the programme changed. And today was just such a day.

As soon as the telephone started ringing, Varenukha would pick up the receiver and lie into it:

"Who? Varenukha? He's not here. He's left the theatre."

"Will you please ring Likhodeyev again," said Rimsky irritably.

"But he isn't at home. I sent Karpov earlier. There's nobody at the apartment."

"The devil knows what's going on," hissed Rimsky, clicking away on the calculating machine.

The door opened, and an usher dragged in a thick bundle of newly printed additional playbills. On the green sheets in large red letters was printed:

TODAY AND EVERY DAY
AT THE VARIETY THEATRE
AN ADDITION TO THE PROGRAMME

PROFESSOR WOLAND

PERFORMANCES OF BLACK MAGIC
WITH ITS COMPLETE EXPOSURE

Stepping back from the playbill he had thrown over the model, Varenukha admired it for a moment and ordered the usher to have all copies pasted up immediately.

"It's good, garish," remarked Varenukha after the usher's departure.

"Well I find this undertaking displeasing in the extreme," grumbled Rimsky, casting malicious looks at the playbill through horn-rimmed spectacles, "and I'm surprised generally at how he's been allowed to put it on!"

"No, Grigory Danilovich, you can't say that, it's a very astute step. The whole point here is the exposure."

"I don't know, I don't know, there's no point here at all, and he'll always go thinking up something of the sort! He could at least have shown us this magician. You, have you seen him? Where he dug him up from the devil only knows!"

It transpired that Varenukha, just like Rimsky, had not seen the magician. The day before, Styopa had come running ("like a madman" in Rimsky's expression) to the Financial Director with a draft agreement already written, had ordered him there and then to copy it out and to issue the money. And this magician had cleared off, and nobody had seen him except Styopa himself.

Rimsky took out his watch, saw that it said five past two, and flew into an absolute fury. Really! Likhodeyev had rung at about eleven o'clock, said he would be arriving in half an hour, and not only had he not arrived, he had also vanished from his apartment!

"All my work's being held up!" Rimsky was now growling, jabbing his finger at a heap of unsigned papers.

"He hasn't fallen under a tram, like Berlioz, has he?" said Varenukha, holding up to his ear a receiver in which ringing tones could be heard, rich, prolonged and completely hopeless.

"That would be a good thing, actually..." said Rimsky, scarcely audibly through his teeth.

At that very moment a woman came into the office wearing a uniform jacket, peaked cap, a black skirt and soft shoes. From a small bag on her belt the woman took a little white square and a notebook and asked:

"Where's Variety? Super-lightning for you. Signature."

Varenukha dashed off some sort of squiggle in the woman's notebook and, as soon as the door had slammed behind her, he opened up the little square.

Having read the telegram, he blinked his eyes a bit and passed the little square to Rimsky.

Printed in the telegram was the following: "Yalta. Moscow. Variety. Today half eleven appeared CID nightshirted trousered bootless mental brunet claimed Likhodeyev Director Variety. Lightning-wire Yalta CID whereabouts Director Likhodeyev."

"Well I never!" exclaimed Rimsky, and added: "Another surprise!"

"A False Dmitry,"* Varenukha said, and began speaking into the mouthpiece of the telephone: "Telegraph Office? The Variety's account. Take a super-lightning... Are you listening?... 'Yalta CID... Director Likhodeyev Moscow. Financial Director Rimsky'..."

Regardless of the communication about the impostor in Yalta, Varenukha once more set about hunting for Styopa on the telephone anywhere and everywhere, and naturally could find him nowhere.

At the precise time when Varenukha, holding the receiver in his hand, was pondering over where else he might phone, that same woman who had also brought the first lightning telegram came in and handed Varenukha a new little envelope. Opening it hurriedly, Varenukha read through what had been printed and then whistled.

"What else?" asked Rimsky with a nervous jerk.

Varenukha handed him the telegram in silence, and the Financial Director saw in it the words: "Implore believe. Cast Yalta by hypnosis Woland. Lightning-wire CID confirmation identity. Likhodeyev".

Rimsky and Varenukha reread the telegram with their heads touching, and when they had reread it, they started staring at one another in silence.

"Citizens!" the woman suddenly grew angry. "Sign for it, and then you can be silent for as long as you like! It's lightning telegrams I'm delivering, you know."

Without taking his eyes off the telegram, Varenukha dashed off a wonky signature in the notebook and the woman disappeared.

"But you were talking to him on the telephone just after eleven?" began the manager in complete bewilderment.

"It's a ridiculous idea!" cried Rimsky stridently. "Whether I was talking to him or not, he cannot be in Yalta now! It's ridiculous!"

"He's drunk…" said Varenukha.

"Who's drunk?" asked Rimsky, and again they both started staring at one another.

Some impostor or madman was sending telegrams from Yalta, of that there was no doubt. But this is what was strange: how ever did the joker in Yalta know Woland, who had arrived in Moscow only yesterday? How did he know about the link between Likhodeyev and Woland?

"'Hypnosis…'" Varenukha repeated a word from the telegram. "How on earth does he know about Woland?" He blinked his eyes a bit and suddenly exclaimed decisively. "No, nonsense, nonsense, nonsense!"

"Where's he staying, this Woland, damn him?" asked Rimsky.

Varenukha got through to the Foreign Tourist Office without delay, and to Rimsky's utter amazement, announced that Woland was staying in Likhodeyev's apartment. After that, having dialled the number of Likhodeyev's apartment, Varenukha spent a long time listening to the rich ringing tones in the receiver. From somewhere in the distance in the midst of those tones a grave, gloomy voice could be heard singing: "…the cliffs, my refuge…"* and Varenukha decided that a voice from a radio play had broken through into the telephone network from somewhere.

"The apartment's not answering," said Varenukha, hanging up the receiver, "perhaps we might try ringing…"

He did not finish the sentence. In the doorway appeared that same woman again, and the two of them, both Rimsky and Varenukha, stood up to meet her, while she took out from her bag this time not a white, but some sort of dark little sheet of paper.

"Now this is getting interesting," said Varenukha through his teeth, while his eyes followed the hastily departing woman. The first to take possession of the sheet was Rimsky.

Against the dark background of the photographic paper the black lines of writing stood out distinctly:

"Proof my handwriting my signature. Wire confirmation establish secret surveillance Woland. Likhodeyev".

Over the twenty years of his work in theatres Varenukha had seen all sorts of things, but here he felt as if his mind were being covered with a shroud, and he did not manage to utter anything but the everyday and, moreover, completely absurd phrase:

"This cannot be!"

But Rimsky acted differently. He rose, opened the door and bellowed through it to the messenger-girl sitting on a stool: "Don't admit anyone except postmen!" and locked the door.

Next he got a heap of papers out of the desk and began painstakingly comparing the thick, left-sloping letters from the photogram with the letters in Styopa's resolutions and in his signatures, complete with a spiralling squiggle. Varenukha, dropping onto the desk, breathed hotly on Rimsky's cheek.

"The handwriting's his," the Financial Director said firmly at last, and Varenukha responded like an echo:

"His."

Peering into Rimsky's face, the manager wondered at the change that had taken place in that face. It was as if the Financial Director, thin as he was, had become still thinner and had even aged, and his eyes in their horn rims had lost their normal prickliness, with not only alarm appearing in them, but even sadness too.

Varenukha went through all the actions a man is supposed to at moments of great astonishment. He ran around the office, he twice raised his arms like a man being crucified, he drank a whole glass of yellowish water from the carafe, and he exclaimed:

"I don't understand! I don't understand! I do not un-der-stand!"

And Rimsky looked out of the window, thinking hard about something. The Financial Director's position was a very difficult one. There was a requirement to devise, here and now, on the spot, ordinary explanations for extraordinary phenomena.

Narrowing his eyes a little, the Financial Director pictured Styopa, in his nightshirt and bootless, clambering at around eleven thirty that day into some unprecedented super-high-speed aeroplane, and then him, Styopa, again, and also at eleven thirty, standing in his socks at the aerodrome in Yalta… The devil knew what was going on!

Perhaps it had not been Styopa who had spoken to him on the

telephone today from his very own apartment? No, it had been Styopa talking! He wasn't the one not to know Styopa's voice! And even if it had not been Styopa talking today, it had after all been no further back than yesterday, towards evening, that Styopa had come from his own office into this very office with that idiotic agreement and had irritated the Financial Director with his frivolity. How could he have gone away or flown off without saying anything at the theatre? And even if he had flown off yesterday evening, he would not have arrived by midday today. Or would he?

"How many kilometres to Yalta?" asked Rimsky.

Varenukha ceased his running and yelled:

"Thought of it! Thought of it already! To Sevastopol by rail is about fifteen hundred kilometres. And to Yalta add on another eighty kilometres. Well, by air, of course, it's less."

Hm... Yes... There could be no question of any trains. But what then? A fighter plane? Who'd allow a bootless Styopa into what kind of fighter plane? Why? Perhaps he took his boots off after flying into Yalta? The same thing: why? And he wouldn't be allowed into a fighter plane even with his boots on! And anyway, a fighter plane was neither here nor there. It had been written, after all, that he had appeared at the CID at half-past eleven in the morning, but he'd been speaking on the telephone in Moscow... permit me... here the face of his watch arose before Rimsky's eyes... He was trying to recall where the hands had been. Shocking! It was at twenty past eleven. So what's the upshot then? If one assumes that instantly after the conversation Styopa had dashed to the aerodrome and reached it in, say, five minutes, which is also, incidentally, unthinkable, then the upshot is that the aeroplane, after getting under way at once, had, in five minutes, covered more than a thousand kilometres. In an hour, therefore, it covers more than twelve thousand kilometres!! That cannot be, and so he is not in Yalta.

So what remains? Hypnosis? There is no such hypnosis on earth that could fling a man a thousand kilometres! Accordingly, is he imagining he's in Yalta? Maybe he is indeed imagining it, but is the Yalta CID imagining it too?! Well, no, excuse me, that doesn't happen!... But they're sending telegrams from there, aren't they?

The Financial Director's face was absolutely terrible. At this time the door handle was being turned and tugged from without, and the messenger-girl could be heard shouting desperately outside the doors:

"You can't! I won't let you in! You'll have to kill me first! There's a meeting!"

Rimsky gained control of himself as best he could, picked up the telephone receiver and said into it:

"I want to make a call of priority urgency to Yalta."

"Clever!" exclaimed Varenukha in his mind.

But the call to Yalta did not take place. Rimsky hung up the receiver and said:

"As if on purpose, the line's out of order."

It was evident that for some reason the damage to the line had particularly upset him and even made him pause for thought. After a little think he again took hold of the receiver with one hand, and with the other began noting down what he said into the receiver:

"Take a super-lightning. The Variety. Yes. Yalta. The CID. Yes. 'Today around eleven thirty Likhodeyev spoke me telephone Moscow, stop. Afterwards not come work and unable find him telephones, stop. Handwriting confirmed, stop. Surveillance named artiste undertaken. Financial Director Rimsky'."

"Very clever!" thought Varenukha, but he had not had time to have a proper think before these words ran through his head: "It's stupid! He can't be in Yalta!"

Rimsky, in the meantime, had done the following: put all the telegrams that had been received and a copy of his own neatly together into a bundle, placed the bundle in an envelope, stuck it down, inscribed a few words on it and entrusted it to Varenukha, saying:

"Deliver this personally, Ivan Savelyevich, right away. Let them sort it out there."

"Now that really is clever!" Varenukha thought, and he put the envelope away in his briefcase. Then he once again dialled the number of Styopa's apartment on the telephone, just in case, listened closely, and began joyfully and mysteriously winking and pulling faces. Rimsky craned his neck.

"Can I speak to the artiste Woland?" asked Varenukha sweetly.

"He's busy," the receiver replied in a jangling voice, "who is it enquiring?"

"The manager of The Variety, Varenukha."

"Ivan Savelyevich?" the receiver exclaimed joyfully. "Dreadfully pleased to hear your voice! How are you?"

"*Merci*," replied Varenukha in astonishment, "and who am I talking to?"

"His assistant, assistant and interpreter, Korovyev," the receiver crackled, "entirely at your service, dearest Ivan Savelyevich! Do with me as you will. And so?"

"Forgive me, but is Stepan Bogdanovich Likhodeyev at home just now?"

"Alas, he isn't! He isn't!" cried the receiver. "He's gone away."

"Where to?"

"Into the country for a drive."

"Wh... what? Dr... drive?... And when will he be back?"

"He said, 'I'll get a breath of fresh air and be back'!"

"Right..." said Varenukha in bewilderment, "*merci*. Be so kind as to tell Monsieur Woland that his performance today is in part three."

"Certainly. Of course. Absolutely. Immediately. Most definitely. I'll tell him," the receiver rapped out jerkily.

"All the best," said Varenukha in surprise.

"Please accept," said the receiver, "my very best, warmest greetings and wishes! Success! Good luck! Perfect happiness! Best!"

"Well, of course! Like I said!" shouted the manager in excitement. "No Yalta whatsoever, he's gone off to the country!"

"Well, if that's so," began the Financial Director, turning white with anger, "then that really is the sort of swinish trick there's no name for!"

At this point the manager jumped up into the air and shouted in such a way that Rimsky gave a start:

"Now I remember! Now I remember! A café called 'Yalta' has opened in Pushkino selling meat pasties! Everything becomes clear! He's gone there, got drunk, and now he's sending telegrams from there!"

"Well, this really is too much," Rimsky replied with a tic in his cheek, and in his eyes there burned a genuine, serious malice, "well then, this trip is going to cost him dear!" Suddenly he faltered and added uncertainly: "But then how, I mean, the CID..."

"That's nonsense! His own little jokes," the expansive manager interrupted and asked: "And the packet, shall I take it?"

"Definitely."

And again the door opened, and that same woman came in... "Her!" thought Rimsky, with anguish for some reason. And they both rose to meet the postwoman.

In the telegram this time were the words:

"Thanks confirmation. Send me five hundred urgently CID. Flying Moscow tomorrow. Likhodeyev".

"He's out of his mind..." said Varenukha weakly.

But Rimsky jangled a key, took the money from a drawer in the safe, counted off five hundred roubles, rang the bell, entrusted the money to a messenger and sent him to the telegraph office.

"Pardon me, Grigory Danilovich," said Varenukha, unable to believe his eyes, "I don't think it's a good idea to send the money."

"It'll come back," responded Rimsky quietly, "but he's going to pay dearly for this little picnic." And indicating Varenukha's briefcase, he added: "Go, Ivan Savelyevich, don't delay."

And Varenukha ran out of the office with the briefcase.

He went down to the ground floor and, seeing the longest of queues at the box office, he learnt from the cashier that she was expecting the house to be full in an hour's time, because the public had simply poured in just as soon as it had seen the additional playbill; he ordered the cashier to reserve from sale the thirty best seats in the boxes and the stalls, and then, slipping out of the box office, and there beating off the importunate complimentary ticket seekers as he went, he dived into his little office to grab his cap. At that moment the telephone started crackling.

"Yes!" cried Varenukha.

"Ivan Savelyevich?" the receiver enquired in the most repellent nasal voice.

"He's not in the theatre!" Varenukha was about to cry, but the receiver immediately interrupted him:

"Don't act the fool, Ivan Savelyevich, just listen. Don't take those telegrams anywhere and don't show them to anyone."

"Who's this speaking?" roared Varenukha. "Stop these tricks, Citizen! You'll be detected straight away! Your number?"

"Varenukha," still that same vile voice responded, "do you understand Russian? Don't take the telegrams anywhere."

"Ah, so you're not giving up?" shouted the manager in fury. "Well, look out then! You'll pay for this!" He shouted out some further threat, but fell silent, because he sensed there was no longer anyone listening to him in the receiver.

At this point it somehow began getting dark quickly in the little

111

office. Varenukha ran out, slammed the door behind him and headed through the side entrance into the summer garden.

The manager was excited and full of energy. After the insolent telephone call he was in no doubt that a band of hooligans was playing dirty tricks, and that these tricks were connected to Likhodeyev's disappearance. A desire to expose the villains was choking the manager, and, strange as it might seem, there arose in him a sense of anticipation of something pleasant. This can happen when a man seeks to become the centre of attention, to bear some sensational piece of news.

In the garden the wind blew into the manager's face and filled his eyes with sand, as though blocking his path, as though in warning. On the first floor a window frame slammed so hard the panes almost flew out, and there was an alarming rustling in the tops of the maples and limes. It grew darker and fresher. The manager wiped his eyes and saw that a yellow-bellied storm cloud was crawling low over Moscow. A deep grumbling began in the distance.

No matter how much of a hurry Varenukha was in, an insuperable desire drew him to pop into the summertime public convenience for a second to check in passing whether the electrician had put a bulb in behind the grille.

After running past the shooting gallery, Varenukha entered the dense thicket of lilac bushes in which stood the bluish building of the public convenience. The electrician had proved to be a thorough man, for a bulb beneath the roof in the men's section already had the metal grille fitted over it, but the manager was distressed by the fact that even in the darkness before the storm it was possible to make out that the walls were covered in writing in charcoal and pencil.

"Well, whatever is this for a..." the manager was about to begin, when suddenly he heard a voice behind him purring:

"Is that you, Ivan Savelyevich?"

Varenukha gave a start, turned around and saw before him some short fat man with the physiognomy, as it appeared, of a cat.

"It's me," replied Varenukha inimically.

"Very, very pleased to meet you," responded the fat, cat-like man in a squeaky voice, and suddenly, swinging around, he clapped Varenukha on the ear so hard that the cap flew off the manager's head and vanished without trace into the opening of a toilet seat.

The fat man's clap made the whole toilet light up for a moment with a flickering light, and a clap of thunder echoed it in the sky. Then there was another flash, and a second man appeared before the manager – small, but with athletic shoulders, flaming red hair, a cataract in one eye and a fang in his mouth. This second one, evidently being left-handed, whacked the manager's other ear. In response there was once again a crash in the sky, and torrential rain tumbled down onto the toilet's wooden roof.

"What is it, Comra…" the manager whispered, half out of his mind, but realizing straight away that the word "Comrades" was not at all suitable for bandits who had attacked a man in a public convenience, he croaked: "Citiz…" then grasped that they did not deserve this appellation either, and received a third terrible blow from who knows which of the two, so that blood gushed out of his nose onto his *tolstovka*.

"What have you got in your briefcase, you parasite?" the one like a cat cried shrilly. "Telegrams? And were you warned over the phone not to take them anywhere? Were you warned, I'm asking you?"

"I war… were… werned…" replied the manager, gasping for breath.

"And you still ran along? Give the briefcase here, you scum!" cried the second one in that same nasal voice that had been heard in the telephone, and he wrenched the briefcase out of Varenukha's shaking hands.

And together they picked the manager up by the arms, dragged him out of the garden and tore down Sadovaya with him. The thunderstorm was raging at full power, the water was being hurled down into the drain-holes with a crashing and a howling, everywhere there was a bubbling, waves were swelling, it lashed down from roofs, missing the pipes, its foaming torrents running out from gateways. Everything living had cleared off out of Sadovaya, and there was no one to save Ivan Savelyevich. Jumping through murky rivers and lit up by streaks of lightning, in one second the bandits had dragged the half-dead manager as far as building No. 302 *bis*, and had flown with him into the gateway where two barefooted women were pressed up against the wall, holding their shoes and stockings in their hands. Then they dashed into entrance No. 6, and Varenukha, close to madness, was carried up to the fourth floor and thrown onto the ground in the semi-darkness of the very familiar hallway of Styopa Likhodeyev's apartment.

Here both brigands scarpered, and in their place there appeared in the hallway a completely naked girl – red-haired, with burning phosphoric eyes.

Varenukha realized that this was the most terrible thing of all that had happened to him and, starting to moan, he recoiled towards the wall. But the girl came right up close to the manager and put the palms of her hands on his shoulders. Varenukha's hair stood up on end, because even through the cloth of his *tolstovka*, cold and soaked with water, he felt that these hands were still colder, that they were cold with the cold of ice.

"Let me give you a kiss," said the girl tenderly, and the shining eyes were right next to his eyes. Then Varenukha fainted away and did not feel any kiss.

11

Ivan Splits in Two

THE WOOD ON THE OPPOSITE BANK OF THE RIVER, lit up just an hour before by the May sunshine, had grown muddy, become blurred, and dissolved.

The water was coming down outside the window in an unbroken sheet. In the sky, filaments kept on flashing out, the sky would split open, the patient's room was flooded with a flickering, frightening light.

Ivan quietly wept, sitting on the bed and gazing at the muddy river boiling and bubbling. At every clap of thunder he cried out piteously and covered his face with his hands. The sheets of paper Ivan had covered in writing lay scattered on the floor. They had been blown down there by the wind that had flown into the room just before the start of the thunderstorm.

The poet's attempts to compose a statement regarding the terrible consultant had come to nothing. As soon as he had got a stub of pencil and paper from the fat medical attendant, whose name was Praskovya Fyodorovna, he had rubbed his hands together in a businesslike way and hurriedly settled himself at the table. The beginning he had depicted quite boldly:

"To the police. The statement of MASSOLIT member Ivan Nikolay-evich Bezdomny. Yesterday evening I arrived with the deceased M.A. Berlioz at Patriarch's Ponds..."

And immediately the poet got into a tangle, mainly because of the word "deceased". It came out as some sort of nonsense right from the start: how do you mean – arrived with the deceased? The deceased don't go walking around! Who knows, they might indeed take him for a madman!

Thinking like that, Ivan Nikolayevich began amending what he had written. The result was the following: "...with M.A. Berlioz, subsequently deceased..." Nor did this satisfy the author. He had to use a third wording, and that turned out even worse than the first two: "...Berlioz, who fell under a tram..." and here that composer of the same name that no one knew started bothering him too, and he had to insert "... not the composer..."

After much agonizing over the two Berliozes, Ivan crossed everything out and decided to begin with something very powerful straight away, so as to attract the attention of the person reading at once, and he wrote that the cat had boarded a tram, and then went back to the episode with the severed head. The head and the consultant's prediction set him thinking about Pontius Pilate, and for greater persuasiveness Ivan decided to set out in full the entire story of the Procurator right from the moment when he emerged wearing the white cloak with the blood-red lining into the colonnade of Herod's palace.

Ivan worked diligently, and he would cross through what he had written, and insert new words, and he even tried to draw Pontius Pilate, and then the cat on its hind legs. But the drawings did not help either, and the further he went, the more muddled and incomprehensible the poet's statement became.

By the time a frightening storm cloud with billowing edges appeared from afar and covered the wood, and the wind blew, Ivan felt his strength had gone and he could not control the statement, and he did not bother picking up the sheets of paper that had scattered all around, but began crying quietly and bitterly.

The good-natured medical attendant Praskovya Fyodorovna called in on the poet during the thunderstorm, grew alarmed when she saw he was crying, closed the blind so that the lightning flashes did not frighten the patient, picked the sheets of paper up from the floor and ran off with them to fetch a doctor.

The latter came, gave Ivan an injection in the arm, and assured him he would not cry any more, that it would all be over now, it would all change and would all be forgotten.

The doctor proved right. Soon the wood across the river had become its former self. It stood out sharply to the very last tree under a sky that had cleared to its former perfect blue, while the river had grown calm. The anguish had started to leave Ivan immediately after the injection, and now the poet lay calmly and gazed at the rainbow that had stretched itself across the sky.

It continued thus until the evening, and he did not even notice how the rainbow melted away, and how the sky grew sad and colourless, and how the wood blackened.

After drinking his fill of hot milk, Ivan again lay down and was surprised himself at how his thoughts had changed. The damned diabolical cat had somehow mellowed in his memory, the severed head frightened him no more, and, abandoning thoughts of the head, Ivan started reflecting on how, as a matter of fact, it was not at all bad at the clinic, that Stravinsky was a clever chap and a celebrity, and it was extremely pleasant having dealings with him. The evening air, what's more, was both sweet and fresh after the thunderstorm.

The mental asylum was falling asleep. In the quiet corridors the white pearl lamps went out, and in their place, following the routine, weak blue night lights lit up, and more and more rarely could the cautious little footsteps of the medical attendants be heard on the rubber mats of the corridor outside the doors.

Now Ivan lay in sweet languor and cast looks first at the bulb under the lampshade pouring a softened light from the ceiling, then at the moon coming out from behind the black wood, and he conversed with himself.

"Why precisely did I get so agitated about Berlioz falling under a tram?" reflected the poet. "In the final analysis, to hell with him! Who am I, when it comes down to it, godfather to his child or an in-law? If you give the question a proper airing, it emerges that, in essence, I didn't even really know the dead man. Truly, what did I know about him? Nothing at all, except that he was bald and terribly eloquent. And then, Citizens," Ivan continued his speech, addressing someone or other, "here's what we'll look into: do explain why it was I went mad at that enigmatic consultant, magician and professor with the one empty and the one black eye? What was the point of that whole absurd pursuit of him, wearing long johns and with a candle in my hands, and then the ridiculous malarkey in the restaurant?"

"But, but, but," the former Ivan suddenly said sternly to the new Ivan from somewhere, perhaps inside, perhaps right by his ear, "he did after all know in advance about the fact that Berlioz's head would be cut off, didn't he? How could you not get agitated?"

"What are you talking about, Comrades!" the new Ivan retorted to the old, former Ivan. "That it's all a dirty business can be grasped even by a child. He's an exceptional and mysterious personality, one hundred per cent. But then it's that precisely that's the most interesting bit! A man was personally acquainted with Pontius Pilate, whatever could you want more interesting than that? And instead of kicking up the most stupid row at Patriarch's, wouldn't it have been cleverer to ask politely about what happened afterwards to Pilate and that arrested man, Ha-Nozri? But I got started on the devil knows what! An important event, truly – the editor of a magazine got run over! So what of it, will the journal be closed down or something? Well, what can be done? Man is mortal, and, as was rightly said, suddenly mortal. Well, may he rest in peace! So there'll be a different editor, and perhaps he'll even be still more eloquent than the previous one."

After dozing a little, the new Ivan asked venomously of the old Ivan: "So who do I turn out to be in that case?"

"A fool!" a bass not belonging to either of the Ivans, and extremely like the bass of the consultant, said distinctly from somewhere.

For some reason not taking offence at the word "fool", and even being pleasantly surprised by it, Ivan grinned and, half asleep, fell quiet. Sleep was stealing up on Ivan, and he had already imagined that he saw the palm tree on the elephantine leg, and that the cat had passed by – not frightening, but jolly – and, in short, sleep was right on the point of enveloping Ivan, when suddenly the grille travelled soundlessly aside, and on the balcony there appeared a mysterious figure, hiding from the moonlight, that wagged its finger at Ivan.

Without any fear at all, Ivan raised himself on the bed and saw there was a man on the balcony. And this man, pressing a finger to his lips, whispered:

"Shhh!"

117

12

Black Magic and its Exposure

A SMALL MAN IN A HOLEY YELLOW BOWLER HAT, with a pear-shaped, raspberry-coloured nose and wearing checked trousers and patent-leather boots, rode out onto the stage of The Variety on an ordinary two-wheeled bicycle. To the strains of a foxtrot he made a circuit, and then uttered a triumphant shriek, which made the bicycle rear up. Having travelled some distance on one wheel, the little man turned upside down, contrived while on the move to unscrew the front wheel and launch it into the wings, and then continued on his way on one wheel, turning the pedals with his hands.

A plump blonde in a leotard and a little skirt, spangled with silver stars, rode out on a tall metal mast with one wheel and a saddle at the top and began riding round in a circle. Meeting up with her, the little man emitted cries of greeting and removed the bowler hat from his head with his foot.

Finally, a wee mite, a little fellow of about eight with an old man's face, rolled up and began darting between the adults on a minute two-wheeler with a huge car horn attached to it.

After doing several loops, the whole company, to the alarming roll of a drum from the orchestra, rode up to the very edge of the stage, and the spectators in the front rows gasped and leant back, because it seemed to the audience that the entire trio with their machines would fall with a crash into the orchestra pit.

But the cycles stopped at precisely the moment when the front wheels were already threatening to slip off into the abyss and onto the heads of the musicians. With a loud cry of "Up!" the cyclists leapt off their machines and, bowing, took their leave, with the blonde blowing kisses to the audience and the wee mite sounding a funny call on his horn.

The applause shook the building, the blue curtain set off from both sides and hid the cyclists, the green lights by the doors with the inscription "EXIT" went out, and in the web of trapezes beneath the dome, white spheres lit up like the sun. The interval before the final part had begun.

The only person not interested to any extent in the wonders of the cycling art of the Giulli family was Grigory Danilovich Rimsky. He sat in complete solitude in his office, biting his thin lips, and a spasm kept on passing over his face. To the extraordinary disappearance of Likhodeyev had been added the completely unforeseen disappearance of the manager, Varenukha.

Rimsky knew where he had gone, but he had gone and... had not come back! Rimsky was shrugging his shoulders and whispering to himself:

"But what for?!"

And it was a strange thing: for a businesslike man such as the Financial Director it was, of course, the simplest thing of all to telephone the place for which Varenukha had set out and discover what had befallen him, and yet he had been unable, until ten o'clock in the evening, to compel himself to do it.

But at ten, positively using force upon himself, Rimsky took the receiver from the apparatus, and at that point found out that his telephone was dead. A messenger reported that the other telephones in the building were faulty too. This event, unpleasant, of course, but not supernatural, for some reason completely stunned the Financial Director, but at the same time delighted him too: the need to phone receded.

At the time when a red lamp above the Financial Director's head flared up and started flashing to proclaim the start of the interval, a messenger came in and announced that the foreign artiste had arrived. The Financial Director came over unwell for some reason, and, now quite definitely gloomier than a storm cloud, he set off into the wings to greet the touring performer, since there was no one else there to greet him.

From the corridor, where the warning bells were already crackling, the curious, under various pretexts, were glancing into the large dressing room. Here were conjurors in bright oriental robes and turbans, a skater in a white knitted jacket, a storyteller, white with powder, and a make-up artist.

The newly arrived celebrity struck everyone with the unprecedented length of his wonderfully cut tailcoat and the fact that he had turned up in a black half-mask. But most surprising of all were the black magician's two companions: a lanky man in checks wearing a cracked pince-nez, and a fat black cat who, upon entering the dressing room on his hind legs, sat down on a couch, perfectly relaxed, squinting at the bare bulbs of the make-up mirror.

Rimsky tried to portray a smile, which made his face look sour and angry, and he exchanged bows with the silent magician sitting on the couch beside the cat. There was no handshake. And yet the unduly familiar man in checks introduced himself to the Financial Director, calling himself "their assistant". This circumstance surprised the Financial Director, and, once again, unpleasantly: there was absolutely no mention in the contract of any assistant.

Very stiffly and drily Grigory Danilovich enquired of the man in checks, who had come upon him like a bolt from the blue, where the artiste's equipment was.

"Celestial diamond of ours, most precious Mr Director," the magician's assistant replied in a jangling voice, "our equipment is always with us. Here it is! *Eins, zwei, drei!*" And, twirling his gnarled fingers around in front of Rimsky's eyes, he suddenly pulled out from behind the cat's ear Rimsky's very own gold watch and chain, which had previously been in the Financial Director's waistcoat pocket, beneath his buttoned jacket, and with the chain passed through a buttonhole.

Rimsky grabbed involuntarily at his stomach, those present gasped, and the make-up artist, who was looking in through the door, quacked approvingly.

"Your watch? Please have it," said the man in checks with a free-and-easy smile, and handed the bewildered Rimsky his property on a dirty palm.

"Don't get on a tram with anyone like that," the storyteller whispered quietly and cheerily to the make-up artist.

But then the cat performed a stunt rather slicker than the trick with another person's watch. Rising unexpectedly from the couch, he went over to the little dressing table on his hind legs, pulled the stopper from a carafe with his front paw, poured some water into a glass, drank it, fitted the stopper back in place and wiped his whiskers with a make-up cloth.

At this point nobody even gasped, they just opened their mouths wide, and the make-up artist whispered admiringly:

"Wow, class!"

At that moment the bells began clanging in warning for the third time, and, excited and looking forward to an interesting act, everyone flocked out of the dressing room.

A minute later the lights were put out in the auditorium, the footlights flared up and gave a reddish glow to the bottom of the curtain, and in the illuminated gap in the curtain there appeared before the audience a plump man with a clean-shaven face, as cheerful as a child, in a crumpled tailcoat and less than fresh linen. It was the compère, George Bengalsky, well known to the whole of Moscow.

"And so, Citizens," Bengalsky began, smiling his infantile smile, "appearing before you now will be..." here Bengalsky interrupted himself and continued with a different intonation: "I see the size of the audience has increased still further for the third part of the show. Half the city is with us today! A few days ago I happen to meet a friend, and I say to him: 'Why don't you come and see us? Half the city was with us yesterday!' And he answers me: 'Well I live in the other half!'" Bengalsky paused, expecting an explosion of laughter to take place, but since nobody laughed, he continued: "...And so, the renowned foreign artiste Monsieur Woland will be appearing with a performance of black magic. Well, you and I understand," here Bengalsky smiled a wise smile, "that there's no such thing on earth at all and it's nothing other than a superstition, it's simply that the maestro Woland has a command of the art of conjuring at the highest level, as will be evident from the most interesting part, that is, the exposure of that art, and since we are as one in being in favour of both the art and its exposure, we shall call on Mr Woland!"

Having uttered all this drivel, Bengalsky joined both hands palm to palm and started waving them in welcome into the slit in the curtain, as a result of which, with a quiet swish, it duly parted and moved aside.

The entrance of the magician with his lanky assistant and the cat, who stepped onto the stage on his hind legs, delighted the audience.

"An armchair for me," ordered Woland in a low voice, and in the same second, from who knows where and how, on the stage there appeared an armchair in which the magician duly sat down. "Tell me, dear Fagot," Woland enquired of the buffoon in checks, who evidently bore another name apart from Korovyev, "what's your opinion, the population of Moscow has altered significantly, has it not?"

The magician looked at the audience, which had fallen quiet, stunned by the appearance of the armchair out of thin air.

"Quite so, Messire," replied Fagot-Korovyev in a low voice.

"You're right. The people of this city have altered greatly... outwardly, I mean, like the city itself, by the way. The costumes, needless to say, but those... what are they called... trams, cars have appeared..."

"Buses," prompted Fagot deferentially.

The audience listened attentively to this conversation, supposing it to be a prelude to the magic tricks. The wings were packed with artistes and stagehands, and among their faces could be seen the tense, pale face of Rimsky.

The physiognomy of Bengalsky, who had taken shelter at the side of the stage, started to express bewilderment. He raised an eyebrow just a very little and, taking advantage of a pause, began to speak:

"The foreign artiste is expressing his admiration for Moscow, which has grown up in a technological respect, and also for the Muscovites," and here Bengalsky smiled twice, first to the stalls, and then to the gallery.

Woland, Fagot and the cat turned their heads in the direction of the compère.

"Did I really express admiration?" the magician asked Fagot.

"Not at all, Messire, you expressed no admiration," the latter replied.

"So what ever is that man saying?"

"He simply lied!" the assistant in checks declared sonorously, for the whole theatre to hear, and, turning to Bengalsky, he added: "Congratulations, Citizen, on lying!"

There was a splash of tittering from the gallery, while Bengalsky gave a start and opened his eyes wide.

"But of course, I'm not so much interested in buses, telephones and other..."

"Equipment!" prompted the man in checks.

"Absolutely correct, thank you," said the magician slowly in a heavy bass, "as in the much more important question: have the people of this city altered inwardly?"

"Yes, that's the most important question, sir."

In the wings they started exchanging glances and shrugging their shoulders, Bengalsky stood red-faced, while Rimsky was pale. But at this point, as though having guessed at the unease that was developing, the magician said:

"However, we've talked too much, dear Fagot, and the audience is starting to get bored. Show us something nice and simple to begin with."

The auditorium stirred in relief. Fagot and the cat went in different directions along the footlights. Fagot clicked his fingers and gave a raffish cry:

"Three, four!" and caught a pack of cards from out of thin air, shuffled it and sent it in a ribbon towards the cat. The cat caught the ribbon and sent it back again. The satin snake snorted, Fagot opened his mouth wide like a baby bird and swallowed the whole of it, card by card.

After that, the cat took a bow, scraping his right hind paw, and provoked an unbelievable round of applause.

"Class! Class!" they cried in admiration in the wings.

But Fagot jabbed a finger at the stalls and announced:

"That pack is now to be found, respected Citizens, on Citizen Parchevsky in row seven, right between a three-rouble note and a court summons on the matter of alimony payments to Citizeness Zelkova."

People began stirring in the stalls, half-rising from their seats, and finally a citizen who was indeed called Parchevsky, perfectly crimson in amazement, extracted the pack from his wallet and started jabbing it into the air, not knowing what to do with it.

"You keep it as a memento!" cried Fagot. "Not for nothing did you say over dinner yesterday, that if it weren't for poker, your life in Moscow would be utterly unbearable."

"That's an old joke," was heard from the gods, "that fellow in the stalls is one of their troupe."

"Do you suppose so?" yelled Fagot, squinting at the gallery. "In that case you too are in the same gang as us, because you have a pack in your pocket!"

A movement took place in the gods and a joyful voice was heard:

"It's true! He has! Here, here... Hang on! But they're ten-rouble notes!"

Those sitting in the stalls turned their heads. In the gallery a perturbed citizen had discovered in his pocket a wad, bound together in the way used by banks and with an inscription on the cover: "One thousand roubles".

His neighbours were leaning on him, and he in amazement was picking at the cover with a fingernail, trying to ascertain whether these were genuine ten-rouble notes or some sort of magic ones.

"Honest to God, they're genuine! Tenners!" they cried joyfully from the gods.

"Play some cards like that with me too," a fat man requested cheerfully in the middle of the stalls.

"*Avec plaisir!*"* responded Fagot. "But why on earth with just you? Everyone will play an active part!" and he commanded: "Please look up! One!" In his hand there appeared a pistol, and he cried: "Two!" The pistol was jerked upwards. He cried: "Three!" There was a flash, a bang, and immediately, from beneath the dome, fluttering between the trapezes, white notes began falling into the auditorium.

They span, they carried sideways, they piled up in the gallery, they were diverted into the orchestra pit and onto the stage. After a few seconds the rain of money, growing ever thicker, reached the seats, and the audience began catching the notes.

Hundreds of arms were raised, the audience looked through the notes at the lighted stage and saw the most true and righteous watermarks. The smell too left no doubt: it was the smell, comparable to nothing in its charm, of freshly printed money. At first merriment, and then amazement gripped the whole theatre. Everywhere the word "tenners, tenners" was buzzing, exclamations of "oh, oh!" could be heard, and merry laughter. Some were already crawling in the aisles, groping under the chairs. Many were standing on the seats, catching the flighty, whimsical notes.

Bewilderment gradually began to be expressed on the faces of the police, while the artistes started pushing forward unceremoniously out of the wings.

In the dress circle a voice was heard: "What are you doing, snatching? That's mine! It was coming towards me!" And another voice: "Just you stop pushing, I'll give you such a shove myself!" And suddenly a slap was heard. A policeman's helmet immediately appeared in the dress circle and someone was led out of the dress circle.

In general, the excitement was growing, and there is no knowing what would have sprung from it all if Fagot had not stopped the rain of money by suddenly blowing into the air.

Two young men exchanged meaningful and merry looks, left their seats and headed directly for the bar. The theatre was abuzz, the eyes of the entire audience were shining with excitement. No, no, there is no knowing what would have sprung from it all if Bengalsky had not found some strength within himself and stirred. Trying to take a good, firm hold on himself, he rubbed his hands out of habit and in the most sonorous of voices he began speaking thus:

"There, Citizens, we have just now seen an instance of so-called mass hypnosis. A purely scientific experiment providing the best possible proof that there are no miracles or magic. Let's ask maestro Woland to expose this experiment for us. You will now, Citizens, see those notes, ostensibly banknotes, disappear just as suddenly as they appeared."

At this point he started to applaud, but in complete isolation, and as he did so there was a confident smile playing on his face, yet that confidence was by no means there in his eyes, in which was expressed rather supplication.

The audience did not like Bengalsky's speech. Complete silence fell, which was interrupted by the checked Fagot.

"That is once again an instance of so-called lying," he declared in a loud, goat-like tenor, "the notes, Citizens, are genuine!"

"Bravo!" a bass abruptly roared somewhere high up.

"Incidentally, I'm fed up with this fellow," here Fagot indicated Bengalsky. "He pokes his nose in where he's not asked all the time and spoils the show with false observations. Now, what should we do with him?"

"Rip his head off!" someone said sternly from the gallery.

"What's that you say? Huh?" Fagot immediately responded to this outrageous suggestion. "Rip off his head? That's an idea! Behemoth!" he cried to the cat. "Do it! *Eins, zwei, drei!*"

And an unprecedented thing occurred. The black cat's fur stood up on end and he gave a harrowing miaow. Then he compressed himself into a ball and, like a panther, leapt straight onto Bengalsky's chest, and from there skipped onto his head. With a grumbling noise, the cat caught hold of the compère's sparse *chevelure* with his chubby paws and, with a savage howl, in two turns he pulled that head right off the plump neck.

Two and a half thousand people in the theatre cried out as one. Fountains of blood from the torn arteries in the neck beat upwards and drenched both the dicky and the tailcoat. The headless body shuffled its feet in an absurd sort of way and sat down on the floor. Women's hysterical cries could be heard in the auditorium. The cat passed the head to Fagot, the latter raised it up by the hair and showed it to the audience, and the head shouted desperately for the whole theatre to hear:

"A doctor!"

"Are you going to spout all sorts of nonsense in future?" Fagot asked threateningly of the crying head.

"I won't do it any more!" wheezed the head.

"For God's sake, stop tormenting him!" a woman's voice suddenly resounded from a box, drowning the din, and the magician turned his face in the direction of this voice.

"So then, Citizens, be forgiven, should he?" asked Fagot, addressing the auditorium.

"Forgive him! Forgive him!" rang out at first individual and primarily women's voices, but then they merged into a single choir with the men's.

"What is your command, Messire?" Fagot asked the masked one.

"Well," the latter replied pensively, "they're the same as any other people. They like money, but that was always the case, you know... Mankind likes money, no matter what it might be made of, whether of leather, whether of paper, of bronze or gold. So, they're frivolous... well... and mercy sometimes knocks at their hearts... ordinary people... All in all they're reminiscent of the previous ones... it's just the housing question that's spoiled them..." and in a loud voice he ordered: "Put the head on."

The cat, taking good and careful aim, plonked the head onto the neck, and it settled exactly in its place as though it had not even been away anywhere. And the main thing was, there was not even any scar left on the neck. The cat brushed off Bengalsky's tailcoat and the shirt front with his paws, and the traces of blood vanished from them. Fagot raised the seated Bengalsky to his feet, shoved a wad of ten-rouble notes into the pocket of his tailcoat and sent him packing from the stage with the words:

"Get out of here! It's more fun without you."

Gazing around foolishly and staggering, the compère only got as far as the fire-post, and there he had a bad turn. He let out a piteous cry:

"My head, my head!"

Rimsky, among others, rushed up to him. The compère was crying, trying to catch something in the air in his hands, and muttering:

"Give my head back! Give it back! Take my apartment, take my pictures, only give me back my head!"

A messenger ran off for a doctor. They tried to lay Bengalsky down on a couch in a dressing room, but he started fighting them off and became violent. An ambulance had to be called. When the unfortunate compère had been taken away, Rimsky ran back to the stage and saw that new wonders were taking place upon it. Yes, incidentally, it may have been at this time or maybe a little earlier, only the magician, together with his faded armchair, had vanished from the stage, and moreover, it has to be said, the audience had completely failed to notice it, distracted by the extraordinary things that Fagot had unfurled on the stage.

And Fagot, having sent the traumatized compère on his way, had made this announcement to the audience:

"Now we've got rid of that pain in the neck, let's open a ladies' boutique!"

And the floor of the stage was immediately covered with Persian carpets, huge mirrors appeared, lit from the sides by greenish strip lights, and between the mirrors – showcases, and in them the audience in cheerful stupefaction saw women's dresses of various colours and styles from Paris. That was in just some of the showcases. And in the others there appeared hundreds of women's hats, both with feathers and without feathers, both with clasps and without them, and hundreds of shoes – black, white, yellow, leather, satin, suede, both with straps and with little stones. Between the shoes there appeared boxes of perfume, mountains of handbags made of antelope leather, of suede, of silk, and between them – whole heaps of the small, chased gold, oblong holders in which lipstick is sometimes found.

A red-haired girl in black evening dress, who had appeared from the devil knows where, a nice girl in every way – had a weird scar on her neck not spoilt her – began smiling a proprietorial smile by the showcases.

Fagot announced with a sugary grin that the firm was carrying out a completely free exchange of ladies' old dresses and footwear for Parisian fashions and also Parisian footwear. He added the same regarding handbags and so on.

The cat began scraping a hind paw, and at the same time making with a fore paw gestures of the sort characteristic of doormen opening a door.

Sweetly, albeit a little hoarsely and with a burr, the girl started singing something scarcely comprehensible, but, judging by the women's faces in the stalls, very seductive:

"Guerlain, Chanel No. 5, Mitsuko, Narcisse Noir, evening dresses, cocktail dresses..."

Fagot was writhing around, the cat was bowing, the girl was opening the glass showcases.

"Please!" Fagot yelled. "Without any inhibitions or ceremony!"

The audience was excited, but nobody as yet dared to go onto the stage. Finally a brunette left row ten of the stalls and, smiling in a way that said it was absolutely all the same to her and she didn't really care, went forward and up a side stairway onto the stage.

"Bravo!" exclaimed Fagot. "I welcome the first customer! Behemoth, an armchair! Let's start with footwear, madam!"

The brunette sat down in an armchair and Fagot immediately tossed out onto the carpet in front of her a whole pile of shoes. The brunette took off her right shoe, tried on a lilac one, stamped her foot into the carpet and examined the heel.

"They won't be too tight, will they?" she asked pensively. To that Fagot exclaimed resentfully:

"Oh, come, come!" and the cat miaowed in resentment.

"I'll take this pair, monsieur," said the brunette with dignity, putting on the left shoe as well.

The brunette's old shoes were thrown away behind the curtain, and she herself proceeded that way too, accompanied by the red-haired girl and Fagot, who was carrying several fashionable dresses on his small shoulders. The cat fussed about, helping, and for greater show hung a measuring tape around his neck.

A minute later the brunette emerged from behind the curtain in such a dress that a sigh rolled right across the stalls. The courageous woman, who had grown prettier to an amazing degree, stopped by a mirror, moved her bared shoulders, touched at the hair on the back of her head, and bent her body, trying to get a look behind her back.

"The firm requests you to accept this as a memento," said Fagot, and handed the brunette an open box with a flacon.

"*Merci*," replied the brunette haughtily and went down the steps into the stalls. As she went, members of the audience leapt up to get a touch of the box.

And it was at this point that people completely lost control, and from all sides women set off for the stage. In the general sound of excited voices, giggles and sighs a man's voice was heard: "I'm not letting you!" and a woman's: "Despot and philistine! Stop breaking my arm!" The women disappeared behind the curtain, left their dresses there and came out in new ones. On stools with gilt legs sat a whole row of ladies, energetically stamping newly shod feet into the carpet. Fagot was kneeling down and being active with a metal shoehorn, the cat, exhausted beneath piles of handbags and shoes, dragged himself from showcase to stools and back again, the girl with the disfigured neck now appeared, now disappeared, and got to the point where she started rattling on completely in French, and the amazing thing was that all the women understood her straight away, even those of them who did not know a single word of French.

General astonishment was caused by the man who wormed his way onto the stage. He announced that his wife had flu, and so he was asking for something to be passed on to her through him. And as proof of the fact that he really was married the citizen was prepared to produce his passport. The caring husband's declaration was greeted with loud laughter, Fagot yelled out that he believed him as he would believe himself, even without the passport, and handed the citizen two pairs of silk stockings, and the cat added a case with a lipstick from himself.

Women who were late coming forward were bursting to get onto the stage, and from the stage there was a flow of lucky females in ball dresses, in pyjamas with dragons on them, in formal business suits, in nice little hats tilted over one eyebrow.

Then Fagot announced that on account of the late hour the shop was closing in exactly one minute, until the next evening, and an unbelievable commotion started up on the stage. Women hurriedly grabbed shoes without trying them on. One tore behind the curtain like a hurricane, there threw off her costume and took possession of the first thing that came to hand – a silk dressing gown covered in huge bouquets – and managed to pick up two boxes of perfume besides.

After exactly a minute a pistol shot cracked out, the mirrors vanished, the showcases and stools disappeared, the carpet melted into thin air, as did the curtain too. Last to vanish was the great high mountain of old dresses and footwear, and the stage again became stark, empty and bare.

And it was here that a new character got involved in things.

A pleasant, sonorous and very insistent baritone was heard from box No. 2:

"It is nonetheless desirable, Citizen artiste, that you should without delay expose before the audience the technique of your tricks, in particular the trick with the banknotes. Also desirable is the return of the compère to the stage. His fate is worrying the audience."

The baritone belonged to none other than the evening's guest of honour, Arkady Apollonovich Sempleyarov, the Chairman of the Acoustics Commission of Moscow Theatres.

Arkady Apollonovich was in the box with two ladies: one elderly, expensively and fashionably dressed, and the other, young and pretty, dressed rather more simply. The first of them, as soon became clear when the statement was being drawn up, was Arkady Apollonovich's wife, and the second was a distant relative of his, a novice, but promising actress who had arrived from Saratov and was staying in Arkady Apollonovich and his wife's apartment.

"Pardon me!" responded Fagot. "My apologies, there's nothing to expose here, everything's clear."

"No, I'm sorry! Exposure is absolutely essential. Without it your brilliant turns will leave a distressing impression. The watching mass demands an explanation."

"The watching mass," the rude clown interrupted Sempleyarov, "doesn't seem to have made any declaration. But, taking into consideration your deeply respected desire, Arkady Apollonovich, so be it, I shall perform an exposure. But to do that, will you allow me one more tiny little turn?"

"Why of course," replied Arkady Apollonovich patronizingly, "but there should without fail be an exposure!"

"Yes, sir, yes, sir. And so, may I ask you where you were yesterday evening, Arkady Apollonovich?"

At this inappropriate and even perhaps boorish question, Arkady Apollonovich changed countenance, and changed very seriously too.

"Arkady Apollonovich was at a meeting of the Acoustics Commission yesterday evening," declared Arkady Apollonovich's wife very haughtily, "but I don't understand what that has to do with magic."

"*Oui, madame*,"* confirmed Fagot. "Naturally you don't understand. And as to a meeting, you're utterly deluded. After leaving for the meeting referred to, which, by the way, wasn't even arranged for yesterday, Arkady Apollonovich let his driver go by the building of the Acoustics Commission at Pure Ponds," (the whole theatre had fallen silent) "and went himself in a bus to Yelokhovskaya Street to visit

Militsa Andreyevna Pokobatko, an actress from the District Travelling Theatre, and spent about four hours at her apartment."

"Oh!" somebody exclaimed with a note of suffering in the absolute silence.

But Arkady Apollonovich's young relative suddenly broke into low and terrible laughter.

"I see it all!" she exclaimed. "And I'd already been suspecting it for a long time. Now it's clear to me why that third-rater got the part of Louisa!"*

And with a sudden swing of her arm, she struck Arkady Apollonovich on the head with a short, fat, lilac umbrella.

And the ignoble Fagot, who was also Korovyev, cried out:

"There, estimable Citizens, is one instance of the exposure that Arkady Apollonovich so insistently sought!"

"How could you have dared, you good-for-nothing, to touch Arkady Apollonovich?" Arkady Apollonovich's wife asked menacingly, rising in the box to her full, gigantic height.

A second short tide of satanic laughter took hold of the young relative.

"If there's anyone," she replied, chuckling, "then I'm the one who can dare to touch him!" and there rang out for a second time the dry crack of the umbrella rebounding off Arkady Apollonovich's head.

"Police! Seize her!" Sempleyarov's wife cried out in such a terrible voice that the hearts of many turned cold.

And at this point too, the cat leapt out towards the footlights and suddenly roared in a human voice for the whole theatre to hear:

"The show's over! Maestro! Saw out a march!"

The conductor, half out of his mind and not aware of what he was doing, waved his baton, and the orchestra started not to play, and not even to crash out, and not even to strike up, but indeed, in the cat's loathsome expression, to saw out some incredible march, unlike anything on earth in its abandon.

It seemed for an instant as if sometime in the past, beneath southern stars in a *café chantant*, some scarcely comprehensible, purblind, but very dashing words had been heard to this march:

His Royal Majesty the King
Admired domestic fowl

And took under his ample wing
The cutest girls in town!!!*

Yet perhaps there had been none of these words at all, but there had been others to the same music, and extremely indecent ones too. That is not important; the important thing is that after all this, something like Babel started up at The Variety. The police were running to the Sempleyarovs' box, the curious were climbing onto the barrier, hellish explosions of laughter were heard, and mad cries, drowned out by the golden ringing of the cymbals from the orchestra.

And it could be seen that the stage had suddenly emptied, and that the swindler Fagot, as well as the insolent great tomcat Behemoth, had melted into thin air, vanished, just as the magician in the armchair with the faded upholstery had vanished earlier on.

13

The Coming of the Hero

A ND SO, AN UNKNOWN MAN wagged his finger at Ivan and whispered: "Shhh!"

Ivan lowered his legs from the bed and peered. Looking cautiously into the room from the balcony was a clean-shaven, dark-haired man of approximately thirty-eight, with a sharp nose, anxious eyes and a lock of hair hanging down over his forehead.

Having satisfied himself that Ivan was alone, and after listening intently, the mysterious visitor grew bold and entered the room. At this point Ivan saw that the visitor was dressed in hospital things. He was wearing underclothes, and slippers on sockless feet, and a brown dressing gown was thrown over his shoulders.

The visitor winked at Ivan, put a bunch of keys away in his pocket, enquired in a whisper: "May I sit down?" and, receiving an affirmative nod, settled in an armchair.

"How on earth did you get in here?" Ivan asked in a whisper, obeying the lean, wagging finger. "The balcony grilles are on locks, aren't they?"

"The grilles are on locks," confirmed the guest, "but Praskovya Fyodorovna, the nicest person, is yet, alas, absent-minded. I pinched a bunch of keys from her a month ago and thus acquired the capacity for getting out onto the shared balcony, which stretches around the entire floor, and thus of sometimes calling on a neighbour."

"If you can get out onto the balcony, then you can get away. Or is it too high?" Ivan wondered.

"No," replied the guest firmly, "I can't get away from here, not because it's too high, but because I've got nowhere to get away to." And after a pause he added: "And so, we're stuck in here?"

"We are," replied Ivan, peering into the stranger's brown and very restless eyes.

"Yes…" here the guest suddenly grew anxious, "but I hope you're not violent? Because I can't endure noise, you know, and trouble and the use of force and all that sort of thing. I find people's cries particularly hateful, whether it be a cry of suffering, of rage, or some other kind of cry. Reassure me, say you're not violent?"

"In a restaurant yesterday I socked a fellow in the snout," the transfigured poet confessed manfully.

"The reason?" asked the guest sternly.

"To be honest, without reason," replied Ivan, embarrassed.

"Disgraceful," the guest censured Ivan, and added: "And besides, what are you doing, expressing yourself like that: socked in the snout? I mean, there's no knowing what the person actually has, a snout or a face. But it's quite likely a face, you know, after all. So using fists, you know… No, you give that up, and for good."

Having told Ivan off in this way, the guest enquired:

"Profession?"

"Poet," Ivan admitted, unwillingly for some reason.

The visitor was distressed.

"Oh, how unlucky I am!" he exclaimed, but immediately pulled himself up, apologized and asked: "And what's your name?"

"Bezdomny."

"Oh dear, oh dear…" said the guest, frowning.

"What's the matter then, don't you like my poems?" asked Ivan curiously.

"Not one little bit."

"What have you read?"

"I've not read any of your poems!" exclaimed the visitor edgily.

"So how can you say?"

133

"Well, what's the problem?" replied the guest. "It's not as though I haven't read any others. Still… a miracle, perhaps? All right, I'm prepared to take it on trust. Are your poems any good, tell me yourself?"

"Monstrous!" Ivan suddenly pronounced boldly and candidly.

"Don't write any more!" requested the visitor imploringly.

"I promise and swear to it!" Ivan pronounced solemnly.

The oath was sealed with a handshake, and at this point the sounds of soft footsteps and voices carried in from the corridor.

"Shh," whispered the guest and, slipping out onto the balcony, he closed the grille behind him.

Praskovya Fyodorovna glanced in and asked how Ivan was feeling, and whether he wished to sleep in the dark or with the light on. Ivan asked for the light to be left on, and, after wishing the patient good night, Praskovya Fyodorovna withdrew. And when all had gone quiet, the guest returned once more.

He informed Ivan in a whisper that someone new had been brought to room 119, a fat man with a crimson physiognomy, who was muttering all the time about some sort of foreign currency in the ventilation and swearing that unclean spirits had moved into their building on Sadovaya.

"He's cursing Pushkin like nothing on earth and shouting all the time: 'Kurolesov, *bis*, *bis*!'" said the guest, twitching uneasily. Calming himself, he sat down and said: "But still, never mind him," and continued his conversation with Ivan: "So why is it you've ended up in here?"

"Because of Pontius Pilate," replied Ivan with a gloomy look at the floor.

"What?!" the guest cried, forgetting caution, then stopped his mouth with his own hand. "Amazing coincidence! Please tell me, I implore you!"

For some reason Ivan felt confidence in the stranger, and, initially halting and shy, but then growing bolder, he began to recount the previous day's incident at Patriarch's Ponds. Yes, Ivan Nikolayevich found a grateful listener in the person of the mysterious abductor of keys! The guest did not dress Ivan up as a madman, manifested the greatest interest in what he was being told, and, as the tale developed, he finally went into raptures. He kept on interrupting Ivan with exclamations:

"Well, well, carry on, carry on, I implore you! Only for the sake of all that's holy, don't leave anything out!"

Ivan was indeed missing nothing out, he himself found it easier to tell it that way, and gradually he got to the moment when Pontius Pilate in a white mantle with a blood-red lining emerged onto the balcony.

The guest then put his hands together in prayer and whispered:

"Oh, how right I got it! Oh, how right I got it all!"

The listening man accompanied the description of Berlioz's terrible death with an enigmatic remark, and malice flared up in his eyes:

"One thing I regret, that it wasn't the critic Latunsky or the writer Mstislav Lavrovich in place of this Berlioz." And frenziedly, yet soundlessly he exclaimed: "Carry on!"

The cat paying the conductress amused the guest greatly, and he choked with quiet laughter watching Ivan, excited by the success of his narrative, hopping on his haunches, portraying the cat with the ten-copeck piece beside his whiskers.

"And so," Ivan concluded, after recounting the occurrence at Griboyedov and growing sad and misty-eyed: "I ended up here."

The guest put his hand sympathetically on the poor poet's shoulder and spoke thus:

"Unhappy poet! But, my dear fellow, you yourself are to blame for everything. You shouldn't have behaved so casually, even somewhat insolently with him. And now you've paid for it. And you ought to say thank you for getting away with it all comparatively cheaply too."

"But who on earth is he, in the end?" asked Ivan, shaking his fists in excitement.

The guest peered at Ivan and answered with a question:

"You won't become disturbed, no? We're all unreliable people here… We won't have a doctor being called, injections and all sorts of other trouble?"

"No, no!" exclaimed Ivan. "Tell me, who is he?"

"Very well then," replied the guest, and said weightily and distinctly: "Yesterday at Patriarch's Ponds you met with Satan."

As he had promised, Ivan did not become disturbed, but he was nonetheless very greatly shaken.

"That cannot be! He doesn't exist!"

"For pity's sake! You of all people can't say that. You were evidently one of the first to suffer at his hands. You're stuck here, as you yourself understand, in a psychiatric clinic, but you keep on talking about his not existing. That is truly strange."

Confused, Ivan fell silent.

"As soon as you began describing him," continued the guest, "I already started to guess who you'd had the pleasure of chatting with yesterday. And truly, I'm amazed at Berlioz. Well, you, of course, are an innocent," here the guest apologized again, "but he, from all I've heard of him, had at least read something, after all! The very first things this Professor said dispelled any doubts I had. It's impossible not to recognize him, my friend! But then you're... you must again forgive me, I'm not mistaken, am I, you're an ignorant man?"

"Indisputably," agreed the unrecognizable Ivan.

"Right... I mean, even the face you described... different eyes, the brows! Forgive me, but perhaps you haven't even heard the opera *Faust*?"*

For some reason Ivan got most terribly embarrassed, and with a burning face he began mumbling something about some trip to a sanatorium in Yalta...

"Right, right... it's not surprising! But Berlioz, I repeat, amazes me... He's not only a well-read man, but a very cunning one too. Although in his defence I ought to say that Woland can, of course, throw dust in the eyes even of someone still more cunning."

"What?!" cried Ivan in his turn.

"Quiet!"

Ivan swung his palm and slapped it against his forehead and began to croak:

"I see, I see. He had the letter 'W' on his visiting card. Dearie, dearie me, there's a thing!" he was silent for a time in his confusion, peering at the moon that was floating beyond the grille, and then he began: "So therefore he really could have been with Pontius Pilate? He'd already been born then, hadn't he? And they call me a madman!" added Ivan, pointing at the door in indignation.

A bitter line revealed itself by the guest's lips.

"Let's look the truth in the eye," and the guest turned his face in the direction of the nocturnal heavenly body that was racing through a cloud. "Both you and I are madmen, why deny it! Do you see, he shook you, and you went off your head, because you're clearly the suitable type for it. But what you say did indisputably happen in reality. And yet it's so extraordinary, that even Stravinsky, a psychiatrist of genius, did not, of course, believe you. Did he look at you?" (Ivan nodded.) "The man you spoke to was both with Pilate, and at breakfast with Kant, and now he's come to Moscow."

"But I mean, he'll get up to the devil knows what here! Mustn't he be caught somehow?" inside the new Ivan, the former Ivan did after all raise his head, not entirely confidently, but not yet finally done for.

"You've already tried, and that's enough from you," responded the guest ironically, "and I don't advise others to try either. But that he will get up to things, you can rest assured of that. Oh dear, oh dear! How annoyed I am that it was you who met him and not me! Even if I'm all burnt out and the coals are covered in ash, still I swear I'd give Praskovya Fyodorovna's bunch of keys in return for that meeting, for I've got nothing else to give. I'm a beggar!"

"And what do you want him for?"

The guest grieved and twitched for a long time, but finally spoke:

"You see, what a strange thing it is, I'm stuck in here for the very same reason that you are, precisely because of Pontius Pilate." At this point the guest looked around fearfully and said: "The thing is that a year ago I wrote a novel about Pilate."

"You're a writer?" asked the poet with interest.

The guest's face darkened and he shook his fist at Ivan, then said:

"I'm the Master," he became stern and took from his dressing-gown pocket a thoroughly soiled black hat with the letter "M" embroidered on it in yellow silk. He put this hat on and showed himself to Ivan both in profile and full face to prove that he was the Master. "She sewed it for me with her own hands," he added mysteriously.

"And what is your name?"

"I no longer have a name," the strange guest replied in gloomy scorn, "I rejected it, as I did everything else in life generally. Let's forget about it."

"Then at least tell me about the novel," Ivan requested tactfully.

"As you wish. My life, it should be said, has turned out in a not entirely ordinary way," began the guest.

…A historian by education, just two years ago he had been working in one of Moscow's museums, and as well as that had been doing translations.

"From what language?" asked Ivan with interest.

"I know five languages besides my own," the guest replied, "English, French, German, Latin and Greek. Well, and I read a little Italian too."

"How about that!" Ivan whispered enviously.

The historian lived a solitary life, having no relatives anywhere and having almost no acquaintances in Moscow. And, just think, one day he won a hundred thousand roubles.

"Imagine my astonishment," the guest in the black hat whispered, "when I put my hand in the basket of dirty washing, and lo and behold: it has the same number on it as is in the newspaper! A bond," he explained, "I was given it at the museum."

Having won a hundred thousand, Ivan's enigmatic guest acted thus: bought books, gave up his room on Myasnitskaya...

"Ooh, what a damned hole" he growled.

...And he rented two rooms from the owner in the basement of a little private house in a garden square in a side street near the Arbat. He gave up his work at the museum and began composing a novel about Pontius Pilate.

"Ah, that was a golden age!" the narrator whispered, his eyes shining. "A completely self-contained little apartment, and an entrance hall as well, and a sink with water in it," he emphasized for some reason with especial pride, "and little windows just above the pathway leading from the gate. Opposite, four paces away, by the fence, there was a lilac, a lime and a maple. Dear, dear, dear! In winter I'd very rarely see anybody's black feet at the window or hear the crunch of the snow beneath them. And the fire burned eternally in my little stove! But suddenly the spring came, and through the murky window panes I saw the lilac bushes, at first bare, and later clothing themselves in greenery. And it was then, last spring, that something much more delightful happened than getting a hundred thousand roubles, and that, you must agree, is a huge sum of money!"

"That's true," acknowledged Ivan, who was listening attentively.

"I'd opened the little windows and was sitting in the second, absolutely tiny room," the guest began measuring it out with his arms, "like this – a couch, and opposite – another couch, and between them a little table, and on it a splendid night light, and further towards the window – books, here a small desk, and in the first room – a huge room, fourteen square metres – books, more books and the stove. Oh, what an ambience I had! There was an extraordinary scent of lilac! And exhaustion was making me light-headed, and Pilate was racing to its end..."

"The white mantle, the red lining! I understand!" exclaimed Ivan.

"Exactly so! Pilate was racing to its end, to its end, and I already knew that the last words of the novel would be: '...The fifth Procurator of Judaea, the horseman Pontius Pilate.' Well, naturally, I'd go out for walks. A hundred thousand is a huge sum, and I had a splendid suit. Or I'd set off for dinner in some cheap restaurant. There was a wonderful restaurant on the Arbat, I don't know if it still exists now."

At this point the guest's eyes opened wide, and he continued whispering, gazing at the moon:

"She was carrying some disgusting, alarming yellow flowers in her hands. The devil knows what they're called, but for some reason they're the first to appear in Moscow. And those flowers stood out very distinctly against her black spring coat. She was carrying yellow flowers! Not a good colour. She turned off Tverskaya into a side street, and at that point she turned around. Well, you know Tverskaya? Thousands of people were walking along Tverskaya, but I guarantee that she saw me alone, and looked not exactly anxiously, but rather even painfully somehow. And I was struck not so much by her beauty, as by the extraordinary solitude that no one saw in her eyes!

"Obeying that yellow sign, I turned into the side street as well and followed in her footsteps. We walked wordlessly down the winding, boring street, I down one side, and she down the other. And imagine, there wasn't a soul in the street. I was in torment, because it seemed to me it was essential to talk to her, and I was worried that I wouldn't utter a single word, and she'd go away, and I'd never see her again.

"And just imagine, suddenly it was she who spoke:

"'Do you like my flowers?'

"I remember distinctly the way her voice sounded, quite low, but with breaks in it, and, however silly, there seemed to be an echo in the side street, and it reverberated off the dirty yellow wall. I quickly crossed over to her side and, going up to her, replied:

"'No.'

"She looked at me in surprise, and suddenly, and completely unexpectedly, I realized it was specifically this woman I had loved all my life! There's a thing, eh? You'll say I'm mad, of course?"

"I'm not saying anything," exclaimed Ivan, and added: "I beg of you, do carry on!"

And the guest continued:

"Yes, she looked at me in surprise, and then, after looking, asked this:

"'Do you not like flowers generally?'

"In her voice, as it seemed to me, there was animosity. I walked alongside her, trying to keep in step, and, to my surprise, didn't feel myself constrained at all.

"'No, I like flowers, only not that kind,' I said.

"'What kind, then?'

"'I like roses.'

"At that point I regretted what I had said, because she smiled guiltily and threw her flowers into the gutter. Somewhat bewildered, I picked them up nonetheless and handed them to her, but she grinned and pushed the flowers away, and I carried them in my hands.

"We walked like that in silence for some time until she took the flowers from my hands and threw them onto the roadway, then she passed her hand in its black, bell-mouthed glove through my arm, and we went on side by side."

"Carry on," said Ivan, "and please don't leave anything out."

"Carry on?" queried the guest. "Well, but you can guess for yourself how it carried on." He suddenly wiped away an unexpected tear with his right sleeve and continued: "Love leapt out in front of us, as a murderer leaps out from under the ground in a side street, and it struck us both at once. Lightning strikes like that, a Finnish knife strikes like that! She, however, subsequently claimed that it wasn't like that, that we had, of course, loved one another for ever such a long time without knowing, and never seeing one another, and that she had lived with another man... and I too, at that time... with that... what's her name..."

"Who?" asked Bezdomny.

"With that... um... with that... um..." the guest replied, and started clicking his fingers.

"You were married?"

"Well yes, that's why I'm clicking... To that... Varenka... Manech-ka... No, Varenka... a striped dress as well, the museum... Still, I don't remember.

"And so she said she'd come out with yellow flowers in her hands that day so that I'd finally find her, and that if it hadn't happened, she'd have poisoned herself, because her life was empty.

"Yes, we were instantly struck by love. I knew it that same day, just an hour later, when, without noticing the city, we found ourselves on the embankment by the Kremlin wall.

"We talked as though we'd parted the day before, as though we'd known one another for many years. We agreed to meet the next day in the same place, on the Moscow River, and we did. The May sun shone for us. And soon, soon, that woman became my secret wife.

"She came to me every day, and I'd begin waiting for her first thing in the morning. The waiting expressed itself in my moving objects around on the table. Within ten minutes I'd sit down by the window and start listening out for the ramshackle old gate to go bang. And how curious: until my meeting with her, very few people came into our yard, or to put it simply, nobody did, but now it seemed to me that the city was focused on it. The gate would go bang, my heart would go bang, and, imagine, on the level of my face, outside the window, without fail somebody's dirty boots. A grinder. So who in our building needs a grinder? To grind what? What knives?

"She'd come through the gate once, but before that I'd have experienced my heart pounding no fewer than ten times, I'm not lying. And later on, when it was her time, and the hand on the clock was showing midday, it never actually stopped banging until, without any banging, almost completely noiselessly, her shoes with black suede decorative bows, fastened with steel buckles, drew level with the window.

"Sometimes she'd play a trick and, delaying by the second window, she'd tap the toe of her shoe on the pane. That same second I'd be at the window, but the shoe would vanish, the black silk blocking out the light would vanish – I'd go and open the door to her.

"Nobody knew of our liaison, I can vouch for that, though that's never ever the way it is. Her husband didn't know, acquaintances didn't know. In the little old detached house, where that basement belonged to me, people did know, of course, they saw some woman visiting me, but they didn't know her name."

"And who is she?" asked Ivan, interested in the love story in the highest degree.

The guest made a gesture signifying that he would never tell that to anyone, and continued his story.

It became known to Ivan that the Master and the stranger had come to love one another so deeply that they became completely inseparable. And Ivan could already clearly picture to himself the two rooms in the basement of the detached house, in which it was always twilight because of the lilac and the fence. The shabby red furniture, the bureau, on it a clock that chimed every half-hour, and the books, books from the painted floor to the smoke-blackened ceiling, and the stove.

Ivan learnt that his guest and his secret wife came to the conclusion as early as the first days of their liaison that it was fate itself that had brought them together on the corner of Tverskaya and the side street, and that they were made for each other for ever.

Ivan learnt from the guest's narrative how the lovers used to spend the day. She would arrive and, first and foremost, put on an apron, and in the narrow entrance hall, which housed the sink that the poor sick man was for some reason proud of, she would light the paraffin stove on the wooden table and cook breakfast, and lay it on the oval table in the first room. When the May thunderstorms were under way, and the water rolled noisily past the myopic windows into the gateway, threatening to flood the final refuge, the lovers heated up the stove and baked potatoes in it. The steam would billow from the potatoes, the black potato skin stained their fingers. Laughter was heard in the little basement, and after the rain the trees in the garden threw off their broken twigs and their white tassels.

When the thunderstorms ended and the stifling summer arrived, the long-awaited roses they both loved appeared in a vase. The one who called himself the Master worked feverishly on his novel, and the novel absorbed the unknown woman too.

"Truly, there were times I began to be jealous of her attachment to it," the nocturnal guest who had come from the moonlit balcony whispered to Ivan.

Thrusting her slender fingers with their sharply pointed nails into her hair, she would endlessly read over what had been written, and after reading it over, would spend time sewing that hat. Sometimes she would squat by the lower shelves or stand on a chair to reach the top ones and wipe the hundreds of dusty spines with a cloth. She promised fame, she urged him on, and it was at this point she started calling him the Master. She impatiently awaited the final words that had already been promised about the fifth Procurator of Judaea, repeating individual phrases she liked in a loud, sing-song voice, and said that this novel was her life.

It was finished in August, was given to some obscure typist, and she typed it up in five copies. And finally the hour came when it was necessary to abandon the secret refuge and emerge into life.

"And I emerged into life, holding it in my hands, and then my life ended," the Master whispered, and hung his head, and it was for a long time that the sad black hat with the yellow letter "M" shook. He took his story further, but it became rather incoherent. Only one thing was it possible to understand, that some sort of catastrophe then befell Ivan's guest.

"I found myself in the world of literature for the first time, but now, when everything's already over and my ruin's clear to see, I remember it with horror!" the Master whispered solemnly and raised his hand. "Yes, he really shocked me, oh, how he shocked me."

"Who?" whispered Ivan scarcely audibly, fearful of interrupting the agitated narrator.

"The editor, that's what I'm saying, the editor. Yes, so he read it. He looked at me as if my cheek had swollen up with an abscess, kind of squinted into the corner and even tittered in embarrassment. He needlessly crumpled the manuscript and quacked. The questions he asked me seemed mad to me. Without saying a thing about the essence of the novel, he asked me who I was and where I'd sprung from, had I been writing long, and why nothing had been heard of me before, and even posed, from my point of view, an utterly idiotic question: who was it that had given me the idea of composing a novel on such a strange subject?

"Finally I got sick of him, and I asked him straight out, would he be publishing the novel or would he not?

"At this point he began making a fuss, started mumbling something or other, and declared that he couldn't decide that question himself, that the other members of the editorial board had to familiarize themselves with my work, namely, the critics Latunsky and Ariman and the writer Mstislav Lavrovich. He asked me to come in two weeks' time.

"I came in two weeks' time, and was seen by some girl with eyes that squinted in towards her nose from her constant lying."

"That's Lapshonnikova, the publishers' secretary," said Ivan with a grin, knowing well the world that his guest was describing so irately.

"Perhaps," snapped the latter, "and so I got my novel back from her, already pretty soiled and tattered. Trying not to let her eyes meet mine, Lapshonnikova informed me that the publishers had supplies of material for two years ahead, and for that reason the question of publishing my novel, as she expressed herself, 'didn't arise'. What do I remember after that?" muttered the Master, rubbing his temples. "Yes, fallen red petals on the title page, and also my girl's eyes. Yes, I remember those eyes."

Ivan's guest's story was becoming more and more muddled, was more and more full of omissions. He said something about slanting rain and despair in the basement refuge, of how he had gone somewhere else. He cried out in a whisper that he did not blame her in the least, the one who had pushed him into the struggle, oh no, he did not blame her!

"I remember, I remember that damned insert in the newspaper," muttered the guest, drawing a newspaper page in the air with a finger of each hand, and Ivan guessed from the subsequent muddled phrases that some other editor had printed a big extract from the novel of the one who called himself the Master.

Later on, as Ivan heard, something sudden and strange occurred. One day, the hero opened up a newspaper and saw an article in it by the critic Ariman, which was called 'An Enemy Sortie', where Ariman warned all and sundry that he, that is, our hero, had made an attempt to sneak into print an apologia for Jesus Christ.

"Ah, I remember, I remember!" exclaimed Ivan. "But I've forgotten what your name is!"

"I repeat, let's leave my name aside, it no longer exists," replied the guest. "And that's not the point. A day later in another newspaper another article came to light, signed by Mstislav Lavrovich, where its author suggested striking, and striking hard, against pilatism and the icon-dauber who had taken it into his head to sneak it (that damned word again!) into print.

"Dumbfounded by this unheard-of word, 'pilatism', I opened up a third newspaper. Here there were two articles: one by Latunsky, and the other signed with the initials 'M.Z.'. I can assure you that the works of Ariman and Lavrovich could have been considered a joke compared with what Latunsky had written. It's enough to tell you that Latunsky's article was called 'A Militant Old Believer'.* I got so carried away with reading the articles about me that I didn't notice her appearing in front of me (I'd forgotten to close the door) with a wet umbrella in her hands and with newspapers that were wet as well. Her eyes were exuding fire, her hands were trembling and cold. First of all she rushed to kiss me, then, in a hoarse voice and banging her hand on the table, she said she would poison Latunsky."

Ivan gave an embarrassed sort of grunt, but said nothing.

"The joyless days of autumn arrived," the guest continued, "the monstrous failure with the novel seemed to have taken a part of my soul out of me. In essence, there was nothing else for me to do, and I lived from one meeting with her to the next. And it was at this time that something happened to me. The devil knows what, but Stravinsky probably worked it out long ago. Namely, I was overcome with melancholy and various presentiments appeared. The articles, note, didn't cease. I laughed at the first of them. But the more of them appeared, the more my attitude to them changed. The second stage was the stage of surprise. Something uncommonly false and uncertain could be sensed in literally every line of those articles, despite their menacing and certain tone. I constantly had the impression, and I couldn't free myself of it, that the authors of those articles weren't saying what they wanted to say, and that was precisely what aroused their fury. And then, imagine, a third stage began – of fear. No, not fear of those articles, you should understand, but fear regarding other things that had nothing whatsoever to do with them or with the novel. So, for example, I began to be afraid of the dark. In short, the stage of mental illness began. It seemed to me, particularly as I was falling asleep, that the tentacles of some highly flexible, cold octopus were stealing directly, straight towards my heart. And I had to sleep with the light on.

"My beloved changed greatly (of course, I didn't tell her about the octopus, but she could see there was something bad happening to me), she grew thin and pale, stopped laughing, and kept on asking me to forgive her for advising me to print the extract. She said I should drop everything and go away to the south, to the Black Sea, spending all the money that remained of the hundred thousand on the trip.

"She was very insistent, and so as not to quarrel (something told me I wouldn't have to go away to the Black Sea), I promised her I'd do it in a few days' time. But she said she'd get me the ticket herself. Then I took out all my money, around ten thousand roubles, that is, and handed it over to her.

"'Why so much?' she asked in surprise.

"I said something about being afraid of thieves and asked her to take care of the money until my departure. She took it, put it away in her handbag, started kissing me and saying it would be easier for her to die than leave me alone in such a state, but that she was expected, she was submitting to necessity, she would come the next day. She begged me not to be afraid of anything.

"It was at dusk, in mid-October. And she left. I lay down on the couch and fell asleep without lighting the lamp. I was woken up by the sensation that the octopus was there. Fumbling in the dark, I just about managed to light the lamp. My pocket watch showed two o'clock in the morning. I'd lain down falling ill, and woken up sick. It suddenly seemed to me that the autumn darkness would knock out the window panes, pour into the room, and I'd choke in it, as though in ink. I got up like a man no longer in control of himself. I cried out, and the idea came to me of running to somebody, if only to my landlord upstairs. I struggled with myself like a madman. I had the strength to get as far as the stove and stir up the firewood inside it. When it began to crackle and the door began rattling, I seemed to feel a little better. I rushed into the hall and lit the light there, found a bottle of white wine, uncorked it and started drinking the wine out of the bottle. This dulled the fear somewhat, at least to the extent that I didn't run to the landlord, I returned to the stove. I opened the door so that the heat began scorching my face and hands, and whispered:

"'Sense that I've had a calamity... Come, come, come!...'

"But no one came. The fire was roaring in the stove, the rain was lashing at the windows. Then the final thing happened. I took out of the desk drawer the heavy copies of the novel and the draft notebooks and started to burn them. It's terribly hard to do, because paper covered in writing burns unwillingly. Breaking my nails, I ripped the notebooks apart, put them in upright between the logs and ruffled the leaves with the poker. Ash would get the better of me at times and quench the flame, but I struggled with it, and while resisting stubbornly, the novel was nonetheless perishing. Familiar words flashed before me, a yellow colour rose inexorably up the pages from bottom to top, but even there the words stood out all the same. They disappeared only when the paper was blackening, and I would finish them off furiously with the poker.

"At this time someone began quietly scratching at the window. My heart leapt, and, loading the last notebook into the fire, I rushed to open up. Brick steps led from the basement to the door to the yard. Stumbling, I ran up to it and quietly asked:

"'Who's there?'

"And a voice, her voice, answered me:

"'It's me...'

"Without knowing how, I managed the chain and the key. No sooner had she stepped inside than she fell against me, all wet, with wet cheeks and bedraggled hair, shivering. The only word I could utter was:

"'You... you?' and my voice broke, and we ran down the steps. She freed herself of her overcoat in the hall, and we quickly went into the first room. She gave a quiet cry, and with her bare hands threw out of the stove onto the floor the last of what remained there, a bundle that had started burning from the bottom up. Smoke immediately filled the room. I stamped the fire out with my feet, while she fell onto the couch and burst into uncontained and convulsive sobbing.

"When she'd quietened down, I said:

"'I'd come to hate that novel, and I'm afraid. I'm ill. I'm frightened.'

"She got up and spoke:

"'God, how ill you are. Why is this, why? But I'll save you, I'll save you. What ever is it?'

"I could see her eyes, puffed up from the smoke and from crying, could feel her cold hands stroking my forehead.

"'I'll cure you, I will,' she muttered, boring into my shoulders, 'you'll rewrite it. Why oh why didn't I keep one copy myself!'

"She bared her teeth in rage and said something else indistinct. Then, with lips compressed, she set about collecting and smoothing out the scorched sheets. It was some chapter from the middle of the novel, I don't remember which. She put the sheets carefully together, wrapped them in paper and tied them with a ribbon. Her every action showed she was full of resolution and had regained her self-control.

She demanded some wine and, after having a drink, began speaking more calmly.

"'This is how you have to pay for lying,' she said, 'and I don't want to lie any more. I'd even stay here with you now, but I don't want to do it this way. I don't want it to remain in his memory for ever that I ran away from him at night. He never did me any harm... He was called out suddenly, there's a fire at his factory. But he'll soon be back. I'll have things out with him tomorrow morning, I'll say I love someone else, and I'll return to you for ever. Answer me, perhaps you don't want that?'

"'My poor, poor girl,' I said to her, 'I won't allow you to do it. Things won't be going well for me, and I don't want you to perish along with me.'

"'That reason alone?' she asked, and brought her eyes up close to mine.

"'That alone.'

"She became terribly animated, leant up against me, winding her arms around my neck, and said:

"'I'll perish along with you. In the morning I'll be here with you.'

"And so the last thing I remember in my life is a strip of light from my hallway, and in that strip of light an unwound strand of hair, her beret and her eyes full of resolution. I remember too a black silhouette on the outer doorstep and a white bundle.

"'I'd see you on your way, but I no longer have the strength to come back alone, I'm afraid.'

"'Don't be afraid. Be patient for a few hours. Tomorrow morning I'll be here with you.'

"And those were her last words in my life... Shhh!" the sick man suddenly cut himself short and raised a finger. "It's a restless moonlit night tonight."

He hid on the balcony. Ivan heard wheels driving down the corridor, and somebody uttered a weak sob or cry.

When everything had gone quiet, the guest returned and announced that room 120 had gained a resident too. Someone had been brought in, and he kept on asking for his head to be returned. Both men paused in silent alarm, but, calming themselves, they returned to the interrupted story. The guest was about to open his mouth, but the night was indeed a restless one. Voices were still audible in the corridor, and the guest began speaking into Ivan's ear so quietly that what he said became known to the poet alone, with the exception of the first phrase:

"A quarter of an hour after she left me, there was a knock on my window…"

The sick man was evidently greatly agitated by what he whispered into Ivan's ear. Spasms kept on passing over his face. Fear and fury swam and raged in his eyes. The narrator pointed his hand somewhere in the direction of the moon, which was already long gone from the balcony. Only when various sounds from without stopped carrying in to them did the guest move away from Ivan and begin speaking a little louder:

"Yes, and so, in mid-January, at night, in the same overcoat, but with the buttons torn off, I was huddled against the cold in my little yard. Behind me were snowdrifts which hid the lilac bushes, while in front of me, low down, were my little windows, feebly lit and with the curtains closed. I fell down by the first of them and listened closely – a gramophone was playing in my rooms. That's all I could hear, but I couldn't see anything. I stood there for a little, then went out of the gate into the lane. There was a blizzard blowing in it. A dog that got caught up under my feet gave me a fright, and I ran over to the other side away from it. The cold and the fear that had become my constant companion were working me into a frenzy. There was nowhere for me to go, and it would have been simplest of all, of course, to throw myself under a tram in the street into which my lane emerged. From afar I could see those ice-covered crates, filled with light, and hear their loathsome grating on the frost. But, my dear neighbour, the whole thing was that fear had a hold on every cell of my body. And I was afraid of the tram in exactly the same way as I was of the dog. No, there's no illness in this building worse than mine, I can assure you."

"But you could have let her know," said Ivan, sympathizing with the poor sick man, "and besides, she has your money, doesn't she? She has kept it, of course, hasn't she?"

"Be in no doubt about that, of course she's kept it. But you evidently don't understand me. Or rather, I've lost the capacity I once had for describing something. I don't feel regret for it, though, as it'll be of no further use to me. Before her," the guest looked reverentially into the darkness of the night, "would have dropped a letter from the madhouse. How can you send letters from such an address? A mental patient? You're joking, my friend! Make her unhappy? No, I'm not capable of that."

Ivan could not object to this, but the taciturn Ivan felt sympathy for his guest, felt pity for him. And the latter nodded his head in its black hat in the torment of his memories and spoke thus:

"The poor woman... Still, I'm hopeful she's forgotten me..."

"But you may recover..." said Ivan timidly.

"I'm incurable," replied the guest calmly, "when Stravinsky says he'll return me to life, I don't believe him. He's humane, and simply wants to comfort me. Still, I don't deny I'm much better now. Yes, now where was it I stopped? The frost, those flying trams... I knew this clinic had already opened, and I set off for it on foot across the entire city. Madness! Out of town I'd probably have frozen to death, but I was saved by chance. Something had broken down in a truck, and I approached the driver, this was about four kilometres outside the city gates, and, to my surprise, he took pity on me. The vehicle was on its way here. And he drove me. I escaped with frostbitten toes on my left foot. But that was cured. And so I've been here more than three months. And do you know, I find that it's really not at all bad here. You don't have to make great plans for yourself, dear neighbour, truly! Me, for example, I wanted to travel the entire globe. Oh well, it turns out that's not meant to be. I see only an insignificant part of that globe. I don't think it's the very best there is upon it, but, I repeat, it's not so very bad. Now summer's on its way to us, and ivy will entwine the balcony, so Praskovya Fyodorovna promises. The keys have broadened my possibilities. There'll be the moon at night. Ah, it's gone! It's getting cooler. The night's slipping past midnight. Time for me to go."

"Tell me, what happened to Yeshua and Pilate next," asked Ivan, "I beg you, I want to know."

"Oh no, no!" replied the guest, twitching painfully, "I can't remember my novel without a shudder. And your acquaintance from Patriarch's would have done it better than me. Thank you for the chat. Goodbye."

And before Ivan could come to his senses, the grille closed with a quiet clang, and the guest disappeared.

14

Praise Be to the Cockerel!

H IS NERVES COULDN'T TAKE IT, as they say, and Rimsky did not wait for the compilation of the report to be finished to escape to his office. He sat at the desk and gazed with inflamed eyes at the magical ten-rouble notes that lay in front of him. The Financial Director was at his wits' end. From outside there came a steady hum. The audience was streaming out of the building of The Variety onto the street. To the Financial Director's extremely sharpened hearing there suddenly came the distinct trilling of the police. In itself it never ever promises anything pleasant. And when it was repeated, and another trill, more imperious and prolonged, stepped in to assist it, and then clearly audible cackling joined in with it too, and even some sort of whooping, the Financial Director immediately realized that something else scandalous and foul had happened in the street. And that no matter how much one might want to brush it aside, it had the closest connection with the disgusting performance put on by the black magician and his assistants. The sensitive Financial Director was not in the least mistaken.

As soon as he glanced out of a window that looked out onto Sadovaya, his face twisted and he did not so much whisper as hiss:

"I knew it!"

In the bright light of the very powerful street lights he saw on the pavement down below him a lady wearing just a violet-coloured camisole and knickers. On the lady's head there was, true, a hat, and in her hands an umbrella.

Around this lady, who was in a state of utter confusion, now squatting down, now bursting to run off somewhere, there was a restless crowd letting out that same raucous laughter that had sent a shiver down the Financial Director's spine. Some citizen was throwing himself around beside the lady, tearing off his summer coat and, in his agitation, completely failing to cope with the sleeve in which his arm had got caught.

Cries and roars of laughter could be heard from another spot too – namely, from the left doorway, and, turning his head in that direction, Grigory Danilovich saw another lady wearing pink underwear. She jumped from the road onto the pavement, seeking to hide in the doorway, but the people flowing out were blocking her path, and the poor victim of her own frivolity and passion for fancy clothes, tricked by the vile Fagot's crew, dreamt of only one thing – being swallowed up by the ground. A policeman was heading towards the unfortunate woman, drilling the air with his whistling, and hurrying along behind the policeman were some extremely cheerful young men wearing caps. It was they who were emitting that raucous laughter and the whoops.

A thin, moustachioed cab driver flew up to the first undressed woman and reined in his bony, worn-out horse with a flourish. The face of the man with the moustache was grinning joyfully.

Rimsky hit himself on the head with his fist, spat and leapt back from the window.

He sat by the desk for a little while, listening intently to the street. The whistling reached a crescendo in various spots and then began to die away. The scandal, to Rimsky's surprise, was wound up unexpectedly quickly.

The time was coming to act, the bitter cup of responsibility had to be drunk. The telephones had been repaired during the third part of the show, and he had to ring and report what had happened, ask for help, lie his way out of it, blame everything on Likhodeyev, shield himself and so on. Hell and damnation!

Two times the distressed Director put his hand on the receiver, and twice he took it off again. And suddenly, in the deathly hush of the office, the telephone burst out ringing itself, right in the Financial Director's face, and he flinched and turned cold. "My nerves are well and truly frayed, though," he thought, and picked up the receiver. Immediately he recoiled from it and went whiter than paper. A quiet, and at the same time insinuating and depraved female voice had whispered into the receiver:

"Don't phone anyone, Rimsky, or there'll be trouble…"

At once the receiver was deserted. Feeling gooseflesh on his back, the Financial Director put the receiver down and for some reason looked around at the window behind his back. Through the branches of a maple, sparse and still barely covered in greenery, he saw the moon flying in a transparent little cloud. Riveted for some reason by the branches, Rimsky looked at them, and the more he looked, the more and more powerfully was he gripped by terror.

Making an effort with himself, the Financial Director finally turned away from the moonlit window and got up. There could not possibly be any more talk of ringing, and now the Financial Director thought of only one thing – how he could leave the theatre quickly.

He listened intently: the theatre building was silent. Rimsky realized that he had long been alone on the entire first floor, and at that thought a child's insuperable terror took hold of him. He could not think without a shudder of the fact that he would now have to walk alone along the empty corridors and go down the staircases. He feverishly grabbed the hypnotist's ten-rouble notes from the desk, put them away in his briefcase and coughed, to give himself just a little bit of encouragement. The cough came out rather hoarse and weak.

And here it seemed to him that from under the office door there was a sudden breath of rather putrid dampness. A shiver ran down the Financial Director's back. And at that point a clock struck unexpectedly too, and began chiming midnight. And even the chimes elicited a shiver in the Financial Director. But his heart sank completely when he heard a Yale key turning gently in the lock of the door. Clutching on to his briefcase with moist, cold hands, the Financial Director felt that if this rustling in the keyhole continued any longer, he would be unable to contain himself and would emit a piercing cry.

Finally the door yielded to someone's efforts, opened up, and noiselessly into the office came Varenukha. Rimsky sat down in an armchair exactly as he had been standing, because his legs buckled. Filling his chest with air, he smiled an ingratiating sort of smile and said quietly:

"God, how you frightened me..."

Yes, that sudden appearance might have frightened absolutely anyone, and nonetheless at the same time it was a great joy: one end, at least, had emerged in this tangled business.

"Well, hurry up and talk then! Well! Well!" croaked Rimsky, clutching at that end. "What does it all mean?!"

"Forgive me, please," the man who had entered responded in a muffled voice, closing the door, "I thought you'd already left."

And without taking off his cap, Varenukha went over to an armchair and sat down on the other side of the desk.

It must be said that a slight oddity was evident in Varenukha's reply, and it immediately stung the Financial Director, capable in his sensitivity of competing with any of the world's best seismographic stations. How could that be? Whatever was Varenukha on his way into the Financial Director's office for, if he assumed he was not there? He has his own office, after all. That's the first thing. And the second thing is: no matter which entrance Varenukha had used to enter the building, he must unavoidably have encountered one of the night-time duty staff, and all of them had been informed that Grigory Danilovich would be detained in his office for a certain time.

But the Financial Director did not bother pondering long on the subject of this oddity. There were other things to worry about.

"Why on earth didn't you ring? What's the meaning of all this foolishness about Yalta?"

"Well, just what I said," replied the manager, smacking his lips as though he were suffering from toothache, "he's been found in a tavern in Pushkino."

"What do you mean, in Pushkino?! Isn't that just outside Moscow? But the telegrams are from Yalta?!"

"Yalta's got damn all to do with it! He plied the Pushkino telegraphist with drink, and the two of them started getting up to no good, including sending telegrams marked 'Yalta'."

"Aha... Aha... Well, all right, all right..." Rimsky did not so much say as sort of sing. His eyes lit up with a nice yellow light. There took shape in his head the festive picture of Styopa's ignominious dismissal. Liberation! The Financial Director's long-awaited liberation from that disaster in the person of Likhodeyev! And perhaps Stepan Bogdanovich would get something even rather worse than dismissal... "The details!" said Rimsky, banging a blotter on the desk.

And Varenukha began recounting the details. As soon as he had arrived where he had been sent by the Financial Director, they had seen him immediately and heard him out in the most attentive fashion. Of course, nobody had even entertained the thought that Styopa might be in Yalta. Everyone had agreed straight away with Varenukha's assumption that Likhodeyev was, of course, in the 'Yalta' at Pushkino.

"And where is he now?" the agitated Financial Director interrupted the manager.

"Well, where else would he be?" replied the manager with a crooked grin. "Naturally, at the sobering-up station."

"Right, right! Ah, thank you!"

But Varenukha continued his narrative. And the more he narrated, the more vividly there opened up before the Financial Director the great long chain of Likhodeyev's loutish and disgraceful actions, and each succeeding link in that chain was worse than the one preceding it. What about, say, merely the drunken dancing, when he was locked in an embrace with the telegraphist on the patch of grass in front of the Pushkino telegraph office to the sounds of some idle accordion. The racing after some citizenesses, who squealed in horror! The attempt to have a fight with the barman at the 'Yalta' itself! The strewing of spring onions all over the floor of that same 'Yalta'. The smashing of eight bottles of dry white Ai-Danil.* The breaking of the meter of the taxi driver who didn't want to let Styopa into his vehicle. The threat to arrest the citizens who tried to put a stop to Styopa's foul behaviour... In short, a horror story!

Styopa was well known in Moscow's theatrical circles, and everyone was aware that the man was no bowl of cherries. But nevertheless, what was being related by the manager about him was too much, even for Styopa. Yes, too much. Far too much even...

Rimsky's sharp eyes cut into the face of the manager across the desk, and the more the latter spoke, the gloomier those eyes became. The more lifelike and colourful became the foul details with which the manager adorned his tale, the less the Financial Director believed the narrator. And when Varenukha reported that Styopa had thrown restraint aside to such an extent that he had tried to offer resistance to those who had come for him in order to return him to Moscow, the Financial Director already knew for sure that everything he was being told by the manager who had returned at midnight, everything was a lie! A lie from the first word to the last.

Varenukha had not been to Pushkino, and Styopa himself had not been in Pushkino either. There had been no drunken telegraphist, there had been no broken glass in the tavern, Styopa had not been bound with ropes... there had been none of it.

As soon as the Financial Director became firmly convinced that the manager was lying to him, terror began to spread through his entire body, starting at his feet, and twice more the Financial Director imagined a breath of putrid malarial dampness blowing across the floor. Without for an instant taking his eyes off the manager, who was going into strange sorts of contortions in the armchair as he continually strove not to emerge from out of the blue shadow of the table lamp, and shielded himself, in a surprising way somehow, with a newspaper from the light of the bulb that was ostensibly bothering him, the Financial Director thought about only one thing: what on earth did it all mean? Why was the manager, whose return to him had been far too late, lying to him so brazenly in the deserted and silent building? And the consciousness of danger, unknown but terrible danger, began wracking the Financial Director's soul. Pretending not to notice the manager's wiles and his tricks with the newspaper, the Financial Director examined his face, hardly listening any longer to the yarn Varenukha was spinning. There was something that was still more inexplicable than the slanderous story, invented for an unknown reason, about the escapades in Pushkino, and that something was the change in the appearance and in the manners of the manager.

No matter how the latter drew the duck's peak of his cap down over his eyes to throw a shadow on his face, no matter how he twisted the sheet of newspaper around, the Financial Director managed to make out a huge bruise on the right side of his face just beside his nose. Apart from that, the normally full-blooded manager was now pale with a chalky, unhealthy pallor, while – on a stifling night – an old striped muffler was for some reason wound around his neck. And if to this had been added the disgusting manner of sucking in and smacking his lips that had appeared in the manager during the period of his absence, the abrupt change of voice, which had become muffled and coarse, the furtiveness and cowardliness in the eyes, it could boldly have been said that Ivan Savelyevich Varenukha had become unrecognizable.

Something else was causing the Financial Director burning disquiet, but what precisely he could not understand, no matter how he strained his inflamed brain, no matter how much he peered at Varenukha. One thing he could assert, that there was something unprecedented, unnatural in this combination of the manager and the very familiar armchair.

"Well, they finally overcame him, loaded him into a vehicle," Varenukha was droning, glancing out from behind the sheet and covering up the bruise with his palm.

Rimsky suddenly reached out his hand and, as if without thinking,

156

and at the same time playing on the desk with his fingers, he pressed the button of the electric bell with his palm, then froze. In the empty building the sharp signal would be bound to be heard. But that signal did not ensue, and the button sank lifelessly into the wood of the desk. The button was dead, the bell not working.

The Financial Director's cunning had not escaped Varenukha, who asked, wincing, and with a flash of obviously malicious fire in his eyes:

"What are you ringing for?"

"I did it without thinking," the Financial Director replied in a muffled voice, jerked his hand back and, in his turn, asked shakily: "What's that on your face?"

"The car swerved, I hit myself on the door handle," replied Varenukha, averting his eyes.

"He's lying!" the Financial Director exclaimed inwardly. And at this point his eyes suddenly became rounded and quite mad, and he fixed them on the back of the armchair.

Behind the armchair, on the floor, lay two intersecting shadows, one weak and grey, the other rather denser and blacker. Distinctly visible on the floor was the shadow of the back of the armchair and its tapering legs, but above the chair back on the floor there was no shadow from Varenukha's head, and equally, the manager's legs were not there under the legs.

"He's not casting a shadow!" Rimsky gave a mental cry of despair. He was struck by the shivers.

Varenukha glanced round furtively behind the back of the armchair, following Rimsky's mad gaze, and realized he had been found out.

He rose from the armchair (and the Financial Director did the same) and took a step away from the desk, squeezing his briefcase in his arms.

"Guessed, damn you! Always were bright," Varenukha said, smirking maliciously right in the Financial Director's face, and he leapt back unexpectedly from the armchair to the door and quickly pushed down the button on the Yale lock. The Financial Director glanced round despairingly, retreating towards the window that looked into the garden, and in that window, flooded with moonlight, he saw the face of a naked girl pressed up against the glass and her bare arm thrust in through the transom and trying to undo the lower catch. The upper one was already undone.

It seemed to Rimsky that the light in the table lamp was going out and the desk was leaning over. An icy wave poured over Rimsky, but, fortunately for him, he mastered himself and did not fall. What remained of his powers was sufficient for him not to shout, but to whisper:

"Help…"

Varenukha, guarding the door, was jumping about beside it, hanging in the air and rocking about in it for long periods of time. He waved bent fingers in Rimsky's direction, hissed and smacked his lips, winking at the girl in the window.

The latter began to hurry, thrust her red-haired head through the transom, stretched her arm out as far as she could, started scratching with her nails at the lower latch and shaking the frame. Her arm began to lengthen as if it were elastic, and became covered in the green colour of a corpse. Finally the green fingers of the dead woman clasped the head of the latch, turned it, and the frame started to open. Rimsky gave a feeble cry, leant up against the wall and put his briefcase out in front of him like a shield. He understood that his end had come.

The frame flew wide open, but instead of the freshness of the night and the scent of the limes, into the room burst the smell of the cellar. The deceased woman stepped onto the window sill. Rimsky could distinctly see patches of putrefaction on her breast.

And at that moment the joyful, unexpected cry of a cockerel reached the garden from the low building behind the shooting range where the birds that took part in the acts were kept. The strident trained cockerel was blaring out its proclamation that the dawn was rolling towards Moscow from the east.

Wild fury distorted the girl's face, she emitted a hoarse curse, and by the doors Varenukha shrieked and collapsed out of the air onto the floor.

The cockerel's cry was repeated, the girl snapped her teeth together, and her red hair stood up on end. With the cockerel's third cry she turned and flew out. And in her wake, jumping up and stretching out horizontally in the air, Varenukha, reminiscent of a flying cupid, floated slowly over the desk and out of the window.

White as snow, without a single black hair, the old man who had just recently been Rimsky ran up to the door, released the latch, opened the door and rushed off down the dark corridor. At the turn onto the staircase, moaning in terror, he fumbled for the light switch and the staircase was lit up. On the stairs the shaking, trembling old man fell down, imagining that Varenukha had collapsed on him gently from above.

When he had run down, Rimsky saw the man on duty asleep on a chair by the box office in the vestibule. Rimsky stole past him on tiptoe and slipped out through the main door. Outside he felt a little better. He came to his senses to the extent that, taking his head in his hands, he managed to grasp that his hat had remained in the office.

It stands to reason that he did not return for it, but, gasping for breath, started running across the wide road to the opposite corner by the cinema, beside which a dim little reddish light could just be made out. A minute later he was already beside it. No one had managed to beat him to the vehicle.

"Make the express train to Leningrad and I'll give you a tip," said the old man, breathing heavily and holding on to his heart.

"I'm going to the garage," the driver replied with hatred, and turned away.

Then Rimsky undid his briefcase, pulled fifty roubles out of it and held them out to the driver through the open front window.

A few moments later the jangling vehicle was flying like a whirlwind along the ring road of Sadovaya. The fare was being tossed about on his seat, and in the sliver of mirror hanging in front of the driver Rimsky could see now the driver's joyful eyes, now his own mad ones.

Leaping from the vehicle in front of the station building, Rimsky shouted to the first person he came across wearing a white apron and with a badge:

"First category, one, I'll give you thirty," he was crumpling up ten-rouble notes as he took them out of his briefcase, "if there's no first, then second, if there's none, take hard carriage."

The man with the badge, glancing round at the illuminated clock, tore the notes from Rimsky's hands.

Five minutes later, the express train disappeared from beneath the station's glass dome and vanished completely in the darkness. Along with it vanished Rimsky too.

15

Nikanor Ivanovich's Dream

I T'S NOT HARD TO GUESS that the fat man with the crimson physiognomy who was put in room No. 119 was Nikanor Ivanovich Bosoi.

He got to Professor Stravinsky not immediately, however, but after having spent some time beforehand in another place.

From that other place there remained but little in Nikanor Ivanovich's recollection. There were memories of only a desk, a cupboard and a couch.

A conversation had been entered into there with Nikanor Ivanovich, before whose eyes things had somehow grown dim because of rushes of blood and mental excitement, but the conversation had turned out a strange, muddled sort of one, or to put it more accurately, had not turned out at all.

The very first question that was put to Nikanor Ivanovich was this:

"Are you Nikanor Ivanovich Bosoi, Chairman of the House Committee of No. 302 *bis* on Sadovaya?"

To this, laughing a terrible laugh, Nikanor Ivanovich replied literally thus:

"I'm Nikanor, of course I'm Nikanor! But whatever sort of darned Chairman am I?"

"How's that, then?" Nikanor Ivanovich was asked with a narrowing of the eyes.

"It's just that if," he replied, "I'm the Chairman, I should have established straight away that he was an unclean spirit. I mean, what's all this? The pince-nez cracked... all in rags... How can he be an interpreter for a foreigner!"

"Who are you talking about?" Nikanor Ivanovich was asked.

"Korovyev!" Nikanor Ivanovich exclaimed. "He's put up in our building in apartment No. 50! Write it down: Korovyev. He must be caught immediately! Write it down: entrance No. 6, that's where he is."

"Where did you get the foreign currency?" Nikanor Ivanovich was asked cordially.

"The true God, Almighty God," Nikanor Ivanovich began, "sees all, and it serves me right. I never held it in my hands and never had an inkling what hard currency was! The Lord will punish me for my iniquity," Nikanor Ivanovich continued with feeling, now buttoning his shirt, now unbuttoning it, now crossing himself, "I took bribes! I did, but I took them in our Soviet money! I gave out registrations for money, I don't argue, it happened. Our secretary Prolezhnev's a fine one too, he's a fine one as well! Let's put it bluntly, we're all thieves in the House Management Committee. But I didn't take any foreign currency!"

At the request not to play the fool, but to tell how the dollars had got into the ventilation shaft, Nikanor Ivanovich got down on his knees and rocked forward, opening his mouth wide, as though wishing to swallow a block of the parquet.

"Do you wish me," he moaned, "to eat the ground to show I didn't take it? And Korovyev – he's a devil!"

All patience has its limits, and the voice at the desk was now raised, and a hint given to Nikanor Ivanovich that it was time for him to start speaking the language of a human being.

At this point the room with the couch was filled with a wild roar from Nikanor Ivanovich, who had leapt up from his knees:

"There he is! There he is behind the cupboard! There he is grinning! And it's his pince-nez... Hold him! Exorcize the room!"

The blood ebbed away from Nikanor Ivanovich's face; trembling, he made the sign of the cross in the air, rushed to the door and back again, started chanting some prayer or other and, finally, began spouting complete rubbish.

It had become quite clear that Nikanor Ivanovich was no good for conversation of any kind. He was led out and put in a separate room, where he calmed down somewhat and only prayed and sobbed.

A journey was made, of course, to Sadovaya, and apartment No. 50 was visited. But no Korovyev was found there, and no one in the building either knew or had seen any Korovyev. The apartment occupied by the late Berlioz and Likhodeyev, who had gone away to Yalta, was empty, and in the study the wax seals hung peacefully, unharmed by anyone, on the cabinets. And with that an exit was made from Sadovaya, and along with those exiting, moreover, there left the dismayed and depressed secretary of the House Management Committee, Prolezhnev.

In the evening Nikanor Ivanovich was delivered to Stravinsky's clinic. There he behaved so restlessly that, in accordance with Stravinsky's practice, he had to be given an injection, and only after midnight did Nikanor Ivanovich fall asleep in room 119, occasionally emitting a pained moan of suffering.

But the more it went on, the easier his sleep became. He stopped rolling around and groaning, his breathing became easy and even, and he was left on his own.

Then Nikanor Ivanovich was visited by a dream, at the root of which were undoubtedly his difficult experiences of the day. It began with Nikanor Ivanovich dreaming that people of some sort with golden trumpets in their hands were leading him, very ceremoniously too, up to some big, varnished doors. At these doors his companions played what seemed to be a fanfare for Nikanor Ivanovich, and then a booming bass from the heavens said cheerfully:

"Welcome, Nikanor Ivanovich! Hand in the foreign currency!"

Extremely surprised, Nikanor Ivanovich saw a black loudspeaker above him.

Next he found himself for some reason in the auditorium of a theatre, with crystal chandeliers shining beneath the gilt ceiling, and argands on the walls. All was as it should be, as in a theatre small in size, but very sumptuous. There was a stage hidden behind a velvet curtain – which had, scattered across its dark-cherry ground like little stars, images of enlarged gold ten-rouble pieces on it – there was a prompt box and even an audience.

Nikanor Ivanovich was surprised at the fact that all of this audience was of the same sex – male – and for some reason all had beards. Apart from that, it was striking that there were no seats in the auditorium, and the whole of the audience was sitting on the floor, which was magnificently polished and slippery.

Confused in the new and numerous company, Nikanor Ivanovich vacillated for a little while, then followed the general example and sat himself down cross-legged on the parquet, finding room between some red-bearded man in the best of health and another citizen, pale and excessively hairy. None of those sitting down paid any attention to the newly arrived spectator.

At this point the soft ringing of a little bell was heard, the light in the auditorium went out, the curtain parted, and a lighted stage was revealed with an armchair, a table – on which was a little gold bell – and a blind, black velvet backdrop.

Out of the wings at this point came an artiste in a dinner jacket, smooth-shaven and with a parting in his hair, young and with very pleasant facial features. The people in the auditorium perked up, and everyone turned towards the stage. The artiste went up to the prompt box and rubbed his hands.

"Are you sitting down?" he asked in a soft baritone, and smiled into the auditorium.

"We are, we are," a choir of tenors and basses answered him from the auditorium.

"Hm..." the artiste began pensively, "and how is it you don't get fed up with it, I don't understand? Everyone else is acting normally, they're walking around the streets now, enjoying the spring sunshine and the warmth, while you're hanging about here on the floor in a stuffy auditorium! Is the programme really so interesting? However, each to his own," the artiste concluded philosophically.

Then he altered both the timbre of his voice, and the intonations, and announced cheerfully and sonorously:

"And so, the next act in our programme is Nikanor Ivanovich Bosoi, Chairman of a House Committee and manager of a dietetic canteen. Nikanor Ivanovich, please!"

The reply to the artiste was friendly applause. The astonished Nikanor Ivanovich opened his eyes wide, but the compère, shielding himself from the glare of the footlights with his hand, found him with his gaze among the seated men and beckoned him affectionately onto the stage with a finger. And Nikanor Ivanovich, without knowing how, found himself on the stage. The light of coloured lamps struck him in the eyes from below and from the front, which made the auditorium and the audience immediately disappear into the darkness.

"Come on then, Nikanor Ivanovich, set us an example," the young artiste began cordially, "and hand in your foreign currency."

Silence fell. Nikanor Ivanovich took a deep breath and began quietly: "I swear to God that..."

But he had not had time to utter the words before the whole auditorium broke out in cries of indignation. Nikanor Ivanovich grew flustered and fell quiet.

"So far as I've understood you," began the programme's presenter, "you wanted to swear to God that you have no foreign currency?" And he looked at Nikanor Ivanovich sympathetically.

"Exactly so, I haven't got any," replied Nikanor Ivanovich.

"Right," responded the artiste, "well, forgive my indelicacy: where, then, did the four hundred dollars come from that were discovered in the toilet of the apartment, the sole inhabitants of which are you and your spouse?"

"The magic ones!" someone in the dark auditorium said with evident irony.

"Exactly so, the magic ones," Nikanor Ivanovich replied timidly to an indeterminate quarter, not exactly to the artiste, not exactly to the dark auditorium, and elucidated: "The unclean spirit, the interpreter in checks left them there deliberately."

And again the auditorium let out an indignant roar. When silence fell, the artiste said:

"These are the kind of La Fontaine fables* I have to listen to! Four hundred dollars were left deliberately! Now all of you here are speculators in foreign currency, and I turn to you as experts: is this something conceivable?"

"We're not speculators," individual offended voices rang out in the theatre, "but it's inconceivable."

"I'm with you completely," said the artiste firmly, "and I ask you: what might be left deliberately?"

"A baby!" cried someone from the auditorium.

"Absolutely correct," confirmed the programme's presenter, "a baby, an anonymous letter, a political leaflet, an infernal machine, all sorts of other things, but four hundred dollars no one would think of leaving deliberately, for no one in the whole of nature is such an idiot." And, turning to Nikanor Ivanovich, the artiste added reproachfully and sadly: "You've distressed me, Nikanor Ivanovich! And I was relying on you. And so our act has been a failure."

Whistling rang out in the auditorium, directed at Nikanor Ivanovich.

"He's a foreign currency speculator!" people in the auditorium were calling out. "Because of the likes of him, we, the innocent, suffer too!"

"Don't criticize him," said the compère gently, "he'll repent." And, turning blue eyes filled with tears to Nikanor Ivanovich, he added: "Well, go back to your place, Nikanor Ivanovich."

After that the artiste rang the little bell and announced loudly:

"Interval, scoundrels!"

The shaken Nikanor Ivanovich, who, unexpectedly for himself, had become a participant in some sort of theatrical programme, again found himself in his place on the floor. At this point he dreamt that the auditorium was plunged into total darkness and that burning red words sprang out on the walls: "Hand in foreign currency!" Then the curtain opened again and the compère gave the invitation:

"Please come up onto the stage, Sergei Gerardovich Dunchil."

Dunchil proved to be a fine-looking, but very neglected man of about fifty.

"Sergei Gerardovich," the compère addressed him, "you've been sitting here now for a month and a half, stubbornly refusing to hand in your remaining foreign currency, at a time when the country needs it and it's of no use whatsoever to you, and yet you're nonetheless unyielding. You're an educated man, you understand all this perfectly well, and still you don't want to take any conciliatory steps."

"Unfortunately, there's nothing I can do, since I don't have any more foreign currency," replied Dunchil calmly.

"So you don't have, at the very least, any diamonds?" asked the artiste.

"No diamonds either."

The artiste hung his head and fell deep in thought, and then he clapped his hands. A middle-aged lady came out onto the stage from the wings, fashionably dressed, that is, wearing a coat with no collar and a tiny little hat. The lady had an alarmed air, but Dunchil looked at her without twitching an eyebrow.

"Who is this lady?" the programme's presenter asked Dunchil.

"It's my wife," replied Dunchil with dignity, and looked at the lady's long neck with a certain disgust.

"We've disturbed you, Madame Dunchil," the compère referred himself to the lady, "regarding this: we wanted to ask you if your spouse still has any foreign currency?"

"He handed everything in then," replied Madame Dunchil anxiously.

"So," said the artiste, "well then, if that's so, then so be it. If he handed everything in, then we're required to part with Sergei Gerardovich immediately, what can one do! If you wish, you can leave the theatre, Sergei Gerardovich," and the artiste made a regal gesture.

Calmly and with dignity, Dunchil turned and went towards the wings.

165

"One moment!" the compère stopped him. "Permit me in parting to show you one more act from our programme," and again he clapped his hands.

The black rear curtain parted, and out onto the stage came a beautiful young girl in a ball gown, holding in her hands a little gold tray, on which there lay a thick wad, tied with a sweet ribbon, and a diamond necklace, from which blue, yellow and red lights bounced off in all directions.

Dunchil took a pace backwards, and pallor covered his face. The auditorium froze.

"Eighteen thousand dollars and a necklace worth forty thousand in gold," the artiste announced triumphantly, "was being kept by Sergei Gerardovich in the town of Kharkov, in the apartment of his mistress, Ida Gerkulanovna Vors, whom we have the pleasure of seeing before us, and who kindly helped to bring to light these treasures, priceless, but pointless in the hands of a private individual. Thank you very much, Ida Gerkulanovna."

The beauty flashed her teeth in a smile and fluttered her thick eyelashes.

"But beneath your mask of utter dignity," the artiste referred himself to Dunchil, "is concealed an avaricious spider, a shocking gloommonger and liar. Over a month and a half you have exasperated everyone with your dull obstinacy. So go home now, and let the hell your spouse will give you be your punishment."

Dunchil rocked and seemed to want to fall, but someone's sympathetic arms caught him up. At this point the front curtain tumbled down and hid all those who were on the stage.

Furious applause shook the auditorium to such a degree that it seemed to Nikanor Ivanovich as though the lights in the chandeliers had started jumping. And when the front curtain went up, there was no longer anyone on the stage apart from the solitary artiste. He cut short a second volley of applause, bowed and began to speak:

"In the person of that Dunchil, a typical ass appeared before you in our programme. I had the pleasure of saying yesterday, after all, that the secret holding of foreign currency was a senseless business. Nobody can use it, not under any circumstances, I assure you. Take that Dunchil, for example. He gets a magnificent salary and wants for nothing. He has a splendid apartment, a wife and a beautiful mistress. But oh no! Instead of handing in the foreign currency and stones and living quietly and peacefully, without any unpleasantness, that mercenary buffoon has got himself exposed in front of everyone after all, and, as a special treat, has incurred the most major domestic unpleasantness. And so, who's handing things in? No takers? In that event, the next act in our programme – the well-known dramatic talent, the specially invited actor Savva Potapovich Kurolesov, will perform an extract from *The Miserly Knight* by the poet Pushkin."*

The promised Kurolesov was not long in appearing on the stage and proved to be a strapping and fleshy, clean-shaven man in a white tie and tails.

Without any words of introduction, he pulled a gloomy face, knitted his brows and began in an unnatural voice, looking askance at the little gold bell:

"Just as a youthful rake awaits his meeting
With some debauched and devious young woman..."

And Kurolesov related many bad things about himself. Nikanor Ivanovich heard Kurolesov admit to how some unfortunate widow knelt howling before him in the rain but failed to touch the actor's hard heart.

Before his dream, Nikanor Ivanovich did not know the works of the poet Pushkin at all, but he knew the man himself very well, and several times daily uttered phrases such as: "And who's going to pay for the apartment – Pushkin?" or "I suppose it was Pushkin that unscrewed the light bulb on the stairs?" or "Pushkin, I suppose, is going to be buying the oil?"

Now, after becoming acquainted with one of his works, Nikanor Ivanovich grew sad, imagined the woman on her knees with the orphans in the rain, and involuntarily thought: "This Kurolesov is a right one, though!"

And the latter, ever raising his voice, continued to repent, and muddled Nikanor Ivanovich up completely, because he suddenly started addressing someone who was not on the stage, and he himself went and answered in place of this absent person, calling himself, in so doing, first "Sire", then "Baron", first "father", then "son", first using formal terms, and then intimate ones.

Nikanor Ivanovich understood only one thing, that the actor died a nasty death, crying: "The keys! My keys!" and after that falling on the floor, wheezing and carefully pulling off his tie.

Having died, Kurolesov rose, shook the dust off the dress-suit trousers, bowed, smiling a false smile, and withdrew to muted applause. And the compère began thus:

"We have listened to *The Miserly Knight* in a remarkable performance by Savva Potapovich. That knight was hoping that playful nymphs would come running to him, and that a lot of other pleasant things of the same sort would take place. But, as you see, none of it happened, no nymphs came running to him, and the Muses failed to pay tribute to him, and he didn't erect any edifices, but on the contrary, came to a very unpleasant end – died, damn him, of a stroke on top of his chest of foreign currency and stones. I warn you that something of the sort will happen to you too, if perhaps not worse, unless you hand in your foreign currency!"

Whether it was Pushkin's poetry that made such an impression or the prosaic speech of the compère, only suddenly a shy voice rang out from the auditorium:

"I'm handing in my foreign currency."

"Please come up onto the stage," was the compère's polite invitation as he peered into the dark auditorium.

And on the stage appeared a blond citizen of small stature, who, to judge by his face, had not shaved for about three weeks.

"I'm sorry, what's your name?" inquired the compère.

"Nikolai Kanavkin," the man who had appeared responded shyly.

"Ah! Pleased to meet you, Citizen Kanavkin. And so?"

"I'm handing it in."

"How much?"

"A thousand dollars and twenty gold ten-rouble pieces."

"Bravo! Is that all there is?"

The presenter of the programme stared straight into Kanavkin's eyes, and to Nikanor Ivanovich it even seemed that from his eyes spurted rays that pierced right through Kanavkin like X-rays. The audience stopped breathing.

"I believe you!" the artiste finally exclaimed, and extinguished his gaze. "I believe you! Those eyes are not lying. You know, how many times have I told you that your basic error consists in underestimating the significance of a man's eyes? You must understand that the tongue can conceal the truth, but the eyes – never! You're asked a sudden question, you don't even give a start, in one second you're in control of yourself and know what needs to be said to cover up the truth, and you speak most convincingly, and not a single line on your face will move, but, alas, stirred up by the question, for an instant the truth springs from the bottom of your soul into your eyes, and it's all over. It's noted, and you're caught!"

After uttering this very convincing speech, with great fervour too, the artiste enquired affectionately of Kanavkin:

"And where is it hidden?"

"At Porokhovnikova's – she's my aunt – on Prechistenka…"

"Ah! That's… hang on… that's at Klavdia Ilyinichna's, is it?"

"Yes."

"Ah, yes, yes, yes, yes! A little detached house? A little front garden opposite too? Of course, I know it, I know it! And where is it you've hidden it away there?"

"In the cellar in an empty Einem* tin…"

The artiste clasped his hands together.

"Have you ever seen anything like it?" he exclaimed in distress. "But it'll get covered in mould there, won't it, it'll get damp! Now is it conceivable to entrust foreign currency to such people? Eh? Just like children, honest to God!"

Kanavkin himself realized he was at fault and had made a botch of things, and he hung his tufted head.

"Money," continued the artiste, "should be kept in the State Bank, in special dry and well-guarded premises, and not under any circumstances in an aunt's cellar where it can, in particular, be damaged by rats! Truly, you should be ashamed of yourself, Kanavkin! After all, you're a grown man."

Kanavkin just did not know what to do with himself, and merely picked at the breast of his jacket with his finger.

"Oh, all right," the artiste softened, "we'll let bygones be bygones…" and he suddenly added unexpectedly: "Yes, by the way… to get it over with all at once… so as not to waste the car journey… this aunt has some as well, doesn't she, eh?"

Kanavkin, who had not expected such a turn of events at all, hesitated, and silence fell in the theatre.

169

"Oh, Kanavkin," said the compère in gentle reproach, "and I'd even praised him! And there you are, without any warning he's gone and started messing things up! This is ridiculous, Kanavkin! I mean, I was just talking about the eyes. I mean, it's clear your aunt has some. Well, why are you tormenting us for nothing?"

"She has!" cried Kanavkin recklessly.

"Bravo!" cried the compère.

"Bravo!" the audience let out a terrible roar.

When quiet had fallen, the compère congratulated Kanavkin, shook his hand, offered to have him driven to his home in the city, and ordered someone in the wings to drop by in the same car for the aunt and to ask her to go and be in the programme at the women's theatre.

"Yes, I meant to ask, did your aunt say where she hides hers?" enquired the compère, cordially offering Kanavkin a cigarette and a lighted match. Lighting up, the latter grinned in a melancholy sort of way.

"I believe you, I believe you," responded the artiste, sighing, "the old skinflint wouldn't tell the devil that, let alone her nephew. Well, all right, we'll try and arouse human feelings in her. Maybe not all the strings have yet rotted in her wretched, moneylender's heart. All the best, Kanavkin!"

And a happy Kanavkin left. The artiste enquired whether there were any others wishing to hand in foreign currency, but got silence in reply.

"A funny lot, honest to God!" said the artiste, shrugging his shoulders, and he was hidden by the curtain.

The lamps went out, and for some time there was darkness, and in it, from afar, could be heard a nervous tenor voice singing:

> "Great piles of gold are lying there,
> And yes, they all belong to me."*

Then, twice, muffled applause reached them from somewhere.

"Some little lady's handing it over in the women's theatre," Nikanor Ivanovich's red-bearded neighbour unexpectedly spoke up, and added with a sigh: "Ah, if it weren't for my geese! I've got fighting geese in Lianozov, my dear man... I'm afraid they'll die without me. A fighting bird's a delicate thing, it needs looking after... Ah, if it weren't for the geese! And I'm not going to be impressed by Pushkin," and again he began sighing.

At this point the auditorium was lit up brightly, and Nikanor Ivanovich started dreaming that chefs in white hats with serving spoons in their hands poured into the auditorium from all the doors. Young chefs dragged a vat of soup and a big tray of sliced black bread into the auditorium. The audience grew animated. The cheery chefs darted in and out among the theatre-goers, pouring the soup into dishes and handing out the bread.

"Have some dinner, lads," shouted the chefs, "and hand in your foreign currency! Why should you sit here to no purpose? Who wants to eat this skilly! You could go home, have a proper drink, a bite to eat, lovely!"

"Well, here's an example, what are you stuck here for, Dad?" a fat chef with a crimson neck addressed Nikanor Ivanovich directly, holding out to him a bowl in which a solitary cabbage leaf was floating in some liquid.

"I've got none! None! None!" shouted Nikanor Ivanovich in a terrible voice. "Do you understand, none!"

"None?" the chef roared in a threatening bass. "None?" he asked in a gentle female voice. "None, none," he began muttering reassuringly, turning into the medical attendant, Praskovya Fyodorovna.

She was gently shaking Nikanor Ivanovich, who was moaning in his sleep, by the shoulder. Then the chefs melted away, and the theatre with the curtain disintegrated. Through his tears Nikanor Ivanovich made out his room in the clinic and two people in white coats, yet not the excessively familiar chefs, thrusting themselves and their advice at people, at all, but rather doctors, and still that same Praskovya Fyodorovna, who held in her hands not a bowl, but a little dish covered with gauze with a syringe lying on it.

"I mean, what is all this," said Nikanor Ivanovich bitterly while being given the jab, "I've got none and that's that! Let Pushkin hand in his foreign currency to them. I've got none!"

"No, you've got none," kind-hearted Praskovya Fyodorovna reassured him, "and what can't be cured must be endured."

Nikanor Ivanovich felt better after the injection, and he fell into a sleep without any dreams.

But thanks to his cries, alarm was transmitted to room 120, where the patient woke up and began searching for his head, and to room 118, where the unknown Master became worried and wrung his hands in anguish, gazing at the moon and remembering the last night of his life, bitter and autumnal, the strip of light from under the door and the unwound hair.

Alarm flew from room 118 along the balcony to Ivan, and he woke up and started crying.

But a doctor quickly calmed all who were alarmed, all who were sick in the head, and they started to fall asleep. Ivan dropped off latest of all, when it was already getting light above the river. After medicine that impregnated the whole of his body, sedation came to him like a wave that covered him. His body became lighter, and a warm breeze of drowsiness blew around his head. He fell asleep, and the last thing he heard while awake was the pre-dawn chirping of the birds in the wood. But they soon fell quiet, and he began to dream that the sun was already sinking over Bald Mountain, and the mount was cordoned off by a double cordon…

16

The Execution

THE SUN WAS ALREADY SINKING over Bald Mountain, and the mount was cordoned off by a double cordon.

The cavalry *ala* which had cut across the Procurator's path at about midday had emerged at a trot towards the city's Hebron Gate. The way had already been prepared for it. The foot soldiers of the Cappadocian Cohort had crushed back to the sides the throngs of people, mules and camels, and the *ala*, trotting and raising white columns of dust up to the sky, came out to the crossroads where two roads met: the southern one leading to Bethlehem, and the north-western one to Jaffa. The *ala* sped down the north-western road. The same Cappadocians were scattered along the edges of the road, and they had driven off to the sides in good time all the caravans hurrying to Yershalaim for the feast. Crowds of pilgrims had abandoned their temporary striped tents, pitched directly on the grass, and stood behind the Cappadocians. After about a kilometre, the *ala* overtook the Second Cohort of the Lightning

Legion and, having covered one more kilometre, was first to arrive at the foot of Bald Mountain. Here it dismounted. The commander split the *ala* up into platoons, and they cordoned off the entire foot of the low hill, leaving free only the one way up it from the Jaffa road.

Some time later the Second Cohort came up to the hill after the *ala*, went up a level higher and girdled the mount like a crown.

Finally the century under the command of Marcus the Rat-catcher approached. It moved, stretched out in two columns along the edges of the road, and between these columns, under the escort of the Secret Guard, there rode in a cart the three condemned men with white boards on their necks, on each of which was written "Villain and rebel" in two languages – Aramaic and Greek.

Behind the condemned men's cart moved others, loaded up with freshly cut poles complete with crosspieces, ropes, spades, buckets and axes. In these carts rode six executioners. Behind them on horseback rode Centurion Marcus, the chief of the Yershalaim Temple guard and that same hooded man with whom Pilate had held a brief conference in a darkened room in the palace.

The procession was completed by a line of soldiers, but behind it there already walked about two thousand of the curious, unafraid of the hellish heat and wishing to attend an interesting spectacle.

The curious from the city were now joined by curious pilgrims, who were allowed unimpeded into the tail of the procession. To the shrill calls of the public criers, who were accompanying it and shouting out what Pilate had shouted around midday, the procession started up Bald Mountain.

The *ala* allowed everyone up to the second level, but the second century allowed up to the top only those who were involved in the execution, and then, manoeuvring quickly, it dispersed the crowd around the whole of the hill, so that it found itself between the infantry cordon above and the cavalry one below. Now it could see the execution through the thin line of foot soldiers.

And so more than three hours had passed since the time when the procession had gone up the hill, and the sun was already sinking over Bald Mountain, but the heat was still unbearable, and the soldiers in both cordons were suffering from it, were bored out of their wits, and in their hearts were cursing the three villains, sincerely wishing them the quickest of deaths.

The little commander of the *ala*, who was at the bottom of the hill by the open path, with his forehead sopping wet and in a white shirt whose back was dark with sweat, kept on going up to the leather bucket in the first platoon, scooping handfuls of water from it, drinking and wetting his turban. Getting some relief from this, he would move away and again begin pacing up and down the dusty road leading to the summit. His long sword banged against his laced leather boot. The commander wanted to set his cavalrymen an example of endurance, but, sparing his soldiers, he allowed them to set up pyramids of lances, stuck into the ground, and to throw white cloaks onto them. And it was under these tents that the Syrians hid themselves from the pitiless sun. The buckets quickly emptied, and cavalrymen from different platoons set off by turns to fetch water from the gully just outside the city where, in the sparse shade of straggly mulberry trees, a rather turbid stream was living out its days in this devilish heat. Here too the horse-holders, trying to catch the shifting shade, stood getting bored, holding the quietened horses.

The soldiers' languor and the abuse they aimed at the villains were understandable. The Procurator's misgivings regarding disturbances that might take place in the hated city of Yershalaim at the time of the execution were fortunately unjustified. And when the fourth hour of the execution got under way, between the two lines, the upper one of infantry and the cavalry at the foot of the hill, there remained, contrary to all expectations, not a single person. The sun had scorched the crowd and driven it back to Yershalaim. Beyond the line of two Roman centuries were to be found just two dogs which had found their way onto the hill for some reason and whose owners were unknown. But they too were worn out by the heat and lay down with their tongues hanging out, breathing hard and paying no attention whatever to the green-backed lizards, the only creatures not afraid of the sun, which darted between the scorching stones and the plants of some sort with large thorns that wound across the earth.

Nobody had made any attempt to take the condemned men by force either in Yershalaim itself, flooded with troops, or here on the cordoned-off hill, and the crowd had returned to the city, for there really was absolutely nothing of interest in this execution, and in the city preparations were already under way for the great Feast of the Passover that would be starting in the evening.

The Roman infantry at the second level suffered even more than the cavalrymen. The only thing Centurion Rat-catcher allowed the soldiers to do was to remove their helmets and cover their heads with white cloths moistened with water, but he kept the soldiers standing and with their spears in their hands. Wearing just such a head-cloth, only not moistened, but dry, he himself strode about not far from the group of executioners, without even removing the detachable silver lions' heads from his shirt, without taking off his scabbard, his sword and knife. The sun beat down directly onto the centurion without doing him any harm, and it was impossible to glance at the lions' heads, for the blinding brilliance of the silver, which seemed to be coming to the boil in the sun, ate away at the eyes.

Neither exhaustion nor displeasure was expressed on Rat-catcher's disfigured face, and it seemed as if the giant centurion had the strength to walk about like this all day, all night and for another day – in short, as much as might be needed: to carry on walking like this, his hands set on his heavy belt with its bronze buckles, to carry on glancing just as sternly now at the poles with the men being executed, now at the soldiers in the line, to carry on kicking away just as indifferently with the toe of a shaggy boot the little flints, or the human bones, bleached by time, that got under his feet.

The hooded man had positioned himself on a three-legged stool not far from the poles and was sitting in placid immobility, though occasionally, out of boredom, scratching away at the sand with a little twig.

What was said about there not being a single man beyond the line of legionaries is not entirely true. One man there was, but simply he was not visible to all. He had positioned himself not on the side where the path up the hill was open and from which it was most convenient of all to see the execution, but on the northern side, where the hill was not gently sloping and accessible, but uneven, where there were both cavities and crevices, where, clinging on in a cranny to the waterless earth, cursed by the sky, a sick little fig tree was trying to live.

It was precisely beneath it, although it gave no shade at all, that this sole spectator not participating in the execution had established himself and had been sitting on a rock from the very start, that is, for more than three hours now. Yes, to see the execution he had chosen not the best, but the worst position. But the poles were nonetheless visible from there too, as were also visible beyond the line the two glinting spots on the chest of the centurion – and that, for a man who clearly wished to remain unnoticed and undisturbed by anyone, was evidently perfectly sufficient.

But some four hours earlier, at the start of the execution, this man had been behaving quite differently and could have been noticed very easily, which was probably the very reason why he had now altered his behaviour and gone off by himself.

Then, as soon as the procession had gone up to the very top beyond the line, that was when he had appeared for the first time and, moreover, like an obvious latecomer. He had been breathing hard and had not walked, but had run and jostled his way up the hill, and, seeing that the line had closed up before him, as before everyone else too, he had made a naive attempt, pretending not to understand the irritated cries, to break through between the soldiers to the very place of execution, where the condemned men were already being removed from the cart. For that he had been dealt a heavy blow on the chest with the blunt end of a spear, and had leapt back from the soldiers with a cry, though not of pain, but of despair. He had cast a gaze that was dull and indifferent to everything over the legionary who had struck him, like a man insensitive to physical pain.

Coughing and gasping for breath, and clutching at his chest, he had run all around the hill, striving to find some gap in the line where he could slip through on the northern side. But it was already too late. The ring had closed. And this man with a face contorted by grief had been forced to renounce his attempts to break through to the carts from which the posts had already been removed. These attempts would have led to nothing except his being seized, and being detained on this day did not enter into his plans in any way at all.

And so he had moved aside to the cranny, where it was quieter and nobody bothered him.

Now, sitting on a rock, this black-bearded man, with his eyes suppurating from the sun and lack of sleep, was miserable. At times he would sigh, opening up his worn tallith, that had turned in his wanderings from blue to dirty-grey, and would bare his chest, bruised by the spear, down which dirty sweat was flowing; then in unbearable torment he would raise his eyes to the sky, watching the three carrion crows which had already been floating in big circles on high for a long time now in expectation of an imminent feast; then he would fasten his hopeless gaze on the yellow earth, and see upon it the partly destroyed skull of a dog and the lizards running around it.

The man's sufferings were so great that at times he would start talking to himself.

"Oh, I'm an idiot!" he muttered, swaying about on the rock in mental pain and scratching his swarthy chest with his fingernails. "An idiot, a foolish woman, a coward! Carrion's what I am, not a man!"

He would fall quiet, his head would sink, then, after drinking warm water from a wooden flask, he would revive once more and grab now at his knife, hidden beneath the tallith on his chest, now at the piece of parchment lying before him on a rock alongside a stick and a phial of ink.

Some entries had already been jotted down on this parchment:

"The minutes hurry by, and I, Levi Matthew, am on Bald Mountain, but death has not yet come!"

Next:

"The sun is declining, but death has not come."

Now Levi Matthew wrote this hopeless note with the sharp stick:

"God! Why are you angry with him? Send him death."

After writing this down, he gave a tearless sob, and again his fingernails covered his chest with wounds.

The reason for Levi's despair was the terrible misfortune that had befallen Yeshua and him and, besides that, the grave error that he, Levi, had, in his opinion, made. Two days before, in the afternoon, Yeshua and Levi had been in Bethany, not far from Yershalaim, where they had been the guests of a market gardener who had been extremely impressed with Yeshua's sermons. All morning the two guests had worked in the market garden, helping their host, and towards evening they had been intending to walk through the cool of the day to Yershalaim. But Yeshua had suddenly been in a hurry for some reason, had said he had urgent business in the city, and had gone off alone at about midday. And it was this that had been Levi Matthew's first error. Why oh why had he let him go alone!

It had not been Matthew's lot to walk to Yershalaim that evening. He had been struck down by some unexpected and terrible ailment. He had got the shakes, his body had filled with fire, his teeth had begun chattering and he had been continually asking for something to drink.

He had not been able to go anywhere. He had collapsed onto a mat in the market gardener's shed and lain there until dawn on Friday, when the illness had released Levi just as unexpectedly as it had fallen upon him. Although he had still been weak and his legs had been trembling, he had taken his leave of his host and set off for Yershalaim, tormented by some presentiment of calamity. There he had learnt that his presentiment had not deceived him. The calamity had occurred. Levi had been in the crowd and had heard the Procurator announce the sentence.

When they had set off for the mount with the condemned men, Levi Matthew had been running alongside the file of soldiers in the crowd of curious people, trying in some inconspicuous way at least to let Yeshua know that he, Levi, was there with him, that he had not abandoned him on his final journey and that he was praying for death to overtake Yeshua as quickly as possible. But Yeshua, of course, looking into the distance to where he was being taken, had not seen Levi.

And then, when the procession had gone about half a kilometre along the road, Matthew, who was being pushed about in the crowd right by the column of soldiers, had had a simple but brilliant idea, and immediately, in his impulsiveness, had heaped curses upon himself for it not having occurred to him earlier. The soldiers were not walking in a closely packed column. There were gaps between them. Using great agility and very accurate calculation, he could bend down and jump between two legionaries, burst through to the cart and leap up onto it. Then Yeshua would be saved from his sufferings.

One moment was sufficient to strike Yeshua in the back with a knife, crying out to him: "Yeshua! I'm saving you and going along with you! I, Matthew, your faithful and only disciple!"

And if God blessed him with one more free moment, he could have time to stab himself too, avoiding death on a pole. The latter point, however, was of little interest to Levi, the former tax-collector. He was indifferent to how he might perish. He wanted one thing: for Yeshua, who had not done anybody the slightest harm in his whole life, to avoid torture.

The plan was a very good one, but the fact of the matter was that Levi had no knife with him. Nor did he have a single coin either.

In a fury with himself, Levi made his way out of the crowd and ran back to the city. In his burning head there leapt just the one feverish thought of how to get hold of a knife in the city immediately and in any way at all, and be in time to catch up with the procession.

He ran as far as the city gates, manoeuvring through the crush of caravans being sucked into the city, and saw on his left-hand side the open door of a wretched little shop where they sold bread. Breathing hard after the run down the scorching road, Levi got himself under control, went into the shop very steadily, greeted the shopkeeper standing behind the counter, asked her to get down from the top shelf a round loaf which for some reason he liked more than the others, and, when she had turned around, he took silently and quickly from the counter something that could not have been any better – a long bread-knife, sharp as a razor – and immediately rushed out of the shop.

A few minutes later he was once again on the Jaffa road. But the procession was no longer to be seen. He started running. From time to time he had to collapse right into the dust and lie motionless to recover his breath. And thus he lay, amazing passers-by on mules and people going to Yershalaim on foot. He lay listening to the way his heart was thumping not only in his chest, but in his head and ears too. When he had recovered his breath a little, he would jump up and carry on running, but ever slower and slower. When he finally caught sight of the long procession raising dust in the distance, it was already at the foot of the hill.

"Oh, God!" groaned Levi, realizing he was going to be too late. And he was too late.

When the fourth hour of the execution had elapsed, Levi's sufferings reached their highest degree, and he flew into a frenzy. Getting up from the rock, he flung the knife he had stolen, as he now thought, in vain to the ground, stamped on his flask, depriving himself of water, threw off the keffiyeh from his head, grabbed hold of his wispy hair and began cursing himself.

He cursed himself, calling out senseless words, he snarled and spat, reviled his father and mother, who had brought forth an idiot into the world.

Seeing that curses and abuse had no effect and nothing in the blaze of the sun was changing as a result, he clenched his dry fists, screwed up his eyes and raised them to the sky, to the sun, which was slipping ever lower, lengthening the shadows, and leaving to fall into the

Mediterranean Sea, and he demanded of God an immediate miracle. He demanded that God at once send death to Yeshua.

Opening his eyes, he satisfied himself that all on the hill was unchanged, except for the fact that the burning spots on the chest of the centurion had gone out. The sun was sending its rays into the backs of the men being executed, who had their faces turned towards Yershalaim. Then Levi shouted:

"I curse you, God!"

In a hoarsened voice he shouted of how he had become convinced of God's injustice and of how he did not mean to trust him any more.

"You're deaf!" Levi snarled. "If you weren't deaf, you'd hear me and kill him right away!"

Levi waited with his eyes screwed up for the fire that would fall on him from the sky and strike *him*. This did not happen and, keeping his eyelids tightly shut, Levi continued to call out caustic and offensive speeches at the sky. He shouted of his total disenchantment and of there being other gods and religions. No, another god would not have allowed it, would never have allowed a man like Yeshua to be burnt on a pole by the sun.

"I was wrong!" shouted Levi, completely hoarse. "You are the god of evil! Or have your eyes been completely blinded by smoke from the Temple's incense-burners, and have your ears ceased to hear anything other than the trumpet sounds of the priests? You are not the Almighty God. You are a black god. I curse you, god of scoundrels, their patron and soul!"

At this point something blew into the former tax-collector's face, and something started to rustle beneath his feet. It blew again, and then, opening his eyes, Levi saw that everything in the world, under the influence of his curses or for some other reasons, had changed. The sun had disappeared without having reached the sea in which it sank each evening. The storm cloud which had swallowed it was climbing steadily and threateningly across the sky from the west. Its edges were already boiling up in white foam, the smoky black belly had a yellow lustre. The cloud was grumbling, and from time to time fiery threads tumbled out of it. Along the Jaffa road, along the barren Valley of Gion, pillars of dust, driven by the wind that had got up so suddenly, were flying above the tents of the pilgrims.

Levi fell silent, trying to grasp whether the storm that would shortly cover Yershalaim would bring any change in the fate of the unfortunate

Yeshua. And straight away, looking at the threads of fire that were cutting the cloud open, he began asking for the lightning to strike Yeshua's pole. Looking in repentance at the clear sky, not gobbled up as yet by the cloud, where the carrion crows were banking away to escape the storm, it occurred to Levi that he had been madly hasty with his curses: God would not listen to him now.

Having turned his gaze to the foot of the hill, Levi became riveted to the spot where the cavalry regiment had deployed and was stationed, and saw that significant changes had taken place there. From his high position, Levi was able to make out very well the way the soldiers were bustling about, pulling their lances out of the ground and throwing their cloaks over themselves, the way the horse-holders were jogging towards the road, leading the black horses by the reins. The regiment was moving off, that was clear. Using his hand to shield himself from the dust beating into his face, and spitting the dust out, Levi tried to grasp what the cavalry getting ready to leave might mean. He shifted his gaze a little higher and made out a small figure in a purple military chlamys which was going up towards the area of execution. And at this point the presentiment of a happy ending made the former tax-collector's heart turn cold.

The man going up the hill in the fifth hour of the villains' sufferings was the Commander of the Cohort, who had galloped here from Yershalaim accompanied by an orderly. The line of soldiers opened at a gesture from Rat-catcher, and the centurion saluted the tribune. The latter, leading Rat-catcher aside, whispered something to him. The centurion saluted a second time and moved towards the group of executioners sitting on the rocks at the foot of the poles, while the tribune directed his steps towards the one sitting on the three-legged stool, and the seated man rose politely to meet the tribune. And the tribune said something to him in a low voice, and they both went towards the poles. They were joined by the chief of the Temple guard too.

Looking askance in disgust at the dirty rags lying on the ground by the poles, rags that had recently been the criminals' clothes and that the executioners had refused, Rat-catcher called two of the latter aside and ordered:

"Follow me!"

From the nearest pole came a hoarse, senseless song. Towards the end of the third hour of the execution, the man hanging on it, Gestas, had gone mad from the flies and the sun, and was now quietly singing something about grapes, but he would still shake his turbanned head from time to time, and then the flies would rise sluggishly from his face and return to it once again.

Dismas on the second pole suffered more than the other two, because he had not been overcome by oblivion, and he shook his head frequently and rhythmically, now to the right, now to the left, to strike his ears against his shoulders.

More fortunate than the other two was Yeshua. In the very first hour he began to be struck by swoons, and later he fell into oblivion, hanging his head in its uncoiled turban. He was therefore completely plastered with flies and gadflies, such that his face had disappeared under a black, moving mask. At the groin, and on the stomach and under the armpits fat gadflies sat and sucked on the yellow, naked body.

Obeying the gestures of the hooded man, one of the executioners took a spear, and the other brought a bucket and sponge to the pole. The first of the executioners raised the spear and tapped with it, first on one, then on the other of Yeshua's arms, which were stretched out and tied with ropes to the crossbar of the pole. The body with its protruding ribs shuddered. The executioner drew the end of the spear over his stomach. Then Yeshua lifted his head, and with a buzzing the flies moved off, and the face of the hanged man was revealed, swollen with bites, with bloated eyes, an unrecognizable face.

Ungluing his eyelids, Ha-Nozri glanced down. His eyes, usually clear, were now rather lacklustre.

"Ha-Nozri!" said the executioner.

Ha-Nozri moved his swollen lips and responded in a hoarse, villainish voice:

"What do you want? Why have you come over to me?"

"Drink!" said the executioner, and the sponge soaked in water on the end of the spear rose to Yeshua's lips. There was a flash of joy in the latter's eyes, he pressed against the sponge and began greedily taking in the moisture. The voice of Dismas was heard from the next pole:

"Injustice! I'm just as much a villain as he is!"

Dismas strained, but could not move, his arms were held in three places on the crosspiece by rings of rope. He pulled in his stomach, stuck his fingernails into the ends of the crosspieces and held his head turned towards Yeshua's pole; malice burned in Dismas's eyes.

A cloud of dust covered the area of execution, it grew much darker. When the dust had whirled away, the centurion cried:

"Silence on the second pole!"

Dismas fell silent. Yeshua tore himself away from the sponge and, trying to make his voice sound gentle and convincing, but without achieving it, he requested the executioner hoarsely:

"Give him a drink."

It was getting ever darker. Speeding towards Yershalaim, the storm cloud had spilt over half the sky, and white boiling clouds rushed on ahead, impregnated with the black moisture and the fire of the storm cloud. There was a flash and a clap right above the hill. The executioner took the sponge from the spear.

"Praise the magnanimous Hegemon!" he whispered solemnly, and gently pricked Yeshua in the heart. The latter jerked, whispered:

"Hegemon..."

Blood ran down his stomach, his lower jaw jerked spasmodically, and his head drooped.

At the second clap of thunder the executioner was already giving Dismas a drink, and with the same words:

"Praise the Hegemon!" he killed him too.

Gestas, bereft of reason, cried out in fright as soon as the executioner came near him, but when the sponge touched his lips, he snarled something and sank his teeth into it. A few seconds later his body sagged too, as far as the ropes would allow.

The hooded man followed in the footsteps of the executioner and the centurion, and he was followed by the chief of the Temple guard. Stopping at the first pole, the hooded man carefully examined the bloodied Yeshua, touched his foot with a white hand and said to his companions:

"Dead."

The same thing was repeated at the other two poles as well.

After this the tribune made a sign to the centurion and, turning, started to leave the summit together with the chief of the Temple guard and the hooded man. Semi-darkness had descended, and lightning was furrowing the black sky. Fire suddenly spurted out of it, and the centurion's cry: "Cordon, fall out!" was drowned in thunder. The happy soldiers made haste to run down the hill, putting on their helmets.

Darkness covered Yershalaim.

The torrential rain struck suddenly and caught the centuries halfway down the hill. The water poured down so terribly that, as the soldiers ran downwards, raging streams were already rushing in pursuit of them. The soldiers slid and fell on the sodden clay, as they hurried onto the even road, along which – already scarcely visible in the shroud of water – the cavalry, soaked to the skin, was leaving for Yershalaim. A few minutes later, in the smoking broth of the storm, water and fire on the hill, one man remained.

Brandishing the knife that had not been stolen in vain, falling off slippery ledges, grabbing hold of whatever came to hand, sometimes crawling on his knees, he was striving towards the poles. Now he would disappear in the utter gloom, now suddenly be illuminated by flickering light.

Already ankle-deep in water when he reached the poles, he tore off his tallith, saturated and heavy with water, to remain in just his shirt, and fell at Yeshua's feet. He cut through the ropes at the shins, got up onto the lower crosspiece, embraced Yeshua, and freed his arms from the upper bonds. Yeshua's naked, damp body collapsed onto Levi and knocked him to the ground. Levi immediately wanted to hoist it up onto his shoulders, but some idea stopped him. He left the body on the ground in the water with its head tossed back and arms thrown apart, and ran on legs that slipped about in the clayey slush to the other poles. He cut through the ropes on those as well, and the two bodies collapsed onto the ground. A few minutes passed, and on the summit of the hill there remained only those two bodies and three empty poles. The water was beating against the bodies and turning them around.

At this time neither Levi nor the body of Yeshua was any longer on the summit of the hill.

17

A Day with no Peace

O N FRIDAY MORNING, that is, the day after the accursed performance, none of The Variety's available office personnel – the accountant, Vasily Stepanovich Lastochkin, two accounts clerks, three typists, the two cashiers, the messengers, ushers and cleaners – in short, none of those available were busy working at their posts; they were all sitting on the sills of the windows looking out onto Sadovaya and watching what was going on by The Variety's wall. Beside the wall in two lines crawled a queue, several thousand strong, the tail of which was to be found on Kudrinskaya Square. At the head of the queue stood approximately two dozen ticket touts, well-known in Moscow's theatrical world.

The queue's behaviour was very agitated, attracting the attention of the citizens streaming past, and it was busy discussing the stirring stories about the previous day's unprecedented performance of black magic. Those same stories had got the accountant, Vasily Stepanovich, who had not been at the show the day before, into a state of the greatest confusion. The ushers had been recounting God knows what, including how after the end of the celebrated performance there had been some citizenesses running around in the street in an indecent state, and other things of the kind. Quiet and modest Vasily Stepanovich only blinked his eyes as he listened to tall stories about all these wonders, and simply did not know what he should do, but at the same time something did need to be done, and specifically by him, since he now turned out to be the senior person in the entire Variety team.

By ten o'clock in the morning, the queue of those thirsting for tickets had swollen to such an extent that rumours of it had reached the police, and details were dispatched with amazing speed, both unmounted and mounted, which did bring the queue to order somewhat. However, a snake a kilometre long, even when standing in good order, already in itself represented a great temptation, and it was getting citizens on Sadovaya into a state of utter astonishment.

This was outside, while inside The Variety things were very much amiss as well. From very early in the morning, the telephones had started ringing and had then rung continually in Likhodeyev's office, Rimsky's office, the accounts office, the box office and Varenukha's office. Vasily Stepanovich had at first given some answer, the cashier had answered too, the ushers had mumbled something into the telephone, but then they had completely stopped answering, because to the questions about where Likhodeyev, Varenukha and Rimsky were, there was absolutely no answer. At first they tried getting away with "Likhodeyev's at his apartment", but the people ringing in replied that they had phoned the apartment, and the apartment said Likhodeyev was at The Variety.

An agitated lady telephoned and started demanding Rimsky; she was advised to ring his wife, at which, breaking into sobs, the receiver replied that it was his wife and that Rimsky was nowhere to be found. There was some sort of nonsense under way. The cleaner had already told everyone that, when turning up at the Financial Director's office to do the cleaning, she had seen that the door was wide open, the lights were on, the window looking onto the garden was broken, the armchair was lying on the floor and there was no one there.

After ten o'clock Madame Rimskaya burst into The Variety. She was sobbing and wringing her hands. Vasily Stepanovich lost his head completely and did not know what to advise her. And at half-past ten the police appeared. Their very first, and perfectly reasonable question was:

"What's going on here, Citizens? What's the matter?"

The team retreated, putting forward the pale and agitated Vasily Stepanovich. He was obliged to call a spade a spade and admit that The Variety's administration, in the persons of the Director, the Financial Director and the Manager, had disappeared, and their whereabouts were unknown; that the compère, after the previous day's performance, had been taken away to a psychiatric clinic; and that, to put it briefly, that previous day's performance had been a downright scandalous performance.

The sobbing Madame Rimskaya, after she had been calmed as far as she could be, was sent home, and most interest of all was shown in the cleaner's story about what a state the Financial Director's office had been found in. The staff were asked to go to their posts and get on with their work, and a short time later there appeared in The Variety building an investigation team accompanied by a sharp-eared, muscular dog the colour of cigarette ash and with extremely intelligent eyes. Gossip immediately spread among the staff of The Variety about the dog being none other than the renowned Ace of Diamonds. And it was indeed him. His behaviour amazed everyone. As soon as Ace of Diamonds ran into the Financial Director's office, he began growling, baring monstrous yellowish fangs, then he lay down on his belly and with an anguished sort of expression in his eyes he began crawling towards the broken window. Overcoming his terror, he suddenly leapt up onto the window sill and, stretching his sharp face up into the air, he set up a wild and furious howling. He did not want to leave the window, he growled and quivered and strained to jump out.

The dog was led out of the office and let loose in the vestibule, from there he went out through the main entrance into the street and led those following him towards the taxi rank. Beside it he lost the trail he had been following. After that, Ace of Diamonds was led away.

The investigation team settled into Varenukha's office, and it was there that those of The Variety's staff who had been witnesses to the previous day's events during the performance began to be summoned by turns. It should be said that at every step of the way the investigation team was obliged to overcome unforeseen difficulties. The thread kept on breaking in their hands.

Had there been playbills? There had. But during the night they'd been pasted over with new ones, and now there wasn't a single one, not to save your life! Where had this magician fellow sprung from? Well, that's anybody's guess. So an agreement must have been concluded with him?

"One would assume so," replied the agitated Vasily Stepanovich.

"And if one was concluded, then it ought to have gone through the accounts office?"

"Most definitely," replied Vasily Stepanovich in agitation.

"Well, where is it then?"

"Not here," replied the accountant, turning paler and paler and spreading his hands. And indeed, neither in the accounts office files, nor in the Financial Director's, nor in Likhodeyev's, nor in Varenukha's were there any traces of an agreement.

What was this magician's name? Vasily Stepanovich didn't know, he hadn't been at the performance yesterday. The ushers didn't know, the ticket cashier knitted and knitted her brow, thought and thought, and finally said:

"Wo... Woland, maybe."

But perhaps not Woland? Perhaps not Woland. Perhaps Faland.

It turned out that at the Foreigners' Bureau precisely nothing had been heard about any Woland, nor, equally, about Faland the magician either.

Karpov, the messenger, gave the information that this magician fellow had apparently put up in Likhodeyev's apartment. A visit was, of course, immediately paid to the apartment. There proved to be no magician there. No Likhodeyev himself either. No maid Grunya, and where she'd got to nobody knew. No Chairman of the Management Committee Nikanor Ivanovich, no Prolezhnev!

Something quite extraordinary was emerging: all the senior administrators had disappeared, yesterday there had been a strange, scandalous performance, but who had carried it out and at whose behest was unknown.

Yet in the meantime it was getting on for midday, when the box office was due to open. But of that, of course, there could be no question! A huge piece of cardboard was immediately hung up on the doors of The Variety with the inscription: "Today's show cancelled". Agitation began in the queue, beginning at its head, but after getting a little agitated, the queue started to fall apart all the same, and after approximately an hour there remained not a trace of it on Sadovaya. The investigation team departed to continue its work in another place, the staff were allowed to go, with only the security men left in place, and the doors of The Variety were locked.

The accountant Vasily Stepanovich had to carry out two tasks urgently. Firstly, going to the Commission for Spectacles and Light Entertainments with a report of the previous day's happenings, and secondly, paying a visit to the Spectacles' Finance Department to deposit the previous day's takings – 21,711 roubles.

The thorough and efficient Vasily Stepanovich packed the money up in newspaper, criss-crossed the package with string, stowed it away in his briefcase, and, with an excellent knowledge of the official instructions, headed, of course, not for the bus or the tram, but for the taxi rank.

No sooner did the drivers of three vehicles catch sight of a passenger hurrying to the rank with a tightly packed briefcase, than all three drove away empty from right under his nose, for some reason looking round angrily as they did so.

Stunned by this occurrence, the accountant stood for a long time rooted to the spot, trying to grasp what it might mean.

After two or three minutes an empty vehicle drove up, and the driver immediately pulled a face as soon as he saw the passenger.

"Is the vehicle free?" asked Vasily Stepanovich, coughing in amazement.

"Show us your money," replied the driver with venom, not looking at the passenger.

More and more surprised, the accountant, clutching the precious briefcase under his arm, pulled a ten-rouble note from his wallet and showed it to the driver.

"Not going!" said the latter curtly.

"I'm sorry…" the accountant tried to begin, but the driver interrupted him.

"Got any threes?"

The utterly confused accountant took two three-rouble notes from his wallet and showed them to the driver.

"Get in," the latter cried, and slammed down the flag of the meter so hard he almost broke it. "Let's go."

"Have you not got any change, or something?" asked the accountant timidly.

"My pocket's full of change!" yelled the driver, and his bloodshot eyes were reflected in the mirror. "The third instance I've had today. And others have had the same thing too. Some son of a bitch gives me a ten-rouble note, I give him change – four-fifty… He gets out, the bastard! Five minutes later I take a look, and instead of the ten-rouble note there's the label from a bottle of Narzan!" Here the driver uttered several unprintable words. "Another – the other side of Zubovskaya. A ten-rouble note. I give him three roubles change. Off he went! I put my hand in my purse, and out flies a bee – stings me on the finger! Oh, you!…" again the driver stuck in some unprintable words. "But the ten-rouble note's gone. Yesterday in that Variety (unprintable words) some scumbag of a conjuror did a show with ten-rouble notes (unprintable words)…"

The accountant was stupefied, shrank down and put on an appearance of hearing the very words "The Variety" for the first time, but he thought to himself: "Well I never!"

Arriving at his destination and settling up all right, the accountant entered the building and headed down the corridor to where the manager's office was, and while on his way he already realized he had come at a bad time. Some sort of turmoil reigned in the Spectacles Commission office. A messenger-girl ran past the accountant with her headscarf slipping down the back of her head and her eyes bulging.

"Gone, gone, gone, my dears!" she cried, addressing who knows who. "The jacket and trousers are there, but there's nothing inside the jacket!"

She disappeared through a door, and immediately after her the sounds of crockery being broken were heard. Out of the secretary's room ran the manager of the Commission's first section, but he was in such a state that he failed to recognize the accountant and disappeared without a trace.

Shaken by all this, the accountant went as far as the secretary's room, which was the ante-room of the Chairman of the Commission's office, and here he was totally shocked.

From behind the closed door of the office came a threatening voice, undoubtedly belonging to Prokhor Petrovich, the Chairman of the Commission. "Giving someone a wigging, is he?" thought the perturbed accountant, and, looking around, he saw something else: in a leather armchair, with her head thrown against its back, sobbing uncontrollably, with a wet handkerchief in her hand, there lay, with her legs stretched out almost to the middle of the room, Prokhor Petrovich's personal secretary, the beautiful Anna Richardovna.

The whole of Anna Richardovna's chin was smeared with lipstick, while down her peachy cheeks ran black streams of fermented mascara from her eyelashes.

Seeing that someone had come in, Anna Richardovna leapt up, rushed over to the accountant, grabbed hold of the lapels of his jacket, and began shaking the accountant and shouting:

"Thank God! At least one brave man's been found! Everyone's run away, everyone's betrayed us! Let's go, let's go in to him, I don't know what to do!" And, continuing to sob, she dragged the accountant into the office.

When he got into the office, the first thing the accountant did was to drop his briefcase, and all the thoughts in his head were turned upside down. And, it must be said, there was good reason.

At the huge desk with its massive inkstand sat an empty suit, drawing a dry pen, undipped in ink, across a sheet of paper. The suit had a tie on, from the pocket of the suit protruded a fountain pen, but above the collar there was neither neck, nor head, just as the wrists did not emerge from the cuffs either. The suit was engrossed in work and completely failed to notice the commotion that reigned all around. Hearing that someone had come in, the suit leant back in its armchair, and above the collar there resounded the voice, well-known to the accountant, of Prokhor Petrovich:

"What is it? I mean, it does say on the doors that I'm seeing no one."

The beautiful secretary screamed and, wringing her hands, exclaimed:

"Do you see? You see?! He's gone! Gone! Bring him back, bring him back!"

At this point someone pushed in through the office door, groaned and rushed off out. The accountant sensed that his legs had started trembling, and he sat down on the edge of a chair, but did not forget to pick up his briefcase. Anna Richardovna leapt around the accountant, pulling at his jacket and crying out:

"I always, always stopped him when he was cursing! Now this is where his cursing's got him!" Here the beauty ran up to the desk and in a tender, musical voice, a little nasal after her crying, exclaimed: "Prosha! Where are you?"

"Who are you calling 'Prosha'?" the suit enquired haughtily, falling back still deeper in the armchair.

"Doesn't recognize me! He doesn't recognize me! Do you understand?" the secretary sobbed out.

"I'll ask you not to sob in the office!" said the irascible striped suit, now getting cross, and with its sleeve it pulled a fresh wad of papers towards itself with the clear aim of putting instructions on them.

"No, I can't look at it, no, I can't!" Anna Richardovna shouted, and ran out into the secretary's room, and like a bullet the accountant ran out after her too.

"Imagine, I'm sitting there," Anna Richardovna recounted, shaking in agitation and once again grabbing hold of the accountant's sleeve, "and in comes a cat. Black and massive, like a behemoth. Of course, I shout at him, 'Shoo!' He's off, but in his place in comes a fat man, and he has a cat's face too, and he says: 'Whatever is it you're doing, Citizeness, shouting "Shoo" at visitors?' And he strolls straight in to Prokhor Petrovich. Of course, I'm after him, shouting: 'Are you out of your mind?' But the cheeky thing's straight in to Prokhor Petrovich and sits down in the armchair opposite him! Well and he... he's a man with the kindest of hearts, but he is highly strung. Flew into a rage! I can't deny it. He's an excitable man, works like an ox – he flew into a rage. 'What are you doing,' he says, 'pushing in unannounced?' And that saucy thing, imagine, he's sprawling in the armchair and says with a smile: 'I've come,' he says, 'to have a chat with you about a little matter of business.' Prokhor Petrovich flew into a rage again: 'I'm busy!' And the other one, just think, replies: 'You're not busy at all...' Eh? Well, at this point, of course, Prokhor Petrovich's patience really was exhausted, and he exclaimed: 'What on earth is all this? Well, I'll go to the devil, get him out of here.' And the other one, just imagine, smiles and says: 'You want to go to the devil? Well, that can be arranged!' And bang! I didn't have time to cry out, I look, and the one with the cat's face has gone, and si... sitting there's... a suit... Whaaa!..." Anna Richardovna started howling, stretching out her mouth, which had completely lost any sort of outline.

Choking on her sobs, she caught her breath, but began spouting something utterly absurd:

"And it writes and writes and writes! It's enough to drive you mad! It talks on the phone! A suit! Everyone's run off, like rabbits."

The accountant just stood and shook. But here fate came to his aid. Into the secretary's room with a calm, businesslike gait came the police in the figures of two men. On seeing them the beauty began sobbing even more, jabbing her hand at the office door.

"Let's not go sobbing, Citizeness," said the first one calmly, and the accountant, feeling he was completely superfluous here, slipped out of the secretary's room, and a minute later was already in the fresh air. There was a sort of draught in his head, there was a howling, as if in a chimney, and in this howling could be heard scraps of the usher's stories about the cat which had taken part in the performance the previous day. "Oh-ho-ho! Could this possibly be our little pussy cat?"

Having got no sense out of the Commission, the conscientious Vasily Stepanovich decided to look in at its branch office which was located in Vagankovsky Lane. And in order to calm himself a little, he made the journey to the branch office on foot.

The Municipal Spectacles' branch office was located in a detached house, peeling with age, in the depths of a courtyard, and was renowned for its porphyry columns in the vestibule.

Yet it was not the columns that amazed the branch office's visitors that day, but what was happening beneath them.

Several visitors stood rooted to the spot and gazing at a weeping young lady who was sitting at a little table on which lay the special entertainment literature the young lady was selling. At the given moment the young lady was not offering anyone any of this literature, and was only waving away sympathetic questions, but at this time from both above and below, and from the sides, from all sections of the branch office, the ringing of telephones was pouring forth, with at least twenty sets letting rip.

After having a little weep, the young lady suddenly gave a start and cried hysterically:

"Here it comes again!" and in a tremulous soprano she unexpectedly started to sing:

Glorious sea, sacred Baikal...*

A messenger who had appeared on the staircase shook his fist at someone and started singing along with the young lady in an unsonorous, lacklustre baritone:

Glorious the ship, the omul barrel!...

The messenger's voice was joined by voices in the distance, the choir began to spread, and finally the song started thundering in every corner of the branch office. In the nearest room, No. 6, where the auditing department was located, somebody's powerful, slightly hoarse, low bass stood out in particular. The choir was accompanied by the intensifying crackling of the telephone sets.

Hey, Barguzin,* make the waves roll!...

yelled the messenger on the staircase.

Tears were running down the girl's face, she was trying to clench her teeth, but her mouth was opening of its own accord, and an octave higher than the messenger she sang:

The lad hasn't got far to travel!

The silent visitors to the branch office were amazed by the fact that the choristers, scattered in various spots, sang very much in time, as though the whole choir were standing and not taking its eyes off an invisible conductor.

Passers-by in Vagankovsky stopped by the courtyard railings, wondering at the merriment that reigned in the branch office.

As soon as the first verse came to an end, the singing suddenly died down, again as if in response to a conductor's baton. The messenger swore quietly and disappeared.

At this point the main doors opened and in them appeared a citizen in a summer coat, from beneath which there protruded the skirts of a white coat, and with him a policeman.

"Take measures, Doctor, I beg of you!" cried the girl hysterically.

The branch secretary ran out onto the staircase and, evidently burning with shame and embarrassment, began falteringly:

"You see, Doctor, we have a case of some sort of mass hypnosis... So it's essential..." he failed to finish the phrase, began choking on his words and suddenly started singing in a tenor voice:

Shilka and Nerchinsk...*

"Fool!" the girl managed to cry, yet did not explain whom she was abusing, but instead brought out a violent roulade, and herself began singing about Shilka and Nerchinsk.

"Take yourself in hand! Stop singing!" the doctor addressed the secretary.

It was abundantly clear that the secretary would himself have given anything to stop singing, but stop he could not, and, together with the choir, he brought to the ears of passers-by in the lane news of the fact that he had not been touched in the wilds by the voracious beast, and the riflemen's bullet had failed to catch up with him!

As soon as the verse had ended, the girl was the first to get a dose of tincture of valerian from the doctor, and then he ran after the secretary to the others to give them a drop as well.

"Forgive me, young Citizeness," Vasily Stepanovich suddenly addressed the girl, "has a black cat been to see you?"

"What do you mean, a cat?" shouted the girl in anger. "We've got an ass here in the branch, an ass!" and, adding to this: "Let him hear! I'll tell everything," she did indeed tell of what had happened.

It turned out that the manager of the Municipal Branch, who had (according to the girl) "completely messed up Light Entertainment", suffered from a mania for organizing all sorts of clubs.

"Pulling the wool over his superiors' eyes!" yelled the girl.

In the course of a year the manager had succeeded in organizing a club for the study of Lermontov,* a chess and draughts club, a ping-pong club and a horse-riding club. In time for the summer he was threatening to organize a freshwater boat club and a climbing club.

And so today in the lunch break, he comes in, the manager...

"And leads in by the arm some son of a bitch," recounted the girl, "who'd appeared from who knows where in horrible check trousers and with a cracked pince-nez and... an utterly unspeakable face!"

And there and then, according to the girl's account, he had introduced him to all the diners in the branch canteen as a distinguished expert in the organization of choral clubs.

The faces of the future climbers had grown gloomy, but the manager had immediately called upon everyone to cheer up, and the expert had cracked jokes and made witticisms and given sworn assurances that the singing took the tiniest bit of time, but that there was, incidentally, a coachload of benefit from the singing.

Well, of course, as the girl reported, the first to jump forward were Fanov and Kosarchuk, well-known as the branch toadies, declaring that they were signing up. At that point the remainder of the staff became convinced that the singing could not be avoided, and they too were obliged to sign up for the club. They decided to sing in the lunch break, for all the rest of the time was taken up by Lermontov and draughts. The manager, to set an example, declared that he was a tenor, and thereafter everything happened as if in a nasty dream. The expert choirmaster in checks yelled out:

"Doh-mi-sol-doh!" he pulled the shyer ones out from behind the cupboards where they were trying to escape the singing, told Kosarchuk he had perfect pitch, began to whine and whimper, asked everyone to humour an old precentor and songster, and tapped a tuning fork on his fingers, begging them to bash out 'The Glorious Sea'.

They bashed it out. And bashed it out splendidly. The one in checks really did know his business. They finished singing the first verse. At this point the precentor excused himself, saying: "I'll just be a minute!" and... vanished. They thought he really would be back in a minute. But ten minutes passed and he was not back. The branch staff were gripped by joy – he had disappeared.

And suddenly, somehow of their own accord, they started singing the second verse. Kosarchuk, who did not actually have perfect pitch, perhaps, but did have quite a pleasant high tenor, took everyone with him. They sang the verse through. No precentor! They moved to their various seats, but had not managed to sit down before, against their will, they started singing. Stopping – there was no chance of that. They would be quiet for two or three minutes and then bash it out again! Be quiet – bash it out! At that point they realized they were in trouble. The manager locked himself in his office in shame.

Here the girl's story was interrupted. The valerian had not helped at all.

A quarter of an hour later three trucks drove up to the railings on Vagankovsky and the entire personnel of the branch office with the manager at their head was loaded onto them.

As soon as the first truck shook through the gates and drove out into the lane, the staff, standing on its open back and holding onto one another's shoulders, opened their mouths wide, and the whole lane resounded to the popular song. The second truck joined in, and the third one after it too. And like that they set off. Passers-by, hurrying about their business, cast only fleeting glances at the trucks and were not in the least surprised, supposing that it was an excursion driving out of town. They were, indeed, driving out of town, only not on an excursion, but to Professor Stravinsky's clinic.

Half an hour later, the accountant, who had lost his head completely, reached the Spectacles' Finance Department, hoping finally to rid himself of the official money. Having already learnt from experience, he first of all glanced cautiously into the elongated hall where the staff sat behind frosted glass panes with gold inscriptions. The accountant found no signs of alarm or disturbance here. It was quiet, as it is supposed to be in a respectable establishment.

Vasily Stepanovich poked his head in at the window above which was written "Receipt of monetary sums", said hello to some clerk he did not know, and asked politely for a paying-in slip.

"What do you want it for?" asked the clerk at the window.

The accountant was astonished.

"I want to pay in a sum of money. I'm from The Variety."

"One moment," the clerk replied, and instantly closed the gap in the glass with a grille.

"Strange!" thought the accountant. His astonishment was perfectly natural. This was the first time in his life he had encountered such a situation. Everyone knows how hard it is to get hold of money; obstacles to that are always to be found. Yet in the accountant's thirty years' practical experience there had never been an instance when anyone, be it an official or a private individual, had found difficulty in accepting money.

But finally the grille moved aside, and the accountant again pressed up against the window.

"And have you got a lot?" asked the clerk.

"Twenty-one thousand, seven hundred and eleven roubles."

"Oho!" replied the clerk, ironically for some reason, and he reached a slip of green paper out to the accountant.

Knowing the form well, the accountant completed it in an instant and started untying the string on the package. When he had unpacked his cargo, his eyes suddenly blurred, and he moaned something in a painful way.

Foreign money had flashed before his eyes. There were wads here of Canadian dollars, English pounds, Dutch guilders, Latvian latts, Estonian crowns...

"There he is, one of those jokers from The Variety," a threatening voice was heard above the numbed accountant. And Vasily Stepanovich was immediately arrested.

18

Luckless Callers

A T THE VERY TIME when the diligent accountant was speeding in the taxi to run up against the writing suit, from the reserved berths of soft carriage No. 9 of the Kiev-Moscow train there emerged, amongst others, a respectable passenger with a small imitation-leather suitcase in his hand. This passenger was none other than the uncle of the late Berlioz, Maximilian Andreyevich Poplavsky, an economic planner who lived in Kiev on what was formerly Institutskaya Street. The reason for Maximilian Andreyevich's arrival in Moscow was the telegram he had received late in the evening two days before with the following content:

Tram just killed me at Patriarch's.
Funeral Friday afternoon three. Come. Berlioz.

Maximilian Andreyevich was considered, and deservedly so, one of the cleverest men in Kiev. But even the cleverest man can be nonplussed by a telegram like that. Since someone is wiring that he's been killed, it's clear that he hasn't been fatally killed. But why on earth the funeral then? Or, being in a very bad way, does he foresee that he will die? That's possible, but this precision is odd in the highest degree – however does he know, after all, that he's going to be buried on Friday at three o'clock in the afternoon? An amazing telegram.

However, that's why clever men are clever, to sort out tangled things. Very simple. An error had occurred, and the telegram had been transmitted in corrupted form. Without doubt, the word "me" had got in there from another telegram instead of the word "Berlioz", which had got in at the end of the telegram. With such a correction the meaning of the telegram became clear, albeit, of course, tragic.

When the explosion of grief, which shocked Maximilian Andreyevich's wife, had abated, he immediately started preparing to go to Moscow.

It is necessary to reveal a secret of Maximilian Andreyevich's. No argument, he did feel sorry for his wife's nephew, who had perished in the prime of life. But, of course, as a businessman, he understood that there was no particular need for his presence at the funeral. And nevertheless, Maximilian Andreyevich was in a great hurry to get to Moscow. Whatever was the matter? One thing – the apartment. An apartment in Moscow! That is serious. There is no knowing why, but Maximilian Andreyevich did not like Kiev, and the idea of a move to Moscow had been gnawing away at him so much of late that he had even started sleeping badly.

He was not delighted by the Dnieper overflowing in the spring, when, flooding the islands along the low shores, the water would merge with the horizon. He was not delighted by the view, stunning in its beauty, that opened up from the pedestal of the monument to Prince Vladimir.* He was not cheered by the patches of sunlight playing on the brick paths of Vladimir's Hill in the spring. He wanted none of this, he wanted one thing – to move to Moscow.

Notices in the newspapers about the exchange of an apartment on

Institutskaya Street in Kiev for less floor-space in Moscow brought no result. No takers were to be found, and if they occasionally did turn up, their proposals were unscrupulous.

The telegram shook Maximilian Andreyevich. It was a moment which it would be a sin to miss. Businessmen know that such moments are not repeated.

In short, regardless of any difficulties, he needed to succeed in inheriting the nephew's apartment on Sadovaya. Yes, it was complicated, very complicated, but he needed to get over the complications at all costs. The experienced Maximilian Andreyevich knew that the first and indispensable step towards it should be the following step: he needed, if only temporarily, to be registered in the deceased nephew's three rooms.

On Friday afternoon, Maximilian Andreyevich entered the door of the room in which was located the House Management Committee of building No. 302 *bis* on Sadovaya Street in Moscow.

In the narrow little room, where on the wall there hung a poster representing in a number of pictures the ways of resuscitating those who have drowned in the river, sat an unshaven middle-aged man with anxious eyes in total solitude at a wooden desk.

"Can I see the Chairman of the Committee?" the economic planner enquired politely, taking off his hat and standing his suitcase on an empty chair.

For some reason this seemingly quite simple question upset the seated man, so that he even changed countenance. Narrowing his eyes in alarm, he mumbled indistinctly that the Chairman was not there.

"Is he in his apartment?" asked Poplavsky. "I have the most urgent business."

The seated man again replied very incoherently. But it could nevertheless be inferred that the Chairman was not in his apartment.

"And when will he be here?"

The seated man made no reply to this, and he looked out of the window with a kind of anguish.

"Aha!" the clever Poplavsky said to himself, and enquired about the secretary.

The strange man at the desk even turned crimson from tension and again said indistinctly that the secretary was not there either... when he would be coming was unknown and... that the secretary was ill...

"Aha!" Poplavsky said to himself. "But is there *somebody* here from the Committee?"

"Me," the man responded in a weak voice.

"You see," Poplavsky began impressively, "I am the sole heir of the late Berlioz, my nephew, who perished, as you know, at Patriarch's, and I am duty-bound, in accordance with the law, to accept the legacy, consisting of our apartment No. 50..."

"I know nothing about it, Comrade..." the man interrupted miserably.

"But permit me," said Poplavsky in a sonorous voice, "you are a member of the Committee and are duty-bound..."

And at this point some sort of citizen entered the room. At the sight of the man who had entered, the man sitting at the desk turned pale.

"Committee member Pyatnazhko?" the man who had entered asked the seated man.

"Me," the latter replied, scarcely audibly.

The man who had entered whispered something to the seated man, and the latter, utterly downcast, rose from his chair, and a few seconds later Poplavsky remained alone in the Committee's empty room.

"Oh dear, what a complication! Just what was needed, that they should all at once be..." thought Poplavsky in annoyance, cutting across the asphalt courtyard and hurrying to apartment No. 50.

As soon as the economic planner rang, the door opened and Maximilian Andreyevich went into the semi-darkness of the entrance hall. He was somewhat surprised by the fact that it was unclear who had let him in: there was nobody in the hall, apart from the most enormous black cat sitting on a chair.

Maximilian Andreyevich coughed a little, stamped his feet a little, and then the study door opened and Korovyev came out into the hall. Maximilian Andreyevich bowed to him politely, but with dignity, and said:

"My name is Poplavsky. I am the uncle..."

But he had not managed to finish speaking before Korovyev grabbed a dirty handkerchief from his pocket, buried his nose in it and started crying.

"...of the late Berlioz..."

"Of course, of course," Korovyev interrupted, removing the handkerchief from his face. "As soon as I looked at you I guessed it was you!" At this point he started to shake with tears and began crying out: "What a calamity, eh? I mean, what on earth's going on? Eh?"

"Run over by a tram?" asked Poplavsky in a whisper.

"Completely!" cried Korovyev, and the tears ran from under his pince-nez in torrents. "Completely! I was a witness. Can you believe it – bang! The head – off! The right leg – crunch, in half! The left – crunch, in half! That's where those trams can get you!" And, evidently lacking the strength to hold himself in check, Korovyev dipped his nose against the wall beside the mirror and began shaking with sobs.

Berlioz's uncle was sincerely struck by the unknown man's behaviour. "There, and they say there are no warm-hearted people nowadays!" he thought, sensing that his own eyes were beginning to itch. At the same time, however, an unpleasant little cloud raced up into his soul, and at once the thought flashed by like a snake about whether this warm-hearted man had not already been registered in the apartment of the deceased, for instances even of that kind of thing had been known.

"Forgive me, were you a friend of my deceased Misha?" he asked, wiping his dry left eye with his sleeve, while studying the grief-stricken Korovyev with his right. But the latter burst into such sobs that it was impossible to understand anything other than the repeated words "crunch – and in half!" When he had had his fill of sobbing, Korovyev finally unstuck himself from the wall and said:

"No, I've had enough! I'll go and take three hundred drops of valerian ether!…" And, turning a thoroughly tear-stained face to Poplavsky, he added: "There you have them, those trams!"

"I'm sorry, did you send me a telegram?" asked Maximilian Andrey-evich, tormented by thoughts of who this amazing crybaby might be.

"It was him!" Korovyev replied, and pointed a finger at the cat.

Poplavsky opened his eyes wide, assuming he had misheard.

"No, I haven't got the strength, I can't stand it," continued Korovyev, sniffing, "I only have to remember: the wheel on the leg… one wheel weighs about a hundred and sixty kilos… Crunch!… I'll go and lie down in bed, find oblivion in sleep," and at that point he disappeared from the hall.

But the cat stirred, jumped down from the chair, stood up on his hind legs, put his forelegs akimbo, opened up his mouth and said:

"Well, I sent the telegram. And what of it?"

Maximilian Andreyevich's head immediately began to spin, he lost the power of his arms and legs, he dropped the suitcase and sat down on a chair opposite the cat.

"I'm asking in Russian, I think," said the cat sternly, "and what of it?"

But Poplavsky gave no reply.

"Passport!"* yapped the cat, and reached out a chubby paw.

Not grasping anything, nor seeing anything except the two sparks burning in the cat's eyes, Poplavsky pulled his passport out of his pocket like a dagger. The cat took a pair of spectacles with thick black frames from the looking-glass table, put them on his face, which made him even more imposing, and removed the passport from Poplavsky's twitching hand.

"Now, I wonder if I'll faint or not?" thought Poplavsky. Korovyev's sobbing could be heard from afar, and the whole entrance hall was filled with the smell of ether, valerian and some other nauseating muck.

"What department issued the document?" asked the cat, peering at a page. No reply ensued.

"Four hundred and twelve," said the cat to himself, moving his paw across the passport, which he was holding upside down, "well yes, of course! I know that department! They issue passports to absolutely anyone! Whereas I, for example, wouldn't issue one to somebody like you! Not for anything would I issue one! I'd take just one look at your face and instantly refuse!" The cat got so angry that he flung the passport onto the floor. "Your attendance at the funeral is cancelled," the cat continued in an official voice, "be so kind as to leave for your place of residence." And he bellowed through the door: "Azazello!"

At his call there ran out into the entrance hall, limping slightly, a small red-headed man wearing close-fitting black tights with a knife stuck in a leather belt, a yellow fang and a cataract in the left eye.

Poplavsky felt he was short of air; he rose from the chair and backed away, holding on to his heart.

"Azazello, see him out!" the cat ordered, and left the entrance hall.

"Poplavsky," the one who had entered said quietly through his nose, "I hope everything's already clear?"

Poplavsky nodded his head.

202

"Return immediately to Kiev," continued Azazello, "stay there as quiet as a mouse, and don't dream of any apartments in Moscow, understood?"

This little creature, who was reducing Poplavsky to mortal terror with his fang, knife and blind eye, only came up to the economist's shoulder, but he operated energetically, smoothly and in an organized way.

First of all he picked up the passport and handed it to Maximilian Andreyevich, and the latter took the little book with a dead hand. Then the one named Azazello picked up the suitcase with one hand, threw the door open with the other, and, taking Berlioz's uncle by the arm, he led him out onto the staircase landing. Poplavsky leant against the wall. Without a key Azazello opened the suitcase, took out of it a huge roast chicken with one leg missing wrapped in a greasy newspaper, and put it on the landing. Then he pulled out two sets of underwear, a razor strop, some book or other and an etui, and kicked it all down into the stairwell, apart from the chicken. The emptied suitcase flew the same way. It could be heard hitting the bottom with a crash, and, to judge by the sound, its lid flew off.

Then the red-headed villain grabbed the chicken by the leg and struck Poplavsky flat-ways on the neck with the whole thing, a blow so hard and terrible that the body of the chicken broke off, while the leg remained in Azazello's hands. Everything was in confusion in the Oblonskys' house,* as the renowned writer Leo Tolstoy rightly expressed himself. And he would have said just the same in the given instance too. Yes! Everything was in confusion in Poplavsky's eyes. A long spark flew by in front of his eyes, then it was replaced by some funeral-black snake which for a moment extinguished the May day – and Poplavsky flew down the staircase, holding the passport in his hand. Reaching the turn, he knocked out a pane of glass in the window on the next landing with his foot and ended up sitting on a step. The legless chicken bounced past him and fell down into the stairwell. Azazello, who had stayed upstairs, picked the chicken leg clean in an instant and stuck the bone into the small side pocket of his tights, then he returned to the apartment and shut the door behind him with a crash.

At this time there began to be heard from below the cautious steps of a man ascending.

Having run down another flight, Poplavsky sat on a little wooden bench on the landing and caught his breath.

A tiny little elderly man with an extraordinarily sad face, wearing an ancient tussore suit and a straw boater with a green ribbon, stopped beside Poplavsky on his way up the stairs.

"Permit me to ask you, Citizen," enquired the man in tussore sadly, "where's apartment No. 50?"

"Further up!" Poplavsky replied curtly.

"I'm most humbly grateful to you, Citizen," the little man said, just as sadly, and went on up, while Poplavsky rose and ran down the stairs.

The question arises, was it to the police Maximilian Andreyevich was hurrying, to complain about the villains who had used savage violence on him in broad daylight? No, not under any circumstances, that can be said with certainty. Going to the police and saying something like: "Just now a cat wearing spectacles was reading my passport, and then a man in tights with a knife..." no, Citizens, Maximilian Andreyevich really was a clever man!

He was already downstairs, and right by the street door he caught sight of a door leading into some sort of cubbyhole. The glass in this door had been knocked out. Poplavsky put the passport in his pocket and looked around, hoping to catch sight of the things that had been thrown away. But there was no trace of them. Poplavsky even marvelled himself at how little this distressed him. He was absorbed by another interesting and seductive idea – to test out the accursed apartment once more on that little man. Indeed: since he was asking about where it was, that means he was going there for the first time. Therefore he was now heading straight into the clutches of the company that had ensconced itself in apartment No. 50. Something told Poplavsky that that little man would be coming out of that apartment very soon. Maximilian Andreyevich, of course, no longer intended going to any funeral of any nephew, and there was ample time until the train to Kiev. The economist glanced around and dived into the cubbyhole.

At this time a door banged far above. "That's him gone in..." thought Poplavsky with a sinking heart. It was cool in the cubbyhole, and it smelt of mice and boots. Maximilian Andreyevich settled down on a stump of wood and decided to wait. The position was convenient, as the street door of entrance No. 6 was directly visible from the cubbyhole.

The wait, however, was longer than the Kievan supposed. The stair-case was for some reason continually deserted. Everything was clearly audible, and finally on the fourth floor a door banged. Poplavsky froze. Yes, his little steps. "He's coming down." A door opened a floor lower. The little steps died away. A woman's voice. The voice of the sad little man... yes, that's his voice... Said something like "Leave me, for Christ's sake..." Poplavsky's ear was sticking out of the broken pane. That ear caught a woman's laughter, rapid and lively steps coming down, and there was a brief glimpse of a woman's back. This woman, with a green oilskin bag in her hands, went out of the doorway and into the courtyard. And the little steps of the little man resumed. "Strange! He's going back to the apartment! Perhaps he's one of that gang himself? Yes, going back. There they are again, opening the door upstairs. Well then, we'll wait some more."

This time the wait was not a long one. The sounds of a door. Little steps. The little steps died away. A desperate cry. A cat miaowing. Rapid, staccato little steps, down, down, down!

Poplavsky's wait was over. Crossing himself and muttering something, the sad little man flew past, without his hat, with an absolutely demented face, a scratched bald patch and in absolutely sopping trousers. He started tearing at the handle of the street door, unaware in his terror of which way it opened – outwards or inwards – finally won control of it and flew out into the courtyard into the sunshine.

The testing of the apartment had been carried out. Thinking no more of either his late nephew or the apartment, shuddering at the thought of the danger he had been subjected to, Maximilian Andreyevich, whispering just two words: "Everything's clear! Everything's clear!" ran out into the courtyard. A few minutes later a trolleybus was carrying the economic planner away in the direction of the Kiev Station.

But while the economist had been sitting in the cubbyhole downstairs, the most unpleasant incident had befallen the little man. The little man was the barman at The Variety and was called Andrei Fokich Sokov. While the investigation had been going on at The Variety, Andrei Fokich had kept himself aloof from all that was happening, and only one thing had been noticed, that he had become even sadder than he always was generally, and, apart from that, had been asking the messenger Karpov about where the visiting magician had put up.

And so, parting with the economist on the landing, the barman had got to the fourth floor and rung at apartment No. 50.

The door was opened to him at once, but the barman gave a start, backed away and did not immediately go in. This was understandable. The door was opened by a girl who was dressed in nothing except for a coquettish little lace apron and a white cap on her head. She did have little golden shoes on her feet, though. The girl was notable for an impeccable figure, and the sole defect in her appearance might have been considered the crimson scar on her neck.

"Well then, come in, since you've rung!" said the girl, fixing green, dissolute eyes on the barman.

Andrei Fokich groaned, started blinking his eyes, and stepped into the entrance hall, taking off his hat. At that moment right there in the hall, the telephone rang. The shameless maid, putting one foot on a chair, took the receiver off the hook and said into it:

"Hello!"

The barman did not know where to look, shifted from one foot to the other and thought: "What a maid the foreigner's got! Well I'll be blowed, what muck!" And to protect himself from the muck he started casting sidelong glances in different directions.

In semi-darkness, the whole of the large entrance hall was cluttered up with unusual objects and attire. Thus a funeral-black cloak lined with flame-coloured material was thrown over the back of a chair, and on the looking-glass table lay a long sword with a gleaming gold hilt. Three swords with silver hilts stood in the corner just as simply as any umbrellas or walking sticks. And on a deer's antlers hung berets with eagle feathers.

"Yes," the maid was saying into the telephone, "what? Baron Maigel? Go ahead. Yes! The artiste is in today. Yes, he'll be glad to see you. Yes, guests… Tails or black jacket. What? For twelve midnight." Finishing the conversation, the maid hung up the receiver and addressed the barman. "What do you want?"

"It's essential I see the citizen artiste."

"What? Him himself, really?"

"Him," answered the barman sorrowfully.

"I'll ask," said the maid, visibly wavering, and, opening the door of the late Berlioz's study a little, she announced: "Sir knight, there's a little man has turned up here who says he needs Messire."

"Let him go in, then," the exhausted voice of Korovyev rang out from the study.

"Go through into the living room," said the girl, as simply as if she had been dressed like a normal person; she set the door into the living room ajar, and she herself left the hall.

When he had gone into where he had been invited, the barman even forgot about his business, so struck was he by the decoration of the room. Through the coloured glass of the large windows (the fancy of the jeweller's wife who had disappeared without trace) poured an extraordinary light, like that in a church. In the huge old fireplace, despite the hot spring day, firewood was blazing. And yet at the same time it was not in the least hot in the room, on the contrary even, the man entering was gripped by damp as though from a cellar. On a tiger skin in front of the fireplace, screwing his eyes up good-humouredly at the fire, sat a huge black cat. There was a table, glancing at which the God-fearing barman winced: the table was covered with church brocade. On the brocade tablecloth stood a multitude of bottles – rounded, covered in mould and dust. Amidst the bottles gleamed a dish, and it was immediately clear that this dish was of pure gold. By the fireplace a little red-headed man with a knife in his belt was roasting pieces of meat on a long steel sword, and the juice was dripping into the fire, and the smoke was departing into a flue. There was a smell not only of roasted food, but also of some very powerful perfume and of incense, which made the barman, who already knew from the newspapers about Berlioz's death and about his place of residence, wonder fleetingly about whether, who knows, they might have been holding a memorial service for Berlioz – a thought he immediately drove off, however, as patently absurd.

The stunned barman unexpectedly heard a heavy bass.

"Well, sir, how can I be of assistance to you?"

And it was at this point that the barman detected in the shadows the one that he needed.

The black magician was sprawled on some immense couch, low and with cushions scattered all over it. As it seemed to the barman, the artiste was wearing only black underwear and shoes with pointed toes, also black.

"I," began the barman bitterly, "am the manager of The Variety Theatre bar..."

The artiste stretched forward his hand, on the fingers of which were sparkling stones, as though to block the barman's mouth, and he started to speak with great ardour:

"No, no, no! Not a word more! Not under any circumstances, not ever! I won't have so much as a bite to eat in your bar! I passed by your counter yesterday, my esteemed man, and am even now unable to forget either the sturgeon or the mare's cheese. My dear man! Mare's cheese doesn't come in a green colour, somebody has duped you there. It's supposed to be white. And what about the tea? I mean, it's just slops. With my own eyes I saw some slovenly girl pouring unboiled water from a bucket into your enormous samovar and continuing in the meantime to pour out the tea. No, my good man, you can't do things like that!"

"Excuse me," began Andrei Fokich, stunned by this sudden attack, "I've not come about that, and the sturgeon's got nothing to do with it."

"How can it have nothing to do with it, if it was off!"

"They sent us sturgeon that was second-quality fresh," announced the barman.

"My dear fellow, that's nonsense!"

"What's nonsense?"

"Second-quality fresh – that's what's nonsense! There's only one quality freshness – first-quality, and that's first and last too. And if the sturgeon's second-quality fresh, then that means it's rotten!"

"Excuse me," the barman was about to begin again, not knowing how to escape from the artiste finding fault with him.

"I can't excuse you," the latter said firmly.

"I've not come about that," said the barman, completely distraught.

"Not about that?" said the foreign magician in surprise. "But then what else could have brought you to me? If memory serves, of people close to you by profession, I've associated with just the one female sutler, but even that was long ago, before you'd yet appeared in the world. However, I'm delighted. Azazello! A stool for the gentleman who manages the bar!"

The one who was roasting the meat turned around, horrifying the barman with his fangs in so doing, and deftly handed him one of the dark, low, oak stools. There were no other seats in the room.

The barman said:

"I'm most humbly grateful," and lowered himself onto the little bench. Its rear leg immediately broke with a crack, the barman gasped, and he hit his backside very painfully on the floor. In falling, he caught another little bench that was standing in front of him with his foot, and from it overturned a full goblet of red wine onto his trousers.

The artiste exclaimed:

"Ouch! Have you hurt yourself?"

Azazello helped the barman up and handed him a second seat. In a voice filled with woe the barman declined the host's suggestion that he take off his trousers and dry them in front of the fire, and, feeling unbearably awkward in his wet underwear and clothes, he sat down warily on the second seat.

"I like sitting low down," began the artiste, "it's not so dangerous falling from something low. Yes, and so, did we stop at the sturgeon? My dear fellow! Freshness, freshness, freshness, that's what any barman's motto ought to be. Here, would you like a taste..."

At this point, in the crimson light from the fireplace there was a flash from the sword in front of the barman, and Azazello laid out on a gold plate a hissing piece of meat, poured lemon juice onto it and handed the barman a gold, two-pronged fork.

"I'm... most humbly..."

"No, no, try it!"

Out of politeness the barman put the morsel in his mouth, and immediately realized he was chewing something really very fresh and, most importantly, extraordinarily tasty. But while chewing his way through the fragrant, juicy meat, the barman almost choked and almost fell over for a second time. A large, dark bird flew in from the next room and gently glanced the barman's bald patch with its wing. Settling on the mantelpiece next to the clock, the bird turned out to be an owl. "O Lord God!" thought Andrei Fokich, who was highly strung, like all barmen. "A nice apartment, this is!"

"A goblet of wine? White, red? Which country's wine do you prefer at this time of day?"

"Most humbly... I don't drink."

"You should! So would you like a game of dice? Or do you like some other games? Dominoes, cards?"

"I don't gamble," the barman responded, already exhausted.

"That's really bad," concluded his host, "say what you will, but there's something evil lurking in men who avoid wine, games, the society of delightful women, table talk. Such people are either gravely ill or secretly hate those around them. True, exceptions are possible.

Among those who have sat down with me at the banqueting table, there have sometimes been some astonishing scoundrels! And so, I'm listening to why you're here."

"Yesterday you were so good as to do some tricks..."

"I?" exclaimed the magician in amazement. "Have mercy. That really doesn't become me somehow!"

"Sorry," said the barman, taken aback, "but, you know... the black magic performance..."

"Ah, well yes, well yes! My dear! I'll let you into a secret: I'm not an artiste at all, I simply wanted to see Muscovites en masse, and it was most convenient of all to do that at the theatre. And so my suite," he nodded in the direction of the cat, "went and arranged that performance, while I only sat and looked at the Muscovites. But don't change countenance, just say what it was in connection with the performance that has brought you to see me?"

"If you'd be so kind as to see, among other things, there were notes flying down from the ceiling..." the barman lowered his voice and glanced around shyly, "well, and they all got grabbed. And then this young man comes into my bar, gives me a ten-rouble note, I give him eight-fifty change... then another..."

"Also a young man?"

"No, elderly. A third, a fourth... I keep on giving change. But today I started checking the till, and look at that, instead of the money there's chopped-up paper. The bar's lost out to the tune of a hundred and nine roubles."

"Oh dear!" exclaimed the artiste. "But surely they didn't think they were genuine banknotes? I can't concede the notion that they did it knowingly."

The barman took a wry and melancholy sort of glance around, but said nothing.

"Surely not swindlers?" the magician asked his guest in alarm. "Surely there aren't swindlers amongst the Muscovites?"

The barman smiled so bitterly in reply, that any doubts fell away: yes, there were swindlers amongst the Muscovites.

"That is base!" said Woland indignantly. "You're a poor man... I mean, are you – a poor man?"

The barman drew his head down into his shoulders so that it became clear he was a poor man.

"How much do you have in savings?"

The question was asked in a sympathetic tone, but all the same, such a question cannot help but be deemed indelicate. The barman faltered.

"Two hundred and forty-nine thousand roubles in five Savings Banks," a cracked voice responded from the neighbouring room, "and at home under the floor two hundred gold tenners."

It was as if the barman had become glued to his stool.

"Well, of course, that's no sum at all," said Woland condescendingly to his guest, "but you don't really need even that, though. When are you going to die?"

Now at this the barman grew indignant.

"No one knows that, and it's of no concern to anyone," he replied.

"Oh right, no one knows," still that same horrid voice was heard from the study, "you'd think it was Newton's binomial theorem!* He's going to die of liver cancer in nine month's time, in February next year, in the First Moscow University Clinic, ward four."

The barman's face turned yellow.

"Nine months," Woland counted pensively, "two hundred and forty-nine thousand... That works out in round figures at twenty-seven thousand a month? Not very much, but enough for a modest life... And there's those tenners as well..."

"He won't be able to realize the tenners," still that same voice butted in, turning the barman's heart to ice, "the building will be demolished immediately after Andrei Fokich's death, and the tenners will be sent to the State Bank."

"And I wouldn't advise you to go into the clinic either," continued the artiste, "what's the sense of dying in a hospital ward to the groans and wheezing of the terminally ill? Isn't it better to spend those twenty-seven thousand on organizing a banquet, and, taking poison, to move to the other side to the sounds of strings, surrounded by intoxicated beauties and spirited friends?"

The barman sat motionless and much aged. Dark rings surrounded his eyes, his cheeks had sagged, and his lower jaw had dropped.

"However, we've got carried away," exclaimed the host. "To business! Show me your chopped-up paper."

The agitated barman pulled a wad from his pocket, unwrapped it and was rooted to the ground. In the fragment of newspaper lay ten-rouble notes.

"You really are unwell, my dear," said Woland, shrugging his shoulders. With a wild smile, the barman rose from the stool.

"And," he said falteringly, "and if they, you know, again…"

"Hm…" the artiste fell deep into thought, "well, come and see us again, then. You're always welcome! Pleased to meet you."

And at this point Korovyev leapt out of the study, seized hold of the barman's hand, and began shaking it and begging Andrei Fokich to pass on greetings to absolutely everyone. With a poor grasp of what was happening, the barman moved off into the entrance hall.

"Hella, see him out," cried Korovyev.

And again that naked redhead was in the hall! The barman squeezed his way past to the door, squeaked, "Goodbye," and set off like a drunken man. After going a little way down the stairs, he stopped, sat down on the steps, took out the wad, checked it – the ten-rouble notes were in place. At that point a woman with a green bag emerged from an apartment with a door onto this landing. Seeing a man sitting on the step and gazing dimwittedly at some ten-rouble notes, she smiled and said pensively:

"What's this building of ours coming to… This one's drunk first thing in the morning too. The glass has been knocked out on the staircase again!" After peering a little more closely at the barman, she added: "Hey, Citizen, you're rolling in tenners there! Why not share them with me, eh?"

"You leave me alone, for Christ's sake," the barman took fright and swiftly hid the money. The woman burst out laughing:

"Oh, go to the devil, you old skinflint! I was joking…" and she went downstairs.

The barman rose slowly, raised his hand to straighten his hat, and discovered that it was not on his head. He was terribly reluctant to return, but it grieved him to lose the hat. After a little wavering he did nonetheless go back and ring the bell.

"What do you want now?" the accursed Hella asked him.

"I forgot my hat," whispered the barman, jabbing at his bald pate. Hella turned around, the barman mentally spat and closed his eyes. When he opened them, Hella was handing him his hat and a sword with a dark hilt.

"It's not mine," the barman whispered, pushing the sword away and quickly putting on the hat.

"You came without a sword, did you?" asked Hella in surprise.

The barman growled something and quickly went downstairs. His head felt uncomfortable for some reason and too warm with the hat on; he took it off and, jumping in terror, let out a quiet cry. In his hands was a velvet beret with a tattered cockerel's feather. The barman crossed himself. At the same moment the beret miaowed, turned into a black kitten and, leaping back onto Andrei Fokich's head, sank all its claws into his bald pate. Emitting a cry of despair, the barman went careering downstairs, while the kitten fell off his head and belted up the staircase.

Bursting out into the fresh air, the barman trotted across to the gates and left for ever the devilish building of No. 302 *bis*.

What happened to him next is tremendously well-known. Bursting out of the gateway, the barman glanced around rather wildly as though looking for something. A minute later he was in the chemist's on the other side of the street. As soon as he uttered the words: "Tell me, please..." the woman behind the counter exclaimed:

"Citizen! Your whole head's covered in cuts!"

In five minutes' time the barman was bandaged up in gauze; he had learnt that the best specialists in liver disease were considered to be Professors Bernadsky and Kuzmin, had asked who was nearer, had lit up with joy on learning that Kuzmin lived literally across the courtyard in the little white detached house, and a couple of minutes later he was inside that little house.

The little place was ancient, but very, very cosy. The barman recalled that the first person he came across was a little old nursemaid who wanted to take his hat from him, but since he turned out not to have a hat, the nanny, chewing on an empty mouth, went away somewhere.

In her place by the mirror and, he thought, underneath some sort of arch, there was a middle-aged woman who immediately said he could make an appointment only for the nineteenth, no sooner. The barman grasped at once where salvation lay. Looking with a failing eye to beyond the arch, where three people were waiting in what was obviously some sort of ante-room, he whispered:

"Fatally ill..."

The woman gave the barman's bandaged head a puzzled look, wavered, said, "All right then..." and let the barman through the arch.

At the same instant the door opposite opened; in it there was the gleam of a gold pince-nez, and the woman in the white coat said:

"Citizens, this patient will be going in out of turn."

And the barman had not had time to look around before he found himself in Professor Kuzmin's office. There was nothing frightening, grand or medical in this elongated room.

"What's the matter with you?" asked Professor Kuzmin in a pleasant voice, giving the bandaged head a look of some alarm.

"I've just learnt from reliable hands," replied the barman, casting wild glances at some photographic group portrait behind glass, "that in February next year I'm going to die of liver cancer. I'm begging you to stop it."

Remaining seated, Professor Kuzmin simply recoiled against the high leather Gothic back of his armchair.

"Forgive me, I don't understand you… what, have you been to a doctor? Why is your head bandaged?"

"What do you mean, a doctor? If you'd only seen that doctor!…" the barman replied, and his teeth suddenly began chattering. "And pay no attention to my head, it has no relevance. You can spit on my head, it's got nothing to do with it. The liver cancer, please stop it."

"But permit me, who was it that told you?"

"Believe him!" requested the barman ardently. "He knows!"

"I don't understand a thing," said the Professor, shrugging his shoulders and rolling away from the desk with the armchair. "How can he possibly know when you're going to die? Especially if he isn't a doctor!"

"In ward four," replied the barman.

Here the Professor looked at his patient, at his head, at his damp trousers, and thought: "That's all I needed! A madman!" He asked:

"Do you drink vodka?"

"Never touched the stuff," replied the barman.

A minute later he was undressed, lying on a cold, oilskin couch, and the Professor was kneading his stomach. At this point, it should be said, the barman grew significantly more cheerful. The Professor stated categorically that now, at the present moment at least, the barman had no signs of cancer. But since that was how things were… since he was scared, and some charlatan had frightened him, all the tests needed to be done…

The Professor scribbled on some slips of paper, explaining where to go, what to take. Besides that he gave him a note to Professor Buryé,

214

a neuropathologist, explaining to the barman that his nerves were in total disarray.

"How much do I owe you, Professor?" asked the barman in a tender and quavering voice, pulling out his fat wallet.

"As much as you like," replied the Professor curtly and drily.

The barman took out thirty roubles and laid them out on the desk, and then, unexpectedly gently, as though operating with a cat's paw, he put on top of the ten-rouble notes a little clinking column in a piece of newspaper.

"And what's that?" asked Kuzmin, twirling up his moustache.

"Don't be picky, Citizen Professor," whispered the barman, "I'm begging you – stop the cancer."

"Take your gold away at once," said the Professor, proud of himself, "you'd do better to look after your nerves. Give your urine in for testing tomorrow, don't drink a lot of tea and eat without any salt at all."

"No salt even in my soup?" asked the barman.

"No salt in anything," ordered Kuzmin.

"Oh dear!…" exclaimed the barman mournfully, gazing with emotion at the Professor, taking his tenners and backing away towards the door.

The Professor had few patients that evening, and with the approach of dusk the last one left. While taking off his white coat, the Professor glanced at the spot where the barman had left the ten-rouble notes and saw that there were no ten-rouble notes there, but instead there lay three labels from bottles of Abrau Durso.

"The devil knows what's going on!" muttered Kuzmin, dragging the skirt of his white coat across the floor and fingering the bits of paper. "It turns out he's not just a schizophrenic, but a cheat as well! But I can't understand what he wanted from me? Surely not a note for a urine test? Oh! He's stolen the overcoats!" And the Professor rushed into the ante-room, with one sleeve of his white coat on again. "Ksenya Nikitishna!" he cried shrilly in the doorway of the ante-room. "Take a look, are the overcoats safe?"

All the overcoats proved to be safe. But on the other hand, when the Professor returned to the desk, having finally torn off the white coat, it was as if he had taken root in the parquet beside the desk, with his gaze riveted to his desk. On the spot where the labels had been lying sat an orphaned black kitten with an unhappy little face, miaowing over a saucer of milk.

"Wha-at is all this, permit me? This is just..." Kuzmin felt the back of his head turn cold.

At the Professor's quiet and piteous cry Ksenya Nikitishna came running and completely reassured him, saying straight away that it was, of course, one of the patients that had abandoned the kitten, that this happened to professors not infrequently.

"They probably lead a life of poverty," Ksenya Nikitishna explained, "whereas we, of course..."

They started to think and guess who might have abandoned it. Suspicion fell upon the old woman with a stomach ulcer.

"Her, of course," said Ksenya Nikitishna, "she thinks like this: I'm going to die anyway, but I feel sorry for the little kitten."

"But permit me!" cried Kuzmin. "And what about the milk?! Did she bring that as well? The saucer, eh?"

"She brought it in a little phial and poured it into the saucer here," Ksenya Nikitishna explained.

"In any case, take both the kitten and the saucer away," said Kuzmin, and he himself accompanied Ksenya Nikitishna as far as the door. When he returned, the situation changed.

While hanging his white coat on its nail, the Professor heard loud laughter in the courtyard; he glanced out, naturally, and was struck dumb. A lady wearing just a petticoat was running across the courtyard to the little outhouse opposite. The Professor even knew what she was called – Maria Alexandrovna. It was a little boy that was chuckling.

"What's this?" said Kuzmin scornfully.

At that point, on the other side of the wall, in the Professor's daughter's room, the gramophone started playing a foxtrot, 'Hallelujah', and at the same instant the chirping of a sparrow was heard behind the Professor's back. He turned around and saw a large sparrow hopping about on his desk.

"Hm... steady..." thought the Professor, "it flew in as I was moving away from the window. Everything's in order!" the Professor told himself, while sensing that everything was in complete disorder, and mainly, of course, because of this sparrow. When he looked at it closely, the Professor was immediately convinced that this sparrow was not an entirely ordinary sparrow. The filthy little sparrow was slightly lame in the left leg and, behaving in a blatantly affected way, it was dragging it, working in syncopation, in short – it was dancing the foxtrot to the sounds of the gramophone like a drunk at a bar. It was being as rude as it knew how, casting insolent looks at the Professor.

Kuzmin's hand went down onto the telephone, and he was ready to ring his college contemporary Buryé to ask what sparrows like this signified at the age of sixty, when your head suddenly started spinning too.

The sparrow, meanwhile, had sat down on the inkstand – a gift – had defecated into it (I'm not joking!), had then flown up and hung in the air, then had pecked with all its might, as if with a beak of steel, at the glass of the photograph of the entire university graduation class of '94, had smashed the glass to smithereens and had then flown away through the window.

The Professor changed the number on the telephone, and instead of ringing Buryé, he rang the leeches' bureau, said it was Professor Kuzmin speaking and that he was asking for some leeches to be sent to his house immediately.

After placing the receiver on the lever, the Professor again turned to the desk and immediately emitted a shriek. At the desk, wearing the headscarf of a Sister of Mercy,* sat a woman with a small bag bearing the inscription "leeches". The Professor shrieked when he peered into her mouth. It was a man's mouth, crooked, stretching to the ears, with a single fang. The sister's eyes were dead.

"I'll tidy up the money," said the sister in a man's bass, "it has no business lying around here." With a bird's leg she raked up the labels and began melting into thin air.

A couple of hours passed. Professor Kuzmin sat in his bedroom on the bed, and there were leeches hanging on his temples, behind his ears and on his neck. On a silk quilt at Kuzmin's feet sat grey-whiskered Professor Buryé, gazing sympathetically at Kuzmin and comforting him that it was all nonsense. At the window it was already night.

What queer things happened thereafter in Moscow that night we do not know and, of course, will not be trying to find out – particularly as the time is coming for us to move on to the second part of this true narrative. Follow me, Reader!

Part Two

19

Margarita

F OLLOW ME, Reader! Who told you there is no genuine, true, everlasting love in the world? Let the liar's vile tongue be cut off!

Follow me, my Reader, and only me, and I shall show you such love!

No! The Master was mistaken in the hospital when he told Ivanushka with bitterness at that hour when the night was slipping past midnight that she had forgotten him. That could not have been. Of course she had not forgotten him.

First of all we shall reveal the secret which the Master did not wish to reveal to Ivanushka. His beloved was called Margarita Nikolayevna. All the Master said about her to the poor poet was the absolute truth. He described his beloved accurately. She was beautiful and clever. To this must be added one thing more: it can be said with certainty that many women would have given absolutely anything to exchange their lives for the life of Margarita Nikolayevna. Childless thirty-year-old Margarita was the wife of a very major specialist, who had, in addition, made a most important discovery of national significance. Her husband was young, handsome, kind, honest, and adored his wife. Margarita Nikolayevna and her husband together occupied the entire upper part of a splendid detached house, set in a garden in one of the side streets near the Arbat. An enchanting place! Anyone can satisfy himself of it, should he desire to head into that garden. Let him ask me, I'll tell him the address, I'll point out the way – the house is still intact to this day.

Margarita Nikolayevna was not in need of money. Margarita Nikolayevna could buy anything she liked. Among her husband's acquaintances there were some interesting people. Margarita Nikolayevna never touched a Primus. Margarita Nikolayevna did not know the horrors of living in a shared apartment. In short... was she happy? Not for one minute! Ever since she had married as a nineteen-year-old and found herself in the detached house, she had not known happiness. Gods, my gods! Whatever did this woman need?! What did she need, this woman in whose eyes there always burned some incomprehensible little fire? What did she need, this witch with a slight squint in one eye who adorned herself that time in spring with mimosas? I don't know. It's unknown to me. Obviously she was telling the truth, she needed him, the Master, and not by any means a Gothic house, nor a private garden, nor money. She loved him, she was telling the truth.

Even I, the truthful narrator, but an outside observer, feel my heart contract at the thought of what Margarita experienced when she arrived the next day at the Master's little house – fortunately, without having managed to talk things over with her husband, who had not returned at the appointed time – and learnt that the Master was no longer there. She did everything to find something out about him, and, of course, she found out precisely nothing. Then she returned to her house and began living in her former place.

But as soon as the dirty snow disappeared from the pavements and the roadways, as soon as there was a breath of the rather muggy, restless wind of spring through the transom windows, Margarita Nikolayevna began pining more than in the winter. She often cried in secret, crying long and bitterly. She did not know whom she loved: someone alive or dead. And the longer the desperate days went on, the more often the thought came to her, and particularly in the twilight, that she was tied to someone who was dead.

She either had to forget him, or die herself. Such a life just can't be dragged out. It can't! Forget him, whatever the cost – forget! But he won't be forgotten, that's the trouble.

"Yes, yes, yes, the same sort of mistake!" said Margarita, sitting by the stove and gazing at the fire, lit in memory of the fire that had burned then, when he had been writing Pontius Pilate. "Why did I leave him then, in the night? Why? It's madness, isn't it! I was honest, I returned the next day, as I'd promised, but it was already too late. Yes, like the unhappy Levi Matthew, I returned too late!"

All these words were, of course, absurd, because what would in fact have changed if she had remained that night with the Master? Would she really have saved him? Ridiculous! we would exclaim, but we won't do that in front of a woman reduced to despair.

That same day when all sorts of absurd commotion was taking place, brought about by the appearance in Moscow of the black magician, on the Friday when Berlioz's uncle was banished back to Kiev, when the accountant was arrested, and a multitude of other very silly and incomprehensible things took place too, Margarita woke up around midday in her bedroom, which looked out through the skylight onto the house's turret.

On waking up, Margarita did not start crying, as was often the case, because she had woken up with a premonition that today something would finally happen. Having had this premonition, she began warming and nurturing it in her soul, afraid that it might abandon her.

"I believe it!" whispered Margarita solemnly. "I believe it! Something will happen! It can't fail to happen, because why, after all, have I been sent a lifetime of torment? I admit the fact that I lied and deceived and lived a secret life, hidden from the world, but all the same, that cannot be punished so cruelly. Something is bound to happen, because it cannot be that something drags on for ever. And besides, my dream was a prophetic one, I guarantee it."

Thus whispered Margarita Nikolayevna, gazing at the crimson, sundrenched curtains, dressing uneasily, combing her short, waved hair in front of the triple mirror.

The dream that Margarita had dreamt that night really was unusual. The thing is that during her winter torment she had never seen the Master in her dreams. He would leave her alone in the night, and she was tormented only in the hours of daylight. But now she had dreamt of him.

Margarita had dreamt of a locality unknown to her – hopeless, dreary, beneath an overcast early spring sky. She dreamt of this scraggy, racing grey sky, with beneath it a soundless flock of rooks. Some rough little bridge, beneath it a turbid spring rivulet. Joyless, beggarly, half-bare trees. A solitary aspen, and, further off, between the trees, beyond some sort of vegetable patch, a little log cabin, perhaps a detached cookhouse, perhaps a bathhouse, perhaps the devil knows what. All around is somehow lifeless, and so dreary that there is a real urge to hang oneself on that aspen by the bridge. Not a breath of breeze, not a cloud stirring and not a living soul. What a hellish spot for a living person!

And then, imagine, the door of the log cabin swings wide open, and he appears. Quite far off, but distinctly visible. He is ragged, what he is wearing cannot be made out. Hair tousled, unshaven. The eyes sick, alarmed. He is beckoning to her with his hand, calling. Choking in the lifeless air, Margarita had set off running over the hummocks towards him, and at that moment had woken up.

"That dream can signify only one of two things," Margarita Nikolay-evna reasoned to herself, "if he's dead and beckoned to me, that means he was coming for me, and I shall soon die. That's a very good thing, because then there'll be an end to my torment. Or he's alive, and then the dream can signify only one thing, that he's remembering himself to me! He wants to say we shall see one another again. Yes, we shall see one another very soon!"

Still in the same excited state, Margarita got dressed and began suggesting to herself that, in essence, everything was taking shape very opportunely, and you needed to know how to seize such opportune moments and exploit them. Her husband had gone away on a business trip for three whole days. She had been left to her own devices for a period of three days, nobody would prevent her from thinking about anything she wanted, dreaming about whatever she pleased. All five rooms on the top floor of the house, this whole apartment, which would have been the envy of tens of thousands of people in Moscow, was completely at her disposal.

However, having got freedom for three whole days, the place Marga-rita chose out of the whole of this luxurious apartment was far from the best. After drinking her fill of tea, she went off to a dark room without windows, where suitcases and various old things were kept in two large cupboards. Squatting down, she opened the bottom drawer of the first of them, and from under a heap of silk scraps she got out the only thing of value she had in life. In Margarita's hands was an old, brown leather album, in which there was a photograph of the Master, a Savings Bank book with a deposit of 10,000 in his name, the petals of a dried rose pressed between sheets of ricepaper, and part of a notebook a whole quire in length, covered in typewriting and with its bottom edge scorched.

Returning with these riches to her bedroom, Margarita Nikolayevna set the photograph up on the triple mirror and sat for about an hour, holding the fire-damaged notebook on her knees, leafing through it and rereading what, after the burning, had neither beginning nor end: "…The darkness that had come from the Mediterranean Sea covered the city the Procurator hated. The suspension bridges joining the Temple to the terrible Tower of Antonia disappeared, the abyss descended from the sky and poured over the winged gods above the hippodrome, the Hasmonean Palace with its embrasures, the bazaars, the caravanserais, the lanes, the ponds… Yershalaim, the great city, vanished as if it had never existed on earth…"

Margarita wanted to read further, but there was nothing further except an uneven, charred fringe.

Wiping away her tears, Margarita Nikolayevna finished with the notebook, put her elbows on the dressing table and sat for a long time, reflected in the mirror, not taking her eyes off the photograph. Then her tears dried. Margarita collected her property neatly together, and a few minutes later it was buried once again beneath the bits of silk, and the lock closed with a clang in the dark room.

Margarita Nikolayevna was in the hall, putting on her coat to go out for a walk. Her beautiful maid Natasha enquired about what she should do for the main course, and, getting the reply that it was all the same, to amuse herself she entered into conversation with her mistress and began telling her God knows what, such as how at the theatre the day before a conjuror had performed such tricks that everyone had gasped, he had given out for free to everyone two flacons of foreign perfume each, and stockings for free, and then, when the performance had ended, the audience had gone out into the street and – hey presto! – everyone had turned out to be naked! Margarita Nikolayevna collapsed onto the chair under the mirror in the hall and roared with laughter.

"Natasha! You should be ashamed of yourself," said Margarita Nikolayevna, "you're a literate, intelligent girl; people in queues tell the devil knows what lies, and you go repeating them!"

Natasha flushed red and objected with great fervour that they weren't lying one bit and that she herself had personally seen in a grocer's on the Arbat that day a citizeness who had come into the grocer's wearing shoes, but when she had gone to the till to pay, her shoes had disappeared from her feet and she had been left in just her stockings. Eyes popping out and a hole in the heel! And those shoes had been magic ones from that same performance.

"And she left like that?"

225

"She left like that!" Natasha cried out, blushing more and more at not being believed. "And yesterday, Margarita Nikolayevna, the police took in about a hundred people during the night. Citizenesses from this show were running down Tverskaya in just their knickers."

"Well, it was Darya telling you, of course," said Margarita Nikolayevna, "I've been noticing for a long time now that she's a dreadful liar."

The funny conversation ended with a pleasant surprise for Natasha. Margarita Nikolayevna went into the bedroom and came out of it holding in her hands a pair of stockings and a flacon of eau de Cologne. Telling Natasha that she wanted to perform a trick as well, Margarita Nikolayevna presented her with both the stockings and the bottle and said that she asked only one thing of her – not to run down Tverskaya in just the stockings, and not to listen to Darya. With an exchange of kisses, the mistress and the maid parted.

Reclining against the comfortable soft back of a seat in a trolleybus, Margarita Nikolayevna rode down the Arbat, at times thinking her own thoughts, at times listening in on what the two citizens sitting in front of her were whispering.

And they, occasionally turning around warily in case somebody might hear, were whispering to one another about some sort of nonsense. The hefty, meaty one with lively little piggy eyes sitting by the window was telling his small neighbour quietly about how a coffin had had to be covered with a black bedspread…

"It's not possible!" whispered the small one in shock. "That's something unheard of… And whatever action did Zheldybin take?"

Amid the steady drone of the trolleybus the words could be heard from the window:

"The CID… a scandal… well, simply mysticism!"

From these fragmentary little pieces Margarita Nikolayevna somehow put together something coherent. The citizens were whispering about how some dead man – but who, they had not said – had that morning had his head stolen from his coffin! And so it was because of that, that this Zheldybin was now so anxious. And the two that were whispering in the trolleybus were also linked in some way with the dead man who had been robbed.

"Will we have time to pop in for some flowers?" the small one was worrying. "You say the cremation's at two?"

Finally Margarita Nikolayevna grew tired of listening to this mysterious prattling about a head stolen from a coffin, and she rejoiced that it was time for her to get off.

A few minutes later Margarita Nikolayevna was already sitting on one of the benches beneath the Kremlin wall, and had positioned herself in such a way that the Manège could be seen.

Margarita was squinting in the bright sunlight, remembering that night's dream, remembering how exactly a year ago, to the day and to the hour, she had sat beside him on this very same bench. He was not there next to her today, but Margarita Nikolayevna was still conversing with him in her mind. "If you've been exiled, then why on earth don't you let me know about you? After all, people do let others know. Have you stopped loving me? No, I don't believe that somehow. So that means you were exiled and have died... Then let me go, I beg of you, give me the freedom to live at last, to breathe in the air!" Margarita Nikolayevna replied to herself on his behalf: "You are free... Am I really holding you back?" Then she objected to him: "No, what sort of answer is that? No, you get on out of my memory, then I shall be free."

People were walking past Margarita Nikolayevna. Some man gave the well-dressed woman a sidelong glance, attracted by her beauty and solitude. He coughed and sat down on the very end of that same bench on which Margarita Nikolayevna was sitting. Plucking up courage, he began to speak.

"Decidedly good weather today..."

But Margarita gave him such a gloomy look that he rose and left.

"And there's an example," said Margarita mentally to the one who possessed her, "why, precisely, did I drive that man off? I'm bored, and there's nothing wrong with that Lovelace,* except perhaps for just that silly 'decidedly'. Why am I sitting alone beneath the wall like an owl? Why am I excluded from life?"

She became quite sad and downcast. But suddenly at this point that same wave of expectation and excitement from the morning hit her in the chest. "Yes, it will happen!" The wave hit her a second time, and at this point she realized it was a wave of sound. More and more distinctly through the noise of the city could be heard the approaching beats of a drum and the sounds of trumpets, a little out of tune.

First to appear was a mounted policeman riding at a walk past the railings of the park with three men on foot behind him. Then a truck driving slowly and carrying musicians. And next – a slow-moving, brand-new open funeral car, upon it a coffin, covered in wreaths, and, at the corners of the platform, four people standing: three men and one woman.

Even at a distance Margarita discerned that the faces of the people standing in the funeral car and accompanying the deceased on his last journey were somehow strangely perplexed. This was particularly noticeable in respect of the citizeness standing at the left rear corner of the motor-hearse. It was as if this citizeness's fat cheeks were being burst still wider apart from within by some piquant secret, and in her small, puffy eyes ambiguous little lights were sparkling. It seemed that at any minute, just a little longer, and the citizeness, unable to stand it, would wink at the deceased and say: "Have you ever seen anything like it? It's simply mysticism!" The mourners on foot had just the same perplexed faces too, as, approximately three hundred in number, they walked slowly behind the funeral car.

Margarita's eyes followed the procession, and she listened to the doleful bass drum producing that same repeated "boom boom boom" as it faded into the distance, and she thought: "What a strange funeral! And how depressing that 'boom' is! Oh, I'd truly pawn my soul to the Devil just to find out if he's alive or not! I wonder who that is they're burying with such amazing faces?"

"Berlioz, Mikhail Alexandrovich," a somewhat nasal male voice was heard beside her, "the Chairman of MASSOLIT."

Surprised, Margarita Nikolayevna turned and saw sitting on her bench a citizen who had evidently joined her noiselessly at the time when Margarita had been engrossed in looking at the procession and, it must be assumed, had absent-mindedly asked her last question out loud.

The procession had in the meantime started coming to a halt, probably held up by traffic lights ahead.

"Yes," the unknown citizen continued, "they're in an amazing mood. Carrying the deceased, but thinking only about where his head's got to."

"What head?" asked Margarita, peering at her unexpected neighbour. This neighbour turned out to be small in stature with fiery red hair and a fang, wearing starched linen, a striped suit of good quality, patent-leather shoes and with a bowler hat on his head. His tie was bright. The surprising thing was that sticking out of the pocket where men usually carry a handkerchief or a fountain pen, this citizen had a picked chicken bone.

"Yes, if you'd be so kind as to see," the red-headed man explained, "this morning in the Griboyedov hall the deceased man's head was pinched from the coffin."

"How can that possibly be?" asked Margarita involuntarily, at the same time remembering the whispering in the trolleybus.

"The devil knows how!" replied the red-headed man casually. "Though I suggest it wouldn't be a bad idea to ask Behemoth about it. The way it was nicked was awfully clever. Such a huge scandal! And the main thing is, it's not clear who needs it, the head, or what for!"

No matter how preoccupied Margarita Nikolayevna was with her own business, she was nonetheless struck by the strange gibberish of the unknown citizen.

"Permit me!" she suddenly exclaimed. "What Berlioz? Is this what was in the papers today..."

"Of course, of course..."

"So those are writers following the coffin, then?" Margarita asked, and suddenly bared her teeth.

"Well, naturally, they are!"

"And do you know them to look at?"

"To the very last one," replied the red-headed man.

"Tell me," began Margarita, and her voice became muffled, "is the critic Latunsky among them?"

"How can he possibly fail to be there?" replied the red-headed man. "There he is, on the end of the fourth row."

"Is that the blond?" asked Margarita, narrowing her eyes.

"Ash-grey hair... See, he's raised his eyes skywards."

"Looks like a Catholic priest?"

"That's him!"

Margarita asked no more, peering at Latunsky.

"And you, as I see," began the red-headed man, smiling, "hate this Latunsky."

"I hate someone else as well," Margarita replied through her teeth, "but talking about it's of no interest."

At this time the procession moved on, and stretched out behind those on foot were for the most part empty cars.

"Well, of course, what is there of interest here, Margarita Nikolay-evna!"

Margarita was surprised:

"You know me?"

Instead of a reply, the red-headed man removed his bowler hat and took it in his outstretched hand.

"A real villain's face!" thought Margarita, scrutinizing her interloc-utor of the street.

"But I don't know you," said Margarita drily.

"How on earth would you know me? But at the same time, I'm sent to you on a little business matter."

Margarita turned pale and recoiled.

"You should have started with that straight away," she began, "with-out spinning the devil knows what kind of a story about a severed head! Do you want to arrest me?"

"Nothing of the kind," exclaimed the red-headed man, "what's this about: if he's started talking, then there's bound to be an arrest! Simply I have some business with you."

"I don't understand a thing, what business?"

The red-headed man glanced around and said mysteriously:

"I was sent to invite you to pay a call this evening."

"What are you rambling on about, what call?"

"On a very distinguished foreigner," said the red-headed man mean-ingfully, screwing up his eye.

Margarita grew very angry.

"A new breed's appeared: the street pimp!" she said, rising to leave.

"Thank you very much for errands like this!" the red-headed man ex-claimed, offended, and growled at Margarita's departing back: "Idiot!"

"Swine!" she responded, turning around, and straight away she heard behind her the red-headed man's voice:

"'The darkness that had come from the Mediterranean Sea covered the city the Procurator hated. The suspension bridges joining the Temple to the terrible Tower of Antonia disappeared, the abyss descended from the sky and poured over the winged gods above the hippodrome, the Hasmonean Palace with its embrasures, the bazaars, the caravanserais, the lanes, the ponds... Yershalaim, the great city, vanished as if it had never existed on earth…' So just get lost with your scorched notebook and dried rose! Sit here alone on the bench and implore him to let you go free, to let you breathe the air, to get out of your memory!"

White-faced, Margarita returned to the bench. The red-headed man gazed at her with narrowed eyes.

"I don't understand a thing," Margarita Nikolayevna began quietly, "you could just find out about the sheets of paper… get in, spy… Natasha's been bribed, yes? But how could you have found out my thoughts?" She pulled a face with an air of suffering and added: "Tell me, who are you? What organization are you from?"

"How boring this is," the red-headed man grumbled, then began to speak louder: "Forgive me, I mean, I told you I'm not from any organization at all. Sit down, please."

Margarita obeyed unquestioningly, but, sitting down, all the same asked again:

"Who are you?"

"Well, all right, I'm called Azazello, but that doesn't mean anything to you anyway, does it?"

"And will you tell me how you found out about the sheets of paper and about my thoughts?"

"I won't," replied Azazello drily.

"But do you know anything about him?" Margarita whispered imploringly.

"Well, let's say I do."

"I beg you, tell me just one thing: is he alive? Don't torment me!"

"Oh, he's alive, he's alive," Azazello responded unwillingly.

"God!"

"Please, no agitation or crying out," said Azazello, frowning.

"Forgive me, forgive me," mumbled the now submissive Margarita, "I got angry with you, of course. But you must agree, when a woman's invited in the street to pay a call somewhere… I have no prejudices, I assure you," Margarita grinned cheerlessly, "but I never see any foreigners, I have no desire whatsoever to associate with them… and apart from that, my husband… My drama lies in the fact that I live with a man I don't love, but I consider ruining his life an unworthy thing. I've seen nothing from him but kindness…"

Azazello heard out this incoherent speech with evident boredom.

"Can I ask you to be quiet for a minute?"

Margarita submissively fell quiet.

"I'm inviting you to see a perfectly harmless foreigner. And not a single soul will know about the visit. Now I can vouch to you for that."

"And what does he want me for?" Margarita asked, fishing.

"You'll find out about that later."

"I understand. I have to give myself to him," Margarita said pensively.

At this Azazello snorted in a haughty sort of way and replied thus:

"That would be the dream, I can assure you, of any woman in the world," a chuckle distorted Azazello's ugly mug, "but I'll have to disenchant you, it won't happen."

"What sort of a foreigner is this?!" Margarita exclaimed so loudly in her confusion that people walking past the bench turned around towards her. "And what do I gain from going to see him?"

Azazello leant towards her and whispered meaningfully:

"Well, you have a great deal to gain... You can exploit the opportunity..."

"What?" exclaimed Margarita, and her eyes became rounded. "If I understand you correctly, you're hinting that I can find out about him there?"

Azazello nodded his head in silence.

"I'm going!" Margarita exclaimed forcefully, and seized Azazello by the arm. "I'm going anywhere you like!"

Puffing in relief, Azazello reclined against the back of the bench, covering with his back the word carved out on it in large letters "*Nyura*", and began saying ironically:

"Difficult people, these women!" he thrust his hands into his pockets and stretched his legs way out in front of him. "Why, for example, was I sent on this matter? Behemoth could have come; he's charming..."

Margarita began with a crooked and bitter smile:

"Will you stop mystifying me and tormenting me with your riddles... I'm an unhappy person, you know, and you're exploiting it. I'm getting myself into some strange business, but, I swear, it's only because of your luring me with your words about him! My head's spinning from all these incomprehensible things..."

"No dramas, no dramas," Azazello responded, grimacing, "you have to put yourself in my position too. Giving the manager one in the clock, or throwing the uncle out of the house, or shooting and wounding someone, or some other trifle of the sort, that's my real speciality, but talking to women in love – your humble servant! I mean, I've already been half an hour trying to talk you round. So you're coming?"

"I am," Margarita Nikolayevna replied simply.

"Then be so kind as to have this," said Azazello, and taking from his pocket a little round gold canister, he reached it out to Margarita with the words: "Come on, put it away, or else passers-by are looking. It'll come in handy, Margarita Nikolayevna, grief has aged you a fair bit over the last six months," Margarita flared up, but made no reply, and Azazello continued: "This evening at exactly half-past nine, be so kind as to strip naked and rub this ointment into your face and your entire body. Do whatever you like after that, but don't go far from the telephone. At ten I shall ring you and tell you everything that's necessary. You won't have to worry about anything, you'll be delivered where necessary, and you won't be caused any anxiety. Clear?"

Margarita was silent for a moment then replied:

"Clear. This thing is made of pure gold, it's obvious from the weight. Well, so what, I understand perfectly well that I'm being bribed and dragged into some shady business for which I'll pay dearly."

"What is this about," Azazello all but began to hiss, "are you starting again?"

"No, wait!"

"Give the cream back!"

Margarita squeezed the canister tighter in her hand and continued:

"No, wait... I know what I'm doing. But I'm doing everything because of him, because I have no more expectations of anything in the world. But I want to say to you that, if you destroy me, you'll be ashamed of yourself! Yes, ashamed! I perish because of love," and, striking herself on the breast, Margarita glanced at the sun.

"Give it back," cried Azazello in fury, "give it back, and to hell with it all! Let them send Behemoth!"

"Oh no!" exclaimed Margarita, amazing the passers-by. "I agree to everything, I agree to perform this comedy with the rubbing in of the ointment, I agree to go the devil knows how far! I won't give it back!"

"Bah!" Azazello suddenly yelled, and, goggling at the railings of the garden, started pointing his finger at something.

Margarita turned in the direction Azazello was pointing, but did not discover anything in particular there. Then she turned back to Azazello, wanting to get an explanation for that absurd "Bah!" but there was no one to give the explanation: Margarita Nikolayevna's mysterious interlocutor had vanished.

Margarita quickly put her hand into her handbag, where she had put the canister away before that cry, and checked it was still there. Then, not reflecting on anything, Margarita hurriedly ran off out of the Alexandrovsky Garden.

20

Azazello's Cream

THE FULL MOON HUNG in the clear evening sky, visible through the boughs of the maple. The limes and acacias had covered the earth in the garden with a complex design of dark patches. The triple window in the skylight, open, but with the blind drawn, shone with a furious electric light. In Margarita Nikolayevna's bedroom all the lights were burning and illuminating the complete disarray in the room.

On the blanket on the bed lay camisoles, stockings and linen, and crumpled linen was scattered simply on the floor alongside a packet of cigarettes which had been squashed in agitation. Shoes stood on the bedside table alongside an unfinished cup of coffee and an ashtray in which a cigarette stub was smoking. On the back of a chair hung a black evening dress. The room smelt of perfume. Besides that, the smell of a burning hot iron was carrying from somewhere.

Margarita Nikolayevna was sitting in front of the cheval glass wearing just her bathrobe, thrown onto her naked body, and black suede shoes. Her watch on a gold bracelet lay in front of Margarita Nikolayevna alongside the canister she had got from Azazello, and Margarita did not take her eyes off the watch face. At times it began to seem to her that the watch had broken and the hands were not moving. But they were moving, albeit very slowly, as though sticking, and finally the long hand fell on the twenty-ninth minute after nine. Margarita's heart gave a terrible thump, and so she could not even lay hands on the canister at once. Getting herself under control, Margarita opened it and saw in the canister some greasy, yellowish cream. It seemed to her to smell of marsh slime. With the tip of a finger Margarita put a little dab of the cream onto her palm, at which there was a stronger smell of marsh grasses and the forest, and then began rubbing the cream into her forehead and cheeks with her palm.

The cream spread easily and, as it seemed to Margarita, evaporated straight away. After a few bouts of rubbing in, Margarita glanced in the mirror and dropped the canister right on the glass of the watch, which covered it in cracks. Margarita closed her eyes, then took another glance and burst into roars of wild laughter.

Her eyebrows, plucked along their edges with pincers into a thread, had thickened and lay in black, even arcs above eyes that had turned green. The fine vertical crease that cut across the bridge of her nose and had appeared then, in October, when the Master had disappeared, had vanished without trace. The yellow shadows by her temples had vanished as well, and the two scarcely noticeable little networks at the outer corners of her eyes. The skin of her cheeks had filled with an even pink colour, her forehead had become white and unblemished, while the hairdresser's waves in her hair had come out.

Thirty-year-old Margarita was gazed at from the mirror by a naturally curly, black-haired woman of about twenty who was roaring with unrestrained laughter and baring her teeth.

When she had finished laughing, Margarita slipped out of her robe in a single leap, scooped up the light, greasy cream liberally and with firm strokes started rubbing it into the skin of her body, which immediately turned pink and began to glow. Then instantly, as if a needle had been snatched from her brain, the temple that had been aching all evening after the meeting in the Alexandrovsky Garden quietened down, the muscles of her arms and legs strengthened, and then Margarita's body lost its weight.

She gave a little jump and hung in the air a little way above the rug, then she slowly began to be drawn downwards, and dropped.

"What a cream! What a cream!" cried Margarita, dropping into an armchair.

The rubbing-in changed her not only outwardly. In the whole of her now, in every particle of her body there boiled a joy which she could feel like little bubbles that stung her entire body. Margarita felt herself free, free from everything. Apart from that, she realized with complete clarity that what had happened was precisely what her premonition had already told her about that morning, and she was leaving the house and her former life for ever. But all the same, there broke away from that former life one thought about just one last duty needing to be carried out before the start of something new and extraordinary that was drawing her upwards into the air. And as she was, naked, she ran over to her husband's study, continually taking off into the air, and, putting the light on in the room, she rushed to the desk. On a sheet torn from a notepad, without making any corrections, quickly and in large letters she wrote a note in pencil:

Forgive me, and forget me as soon as possible. I'm leaving you for ever. Don't look for me, it's useless. The sorrow and calamities that have struck me have made me become a witch. I must go. Farewell.

Margarita

With her soul completely unburdened, Margarita flew into the bedroom, and Natasha ran in there too, right behind her, loaded with things. And all those things, a dress on a wooden hanger, lace shawls, blue silk shoes on trees and a belt – all this was immediately scattered onto the floor, and Natasha clasped her freed hands together.

"Well, do I look good?" Margarita Nikolayevna cried loudly in a hoarse voice.

"How on earth?" whispered Natasha, backing away. "How do you do that, Margarita Nikolayevna?"

"It's the cream! The cream, the cream!" Margarita replied, pointing towards the glittering gold canister, and twirling around in front of the mirror.

Forgetting about the crumpled dress lying on the floor, Natasha ran up to the cheval glass and stared with greedy, burning eyes at the remainder of the ointment. Her lips were whispering something. She again turned to Margarita and said with a sort of reverence:

"What skin, eh! What skin! Margarita Nikolayevna, your skin's glowing, you know!" But at this point she remembered herself, ran over to the dress, picked it up and began shaking it down.

"Leave it! Leave it!" Margarita cried to her. "To hell with it, leave it all! But no, take it for yourself as a memento. Take it as a memento, I say. Take everything there is in the room!"

As though half out of her mind, Natasha looked at Margarita for a time without moving, then she threw her arms around her neck, kissing her and crying:

"Satin! Glowing! Satin! And your eyebrows, what eyebrows!"

"Take all the rags, take the perfume and drag it all off to your trunk, hide it away," cried Margarita, "but don't take the valuables, or else you'll be accused of stealing!"

Natasha raked together into a bundle whatever came to hand – dresses, shoes, stockings and underwear – and ran off out of the bedroom.

At that moment from an open window somewhere on the other side of the lane, a thunderous, virtuoso waltz burst out and took flight, and the puffing of a car driving up to the gates was heard.

"Azazello will soon be ringing!" exclaimed Margarita, listening to the waltz pouring forth in the lane. "He'll be ringing! And the foreigner's harmless. Yes, I realize now that he's harmless!"

The car began making a noise, moving off from the gates. The side gate banged, and footsteps were heard on the flagstones of the path.

"It's Nikolai Ivanovich, I recognize him by his footsteps," thought Margarita, "I ought to do something very funny and interesting to say goodbye."

Margarita tore the blind aside and sat down on the window sill sideways on, clasping her arms around her knee. The moonlight licked her right side. Margarita raised her head towards the moon and pulled a pensive and poetic face. The footsteps tapped a couple of times more and then suddenly fell quiet. After admiring the moon a little more, and sighing for the sake of decency, Margarita turned her head towards the garden and did indeed see Nikolai Ivanovich, who lived on the bottom floor of that same house. Nikolai Ivanovich was flooded with bright moonlight. He was sitting on a bench, and everything pointed to his having dropped onto it suddenly. The pince-nez on his face had somehow gone askew, and he was squeezing his briefcase in his arms.

"Ah, hello, Nikolai Ivanovich," said Margarita in a sad voice, "good evening! Have you come from a meeting?"

Nikolai Ivanovich made no reply to this.

"Well I'm sitting here alone, as you can see," continued Margarita, leaning out into the garden a little more, "pining, gazing at the moon and listening to the waltz."

237

Margarita passed her left hand over her temple, adjusting a strand of hair, then said angrily:

"This is impolite, Nikolai Ivanovich! After all, I am a lady, in the end! It's rude not to answer, you know, when you're being spoken to!"

Nikolai Ivanovich, visible in the moonlight down to the last button on his grey waistcoat, to the last little hair in his light little wedge-shaped beard, suddenly grinned a wild grin, rose from the bench, and, obviously beside himself with embarrassment, instead of doffing his hat, waved his briefcase to one side and bent his legs, as though intending to drop into a squat.

"Oh, what a boring sort you are, Nikolai Ivanovich!" Margarita continued. "I'm so fed up with the lot of you in general, I just can't tell you, and I'm so happy to be parting with you! To hell with you!"

At that moment, behind Margarita's back in the bedroom the telephone let out a peal. Margarita darted away from the window sill and, forgetting about Nikolai Ivanovich, grabbed the receiver.

"Azazello speaking," came the words in the receiver.

"Dear, dear Azazello!" exclaimed Margarita.

"It's time! Fly out," Azazello began in the receiver, and it was audible in his tone that he found Margarita's sincere, joyous impulse pleasing, "and when you're flying over the gates, cry 'Invisible!' Next fly about over the city for a while to get used to it, and then fly south, out of the city, and straight to the river... You're expected!"

Margarita hung up the receiver, and at that point in the next room something started stumping about woodenly and beating at the door. Margarita threw it open, and a broom with the bristles uppermost flew dancing into the bedroom. It was beating out a tattoo on the floor with its end, kicking out and straining towards the window. Margarita shrieked in delight and leapt up astride the broom. Only at this point did it flash through the rider's mind that in all this commotion she had forgotten to get dressed. She galloped over to the bed and grabbed the first thing that came to hand, some pale-blue nightshirt. Waving it up in the air like a standard, she flew out of the window. And the waltz struck up more lustily over the garden.

Margarita slipped down from the window and saw Nikolai Ivanovich on the bench. It was as if he had frozen on it and was listening in complete stupefaction to the cries and the clatter that were carrying from the lighted bedroom of the residents upstairs.

"Farewell, Nikolai Ivanovich!" shouted Margarita, dancing about in front of Nikolai Ivanovich.

The latter gasped and began crawling along the bench, pulling himself across it with his hands and knocking his briefcase off onto the ground.

"Farewell for ever! I'm flying away!" shouted Margarita, drowning out the waltz. At this point she grasped that the nightshirt was of no use to her, was unnecessary, and, breaking into sinister laughter, she covered Nikolai Ivanovich's head with it. The blinded Nikolai Ivanovich crashed from the bench onto the bricks of the path.

Margarita turned to take a last look at the house where she had been so long in torment and in the blazing window saw Natasha's face, contorted in astonishment.

"Farewell, Natasha!" Margarita cried, and jerked the broom up. "Invisible! Invisible!" she cried, even louder, and between the branches of the maple, that whipped her across the face, she flew over the gates, flew out into the lane. And in her wake flew the waltz, which had now gone completely mad.

21

The Flight

INVISIBLE AND FREE! Invisible and free! After flying down her own lane, Margarita found herself in another one that sliced across the first at a right angle. In one moment she had cut across this patched, darned, long and crooked lane, with the rickety door of the oil shop where they sell paraffin by the mug and a liquid to combat parasites in flasks, and at that point she recognized that, even being completely free and invisible, she must all the same be just a little prudent in her enjoyment too. Only because by some miracle she braked did she not crash to her death into the old leaning lamp post on the corner. Turning away from it, Margarita squeezed the broom a little tighter and began to fly more slowly, peering at the electric wires and the signs hanging out across the pavement.

A third lane led straight to the Arbat. Here Margarita began to feel perfectly comfortable with controlling the broom, realized that it obeyed the slightest touch of the hands or legs, and that, while flying over the city, it was necessary to be very attentive and not too boisterous. Apart from that, it had become quite obvious even in the lane that passers-by could not see the flying woman. Nobody craned their necks, cried, "Look, look!", shied away, screamed or fainted, or roared with wild laughter.

Margarita flew soundlessly, very slowly and low, at about the level of the first floor. But even flying slowly, by the very exit onto the blindingly illuminated Arbat, she made a slight misjudgement and struck her shoulder against some illuminated disk on which was drawn an arrow. This angered Margarita. She checked the obedient broom, flew off to one side, and then, suddenly hurling herself at the disk, she smashed it to smithereens with the tip of the broom. Splinters fell with a crash, passers-by shied away, someone somewhere began whistling, while Margarita, having done this unnecessary deed, burst out laughing. "I have to be even more careful on the Arbat," thought Margarita, "there's so much stuff entangled here, you can't make anything of it." She set about diving between the wires. Below Margarita swam the roofs of trolleybuses, buses and motor cars, and along the pavements, as it seemed to Margarita from above, there swam rivers of caps. Streams separated out from these rivers and flowed into the fiery jaws of all-night shops.

"Ooh, what a jumble!" Margarita thought angrily. "You can't turn around here." She cut across the Arbat, rose higher, up to the third floors, and, past the blindingly shining tubes on the theatre building on a corner, she sailed into a narrow lane of tall apartment blocks. All the windows in them were open, and everywhere in the windows radio music could be heard. Out of curiosity Margarita glanced into one of them. She saw a kitchen. Two Primus stoves were roaring on the hob, and beside them two women with spoons in their hands stood quarrelling.

"You need to turn the toilet light off after you, that's what I'm telling you, Pelageya Petrovna," said a woman with a saucepan containing eats of some sort in front of her, from which the steam was pouring, "or else we'll apply for you to be evicted!"

"You're a fine one to talk," the other replied.

"You're both fine ones," said Margarita sonorously, crossing over the window sill into the kitchen. Both squabbling women turned at the voice, and froze with their dirty spoons in their hands. Margarita carefully reached her arm between them, and turned the taps on both Primuses, putting them out. The women gasped and opened their mouths. But Margarita was already bored in the kitchen and flew out into the lane.

At its end her attention was attracted by the sumptuous hulk of an eight-storey, evidently newly built block. Margarita descended and, landing, saw that the façade of the house was faced with black marble, that the doors were wide, that behind their glass could be seen the cap with a gold galloon and the buttons of a doorman, and that above the door the inscription was traced out in gold: "House of Dramwrit".

Margarita squinted at the inscription, trying to grasp what the word "Dramwrit" could mean. Taking the broom under her arm, Margarita went in through the entrance, hitting the surprised doorman with the door, and saw on the wall beside the lift a huge black board, and written out on it in white lettering the numbers of the apartments and the names of the tenants. The inscription crowning the list, "House of Dramatists and Writers", made Margarita emit a heartfelt, predatory shriek. Rising a little higher in the air, she began reading the names rapaciously: Khustov, Dvubratsky, Kvant, Beskudnikov, Latunsky...

"Latunsky!" Margarita began screaming. "Latunsky! But it was him, wasn't it... It was him that destroyed the Master!"

The doorman by the doors gazed at the black board with his eyes popping out, and even jumped up and down in surprise, trying to understand such a wondrous thing: why was it that the list of tenants had started screaming all of a sudden?

But by this time Margarita was already going swiftly up the stairs, repeating in a kind of rapture:

"Latunsky – 84... Latunsky – 84..."

Here's 82 to the left, 83 to the right, higher still, to the left – 84. Here! And here's his card – "O. Latunsky".

Margarita leapt off the broom and her heated soles were pleasantly cooled by the stone landing. Margarita rang once, then again. But nobody opened up. Margarita began pressing the button more firmly and could hear for herself the din that kicked up inside Latunsky's apartment. Yes, the resident of apartment No. 84 on the seventh floor should be grateful to the late Berlioz to his dying day for the fact that the Chairman of MASSOLIT had fallen under a tram, and for the fact that the memorial meeting had been arranged for that very evening. The critic Latunsky was born under a lucky star. It saved him from a meeting with Margarita, who had become a witch that Friday.

Nobody opened up. Then Margarita flew downstairs at full speed; counting off the floors, she reached the bottom, tore out into the street and, looking up, counted off and checked the floors from the outside, trying to grasp which windows were actually those of Latunsky's apartment. There was no doubt that it was the five dark windows at the corner of the building on the seventh floor. Having satisfied herself of this, Margarita rose into the air, and a few seconds later was going through an open window into an unlit room in which there was only a narrow little path of silvery moonlight. Margarita ran down it and felt for the light switch. A minute later the whole apartment was lit up. The broom was standing in a corner. After making sure that no one was at home, Margarita opened the door onto the staircase and checked whether the card was there. The card was in place, Margarita was where she needed to be.

Yes, they say the critic Latunsky turns pale even now when he remembers that terrible evening, and even now pronounces the name of Berlioz with reverence. There is absolutely no knowing what dark and foul criminal acts might have marked that evening – on her return from the kitchen there was a heavy hammer in Margarita's hands.

Naked and invisible, the flying woman was restraining and urging herself on, and her hands were trembling with impatience. Taking careful aim, Margarita struck the keys of the grand piano, and the first plaintive howl spread throughout the entire apartment. The utterly innocent Bäcker cabinet instrument cried out frenziedly. Its keyboard was collapsing, the ivory caps were flying in all directions. The instrument droned, howled, wheezed, rang. With the sound of a pistol shot the polished upper sounding board split under a hammer-blow. Breathing hard, Margarita tore and crumpled the strings with the hammer. Finally, tired, she fell back and plopped into an armchair to regain her breath.

Water was making a terrible noise in the bathroom, and in the kitchen too. "It seems to have started spilling onto the floor already…" thought Margarita, and added out loud:

"However, it's no good sitting around."

A stream was already running from the kitchen into the corridor. Splashing her bare feet in the water, Margarita carried buckets of water from the kitchen to the critic's study and poured it out into the desk drawers. Then, after breaking up the doors of the cabinet in that same study with the hammer, she rushed into the bedroom. Having smashed the mirrored wardrobe, she pulled the critic's suit out of it and drowned it in the bath. The inkpotful of ink that she had seized in the study she poured out into the luxuriantly plumped-up double bed in the bedroom. The destruction she was effecting gave her burning enjoyment, but at the same time it constantly seemed to her that the results were turning out rather meagre. And so she began doing anything and everything. She smashed the pots of ficus plants in the room where the piano was. Without finishing the job, she returned to the bedroom and cut up the sheets with a kitchen knife and smashed the glass in the photograph frames. She felt no tiredness, only the sweat ran down her in streams.

At this time in apartment No. 82, underneath Latunsky's apartment, the dramatist Kvant's maid was drinking tea in the kitchen, perplexed by the fact that there was some sort of crashing, running around and ringing noises coming from above. Tilting her head up to the ceiling, she suddenly saw that before her eyes it was exchanging its white colour for a kind of deathly bluish one. The stain was spreading wider before her eyes, and suddenly drops swelled out upon it. The maid sat for a minute or two, wondering at such a phenomenon, until finally genuine rain began falling from the ceiling and started tapping on the floor. At this point she leapt up and put a basin under the streams, which did not help in the least, since the rain had spread wider and started spilling onto both the gas hob and the dresser. Then, with a cry, Kvant's maid ran out of the apartment onto the stairs, and straight away in Latunsky's apartment the ringing of the telephone began.

"Well, they've started ringing... Time to get ready to go," said Margarita. She sat on the broom, listening to a female voice shouting through the chink in the door:

"Open up, open up! Dusya, open up! Is your water leaking, or something? It's come through to us!"

Margarita went up by a metre and hit the chandelier. Two bulbs blew, and pieces of hanging glass flew in all directions. The cries in the chink in the door ceased, the clatter of feet was heard on the stairs. Margarita floated through the window, found herself outside the window, took a gentle swing and struck the glass with the hammer. It gave a sob, and the splinters cascaded down the marble-faced wall. Margarita rode to the next window. Far below, people started running along the pavement, and of the two cars standing by the entrance one began to hum and drove away.

Finishing with Latunsky's windows, Margarita floated to the apartment next door. The blows became more frequent, the lane was filled with a ringing and a crashing. The doorman ran out from entrance No. 1, looked up, wavered a little, evidently not immediately grasping what he should do, stuck a whistle in his mouth and began whistling furiously. Having smashed the last pane of glass on the seventh floor with particular fervour to the sound of this whistle, Margarita descended to the sixth and started shattering the glass there.

Frustrated by his lengthy inactivity behind the plate-glass doors of the entrance, the doorman was putting his heart and soul into his whistling, and was, moreover, following Margarita exactly, as though accompanying her. In the pauses when she was flying from window to window, he was taking in air, and each time Margarita struck, he, blowing out his cheeks, would burst out and drill the night air to the very sky.

His efforts, in conjunction with the efforts of the infuriated Margarita, produced great results. Inside the building there was panic. Window panes that were still intact were thrown wide open, people's heads appeared in them and then hid straight away, and open windows, on the contrary, were closed. In the buildings opposite, against lighted backgrounds there appeared in the windows the dark silhouettes of people trying to understand why the windows in the new Dramwrit building were breaking without any reason.

In the lane folk were running to the Dramwrit building, while inside it people were making a clatter on all the staircases, rushing about without any sense or purpose. Kvant's maid was shouting to those running up and down the stairs that they had been flooded, and she was soon joined by Khustov's maid from apartment No. 80, located beneath Kvant's apartment. At the Khustovs' it had gushed from the ceiling both in the kitchen and in the toilet. Finally at the Kvants' a huge layer of plaster came down from the ceiling in the kitchen and smashed all the dirty crockery, after which genuinely torrential rain began: it poured from the squares of sagging wet lathing as though from a bucket. Then shouting began from the staircase of entrance No. 1. Flying past the penultimate window on the third floor, Margarita glanced into it and saw a man who had pulled on a gas mask in his panic. Striking his window pane with the hammer, Margarita scared him off, and he disappeared from the room.

And then the savage devastation unexpectedly ceased. Slipping down to the second floor, Margarita glanced into the end window with its flimsy, dark blind drawn. A weak little light was burning under a shade in the room. A boy of about four was sitting in a small bed with sides made of netting and listening out in fright. There were no adults in the room. Everyone had evidently run out of the apartment.

"They're breaking the windows," the boy said, and called: "Mama!"

No one responded, and then he said:

"Mama, I'm scared."

Margarita threw the blind aside and flew through the window.

"I'm scared," the boy repeated, and started trembling.

"Don't be scared, don't be scared, little one," said Margarita, trying to soften her criminal voice which had grown hoarse in the wind, "it was some boys breaking windows."

"With a catapult?" the boy asked, ceasing to tremble.

"Yes, with a catapult," Margarita confirmed, "now you go to sleep!"

"It's Sitnik," said the boy, "he's got a catapult."

"Well of course it's him!"

The boy gave a sly look somewhere off to one side and asked:

"And where are you, lady?"

"I'm not here," replied Margarita, "I'm in your dream."

"That's what I thought," said the boy.

"You lie down," ordered Margarita, "put your hand under your cheek, and I'll be in your dream."

"Yes, all right, do be in my dream, do," the boy agreed, and immediately lay himself down and put his hand under his cheek.

"I'll tell you a story," Margarita began, and lay a heated hand on his closely cropped head. "There was once a lady. And she had no children, and generally had no happiness either. And so at first she cried for a long time, and then she became wicked..." Margarita fell silent and took her hand away – the boy was asleep.

Margarita gently put the hammer on the window sill and flew out of the window. Beside the building there was a commotion. People were running about on the asphalted pavement, which was littered with broken glass, and yelling something. Policemen could already be glimpsed among them. Suddenly a bell rang, and into the lane from the Arbat rolled a red fire engine with a ladder...

But what happened thereafter was no longer of any interest to Margarita. Taking aim, so as not to catch on any wire, she squeezed the broom quite firmly and in an instant found herself higher than the ill-starred building. The lane beneath her tilted to one side and disappeared downwards. In place of just the lane there appeared beneath Margarita's feet a multitude of roofs, criss-crossed at angles by glittering little roads. The whole of it unexpectedly slipped aside, and the chains of lights blurred and merged.

Margarita made one more spurt, and then the whole throng of roofs was swallowed up by the earth, and instead of it there appeared below a lake of trembling electric lights, and this lake suddenly rose up vertically, and then appeared above Margarita's head, while beneath her feet there shone the moon. Realizing she had turned a somersault, Margarita assumed a normal position and, turning back, saw that the lake had already gone too, and that there, back there behind her, only a pink glow on the horizon remained. It too disappeared in a second, and Margarita saw that she was alone with the moon, which was flying above her and to the left. Margarita's hair had already long been piled up in a heap, and the moonlight whistled as it washed over her body. From the way two rows of infrequent lights down below merged into two unbroken fiery lines, and from the rate at which they vanished behind her, Margarita guessed she was flying at a monstrous speed and was amazed she was not gasping for breath.

After a lapse of a few seconds, far below in the terrestrial blackness a new lake of electric light flared out and rolled up beneath the flying woman's feet, but straight away it started to spiral and was swallowed up by the earth. A few seconds more – exactly the same phenomenon.

"Towns! Towns!" Margarita shouted.

Two or three times after that she saw below her dimly reflective sabres of some sort lying in open black cases, and she grasped that they were rivers.

Turning her head upwards and to the left, the flying woman admired the way the moon was rushing back to Moscow like a mad thing above her, and was at the same time in a strange way standing still, so that distinctly visible upon it was some mysterious, dark shape, perhaps a dragon, perhaps a little humpbacked horse, with its sharp muzzle directed towards the city she had left.

At this point Margarita was seized by the thought that as a matter of fact there was no point in her driving the broom on so frenziedly. That she was depriving herself of the opportunity of examining anything properly, of revelling properly in the flight. Something told her they would wait for her in the place she was flying to and there was no purpose in her being bored at such a mad speed and height.

Margarita bent the bristles of the broom forward so that its tail rose up, and, slowing greatly, she set off right down towards the earth. And this sliding down, as if on an aerial sledge, brought her the greatest enjoyment. The earth rose towards her, and in its black stodge, formless until now, its secrets and delights during a moonlit night were revealed. The earth was moving towards her, and Margarita already had the scent wafting over her of the woods coming into leaf. Margarita flew just above the mists of a dewy meadow, then over a pond. Below Margarita a choir of frogs was singing, and somewhere in the distance was the noise of a train, which for some reason greatly troubled her heart. Margarita soon caught sight of it. It was crawling slowly, like a caterpillar, scattering sparks into the air. After overtaking it, Margarita passed over one more watery mirror, in which a second moon floated past beneath her feet, she descended still further and went on her way, very nearly catching the tops of huge pine trees with her feet.

The harsh noise of the air being ploughed up became audible from behind and began catching up with Margarita. Gradually this noise of something flying like a missile was joined by a woman's raucous laughter, audible at a distance of many kilometres. Margarita glanced round and saw she was being overtaken by some complex dark object. As it caught up with Margarita it was revealed more and more, and it became evident that someone was flying on something's back. And finally it was completely revealed: Margarita was overtaken by the slowing Natasha.

Completely naked, with her tousled hair flying in the air, she was flying on the back of a fat hog, which was clutching a briefcase in its fore trotters and thrashing wildly at the air with its hind ones. Gleaming in the moonlight from time to time and then dying away, a pince-nez that had toppled off the hog's nose was flying alongside it on a cord, and a hat kept on slipping down over the hog's eyes. After having a good close look, Margarita recognized the hog to be Nikolai Ivanovich, and then her raucous laughter began thundering over the wood, mingling with the laughter of Natasha.

"Natashka!" Margarita cried piercingly. "Did you rub the cream on?"

"Darling!" Natasha replied, waking the sleeping pine forest with her cries. "My Queen of France, I rubbed it on his bald spot as well, didn't I, on him as well!"

"Princess!" yelled the hog pathetically, carrying his rider at a gallop.

"Darling! Margarita Nikolayevna!" cried Natasha, racing alongside Margarita. "I confess, I took the cream! I mean, we want to live and fly too! Forgive me, mistress, but I won't return, I won't return, not for anything! Ah, it's great, Margarita Nikolayevna!… He was proposing to me," Natasha started prodding her finger into the neck of the hog, who was puffing in embarrassment, "proposing! What was it you were calling me, eh?" she cried, leaning down to the hog's ear.

"Goddess!" the latter howled. "I can't fly this fast! I could lose some important papers. Natalya Prokofyevna, I protest!"

"To hell with you and your papers!" cried Natasha, roaring with impudent laughter.

"What are you doing, Natalya Prokofyevna! Someone will hear us!" yelled the hog beseechingly.

Flying at a gallop alongside Margarita, Natasha laughed as she told her about what had happened in the house after Margarita Nikolayevna had flown off over the gates.

Natasha confessed that, without touching any of the things she had been given again, she had thrown off her clothes and rushed to the cream and immediately rubbed it on. And the same thing had happened to her as to her mistress. As Natasha, chuckling with joy, was revelling in her magical beauty before the mirror, the door had opened, and Nikolai Ivanovich had appeared before Natasha. He had been agitated, holding Margarita Nikolayevna's nightshirt and his own hat and briefcase in his hands. On seeing Natasha, Nikolai Ivanovich had been stupefied. Getting the better of himself somewhat, all red as a lobster, he had announced that he had considered it his duty to pick the shirt up and bring it in person...

"The things he said, the good-for-nothing!" Natasha screamed with laughter. "The things he said, the things he was enticing me to! The money he was promising! Said Klavdia Petrovna would know nothing about it. What, are you going to say I'm lying?" Natasha cried to the hog, but the latter only turned his snout away in embarrassment.

Getting mischievous in the bedroom, Natasha had put a dab of the cream on Nikolai Ivanovich and had herself been struck dumb in surprise. The face of the respectable downstairs tenant had been reduced to a snout, while his arms and legs had proved to have trotters. Looking at himself in the mirror, Nikolai Ivanovich had started up a desperate and wild howling, but it was already too late. A few seconds later, straddled by a rider, he was flying out of Moscow, the devil knew where to, sobbing with grief.

"I demand the return of my normal appearance!" the hog suddenly wheezed, and started grunting, half frenziedly, half beseechingly. "I don't intend to fly to an illegal assembly! Margarita Nikolayevna, it's your duty to control your maid!"

"Oh, so I'm a maid for you now? A maid?" Natasha exclaimed, pinching the hog's ear. "When I used to be a goddess? What was it you called me?"

"Venus!" the hog replied pathetically, flying over a stream that roared between some rocks, and rustling some hazel bushes as he caught them with his trotters.

"Venus! Venus!" cried Natasha triumphantly, putting one hand on her hip and stretching the other out towards the moon. "Margarita! Queen! Ask for me to be left as a witch! They'll do anything for you, power has been granted you!"

And Margarita responded:

"All right, I promise."

"Thank you!" Natasha cried, and suddenly began shouting sharply and somehow mournfully: "Hey! Hey! Hurry! Hurry! Come on now, speed it up!" With her heels she squeezed the hog's flanks, which had grown thinner in the mad gallop, and he jerked forward so hard that the air was again ripped apart, and a moment later Natasha was already visible up ahead only as a black dot, and then she disappeared completely, and the noise of her flight melted away.

Margarita flew slowly, as before, in a deserted and unfamiliar locality over hills with a sprinkling of infrequent boulders lying between huge, isolated pines. Margarita flew and thought about the fact that she was probably somewhere very far from Moscow. The broom was flying not above the tops of the pines, but already between their trunks, silvered on one side by the moon. The light shadow of the flying woman slid across the earth up ahead – the moon was now shining on Margarita's back.

Margarita sensed the proximity of water and guessed her objective was near. The pines parted, and Margarita quietly rode up through the air towards a chalk cliff. Beyond this cliff, in the shade down below, lay a river. A mist was hanging and catching on the bushes at the bottom of the vertical cliff, but the opposite bank was flat and low-lying. On it, under a solitary group of spreading trees of some sort, a little light from a bonfire was tossing about and some small moving figures could be seen. It seemed to Margarita that some nagging, jolly music was carrying from there. Further on, as far as the eye could see, no signs either of habitation or people were visible on the silvered plain.

Margarita jumped down from the cliff and quickly descended to the water. The water attracted her after the aerial dash. Tossing the broom aside, she took a run up and threw herself into the water head first. Her light body pierced the water like an arrow and threw out a column of water almost as far as the moon itself. The water proved to be warm, like in a bathhouse, and, coming up from the abyss, Margarita swam to her heart's content in complete solitude in that river in the night.

There was nobody near Margarita, but a little further away beyond the bushes splashes and snorting could be heard, somebody was swimming there too.

Margarita ran out onto the bank. Her body was glowing after bathing. She did not feel any tiredness and hopped about joyfully on the moist grass. Suddenly she stopped dancing and was on her guard. The snorting began to get closer, and a fat, naked man clambered out from behind some willow bushes wearing a black silk top hat, cocked onto the back of his head. The soles of his feet were so covered in muddy silt, it seemed as though the bather was wearing black boots. Judging by the way he was puffing and hiccuping, he had had a decent amount to drink, which was also confirmed, moreover, by the fact that the river suddenly began giving off the smell of brandy.

Catching sight of Margarita, the fat man began peering, and then yelled out joyfully:

"What's this? Is it her I see? Claudine,* it's you, isn't it, the merry widow! Are you here too?" and at this point he went to greet her.

Margarita retreated and replied with dignity:

"Go to the devil. I'm not this Claudine of yours! You watch who you're talking to," and, after a moment's thought, she added to her speech a long unprintable oath. All this had a sobering effect on the flippant fat man.

"Oh dear!" he exclaimed quietly, and winced. "Be generous and forgive me, radiant Queen Margot!* I took you for someone else. But it's the brandy that's to blame, curse it!" The fat man dropped onto one knee, held the top hat out to one side, bowed and, mixing Russian phrases with French ones, began babbling some nonsense about the bloody wedding of his friend Guessard in Paris,* and about brandy, and about his being depressed by his sad mistake.

"You might put your trousers on, you son of a bitch," said Margarita, softening.

The fat man grinned joyfully, seeing that Margarita was not angry, and informed her rapturously that he was without his trousers at the present moment only because through forgetfulness he had left them on the river Yenisei where he had been bathing just before, but that he was flying there at once, thankfully it was no distance at all; and then, entrusting himself to her favour and protection, he began retreating backwards, and he continued retreating until he slipped and fell on his back into the water. Yet even as he fell, he maintained on his face, with its fringe of little sideburns, the smile of rapture and devotion.

But Margarita gave a piercing whistle and, straddling the broom, which flew up, she was carried over the river to the opposite bank. The shadow of the chalk hill did not reach to there, and the whole bank was flooded with moonlight.

As soon as Margarita touched the damp grass, the music under the willows struck up louder, and the sheaf of sparks from the bonfire flew up more gaily. Under the willow branches, covered with delicate, fluffy catkins, which were visible in the moonlight, sat two rows of fat-faced frogs, swelling up as though made of elastic and playing a bravura march on wooden pipes. Glowing pieces of rotten wood hung on the willow withes in front of the musicians and lit up the sheet music, and the darting light from the bonfire played on the faces of the frogs.

The march was played in Margarita's honour. The reception given her was the most ceremonial. Transparent water nymphs stopped their round dance above the river and started waving waterweeds to Margarita, and their distantly audible greetings moaned above the deserted, greenish bank. Leaping out from behind the willows, naked witches lined up in a row and began dropping curtsies and bowing as if at court. Someone with the legs of a goat rushed up and kissed her hand, spread a silk cloth out on the grass, enquired as to whether the Queen had enjoyed her bathe, and invited her to lie down and rest.

Margarita did just that. The goat-legged one presented her with a glass of champagne, she drank it and her heart was immediately warmed. Enquiring where Natasha was, she received the reply that Natasha had already finished bathing and had flown on ahead to Moscow on her hog to give advance warning that Margarita would soon be there, and to help prepare a costume for her.

Margarita's short stay beneath the willows was marked by one episode. A whistling rang out in the air, and a black body, clearly missing its target, came down in the water. A few moments later there appeared before Margarita that same fat man with sideburns who had introduced himself so unfortunately on the other bank. He had evidently managed to dash to the Yenisei and back, for he was wearing tails, but was wet from head to toe. The brandy had got him in a fix for a second time: while landing he had, after all, fallen into the water. But he had not lost his smile, and in this unfortunate instance the laughing Margarita did allow him to kiss her hand.

Then everyone began getting ready to leave. The water nymphs finished their dance in the moonlight and melted away. The goat-legged one enquired respectfully of Margarita how she had arrived at the river. Learning she had come riding on a broomstick, he said:

"Oh, but why, that's uncomfortable," and in a trice he had constructed a suspicious sort of telephone from two twigs and demanded of someone that a car be sent this very minute, which was indeed done in one minute. The dun-coloured open car came down on an island, only in the driver's seat there sat not an ordinary-looking driver, but a black, long-nosed rook in an oilskin cap and funnel-shaped gloves. The islet was emptying. The witches, who had flown off, had dissolved in the glow of the moon. The bonfire was burning out, and the coals had a coating of grey cinders.

The man with the sideburns and the goat-legged one helped Margarita into the car, and she dropped onto the wide back seat. The car howled, jumped, and rose up almost to the moon itself, the island disappeared, the river disappeared, and Margarita sped off to Moscow.

22

By Candlelight

THE STEADY DRONE OF THE CAR flying high above the earth lulled Margarita, and the moonlight warmed her pleasantly. Closing her eyes, she gave her face up to the wind and thought with a certain sadness of the unknown river bank she had left, and which, as she sensed, she would never see again. After all the magic and wonders of that evening she could already guess precisely whom she was being taken to visit, but this did not frighten her. The hope that she would be successful there in securing the return of her happiness made her fearless. However, it was not her lot to dream about her happiness in the car for long. Perhaps the rook knew its business well, or perhaps the car was a good one; only soon, opening her eyes, Margarita saw beneath her not the darkness of woodland, but the trembling lake of Moscow's lights. The black bird driving unscrewed the front right-hand wheel while still in flight, then landed the car in some completely unfrequented cemetery in the Dorogomilovo district.

Setting Margarita, who asked about nothing, down beside one of the gravestones along with her broomstick, the rook started the car up and sent it straight into the ravine beyond the cemetery. It fell into it with a crash, and there it perished. The rook saluted respectfully, mounted the wheel and flew away.

Immediately, from behind one of the monuments a black cloak appeared. A fang flashed in the moonlight and Margarita recognized Azazello. With a gesture he invited Margarita to mount the broomstick, he himself leapt onto a long rapier, they both soared up and, seen by no one, in a few seconds landed by building No. 302 *bis* on Sadovaya Street.

As the travelling companions were passing through the gateway, carrying the broomstick and the rapier under their arms, Margarita noticed a man wearing a cap and high boots languishing in it, probably waiting for somebody. Light as Azazello and Margarita's footsteps were, the solitary man heard them and jerked uneasily, unable to understand who was producing them.

A second man, amazingly similar to the first, they encountered by entrance No. 6. And again the same story repeated itself. Footsteps... The man turned uneasily and frowned. And when the door opened and closed, he rushed after the invisible people going in and glanced into the entrance, but nothing, of course, did he see.

A third, an exact copy of the second one and therefore of the first one too, was on duty on the second-floor landing. He was smoking strong cigarettes, and, as she walked past him, Margarita had a fit of coughing. The smoker leapt up from the bench on which he was sitting as though he had been stung, started looking around uneasily, went up to the banister, looked down. By this time Margarita and her escort were already by the doors of apartment No. 50. They did not bother ringing. Azazello opened the door noiselessly with his own key.

The first thing that struck Margarita was the darkness in which she found herself. It was dark, like in a cellar, so that, afraid of stumbling, she involuntarily caught hold of Azazello's cloak. But at this point, in the distance and on high, the light of a little lamp of some sort began to twinkle, and started coming closer. As they walked, Azazello took the broomstick out from under Margarita's arm, and it disappeared without a sound in the darkness. Here they started going up some wide steps, and it began to seem to Margarita that there would be no end to them. She was amazed at how this extraordinary, invisible but very tangible, endless staircase could fit into the entrance hall of an ordinary Moscow apartment. But the ascent ended, and Margarita realized she was standing on a landing. The light came right up close, and Margarita saw the illuminated face of a man, lanky and dark, holding that same lamp in his hand. Those who had already had the misfortune to cross his path during these days, even by the weak light of the little tongue in the lamp, would, of course, have recognized him immediately. It was Korovyev, otherwise known as Fagot.

True, Korovyev's appearance had changed greatly. The twinkling light was reflected not in a cracked pince-nez that should have been thrown out onto the rubbish heap long ago, but in a monocle – true, also cracked. The little moustache on his impudent face was curled up and pomaded, and Korovyev's blackness was very simply explained – he was wearing tails. Only his chest was white.

The magician, precentor, enchanter, interpreter, or the devil knows what really – in a word, Korovyev – bowed and, making a wide sweep through the air with the lamp, invited Margarita to follow him. Azazello disappeared.

"What an amazingly strange evening," thought Margarita, "I was expecting anything, only not this! Has their electricity gone off or something? But the most astonishing thing is the size of this place. How can all this squeeze into a Moscow apartment? Quite simply, there's no way it can!"

However little the light given off by Korovyev's lamp, Margarita realized that she was in an absolutely boundless hall, and, what is more, with a colonnade, dark and, from her first impression, endless. Korovyev stopped beside some sort of little couch, he set his lamp down on some sort of pedestal and invited Margarita with a gesture to sit down, while he positioned himself in a picturesque pose alongside, leaning on the pedestal.

"Allow me to introduce myself to you," Korovyev squeaked. "Korovyev. You're surprised there's no light? An economy, as you thought, of course? Oh no! May the first executioner I come across, perhaps one of those who, a little later on today, will have the honour of kissing your knee, may he chop my head off on this very pedestal if that's the case. Simply Messire doesn't like electric light, and we'll put it on at the very last moment. And then, believe me, there'll be no shortage of it. Maybe it would even be a good thing if there were to be a little less of it."

Margarita liked Korovyev, and his babbling chatter had a soothing effect upon her.

"No," replied Margarita, "more than anything I'm amazed at how all this fits." She waved her arm, thus emphasizing the boundlessness of the hall.

Korovyev grinned sweetly, which made the shadows move in the lines by his nose.

"The simplest thing of all!" he replied. "For those who are really familiar with the fifth dimension it's nothing at all to extend a space to the desired limits. I'll say more, respected madam, to the devil knows what limits! Incidentally," Korovyev continued chattering, "I've known people who've had no idea not only about the fifth dimension, but who've had no idea generally about anything at all, and who have nevertheless done absolute wonders as regards expanding their space. So, for example, one city-dweller, as I've been told, after getting a three-room apartment on Zemlyanoi Bank, without any fifth dimension or other stuff that leaves you at your wit's end, instantly turned it into a four-room apartment by dividing one of the rooms in half with a partition. Thereupon he exchanged that one for two self-contained apartments in different districts of Moscow, one of three, and the other of two rooms. You must agree that there were now five of them. The three-roomed apartment he exchanged for two self-contained ones with two rooms each, and became the owner, as you can see for yourself, of six rooms, scattered, it's true, in total disorder across the whole of Moscow. He was already preparing to produce the final and most brilliant vault, having placed an advertisement in a newspaper about exchanging six rooms in various districts of Moscow for one five-roomed apartment on Zemlyanoi Bank, when, for reasons beyond his control, his activities ceased. It's possible he does have one room now, only I can assure you it isn't in Moscow. There, what a wheeler-dealer, and there's you talking about the fifth dimension!"

Though she had not been the one talking about the fifth dimension – Korovyev himself had been talking about it – Margarita laughed merrily after listening to the story about the adventures of the accommodation wheeler-dealer. Korovyev, though, continued:

"But to business, to business, Margarita Nikolayevna. You're a most intelligent woman and, of course, have already guessed who our host is."

Margarita's heart gave a thump, and she nodded her head.

"Well, right then, right then," said Korovyev, "we're against any sort of mystery or lack of clarity. Every year Messire gives one ball. It's called the Spring Ball of the Full Moon, or the Ball of a Hundred Kings. The number of people!" Here Korovyev took hold of his cheek as though a tooth had started aching. "Still, I hope you'll find that out for yourself. So, then: Messire is a bachelor, as you can, of course, understand for yourself. But a hostess is required," Korovyev spread out his arms, "you must agree, without a hostess…"

Margarita listened to Korovyev, trying not to miss a word; there was a cold feeling beneath her heart, and hopes of happiness were making her head spin.

"A tradition has been established," Korovyev carried on speaking, "the hostess of the ball should without fail bear the name Margarita, firstly, and secondly, she should be locally born. And as you can see, we travel, and are at the present time in Moscow, and, can you believe it," here Korovyev slapped himself on the thigh in despair, "not one is suitable! And, finally, happy fate..."

Korovyev grinned expressively, inclining his torso, and again Margarita's heart turned cold.

"In brief!" exclaimed Korovyev. "Really briefly: will you be so kind as to take this duty upon yourself?"

"I will," Margarita replied firmly.

"It's settled!" said Korovyev and, picking up the lamp, added: "Please follow me."

They set off between the columns and finally made their way out into some other hall, in which for some reason there was a strong smell of lemons, where rustling of some sort could be heard and where something caught Margarita on the head. She flinched.

"Don't be scared," Korovyev soothed Margarita sweetly, taking her by the arm, "Behemoth's contrivances for the ball, nothing more. And in general, Margarita Nikolayevna, I'll permit myself the audacity of advising you not to be afraid of anything at any time. It's unwise. The ball will be sumptuous, I wouldn't think of concealing that from you. We shall see persons, the extent of whose power was in its time extremely great. But truly, when you think of how microscopically small their potentialities were in comparison to the potentialities of the one in whose suite I have the honour to serve, it starts to be funny and even, I would say, sad... And you are yourself, moreover, of royal blood."

"Why of royal blood?" Margarita whispered in fright, pressing up close to Korovyev.

"Ah, my Queen," Korovyev jabbered playfully, "questions of blood are the most complex questions in the world! And if one were to question certain great-grandmothers, and in particular those of them who had a reputation for being meek and mild, the most astonishing secrets would be revealed, respected Margarita Nikolayevna. I shan't err in the slightest if, in talking about this, I refer to a peculiarly shuffled pack of cards. There are things in which class barriers and even the boundaries between states are completely ineffective. I'll give you a hint: one of the queens of France who lived in the sixteenth century would, one must assume, have been very surprised if someone had told her that I, after the passage of many years, would be leading her delightful great-great-great-great-granddaughter by the arm through ballrooms in Moscow. But we've arrived!"

Here Korovyev blew out his lamp and it vanished from his hands, and Margarita saw a strip of light lying on the floor in front of her beneath some sort of dark door. And it was at this door that Korovyev quietly knocked. At this point Margarita became so agitated that her teeth began chattering and a chill ran down her spine.

The door opened. The room proved to be very small. Margarita saw a wide oak bed with creased and crumpled dirty sheets and pillows. In front of the bed stood an oak table with carved legs on which was a candelabrum with sockets in the form of birds' clawed feet. In these seven gold feet burned thick wax candles. Apart from that, on a little table there was a large chessboard with pieces made with unusual skill. On a small threadbare rug stood a low bench. There was one more table with some sort of gold goblet and another candelabrum, the branches of which were made in the form of snakes. The room smelt of sulphur and pitch. Shadows from the lights criss-crossed on the floor.

Among those present Margarita immediately recognized Azazello, now already dressed in a tailcoat and standing by the bedhead. Got up smartly, Azazello no longer resembled the villain in whose guise he had appeared to Margarita in the Alexandrovsky Garden, and he bowed to Margarita extremely gallantly.

A naked witch, that same Hella who had so embarrassed the respectable barman from The Variety, and, alas, that same one who, by great good fortune, had been scared off by the cockerel on the night of the celebrated show, was sitting on a rug on the floor by the bed, stirring something in a saucepan which was belching out sulphurous steam.

In the room apart from them there was also the most enormous great black tomcat, sitting on a high stool in front of the chess table and holding a knight in his right paw.

Hella rose and bowed to Margarita. The cat did the same too, slipping down from the stool. While scraping his right hind leg, he dropped the knight, and crawled after it underneath the bed.

Frozen to the spot in terror, Margarita somehow made all this out in the treacherous shadows from the candles. Her gaze was drawn to the bed, on which sat the one whom poor Ivan had been trying to convince, still very recently at Patriarch's, that the Devil did not exist. It was this non-existent one that sat on the bed.

Two eyes were firmly fixed on Margarita's face: the right one, with a gold spark in its depths, that drilled through to the bottom of anyone's soul, and the left one, empty and black, like the narrow eye of a needle, like the entrance to a bottomless well of all kinds of darkness and shadows. Woland's face was twisted to one side, the right-hand corner of his mouth was drawn downwards, and on his high, bald brow deep wrinkles had been incised parallel to his sharp eyebrows. It was as if the skin on Woland's face had been burnt for ever by the sun.

Woland was sprawled out wide on the bed, and he was dressed in just a long nightshirt, dirty and patched on the left shoulder. One bare leg he had bent up beneath him, the other he had stretched out onto a bench. And the knee of this dark leg was being rubbed with some smoking ointment by Hella.

Margarita also made out – on a gold chain on Woland's exposed, hairless chest – a beetle, skilfully carved out of dark stone and with characters of some sort on its back. On a heavy base next to Woland on the bed stood a strange globe that seemed to be alive and was lit up on one side by the sun.

The silence lasted several seconds. "He's studying me," Margarita thought, and with an effort of will tried to control the trembling in her legs.

Finally Woland began to speak, smiling, which made his sparkling eye seem to flare up:

"I greet you, my Queen, and beg you to forgive me my domestic attire."

Woland's voice was so low that on some syllables it was drawn out into a hoarse wheeze.

Woland picked up a long sword from the bedding, bent down, moved it about under the bed and said:

"Come out! The game's cancelled. Our guest has arrived."

"Not at all," Korovyev whistled anxiously in Margarita's ear like a prompter.

"Not at all..." Margarita began.

"Messire..." Korovyev breathed into her ear.

"Not at all, Messire," Margarita replied quietly but clearly, getting the better of herself, and added with a smile: "I implore you not to interrupt the game. I imagine the chess magazines would pay pretty good money if they had the opportunity to publish it."

Azazello gave a quiet quack of approval, while Woland, gazing attentively at Margarita, remarked as though to himself:

"Yes, Korovyev's right. How peculiarly the pack is shuffled! Blood!"

He stretched out his hand and beckoned Margarita towards him. She approached, not feeling the floor beneath her bare feet. Woland placed his hand, heavy as though of stone, and at the same time hot like fire, on Margarita's shoulder, jerked her towards him and sat her down on the bed next to him.

"Well, now if you're so charmingly courteous," he said, "and I expected nothing different, then we won't stand on ceremony." He again bent down towards the edge of the bed and shouted: "Will this farce underneath the bed be going on much longer? Come out, you damned *Gans*!"*

"I can't find the knight," the cat responded from under the bed in a strangulated and insincere voice, "he's galloped off somewhere, and instead of him I keep coming across some frog."

"Do you imagine you're at a fairground?" asked Woland, pretending to be angry. "There was no frog under the bed! Keep these cheap tricks for The Variety. If you don't appear straight away, we'll consider you to have resigned, you damned deserter."

"Not at any price, Messire!" the cat yelled, and that same second crawled out from under the bed, holding the knight in his paw.

"May I introduce..." Woland was about to begin, but then interrupted himself: "No, I can't bear to look at this buffoon. Look what he's turned himself into under the bed!"

Standing on his hind legs and covered in dust, the cat was meanwhile bowing in greeting before Margarita. Around the cat's neck there was now a white dress tie, done up in a bow, and on his chest a lady's mother-of-pearl opera glass on a strap. In addition, the cat's whiskers were gilt.

"Now what's all this!" exclaimed Woland. "Why have you gilded your whiskers? And why the devil do you need a tie if you've got no trousers on?"

"A cat isn't meant to wear trousers, Messire," replied the cat with great dignity. "Perhaps you'll require me to don boots as well? Only in fairy tales is there a puss in boots, Messire. But have you ever seen anyone at a ball without a tie? I don't intend finding myself in a comical situation and risking being thrown out on my ear! Everyone adorns himself in whatever way he can. Consider what has been said to apply to the opera glass too, Messire!"

"But the whiskers?"

"I don't understand why," retorted the cat drily, "when shaving today, Azazello and Korovyev could sprinkle themselves with white powder, and in what way it's better than the gold? I've powdered my whiskers, that's all! It would be a different matter if I'd shaved! A shaved cat – now that really is a shocker, I'm happy to admit it a thousand times. But in general," here the cat's voice quavered touchily, "I can see there's a certain amount of fault-finding being applied to me, and I can see there's a serious problem before me – should I attend the ball at all? What will you say to me on that score, Messire?"

And the cat puffed himself up in resentment to such an extent that one second more, it seemed, and he would burst.

"Oh, the rogue, the rogue," said Woland, shaking his head, "every time he's in a hopeless position in the game he starts talking to distract you, like the very worst charlatan on the bridge. Sit down immediately and stop this verbal diarrhoea."

"I will sit down," replied the cat, sitting down, "but I must object with regard to the final point. My speeches are by no means diarrhoea, as you're so good as to express yourself in the presence of a lady, but a series of soundly packaged syllogisms, which would be appreciated on their merits by such connoisseurs as Sextus Empiricus,* Martianus Capella* or even, who knows, Aristotle himself."

"The king's in check," said Woland.

"As you will, as you will," responded the cat, and began looking at the board through the opera glass.

"And so," Woland turned to Margarita, "may I introduce you, *donna*,* to my suite. This one playing the fool is Behemoth the cat. Azazello and Korovyev you've already met, but let me introduce my

261

maidservant Hella. Efficient, quick on the uptake, and there's no service she couldn't manage to render."

The beautiful Hella smiled, turning her green-tinged eyes towards Margarita, but without ceasing to scoop up the ointment by the handful and apply it to the knee.

"Well, and that's everyone," Woland concluded, and frowned as Hella gave his knee a particularly firm squeeze, "a small company, as you can see, mixed and unaffected." He fell silent and began turning before him his globe, which was so skilfully made that the blue oceans upon it moved, and a cap lay on the pole, like the real one, of ice and snow.

On the chessboard, meanwhile, a commotion was under way. Utterly distraught, the king in the white cloak was stamping about on his square and throwing his arms up in despair. Three white landsknecht pawns with halberds were looking in dismay at an officer who was brandishing a sword and pointing ahead to where, on adjoining squares, white and black, Woland's black horsemen could be seen on two mettlesome steeds, pawing the squares with their hoofs.

Margarita was extremely intrigued and struck by the fact that the chess pieces were alive.

Moving the opera glass away from his eyes, the cat gently nudged his king in the back. The latter covered his face with his hands in despair.

"Things are looking bad, dear Behemoth," Korovyev said quietly in a venomous voice.

"The position is serious, but by no means hopeless," responded Behemoth, "more than that: I'm absolutely certain of ultimate victory. One has but to analyse the position thoroughly."

He began to carry out this analysis in quite a strange manner, namely, he started pulling faces of some kind and winking at his king.

"Nothing helps," remarked Korovyev.

"Oh!" exclaimed Behemoth. "The parrots have scattered, just what I predicted!"

Indeed, somewhere in the distance the noise of numerous wings could be heard. Korovyev and Azazello rushed out.

"Oh, the devil take you with your bright ideas for the ball!" growled Woland, still not tearing himself away from his globe.

As soon as Korovyev and Azazello had disappeared, Behemoth's winking assumed intensified proportions. The white king finally guessed what was wanted of him. He suddenly pulled off his cloak, dropped it onto the square and fled from the board. The officer threw on the king's abandoned garb and took the king's place.

Korovyev and Azazello returned.

"Twaddle, as always," grumbled Azazello, looking askance at Behemoth.

"I thought I heard something," replied the cat.

"Well then, how much longer is this going to last?" asked Woland. "The king's in check."

"I must have misheard, my *maître*,"* replied the cat, "the king isn't, and can't be in check."

"I repeat, the king's in check."

"Messire," responded the cat in a falsely anxious voice, "you're overtired: the king isn't in check!"

"The king is on square G2," said Woland without looking at the board.

"Messire, I'm horrified!" the cat howled, depicting horror on his face. "There's no king on that square!"

"What's that?" Woland asked in perplexity, and began looking at the board, where the officer standing on the king's square was turning away and shielding himself with his arm.

"Oh, you wretch," said Woland pensively.

"Messire! I turn anew to logic," began the cat, pressing his paws to his chest. "If a player announces the king is in check, but there is, meanwhile, no longer even a trace of him on the board, the check is declared invalid."

"Do you resign, or not?" cried Woland in a terrible voice.

"Allow me to have a think," the cat replied meekly, putting his elbows on the table, burying his ears in his paws and beginning to think. He thought for a long time, and finally said: "I resign."

"Kill the obstinate creature," whispered Azazello.

"Yes, I resign," said the cat, "but I do so solely because I cannot play in an atmosphere of persecution on the part of the envious!" He rose, and the chess pieces climbed into their box.

"Hella, it's time," said Woland, and Hella vanished from the room. "My leg's started hurting, and now there's this ball..." Woland continued.

"Allow me," Margarita requested quietly.

Woland gazed at her intently and moved his knee towards her.

The sludge, hot as lava, burned her hands, but Margarita rubbed it into his knee without making a face, trying not to cause any pain.

"My retainers assert that it's rheumatism," said Woland, not taking his eyes off Margarita, "but I strongly suspect that this pain in the knee was left me as a memento by a charming witch with whom I became closely acquainted in 1571 in the Brocken Mountains, on The Devil's Pulpit."

"Oh, can that really be so!" said Margarita.

"It's nothing! It'll pass in three hundred years or so. I've been advised to use a multitude of medicines, but I stick to granny's methods in the old-fashioned way. That vile old woman, my grandmother, bequeathed some amazing herbs! Incidentally, tell me, do you suffer from anything? Perhaps you have some sadness, some anguish that poisons your soul?"

"No, Messire, there's nothing of that sort," clever Margarita replied, "and now that I'm here with you, I feel absolutely fine."

"Blood's a great thing," Woland said cheerfully to who knows who, and added: "I see my globe interests you."

"Oh yes, I've never seen such a thing."

"It's a nice little thing. To be frank, I don't like the news on the radio. It's always read by girls of some sort who pronounce the place names incomprehensibly. What's more, one in three of them has a slight speech defect, as though such ones are selected deliberately. My globe is much more convenient, especially as I need to know about events precisely. Here, for example, you see this bit of land whose side is washed by the ocean? Look, there it goes, filling with fire. A war has started there. If you move your eyes closer, you'll see the details too."

Margarita bent down towards the globe and saw that the little square of land had expanded, had been painted in many colours and had turned into a sort of relief map. And then she saw the ribbon of a river too, and some sort of settlement beside it. A house which had been the size of a pea grew and became like a matchbox. Suddenly and soundlessly the roof of this house flew upwards, together with a cloud of black smoke, while the walls collapsed, so that nothing remained of the two-storey box other than a little heap from which black smoke poured. Moving her eye still closer, Margarita made out a small female figure lying on the ground and, in a pool of blood beside her, a small child with its arms thrown out.

"And that's that," said Woland, smiling, "it didn't have the time to sin. Abadonna's work is impeccable."

"I wouldn't want to be on the side this Abadonna is against," said Margarita. "Whose side is he on?"

"The longer I talk with you," Woland responded courteously, "the more convinced I am that you're very intelligent. I can reassure you. He is uncommonly impartial and is equally sympathetic to both warring sides. As a consequence of this, the results for both sides are always identical too. Abadonna!" Woland called softly, and at once from out of the wall there appeared the figure of a thin man in dark glasses. These glasses made such a powerful impression on Margarita that, with a little cry, she buried her face in Woland's leg. "Now stop it!" cried Woland. "How nervy modern people are!" He took a swing and slapped Margarita on the back so that a ringing ran through her body. "You can see, can't you, that he's wearing his glasses. What's more, there's never been an instance, nor will there be, of Abadonna appearing before anybody prematurely. And then, finally, I'm here. You're my guest! I simply wanted to show him to you."

Abadonna stood motionless.

"And is it possible for him to take his glasses off for a second?" Margarita asked, nestling up to Woland and shuddering, but now out of curiosity.

"Now that isn't possible," Woland replied seriously, waving his hand at Abadonna, and the latter was gone. "What do you want to say, Azazello?"

"Messire," replied Azazello, "allow me to tell you. There are two strangers here: a beautiful woman, who's snivelling and begging to be left with her mistress, and as well as that, with her, I beg your pardon, is her hog."

"Beautiful women do behave strangely," remarked Woland.

"It's Natasha, Natasha!" exclaimed Margarita.

"Well, leave her with her mistress. And the hog – to the cooks."

"To be stuck?" cried Margarita in fright. "For pity's sake, Messire, it's Nikolai Ivanovich, the tenant downstairs. There's a misunderstanding here, you see, she daubed him with the cream..."

"But forgive me," said Woland, "who's going to stick him, and what the devil for? Let him sit with the cooks, that's all! I can't let him into the ballroom, you must agree!"

"Of course not…" Azazello added, and announced: "Midnight approaches, Messire."

"Ah, good." Woland turned to Margarita: "And so, please… My thanks in advance. Don't get flustered and don't be afraid of anything. Don't drink anything except water, or else you'll become languid and you'll find things difficult. It's time!"

Margarita got up from the rug, and then Korovyev appeared in the doorway.

23

Satan's Grand Ball

M IDNIGHT WAS APPROACHING, they had to hurry. Margarita could see her surroundings vaguely. She remembered candles and some sort of semi-precious stone pool. When Margarita was standing on the bottom of the pool, Hella, with Natasha helping her, poured some sort of hot, thick and red liquid over her. Margarita experienced a salty taste on her lips and realized she was being washed with blood. The bloody mantle gave way to another – thick, transparent, pinkish – and the attar of roses made Margarita's head spin. Then Margarita was thrown onto a crystal couch and they started rubbing her with some sort of large, green leaves until she shone. At this point the cat burst in and started helping. He squatted down by Margarita's feet and began polishing her soles, looking as if he were cleaning boots in the street.

Margarita did not remember who made her shoes from the petals of a pale rose, and how those shoes did themselves up with gold buckles. A force of some kind jerked Margarita up and stood her in front of a mirror, and in her hair there shone a royal crown of diamonds. Korovyev appeared from somewhere and hung on Margarita's chest a heavy effigy on a heavy chain of a black poodle in an oval frame. This adornment was extremely burdensome for the queen. The chain began rubbing on her neck straight away, the effigy drew her into a stoop. But there was something that rewarded Margarita for the discomforts the chain with the black poodle caused her. This was the deference with which Behemoth and Korovyev began to treat her.

"It's all right, all right, all right!" muttered Korovyev by the doors of the room with the pool. "Nothing can be done, you must, must, must... Allow me, my Queen, to give you a final piece of advice. Amongst the guests will be diverse, oh, very diverse people, but no preference, Queen Margot, to anyone! Even if you don't like someone... I realize you won't, of course, express it on your face... No, no, it mustn't be given a thought! He'll notice, he'll notice that very instant! You must immediately like him, like him, my Queen. The hostess of the ball will be rewarded for it a hundredfold. And another thing: don't miss anyone out! A little smile, at least, if there isn't the time to toss them a word, a tiny turn of the head at least. Anything you like, only not inattention. That will make them start to feel rotten..."

At this point, accompanied by Korovyev and Behemoth, Margarita stepped from the room with the pool into complete darkness.

"Me, me," whispered the cat, "I'll give the signal!"

"Go on!" Korovyev replied in the darkness.

"The ball!" screamed the cat piercingly, and straight away Margarita cried out and closed her eyes for several seconds. The ball fell upon her immediately in the form of light and, together with it, sound and smell. Carried off arm in arm with Korovyev, Margarita saw herself in a tropical forest. Red-breasted, green-tailed parrots clung onto lianas, jumped from place to place on them and cried out deafeningly: "I'm enchanted!" But the forest soon ended, and the stifling heat of the bathhouse immediately gave way to the cool of a ballroom with columns of some yellowish, scintillating stone. This hall, just like the forest too, was completely empty, and only by the columns did there stand motionless naked negroes with silver bands on their heads. Their faces turned a dirty brown from anxiety when into the hall flew Margarita with her suite, in which Azazello had appeared from somewhere. Here Korovyev released Margarita's arm and whispered:

"Straight for the tulips!"

A low wall of white tulips grew up in front of Margarita, and beyond it she saw countless lights in shades, and in front of them the white chests and black shoulders of men in tails. Then Margarita realized where the sound of the ball was coming from. The roar of trumpets came down upon her, and the soaring of the violins that burst out from beneath it poured over her body like blood. The orchestra of about a hundred and fifty was playing a polonaise.

When he saw Margarita, a man in tails towering in front of the orchestra turned pale, began to smile, and suddenly, with a wave of his arms, had the entire orchestra rise. Without interrupting the music for a moment, the orchestra, standing, enveloped Margarita in sounds. The man above the orchestra turned away from it and bowed low, throwing his arms out wide, and Margarita, smiling, waved her hand to him.

"No, that's not enough, not enough," whispered Korovyev, "he'll be awake all night. Shout to him: 'I greet you, King of the Waltz!'"

Margarita shouted it and wondered at the fact that her voice, full as a bell, drowned the howling of the orchestra. The man gave a start of happiness and put his left hand up to his chest, continuing to wave his white baton at the orchestra with the right.

"Not enough, not enough," whispered Korovyev, "look to the left at the first violins and give them a nod so that each one of them thinks you've recognized him individually. There are only world-famous celebrities here. Nod to that one at the first stand – that's Vieuxtemps.* That's it, very good. Now on we go!"

"Who's the conductor?" asked Margarita as she flew away.

"Johann Strauss!"* cried the cat. "And may I be hanged on a liana in the tropical forest if such an orchestra has ever played at any ball! I'm the one who invited it! And take note, not one person fell ill, and not one declined."

In the next hall there were no columns, in their place stood walls of red, pink and milky-white roses on one side, and on the other – a wall of double Japanese camellias. Between these walls fountains were already gushing and hissing, and champagne was boiling up in bubbles in three pools, the first of which was a transparent lilac, the second – ruby-coloured, and the third – of crystal. Beside them bustled negroes in scarlet headbands, using silver scoops to fill shallow goblets from the pools. There was a gap in the pink wall, and in the gap, on a stage, a man in red with a swallowtail coat was coming to the boil. In front of him thundered an unbearably loud jazz band. As soon as the conductor saw Margarita he bent down before her so that his arms touched the floor, then he straightened up and cried piercingly:

"Hallelujah!"

He slapped himself on the knee, one, then crossways on the other, two, tore a cymbal from the hands of the last musician in the line and struck it against a column.

Flying off, Margarita could only see that the virtuoso jazzman, struggling against the polonaise blowing at Margarita's back, was hitting the jazzmen on the head with his cymbal, while they cowered in comic horror.

Finally they flew out onto the landing where, as Margarita understood it, she had been met by Korovyev with the lamp in the darkness. Now on this landing her eyes were blinded by the light pouring from bunches of crystal grapes. Margarita was set in place, and beneath her left arm there proved to be a low amethyst pillar.

"You'll be able to put your arm on it if things become very difficult," whispered Korovyev.

Some black-skinned man dropped a cushion with a golden poodle embroidered on it at Margarita's feet and, obeying someone's hands, she set her right leg upon it, bending it at the knee.

Margarita tried to look around. Korovyev and Azazello were standing beside her in ceremonial poses. Next to Azazello were three more young men, who somehow reminded Margarita vaguely of Abadonna. The air at her back was cold. Glancing round, Margarita saw that foaming wine was gushing from a marble wall behind her and flowing down into an icy pool. By her left leg she felt something warm and hairy. It was Behemoth.

Margarita was high up, and a grandiose staircase covered with a carpet went away downwards from beneath her feet. At the bottom, so far off it was as if Margarita were looking the wrong way through binoculars, she could see the most enormous porter's lodge with an absolutely immense fireplace, into whose cold and black jaws a five-ton truck could have driven comfortably. The porter's lodge and the staircase, so flooded in light it was painful for the eyes, were empty. Trumpets now reached Margarita from afar. They stood motionless like this for about a minute.

"So where are the guests?" Margarita asked Korovyev.

"They'll be here, my Queen, they'll be here, they'll be here soon. There'll be no shortage of them. And truly, I'd prefer to be chopping firewood, rather than receiving them here on this landing."

"Never mind chopping firewood," the garrulous cat chimed in, "I'd like to be working as a tram-conductor, and there's absolutely nothing on earth worse than that job!"

"Everything has to be ready in advance, my Queen," Korovyev explained, with his eye flashing through his damaged monocle. "Nothing can be viler than when the first guest to arrive wanders about, not knowing what he's to do, while his lawfully wedded shrew nags him in a whisper because they've arrived before anybody else. Such balls should be thrown out on the rubbish heap, my Queen."

"On the rubbish heap, definitely," confirmed the cat.

"There's no more than ten seconds till midnight," added Korovyev, "it'll be starting at any moment."

Those ten seconds seemed extremely long to Margarita. They had evidently already elapsed, and precisely nothing had happened. But at that point something suddenly fell with a crash into the huge fireplace downstairs, and out from it leapt a gibbet with some half-disintegrated remains bobbing about on it. These remains broke loose from the rope, struck against the floor, and from them there leapt a handsome black-haired man wearing tails and patent-leather shoes. Out of the fireplace ran a small, half-rotted coffin, its lid came off, and out of it fell another set of remains. The handsome man hurried up to them gallantly and offered his bent arm, the second set of remains formed themselves into a flighty naked woman in black shoes and with black plumes on her head, and then both of them, the man and the woman, began hurrying up the staircase.

"The first!" exclaimed Korovyev. "Monsieur Jacques* and his wife. I recommend him to you, my Queen, one of the most interesting men. A confirmed counterfeiter, a traitor to the state, but not at all a bad alchemist. Became famous," Korovyev whispered in Margarita's ear, "for poisoning the king's mistress. And that doesn't happen to everyone, after all! Look how handsome he is!"

Margarita, pale and open-mouthed, looked down and saw both the gibbet and the coffin disappearing in some sort of side entrance in the porter's lodge.

"I'm enchanted!" yelled the cat, right in the face of Monsieur Jacques, who had reached the top of the stairs.

At this time from the fireplace downstairs there appeared a headless skeleton with one arm torn off, which struck itself on the ground and turned into a man in tails.

Monsieur Jacques's wife was already going down on one knee before Margarita and, pale from agitation, was kissing Margarita's knee.

"My Queen..." mumbled Monsieur Jacques' wife.

"The Queen is enchanted!" cried Korovyev.

270

"My Queen…" handsome Monsieur Jacques said quietly.

"We're enchanted," howled the cat.

The young men, Azazello's companions, smiling lifeless but welcoming smiles, were already crowding Monsieur Jacques and his wife away towards the goblets of champagne which the negroes were holding in their hands. Coming up the stairs at the double was a solitary man in tails.

"Count Robert," Korovyev whispered to Margarita, "attractive as ever. Take note, my Queen, how funny – the reverse situation: this one was the lover of a queen and poisoned his wife."*

"We're delighted, Count," exclaimed Behemoth.

Out of the fireplace there fell in succession three coffins, which, one after another, broke open and split apart, followed by someone in a black cloak whom the next to run out of the black jaws struck in the back with a knife. Downstairs a smothered cry was heard. Out of the fireplace ran an almost completely decomposed corpse. Margarita screwed up her eyes, and somebody's hand brought a flacon of white salt up to her nose. It seemed to Margarita to be Natasha's hand. The staircase began to fill up. Already on every step now there were men in tails who seemed from a distance completely identical, and with them naked women, who differed from one another only in the colours of the plumes on their heads and of their shoes.

Approaching Margarita and hobbling in the strange wooden boot on her left leg was a lady with eyes downcast like a nun's, slim, modest, and for some reason wearing a broad green band around her neck.

"Who's the green woman?" Margarita asked mechanically.

"The most charming and respectable lady," whispered Korovyev, "I recommend her to you: Signora Tofana.* She was extremely popular amongst charming young Neapolitan girls, and also the female inhabitants of Palermo, and in particular those who were tired of their husbands. It does sometimes happen, after all, my Queen, that a woman gets tired of her husband…"

"Yes," Margarita replied indistinctly, at the same time smiling at two men in tails who, one after the other, bowed down before her, kissing her knee and her hand.

"Well then," Korovyev contrived to whisper to Margarita, and at the same time to cry to someone: "Duke! A glass of champagne! I'm

271

enchanted! Yes, so then, Signora Tofana would sympathize with the position of those poor women and sell them some sort of water in phials. The wife would pour this water into her husband's soup, he would eat it up, thank her for her kindness and feel marvellous. True, a few hours later he would start feeling very thirsty, then he would go to bed, and a day later the beautiful Neapolitan girl who had fed her husband with soup was as free as the wind in spring."

"And what's that on her leg?" asked Margarita, tirelessly offering her hand to the guests who had overtaken the hobbling Signora Tofana. "And why that green thing on her neck? A withered neck?"

"I'm enchanted, Prince!" cried Korovyev, and at the same time whispered to Margarita: "A beautiful neck, but something unpleasant happened to her in prison. On her leg, my Queen, is a Spanish boot,* and this is why there's the ribbon: when the jailers learnt that around five hundred poorly chosen husbands had left Naples and Palermo for ever, in the heat of the moment they strangled Signora Tofana in prison."

"How happy I am, Black Queen, that this great honour has fallen to me," Tofana whispered like a nun, attempting to go down on one knee. The Spanish boot hindered her. Korovyev and Behemoth helped Tofana to rise.

"I'm delighted," Margarita answered her, at the same time offering her hand to others.

There was now a stream coming up the stairs from down below. Margarita had stopped seeing what was going on in the porter's lodge. She raised and lowered her hand automatically and, baring her teeth monotonously, smiled at the guests. The air on the landing was already abuzz, and from the ballrooms that Margarita had left behind music could be heard like the sea.

"Now this is a boring woman," Korovyev no longer whispered, but said loudly, knowing that in the buzz of voices he would no longer be heard, "adores balls, constantly dreams of complaining about her handkerchief."

Among those ascending, Margarita's gaze caught the one Korovyev was indicating. She was a young woman of about twenty with a figure extraordinary in its beauty, but with eyes somehow anxious and importunate.

"What handkerchief?" asked Margarita.

"She has a lady's maid assigned to look after her," explained Korovyev, "who for thirty years has been putting a handkerchief on her table at bedtime. When she wakes up, the handkerchief's already there. She's already both burned it in the stove and dropped it in the river, but nothing helps."

"What handkerchief?" whispered Margarita, raising and lowering her hand.

"A handkerchief with a little blue border. The thing is that, when she worked in a café, the owner pressed her to join him in the pantry once, and nine months later she gave birth to a boy; she carried him off to the wood and stuffed a handkerchief into his mouth, and then buried the boy in the ground. At the trial she said she had nothing to feed the child with."*

"And so where's the owner of this café?" asked Margarita.

"My Queen," the cat suddenly began squeaking from below, "permit me to ask you: what ever has the owner got to do with it! After all, he didn't smother the baby in the wood!"

Without ceasing to smile and move her right hand up and down, Margarita sank the sharp nails of the left one into Behemoth's ear and whispered to him:

"If you, you scum, allow yourself to get involved in the conversation one more time..."

Behemoth let out a squeal, inappropriate somehow for a ball, and croaked:

"My Queen... My ear'll swell up... Why go and spoil the ball with a swollen ear?... I was speaking legally... from a legal point... I'll be quiet, I'll be quiet... Consider me not a cat, but a fish, only let go of my ear."

Margarita released his ear, and importunate, gloomy eyes were before her.

"I'm happy, Hostess-Queen, to be invited to the Great Ball of the Full Moon."

"And I," Margarita answered her, "am glad to see you. Very glad. Do you like champagne?"

"What are you doing, my Queen?!" Korovyev exclaimed desperately, but soundlessly, in Margarita's ear. "There'll be congestion!"

"I do," said the woman beseechingly, and suddenly began repeating mechanically: "Frieda, Frieda, Frieda! My name is Frieda, O Queen!"

"Well, you get drunk today, Frieda, and don't think about anything," said Margarita.

Frieda reached both arms out to Margarita, but Korovyev and Behemoth caught her by the arms very deftly and she was slipped away into the crowd.

There was now a solid wall of people coming from below, as though they were storming the landing on which Margarita stood. Bare female bodies came up among men in tails. Margarita was being engulfed by their swarthy, and white, and coffee-bean-coloured, and completely black bodies. In hair that was red, black, chestnut, light as flax, precious stones played and danced, and scattered sparks in a downpour of light. And it was as if someone had sprinkled the column of storming men with little drops of light. Diamond studs sprayed light out from their chests. Every second now Margarita could feel the touch of lips on her knee, every second she reached her hand out in front of her for a kiss, her face was tightened into an unmoving mask of greeting.

"I'm enchanted," Korovyev sang monotonously, "we're enchanted... The Queen is enchanted..."

"The Queen is enchanted..." Azazello said nasally at her back.

"I'm enchanted," cried the cat.

"The Marquise..." mumbled Korovyev, "poisoned her father, two brothers and two sisters over their inheritance...* The Queen is enchanted!... Madame Minkina...* Ah, how beautiful! A little highly strung. Why ever did she burn her maid's face with the curling irons? Of course you'll be murdered in such circumstances... The Queen is enchanted!... A moment's attention, my Queen! The Emperor Rudolf,* a wizard and alchemist... Another alchemist – hanged... Oh, and there she is! Oh, what a wonderful brothel she had in Strasbourg!... We're enchanted!... The Moscow dressmaker, we all love her for her inexhaustible imagination... she kept a shop and thought up a terribly funny thing: she bored two round holes in the wall..."

"And the ladies didn't know?" asked Margarita.

"Every single one of them knew, my Queen," replied Korovyev. "I'm enchanted!... That young lad of twenty was remarkable for his strange fantasies even as a child, a dreamer and eccentric. A girl fell in love with him, and he went and sold her into a brothel..."

A river was flowing from below. No end could be seen to that river. Its source, the enormous fireplace, continued to feed it. Thus an hour passed, and a second hour began. At that point Margarita began to notice that her chain had become heavier than it had been. Something strange had happened to her hand as well. Before raising it, Margarita now had to knit her brows. Korovyev's interesting remarks ceased to engage Margarita. Slant-eyed Mongolian faces, and faces white and black became all the same to her, merged at times, and the air between them was for some reason beginning to tremble and shimmer. A sharp pain, as from a needle, suddenly ran through Margarita's right arm and, gritting her teeth, she put her elbow on the pedestal. A sort of rustling, as of wings against walls, could now be heard from the hall behind her, and it was clear that unprecedented hordes of guests were dancing there, and it seemed to Margarita that even the massive marble, mosaic and crystal floors in that wondrous hall were rhythmically pulsating.

Neither Gaius Caesar Caligula,* nor Messalina* could interest Margarita any longer, just as not one of the kings, dukes, cavaliers, suicides, poisoners, gallows-birds and procuresses, jailers and card-sharps, executioners, informers, traitors, madmen, detectives and debauchers could interest her. All their names got mixed up in her head, their faces got stuck together in one enormous flat cake, and just one face alone stayed agonizingly in her memory, fringed with a truly fiery beard, the face of Malyuta Skuratov.* Margarita's legs were buckling, every minute she was afraid of bursting into tears. She was caused the worst suffering by her right knee, the one being kissed. It swelled up and the skin on it turned blue, despite the fact that several times Natasha's hand appeared with a sponge beside the knee and rubbed it with something fragrant. At the end of the third hour Margarita glanced down with utterly hopeless eyes, then gave a joyous quiver: the stream of guests was thinning.

"The laws governing arrival at the ball are identical, my Queen," whispered Korovyev, "the wave will now begin to abate. I swear we are enduring the final minutes. There's the group of playboys from the Brocken. They always arrive last. Oh yes, it's them. Two drunk vampires... is that everyone? Oh no, there's another one. No, two!"

The two last guests were coming up the stairs.

"Now this is someone new," said Korovyev, squinting through his lens. "Oh yes, yes. Azazello once paid him a visit, and over the brandy whispered some advice to him on how he could rid himself of a man of whose exposures he was extremely fearful. And so he ordered an acquaintance, who was dependent upon him, to spray the walls of the man's office with poison."*

"What's his name?" asked Margarita.

"Oh, I really don't know yet myself," replied Korovyev, "you need to ask Azazello."

"And who is it with him?"

"Now that's his most dependably efficient subordinate. I'm enchanted!" Korovyev cried to the last two.

The staircase had emptied. Out of caution they waited a little more. But no one else emerged from the fireplace.

A second later, without understanding how it had happened, Margarita found herself in that same room with the pool, and there, immediately bursting into tears from the pain in her arm and leg, she collapsed straight onto the floor. But Hella and Natasha, comforting her, again drew her under the shower of blood, again massaged her body, and Margarita came to life once more.

"There's more, there's more, Queen Margot," whispered Korovyev, who had appeared beside her, "you need to fly round all the halls so the honoured guests don't feel themselves abandoned."

And Margarita once more flew out of the room with the pool. On the stage behind the tulips where the King of the Waltz's orchestra had been playing, there now raged a simian jazz band. An enormous gorilla with shaggy sideburns and with a trumpet in his hand was dancing ponderously as he conducted. Orang-utans were sitting all in a row, blowing on shining trumpets. Astride their shoulders sat cheerful chimpanzees with accordions. Two hamadryads with manes that looked as if they belonged to lions were playing grand pianos, but those pianos could not be heard in the thunder and squealing and thumping of the saxophones, violins and drums in the paws of gibbons, mandrills and monkeys. On the mirrored floor a countless number of couples, stunning in the agility and neatness of their movements, all spinning in the same direction, moved in a solid wall as though merged into one, threatening to sweep away everything in their path. Live satin butterflies swooped above the dancing hordes, flowers fell from the ceilings. When the electricity went off, myriads of glow-worms started burning in the capitals of the columns, and will-o'-the-wisps floated in the air.

Then Margarita found herself in a pool, monstrous in its dimensions, bordered by a colonnade. A gigantic black Neptune was throwing a broad, pink stream out of his jaws. The intoxicating scent of champagne rose from the pool. Here unconstrained merriment held sway. Laughing ladies threw off their shoes, gave their handbags to their cavaliers or to the negroes who were running about with sheets in their hands, and with a cry made swallow dives into the pool. Foaming pillars were thrown upwards. The crystal bottom of the pool burned with underlighting which shone through the depths of the wine, and the silvery swimming bodies could be seen in it. They leapt out of the pool completely drunk. Loud laughter resounded beneath the columns and thundered like in a bathhouse.

In all this commotion, one completely drunk female face stuck in the memory with its senseless eyes, which even in their senselessness were beseeching, and one word came to mind – "Frieda"!

Margarita's head began to spin from the scent of the wine, and she already meant to leave when the cat played a trick in the pool that detained Margarita. Behemoth performed some sort of magic at Neptune's jaws, and at once the rippling mass of champagne left the pool with a hissing and a crashing, and Neptune began disgorging a wave of a dark-yellow colour that did not sparkle, and did not foam. The ladies, with a squealing and a wailing of: "Brandy!" rushed from the edges of the pool to behind the columns. A few seconds later the pool was full, and the cat, turning over three times in the air, came down into the swelling brandy. He climbed out, blowing and snorting, with a bedraggled tie, having lost the gilding from his whiskers and his opera glass. Only one woman brought herself to follow Behemoth's example, that same practical-joking dressmaker and her cavalier, an unknown young mulatto. They both threw themselves into the brandy, but at that point Korovyev caught Margarita by the arm and they abandoned the bathers.

It seemed to Margarita that she flew over a place where she saw mountains of oysters in enormous stone ponds. Then she was flying above a glass floor, beneath which burned hellish furnaces, with devilish white cooks rushing about between them. Then, already ceasing to grasp anything, she somewhere saw dark cellars, where lamps of some sort were burning, where girls were serving meat that sizzled on red-hot coals, where they drank to her health from large tankards. Then she saw polar bears playing accordions and dancing the Kamarinsky on a stage. A conjuring salamander not burning in a fireplace... And for the second time her strength began to fail.

"One final appearance," Korovyev whispered to her anxiously, "and we're free."

Accompanied by Korovyev, she again found herself in the ballroom, but now there was no dancing in it, and the innumerable throng of guests was crowding between the columns, leaving the middle of the hall free. Margarita did not remember who helped her up onto the raised area that had appeared in the middle of this empty space in the hall. When she had mounted it, to her surprise she heard midnight striking somewhere, which, according to her calculation, had passed a very long time ago. With the last stroke of the clock that could be heard from who knows where, silence fell on the throng of guests.

Then Margarita saw Woland again. He was walking in the company of Abadonna, Azazello and several others resembling Abadonna, black and young. Margarita now saw that opposite her raised area another raised area had been prepared for Woland. But he did not make use of it. Margarita was struck by the fact that Woland had come out for this final grand appearance at the ball looking exactly the same as he had in the bedroom. Still the same dirty, patched nightshirt hung on his shoulders, and his feet were in down-at-heel bedroom slippers. Woland had a sword, but he was using this naked sword as a walking stick and leaning on it.

The limping Woland stopped beside his raised area, and immediately Azazello was before him with a dish in his hands, and on that dish Margarita saw a man's severed head with the front teeth knocked out. The most complete silence continued to reign, and it was broken only by a bell, incomprehensible in these circumstances, which was heard once in the distance, as if from a front entrance.

"Mikhail Alexandrovich," Woland addressed the head quietly, and then the eyelids of the man who had been killed were raised a little, and in the dead face Margarita saw with a shudder living eyes, full of thought and suffering. "Everything came true, didn't it?" Woland continued, gazing into the head's eyes. "Your head was cut off by a woman, the meeting didn't take place, and I'm staying in your apartment. That is fact. And fact is the most obstinate thing in the world. But now we're interested in what happens next, and not in this already accomplished fact. You were always an ardent advocate of the theory that upon the severance of the head, life ceases in a man, he turns to ashes and departs into unbeing. It's pleasant for me to inform you, in the presence of my guests, although they actually serve as proof of a quite different theory, that your theory is both well-founded and witty. However, one theory is worth the same as any other. There's even one amongst them, whereby everyone will receive in accordance with his beliefs.* Let it come to pass! You depart into unbeing, and I shall take joy in drinking to being from the goblet into which you turn."

Woland raised his sword. At once the coverings of the head darkened and shrivelled, then fell away in lumps, the eyes disappeared, and soon Margarita saw on the dish a yellowish skull on a golden stem with emeralds for eyes and pearls for teeth. The lid of the skull opened up on a hinge.

"This second, Messire," said Korovyev, noticing Woland's enquiring look, "he will appear before you. In this deathly silence I can hear the squeaking of his patent-leather shoes and the ringing of the glass he has put down on a table, after drinking champagne for the last time in this life. And here he is."

A new single guest was stepping into the hall and heading towards Woland. In appearance he did not differ in any way from the numerous other male guests, except for one thing: the guest was literally reeling in his agitation, which could be seen even from afar. There were burning blotches on his cheeks, and his eyes darted about in utter alarm. The guest was staggered, and this was perfectly natural: he was amazed by everything, and chiefly, of course, by Woland's costume.

The guest was greeted, however, with tremendous kindness.

"Ah, dearest Baron Maigel," Woland turned with a welcoming smile to the guest, whose eyes were popping out of his head, "I'm happy to introduce you," Woland turned to his guests, "to the most esteemed Baron Maigel, an official of the Entertainments Commission with the job of acquainting foreigners with the sights of the capital."

At this point Margarita froze, for she had suddenly recognized this Maigel. She had come across him several times in Moscow's theatres and restaurants. "Excuse me..." thought Margarita, "so he's died as well, then, has he?" But the matter was cleared up straight away.

"The dear Baron," continued Woland, smiling joyfully, "was so charming that, on learning of my arrival in Moscow, he immediately rang me to offer his services in his specialized field, that is, in acquainting me with the sights. It goes without saying that I was happy to invite him to pay me a visit."

At this time Margarita saw Azazello pass the dish with the skull to Korovyev.

"Yes, incidentally, Baron," said Woland, suddenly lowering his voice intimately, "rumours have spread of your extreme inquisitiveness. They say that, in combination with your no less developed loquaciousness, it has begun attracting general attention. What is more, wicked tongues have already let drop the words – informer and spy. And what is even more, there is a supposition that this will lead you to a sad end in no more than a month's time. And so, to spare you that tiresome wait, we decided to come to your assistance, exploiting the fact that you had invited yourself to pay me a visit with the specific aim of spying out and overhearing everything you could."

The Baron turned paler than Abadonna, who was exceptionally pale by nature, and then something strange happened. Abadonna appeared in front of the Baron and for a second took off his glasses. At the same moment something flashed fire in Azazello's hands, there was a soft noise as of someone clapping their hands, the Baron began falling backwards, and scarlet blood spurted from his chest and spilt onto his starched shirt and waistcoat. Korovyev put the goblet under the gushing stream and handed the filled goblet to Woland. The Baron's lifeless body was at this time already on the floor.

"I drink to your health, gentlemen," said Woland softly and, raising the goblet, touched it lightly with his lips.

Then a metamorphosis took place. The patched shirt and the down-at-heel slippers vanished. Woland was now in some sort of black chlamys with a steel sword at his hip. He approached Margarita rapidly, offered her the goblet and said imperiously:

"Drink!"

Margarita's head span, she reeled, but the goblet was already at her lips, and some people's voices – but whose she failed to make out – whispered in both her ears:

"Don't be afraid, my Queen, the blood seeped away into the ground long ago. And bunches of grapes already grow in the spot where it was spilt."

Margarita took a gulp without opening her eyes, and a sweet current ran through her veins, and a ringing began in her ears. It seemed to her that deafening cockerels were crying, that somewhere a march was playing. The crowds of guests started to lose their shape. Both the men in tails and the women collapsed into dust. Decay enveloped the hall before Margarita's eyes, the smell of the burial vault began to flow over it. The columns collapsed, the lights went out, everything shrivelled, and all the fountains, the tulips and the camellias were no more. And there was simply what there was – the modest living room of the jeweller's wife, and from the door into it, which was slightly ajar, there fell a strip of light. And it was into that partly open door that Margarita went.

24

The Extraction of the Master

WOLAND'S BEDROOM was as it had been before the ball. Woland was sitting on the bed in his nightshirt, only Hella was not rubbing his leg, and on the table where they had been playing chess before, dinner was being laid. Korovyev and Azazello had taken off their tailcoats and were sitting by the table, and next to them, of course, was the cat, who had not wanted to part with his tie, even if it had turned into the most perfectly dirty rag. Margarita staggered up to the table and leant on it. Then Woland beckoned her towards him, as he had before, and indicated she should sit down next to him.

"Well then, did they really tire you out?" Woland asked.

"Oh no, Messire," Margarita replied, but scarcely audibly.

"*Noblesse oblige*,"* remarked the cat, and poured Margarita some transparent liquid into a wineglass.

"Is that vodka?" asked Margarita weakly.

The cat gave a little jump on his chair in resentment.

"For pity's sake, my Queen," he wheezed, "would I really permit myself to pour vodka for a lady? This is pure alcohol!"

Margarita smiled and made an attempt to move the glass away from her.

"Drink without fear," said Woland, and Margarita immediately took the glass in her hands. "Hella, sit down," Woland ordered, and explained to Margarita: "The night of the full moon is a festive night, and I dine in the close company of my retinue and servants. And so, how do you feel? How did that exhausting ball go?"

"Stunningly!" trilled Korovyev. "Everyone is charmed, infatuated, overwhelmed! So much tact, so much savoir-faire, fascination and allure!"

Woland raised his glass in silence and clinked it with Margarita's. Margarita drank her drink obediently, thinking that the alcohol would be the end of her straight away. But nothing bad happened. The warmth of life began running through her stomach, something knocked gently at the back of her head, her powers returned, as though she had got up after a long, refreshing sleep, and what is more, she felt the hunger of a wolf. And at the recollection that she had eaten nothing since the previous morning, it flared up still more. She started greedily swallowing down caviar.

Behemoth cut off a piece of pineapple, put salt and pepper on it, ate it, and after that knocked back a second glass of alcohol so raffishly that everyone started clapping.

After the second glass that Margarita drank, the candles in the candelabra flared up brighter, and the flame in the fireplace grew stronger. Margarita felt no intoxication. Biting into meat with her white teeth, Margarita revelled in the juice flowing out of it, and at the same time watched Behemoth spreading mustard on an oyster.

"Put some grapes on the top as well," said Hella quietly, poking the cat in the side.

"I'll request you not to give me lessons," replied Behemoth, "I've sat at a table before, don't you worry, I've sat at a table."

"Ah, how pleasant it is to have dinner like this, with a fireplace, nice and simple," Korovyev jangled, "in the close circle..."

"No, Fagot," the cat objected, "a ball has its own charm and grand scale."

"There's no charm there, and no grand scale either, and those stupid bears, and the tigers in the bar almost gave me a migraine too with their roaring," said Woland.

"I obey, Messire," said the cat, "if you find there to be no grand scale, I'll immediately start to be of the same opinion too."

"You watch it!" Woland replied to this.

"I was joking," said the cat meekly, "but as far as the tigers are concerned, I'll order them to be roasted."

"You can't eat tigers," said Hella.

"You think so? Then please listen," the cat responded and, narrowing his eyes in pleasure, he told of how he once roamed in the wilderness for a period of nineteen days, and the only thing he had to eat was the meat of a tiger he killed. Everyone listened with interest to this engaging narrative, and when Behemoth had finished it, everyone exclaimed in unison:

"Lies!"

"And the most interesting thing about those lies," said Woland, "is the fact that they're lies from the first word to the last."

"Oh really? Lies?" the cat exclaimed, and everyone thought he would start protesting, but he only said quietly: "History will judge us."

"But tell me," said Margot, who had revived after the vodka, turning to Azazello, "did you shoot him, that ex-Baron?"

"Naturally," replied Azazello, "how ever could he not be shot? He has to be shot without fail."

"I got so agitated!" exclaimed Margarita. "It happened so unexpectedly."

"There's nothing unexpected about it," objected Azazello, but Korovyev started howling and moaning:

"How could you fail to be agitated? I was shaking in my boots myself! Bang! There! The Baron's over onto his side!"

"I almost went into hysterics," added the cat, licking the caviar spoon clean.

"This is what I don't understand," said Margarita, and golden sparks from the cut glass were dancing in her eyes, "was it really the case that the music, and the clatter of the ball generally, wasn't audible outside?"

"Of course it wasn't audible, my Queen," explained Korovyev, "it needs to be done in such a way that it isn't audible. It needs to be done pretty carefully."

"Well yes, yes… Or else, after all, the fact is, that man on the stairs… When Azazello and I were going past… And the other one by the entrance… I think he was keeping watch on your apartment…"

"That's right, that's right!" cried Korovyev. "That's right, dear Margarita Nikolayevna! You confirm my suspicions! Yes, he was keeping watch on the apartment! I myself was going to take him for an absentminded *privat-docent* or a man in love, pining on the stairs. But no, no!

Something was gnawing at my heart! Ah, he was keeping watch on the apartment! And the other one by the entrance too! And the one that was in the gateway, the same thing!"

"And won't that be interesting, if they come to arrest you?" asked Margarita.

"They're sure to come, charming Queen, they're sure to!" replied Korovyev. "I sense it in my heart that they'll come. Not now, of course, but in their own time they'll come without fail. But I suspect there'll be nothing of interest."

"Oh, how anxious I was when that Baron fell," said Margarita, evidently still worrying about the murder, something she had seen for the first time in her life. "I expect you shoot very well?"

"Sufficiently," replied Azazello.

"And at how many paces?" Margarita asked Azazello a not entirely clear question.

"It depends at what," Azazello replied reasonably, "it's one thing to hit the critic Latunsky's window with a hammer, and quite another thing to hit him himself in the heart."

"In the heart!" exclaimed Margarita, for some reason touching her own heart. "In the heart!" she repeated in a muffled voice.

"Who's this critic Latunsky?" asked Woland, narrowing his eyes at Margarita.

Azazello, Korovyev and Behemoth cast their eyes down modestly somehow, and Margarita, blushing, replied:

"There's one such critic. This evening I smashed up the whole of his apartment."

"There's a thing for you! But why?"

"He, Messire," Margarita explained, "destroyed a certain Master."

"And why ever did you go to the trouble yourself?" asked Woland.

"Allow me, Messire!" exclaimed the cat joyfully, leaping up.

"You just sit still," growled Azazello, getting up, "I'll go myself right now…"

"No!" exclaimed Margarita. "No, I beg you, Messire, there's no need for that!"

"As you wish, as you wish," replied Woland, and Azazello sat down in his chair.

"So, where did we stop, precious Queen Margot?" said Korovyev. "Ah yes, the heart. He'll hit the heart," Korovyev stretched out his long finger in Azazello's direction, "as you choose, any auricle of the heart or any of the ventricles."

Margarita did not understand at first, but when she had understood she exclaimed in surprise:

"But they're covered up, aren't they!"

"My dear," Korovyev jangled, "that's the very thing, that they're covered up! That's what the whole point is! Anyone can hit an object that's exposed!"

Korovyev took from a drawer in the table the seven of spades and offered it to Margarita, asking her to mark one of the spots with her nail. Margarita marked the one in the top right-hand corner. Hella hid the card under a pillow, crying:

"It's ready!"

Azazello, who was sitting facing away from the pillow, took out of the pocket of his dress-suit trousers a black automatic pistol, put its barrel on his shoulder and, without turning towards the bed, fired a shot, eliciting merry fright in Margarita. The seven was pulled out from under the pillow he had shot through. The spot that had been marked by Margarita had a hole in it.

"I wouldn't want to meet with you when you have a revolver in your hands," said Margarita, throwing coquettish glances at Azazello. She had a passion for all people who are first-class at doing something.

"Precious Queen," squeaked Korovyev, "I don't recommend anyone to meet with him, even if he doesn't have any revolver in his hands at all! I give you the word of honour of a former precentor and choir leader that no one would congratulate the person he met."

The cat had sat frowning during the shooting experiment, and suddenly he declared:

"I undertake to break the record with the seven."

Azazello snarled something in reply to this. But the cat was persistent, and demanded not one, but two revolvers. Azazello took a second revolver from the other back pocket of his trousers and, with a scornful twist of his mouth, held it out with the first one to the braggart. Two spots were marked on the seven. The cat spent a long time in preparation with his back turned to the pillow. Margarita sat with her fingers stuck in her ears and gazed at the owl drowsing on the mantelpiece. The cat fired both revolvers, after which Hella immediately screamed, the dead owl fell from the fireplace, and the broken clock stopped. With a howl,

Hella, one of whose hands was bloodied, seized hold of the cat's fur, and he of her hair in reply, and, curled up in a ball, they began rolling around the floor. One of the glasses fell from the table and broke.

"Pull this crazy she-devil off me!" the cat howled, trying to beat Hella, who was sitting astride him, off. The combatants were separated, Korovyev blew on Hella's wounded finger and it healed over.

"I can't shoot when people are distracting me by talking!" shouted Behemoth, and tried to fit back into place the huge tuft of fur that had been torn out of his back.

"I bet," said Woland, smiling at Margarita, "he played that trick on purpose. He's a decent shot."

Hella and the cat made up, and as a token of this reconciliation they kissed. The card was taken out from under the pillow and checked. Not a single spot, apart from the one that had been shot through by Azazello, had been touched.

"That cannot be," the cat affirmed, looking through the card against the light of a candelabrum.

The jolly dinner continued. The candles were guttering in the candelabra, the dry, fragrant warmth from the fireplace was spreading around the room in waves. The sated Margarita was enveloped by a feeling of bliss. She watched the blue-grey rings from Azazello's cigar drift off into the fireplace and the cat catching them on the tip of a sword. She did not want to go anywhere, although it was, by her calculations, already late. From all the indications, the time was approaching six in the morning. Taking advantage of a pause, Margarita turned to Woland and said timidly:

"It's probably time I went... It's late..."

"Where are you hurrying off to?" asked Woland politely, but rather drily. The others remained silent, pretending they were captivated by the smoke rings from the cigar.

"Yes, it's time," repeated Margarita, utterly confused by this, and she turned around, as though looking for a wrap or a cloak. Her nakedness suddenly began to inhibit her. She rose from the table. Woland silently took his threadbare and soiled dressing gown from the bed, and Korovyev threw it onto Margarita's shoulders.

"I thank you, Messire," Margarita said, scarcely audibly, and looked at Woland enquiringly. He in reply smiled at her politely and indifferently. Immediately somehow a black melancholy surged up towards

Margarita's heart. She felt herself deceived. Evidently no one was intending to offer her any reward for all her services at the ball, just as no one was stopping her going either. But at the same time it was perfectly clear to her that there was nowhere else for her to go from here. A fleeting thought about having to return to her detached house caused her an inner explosion of despair. Should she herself ask, then, as Azazello had temptingly advised in the Alexandrovsky Garden? "No, not for anything!" she said to herself.

"All the best, Messire," she pronounced out loud, while thinking: "If only I can get out of here, then I'll just get myself to the river and drown myself."

"Sit down," Woland suddenly said imperiously.

Margarita changed countenance and sat down.

"Perhaps you want to say something in farewell?"

"No, nothing, Messire," Margarita answered with pride, "except that if you still need me, I am willingly prepared to do anything you like. I'm not in the least tired and had great fun at the ball. So that even if it had carried on for longer, I would have willingly presented my knee for thousands of gallows-birds and murderers to kiss." Margarita was gazing at Woland as if through a shroud, and her eyes were filling with tears.

"Correct! You're absolutely right!" cried Woland in a booming and terrible voice. "That's the way!"

"That's the way!" Woland's suite repeated like an echo.

"We've been testing you," said Woland, "never ask for anything! Never anything, and especially of those who are more powerful than you. They'll make the offer themselves and give everything themselves. Take a seat, proud woman." Woland tore the heavy dressing gown off Margarita, and again she found herself sitting next to him on the bed. "And so, Margot," Woland continued, softening his voice, "what do you want in return for being my hostess today? What do you desire in return for going naked through the ball? What price do you put on your knee? What were the damages caused by my guests, to whom you have just now given the name of gallows-birds? Speak! And do speak now without inhibitions, for it was I who made the offer."

Margarita's heart began thumping, she heaved a heavy sigh and began trying to grasp something.

"Well, come on, don't be shy!" Woland encouraged her. "Arouse your fantasy, spur it on! Being at the scene of the murder of that arrant villain of a Baron alone makes someone worthy of a reward, especially if that someone is a woman. Well?"

Margarita caught her breath, and she was already meaning to utter the cherished words she had prepared in her soul, when suddenly she turned pale and opened her mouth and eyes wide. "Frieda! Frieda! Frieda!" someone's importunate, beseeching voice shouted in her ears. "My name is Frieda!" And, stumbling over the words, Margarita began to speak:

"So therefore... I can ask... one thing?"

"Demand, demand, my *donna*," replied Woland with a knowing smile, "demand one thing."

Oh, how cunningly and distinctly did Woland emphasize it, repeating Margarita's own words – "one thing"!

Margarita sighed once again and said:

"I want Frieda to stop being given the handkerchief with which she smothered her child."

The cat raised his eyes skywards and sighed noisily, but said nothing, obviously remembering his ear being twisted at the ball.

"In view of the fact," began Woland with a grin, "that the possibility of your having received a bribe from that idiot Frieda is, of course, completely ruled out – that would, after all, be incompatible with your queenly dignity – I really don't know what to do. One thing remains, I suppose – to stock up with rags and stop up all the cracks in my bedroom with them!"

"What are you talking about, Messire?" wondered Margarita, after hearing out these truly incomprehensible words.

"I agree with you entirely, Messire," the cat butted into the conversation, "rags, precisely!" and the cat struck his paw on the table in irritation.

"I'm talking about charity," Woland explained his words without taking his fiery eye off Margarita. "It sometimes crawls in quite unexpectedly and insidiously through the narrowest of cracks. And that's why I'm talking about rags."

"And I'm talking about the same thing too!" the cat exclaimed, and leant away from Margarita just in case, covering his sharp ears with paws smeared in pink cream.

"Go away," Woland said to him.

"I've not had any coffee yet," the cat replied, "how can I possibly go away? On a festive night, Messire, are guests at the table really to be divided into two sorts? Some are first, while others, as that sad skinflint of a barman expressed himself, are second-quality fresh?"

"Be quiet," Woland ordered him, and, turning to Margarita, asked: "To all appearances, you're an exceptionally good person? A highly moral person?"

"No," Margarita replied forcefully, "I know you can only be spoken with frankly, and I'll tell you frankly: I'm a frivolous person. I interceded with you on Frieda's behalf only because I was incautious enough to give her firm hope. She's waiting, Messire, she believes in my power. And if she is deceived, I find myself in a terrible position. I won't have any peace for the rest of my life. Nothing can be done! It's just turned out this way."

"Ah," said Woland, "that's understandable."

"So will you do that?" Margarita asked quietly.

"Under no circumstances," replied Woland. "The fact of the matter is, dear Queen, that there's been a little confusion here. Each department should deal with its own affairs. I don't deny our potentialities are quite great, they are much greater than some not very perspicacious people suppose..."

"Yes, really much greater," the cat put in, unable to restrain himself, evidently proud of these potentialities.

"Be quiet, the devil take you!" Woland said to him and, turning to Margarita, continued: "Only what's the sense of doing what is supposed to be done by another, as I expressed myself, department? And so I'm not going to do that, you'll do it yourself."

"And will what I say really be carried out?"

Azazello squinted his one eye ironically at Margarita, gave his red-haired head an imperceptible turn and snorted.

"Get on and do it, what a pain," Woland muttered and, turning the globe, began peering at some detail on it, evidently also busy with another matter during his conversation with Margarita.

"Well, Frieda..." Korovyev prompted.

"Frieda!" cried Margarita piercingly.

The door flew open, and a woman with frenzied eyes, who was tousle-haired and naked, but no longer showed any signs of drunkenness, ran into the room and stretched out her arms to Margarita, and the latter said majestically:

"You are forgiven. You will no longer be offered the handkerchief."

A wail was heard from Frieda, she fell face down on the floor and stretched out in the shape of a cross before Margarita. Woland waved his hand, and Frieda disappeared from view.

"I thank you, farewell," Margarita said, and rose.

"Well then, Behemoth," began Woland, "we don't want to profit from the act of an impractical person on a festive night," and he turned round to Margarita, "and so that doesn't count, after all, I didn't do anything. What do you want for yourself?"

Silence fell, and it was broken by Korovyev, who began whispering in Margarita's ear:

"Diamond *donna*, this time I advise you to be a little more sensible! Otherwise fortune may slip away, you know."

"I want my lover, the Master, returned to me at once, this second," said Margarita, and her face was contorted by a spasm.

At this point the wind burst into the room so that the flames of the candles in the candelabra lay flat, the heavy curtain over the window moved aside, the window flew open, and on high in the distance was revealed the full moon, not of the morning, but of midnight. A greenish handkerchief of nocturnal light from the window sill lay on the floor, and in it appeared Ivanushka's nocturnal guest who called himself the Master. He was in his hospital attire – a dressing gown, slippers and the little black hat with which he never parted. His unshaven face twitched in a grimace, he looked askance at the light of the candles with madly fearful eyes, and a stream of moonlight seethed around him.

Margarita recognized him at once, groaned, clasped her hands together and ran up to him. She kissed him on the forehead, on the lips, pressed up against his prickly cheek, and the tears she had long been holding back now ran in streams down her face. She uttered only one word, repeating it senselessly:

"You... you... you..."

The Master pushed her away from him and said in a muffled voice:

"Don't cry, Margot, don't torment me. I'm seriously ill." He grabbed at the window sill with his hand as though meaning to leap up onto it and flee, he bared his teeth, peering at the seated figures, and cried: "I'm frightened, Margot! My hallucinations have started again..."

Margarita was being suffocated by her sobbing and she whispered, choking on the words:

"No, no, no... don't be afraid of anything... I'm with you... I'm with you..."

Deftly and unnoticed, Korovyev shoved a chair towards the Master, and the latter sank onto it, while Margarita dropped to her knees, pressed up against the sick man's side, and fell quiet in that position. She had not noticed in her agitation that her nakedness had somehow suddenly come to an end, that she was now wearing a black silk cloak. The sick man lowered his head and started looking at the ground with sullen, sick eyes.

"Yes," began Woland after a silence, "he's been given a good going over." He ordered Korovyev: "Give this man something to drink, sir knight."

Margarita entreated the Master in a trembling voice:

"Have a drink, have a drink! Are you afraid? No, no, believe me, they'll help you!"

The sick man took the glass and drank what was in it, but his hand shook, and the emptied glass broke at his feet.

"That's good luck! That's good luck!" Korovyev began whispering to Margarita. "Look, he's already coming to his senses."

The sick man's gaze had, indeed, already become less wild and troubled.

"But is it you, Margot?" asked the moonlight guest.

"Have no doubts, it's me," replied Margarita.

"Some more!" ordered Woland.

After the Master had drained a second glass, his eyes became lively and sensible.

"Well then, that's a different matter," said Woland, narrowing his eyes, "now we'll have a talk. Who are you?"

"I'm nobody now," replied the Master, and his mouth twisted in a smile.

"Where have you come from just now?"

"From the asylum. I'm mentally ill," the newcomer answered.

Margarita could not endure these words and burst into tears once more. Then, after wiping her eyes, she exclaimed:

"Dreadful words! Dreadful words! He's the Master, Messire, I'm giving you notice of it! Cure him, he's worthy of it!"

"Do you know who you're talking with now," Woland asked the new arrival, "who you find yourself with?"

291

"I do," replied the Master, "my neighbour in the madhouse was that boy, Ivan Bezdomny. He told me about you."

"Of course, of course," responded Woland, "I had the pleasure of meeting that young man at Patriarch's Ponds. He almost drove me myself mad, trying to prove to me that I don't exist! But do you believe that it really is me?"

"I have to believe it," replied the newcomer, "but it would, of course, be much more comfortable to think of you as the fruit of a hallucination. I'm sorry," added the Master, having a sudden thought.

"Well then, if that's more comfortable, do think it," replied Woland politely.

"No, no!" said Margarita in fright, and she shook the Master by the shoulder. "Come to your senses! It really is him before you!"

The cat got involved here too:

"Well I really am like a hallucination. Pay attention to my profile in the moonlight." The cat wormed his way into a shaft of moonlight and wanted to say something more, but he was asked to be quiet, and with the reply: "Very well, very well, I'm prepared to be quiet. I'll be a quiet hallucination," he fell quiet.

"Now tell me, why does Margarita call you the Master?" asked Woland.

He grinned and said: "It's a forgivable weakness. She's of too high an opinion of a novel that I wrote."

"What's the novel about?"

"The novel's about Pontius Pilate."

At this point the tongues of the candles again began to rock and jump and the crockery on the table began to tinkle. Woland burst out laughing in a thunderous manner, but frightened no one and surprised no one with that laughter. Behemoth for some reason began clapping.

"About what, about what? About whom?" Woland began, when he had stopped laughing. "Right now? That's amazing! And couldn't you find another subject? Let me have a look," Woland reached out his hand with the palm uppermost.

"Unfortunately, I can't do that," replied the Master, "because I burned it in the stove."

"Forgive me, I can't believe it," replied Woland, "it can't be so. Manuscripts don't burn." He turned around to Behemoth and said: "Come on, Behemoth, give the novel here."

The cat instantly leapt up from his chair, and everyone saw he had been sitting on a fat wad of manuscripts. With a bow the cat proffered the top copy to Woland. Margarita started trembling and crying out, once again getting agitated to the point of tears:

"There it is, the manuscript! There it is!"

She rushed to Woland and added in raptures:

"All-powerful one! All-powerful one!"

Woland took the copy proffered him in his hands, turned it around, put it aside, and silently, without a smile, began staring at the Master. But for some unknown reason the latter sank into anguish and unease, got up from his chair, started wringing his hands and, turning to the distant moon, began shuddering and muttering:

"Even at night in the moonlight I have no peace... why have they disturbed me? O gods, gods..."

Margarita seized hold of the hospital dressing gown, nestled up against him, and she herself began muttering in anguish and tears:

"God, why is it the medicine doesn't help you?"

"It's all right, all right, all right," whispered Korovyev, wriggling around beside the Master, "all right, all right... Another glass, and I'll have one with you for company..."

And the glass winked and flashed in the moonlight, and this glass helped. The Master was sat down in his place, and the sick man's face assumed a calm expression.

"Well, everything's clear now," Woland said, and tapped a long finger on the manuscript.

"Perfectly clear," confirmed the cat, forgetting his promise to become a quiet hallucination, "the main thread of this opus is now clear to me through and through. What do you say, Azazello?" he turned to the silent Azazello.

"I say," replied the latter nasally, "it would be a good thing to drown you."

"Be merciful, Azazello," the cat answered him, "and don't give my master that idea. Believe me, I would appear to you every night in just such lunar attire as the poor Master, and I'd nod to you, and beckon you to follow me. How would you feel about that, O Azazello?"

"Well, Margarita," Woland again entered into the conversation, "tell me everything, what do you need?"

Margarita's eyes blazed, and she addressed Woland imploringly:

"Will you permit me to do a little bit of whispering with him?"

Woland nodded, and Margarita, pressing up against the Master's ear, whispered something to him. He could be heard to answer her:

"No, it's too late. I want nothing more in life. Except to see you. But again I advise you to leave me. You'll be done for together with me."

"No, I won't leave you," Margarita replied, and turned to Woland: "I request that you return us to the basement in the lane in the Arbat, and that the lamp should light up, and that everything should again be as it was."

Here the Master began to laugh and, clasping Margarita's head of curls, which had long since come loose, he said:

"Oh, don't listen to the poor woman, Messire. Someone else has been living in that basement for a long time now, and it's never the way, that everything should again be as it was."

He pressed his cheek against his girl's head, embraced Margarita and began muttering: "Poor thing, poor thing…"

"It's never the way, you say?" said Woland. "That's true. But we'll try." And he said: "Azazello!"

There immediately collapsed from the ceiling onto the floor a confused citizen, close to frenzy, in just his underwear, but for some reason with a suitcase in his hands and wearing a cap. The man was quaking and cowering in terror.

"Mogarych?" asked Azazello of the man who had fallen from the sky.

"Aloizy Mogarych," he replied, trembling.

"Was it you who, after reading Latunsky's article about this man's novel, wrote a complaint about him with a report that he kept illegal literature at his home?" asked Azazello.

The newly appeared citizen turned blue and burst into tears of repentance.

"Did you want to move into his rooms?" said Azazello through his nose, as cordially as possible.

The hissing of an enraged cat became audible in the room, and Margarita howled:

"Know a witch, know one!" and she sank her nails into Aloizy Mogarych's face.

There was a commotion.

"What are you doing?" cried the Master in a voice of suffering. "Margot, don't disgrace yourself!"

"I protest, that's no disgrace!" yelled the cat.

Margarita was pulled off by Korovyev.

"I've built in a bath…" cried the bloodied Mogarych, his teeth chattering, and in his horror he began talking stuff and nonsense, "The whitewash alone… the vitriol…"

"Well, it's a good thing that you've built in a bath," said Azazello approvingly, "he needs to take baths." And he shouted "Be off!"

Then Mogarych was turned upside down and borne away through the open window out of Woland's bedroom.

The Master opened his eyes wide, whispering:

"Now that has got to be rather slicker than what Ivan was telling me." Utterly amazed, he looked around and finally said to the cat: "Do forgive me… are you… sir…" he was thrown, not knowing how to address the cat, "are you, sir, the same cat that boarded the tram?"

"I am," the gratified cat confirmed, and added: "It's nice to hear you addressing a cat so politely. For some reason cats are usually spoken to with excessive familiarity, although not a single cat has ever drunk *Bruderschaft** with anyone."

"It seems to me for some reason you're not really a cat…" replied the Master indecisively. "They'll notice I'm missing at the hospital anyway," he added timidly to Woland.

"Oh, why should they notice you're missing!" Korovyev reassured him, and now there were papers and books of some sort in his hands. "Your case history?"

"Yes."

Korovyev flung the case history into the fireplace.

"No document, and there's no person either," said Korovyev with satisfaction, "and is this your house owner's register of tenants?"

"Ye-es."

"Who's registered in it? Aloizy Mogarych?" Korovyev blew on a page of the house register. "Bang, and he's not there, and please note, he never was. And if the owner's surprised, tell him he dreamt of Aloizy. Mogarych? What Mogarych is that? There was no Mogarych." At this point the string-bound book vanished into thin air from Korovyev's hands. "And there it is, already in the owner's desk."

"What you said was right," said the Master, amazed by the slickness of Korovyev's work, "that if there's no document, there's no person either. And to be specific, there's no me, I haven't got a document."

"I'm sorry," exclaimed Korovyev, "that is, to be specific, a halluci-nation, here it is, your document," and Korovyev passed the Master a document. Then he rolled his eyes and whispered sweetly to Margarita: "And here's your property, Margarita Nikolayevna," and he handed Margarita a notebook with scorched edges, a dried rose, a photograph and, with special solicitude, a savings book. "Ten thousand, as you were good enough to put in, Margarita Nikolayevna. We don't want what belongs to someone else."

"I'm more likely to have my paws wither away than so much as touch what belongs to someone else," exclaimed the cat, puffing himself up and dancing on a suitcase to squash down into it all the copies of the ill-starred novel.

"And your document too," Korovyev continued, passing Margarita a document, and then, turning to Woland, he reported deferentially: "That's all, Messire!"

"No, that's not all," replied Woland, tearing himself away from the globe. "Where, my dear *donna*, do you wish your suite to go? I per-sonally don't need it."

At this point Natasha ran in through the open door, naked as she had been before, clasped her hands together and cried to Margarita:

"Be happy, Margarita Nikolayevna!" She started nodding to the Master and again addressed Margarita. "I knew everything about where you were going, you know."

"Maids know everything," remarked the cat, raising his paw mean-ingfully, "it's a mistake to think they're blind."

"What do you want, Natasha?" asked Margarita. "Go back to the house."

"Margarita Nikolayevna, darling," Natasha began imploringly, and got down on her knees, "can you beg them," she gave Woland a side-long glance, "to leave me as a witch? I don't want to go to the house any more! I'm not going to marry either an engineer, or a technician! Monsieur Jacques proposed to me yesterday at the ball." Natasha unclenched her fist and revealed some gold coins.

Margarita turned an enquiring gaze to Woland. He nodded his head. Then Natasha flung her arms around Margarita's neck, smoth-ered her in noisy kisses and, with a cry of triumph, flew off out of the window.

In Natasha's place was Nikolai Ivanovich. He had regained his former human appearance, but was extremely gloomy and possibly even irritated.

"Here's who I'll release with particular pleasure," said Woland, gazing at Nikolai Ivanovich with revulsion, "with exceptional pleasure, to such an extent is he superfluous here."

"I beg you to issue me with a certificate," began Nikolai Ivanovich, looking around wildly, but with great persistence, "as to where I spent the preceding night."

"With what object?" asked the cat sternly.

"With the object of presenting it to the police and to my wife," said Nikolai Ivanovich firmly.

"We don't usually give certificates," replied the cat, frowning, "but for you, so be it, we'll make an exception."

And Nikolai Ivanovich had not had time to collect his thoughts before the bare Hella was sitting at the typewriter and the cat was dictating to her:

"I hereby certify that the bearer, Nikolai Ivanovich, spent the night in question at Satan's ball, being summoned thereto in the capacity of a mode of transport... put in some brackets, Hella! And in the brackets write 'a hog'. Signed – Behemoth."

"What about the date?" squeaked Nikolai Ivanovich.

"We don't put dates, with a date the document will become invalid," the cat responded, dashed off a signature, got hold of a stamp from somewhere, breathed on it in accordance with the rules, printed the word "paid" on the document and handed the document to Nikolai Ivanovich. After that, Nikolai Ivanovich disappeared without trace, and in his place there appeared a new, unexpected man.

"Who's this now?" asked Woland fastidiously, shielding himself from the light of the candles with his hand.

Varenukha hung his head, sighed and said quietly:

"Let me go back. I can't be a vampire. That time with Hella I almost did for Rimsky completely, you know! But I'm not bloodthirsty. Let me go."

"And what sort of ravings are these now?" asked Woland, wrinkling his face. "What Rimsky is this? What sort of nonsense is this now?"

"Please don't trouble yourself, Messire," Azazello responded, and turned to Varenukha: "There's no need to be rude over the phone.

There's no need to lie over the phone. Understood? Will you not do it any more?"

Joy made everything start spinning round in Varenukha's head, his face became radiant and, not remembering what he was saying, he started mumbling:

"With sincere... that is, I'd like to say, Your Ma... immediately after lunch..." Varenukha pressed his hands against his chest and looked at Azazello in supplication.

"All right, go home," the latter replied, and Varenukha melted away.

"Now all of you leave me alone with them," commanded Woland, indicating the Master and Margarita.

Woland's command was carried out instantly. After a period of silence Woland addressed the Master:

"So, it's to the Arbat basement, then? And who's going to write? What about dreams, inspiration?"

"I have no more dreams, and no inspiration either," replied the Master, "nothing around me is of interest except for her," he again put his hand on Margarita's head, "I've been broken, I'm miserable, and I want to go to the basement."

"What about your novel? Pilate?"

"It's hateful to me, that novel," replied the Master, "I've gone through too much because of it."

"I implore you," Margarita requested plaintively, "don't talk like that. What do you torment me for? You know very well I've put my whole life into that work of yours." Turning to Woland, Margarita also added: "Don't listen to him, Messire, he's too worn out."

"But you do need to be describing something, don't you?" said Woland. "If you've exhausted that Procurator, well, start depicting someone else, that Aloizy, for example."

The Master smiled.

"Lapshonnikova won't publish that, and besides, it's of no interest either."

"And what are you going to live on? You'll have to live like beggars, you know."

"Willingly, willingly," the Master replied, and drew Margarita towards him, put his arm around her shoulders and added: "She'll see sense and leave me..."

"I don't think so," Woland said through his teeth, and continued:

"And so, the man who composed the story of Pontius Pilate goes off to a basement with the intention of settling down there by the lamp and living like a beggar?"

Margarita broke away from the Master and began speaking very heatedly:

"I've done all I could, and I whispered the most tempting thing possible to him. But he refused it."

"I know what you whispered to him," retorted Woland, "and that isn't the most tempting thing possible. But I can tell you," he turned to the Master with a smile, "that your novel will yet bring you surprises."

"That's very sad," replied the Master.

"No, no, it's not sad," said Woland, "there won't be anything terrible now. Well, Margarita Nikolayevna, everything's done. Do you have any complaint against me?"

"Not at all, oh, not at all, Messire!"

"Well, please take this from me as a memento," Woland said, and took out from under a pillow a small gold horseshoe strewn with diamonds.

"No, no, no, what ever for!"

"Do you want to argue with me?" asked Woland with a smile.

Since she had no pocket in her cloak, Margarita packed the horseshoe up in a napkin and tightened it with a knot. At this point something astonished her. She looked around at the window in which the moon was shining, and said:

"But here's what I don't understand. What is all this – it's midnight all the time, but it should already have been morning long ago, shouldn't it?"

"It's pleasant just to detain the festive night a little," replied Woland. "Well, I wish you happiness!"

Margarita reached both her hands out to Woland as if in prayer, but did not dare to approach him, and quietly exclaimed:

"Farewell! Farewell!"

"Goodbye," said Woland.

And Margarita in the black cloak and the Master in the hospital dressing gown went out into the corridor of the jeweller's wife's apartment, in which a candle was burning and where Woland's suite awaited them. When they set off out of the corridor, Hella was carrying the suitcase containing the novel and Margarita Nikolayevna's few belongings, and the cat was helping Hella. At the doors of the apartment Korovyev took his leave and disappeared, while the rest set out to accompany them down the stairs. They were empty. As they were crossing the second-floor landing something gave a soft bump, but no one paid it any attention. Right by the outer doors of entrance No. 6 Azazello blew into the air, and no sooner had they emerged into the courtyard, into which the moon did not come, than they saw a man in boots and a cap sleeping on the porch, and evidently sleeping like the dead, and also a large black car standing by the entrance with its headlights off. In the window at the front could be dimly seen the silhouette of a rook.

They were just about to get in when Margarita exclaimed softly in despair:

"Oh God, I've lost the horseshoe!"

"Get into the car," said Azazello, "and wait for me. I'll be back straight away, I'll just look into what's going on here." And off he went, and in through the front door.

This is what was going on: some time before Margarita and the Master and their escorts emerged, a rather withered woman had come out from apartment No. 48, located underneath the jeweller's wife's, with a can and a bag in her hands. It was that same Annushka who on Wednesday, to Berlioz's misfortune, had spilt the sunflower oil by the turnstile.

Nobody knew, and they will probably never find out either, what this woman did in Moscow or what were the means for her existence. All that was known of her was that she could be seen daily either with a can or with a bag, or else with both a bag and a can together, either in the oil shop, or at the market, or at the gates of the building, or on the stairs, but more often than not in the kitchen of apartment No. 48, which was where this Annushka resided. Apart from that, and most of all, it was known that wherever she was or wherever she appeared, a ruckus would straight away begin in that place and, apart from that, that she bore the nickname "The Plague".

Annushka the Plague rose for some reason extremely early, but today something had got her up at an utterly unearthly hour, just after midnight. The key turned in the door, Annushka's nose was poked out of it, and then all of her as a whole was poked out of it as well, she slammed the door behind her and was already about to move off somewhere when a door banged on the upper landing, someone came rolling down the stairs and, running into Annushka, threw her aside in such a way that she struck the back of her head against the wall.*

"Where on earth is the devil taking you in just your underpants?" screamed Annushka, clutching at the back of her head. The man, in just his underwear, with a suitcase in his hands and wearing a cap, answered Annushka with his eyes closed and in a wild, sleepy voice:

"The geyser! The vitriol! The whitewash alone cost a fortune." And, bursting into tears, he roared: "Get out!"

At that point he rushed not further on down the stairs, but back, up to where the glass in the window had been knocked out by the economist's foot, and through that window he flew out upside down into the courtyard. Annushka even forgot about the back of her head, gasped and made for the window herself. She lay down on her stomach on the landing and poked her head out into the yard, expecting to see the man with the suitcase smashed and dead on the asphalt, lit by the courtyard lamp. But on the asphalt in the courtyard there was precisely nothing.

It only remained to assume that the sleepy and strange individual had flown off out of the building like a bird, without leaving any trace of himself. Annushka crossed herself and thought: "Yes indeed, that apartment No. 50! No wonder people are talking! What an apartment!"

She had not had time to finish the thought before the door upstairs slammed again, and a second person ran down from above. Annushka pressed up against the wall and saw some quite respectable citizen with a little beard, but with a very slightly piggish face, as it seemed to Annushka, dart past her and, like the first one, depart the building through the window, also once again without even thinking of smashing himself on the asphalt. Annushka had already forgotten about the purpose of her outing and remained on the stairs, crossing herself, gasping and talking to herself.

A third man, without a little beard, with a round, shaved face and wearing a *tolstovka*, ran out from upstairs a short time later and flitted off through the window in exactly the same way.

It should be said to Annushka's credit that she was inquisitive and decided to wait and see if there would be any new wonders. The door upstairs was opened anew, and now a whole party began descending

301

from above, only not running, but walking in an ordinary way, like everyone does. Annushka ran away from the window, went downstairs to her own door, opened it quickly, hid herself behind it, and in the chink she had left, her eye began twinkling in a frenzy of curiosity.

Some sort of man, perhaps sick, perhaps not, but strange, pale, with a growth of beard, wearing a little black hat and some sort of dressing gown, was coming down, stepping unsteadily. He was being led solicitously by the arm by some lady in, as it seemed to Annushka in the semi-darkness, a black cassock. The lady was perhaps barefooted, perhaps in some kind of transparent, evidently foreign shoes that had been ripped to shreds. Pah! Who cares about the shoes! I mean, the lady's bare! Well, yes, the cassock's thrown directly onto her bare body! "What an apartment!" Everything in Annushka's soul was singing in anticipation of what she would be telling the neighbours.

Behind the strangely dressed lady there followed a completely bare lady with a little suitcase in her hand, and around the little suitcase roamed an enormous black cat. Annushka very nearly squeaked something out loud as she rubbed her eyes.

Bringing up the rear of the procession was a short, one-eyed foreigner with a limp, without a jacket, in a white dress-waistcoat and wearing a tie. This entire party proceeded downstairs past Annushka. At this point something went bump on the landing.

Hearing that the footsteps were dying away, Annushka slipped out from behind her door like a snake, put her can down against the wall, fell onto her stomach on the landing and began groping about. In her hands there proved to be a napkin holding something heavy. Annushka's eyes popped out when she unfolded the little package. Annushka brought the jewel right up to her eyes, and those eyes burned with a positively wolfish fire. A blizzard developed in Annushka's head:

"I don't know anything, I can't tell you anything! To my nephew? Or saw it up into pieces? The stones can be winkled out... And one stone at a time: one to Petrovka, another to the Smolensky Market... And – I don't know anything, I can't tell you anything!"

Annushka hid her find in her bosom, grabbed the can and, putting off her journey into town, was already about to slip back into the apartment, when before her rose up, and the devil knows where he had sprung from, that same one with the white chest without a jacket, and whispered quietly:

"Give me the horseshoe and the napkin."

"What napkin-horseshoe's that?" asked Annushka, feigning most skilfully. "I don't know of any napkin. Are you drunk or something, Citizen?"

With fingers as hard as the handrail of a bus and just as cold, saying nothing more, the white-chested one squeezed Annushka's throat in such a way that he completely cut off all access to her chest for air. The can fell out of Annushka's hands onto the floor. Having kept Annushka without air for some time, the jacketless foreigner removed his fingers from her neck. After gulping down some air, Annushka smiled:

"Ah, the horseshoe?" she began. "This minute! So it's your horseshoe? Yes, I look and it's lying in the napkin... I tidied it away on purpose, so no one picked it up, or else it'd have vanished into thin air later on!"

After getting the horseshoe and the napkin, the foreigner began bowing and scraping before Annushka, shaking her hand firmly and, with the strongest foreign accent, thanking her fervently in such expressions:

"I am most deeply indebted, madam. This horseshoe is dear to me as a memento. And allow me to hand you two hundred roubles for having kept it safe." And he immediately took the money from his waistcoat pocket and handed it to Annushka.

She, smiling desperately, just kept crying out:

"Oh, I'm most humbly grateful! *Merci! Merci!*"

The generous foreigner slid down a whole flight of stairs at a stroke, but before slipping away completely he shouted from down below, yet without his accent:

"If, you old witch, you ever again pick up something belonging to somebody else, hand it in to the police, don't hide it in your bosom!"

Sensing inside her head a ringing noise and a commotion brought on by all these happenings on the stairs, out of inertia Annushka still continued to shout for a long time:

"*Merci! Merci! Merci!*" But the foreigner was already long gone.

The car was gone from the courtyard too. After returning Woland's present to Margarita, Azazello had taken his final leave of her and asked if she was sitting comfortably, while Hella had exchanged full-blooded kisses with Margarita and the cat had kissed her hand; the escorts had waved to the Master, slumped lifeless and motionless in the corner of the seat, waved to the rook and immediately vanished into thin air, not considering it necessary to trouble themselves with the ascent of the stairs. The rook had switched on the headlights and rolled out through the gates past the man sleeping as if dead in the gateway. And the lights of the big black car had disappeared among the other lights on sleepless and noisy Sadovaya.

An hour later in the basement of the little house on one of the lanes in the Arbat, in the first room, where everything was as it had been until that terrible autumn night the year before, at the table, covered with a velvet tablecloth, beneath a lamp with a shade, beside which stood a little vase of lily of the valley, Margarita sat and shed quiet tears, brought on by the shock she had been through and by happiness. A notebook damaged by fire lay before her, and alongside towered a pile of untouched notebooks. The little house was silent. In the small room next door the Master lay in deep sleep on the couch, covered with the hospital dressing gown. His even breathing was soundless.

When she had had her fill of crying, Margarita took up the untouched notebooks and found the place she had been reading through before the meeting with Azazello beneath the Kremlin wall. Margarita did not feel like sleeping. She stroked the manuscript lovingly, as people stroke their favourite cat, and turned it around in her hands, examining it from all sides, now stopping at the title page, now opening it at the end. Suddenly the dreadful thought came to her that this was all wizardry, at any moment the notebooks would disappear from view, she would find herself in her bedroom in the detached house and, on waking up, she would have to go and drown herself. But this was her last terrible thought, an echo of the long sufferings she had been going through. Nothing disappeared, all-powerful Woland was indeed all-powerful, and for as long as she liked, even right through until dawn, Margarita could rustle the pages of the notebooks, look them over, and kiss and read through the words:

"The darkness that had come from the Mediterranean Sea covered the city the Procurator hated... Yes, the darkness..."

25

How the Procurator Tried to Save Judas from Kiriath

T HE DARKNESS THAT HAD COME from the Mediterranean Sea covered
the city the Procurator hated. The suspension bridges joining
the Temple to the terrible Tower of Antonia disappeared, the abyss
descended from the sky and poured over the winged gods above the
hippodrome, the Hasmonean Palace with its embrasures, the bazaars,
the caravanserais, the lanes, the ponds... Yershalaim, the great city,
vanished as if it had never existed on earth. Everything was devoured
by the darkness that frightened every living thing in Yershalaim and
its environs. A strange cloud had carried in from the direction of the
sea towards the end of the fourteenth day of the spring month of
Nisan.

Its belly had already fallen on Bald Skull, where the executioners
had hurriedly stabbed those being executed, it fell on the Temple in
Yershalaim, crawled in smoking streams from its mount and poured
over the Lower Town. It was pouring into windows, driving people
from the winding streets and into the houses. It was in no hurry to
yield its moisture and yielded only light. As soon as the smoking
black broth was ripped apart by fire, the glittering scaly covering of
the great hulk of the Temple would soar upwards out of the pitch
darkness. But it would die down in an instant, and the Temple
would be plunged into the dark abyss. Several times it rose up out
of it and disappeared again, and each time that disappearance was
accompanied by the din of catastrophe.

Other tremulous glimmerings called forth from the abyss the
Palace of Herod the Great, standing in opposition to the Temple on
the western mount, and terrible eyeless golden statues soared towards
the black sky, reaching out their arms to it. But again the heavenly
fire would be concealed and heavy claps of thunder would drive the
golden idols into the darkness.

Torrential rain gushed unexpectedly, and then the thunderstorm
turned into a hurricane. On the very spot where at about midday the
Procurator and the High Priest had been conversing by the marble
bench in the garden, with a bang like that of a cannon a cypress was
broken in two like a cane. Together with watery dust and hail, onto

the balcony beneath the columns were borne plucked roses, magnolia leaves, small branches and sand. The hurricane racked the garden.

At this time there was only one man beneath the columns, and that man was the Procurator.

He was not sitting in an armchair now, but lying on a couch by a small low table, covered with victuals and jugs of wine. Another couch, empty, was on the other side of the table. At the Procurator's feet stretched an untouched red puddle, as if of blood, and the fragments of a smashed jug lay around. The servant who had been setting the table for the Procurator before the thunderstorm had for some reason lost his head under his gaze, become anxious about not having pleased him in some way, and the Procurator, getting angry with him, had smashed the jug onto the mosaic floor, saying:

"Why don't you look me in the face when you're serving? Have you stolen something, then?"

The African's black face had turned grey, mortal terror had appeared in his eyes, he had started trembling, and all but smashed a second jug too, but the Procurator's wrath had for some reason flown away just as quickly as it had come. The African had wanted to rush to pick up the fragments and wipe away the puddle, but the Procurator had waved his hand at him and the slave had run away. But the puddle had remained.

Now, during the hurricane, the African was hiding beside a niche where there stood a statue of a white, naked woman with her head bowed, afraid to show himself at the wrong time, and at the same time fearful too of missing the moment when he might be called by the Procurator.

Lying on the couch in the semi-darkness of the thunderstorm, the Procurator poured wine into his goblet himself, drank in long draughts, at times laid hands on some bread, crumbled it, swallowed it in small pieces, from time to time sucked out some oysters, chewed on a lemon and drank again.

Had it not been for the roar of the water, had it not been for the claps of thunder, which seemed to threaten to flatten the roof of the palace, had it not been for the knocking of the hail, hammering on the steps of the balcony, it would have been possible to hear that the Procurator was muttering something, conversing with himself. And had the inconsistent flickering of the heavenly fire turned into a constant light, an observer might have seen that the Procurator's face, with eyes inflamed by his latest bouts of insomnia and by the wine, expressed impatience, that the Procurator was not only looking at two white roses, drowned in the red puddle, but was constantly turning his face to the garden, towards the watery dust and the sand, that he was waiting for somebody, waiting impatiently.

Some time passed, and the shroud of water before the Procurator's eyes began to thin. However fierce the hurricane might have been, it was weakening. Branches were no longer cracking and falling. The claps of thunder and the flashes were becoming rarer. No longer did there float above Yershalaim a violet coverlet with white trimming, but an ordinary grey rearguard cloud. The storm was being carried down towards the Dead Sea.

It was now already possible to hear individually both the noise of the rain and the noise of the water precipitating down the gutters and straight down the steps of the staircase by which the Procurator had descended in the daytime for the announcement of the sentence in the square. And finally the fountain that had hitherto been drowned out began to be audible too. It was getting lighter. In the grey shroud that was hurrying away to the east, blue windows appeared.

At this point, from afar, through the tapping of the rain, now very light, there came to the ears of the Procurator the weak sounds of trumpets and the rattle of several hundred hoofs. Hearing this, the Procurator shifted, and his face became animated. The *ala* was returning from Bald Mountain. To judge by the sound, it was crossing over that same square where the sentence had been announced.

Finally the Procurator heard both long-awaited footsteps and a slapping on the staircase leading to the upper terrace of the garden directly in front of the balcony. The Procurator stretched out his neck, and his eyes started shining, expressing joy.

Between two marble lions there appeared first a head in a hood, and then an utterly wet man too, in a cloak that clung to his body. It was that same man who had been whispering with the Procurator in a darkened room of the palace before the sentence, and who during the execution had been sitting on a three-legged stool, playing with a little twig.

The man in the hood cut across the garden terrace, taking no notice of the puddles, stepped onto the mosaic floor of the balcony and, raising his hand, said in a pleasant, high voice:

"May the Procurator prosper and be joyful!" The visitor spoke in Latin.

"Ye gods!" exclaimed Pilate. "There's not a dry stitch on you, is there! What a hurricane! Eh? Do please come through to me straight away. Be so kind as to change your clothes."

The visitor threw back his hood, revealing a thoroughly wet head with the hair sticking to the forehead, and, expressing a polite smile on his shaved face, he started off refusing to change his clothes, giving assurances that a little rain could not harm him in any way.

"I'll hear none of it," Pilate replied, and clapped his hands. By so doing he summoned the servants who were hiding from him, and ordered them to take care of the visitor and then to serve a hot dish at once. The Procurator's visitor needed very little time to dry his hair, change his clothes, change his shoes and generally tidy himself up, and he shortly appeared on the balcony in dry sandals, in a dry crimson military cloak and with his hair smoothed down.

At that time the sun had returned to Yershalaim and, before leaving and sinking into the Mediterranean Sea, was sending its farewell rays to the city the Procurator hated and gilding the steps of the balcony. The fountain had completely revived and sang away with all its might, doves had come out onto the sand and were cooing, hopping over broken branches and pecking at something in the wet sand. The red puddle had been wiped up, the pieces of broken pottery cleared away, and there was meat steaming on the table.

"I am listening for the Procurator's orders," said the visitor, approaching the table.

"But you'll hear nothing until you sit down and drink some wine," Pilate replied amiably, and pointed to the other couch.

The visitor lay down, and a servant poured a rich red wine into his goblet. Another servant, leaning carefully over Pilate's shoulder, filled the Procurator's goblet. After that, with a gesture the latter sent both servants away.

While the visitor was drinking and eating, Pilate, sipping wine, looked at his guest from time to time with narrowed eyes. The man who had come to see Pilate was middle-aged, with a very pleasant, rounded and neat face and with a fleshy nose. His hair was an indefinite sort of colour. Now, as it dried, it was getting lighter. The newcomer's nationality would have been hard to establish. The basic thing that defined his face was probably the good-natured expression which was, however, disrupted by the eyes, or rather, not by the eyes, but by the visitor's manner of looking at the person with whom he was talking. The newcomer usually kept his small eyes beneath half-closed eyelids that were rather strange, as though slightly puffy. In the little slits of those eyes there then shone a mild cunning. It must be assumed that the Procurator's guest was inclined to humour. But at times, completely expelling this gleaming humour from the slits, the Procurator's present guest would open his eyelids wide and glance at his interlocutor suddenly and directly, as though with the aim of quickly making out some inconspicuous little blemish on the interlocutor's nose. This would last for one moment, after which the eyelids were lowered again, the slits narrowed, and in them would begin to shine good nature and a cunning intelligence.

The visitor did not refuse a second goblet of wine either, he swallowed several oysters with obvious enjoyment, tried some boiled vegetables and ate a piece of meat.

When he was full up, he praised the wine:

"A splendid vine, Procurator, but is it Falernum?"*

"Cecubum,* thirty years old," the Procurator responded amiably.

The guest put his hand to his heart, refused anything else to eat, declared that he was full. Then Pilate filled his own goblet, and his guest did the same. Both diners poured off some of the wine from their goblets into the dish of meat, and the Procurator pronounced loudly, raising his goblet:

"To us, and to you, Caesar, father of the Romans, the dearest and the best of men!"

After that, they finished the wine, and the Africans cleared the victuals away from the table, leaving the fruits and the jugs there. Once again the Procurator sent the servants away with a gesture and remained alone under the colonnade with his guest.

"And so," Pilate began softly, "what can you tell me about the mood in this city?"

He involuntarily turned his gaze to where, down below, beyond the terraces of the garden, both colonnades and flat roofs were burning out, gilt by the final rays.

"I think, Procurator," his guest replied, "that the mood in Yershalaim is now satisfactory."

"So it can be guaranteed that disorders are no longer a threat?"

"Only one thing in the world," replied the guest, casting affectionate glances at the Procurator, "can be guaranteed – the might of the great Caesar."

"May the gods send him a long life," Pilate joined in at once, "and universal peace." He was silent for a moment, then continued: "So you think the troops can now be withdrawn?"

"I think the Lightning Legion Cohort can leave," replied the guest, and added: "It would be good if, in parting, it marched through the city in procession."

"A very good idea," the Procurator gave his approval, "I'll dismiss it the day after tomorrow and I'll leave myself, and – I swear to you by the Feast of the Twelve Gods,* I swear by the *lares** – I'd give a great deal to do it today!"

"Does the Procurator not like Yershalaim?" asked the guest good-naturedly.

"Mercy me," exclaimed the Procurator with a smile, "there's no more unreliable place on earth. And I'm not talking now about nature! I'm unwell every time I have to come here. And even that wouldn't be such a bad thing. But these feasts – the magi, the wizards, the magicians, these flocks of pilgrims... Fanatics, fanatics! And take just this Messiah alone that they've suddenly started waiting for this year! All you're doing every minute is expecting to be a witness to the most unpleasant bloodshed. Shuffling the troops all the time, reading denunciations and slanders, half of which, what's more, are written against you yourself! You must agree, that is dull. Oh, if it weren't for the imperial service!..."

"Yes, the feasts here are difficult," the guest agreed.

"With all my soul I wish they'd end soon," Pilate added energetically. "I'll finally get the opportunity to return to Caesarea. Can you believe it, this ludicrous structure of Herod's," the Procurator waved his arm the length of the colonnade so it became clear he was talking about the palace, "is positively driving me out of my mind. I can't bear to spend the night in it. The world has never known odder architecture! Yes, but let's get back to business. First of all, this accursed Bar-rabban isn't troubling you?"

And at this point the guest sent his special look towards the Procurator's cheek. But the latter was gazing into the distance with bored eyes, frowning fastidiously and contemplating the part of the city that, lying at his feet, was dying away in the twilight. The guest's look died away too, and his eyelids dropped.

"One must imagine that Bar has now become harmless as a lamb," the guest began, and little wrinkles appeared on his round face. "It's awkward for him to rebel now."

"Too renowned?" asked Pilate with a grin.

"As always, the Procurator has a subtle understanding of the question!"

"But in any event," the Procurator remarked anxiously, and a long, slim finger with the black stone of a ring rose up, "one will have to..."

"Oh, the Procurator can be certain that, while I am in Judaea, Bar won't take a step without men following at his heels."

"Now I feel calm, as, incidentally, I always do when you're here."

"The Procurator is too kind!"

"And now please inform me about the execution," said the Procurator.

"What specifically interests the Procurator?"

"Were there any attempts on the part of the crowd at expressing indignation? That's the most important thing, of course."

"None," replied the guest.

"Very good. Did you yourself establish that death had come?"

"The Procurator can be certain of it."

"And tell me... were they given a drink before being hung on the poles?"

"Yes. But he," here the guest closed his eyes, "refused to drink it."

"Who precisely?" asked Pilate.

"Forgive me, Hegemon!" exclaimed the guest. "Didn't I name him? Ha-Nozri."

"The madman!" said Pilate, for some reason grimacing. Beneath his left eye a vein began to twitch. "Dying of sunburn! Why on earth refuse what's offered in accordance with the law? In what terms did he refuse?"

"He said," replied the guest, again closing his eyes, "he was grateful and attached no blame for his life having been taken away."

"To whom?" Pilate asked indistinctly.

"That, Hegemon, he did not say."

"Did he try to preach anything in the presence of the soldiers?"

"No, Hegemon, he was not verbose on this occasion. The only thing

311

he did say was that he considered one of the most important among human vices to be cowardice."

"In relation to what was it said?" – the guest heard a suddenly cracked voice.

"That was impossible to understand. In general he behaved strangely though, as always."

"What was so strange?"

"All the time he was trying to look into the eyes of those around him, first of one, then of another, and all the time he was smiling a confused sort of smile."

"Nothing more?" asked a hoarse voice.

"Nothing more."

The Procurator banged his goblet, pouring himself some wine. He drained it to the very dregs, then began to speak:

"The point is as follows: although we are unable to discover – at the given time, at least – any admirers or followers of his, it nonetheless cannot be guaranteed that there are none of them at all."

The guest listened attentively with his head bowed.

"And so, to avoid any surprises," continued the Procurator, "I would ask you, immediately and without any fuss, to wipe the bodies of all three executed men from the face of the earth, and to bury them in secret and in silence, so that not a word should be heard of them any more."

"Very well, Hegemon," said the guest, and he rose, saying: "In view of the complexity and responsibility of the matter, allow me to go straight away."

"No, take a seat again," said Pilate, stopping his guest with a gesture, "there are two more questions. Your immense services in the most difficult work in your position as Chief of the Procurator of Judaea's Secret Service give me the pleasant opportunity of reporting about them in Rome."

At this point the guest's face turned pink, he stood up and bowed to the Procurator, saying:

"I merely carry out my duty in the imperial service!"

"But I'd like to ask you," continued the Hegemon, "if you're offered a transfer away from here with a promotion, to refuse it and remain here. Not for anything would I want to part with you. May you be rewarded in some other way."

"I am happy to serve under your command, Hegemon."

"That's very pleasant for me. And so, the second question. It concerns that, what's his name... Judas from Kiriath."

And at this point the guest sent the Procurator his look, and immediately, as is proper, extinguished it.

"They say," the Procurator continued, lowering his voice, "he is supposed to have been given money for having welcomed that mad philosopher so warmly into his home."

"He will be given it," the Chief of the Secret Service quietly corrected Pilate.

"And is it a large sum?"

"That nobody can know, Hegemon."

"Even you?" said the Hegemon, expressing praise through his astonishment.

"Alas, even I," the guest calmly replied. "But that he will be given the money this evening, that I do know. He is summoned to Caipha's palace today."

"Ah, the greedy old man from Kiriath," remarked the Procurator with a smile. "He is an old man, isn't he?"

"The Procurator is never mistaken, but on this occasion he has made a mistake," the guest replied cordially, "the man from Kiriath is a young man."

"You don't say! Can you give me a description of him? A fanatic?"

"Oh no, Procurator."

"Right. Anything else?"

"He's very handsome."

"What else? Does he perhaps have some passion or other?"

"It's hard to know everyone in this huge city so very precisely, Procurator..."

"Oh no, no, Afranius!* Don't belittle your merits."

"He does have one passion, Procurator." The guest made a tiny pause. "A passion for money."

"And what does he do?"

Afranius raised his eyes upwards, thought for a moment and replied: "He works for one of his relatives in a money-changer's."

"Ah, right, right, right." At this point the Procurator fell silent, looked around to see if there was anyone on the balcony, and then said quietly: "Well, the point is this – I have today received information that he is going to be murdered tonight."

313

Here the guest not only threw his look at the Procurator, he even held it there for a little, and after that replied:

"You were too flattering about me, Procurator. I don't think I deserve your report. I don't have this information."

"You are worthy of the very highest reward," the Procurator replied, "but there is such information."

"Might I be so bold as to ask who this information is from?"

"Permit me not to tell you that for the time being, particularly as it is casual, vague and unreliable. But it's my duty to foresee everything. Such is my position, it's my duty above all else to trust my premonitions, for never yet have they deceived me. But the information is that one of Ha-Nozri's secret friends, indignant at this money-changer's monstrous treachery, is arranging with his accomplices to kill him tonight and to drop off the money he receives for his treachery at the High Priest's with a note: 'I am returning the accursed money'."

The Chief of the Secret Service cast no more of his unexpected looks at the Hegemon and carried on listening to him with narrowed eyes, while Pilate continued:

"Just imagine, will it be pleasant for the High Priest to receive such a gift on the night of the feast?"

"Not only not pleasant, Procurator," replied the guest with a smile, "but I expect it will cause a very great scandal."

"I too am of the same opinion myself. And that's why I'm asking you to take the matter up, that is, to take all possible measures for the protection of Judas from Kiriath."

"The Hegemon's command will be carried out," Afranius began, "but I must reassure the Hegemon: the villains' plan is extremely impracticable. I mean, just think about it," the guest turned around as he spoke, and then continued: "track a man down, murder him and on top of that find out how much he was given, and contrive to return the money to Caipha, and all that in one night? Tonight?"

"But he will nonetheless be murdered tonight," Pilate repeated stubbornly, "I have a premonition, I'm telling you! There has never been an instance of it deceiving me," at this point a spasm flitted over the Procurator's face, and he gave his hands a brief rub.

"Yes, sir," the guest responded obediently, rose, stood up straight, and suddenly asked sternly: "So he'll be murdered, Hegemon?"

"Yes," replied Pilate, "and the only hope is that assiduousness of yours that so astonishes everyone."

The guest adjusted the heavy belt beneath his cloak and said:

"I have the honour to wish you to prosper and be joyful."

"Ah yes," Pilate exclaimed softly, "I completely forgot, didn't I! I owe you some money, don't I!"

The guest was astonished.

"Truly, Procurator, you don't owe me anything."

"What do you mean, I don't! During my entrance into Jerusalem, you remember, the crowd of beggars... and I wanted to toss them some money, but I didn't have any, and I took some from you."

"Procurator, that was a trifling matter!"

"Even a trifling matter should be remembered."

At this point Pilate turned around, picked up the cloak lying on the armchair behind him, took out from underneath it a leather pouch and held it out to the guest. The latter bowed as he took it, and hid it away beneath his cloak.

"I await," began Pilate, "a report on the burial, and also on this matter of Judas from Kiriath this very night, do you hear, Afranius, tonight. The guard will be given the order to wake me as soon as you appear. I await you."

"I have the honour," said the Chief of the Secret Service and, turning around, he left the balcony. He could be heard crunching across the wet sand of the terrace, then the tapping of his boots across the marble between the lions was heard, then his legs were cut off, his body, and finally his hood disappeared as well. Only at that point did the Procurator see that the sun had already gone and the dusk had arrived.

26

The Burial

P ERHAPS IT WAS THIS DUSK that was the reason for the Procurator's appearance changing sharply. It was as if he grew visibly older, bent and anxious besides. Once he looked around and for some reason shuddered upon casting a glance at the empty armchair on the back of which lay his cloak. The night of the feast was approaching, the shadows of evening were playing their game, and it probably appeared to the weary Procurator that someone was sitting in the empty armchair. Having admitted faint-heartedness and given the cloak a shake, the Procurator left it alone and started hurrying around the balcony, now rubbing his hands, now hurrying up to the table and grabbing the goblet, now coming to a halt and starting to gaze senselessly at the mosaic on the floor, as though trying to read letters of some sort in it.

For the second time already that day depression was descending on him. Rubbing his temple, in which there remained only a dull, slightly aching memory of the hellish pain of the morning, the Procurator kept on struggling to understand the reason for his spiritual torment. And he quickly realized it, but tried to deceive himself. It was clear to him that he had irrevocably lost something that afternoon, and now he wanted to make amends for what had been lost by some petty and worthless, but, most importantly, belated actions. And his self-deception consisted in the Procurator trying to convince himself that these actions, the present ones of the evening, were no less important than the sentence of the morning. But the Procurator was managing this very badly.

At one of his turns he stopped abruptly and whistled. In response to this whistle a low bark rang out in the dusk, and there leapt out from the garden onto the balcony a gigantic sharp-eared dog with a grey coat, wearing a collar with gilt studs.

"Banga, Banga," cried the Procurator weakly.

The dog rose up on its hind legs, dropped the front ones onto its master's shoulders so that it all but knocked him to the ground, and licked his cheek. The Procurator sat down in his armchair. Banga, with his tongue hanging out and breathing rapidly, lay down by its master's feet, and the joy in the dog's eyes signified that the thunderstorm, the only thing in the world that the fearless dog was afraid of, had ended, and also the fact that it was here again, alongside the man it loved, respected and considered the mightiest in the world, the master of all men, thanks to whom even the dog itself was considered a privileged creature, superior and special. Yet having lain down at his feet, and without even looking at its master, but looking into the darkening garden, the dog immediately realized that a calamity had befallen its master. For that reason it changed its position, got up, came in from the side and put its front paws and head on the Procurator's knees, smearing the bottom of his cloak with wet sand. Banga's actions were probably meant to signify that it was comforting its master and was prepared to meet misfortune together with him. It was attempting to express this both in its eyes, which were turned sidelong towards its master, and in its pricked, wary ears. Thus the two of them, both the dog and the man who loved one another, saw in the night of the feast on the balcony.

At this time the Procurator's guest was extremely busy. After leaving the upper terrace of the garden in front of the balcony, he had gone down the staircase onto the garden's lower terrace, had turned to the right and gone out towards the barracks located on the territory of the palace. It was in these barracks that the two centuries which had come to Yershalaim along with the Procurator for the feasts were quartered, and also the Procurator's Secret Guard, which was commanded by this very guest. The guest did not spend much time in the barracks, no more than ten minutes, but on the expiration of those ten minutes three carts emerged from the barracks' courtyard, loaded with entrenching tools and a barrel of water. The carts were accompanied by fifteen men in grey cloaks, horsemen. Accompanied by them, the carts emerged from the territory of the palace through the rear gates, bore to the west, went out through the gates in the city wall and set off first of all along a track to the Bethlehem road, and then along it to the north; they went as far as the crossroads by the Hebron gates, and then moved down the Jaffa road, along which the procession with the condemned men had passed to the execution in the afternoon. At this time it was already dark, and the moon had appeared on the horizon.

Shortly after the carts had left with the team accompanying them, the Procurator's guest, having changed into a dark, worn tunic, had departed on horseback from the territory of the palace too. The guest had headed not out of the city, but into the city. A little while later he could have been seen riding up to the Tower of Antonia, located in the north and in immediate proximity to the Great Temple. The guest had also spent a very short time in the Tower, and then his trail had come to light in the Lower City, in its crooked and confused streets. The guest had arrived there now riding on a mule.

The guest, who knew the city well, easily found the street that he wanted. It bore the name Greek Street, since several Greek shops were situated on it, including one in which they traded in carpets. The guest stopped his mule by this very shop, dismounted and tied it to a ring by the gates. The shop had already been locked up. The guest went in through the gate which was to be found next to the entrance to the shop and entered a small, square courtyard, surrounded by sheds in the shape of the letter *pokoi*. Turning a corner in the courtyard, the guest found himself by the stone terrace of a house entwined in ivy, and looked around. Both the house and the sheds were dark, the lights had not yet been lit. The guest softly said:

"Niza!"

At this call a door creaked, and in the evening twilight there appeared on the terrace a young woman without a shawl. She bent over the terrace handrail, peering anxiously in her desire to find out who had come. Recognizing the visitor, she began smiling at him cordially, nodded and waved.

"Are you alone?" Afranius asked softly in Greek.

"I am," whispered the woman on the terrace. "My husband left for Caesarea this morning." At this point the woman glanced round at the door and added in a whisper: "But the maidservant's at home." At this point she made a gesture meaning "come in". Afranius glanced round and stepped onto the stone steps. After this, both he and the woman disappeared inside the little house.

Afranius now spent not long at all with this woman – certainly not more than five minutes or so. After that, he left the house and the terrace, pulled his hood down low over his eyes and went out into the street. Lamps were already being lit in the houses at this time, the pre-feast crush of people was still very great, and Afranius on his mule was lost in the stream of passers-by on foot and riding. His route thereafter is known to no one.

But when left alone, the woman that Afranius had called Niza began changing her clothes, and did so very hurriedly. Yet no matter how hard it was for her to find the things she needed in the dark room, she did not light the lamp and did not summon the maidservant. Only after she was prepared and already had a dark shawl on her head was her voice heard in the little house:

"If anyone asks for me, say I've gone to visit Enanta."

The grumbling of the old maidservant was heard in the darkness:

"Enanta? Oh, that Enanta! But your husband forbade you to visit her, didn't he! She's a procuress, that Enanta of yours! I'll tell your husband…"

"Now, now, now, be quiet," Niza responded, and slipped like a shadow out of the little house. Niza's sandals tapped over the stone flags of the little courtyard. Grumbling, the maidservant closed the door onto the terrace. Niza left her home.

At this very time from another lane in the Lower Town – a winding lane, running down in steps towards one of the city ponds, from the gate of an unprepossessing house, the blind side of which backed onto the lane, while the windows looked out onto the courtyard – there emerged a young man with a neatly trimmed little beard wearing a clean white keffiyeh, a new tallith for the feast with tassels at the bottom, and nice new squeaky sandals. The handsome, hook-nosed man, dressed up for the big feast, walked jauntily, overtaking passers-by hurrying home for their festive meal, and watched as one window after another lit up. The young man was heading down the road leading past the bazaar towards the palace of the High Priest Caipha, situated by the foot of the Temple Mount.

Some time later he could be seen entering the gates of Caipha's palace. And some time later still, leaving that courtyard.

After the visit to the palace, in which lamps and torches were already burning, in which the bustle of the feast was under way, the young man started walking even more jauntily, even more joyfully, and began hurrying back to the Lower Town. On that very corner where the street opened into the market square, in the seething and the jostling he was overtaken by a light woman, who walked with a dancing sort of step, wearing a dark shawl drawn right down to her eyes. As she overtook the handsome young man, this woman drew the shawl back a little higher for a moment and cast a glance in the direction of the young man, yet not only did she not slacken her pace, she quickened it, as though trying to give the man she had overtaken the slip.

Not only did the young man notice the woman, no, he recognized her, and when he recognized her, he jumped, stopped, gazing at her back in bewilderment, and immediately set off to catch up with her. All but knocking over a passer-by with a jug in his hands, the young man caught up with the woman and, breathing hard in agitation, called out to her:

"Niza!"

The woman turned and narrowed her eyes, at which cold annoyance was expressed on her face, and answered drily in Greek:

"Ah, is it you, Judas? I didn't recognize you at first. Still, that's a good thing. We have a superstition that a person who isn't recognized gets rich."

So agitated that his heart began jumping like a bird under a black shawl, Judas asked with a catch in his voice and in a whisper, fearing that passers-by might hear:

"Where ever are you going, Niza?"

"And why do you need to know that?" replied Niza, slackening her pace and gazing at Judas haughtily.

Then certain childish intonations became audible in Judas's voice, and he started whispering in dismay:

"But what do you mean? We made arrangements, didn't we? I wanted to come and see you. You said you'd be at home all evening..."

"Oh no, no," Niza replied, and stuck out her lower lip capriciously, which made it seem to Judas that her face, the most beautiful face he had ever seen in his life, had become even more beautiful, "I got bored. It's a feast day for you, but what on earth do you expect me to do? Sit and listen to you sighing on the terrace? And be afraid, what's more, that the maidservant will tell my husband about it? No, no – and so I decided to go out of town to listen to the nightingales."

"What do you mean, out of town?" asked the bewildered Judas. "By yourself?"

"Of course, by myself," replied Niza.

"Allow me to accompany you," requested Judas, gasping for breath. His thoughts were in a whirl, he had forgotten everything on earth, and he looked with imploring eyes into Niza's blue ones, which seemed now to be black.

Niza made no reply and increased her pace.

"Why don't you say anything, Niza?" asked Judas piteously, matching his pace to hers.

"And I won't be bored with you?" Niza suddenly asked, and stopped. At this point Judas's thoughts became utterly confused.

"Well, all right," Niza finally softened, "come on."

"But where to, where to?"

"Hang on... let's go into this little courtyard and make arrangements, or else I'm afraid someone I know will see me, and then they'll say I was with my lover in the street."

And at that point Niza and Judas disappeared from the bazaar. They were whispering in the gateway of some courtyard.

"Go to the olive estate," whispered Niza, pulling the shawl down over her eyes and turning away from some man who was going through the gateway with a bucket, "to Gethsemane, beyond Kidron, got it?"

"Yes, yes, yes."

"I'll go on ahead," continued Niza, "but don't you follow on my heels, you go separately from me. I'll go off in front... When you cross the stream... you know where the grotto is?"

"I know, I know..."

"You'll go up past the olive press and turn towards the grotto. I'll be there. Only don't you dare come after me immediately, have patience, wait here." And with these words Niza went out from the gateway as though she had never been talking with Judas.

Judas stood alone for some time, trying to collect his scattered thoughts. Among them was the thought of how he would explain his absence from his family's festive meal. Judas stood thinking up some sort of lie, but in his agitation he failed to consider or prepare anything properly, and his legs carried him away out of the gateway by themselves, without his volition.

Now he had altered his route, he was no longer heading for the Lower Town, but had turned back towards Caipha's palace. The feast had already entered the city. Not only were lights twinkling in the windows around Judas, but doxologies could already be heard. The final latecomers were driving their donkeys along, whipping them on and shouting at them. His legs carried Judas by themselves, and he did not notice the terrifying, moss-covered Towers of Antonia fly past him, he did not hear the roar of trumpets in the fortress, he paid no attention to the mounted Roman patrol with a torch that flooded his path with a disquieting light.

After passing the tower, Judas turned and saw that terribly high above the Temple two gigantic five-branched candlesticks had been lit. But even them Judas made out dimly, it seemed to him that over Yershalaim ten lamps, unprecedented in size, had begun to shine, rivalling the light of the single lamp rising ever higher over Yershalaim – the lamp of the moon.

Nothing was of any concern to Judas now, he headed towards the Gethsemane Gate, he wanted to leave the city as quickly as he could. At times it seemed to him that in front of him, among the backs and faces of the passers-by, there was a glimpse of a little dancing figure leading him on. But this was an illusion – Judas understood that Niza had significantly outstripped him. Judas ran past the money-changers' and finally came to the Gethsemane Gate. Burning with impatience, he was nonetheless forced to delay there. Camels were entering the city, and a Syrian military patrol, which Judas cursed inwardly, rode in after them...

But everything comes to an end. The impatient Judas was already outside the city wall. On his left-hand side Judas caught sight of a small graveyard and, beside it, several striped pilgrims' tents. Crossing the dusty road flooded in moonlight, Judas hurried towards the stream of Kidron with the aim of crossing it. The water murmured quietly beneath Judas's feet. Jumping from stone to stone, he finally came out onto the opposite Gethsemane bank, and saw with great joy that the road below the gardens was empty here. Not far away, the crumbling gates of the olive estate were already visible.

After the stifling city Judas was struck by the heavy scent of the spring night. Pouring out over the wall from the garden was a wave of scent of myrtles and acacias from Gethsemane's glades.

Nobody was guarding the gates, there was nobody in them, and a few minutes later Judas was already running beneath the secretive shade of the huge, spreading olives. The road led uphill. Judas climbed, breathing hard, at times coming out of the darkness onto carpets of patterned moonlight, reminding him of the carpets he had seen in the shop belonging to Niza's jealous husband. After some time there was a glimpse in a glade to Judas's left of an olive press with a heavy stone wheel and a stack of barrels of some sort. There was nobody in the garden. Work had stopped at sunset, and now above Judas rolled the thunderous singing of choirs of nightingales.

Judas's goal was at hand. He knew that very soon in the darkness on the right he would begin to hear the quiet whispering of the water falling in the grotto. And so it was, he did hear it. It was becoming ever cooler.

Then he slackened his pace and cried softly:

"Niza!"

But instead of Niza, separating itself from the thick trunk of an olive tree, a thickset male figure jumped out onto the road, and in his hand there was a flash of something that was immediately extinguished. With a weak cry, Judas rushed back, but a second man blocked his path.

The first man, the one who was ahead of him, asked Judas:

"How much have you just been given? Speak, if you want to preserve your life!"

Hope blazed up in Judas's heart, and he exclaimed desperately:

"Thirty tetradrachms! Thirty tetradrachms! I have all I was given with me. Here's the money! Take it, but give me back my life!"

The man who was ahead instantly snatched the purse out of Judas's hands. And at the same moment a knife flew up behind Judas's back and struck the infatuated man like lightning beneath the shoulder blade. Judas was flung forwards, and he threw his hands with their bent fingers out into the air. The man ahead caught Judas on his own knife and plunged it up to the hilt into Judas's heart.

"Ni... za..." said Judas, not in his own high and clear young voice, but in a voice low and reproachful, and he did not emit a single sound more. His body struck the ground so hard that the ground started buzzing.

Then a third figure appeared on the road. This third man wore a hooded cloak.

"Don't linger," he ordered. The murderers quickly packed the purse together with a note, handed them by the third man, into a piece of leather, and criss-crossed it with string. The second man stuck the package in his bosom, and then both murderers hurried off the road in different directions, and the darkness ate them up between the olive trees. But the third man squatted down beside the murdered man and gazed into his face. To the man looking it appeared white as chalk in the shade, and somehow spiritually beautiful.

A few seconds later there was no living person on the road. The lifeless body lay with outstretched arms. The left foot had fallen into a patch of moonlight so that every strap of the sandal was distinctly visible. At this time the entire Garden of Gethsemane thundered with the singing of nightingales. No one knows where the two men who had murdered Judas made for, but the route of the third man in the hood is known. Leaving the path, he headed into a thicket of olive trees, making his way south. He climbed over the garden wall at a distance from the main gates, in its southern corner, where the topmost stones had fallen out of the stonework. Soon he was on the bank of the Kidron. Then he entered the water and made his way through the water for some time, until he saw in the distance the silhouettes of two horses and a man beside them. The horses were also standing in the stream. The water gushed as it washed round their hoofs. The horse-holder mounted one of the horses, the hooded man leapt up onto the other, and they both set off slowly in the stream, and the stones could be heard crunching under the horses' hoofs. Then the horsemen rode out of the water, made their way out onto the Yershalaim bank and set off at a walk beneath the city wall. At this point the horse-holder broke away, galloped on ahead and disappeared from view, while the hooded man stopped his horse, dismounted from it on the deserted road, took off his cloak, turned it inside out, took out from under the cloak a flat helmet without plumage and put it on. Now there leapt up onto the horse a man in a military chlamys and with a short sword at his hip. He touched the reins and the fiery horse set off at a trot, shaking the rider about. The journey was not a long one – the horseman was approaching Yershalaim's southern gate.

Under the archway of the gate the restless flames of torches danced and leapt. The soldiers on watch from the Lightning Legion's second century were sitting on stone benches playing dice. On seeing the military man riding in, the soldiers leapt up from their seats; he waved to them and entered the city.

The city was flooded with festive lights. The flames of lamps were playing in all the windows, and doxologies rang out from everywhere, merging into a discordant choir. Glancing occasionally into windows that looked out into the street, the horseman could see people at festive tables, on which there lay kid's meat and where goblets of wine stood between dishes of bitter herbs. Whistling some quiet little song, the horseman made his way at an unhurried trot along the deserted streets of the Lower Town, heading for the Tower of Antonia, casting occasional glances at the five-branched candlesticks, never seen anywhere before in the world, that burned above the Temple – or at the moon, which hung even higher than the five-branched candlesticks.

The palace of Herod the Great took no part at all in the celebration of the Passover night. In the south-facing ancillary chambers of the palace, where the officers of the Roman Cohort and the Legate of the Legion were accommodated, lights were shining, and there was a sense of some sort of movement and life there. But the front, the official part – where the single and unwilling resident of the palace, the Procurator, was – seemed in its entirety, with its colonnades and golden statues, to have gone blind beneath the brightest of moons. Here, inside the palace, gloom and silence held sway. And the Procurator, just as he had said to Afranius, had had no desire to go inside. He had ordered a bed to be prepared on the balcony, in the same place where he had eaten dinner and had that morning conducted the interrogation. The Procurator had lain down on the couch that had been prepared, but sleep had had no desire to come to him. The bared moon hung high in the clear sky, and the Procurator did not take his eyes off it over the course of several hours.

At about midnight sleep finally took pity on the Hegemon. With a convulsive yawn, the Procurator undid and threw off his cloak, took off the belt that engirdled his shirt with a broad steel knife in a sheath, put it in the armchair by the couch, took off his sandals and stretched out. Banga immediately got up onto his bed and lay down beside him, head to head, and, putting his hand on the dog's neck, the Procurator finally closed his eyes. Only then did the dog fall asleep too.

The couch was in semi-darkness, hidden from the moon by a column, but from the steps of the porch to the bed stretched a ribbon of moonlight. And as soon as the Procurator lost connection with what was around him in reality, he immediately moved off along the shining path and went up it straight towards the moon. He even burst out laughing in happiness in his sleep, so splendid and unique had everything turned out on the transparent blue path. He walked, accompanied by Banga, and next to him walked the vagrant philosopher. They argued about something very complex and important, and neither one of them could defeat the other. They did not agree with one another about anything, and because of that their argument was particularly interesting and interminable. It goes without saying that the execution that day proved to be the most complete misunderstanding – after all, the philosopher who had thought up such an incredibly absurd thing as the idea that all people were good was here, walking along next to him, therefore he was alive. And, of course, it would be absolutely awful even to think that such a man could be executed. There had been no execution!

None! And that was the delightful thing about that journey up the stairway of the moon.

There was as much free time as was necessary, and the storm would come only towards evening, and cowardice was undoubtedly one of the most terrible vices. So said Yeshua Ha-Nozri. No, philosopher, I disagree with you: it is *the* most terrible vice!

So, for example, the present Procurator of Judaea, the former tribune of a legion, had not been a coward then, had he, in the Valley of the Virgins, when the frenzied Teutons had almost torn Rat-catcher the Giant to pieces. But forgive me, philosopher! Surely you, with your intelligence, can't concede the notion that, because of a man who has committed a crime against Caesar, the Procurator of Judaea would ruin his career?

"Yes, yes," Pilate moaned and sobbed in his sleep.

Of course he would ruin it. That morning he would not yet have ruined it, but now, in the night, after weighing everything up, he was prepared to ruin it. He would do anything to save from execution the mad dreamer and doctor who was guilty of absolutely nothing.

"We shall always be together now," he was told in his sleep by the ragged vagrant philosopher who had crossed the path, who knows how, of the horseman with the golden lance. "If there is one – then that means the other is there too. If I am remembered – you too will be remembered straight away! I, a foundling, the son of unknown parents, and you, the son of the astrologer-king and the miller's daughter, the beautiful Pila."*

"Yes, don't you forget, you remember me, the astrologer's son, in your prayers," Pilate requested in his sleep. And, securing a nod from the beggar from En-Sarid walking next to him in his sleep, the cruel Procurator of Judaea cried and laughed with joy in his sleep.

All this was good, but all the more terrible was the Hegemon's awakening. Banga started growling at the moon, and the blue path ahead of the Procurator, slippery, as though smeared with oil, vanished. He opened his eyes, and the first thing he remembered was that the execution had taken place. The first thing the Procurator did was to catch hold of Banga's collar with a customary gesture, then with painful eyes he began searching for the moon and saw it had moved a little to one side and become silvery. Its light was interrupted by an unpleasant, restless light playing on the balcony right before his eyes.

A torch was glowing and smoking in the hands of the centurion Rat-catcher. The man holding it was looking askance in terror and with malice at the dangerous beast which had readied itself to pounce.

"Let him be, Banga," said the Procurator in a sick voice, and coughed. Shielding himself from the flame with his hand, he continued: "Even at night, even in the moonlight I have no peace. O gods! You have a bad job too, Marcus. You maim soldiers…"

Marcus gazed at the Procurator in the greatest astonishment and the latter came to his senses. To gloss over the uncalled-for words, uttered while only half awake, the Procurator said:

"Don't take offence, Centurion. My position, I repeat, is even worse. What do you want?"

"The Chief of the Secret Guard is here to see you," Marcus calmly informed him.

"Call him in, call him in," the Procurator ordered, clearing his throat with a cough, and started feeling for his sandals with his bare feet. The flame began playing on the columns and the centurion's *caligae* began tapping across the mosaic. The centurion went out into the garden.

"Even in the moonlight I have no peace," the Procurator said to himself, grinding his teeth.

On the balcony in the centurion's place there appeared a hooded man.

"Banga, let him be," the Procurator said quietly, and squeezed the top of the dog's head.

Before starting to speak, Afranius, as was his custom, looked around and moved away into the shadows, and, satisfying himself that, apart from Banga, there was no one else on the balcony, said quietly:

"Please put me on trial, Procurator. You have proved right. I was unable to keep Judas from Kiriath safe, he's been murdered. I request a trial and dismissal."

It seemed to Afranius that four eyes were gazing at him – a dog's and a wolf's.

Afranius took out from beneath his chlamys a purse stiffened with blood and sealed with two seals.

"This bag of money was thrown by the murderers into the High Priest's house. The blood on this bag is the blood of Judas from Kiriath."

"How much is in there, I wonder?" Pilate asked, leaning towards the bag.

327

"Thirty tetradrachms."

The Procurator grinned and said:

"Not a lot."

Afranius was silent.

"Where is the dead man?"

"That I don't know," the man who was never parted from his hood replied with calm dignity, "we'll begin the search in the morning."

The Procurator gave a start and dropped the strap of his sandal, which would not do up for anything.

"But you know for sure he's dead?"

To this the Procurator got a dry response:

"Procurator, I've been working in Judaea for fifteen years. I began my service in Valerius Gratus's time.* It's not essential for me to see a corpse to say that a man is dead, and I'm reporting to you now that the man they called Judas from the town of Kiriath was murdered several hours ago."

"Forgive me, Afranius," replied Pilate, "I've not woken up properly yet, and that's why I said that. I sleep badly," the Procurator grinned, "and I dream about a moonbeam all the time. It's so ridiculous, imagine it. As if I'm going for a walk along this beam. So, I'd like to know your intentions in this matter. Where do you mean to look for him? Sit down, Chief of the Secret Service."

Afranius bowed, moved an armchair up a little closer to the bed and sat down, making a clatter with his sword.

"I mean to look for him not far from the olive press in the Garden of Gethsemane."

"I see, I see. And why there exactly?"

"As I understand it, Hegemon, Judas was killed not in Yershalaim itself and not somewhere far away from it. He was killed in the vicinity of Yershalaim."

"I consider you an outstanding expert in your field. Well, I don't know how things are in Rome, but in the colonies you have no equal. Explain why?"

"Under no circumstances can I accept the idea," said Afranius softly, "that Judas let himself be caught by some suspicious people or other within the boundaries of the city. You can't kill secretly in the street. So he had to be lured into a cellar somewhere. But the service was already looking for him in the Lower Town and would undoubtedly have found him. But he isn't in the city, I guarantee you that. If he'd been killed far from the city, this package of money couldn't have been dropped off so quickly. He was killed close by the city. They managed to lure him out of the city."

"I cannot comprehend how it could have been done."

"Yes, Procurator, that is the most difficult question in the whole business, and I don't even know whether I shall succeed in solving it."

"It really is mysterious! On the evening of the feast a believer goes off out of town, no one knows why, abandoning the Passover meal, and there he perishes. Who could have lured him out, and with what? Was it a woman that did it?" the Procurator suddenly asked, inspired.

Afranius replied calmly and weightily:

"Under no circumstances, Procurator. That possibility is completely ruled out. Logical reasoning is required. Who had an interest in Judas's death? Vagrant visionaries of some sort, some sort of circle in which, above all, there were no women. To marry, Procurator, money is necessary, to bring a person into the world it's needed too, but to murder a man with the help of a woman, a very large sum of money is needed, and no vagrants have that. There was no woman in this business, Procurator. I'll say more, such an interpretation of the murder can only throw us off the scent, hinder the investigation and get me confused."

"I can see that you're absolutely right, Afranius," said Pilate, "and I only permitted myself to make a suggestion."

"Alas, it's a mistaken one, Procurator."

"But what, what then?" exclaimed the Procurator, peering into Afranius's face with greedy curiosity.

"I presume it's that same thing, money, again."

"A remarkable idea! But who could have offered him money at night, outside of town, and for what?"

"Oh no, Procurator, it's not like that. I have a single supposition, and if it's wrong, I may not find any other explanations." Afranius leant a little closer to the Procurator and finished what he was saying in a whisper: "Judas wanted to hide his money in a secluded place known only to him."

"A very subtle explanation. And that's evidently how the matter stood. Now I understand you: he was lured out not by other people, but by his own thinking. Yes, yes, that's it."

"Right. Judas was mistrustful. He was hiding the money from people."

"Yes, you said, in Gethsemane. But then why you intend looking for him specifically there – that, I confess, I don't understand."

"Oh, Procurator, that's simplest of all. Nobody is going to hide money on the roads, in open and empty places. Judas was neither on the road to Hebron, nor on the road to Bethany. He needed to be in a sheltered, secluded place with trees. It's that simple. And there are no other such places in the vicinity of Yershalaim, apart from Gethsemane. He couldn't have gone far."

"You've completely convinced me. So, what's to be done now?"

"I shall immediately start looking for the murderers who tracked Judas down outside the city, and in the meantime, as I've already told you, I shall myself go on trial."

"Why?"

"My guards lost him at the bazaar in the evening, after he'd left Caipha's palace. How it occurred, I don't understand. This has never happened in my life before. He was put under observation straight after our conversation. But in the bazaar district he slipped off somewhere and made such a strange loop that he escaped without trace."

"Right. I declare to you that I do not consider it necessary to make you stand trial. You did everything you could, and nobody in the world," here the Procurator smiled, "could have managed to do more than you! Punish the agents who lost Judas. But even then, I warn you, I wouldn't want the punishment to be even in the slightest severe. In the end, we did everything to look after this villain! Yes, I forgot to ask," the Procurator wiped his brow, "how ever did they contrive to drop the money off at Caipha's?"

"You see, Procurator... It's not particularly complicated. The avengers passed by the rear of Caipha's palace where the lane lies above the rear courtyard. They threw the package over the wall."

"With a note?"

"Yes, exactly as you supposed, Procurator. Yes, anyway." At this point Afranius broke the seal off the package and showed its interior to Pilate.

"Please, what are you doing, Afranius, those seals are presumably from the Temple, after all!"

"It's not worth the Procurator worrying himself over that question," replied Afranius, closing the package.

"Surely you don't have every seal, do you?" asked Pilate, laughing.

"It cannot be otherwise, Procurator," replied Afranius very severely, without any laughter.

"I can imagine what it was like at Caipha's!"

"Yes, Procurator, it caused very great agitation. I was asked to come immediately."

Even in the semi-darkness Pilate's eyes could be seen flashing.

"That's interesting, interesting..."

"I beg to differ, Procurator, it wasn't interesting. A most dull and exhausting business. At my question as to whether any money had been paid out to anyone in Caipha's palace, I was told categorically that no such thing had happened."

"Oh really? Well, if none was paid out, then none was paid out. The harder it will be to find the murderers."

"Perfectly correct, Procurator."

"Yes, Afranius, here's what's suddenly occurred to me: did he not commit suicide?"

"Oh no, Procurator," Afranius replied, even leaning back in his arm-chair in surprise, "forgive me, but that's utterly improbable!"

"Hah, in this city, anything's probable! I'm prepared to bet that in the shortest time rumours of it will spread throughout the entire city."

At this point Afranius cast his look at the Procurator, had a think and replied:

"It's possible, Procurator."

The Procurator was apparently still unable to drop this question of the murder of the man from Kiriath, although absolutely everything was clear as it was, and, even with a certain dreaminess, he said:

"I'd have liked to see how they killed him, though."

"He was killed with extreme artistry, Procurator," Afranius replied, giving the Procurator some rather ironic looks.

"And how on earth do you know that?"

"Be so kind as to pay attention to the bag," replied Afranius, "I can guarantee you that Judas's blood gushed out like a wave. I've seen some dead men in my time, Procurator!"

"So he won't be rising again, of course?"

"Yes, Procurator, he will be rising again," Afranius replied with a philosophical smile, "when the trumpet of the Messiah that they're expecting here resounds above him. But he won't rise again any earlier."

331

"Enough, Afranius! That question is clear. Let's move on to the burial."

"The executed men have been buried, Procurator."

"Oh, Afranius, putting you on trial would be a crime. You are worthy of the highest reward. How was it?"

Afranius began telling him, and told how at the time when he was himself busy with the matter of Judas, a team of the Secret Guard, led by his deputy, had reached the hill when evening had set in. It had failed to find one of the bodies on the summit. Pilate gave a start and said hoarsely:

"Oh, how on earth did I fail to foresee this!"

"It's not worth worrying, Procurator," said Afranius, and continued his narrative.

They had picked up the bodies of Dismas and Gestas, with their eyes pecked out by predatory birds, and immediately thrown themselves into searching for the third body. It had been found in a very short time. A certain person...

"Levi Matthew," said Pilate, not so much enquiringly as affirmatively.

"Yes, Procurator..."

Levi Matthew had been hiding in a cave on the northern slope of Bald Skull, waiting for darkness. The naked body of Yeshua Ha-Nozri had been with him. When the guard had entered the cave with a torch, Levi had fallen into despair and rage. He had shouted that he had committed no crime and that, by law, any man had the right to bury an executed criminal if he wanted. Levi Matthew had said that he did not wish to part with this body. He had been excited, shouting out something incoherent, at times begging, at times threatening and cursing...

"Did he have to be arrested?" asked Pilate gloomily.

"No, Procurator, no," replied Afranius very reassuringly, "it proved possible to calm the audacious madman by explaining that the body was to be buried."

When he had grasped what had been said, Levi had quietened down, but had announced that he was going nowhere and wanted to participate in the burial. He had said he would not go away, even if they set out to kill him, and he had even offered a bread knife which he had had with him for that purpose.

"Was he driven off?" asked Pilate in a crushed voice.

"No, Procurator, no. My deputy allowed him to participate in the burial."

"Which of your deputies was in charge of this?" asked Pilate.

"Tolmai," replied Afranius, and added in alarm: "Perhaps he made an error?"

"Continue," replied Pilate, "there was no error. All in all, I'm beginning to get a little flustered, Afranius, I'm evidently dealing with a man who never makes any errors. That man is you."

Levi Matthew had been taken in the cart together with the bodies of the executed men, and a couple of hours later they had reached a deserted ravine to the north of Yershalaim. There, working in shifts, the team had in the course of an hour dug out a deep pit and in it buried all three executed men.

"Naked?"

"No, Procurator – the team had taken tunics with them for the purpose. Rings were put on the fingers of the buried men. Yeshua's with one cut in it, Dismas's with two and Gestas's with three. The pit was filled up and covered over with stones. The landmark is known to Tolmai."

"Oh, if only I could have foreseen it!" began Pilate, frowning. "I ought to see this Levi Matthew, you know…"

"He's here, Procurator."

Opening his eyes wide, Pilate gazed at Afranius for some time and then said this:

"I'm grateful to you for everything that's been done in connection with this matter. Tomorrow please send Tolmai to me, tell him in advance that I'm pleased with him, and you, Afranius," here the Procurator took a ring out of the pocket of a belt that was lying on the table and handed it to the Chief of the Secret Service, "please accept this as a memento."

Afranius bowed and said:

"It's a great honour, Procurator."

"Please give rewards to the team that carried out the burial. To the agents who lost Judas, a reprimand. And Levi Matthew to me at once. I need details on the case of Yeshua."

"Very well, Procurator," Afranius responded, and started to retreat, bowing, while the Procurator clapped his hands and shouted:

"Come here to me! A lamp to the colonnade!"

333

Afranius was already moving away into the garden, and behind Pilate's back, lights could already be glimpsed in the hands of the servants. Three lamps appeared on the table in front of the Procurator, and the moonlit night immediately retreated into the garden, as though Afranius had taken it away with him. In place of Afranius, onto the balcony alongside the giant centurion stepped an unknown man, small and skinny. The former, catching the Procurator's glance, immediately retreated into the garden and disappeared.

The Procurator studied the new arrival with greedy and slightly frightened eyes. People look that way at someone of whom they have heard a lot, of whom they have themselves been thinking and who has finally appeared.

The new arrival, getting on for forty, was black, ragged and covered in dried mud, and looked from under his brows, like a wolf. In short, he was very unsightly, and most likely resembled a city beggar, many of whom knock about on the terraces of the Temple or in the bazaars of the noisy and dirty Lower Town.

The silence lasted a long time, and it was broken by the strange behaviour of the man brought before Pilate. He changed countenance, swayed, and, had he not grabbed the edge of the table with a dirty hand, would have fallen.

"What's wrong with you?" Pilate asked him.

"Nothing," Levi Matthew replied, and made a movement as if he had swallowed something. His skinny, bare, dirty neck swelled out, then subsided again.

"What's wrong with you – answer," Pilate repeated.

"I'm tired," Levi replied, and looked gloomily at the floor.

"Sit down," Pilate said, and indicated an armchair.

Levi looked at the Procurator mistrustfully, moved towards the armchair, looked askance in fright at the gold arms, and sat down not in the armchair, but alongside it on the floor.

"Explain, why didn't you sit down in the armchair?" asked Pilate.

"I'm dirty, I'll soil it," said Levi, looking at the ground.

"You'll be given something to eat in a moment."

"I don't want to eat," replied Levi.

"Why ever lie?" asked Pilate quietly. "After all, you haven't eaten all day, or perhaps even longer. Well, all right, don't eat. I summoned you for you to show me the knife you had."

"The soldiers took it away from me when they were bringing me in here," Levi replied, and added gloomily: "You give it back to me, I need to return it to the owner, I stole it."

"Why?"

"To cut the ropes," replied Levi.

"Marcus!" cried the Procurator, and the centurion stepped in beneath the columns. "Give his knife to me."

The centurion took the dirty bread knife out of one of the two cases on his belt, handed it to the Procurator, and himself withdrew.

"And who did you take the knife from?"

"The bread shop by the Hebron Gate, immediately on the left as you enter the city."

Pilate looked at the broad blade, for some reason tried it with his finger to see if the knife was sharp, and said:

"As regards the knife, don't worry, the knife will be returned to the shop. But now I need something else: show me the charter you carry about with you where Yeshua's words are written down."

Levi looked at Pilate with hatred and smiled such an unkind smile that his face was completely disfigured.

"You want to take away everything? The last thing I have as well?" he asked.

"I didn't say 'Hand it over'," replied Pilate, "I said 'Show me'."

Levi rummaged around in his bosom and took out a roll of parchment. Pilate took it, opened it out, spread it out between the lights and, squinting, began studying the barely decipherable ink marks. It was hard to understand these uneven lines, and Pilate frowned and bent right down to the parchment with his finger tracing the lines. Nonetheless, he managed to make out that what was written represented an incoherent series of sayings, dates of some sort, housekeeping notes and fragments of poetry. Pilate read some of it: "There is no death... Yesterday we ate the sweet young figs of spring..."

Grimacing from the strain, Pilate screwed his eyes up and read:

"We shall see the pure river of the water of life... Mankind will look at the sun through transparent crystal..."*

At this point Pilate gave a start. In the last lines of the parchment he made out the words: "greater vice... cowardice".

Pilate rolled the parchment up and with an abrupt movement handed it to Levi.

335

"Take it," he said and, after a short silence, added: "You're a man of books, so far as I can see, and there's no reason for you to go around alone in the clothes of a beggar with no shelter. I have a big library in Caesarea, I'm very rich, and I want to take you into my service. You'll sort out and look after the papyruses, you'll be fed and clothed."

Levi stood up and replied:

"No, I don't want to."

"Why not?" the Procurator asked, his face darkening. "Do you find me unpleasant, are you afraid of me?"

That same nasty smile distorted Levi's face, and he said:

"No, because you'll be afraid of me. You won't find it particularly easy to look me in the face after having killed him."

"Silence," replied Pilate, "take some money."

Levi shook his head in refusal, but the Procurator continued:

"I know you consider yourself Yeshua's disciple, but I can tell you that you've mastered nothing of what he taught you. For if that were the case, you'd be sure to take something from me. Bear in mind that before he died, he said he blamed no one," Pilate raised a finger meaningfully, and Pilate's face was twitching. "And he himself would have taken something without fail. You're cruel, but he wasn't cruel. Where will you go?"

Levi suddenly approached the table, leant both hands upon it and, looking at the Procurator with burning eyes, began whispering to him:

"Know, Hegemon, that I shall murder a certain person in Yershalaim. I want to tell you this so you know there'll be some more blood."

"I know too that there'll be some more of it," replied Pilate, "you haven't surprised me with your words. You want to murder me, of course?"

"I'll have no success in murdering you," Levi replied, baring his teeth in a smile, "I'm not such a stupid man as to count on that, but I shall murder Judas from Kiriath, I shall devote the rest of my life to it."

At this point delight was expressed in the Procurator's eyes, and, beckoning Levi Matthew closer to him with his finger, he said:

"You'll have no success in doing that, don't you trouble yourself. Judas has already been murdered tonight."

Levi jumped back from the table, gazing around wildly, and cried out:

"Who did it?"

"Don't be jealous," Pilate replied with a grin, and rubbed his hands, "I'm afraid he had other admirers besides you."

"Who did it?" Levi repeated in a whisper.

Pilate answered him:

"I did it."

Levi opened his mouth and stared at the Procurator, but the latter said quietly:

"What's been done isn't very much, of course, but all the same, I did it." And he added: "Well, now will you take something?"

Levi had a think, softened, and finally said:

"Give orders for me to be given a piece of clean parchment."

An hour passed. Levi was gone from the palace. Now the silence of dawn was broken only by the quiet noise of the sentries' footsteps in the garden. The moon was rapidly fading, and at the other edge of the sky the little whitish spot of the morning star could be seen. The lamps had gone out ages ago. On the couch lay the Procurator. With his hand under his cheek he was sleeping and breathing soundlessly. Alongside him slept Banga.

Thus the fifth Procurator of Judaea, Pontius Pilate, greeted the dawn of the fifteenth of Nisan.

27

The End of Apartment No. 50

WHEN MARGARITA REACHED THE LAST WORDS of the chapter "... thus the fifth Procurator of Judaea, Pontius Pilate, greeted the dawn of the fifteenth of Nisan", morning had arrived.

Sparrows could be heard conducting a cheerful, excited morning conversation in the branches of the white willow and lime in the little yard.

Margarita rose from the armchair, stretched, and only now did she sense how battered her body was and how she wanted to sleep. It is interesting to note that Margarita's soul was in perfect order. Her thoughts were not in disarray, she was not at all shaken by the fact that she had spent the night supernaturally. She was not disturbed by memories of having been at Satan's ball, of the Master having by some miracle been returned to her, of the novel having risen from the ashes, of everything having proved to be in its place again in the basement in the lane, whence the informer Aloizy Mogarych had been expelled. In short, her acquaintance with Woland had not caused her any psychological damage at all. Everything was as if that was the way it should be.

She went into the next room, checked that the Master was sleeping soundly and peacefully, turned off the unnecessary table lamp, and herself stretched out beneath the opposite wall on the little divan, covered with an old, torn sheet. A minute later she was asleep, and that morning she had no dreams. The rooms in the basement were silent, the whole of the private landlord's little house was silent, and it was quiet in the secluded lane.

But at that time, that is, at dawn on Saturday, in one of Moscow's organizations an entire floor was awake, and its windows – which looked out onto a large asphalt-covered square* that special vehicles were cleaning with brushes, driving around slowly and hooting – had all their lights shining, and they cut through the light of the rising sun.

The whole floor was busy with the investigation into the case of Woland, and the lamps had been burning all night in ten offices.

As a matter of fact, the case had been clear ever since the previous day, Friday, when The Variety had had to be closed owing to the disappearance of its administrative staff and the various outrages that had occurred the evening before during the renowned black magic show. But the fact is that, all the time and uninterrupted, ever more new material was coming through to the sleepless floor.

Now the team investigating this strange case that smacked of utterly blatant devilry, with an admixture, what's more, of some sort of hypnotic trickery and utterly clear-cut criminality, was required to mould together all the many-sided and confused events that had taken place in various parts of Moscow into a single lump.

The first person who was obliged to visit the sleepless floor, shining with electricity, was Arkady Apollonovich Sempleyarov, the Chairman of the Acoustics Commission.

After lunch on Friday a ringing had resounded in his apartment, located in the building by the Kamenny Bridge, and a man's voice had asked to speak to Arkady Apollonovich. Arkady Apollonovich's spouse, who had gone to the telephone, replied gloomily that Arkady Apollonovich was unwell, had lain down for a sleep and could not come to the telephone. However, Arkady Apollonovich had to come to the telephone all the same. To the question of who was asking for Arkady Apollonovich, the voice in the telephone replied very briefly who it was.

"This second... right away... this minute..." babbled the usually very haughty spouse of the Chairman of the Acoustics Commission, and like an arrow she flew into the bedroom to get Arkady Apollonovich up from the couch on which he was lying, going through hellish torment at the memory of the previous evening's show and the nocturnal row which had accompanied the expulsion of his niece, the one from Saratov, from the apartment.

True, it was not a second later, yet it was not even a minute, but rather a quarter of a minute later that Arkady Apollonovich, wearing only one slipper on his left foot, and in only his underwear, was already at the telephone, babbling into it:

"Yes, it's me... Very well, very well..."

His spouse, who for these moments had forgotten all the loathsome crimes against fidelity of which the unfortunate Arkady Apollonovich had been found guilty, was leaning out through the door into the corridor with a frightened face, jabbing a slipper in the air and whispering:

"Put the slipper on, the slipper... You'll get a chill in your feet," at which Arkady Apollonovich, waving his wife away with his bare foot and making bestial eyes at her, mumbled into the telephone:

"Yes, yes, yes, of course, I understand... I'm setting out right away..."

Arkady Apollonovich spent the whole evening on that same floor where the investigation was being conducted. The conversation was painful, most unpleasant was the conversation, for he was obliged to tell with the most complete frankness not only about that foul show and the fight in the box, but while he was about it, as really was essential, about both Militsa Andreyevna Pokobatko from Yelokhovskaya Street, and about his niece from Saratov, and about much else, the telling of which caused Arkady Apollonovich inexpressible torment.

It goes without saying that the testimony of Arkady Apollonovich, an intellectual and cultured man who had been a witness of the disgraceful show, a sensible and qualified witness who gave an excellent description of both the mysterious magician in the mask himself, and his two villainous assistants, who had an excellent recollection that the magician's name was definitely Woland, moved the investigation forward significantly. And a comparison of Arkady Apollonovich's testimony with the testimony of others – among whom were several ladies who had suffered after the show (the one in the violet underwear who had shocked Rimsky and, alas, many others) and the messenger, Karpov, who had been sent to apartment No. 50 on Sadovaya Street – to all intents and purposes immediately established the place where the culprit in all these adventures needed to be sought.

Apartment No. 50 was visited, and more than once, and not only was it examined extremely thoroughly, but its walls were tapped over, the fireplace flues were examined and hiding places were sought. However, all these measures produced no result, and on not a single one of the visits to the apartment was it possible to discover anyone in it, although it was perfectly clear that someone had been in the apartment, despite the fact that all the people who were required one way or another to be in charge of questions concerning foreign artistes arriving in Moscow asserted decisively and categorically that there was no black magician Woland in Moscow and neither could there be.

He had registered absolutely nowhere on arrival, had not presented his passport, nor any other documents, contracts or agreements to anyone, and nobody had heard anything about him! The head of the Programming Department of the Spectacles Commission, Kitaitsev, vowed and swore that the vanished Styopa Likhodeyev had not sent to him for approval any performance schedule for any Woland and had not telephoned Kitaitsev with anything about the arrival of this Woland. So that for him, Kitaitsev, it was completely incomprehensible and unknown how Styopa could have permitted such a show at The Variety. And when it was said that Arkady Apollonovich had seen this magician in the show with his own eyes, Kitaitsev only spread his hands and raised his eyes to the sky. And from Kitaitsev's eyes alone it could be seen and boldly stated that he was as pure as crystal.

That Prokhor Petrovich, the Chairman of the Main Spectacles Commission... Incidentally: he returned to his suit immediately after the police entered his office, to the frenzied joy of Anna Richardovna and to the great bewilderment of the police who had been disturbed without reason. Incidentally too: returning to his place, to his grey, striped suit, Prokhor Petrovich gave his full approval to all the resolutions that the suit had appended during his brief absence.

...So then, that Prokhor Petrovich most definitely did not know anything about any Woland.

What was emerging was, say what you like, something unfathomable: thousands of theatre-goers, the entire staff of The Variety and, finally, Arkady Apollonovich Sempleyarov, a most highly educated man, had seen this magician, as well as his accursed assistants, yet at the same time there was no possibility of finding him anywhere. Well, allow me to ask you: had the earth swallowed him up, or something, immediately after his repulsive show, or, as some assert, had he not come to Moscow at all? But if the first view is accepted, there can be no doubt that, when being swallowed up, he took with him the entire top level of The Variety's administration; and if the second, then does it not emerge that the administration of the ill-starred theatre itself, having played some sort of dirty trick beforehand (you only have to remember the broken window in the office and the behaviour of Ace of Diamonds!), had disappeared from Moscow without trace?

You have to give credit to the man who was heading the investigation. Rimsky had disappeared and was found with astonishing speed. He only had to set the behaviour of Ace of Diamonds at the taxi rank beside the cinematograph alongside certain time points, such as when the show had ended and when precisely Rimsky could have disappeared, to send a telegram at once to Leningrad. An hour later the reply came (towards Friday evening) that Rimsky had been found in room No. 412 in the Astoria Hotel, on the third floor, next to the room where the man in charge of the repertoire of one of Moscow's theatres, on tour at the time in Leningrad, was staying, in the very room where, as is well known, there is grey-blue and gold furniture and a splendid bathroom.

Discovered hiding in the wardrobe of room No. 412 of the Astoria, Rimsky was immediately arrested and interrogated in that same Leningrad, after which a telegram arrived in Moscow notifying that the Financial Director of The Variety was not in a responsible state, that he was not giving sensible answers to questions, or did not wish to give them, and was requesting just one thing, that he be hidden away in a reinforced cell and have an armed guard set on him. From Moscow the order was given by telegram to deliver Rimsky under guard to Moscow, in consequence of which on Friday evening Rimsky duly left with the evening train under such a guard.

Towards the Friday evening Likhodeyev's trail was found too. Telegrams with enquiries about Likhodeyev were sent out to every town, and from Yalta a reply was received that Likhodeyev had been in Yalta but had flown out by aeroplane for Moscow.

The only person's trail that could not be picked up was Varenukha's trail. The renowned theatre manager, known to absolutely all of Moscow, had disappeared without trace.

Meanwhile it was necessary to spend time on events in other parts of Moscow too, beyond The Variety Theatre. It was necessary to clear up the extraordinary occurrence with the office workers singing 'The Glorious Sea' (incidentally: Professor Stravinsky managed to set them to rights in the course of two hours by means of subcutaneous injections of some sort), with persons who had been presenting the devil knows what to other persons or organizations in the guise of money, and also with persons who had suffered from such presentations.

As is perfectly understandable, the most unpleasant, the most scandalous and insoluble of all these incidents was the incident of the theft of the deceased writer Berlioz's head directly from the coffin in the Griboyedov hall, carried out in broad daylight.

Twelve men were conducting the investigation, gathering up, as though onto a knitting needle, the accursed stitches of this complicated case, which were scattered all over Moscow.

One of the investigators arrived at Professor Stravinsky's clinic and first and foremost asked for a list to be presented to him of the persons who had entered the clinic in the course of the last three days. Discovered in this way were Nikanor Ivanovich Bosoi and the unfortunate compère whose head had been torn off. Little attention was paid to them, however. It was already easy to establish now that these two were victims of one and the same gang, headed by this mysterious magician. But then Ivan Nikolayevich Bezdomny interested the investigator greatly.

Towards evening on Friday the door of Ivanushka's room, No. 117, opened, and into the room walked a young, round-faced, calm and softly spoken man, not at all like an investigator, but nonetheless one of Moscow's best investigators. Lying on the bed he saw a pale and pinched-looking young man with eyes in which could be read an absence of interest in what was happening around him, with eyes that were turned at times to some place in the distance above his surroundings, at times inwards, into the young man himself.

The investigator introduced himself amicably and said he had dropped in on Ivan Nikolayevich to have a little chat about the events of two days before at Patriarch's Ponds.

Oh, how exultant Ivan would have been if the investigator had come to see him a little earlier, if only, shall we say, in the night-time early on Thursday, when Ivan had been violently and passionately trying to get people to listen to his story about Patriarch's Ponds. Now his dream of helping to catch the consultant had been realized, no longer did he need to run around chasing anyone, they had come to him himself with the specific aim of listening to his tale about what had happened on Wednesday evening.

But, alas, Ivanushka had changed completely in the time that had passed since the moment of Berlioz's death. He was prepared to answer all the investigator's questions willingly and politely, but indifference could be sensed both in Ivan's gaze and in his intonations. The poet was no longer concerned by the fate of Berlioz.

Before the investigator's arrival Ivanushka had been lying drowsing, and certain visions had passed before him. Thus he had seen a city, strange, incomprehensible, nonexistent, with blocks of marble, chiselled colonnades, with roofs gleaming in the sun, with the black, gloomy and pitiless Tower of Antonia, with a palace on the western hill sunk almost to its roofs into the tropical greenery of its garden, with bronze statues burning in the sunset above that greenery, and he had seen Roman centuries, bound in armour, walking beneath the walls of the ancient city.

Before Ivan in his drowsiness there appeared a man, motionless in his armchair, shaved, with a harassed, yellow face, a man in a white mantle with a red lining, gazing with hatred at the luxuriant and alien garden. Ivan also saw a treeless hill with deserted poles with crosspieces.

But what had happened at Patriarch's Ponds interested the poet Ivan Bezdomny no more.

"Tell me, Ivan Nikolayevich, how far were you yourself from the turnstile when Berlioz fell down under the tram?"

A scarcely noticeable smile of indifference touched Ivan's lips for some reason, and he replied:

343

"I was a long way off."

"And this one in checks was right beside the turnstile?"

"No, he was sitting on a bench not far away."

"Do you remember clearly that he didn't approach the turnstile at the moment when Berlioz fell?"

"I do. He didn't. He sat sprawling."

These questions were the investigator's last questions. After them he stood up, reached out a hand to Ivanushka, wished him a speedy recovery, and expressed the hope that he would be reading his poetry again in the near future.

"No," Ivan replied quietly, "I won't be writing any more poetry."

The investigator smiled politely and permitted himself to express his certainty that the poet was now in a state of some depression, but that it would soon pass.

"No," responded Ivan, looking not at the investigator, but into the distance, at the fading horizon, "it will never pass. The poetry I used to write was bad poetry, and now I've realized it."

The investigator left Ivanushka, having got some very important material. Following the thread of events from the end to the beginning, he had finally succeeded in reaching the source from which all the events had started out. The investigator was in no doubt that these events had started with a murder at Patriarch's. Of course, neither Ivanushka, nor this man in checks had pushed the unfortunate Chairman of MASSOLIT under the tram – physically, so to speak, his fall under the wheels had been facilitated by no one. But the investigator was certain that Berlioz had thrown himself under the tram (or had fallen under it) while under hypnosis.

Yes, there was already a lot of material, and it was already known whom to catch and where. But the thing was that there was no possible way of catching them. Someone, it must be repeated, had doubtless been in the thrice accursed apartment No. 50. At times this apartment had answered telephone calls, now in a jabbering voice, now in a nasal one; sometimes a window had been opened in the apartment; what's more, the sounds of a gramophone had been heard from it. But at the same time, on every occasion when they had made for it, absolutely no one had been found inside it. And they had been there more than once already, and at different times of the day. And moreover, they had gone through the apartment with a net checking every corner. The apartment had already been under suspicion for a long time. Not only had the path that led into the courtyard through the gateway been guarded, but so had the rear entrance; moreover a guard had been set on the roof by the chimneys. Yes, apartment No. 50 had been playing up, but it had not been possible to do anything about it.

Thus had the matter dragged on until midnight between Friday and Saturday, when Baron Maigel, wearing evening dress and patent-leather shoes, had proceeded grandly into apartment No. 50 in the capacity of a guest. The Baron could be heard being let into the apartment. Exactly ten minutes after that, without any bells being rung, a visit was made to the apartment, yet not only were the hosts not found in it, but – and this really was altogether weird – not a trace of Baron Maigel was to be discovered in it either.

And so, as has been said, the matter dragged on in this way until dawn on Saturday. At that point some new and very interesting data was added. At the Moscow aerodrome a six-seater passenger plane that had flown in from the Crimea made its landing. Among other passengers, there alighted from it one strange passenger. He was a young citizen with a wild growth of stubble who had not washed for about three days, with inflamed and frightened eyes, without luggage, and dressed somewhat oddly. The citizen was wearing a Caucasian fur hat, a Caucasian felt cloak on top of a nightshirt, and nice, new, only just purchased, blue leather bedroom slippers. As soon as he moved away from the steps down which they descended from the aircraft cabin, he was approached. This citizen was already awaited, and a little while later the unforgettable Director of The Variety, Stepan Bogdanovich Likhodeyev, appeared before the investigating team. He added some more data. Now it became clear that Woland had penetrated The Variety in the guise of an artiste after hypnotizing Styopa Likhodeyev, and had then contrived to throw that same Styopa God knows how many kilometres out of Moscow. Material was thus added, yet things did not become any easier as a result, but rather became perhaps even a tiny bit more difficult, for it was becoming obvious that mastering the sort of character that performs tricks like the one Stepan Bogdanovich had been the victim of would not be so easy. Likhodeyev, by the way, was confined at his own request in a safe cell, and before the investigating team appeared Varenukha, who had just been arrested in his apartment, to which he had returned after an unexplained absence of a period of almost forty-eight hours.

Despite the promise made to Azazello not to lie any more, it was precisely with a lie that the manager began. Although he should not actually be judged too severely for it. After all, Azazello had forbidden him to lie and be rude on the telephone, and in the given instance the manager was conversing without the assistance of that apparatus. With his eyes shifting back and forth, Ivan Savelyevich declared that on Thursday afternoon, in his office at The Variety, he had got drunk on his own, after which he had gone off somewhere, but where, he didn't remember, somewhere else he had drunk some *starka*,* but where, he didn't remember, he had lain about under a fence somewhere, but where, again he didn't remember. Only after the manager was told that by his stupid and foolhardy behaviour he was hindering the investigation of an important case and that he would, of course, answer for it, did Varenukha break into sobs and start to whisper, in a quavering voice and gazing around, that he was lying solely out of terror, fearing the revenge of Woland's gang, in whose hands he had already spent time, and that he asked, prayed, thirsted to be locked up in a reinforced cell.

"What the devil! They're obsessed with this reinforced cell!" growled one of those conducting the investigation.

"These villains have really scared them," said the investigator who had visited Ivanushka.

They calmed Varenukha as best they could, said they would guard him even without any cell, and now at this point it emerged that he had not drunk any *starka* under any fence, but had been beaten by two of them, one with a fang and red hair, and the other one fat...

"Ah, looking like a cat?"

"Yes, yes, yes," the manager whispered, frozen in terror and looking round every second, and he revealed further details of how he had existed for about two days in apartment No. 50 in the capacity of a vampire-cum-spy, and had almost been the cause of the Financial Director Rimsky's death...

At this time, Rimsky, who had been brought on the train from Leningrad, was being led in. However, this psychologically disturbed, grey-haired old man, shaking with terror, in whom it was very hard to recognize the former Financial Director, did not want to tell the truth for anything and proved very stubborn in this respect. Rimsky asserted that he had seen no Hella at the window in his office during the night, and no Varenukha either, simply he had been taken ill, and in his delirium he had left for Leningrad. It goes without saying that the sick Financial Director ended his testimony with a request for his confinement in a reinforced cell.

Annushka was arrested at the moment when she was making an attempt to pass a ten-dollar bill to a cashier in a department store on the Arbat. Annushka's story of people flying out of a window of the building on Sadovaya and of the horseshoe that Annushka, according to her, had picked up to hand in to the police was heard out attentively.

"Was the horseshoe really made of gold and diamonds?" Annushka was asked.

"Do you think I don't know diamonds?" replied Annushka.

"But did he give you ten-rouble notes, as you say?"

"Do you think I don't know ten-rouble notes?" replied Annushka.

"Well, and when was it they turned into dollars?"

"I don't know anything about any dollars, and I've not seen any dollars," replied Annushka shrilly, "we're within our rights! We were given a reward, we're buying cotton material with it..." and at this point she started spouting drivel about how she didn't answer for the House Committee which had brought unclean spirits in on the fourth floor who made life impossible.

At that point the investigator began waving his pen at Annushka, because everyone was thoroughly sick of her, and he signed a pass out for her on green paper, after which, to general satisfaction, Annushka disappeared from the building.

Then there came a whole series of people, one after another, and among them Nikolai Ivanovich, just arrested solely because of the stupidity of his jealous spouse, who had let the police know towards morning that her husband had disappeared. Nikolai Ivanovich did not much surprise the investigating team when he laid out on the table the joke certificate about his having spent the time at Satan's ball. In his stories of how he had borne Margarita Nikolayevna's bare maid the devil knows how far through the air to bathe in the river, and of the appearance at the window of the naked Margarita Nikolayevna that preceded this, Nikolai Ivanovich departed somewhat from the truth. Thus, for example, he did not consider it necessary to mention the fact that he had gone to the bedroom with the discarded nightshirt in his hands and had called Natasha Venus. The way it was according to him,

Natasha flew out of the window, straddled him and dragged him away out of Moscow...

"Yielding to force, I was compelled to submit," Nikolai Ivanovich recounted, and ended his cock-and-bull story with a request that his wife should not be told a word about it. Which he was indeed promised.

Nikolai Ivanovich's testimony made it possible to establish that Margarita Nikolayevna, as well as her maid Natasha too, had disappeared quite without trace. Measures were taken with a view to finding them.

Thus was the morning of the Saturday marked by the investigation, which did not cease for one second. At this time there arose and spread around in the city completely impossible rumours, in which a tiny grain of truth was embellished with the most extravagant lies. It was said that there had been a show at The Variety, after which the whole audience of two thousand had leapt out into the street in their birthday suits, that the printers of a magical kind of fake banknote on Sadovaya Street had been caught, that some gang had kidnapped five managers in the entertainment sector, but that the police had found them all straight away, and much else that one doesn't even want to repeat.

Meanwhile it was getting towards lunchtime, and then the ringing of a telephone resounded in the place where the investigation was being conducted. It was information from Sadovaya that the cursed apartment had again shown signs of life inside it. It was said that its windows had been opened from within, that the sounds of a piano and singing had been carrying from it, and that a black cat had been seen at the window, sitting on the sill and basking in the sun.

At about four o'clock in the hot afternoon a large group of men in civilian clothes alighted from three cars a little before reaching building No. 302 *bis* on Sadovaya Street. Here the large group that had arrived split up into two small ones, whereupon one went through the gateway of the building and across the courtyard straight into entrance No. 6, and the other opened a little door that was usually boarded up and led to the rear entrance, and both began going up different staircases to apartment No. 50.

At this time Korovyev and Azazello, with Korovyev in his usual costume and not at all in festive tails, were sitting in the apartment's dining room, finishing breakfast. Woland was, as usual, in the bedroom, and the cat's whereabouts was unknown. But judging by the clatter of saucepans coming from the kitchen, it could be assumed that that was where Behemoth was, acting the fool as usual.

"Now what are those footsteps on the stairs?" asked Korovyev, playing with a teaspoon in a cup of black coffee.

"It's them coming to arrest us," Azazello replied, and downed a shot of brandy.

"Ah-ah, well, well," was Korovyev's reply to that.

Those coming up the main staircase were meanwhile already on the second-floor landing. There two plumbers of some sort were fiddling with the central-heating radiator. The walking men exchanged an expressive glance with the plumbers.

"Everyone's in," whispered one of the plumbers, tapping away on the pipe with a hammer.

Then the man walking at the front openly took out from under his overcoat a black Mauser, and another, next to him, lock-picks. In general, the men going to apartment No. 50 were properly equipped. Two of them had in their pockets fine, easily unfolded silk nets. Another one had a lasso, another one had gauze masks and ampoules of chloroform.

In one second the front door into apartment No. 50 was open, and all those who had come found themselves in the entrance hall, and the door that slammed in the kitchen at this time showed that the second group from the rear entrance had arrived opportunely too.

This time, success of some sort – if not complete – was to be seen. The men instantly scattered through all the rooms and found nobody anywhere, but on the other hand in the dining room they did discover the remains of an evidently just abandoned breakfast, while on the mantelpiece in the living room, alongside a crystal jug, sat a huge black cat. He held in his paws a Primus stove.

In complete silence the men who had entered the living room contemplated this cat over quite a long time.

"Ye-es... that really is something..." whispered one of the visitors.

"I'm not misbehaving, I'm not bothering anyone, I'm mending the Primus," said the cat with an unfriendly frown, "and I also consider it my duty to warn you that the cat is an ancient and inviolable animal."

"Exceptionally skilled work," whispered one of the men who had come in, but another said loudly and distinctly:

"Well now, you inviolable ventriloquial cat, you step this way, please!"

A silk net unfolded and whirled up, but, to the utter surprise of all, the man throwing it missed and caught with it only the jug which, with a ringing noise, immediately smashed.

"Forfeit!" the cat started yelling. "Hoorah!" And at this point, setting the Primus aside, he pulled a Browning out from behind his back. He instantly aimed it at the man standing nearest to him, but before the cat had had time to shoot there was a flash of fire in the man's hand, and along with the shot from the Mauser the cat fell head first with a thump from the mantelpiece onto the floor, dropping the Browning and letting go of the Primus.

"It's all over," said the cat in a weak voice, and he stretched out languidly in a pool of blood, "step back away from me for a second, let me say goodbye to the earth. O my friend, Azazello!" the cat groaned, pouring out his lifeblood. "Where are you?" The cat turned his failing eyes in the direction of the door into the dining room. "You didn't come to my aid in the hour of unequal battle. You abandoned poor Behemoth, giving him up for a glass of – very good, it's true – brandy! Well then, may my death lie upon your conscience, but I bequeath my Browning to you…"

"The net, the net, the net," an anxious whispering began around the cat. But the net, the devil knows why, had got caught up in someone's pocket and would not come out.

"The only thing that can save a mortally wounded cat," said the cat, "is a swig of petrol…" And, exploiting the confusion, he put his mouth to the round opening in the Primus and had a good drink of petrol. Straight away the blood stopped streaming from under his upper left leg. The cat leapt up alive and well and, clasping the Primus under his arm, he hopped back onto the fireplace with it, and from there, ripping the wallpaper to bits, he climbed up the wall, and a couple of seconds later he was sitting on a metal curtain rail, high above the men who had come in.

In a moment hands had grabbed hold of the curtain and torn it down together with the rail, as a result of which the sunlight gushed into the darkened room. But neither the roguishly recovered cat nor the Primus fell down. Without parting with the Primus, the cat had contrived to leap through the air and jump up onto the chandelier hanging in the centre of the room.

"A stepladder!" came the cry from below.

"I challenge you to a duel!" yelled the cat, flying over their heads on the swinging chandelier, and at this point the Browning proved to be in his paws again, while he had found a place for the Primus between the branches of the chandelier. The cat took aim and, flying like a pendulum over the heads of the visitors, he opened fire on them. Thunder shook the apartment. Fragments of cut glass from the chandelier scattered onto the floor, the mirror on the fireplace cracked into stars, plaster dust began flying, spent cartridge cases began jumping over the floor, the panes in the windows started breaking, petrol began splashing from the bullet-riddled Primus. There could be no question of taking the cat alive now, and in reply the visitors fired accurately and frenziedly from Mausers at his head, his stomach, his chest and his back. The shooting caused panic on the asphalt in the courtyard.

But this shooting lasted a very short time and began dying away on its own. The thing is that it did no harm either to the cat, or to the visitors. Not only did nobody prove to be dead, nobody was even wounded; all, including the cat, remained completely unharmed. One of the visitors, in order to prove it definitively, let about five shots go into the head of the accursed animal, and the cat replied smartly with a whole clip. And it was just the same – it made no impression on anyone. The cat rocked in the chandelier, whose swings kept on decreasing, blowing into the barrel of the Browning for some reason and spitting on his paw. On the faces of those standing in silence below there appeared an expression of total bewilderment. This was the only instance, or one of the only ones, when shooting proved utterly ineffective. It could be assumed, of course, that the cat's Browning was some sort of toy, but that could not possibly have been said of the visitors' Mausers. Even the cat's first wound, of which there had clearly been not the slightest doubt, had been nothing other than a trick and a swinish pretence, just like the drinking of the petrol too.

One more attempt was made to get hold of the cat. The lasso was thrown, it caught on one of the candles and the chandelier broke loose. Its crash seemed to shake the entire frame of the building, but nothing useful came of it. Those present were showered in splinters, but the cat flew through the air and settled high up, just below the ceiling, on the upper part of the gilt frame of the mirror above the fireplace. He did not intend trying to clear off: on the contrary, sitting in relative safety, he started on another speech.

"I'm at a loss to understand," he said from above, "the reasons for my being treated so harshly..."

And here this speech was interrupted at the very outset by a heavy, low voice, coming from no one knew where:

"What's going on in the apartment? I'm being prevented from working."

Another voice, unpleasant and nasal, responded:

"Why, it's Behemoth, of course, the devil take him!"

A third, jangling voice said:

"Messire! It's Saturday. The sun's declining. It's time for us to go."

"I'm sorry, I can't chat any more," said the cat from the mirror, "it's time for us to go." He flung his Browning and knocked out both panes of glass in the window. Then he splashed some petrol down, and that petrol caught fire all by itself, throwing out a wave of flame right up to the ceiling.

The fire started extraordinarily quickly and fiercely somehow, in a way that never happens, even with petrol. Straight away the wallpaper began giving off smoke, the torn-down curtain on the floor began burning, and the frames in the broken windows started to smoulder. The cat tensed like a spring, miaowed, leapt from the mirror over to the window and disappeared through it together with his Primus. Outside, shots rang out. A man sitting on the iron fire escape on the level of the jeweller's wife's windows bombarded the cat as he flew from window ledge to window ledge, heading for the drainpipe at the corner of the building which was built, as has been said, in the shape of the letter *pokoi*. The cat clambered up this pipe onto the roof. There he was bombarded, also unfortunately without success, by the guards keeping watch over the chimneys, and the cat slipped away in the light of the setting sun that was flooding the city.

In the apartment at this time the parquet burst into flames beneath the feet of the visitors, and in the fire, in the place where the cat had lain with the feigned wound, there appeared, growing ever more dense, the corpse of the former Baron Maigel, with its chin jerked upwards and glassy eyes. There was already no chance of pulling it out.

Jumping over the burning blocks of the parquet, slapping their smoking shoulders and chests with the palms of their hands, those in the living room retreated into the study and the entrance hall. Those who were in the dining room and the bedroom ran out across the corridor. Those who had been in the kitchen came running too and dashed into the hall. The living room was already full of fire and smoke. Someone managed to dial the telephone number of the fire station as he went, and shouted briefly into the receiver:

"Sadovaya, 302 *bis*!"

Further delay was impossible. Flame flicked out into the hall. Breathing became difficult.

As soon as the first ribbons of smoke burst out of the broken windows of the enchanted apartment, people's desperate cries were heard in the courtyard:

"Fire! Fire! Fire!"

In different apartments in the building people began shouting into telephones:

"Sadovaya, Sadovaya, 302 *bis*!"

At the same time as the heart-rending ringing of bells on long, red vehicles, racing from all parts of the city, began to be heard on Sadovaya, the people rushing around in the courtyard saw how, together with the smoke, out from a fourth-floor window there flew three dark, seemingly male silhouettes, and one silhouette of a naked woman.

28

The Final Adventures of Korovyev and Behemoth

WHETHER THESE SILHOUETTES EXISTED, or whether they were just the fancy of the terror-stricken residents of the ill-starred building on Sadovaya, cannot, of course, be said for certain. If they did exist, no one knows what their immediate destination was either. Nor can we say where they split up, but we do know that about a quarter of an hour after the start of the fire on Sadovaya there appeared at the mirrored doors of Torgsin* at the Smolensky Market a lanky citizen in a checked suit, and with him a large black cat.

Winding his way deftly between passers-by, the citizen opened the outer door of the shop. But here the small, bony and extremely ill-disposed doorman blocked his path and said irritably:

"You can't come in with cats!"

"I'm sorry," the lanky one began jangling, and put a gnarled hand to his ear, as though hard of hearing, "with cats, you say? And where ever do you see a cat?"

The doorman opened his eyes wide, and with good reason: there was no longer any cat at the citizen's feet, but instead of that, from behind his shoulder, a fat man in a ripped cap, with a face that really did smack a little of a cat, was thrusting himself forward and straining to enter the shop. The fat man had a Primus in his hands.

For some reason the misanthropic doorman did not take to this funny pair of visitors.

"We only sell for foreign currency," he wheezed irritably, looking out from under scraggy, as though moth-eaten, greying eyebrows.

"My dear man," the lanky one began jangling, his eye flashing from a broken pince-nez, "but how on earth do you know I don't have any? Are you judging by my dress? Never do that, most precious custodian! You can be mistaken, and very much so at that. Reread once again if only the story of the renowned Caliph Haroun-al-Rashid.* But in the given instance, casting that story aside for the time being, I'd like to tell you that I shall complain about you to the manager and shall tell him such things about you that you might be obliged to abandon your post between the gleaming mirrored doors."

"Maybe I have a Primus full of foreign currency," the catlike fat man butted irascibly into the conversation too, still trying to barge his way into the shop.

Behind them, customers were already pushing forward and getting angry. Looking at the weird pair with hatred and doubt, the doorman stood aside, and our acquaintances, Korovyev and Behemoth, found themselves inside the shop. Here they first and foremost looked around, and then, in a ringing voice audible in absolutely every corner, Korovyev declared:

"A splendid shop! A very, very good shop!"

The customers turned around from the counters and for some reason looked at the man who had spoken with amazement, although he had every reason to praise the shop.

Hundreds of rolls of cotton cloth in the richest of colours could be seen on squared shelf units. Beyond them were piles of calico and chiffon and cloth for dress suits. Whole stacks of shoeboxes stretched away towards vanishing point, and several citizenesses were sitting on low chairs with their right feet in old, battered shoes, and their left in gleaming new court shoes, which they proceeded to stamp anxiously into the rug. Somewhere in the depths of the shop around a corner, gramophones were singing and playing.

But, passing all these delights by, Korovyev and Behemoth headed straight for the point where the grocery and confectionery departments met. There was a lot of room here, citizenesses in headscarves and berets were not pressing against the counters as in the fabrics department.

A rather short, perfectly square man in horn-rimmed glasses – so well-shaven he was blue, wearing a brand-new hat, uncrumpled and without any stains on the ribbon, a lilac overcoat and gingery kid gloves – was standing by the counter and bellowing something imperiously. A shop assistant in a clean white coat and a blue hat was serving the lilac client. With the sharpest of knives, very similar to the knife stolen by Levi Matthew, he was removing the skin, which looked like a snake's with its silvery shine, from a piece of pink salmon, which was oozing fat.

"And this department's magnificent too," Korovyev solemnly declared, "and the foreigner's a likeable one." He pointed his finger benevolently at the lilac back.

"No, Fagot, no," replied Behemoth pensively, "you're mistaken, old chum. There's something lacking in the lilac gentleman's face, in my view."

The lilac back shuddered, but probably by chance, for the foreigner could not possibly have understood what Korovyev and his companion were saying in Russian.

"Is good?" asked the lilac customer sternly.

"World-class!" replied the shop assistant, coquettishly wiggling the blade of the knife around under the skin.

"Is good, I like, is bad – no," said the foreigner sternly.

"Of course!" replied the shop assistant enthusiastically.

Here our acquaintances moved away from the foreigner with his salmon towards the edge of the confectionery counter.

"It's hot today," Korovyev addressed the red-cheeked young shop girl, and got no reply from her to this. "How much are the mandarins?" Korovyev then enquired of her.

"Thirty copecks a kilo," the shop girl replied.

355

"Everything's so pricey," remarked Korovyev with a sigh, "oh dear, oh dear…" Then he thought for a bit and invited his companion: "Eat up, Behemoth."

The fat man clasped his Primus under his arm, took possession of the mandarin at the top of the pyramid and, gobbling it down there and then with the peel on, he set about a second one.

The shop girl was gripped by deathly horror.

"Are you out of your mind?" she exclaimed, losing her rosiness. "Give me the receipt! The receipt!" and she dropped the sweet tongs.

"My darling, my dear, my beauty," Korovyev began hoarsely, lurching across the counter and winking at the shop girl, "we've got no foreign currency with us today… well, what's to be done! But I swear to you, the very next time, and certainly no later than Monday, we'll pay up in full in readies! We're not far from here, on Sadovaya, where the fire is…"

Having swallowed a third mandarin, Behemoth poked his paw into an intricate construction of chocolate bars and pulled out one at the bottom, as a result of which, of course, it all collapsed, and he swallowed the bar together with the gold wrapping.

While the shop assistants at the fish counter turned to stone with their knives in their hands, the lilac foreigner turned towards the robbers, and it was immediately revealed that Behemoth was wrong: the lilac man did not have something lacking in his face, on the contrary, there was rather something superfluous – drooping cheeks and darting eyes.

Having turned quite yellow, the shop girl cried mournfully for the whole shop to hear:

"Palosich! Palosich!"

Customers from the fabrics department came in a rush at this call, and Behemoth moved away from the confectionery temptations and thrust a paw into a barrel with the inscription "Selected Kerch herring", pulled out a couple of herrings and, swallowing them, spat out the bones.

"Palosich!" the desperate cry behind the confectionery counter was repeated, while behind the fish counter a shop assistant with an imperial beard bawled:

"What do you think you're doing, you scum?!"

Pavel Iosifovich was already hurrying to the scene of the action. He was an imposing man in a clean white coat, like a surgeon, and with a pencil poking out of his pocket. Seeing the tail of a third herring in Behemoth's mouth, he appraised the situation in an instant, understood absolutely everything and, without entering into any debates with the insolent fellows, he waved an arm into the distance and commanded:

"Whistle!"

Out from the mirrored doors onto the corner of Smolensky flew the doorman, and he burst into ill-omened whistling. The customers started to surround the villains, and then Korovyev entered into the matter.

"Citizens!" he cried in a vibrating, thin voice. "What ever is going on? Eh? Permit me to ask you that! A poor man," Korovyev added a quaver into his voice and indicated Behemoth, who had immediately put on a pathetic physiognomy, "a poor man is mending Primuses all day long; he's hungry... and where on earth is he to get foreign currency from?"

Pavel Iosifovich, usually restrained and calm, shouted sternly at this: "You stop that!" and waved into the distance, impatiently now. Then the trills at the doors began to ring out a little more merrily.

But Korovyev, not put off by Pavel Iosifovich's utterance, continued:

"Where from? I'm asking everyone the question! He's wearied by hunger and thirst! He's hot. Well, the hapless fellow took a mandarin to taste. And the total price of that mandarin is three copecks. And here they are already whistling like nightingales in a wood in the springtime, disturbing the police, taking them away from their work. While he can? Eh?" and here Korovyev indicated the fat lilac man, and the greatest anxiety was expressed on the latter's face as a result. "Who's he? Eh? Where's he come from? What for? Were we pining without him, or something? Did we invite him, or something? Of course," twisting his mouth sarcastically, the former precentor was yelling at the top of his voice, "he, you see, in his best lilac suit, he's all swollen up from eating salmon, he's completely stuffed with foreign currency, but what about our Russian fellow, our Russian fellow?! It makes me bitter! Bitter! Bitter!" Korovyev howled, like an usher at an old-time wedding.*

This whole speech, extremely silly, tactless and probably politically dangerous, made Pavel Iosifovich shake with rage, but, strange as it might seem, it could be seen from the eyes of the crowd of customers that had gathered that it had aroused sympathy in very many people!

And when, putting a dirty, torn sleeve to his eye, Behemoth tragically exclaimed: "Thank you, faithful friend, you have taken the part of a man who has suffered!" a miracle occurred. The most respectable, quiet, little old man, dressed poorly, but nice and clean, a little old man who had been buying three almond cakes in the confectionery department, was suddenly transfigured. His eyes flashed with the fire of battle, he turned crimson, flung the little bag of cakes onto the floor and cried: "It's true!" in the thin voice of a child. Then he snatched up a tray, throwing from it the remnants of the chocolate Eiffel Tower that Behemoth had ruined, waved it in the air, pulled off the foreigner's hat with his left hand, and with his right, with all his might, hit the foreigner on his bald head with the flat of the tray. There rang out the sort of sound there is when sheet iron is thrown onto the ground from a truck. The fat man, turning white, collapsed backwards and sat down in the vat of Kerch herring, squirting out from it a fountain of herring brine. And straight away a second miracle too came about. The lilac man, having fallen into the vat, exclaimed in perfect Russian without a trace of any accent: "Murder! Police! I'm being murdered by bandits!" evidently having suddenly mastered in consequence of the shock a language previously unknown to him.

Then the doorman's whistling ceased, and in the crowds of agitated customers there were now glimpses, as they approached, of two policemen's helmets. But just as in a bathhouse they pour water over a bench from a tub, so the perfidious Behemoth poured petrol over the confectionery counter from the Primus, and it burst into flames all by itself. The flame struck upwards and ran along the counter, devouring the pretty paper ribbons on the baskets of fruit. Squealing, the shop girls hastened to escape from behind the counter, and as soon as they had slipped out from behind it, the linen blinds on the windows burst into flames and the petrol on the floor caught fire. Immediately raising a desperate clamour, the customers lurched back out of the confectioner's, crushing Pavel Iosifovich, who was no longer needed, and from behind the fish counter the shop assistants with their sharpened knives trotted in single file towards the doors of the back entrance. The lilac citizen, having extricated himself from the vat, but all covered in herring slush, rolled over the salmon on the counter and followed after them. The glass in the mirrored exit doors began to ring and then rained down, knocked out by the escaping people, while the two villains – both Korovyev, and the glutton Behemoth – were off somewhere, but where, that could not be fathomed. Only later did eyewitnesses who had been present at the start of the fire in Torgsin on Smolensky say that the hooligans had apparently both flown up to just below the ceiling, and there had apparently both burst like balloons. It is doubtful, of course, that that is how it actually was, but what we don't know, we don't know.

But we do know that exactly one minute after the occurrence at Smolensky both Behemoth and Korovyev were already on the pavement of the boulevard, just by Griboyedov's auntie's house. Korovyev stopped by the railings and began:

"Well I never! I mean, this is the writers' house! You know, Behemoth, I've heard a great many good and complimentary things about this house. Turn your attention, my friend, to this house. It's nice to think that, hidden under that roof, a whole host of talents is ripening."

"Like pineapples in hothouses," said Behemoth and, in order better to admire the cream house with the columns, he climbed onto the concrete base of the cast-iron railings.

"Quite right," Korovyev concurred with his inseparable companion, "and a delicious wave of awe floods through your heart when you think that maturing in that house now is the future author of *Don Quixote*,* or *Faust*,* or, the devil take me, *Dead Souls*!* Eh?"

"It's a terrifying thought," Behemoth confirmed.

"Yes," Korovyev continued, "amazing things can be expected from the hotbeds of that house, which has united under its roof several thousand zealots, who have resolved to devote their lives selflessly to the service of Melpomene, Polyhymnia and Thalia.* Can you imagine what a clamour there'll be when one of them, for a start, presents the reading public with *The Government Inspector** or, at the very worst, *Eugene Onegin*!"*

"Very easily," Behemoth confirmed once again.

"Yes," Korovyev continued, and raised a finger anxiously, "but! But, I say, and I repeat it – but! Only if some micro-organism or other doesn't attack these tender hothouse plants, doesn't eat away at their roots, if they don't begin to rot! And that can happen with pineapples! Dear, oh dear, can't it just happen!"

"By the way," Behemoth enquired, poking his round head through a gap in the railings, "what's that they're doing on the veranda?"

"Having lunch," explained Korovyev, "and I can add to that, my friend, that there's a restaurant here that's inexpensive and not at all bad. And I, meanwhile, like any tourist before onward travel, am experiencing the desire to have a bite to eat and to drink down a large, ice-cold mug of beer."

"Me too," replied Behemoth, and both of the villains strode off down the asphalt path beneath the limes straight to the veranda of the unsuspecting restaurant.

A pale and bored citizeness with a ponytail, wearing little white socks and a little beret, also white, was sitting on a bentwood chair at the corner entrance to the veranda where an opening had been made in the greenery of the trellis. In front of her on an extensive kitchen table lay a thick, register-style book in which the citizeness, for unknown reasons, was making a note of those who came into the restaurant. And it was by precisely this citizeness that Korovyev and Behemoth were stopped.

"Your identification cards?" She was looking in surprise at Korovyev's pince-nez, and also at Behemoth's Primus and at Behemoth's torn elbow.

"A thousand apologies, what identification cards?" Korovyev asked in surprise.

"Are you writers?" asked the citizeness in her turn.

"Undoubtedly," Korovyev answered with dignity.

"Your identification cards?" the citizeness repeated.

"My lovely…" Korovyev began tenderly.

"I'm not lovely," the citizeness interrupted him.

"Oh, isn't that a pity," said Korovyev, disenchanted, and continued: "Well, all right, if you don't wish to be lovely, which would have been most pleasant, you don't have to be. So then, to be satisfied that Dostoevsky is a writer, surely it's not necessary to ask for his identification card? Just take any five pages from any of his novels, and you'll be satisfied without any identification card that you're dealing with a writer. I actually suspect that he didn't even have an identification card! What do you think?" Korovyev turned to Behemoth.

"I bet he didn't," the latter replied, standing the Primus on the table next to the book and wiping away the sweat on his smoke-blackened forehead with his hand.

"You're not Dostoevsky," said the citizeness, knocked out of her stride by Korovyev.

"Well, who knows, who knows?" he replied.

"Dostoevsky's dead," said the citizeness, but not very confidently somehow.

"I protest!" exclaimed Behemoth heatedly. "Dostoevsky is immortal!"

"Your identification cards, Citizens," said the citizeness.

"For pity's sake, this is ultimately ridiculous," Korovyev would not give in, "it's not by an identification card at all that a writer is defined, but by what he writes! How do you know what ideas are crowding inside my head? Or in this head?" and he indicated Behemoth's head, from which the latter immediately removed his cap, as if for the citizeness to be better able to examine it.

"Make way, Citizens," she said, already feeling fraught.

Korovyev and Behemoth stepped aside and made way for some writer in a grey suit, in a tieless, white summer shirt, the collar of which lay spread out wide on the collar of his jacket, and with a newspaper under his arm. The writer nodded affably to the citizeness, put some sort of squiggle in the book held out for him as he went, and proceeded onto the veranda.

"Alas, it's not us, not us," Korovyev began sadly, "but him who'll get that ice-cold mug of beer of which you and I, poor rovers, so dreamt. Our position is sad and difficult, and I don't know what to do."

Behemoth only spread his arms and put the cap on his round head with its thick growth of hair, very like the fur of a cat. And at that moment a soft but masterful voice was heard above the citizeness's head:

"Let them in, Sofia Pavlovna."

The citizeness with the book was astonished; in the greenery of the trellis appeared the white tail-suited chest and the wedge-shaped beard of the filibuster. He was looking affably at the two dubious ragamuffins and, even more than that, was making gestures of invitation to them. Archibald Archibaldovich's authority was a thing taken seriously in the restaurant which he managed, and Sofia Pavlovna asked Korovyev obediently:

"What's your name?"

"Panayev,"* he replied politely. The citizen wrote this name down and raised an enquiring gaze to Behemoth.

"Skabichevsky,"* he squeaked, for some reason pointing to his Primus. Sofia Pavlovna wrote that down too, and moved the book towards the

361

visitors for them to put their signatures in it. Korovyev wrote "Skabi-chevsky" opposite the name "Panayev", and Behemoth wrote "Panayev" opposite "Skabichevsky".

Archibald Archibaldovich, stunning Sofia Pavlovna completely with a captivating smile, led the guests to the best table at the opposite end of the veranda where the deepest shade was, to the table beside which the sun was playing merrily in one of the slits in the greenery of the trellis. And Sofia Pavlovna, blinking in astonishment, spent a long time studying the strange entries made in the book by the unexpected visitors.

Archibald Archibaldovich surprised the waiters no less than he had Sofia Pavlovna. He personally moved the chair away from the table, inviting Korovyev to sit down, gave a wink to one, whispered something to another, and the two waiters began making a fuss around the new guests, one of whom put his Primus on the floor next to his now ginger, discoloured boot.

Immediately the old tablecloth with yellow stains disappeared from the table, up in the air flew another, crackling with starch and brilliant white, like a Bedouin's burnous, and Archibald Archibaldovich was already whispering quietly, but very expressively, bending right down to Korovyev's ear:

"What am I to regale you with? I have a very special cured fillet of sturgeon... snatched it away from the architects' congress..."

"Will you... er... let us generally have some hors d'oeuvres... er..." Korovyev mumbled benevolently, stretching out on his chair.

"I understand," replied Archibald Archibaldovich meaningfully, closing his eyes.

Seeing how the restaurant boss treated these most dubious visitors, the waiters abandoned all their doubts and set about things seriously. One was already bringing a match for Behemoth, who had taken a cigarette stub from his pocket and stuck it in his mouth, the other had flown up with green glass ringing and was laying out by the place settings vodka glasses, wine glasses, and the delicate ones from which Narzan goes down so well beneath the awning... no, jumping ahead, let us say: Narzan used to go down so well beneath the awning of the unforgettable Griboyedov veranda.

"I can treat you to a nice fillet of hazel grouse," Archibald Archibald-ovich purred musically. The guest in the cracked pince-nez gave his full approval to the commander of the brig's suggestions and gazed at him graciously through his useless lens.

With the powers of observation characteristic of all writers, the belletrist Petrakov-Sukhovei, dining at the next table with his spouse, who was just finishing off a pork cutlet, noticed Archibald Archibaldovich's attentions and was very, very surprised. And his spouse, a most venerable lady, simply even begrudged the pirate's attitude to Korovyev, and even tapped with her teaspoon as if to say: "Why on earth are we being held up... it's time the ice cream was served! What's going on?"

However, having sent Petrakova a captivating smile, Archibald Archibaldovich directed a waiter to her and did not himself abandon his dear guests. Ah, Archibald Archibaldovich was clever! And perhaps no less observant than the writers themselves. Archibald Archibaldovich knew about the show at The Variety, and about many of the other occurrences of these days, and had heard, but, in contrast to others, had not failed to pay heed to both the word "checked", and the word "cat". Archibald Archibaldovich had guessed at once who his visitors were. And having guessed, naturally had not dreamt of arguing with them. But that Sofia Pavlovna was a fine one! I mean, what a thing to dream up – barring the path onto the veranda to those two! But then what could you expect from her?

Haughtily prodding her teaspoon into the melting ice cream, Petrakova watched with discontented eyes as the table in front of these two men dressed like clowns of some sort filled up with victuals as if by magic. Lettuce leaves that had been washed until they shone were already poking out of a bowl of fresh caviar... another moment, and there appeared on a separate side table, set up specially, a little silver bucket covered in condensation...

Only when satisfied that everything had been done conscientiously, only when there flew up in the hands of the waiters a covered pan in which something was grumbling, did Archibald Archibaldovich allow himself to abandon the two enigmatic visitors, and even then after a prior whisper to them:

"Excuse me! For a moment! I'll see to the fillets personally."

He flew away from the table and disappeared in the restaurant's inner passageway. If some observer could have followed Archibald Archibaldovich's subsequent actions, they would doubtless have seemed to him somewhat enigmatic.

The boss headed not into the kitchen to watch over the fillets at all, but into the restaurant's pantry. He opened it with his key, shut himself in it, carefully, so as not to dirty his cuff, took two weighty pieces of cured sturgeon out of a bin of ice, packed them in newspaper, tied them up neatly with string and put them to one side. Then in the next room he checked whether his summer, silk-lined coat and hat were in their places, and only after that proceeded into the kitchen, where the chef was painstakingly preparing the nice fillets the pirate had promised the guests.

It must be said that in all Archibald Archibaldovich's actions there was nothing at all strange or enigmatic, and only a superficial observer could have considered such actions strange. Archibald Archibaldovich's conduct followed perfectly logically from all that had gone before. Knowledge of the latest events and, chiefly, Archibald Archibaldovich's phenomenal sixth sense suggested to the boss of the Griboyedov restaurant that his two visitors' lunch might well be ample and sumptuous, and yet extremely fleeting. And the sixth sense that had never deceived the former filibuster did not let him down on this occasion either.

At the moment when Korovyev and Behemoth were clinking their glasses of splendid, cold, twice distilled Moscow vodka for the second time, there appeared on the veranda the sweaty and agitated news reporter Boba Kandalupsky, famous in Moscow for his amazing omniscience, who straight away joined the Petrakovs. Putting his swollen briefcase on the table, Boba immediately stuck his lips in Petrakov's ear and began whispering into it some very seductive things. Madame Petrakova, dying of curiosity, put her ear up to Boba's plump, greasy lips as well. And the latter, glancing around occasionally like a thief, kept on whispering and whispering, and individual words could be heard, such as these:

"I swear to you on my honour! On Sadovaya, on Sadovaya," Boba lowered his voice still more, "bullets have no effect! Bullets... bullets... petrol... fire... bullets..."

"Now these liars who spread vile rumours," Madam Petrakova's contralto voice started droning indignantly, and rather louder than Boba would have liked, "now they ought to be brought to light! Well, it's all right, that's what will happen, they'll be sorted out! What dangerous drivel!"

"What do you mean, drivel, Antonida Porfiryevna!" Boba exclaimed, aggrieved by the disbelief of the writer's spouse, and again began hissing: "I tell you bullets have no effect... And now there's a fire...

Through the air they... through the air," Boba hissed, not suspecting the fact that those he was talking about were sitting next to him, enjoying his hissing.

However, that enjoyment soon ceased. Swiftly from the inner passageway of the restaurant onto the veranda emerged three men with tightly belted waists, wearing leather gaiters and with revolvers in their hands. The one in front's cry was ringing and terrifying: "Don't move!" and immediately all three opened fire on the veranda, aiming at Korovyev and Behemoth's heads. Both of those being shot at disappeared into thin air at once, and a column of fire from the Primus struck straight at the awning. It was as if gaping jaws with black edges appeared in the awning and began spreading in all directions. Leaping through them, the fire went right up to the roof of The Griboyedov House. The files of papers lying on the first-floor window sill of the editorial office suddenly burst into flames, and after them the blind caught too, and then, humming as though someone were fanning it, the fire went in columns into the inside of auntie's house.

A few seconds later, down the asphalt paths leading to the cast-iron railings of the boulevard, whence on Wednesday evening the first herald of misfortune, understood by no one, Ivanushka, had come, there now ran writers leaving meals unfinished, waiters, Sofia Pavlovna, Boba, Petrakova and Petrakov. Having left in good time through the side entrance, fleeing nowhere and hurrying nowhere, like the captain who is duty-bound to abandon the burning brig last, Archibald Archibaldovich stood calmly in his silk-lined summer coat with two logs of cured sturgeon under his arm.

29

The Master and Margarita's Fate is Determined

A T SUNSET, HIGH ABOVE THE CITY, on the stone terrace of one of the most beautiful buildings in Moscow, built about a hundred and fifty years before,* there were two figures: Woland and Azazello. They were not visible from the street below, since they were hidden from any unwanted gaze by the balustrade with plaster vases and plaster flowers. But the city was visible to them almost to its very edges.

Woland was sitting on a folding stool, dressed in his black soutane. His long and broad sword was stuck vertically in between two cleft paving slabs of the terrace, so the result was a sundial. The shadow of the sword slowly and inexorably lengthened, crawling towards the black shoes on Satan's feet. With his sharp chin resting on his fist, hunched over on the stool and with one leg bent beneath him, Woland looked fixedly at the boundless assemblage of palaces, gigantic buildings and little hovels doomed to demolition.

Azazello, having parted with his contemporary costume, that is, the jacket, bowler hat and patent-leather shoes, and dressed, just like Woland, in black, was standing motionless not far from his lord and, just like him, was not taking his eyes off the city.

Woland spoke:

"What an interesting city, isn't it?"

Azazello stirred and answered deferentially:

"Messire, I like Rome better."

"Yes, it's a matter of taste," Woland replied.

After some time his voice rang out again:

"And why is there that smoke there, on the boulevard?"

"That's Griboyedov burning," replied Azazello.

"It must be assumed that that inseparable pair, Korovyev and Behemoth, have been there?"

"There is no doubt whatsoever of that, Messire."

Again silence set in, and both of those on the terrace watched, as in west-facing windows in the upper floors of the huge blocks the broken, blinding sun lit up. Woland's eye burned in exactly the same way as one such window, although Woland had his back to the sunset.

But at this point something made Woland turn away from the city and direct his attention towards the round tower which was behind his back on the roof. From its wall emerged a ragged, gloomy, black-bearded man covered in clay, wearing a chiton and home-made sandals.

"Well I never!" exclaimed Woland, looking at the new arrival mockingly. "You least of all might have been expected here! Why have you come, uninvited yet anticipated guest?"

"I've come to see you, spirit of evil and lord of shadows," replied the new arrival, gazing at Woland in unfriendly fashion from under his brows.

"If you've come to see me, then why haven't you offered me your good wishes, former collector of taxes?" said Woland sternly.

"Because I don't wish you to prosper," the new arrival answered impertinently.

"But you'll have to reconcile yourself to it," Woland retorted, and his mouth twisted in a grin, "you've scarcely had time to appear on the roof before you've already come out with something absurd, and I'll tell you what it is – it's your intonations. You pronounced your words as if you don't acknowledge the shadows, or the evil either. Would you be so kind as to give a little thought to the question of what your good would be doing if evil did not exist, and how the earth would look if the shadows were to disappear from it? After all, shadows come from objects and people. There's the shadow from my sword. But shadows can come from trees and from other living things. Do you want to strip the whole earth bare, removing from it all the trees and everything that's alive, because of your fantasy of enjoying naked light? You're stupid."

"I'm not going to argue with you, you old sophist," replied Levi Matthew.

"And you can't argue with me for the reason that I've already mentioned: you're stupid," Woland replied, and asked: "Well, be brief and don't tire me, why have you appeared?"

"He sent me."

"And what did he bid you say to me, slave?"

"I'm not a slave," replied Levi Matthew, his animosity growing more and more, "I'm his disciple."

"You and I are speaking different languages, as always," responded Woland, "but the things we're talking about don't change because of it. And so?"

"He has read the Master's work," said Levi Matthew, "and requests that you take the Master with you and reward him with peace. Surely that's not hard for you to do, spirit of evil?"

"Nothing is hard for me to do," replied Woland, "and you know that very well." He paused, and added: "But why don't you take him in yourselves, to the light?"

"He has not merited light, he has merited peace." Levi pronounced in a sad voice.

"Say that it will be done," Woland replied, and added, with his eye flaring up: "And leave me immediately."

"He asks that you should take the one who loved and suffered for him also," for the first time Levi addressed Woland imploringly.

"There's no chance we would have thought of that without you. Go away."

After that, Levi Matthew vanished, and Woland called Azazello to him and gave him the order:

"Fly to them and arrange everything."

Azazello left the terrace and Woland remained alone.

But his solitude was not long-lasting. The tap of footsteps on the paving slabs of the terrace and animated voices were heard, and Korovyev and Behemoth appeared before Woland. But now the fat one had no Primus and was laden with other objects. Thus, under his arm there was a small landscape in a gold frame, thrown over his arm was a half-scorched chef's smock, and in the other hand he held an entire salmon in its skin and with its tail. Korovyev and Behemoth reeked of burning, Behemoth's face was covered in soot and his cap was half scorched.

"*Salut,** Messire!" cried the irrepressible pair, and Behemoth started waving the salmon.

"You look delightful," said Woland.

"Imagine, Messire," cried Behemoth in excitement and joy, "I was taken for a pillager!"

"To judge by the objects you've brought," replied Woland, casting glances at the little landscape, "you are a pillager."

"Would you believe it, Messire..." began Behemoth in a heartfelt voice.

"No, I wouldn't," replied Woland briefly.

"Messire, I swear I made heroic attempts to save everything that could be saved, and this is all I managed to preserve."

"It would be better if you told me what set Griboyedov on fire," said Woland. Both of them, Korovyev and Behemoth, spread their arms wide, raised their eyes to the sky, and Behemoth exclaimed:

"I can't make it out! We were sitting peaceably, utterly quietly, having a bite to eat..."

"And suddenly – bang, bang!" Korovyev chimed in. "Shots! Mad with terror, Behemoth and I rushed to escape onto the boulevard, our persecutors were behind us, we rushed towards Timiryazev!"*

"But a sense of duty," Behemoth joined in, "overcame our shameful terror and we returned."

"Ah, you returned?" said Woland. "Well, of course, and then the building was burnt to a cinder."

"To a cinder!" Korovyev confirmed mournfully. "That is, literally, Messire, to a cinder, as you were good enough to put it so accurately. Just smouldering timbers!"

"I headed," Behemoth recounted, "for the conference hall – that's the one with the columns, Messire – reckoning on pulling something valuable out. Ah, Messire, my wife, if only I had one, risked being left a widow twenty times! But fortunately, Messire, I'm not married, and I'll tell you straight – I'm happy I'm not married. Ah, Messire, how can one possibly exchange bachelor freedom for a burdensome yoke!"

"Some sort of drivel has begun again," remarked Woland.

"I hear and continue," replied the cat, "yes indeed, here's a little landscape. It was impossible to carry anything more out of the hall, the flame struck me in the face. I ran to the pantry, saved the salmon. I ran to the kitchen, saved the smock. I consider, Messire, that I did all I could, and I don't understand how the sceptical expression on your face is to be explained."

"And what was Korovyev doing at the time you were pillaging?" asked Woland.

"I was helping the firemen, Messire," replied Korovyev, indicating his ripped trousers.

"Ah, if that's the case, then of course, a new building will have to be built."

"It will be built, Messire," responded Korovyev, "I make bold to assure you of that."

"Well then, it just remains to wish that it should be better than the previous one," remarked Woland.

"It will be so, Messire," said Korovyev.

"Believe you me," added the cat, "I'm a regular prophet."

"In any event, we're here, Messire," reported Korovyev, "and we await your instructions."

Woland rose from his stool, went up to the balustrade, and for a long time, in silence, alone, with his back turned to his suite, he gazed into the distance. Then he walked away from the edge, sank onto his stool again and said:

"There will be no instructions – you have carried out all that you could, and for the time being I do not need your services any more. You can rest. A storm will shortly be coming, the final storm, it will

369

complete everything that needs to be completed, and we shall be on our way."

"Very good, Messire," the two clowns replied, and disappeared somewhere behind the round central tower, situated in the middle of the terrace.

The storm of which Woland spoke was already gathering on the horizon. A black cloud rose and cut off half of the sun. Then it covered it completely. It became fresher on the terrace. Some time later still it became dark.

This darkness that had come from the west covered the enormous city. The bridges, the palaces vanished. Everything disappeared, as though it had never been on the earth. One fiery thread ran across the whole sky. Then the city was shaken by a thunderclap. It was repeated, and the storm began. Woland ceased to be visible in its gloom.

30

It's Time! It's Time!*

"YOU KNOW," SAID MARGARITA, "just as you fell asleep last night I was reading about the darkness which came from the Mediterranean Sea... and those idols, ah, the golden idols! For some reason they give me no peace any of the time. I think there'll be rain now too. Do you feel it getting fresher?"

"This is all well and good," replied the Master, smoking and dispersing the smoke with his hand, "and those idols, blow them... but what happens next, that really is unclear!"

This conversation took place at sunset, just at the time when Levi Matthew came to Woland on the terrace. The basement's little window was open, and if anyone had glanced into it, they would have been surprised at how strange those conversing looked. Thrown straight onto Margarita's naked body was a black cloak, and the Master was wearing his hospital linen. This was the case because Margarita had nothing whatsoever to put on, since all her things had remained in the detached house, and though that house was not very far away, there was, of course, no question of her going there and getting her things. And the Master, all of whose suits had been found in the wardrobe, as though the Master had not even been away anywhere, simply did not wish to get dressed, as he elaborated before Margarita the idea that some utter nonsense would begin at any moment. True, he was shaved for the first time since that autumn night (in the clinic his beard had been trimmed with clippers).

The room had a strange look too, and it was very difficult to understand anything in its chaos. On the rug lay manuscripts, and they were on the divan as well. Some book or other was lying with its spine sticking up in the armchair. And the round table was set for dinner, and among the hors d'oeuvres stood several bottles. Where all these victuals and drinks had come from was unknown to both Margarita and the Master. On waking up, they had found all of it already on the table.

Having slept through to sunset on Saturday, both the Master and his girl felt fully strengthened, and there was only one thing to remind them of the previous day's adventures – both felt a slight ache in the left temple. But on the psychological side, very great changes had taken place in both of them, as anyone who could have overheard the conversation in the basement apartment would have been convinced. But there was absolutely nobody to overhear. That was the good thing about this yard, that it was always empty. With every day the increasingly green lime trees and the white willow outside the window were giving off the scent of spring more powerfully, and the beginnings of a breeze were carrying it into the basement.

"Damn it all!" the Master exclaimed unexpectedly. "I mean, it's, just think…" he extinguished the cigarette stub in the ashtray and squeezed his head in his hands. "No, listen, you're an intelligent person and haven't been mad… Are you seriously convinced that yesterday we were with Satan?"

"Perfectly seriously," replied Margarita.

"Of course, of course," said the Master ironically, "and so here we now have instead of one mad person – two! Both the husband and the wife." He raised his hands to the sky and cried: "No, it's the devil knows what, the devil, the devil, the devil!"

Instead of replying, Margarita collapsed onto the divan, began roaring with laughter and kicking her bare feet about, and only then did she exclaim:

"Oh, it's too much! Oh, it's too much! Just take a glance at what you look like!"

While the Master was bashfully pulling up his hospital long johns, Margarita finished chuckling and became serious.

"You unwittingly said something true just now," she began, "the Devil does know what's going on, and the Devil, believe me, will arrange everything!" Her eyes suddenly blazed, she leapt up, began dancing on the spot and started crying out: "How happy I am, how happy I am that I struck a bargain with him! Oh, the Devil, the Devil!... You, my dear, will have to live with a witch!" After this, she rushed to the Master, flung her arms around his neck and began kissing him on the lips, the nose, the cheeks. Locks of unbrushed black hair jumped on the Master, and his cheeks and forehead flared up under the kisses.

"You really have become like a witch!"

"And I don't deny it," Margarita replied, "I am a witch, and I'm very happy about it."

"Well, all right," said the Master, "a witch, so be it. Very fine and splendid! And so I was abducted from the clinic... very nice too! We were returned here, we'll assume that's so as well... We'll even suppose that no one will notice we're missing... But just you tell me, for the sake of all that's holy, on what and how are we going to live? In saying that, it's you I'm concerned about, believe me!"

At that moment there appeared in the window a pair of blunt-toed boots and the bottom part of a pair of pin-striped trousers. Then these trousers bent at the knee, and the daylight was shut out by somebody's weighty backside.

"Aloizy, are you at home?" asked a voice outside the window somewhere up above the trousers.

"There you are, it's starting," said the Master.

"Aloizy?" asked Margarita, going up closer to the window. "He was arrested yesterday. And who is it asking for him? What's your name?"

At the same instant the knees and the backside disappeared and the banging of the gate was heard, after which everything returned to normal. Margarita dropped onto the divan and began laughing so hard that the tears rolled out of her eyes. But when she quietened down, her face changed in the most drastic way, she started speaking seriously and, while speaking, she slid down off the divan, crawled up to the Master's knees and, gazing into his eyes, began stroking his head.

"How you've suffered, how you've suffered, my poor thing! Just I alone know about that. Look, you've got grey threads in your hair and a perpetual line by your lips! My only one, my dear one, don't think about anything. You've had to think too much, and now I'm going to think for you. And I guarantee you, I guarantee, that everything will be dazzlingly good!"

"I'm not afraid of anything, Margot," the Master suddenly answered her, and raised his head, and he seemed to her as he had been when he was composing what he had never seen, but what he had known for certain had been, "and I'm not afraid because I've already been through everything. I've been frightened too much, and can't be frightened by anything more. But I feel sorry for you, Margot, that's the whole point, and that's why I keep going on about one and the same thing. Come to your senses! Why should you wreck your life with a sick man and a beggar? Go back home! I feel sorry for you, and that's why I say this."

"Oh, you, you," Margarita whispered, shaking her tousled head, "oh you unhappy man of little faith. Because of you I stood all last night naked and shaking, I lost my own nature and replaced it with another one, I sat for several months in a dark tiny room and thought about only one thing – about the storm over Yershalaim – I cried my eyes out, and now, when happiness has fallen on us, you're driving me away? Well, all right then, I'll go, but know that you are a cruel man! They've drained your soul!"

A bitter tenderness rose towards the Master's heart, and for some unknown reason he burst into tears with his head buried in Margarita's hair. She, crying, whispered to him, and her fingers jumped on the Master's temples.

"Yes, threads, threads... before my eyes his head's getting covered in snow... ah, my poor head, poor head that has suffered so much! Look how your eyes are! There's a wilderness inside them... And the shoulders, shoulders with a burden... He's maimed, maimed..." Margarita's speech was becoming incoherent, Margarita was shaking from her crying.

Then the Master wiped away her tears, raised Margarita from her knees, stood up and himself said firmly:

"Enough! You've put me to shame. Never again will I permit faint-heartedness and I won't return to this question, rest assured. I know that we're both victims of our mental illness which I've perhaps passed on to you... Well, all right, together we'll bear it too."

Margarita brought her lips close to the Master's ear and whispered:

"I swear to you by my life, I swear by the astrologer's son divined by you, all will be well."

"Well, that's fine, fine," the Master responded, and added with a laugh: "Of course, when people have been completely pillaged, like you and me, they seek salvation from a preternatural force! Well, all right, I'm agreeable to seeking there."

"There you are, there you are, now you're the man you used to be, you're laughing," replied Margarita, "and you can go to the devil with your clever words. Preternatural or not preternatural – isn't it all the same? I'm hungry."

And she dragged the Master by the arm to the table.

"I'm not certain this food won't be swallowed up by the earth in a moment, or won't fly away through the window," he said, quite calm again.

"It won't fly away!"

And at that very moment a nasal voice was heard through the window:

"Peace be unto you."

The Master gave a start, but Margarita, already accustomed to the extraordinary, exclaimed:

"Why, it's Azazello! Ah, how nice that is, how good that is!" And whispering to the Master: "There, you see, you see, they're not abandoning us!" she rushed to open the door.

"At least cover yourself up," the Master cried after her.

"I don't give a fig about that," replied Margarita, already from the corridor.

And there was Azazello, already exchanging bows, greeting the Master, flashing his one eye at him, while Margarita exclaimed:

"Oh, how glad I am! I've never been so glad in my life! But forgive me, Azazello, for being naked!"

Azazello told her not to worry, assured her he had seen not only naked women, but even women with their skin completely stripped off, and sat down willingly at the table, after first putting some sort of package in dark brocade into the corner by the stove.

Margarita poured Azazello some brandy, and he willingly drank it down. The Master, without taking his eyes off him, occasionally gave his own left wrist a surreptitious pinch under the table. But these pinches did not help. Azazello did not dissolve into thin air, and, to tell the truth, there was no need for that at all. There was nothing frightening about the short, rather ginger-haired man, only perhaps the eye with the cataract, but that can happen without any sorcery, after all, and only perhaps the not entirely ordinary clothes – some sort of cassock or cloak – but again, if you think about it seriously, you do come across that sometimes too... The brandy he drank smartly as well, like all good people, by the glassful and without any food. That same brandy started a buzzing in the Master's head, and he began to think:

"No, Margarita's right! Of course, before me sits an envoy of the Devil. I mean, no further back than the night before last I was myself trying to prove to Ivan that he'd met none other than Satan at Patriarch's, and now for some reason I've taken fright at the idea and begun jabbering some stuff about hypnotists and hallucinations. What the devil have hypnotists to do with it?"

He started looking closely at Azazello and became convinced that some sort of constraint could be seen in the latter's eyes, some thought that he was not revealing until the time was ripe. "He's not simply come visiting, he's appeared with some kind of errand," thought the Master.

His powers of observation had not betrayed him.

After drinking his third glass of brandy, which had no effect at all on Azazello, the visitor began speaking thus:

"This is a cosy little basement though, damn it! Only one question arises, what can you do in it, in this little basement?"

"And I say the same thing too," replied the Master with a laugh.

"Why are you alarming me, Azazello?" asked Margarita. "We'll manage somehow!"

"Come, come!" exclaimed Azazello. "I had no thought of alarming you. I myself say 'somehow' too. Yes! I almost forgot... Messire sent you his greetings and also told me to say that he invites you to take a little walk with him, if, of course, you wish to. So what do you say to that?"

Margarita nudged the Master with her foot under the table.

"With great pleasure," the Master replied, studying Azazello, and the latter continued:

"We hope Margarita Nikolayevna won't refuse either?"

"It's a certainty that I won't refuse," said Margarita, and again her foot travelled over the Master's leg.

"The most wonderful thing!" exclaimed Azazello. "Now that I like! One, two, and it's done! Not like back then in the Alexandrovsky Garden."

"Ah, don't remind me, Azazello! I was stupid then. But anyway, you can't be too severe with me for that either – after all, it's not every day you meet up with unclean spirits!"

"I should think not," Azazello confirmed, "if it were every day, that would be a fine thing!"

"I like speed myself too," said Margarita excitedly, "I like speed and being naked... As if from a Mauser – bang! Oh, the way he shoots," exclaimed Margarita, turning to the Master. "A seven under a pillow, and any of the pips!" Margarita was starting to get drunk, which made her eyes flare up.

"And again I'd forgotten," cried Azazello, slapping himself on the forehead, "I've got myself so wound up! Messire sent you a present, didn't he," here he addressed himself specifically to the Master, "a bottle of wine. Please note, it's that same wine which was drunk by the Procurator of Judaea. Falernum wine."

It is perfectly natural that such a rarity elicited a great deal of attention from both Margarita and the Master. Azazello drew out from the piece of dark funeral brocade a jug completely covered in mould. They sniffed the wine, poured it into glasses, looked through it to the light in the window which was disappearing before the storm. They saw everything being stained the colour of blood.

"Woland's health!" exclaimed Margarita, raising her glass.

All three put their lips to their glasses and each took a large gulp. Immediately the pre-storm light began to fade in the Master's eyes, there was a catch in his breathing, and he sensed that the end was coming. He also saw how Margarita, now deathly pale and helplessly reaching out her arms to him, dropped her head onto the table and then slid down onto the floor.

"Poisoner..." the Master still had time to cry. He wanted to seize a knife from the table with which to strike Azazello, but his hand slipped helplessly from the tablecloth, everything surrounding the Master in the basement turned black, and then disappeared altogether. He fell backwards and, as he fell, cut the skin on his temple open on a corner of the top of the bureau.

When the poisoned couple had fallen quiet, Azazello began to act.

First and foremost he threw himself out of the window, and a few moments later he was inside the detached house in which Margarita Nikolayevna used to live. Always precise and thorough, Azazello wanted to check that everything had been carried out as was necessary. And everything proved to be in perfect order. Azazello saw how a gloomy woman awaiting the return of her husband came out of her bedroom, suddenly turned pale, clutched at her heart, and with a helpless cry: "Natasha! Anyone... come here!" she fell on the floor in the living room without reaching the study.

"All in order," said Azazello. A moment later he was beside the prostrate lovers. Margarita lay with her face buried in the rug. With his iron hands Azazello turned her like a doll to face him and peered at her. Before his eyes the poisoned woman's face was changing. Even in the approaching twilight of the storm her temporary witch's squint and the hardness and wildness of her features could be seen to be disappearing. The deceased woman's face lightened and finally softened, and her bared teeth became not predatory, but simply the bared teeth of feminine suffering. Then Azazello unclenched her white teeth and poured into her mouth a few drops of that same wine with which he had poisoned her. Margarita sighed, without Azazello's help began to rise, sat up and asked weakly:

"Why, Azazello, why? What have you done to me?"

She caught sight of the supine Master, shuddered and whispered:

"I didn't expect this... murderer!"

"Not at all, no," replied Azazello, "he'll get up in a minute. Oh dear, why are you so jumpy?"

Margarita believed him at once, so convincing was the voice of the red-haired demon. She leapt up, strong and lively, and helped give the supine man some wine to drink. Opening his eyes, he gave a gloomy look and repeated his last word with hatred:

"Poisoner..."

"Oh dear! Insult is the usual reward for good work," replied Azazello. "Are you really blind? Do recover your sight quickly then!"

At this point the Master rose, looked around with a gaze that was lively and bright, and asked:

"And what does this new thing mean?"

"It means," replied Azazello, "that it's time for us to go. The storm's already rumbling, do you hear it? It's getting dark. The horses are

377

pawing the ground, the little garden's shaking. Say goodbye to the basement, quickly, say goodbye."

"Ah, I understand," said the Master, gazing around, "you've killed us, we're dead. Ah, how clever that is! How timely that is! Now I understand it all."

"Oh, for pity's sake," replied Azazello, "is it you I can hear? Your girl calls you the Master, doesn't she, and you think, don't you, so how can you be dead?* In order to consider yourself alive, is it really absolutely essential to be sitting in a basement with a shirt and hospital long johns on? It's ridiculous!"

"I understand everything you've said," exclaimed the Master, "don't go on! You're a thousand times right!"

"Great Woland," Margarita began to echo him, "great Woland! He devised it much better than I did. Only the novel, the novel," she cried to the Master, "take the novel with you wherever you fly!"

"There's no need," replied the Master, "I remember it by heart."

"But will you not forget a word... not a word of it?" asked Margarita, pressing up against her lover and wiping away the blood on his badly cut temple.

"Don't worry! I shall never forget anything now," he replied.

"Then fire!" exclaimed Azazello. "Fire, from which everything began and with which we end everything."

"Fire!" cried Margarita in a terrible voice. The little window in the basement banged, the blind was blown aside by the wind. There was a brief, merry rumbling in the sky. Azazello thrust his clawed hand into the stove, pulled out a smoking brand and set light to the cloth on the table. Then he set light to a bundle of old newspapers on the divan, and after that to the manuscript and the curtain at the window.

The Master, already intoxicated by the gallop to come, threw some book out onto the table from a shelf, riffled its leaves in the burning tablecloth, and the book flared up in cheerful flame.

"Burn, burn, former life!"

"Burn, suffering!" cried Margarita.

The room was already flickering in crimson columns, and the trio ran out through the doors together with the smoke, went up the stone stairs and found themselves in the little yard. The first thing they saw there was the house owner's cook sitting on the ground, and beside her lay some spilt potatoes and several bunches of onions. The cook's state was understandable. A trio of black horses were snorting by the shed, quivering and pawing up the earth in fountains. Margarita leapt up first, after her Azazello, last the Master. The cook, with a groan, wanted to raise her hand to make the sign of the cross, but Azazello cried threateningly from the saddle:

"I'll cut your hand off!" He whistled, and the horses, breaking the branches of the limes, soared up and pierced a low, black cloud. Immediately smoke poured out from the little window of the basement. From below there carried the cook's weak, pitiful cry:

"We're on fire!"

The horses were already racing above the roofs of Moscow.

"I want to say goodbye to the city," the Master cried to Azazello, who was riding along in front. Thunder devoured the end of the Master's phrase. Azazello nodded his head and set his horse off at the gallop. A cloud was flying headlong to meet the flying riders, but not yet splashing out any rain.

They were flying over a boulevard, they could see the little figures of people running in all directions, sheltering from the rain. The first drops were falling. They flew over some smoke – all that remained of Griboyedov. They flew over the city which was already being flooded in darkness. There were flashes of lightning above them. Later the roofs gave way to greenery. Only then did the rain lash down and turn the flying riders into three huge bubbles in the water.

The sensation of flight was already familiar to Margarita, but not to the Master, and he wondered at how quickly they found themselves at their objective, where, because he had no one else to say goodbye to, the one he wanted to say goodbye to was. He recognized immediately in the shroud of rain the building of Stravinsky's clinic, the river, and the wood he had studied so closely on the other bank. They came down in a clearing in a grove not far from the clinic.

"I'll wait for you here," cried Azazello, clasping his hands together and now lit up by lightning, now disappearing in the grey shroud, "say goodbye, only quickly!"

The Master and Margarita leapt from their saddles and could be glimpsed like watery shadows as they flew off across the clinic garden. In another moment, with an accustomed hand, the Master was moving aside the grille in room No. 117. Margarita followed him. They went in to Ivanushka unseen and unnoticed in the crashing and the howling of the storm. The Master stopped beside the bed.

Ivanushka was lying motionless, just as when he had for the first time observed a storm in the house of his repose. But he was not crying like that time. When he had properly examined the dark silhouette that had burst in on him from the balcony, he rose a little, reached out his hands and said joyfully:

"Ah, it's you! I've been waiting and waiting for you. And here you are, my neighbour."

To this the Master replied:

"I'm here! But, unfortunately, I can no longer be your neighbour. I'm flying away for ever, and I've come to see you only to say goodbye."

"I knew it, I guessed," Ivan replied quietly, and asked: "Did you meet him?"

"Yes," said the Master, "I came to say goodbye to you because you were the only person I'd spoken with recently."

Ivan brightened up, and said:

"It's a good thing that you dropped in here. I'll keep my word, you know, I won't write any more poetry. Something else interests me now," Ivanushka smiled, and his mad eyes looked somewhere past the Master, "I want to write something else. While I've been lying here, you know, I've come to understand a very great deal."

The Master grew agitated at these words and, taking a seat on the edge of Ivanushka's bed, said:

"Now that's good, that's good. You write a sequel about him!"

Ivanushka's eyes flared up.

"Won't you be doing that yourself then?" At this point he hung his head and added pensively: "Ah yes... whatever am I asking," Ivanushka cast a sidelong glance at the floor, then gave a frightened look.

"That's right," said the Master, and his voice seemed to Ivanushka unfamiliar and muffled, "I won't be writing about him any longer. I'll be busy with something else."

A distant whistle cut through the noise of the storm.

"Do you hear?" asked the Master.

"It's the noise of the storm..."

"No, it's me being called, it's time for me to go," the Master explained, and rose from the bed.

"Hang on! One more word," requested Ivan, "did you find her? Did she stay true to you?"

"Here she is," said the Master, and pointed at the wall. The dark Margarita detached herself from the white wall and went up to the bed. She looked at the young man lying there, and grief could be read in her eyes.

"Poor thing, poor thing," Margarita whispered soundlessly, and bent towards the bed.

"What a beautiful woman," said Ivan, without envy, but with sadness and with a kind of quiet emotion, "look how well it's turned out for you. But that's not how it is for me." Here he had a think and added pensively: "But then perhaps it is..."

"It is, it is," Margarita whispered, and leant right down to the supine man, "now I shall kiss you on the forehead, and everything will be as it should be for you... now you just believe me on this score, I've already seen everything, I know everything."

The prostrate young man put his arms around her neck and she kissed him.

"Farewell, disciple," the Master said, scarcely audibly, and began melting into thin air. He vanished, and together with him Margarita vanished too. The balcony grille closed.

Ivanushka fell into disquiet. He sat up on the bed, looked around in alarm, even gave a groan, began talking to himself, rose. The storm was raging ever more violently and had evidently stirred up his soul. He was also worried by the fact that outside the door his hearing, already accustomed to the constant quiet, had picked up anxious footsteps, muffled voices outside the door. Fretting and already quivering, he called:

"Praskovya Fyodorovna!"

Praskovya Fyodorovna was already coming into the room, gazing at Ivan in enquiry and alarm.

"What? What is it?" she asked. "Is the storm worrying you? Well, never mind, never mind... We'll help you right away. I'll call a doctor right away."

"No, Praskovya Fyodorovna, there's no need to call a doctor," said Ivanushka, anxiously gazing not at Praskovya Fyodorovna, but at the wall, "there's nothing in particular the matter with me. I can sort everything out now, don't you worry. It'd be better if you told me," Ivan's request was heartfelt, "what's just happened next door there, in room 118?"

"In 118?" asked Praskovya Fyodorovna in return, and her eyes became shifty. "Nothing's happened there." But her voice was insincere, Ivanushka noted it immediately and said:

"Hey, Praskovya Fyodorovna! You're such a truthful person... Do you think I'll start raging? No, Praskovya Fyodorovna, there'll be none of that. But better tell me straight. I can sense everything through the wall, you know."

"Your neighbour has just died," whispered Praskovya Fyodorovna, powerless to overcome her truthfulness and kindness, and, completely clothed in the glare of the lightning, she gave Ivanushka a frightened look. But nothing terrible happened to Ivanushka. He only raised a finger meaningfully and said:

"I knew it! I can tell you for sure, Praskovya Fyodorovna, that another person has just died in the city too. I even know who," here Ivanushka smiled mysteriously. "It's a woman."

31

On the Sparrow Hills

T HE STORM HAD BEEN CARRIED OFF without a trace, and, flung in an arch across the whole of Moscow, a multicoloured rainbow hung in the sky, drinking water from the Moscow River. On high, on a hill, between two groves of trees, three dark silhouettes could be seen. Woland, Korovyev and Behemoth were sitting on saddled black horses, gazing at the city flung out beyond the river, with the broken sun gleaming in thousands of west-facing windows, and at the gingerbread towers of the Novodevichy Convent.

There was a sudden noise in the air, and Azazello, at the black tail of whose cloak flew the Master and Margarita, came down together with them beside the waiting group.

"It was necessary to disturb you, Margarita Nikolayevna and Master," began Woland after a period of silence. "but don't bear a grudge against me. I don't think you'll regret it. Well then," he turned to the Master alone, "say goodbye to the city. It's time for us to go," and Woland pointed a hand in a black bell-mouthed glove to where innumerable suns were melting the glass beyond the river, where above those suns hung the haze, smoke and steam of the city, brought to a great heat in the course of the day.

The Master threw himself from the saddle, left them sitting there and ran to the brink of the hill. His black cloak dragged over the ground behind him. The Master began looking at the city. In the first moments an aching sadness stole up on his heart, but was very quickly replaced by a slightly sweet alarm, the excitement of the wandering gypsy.

"For ever! I need to make sense of that," the Master whispered, and licked his dry, cracked lips. He began paying careful heed, and noting precisely everything that was happening in his soul. His excitement turned, as it seemed to him, into a sense of profound and deadly grievance. But this was passing, it disappeared and was replaced for some reason by proud indifference, and this by a presentiment of permanent peace.

The group of riders waited for the Master in silence. The group of riders watched the long black figure on the edge of the precipice gesticulating, now lifting his head, as though trying to cast his gaze across the entire city and see beyond its edges, now hanging his head, as though studying the trampled, sorry grass beneath his feet.

The silence was broken by the bored Behemoth.

"Allow me, *Maître*," he began, "to whistle in farewell before the ride."

"You might frighten the lady," replied Woland, "and besides, don't forget that all your disgraceful deeds of today are already done."

"Oh no, no, Messire," responded Margarita, sitting in the saddle like an Amazon, with her arms akimbo and her sharp train hanging down to the ground, "allow him, let him whistle. I'm gripped by sadness before the long journey. It's perfectly natural, isn't it, Messire, even when a person knows that at the end of the journey happiness awaits him? Let him make us laugh, or else I'm afraid this will end in tears, and everything will be spoilt ahead of the journey!"

Woland nodded to Behemoth, the latter became very animated, leapt from the saddle onto the ground, put his fingers in his mouth, puffed out his cheeks and whistled. A ringing began in Margarita's ears. Her horse reared up onto its hind legs, dry branches rained down from the trees in the grove, a whole flock of crows and sparrows took off, a column of dust flew down towards the river, and in a river tram that was passing by the landing stage, several caps were seen to be blown off passengers and into the water.

The whistle made the Master jump, yet he did not turn around, but started gesticulating even more anxiously, raising an arm towards the sky as though threatening the city. Behemoth looked around proudly.

"A whistle, I can't argue," Korovyev remarked condescendingly, "a whistle indeed, but, if one is speaking impartially, a very average whistle!"

"I'm not a precentor, after all," Behemoth, in a huff, replied with dignity, and unexpectedly winked at Margarita.

"Now let me have a try for old time's sake," Korovyev said, and rubbed his hands and blew on his fingers.

"But just mind now, just mind," Woland's stern voice was heard from atop his horse, "nothing liable to maim!"

"Messire, believe me," Korovyev responded, and placed his hand on his heart, "for a joke, solely for a joke…" Here he suddenly stretched himself up, as though he were made of elastic, formed the fingers of his right hand into an intricate sort of shape, wound himself up like a screw, and then, suddenly untwisting, whistled.

This whistle Margarita did not hear, but she did see it, as she was thrown, together with her fiery horse, some twenty metres sideways. Alongside her an oak tree was torn up by the roots, and the earth was covered in cracks right down to the river. A huge strip of the river bank, along with the landing stage and a restaurant, was set down in the river. Its water boiled up, surged up, and the entire river tram was splashed out onto the opposite bank, green and low-lying, with the passengers completely unharmed. To the feet of Margarita's snorting horse was tossed a jackdaw, killed by Fagot's whistle.

The Master was startled by this whistle. He took his head in his hands and ran back to the group of travelling companions awaiting him.

"Well then," Woland addressed him from atop his horse, "have all accounts been settled? Is the farewell complete?"

"Yes, it is," the Master replied, and, calm again, looked Woland directly and boldly in the face.

And then above the hills there rolled out, like the last trumpet, the terrible voice of Woland: "It's time!" and a sharp whistle and chuckle from Behemoth.

The horses tore away, and the riders rose up and galloped off. Margarita could feel her furious horse gnawing and pulling at the curb bit. Woland's cloak was blown up above the heads of the cavalcade, and the darkening firmament of evening began to be covered by this cloak.

When the black pall was drawn aside for a moment, Margarita turned as she rode and saw that not only were there no multicoloured towers behind her with aeroplanes swinging around above them, even the city itself had already long ceased to be there, it had sunk into the earth and left after it only a haze.

32

Forgiveness and Eternal Refuge

G ODS, MY GODS! How sad is the earth at evening! How mysterious are the mists over marshes. Whoever has wandered lost in those mists, whoever has suffered much before death, whoever has flown over that earth, bearing a load beyond his strength, he knows it. A tired man knows it. And without regret he abandons the mists of the earth, its marshes and rivers, he gives himself up into the arms of death with a light heart, knowing that just it alone...

The magic black horses, even they grew tired and carried their riders slowly, and the inescapable night began catching them up. Sensing it behind his back, even the irrepressible Behemoth fell quiet and, with his claws dug into the saddle, he flew silent and serious, with his tail fluffed up.

The black shawl of night began to cover the forests and meadows, somewhere far below the night lit melancholy little lights, no longer now of interest or use to either Margarita or the Master, foreign lights. Night was overtaking the cavalcade, sowing itself upon it from above, and tossing out, now here, now there in the saddened sky, the white specks of stars.

The night was growing denser, flying alongside, grabbing the riders by their cloaks, and in tearing them from their shoulders, exposing deceptions. And when Margarita, fanned by the cool wind, opened her eyes, she saw how the appearance of all those flying to their objective was changing. And when the crimson full moon started out from behind the edge of a forest to meet them, all deceptions vanished, sorcerous, impermanent clothing fell off into a marsh and was lost in mists.

It is unlikely that Korovyev-Fagot, the self-proclaimed interpreter for the mysterious consultant who had no need of any translations, would now have been recognized in the one who flew immediately alongside Woland now to the right hand of the Master's girl. In place of the one who in tattered circus clothes had quit the Sparrow Hills under the name of Korovyev-Fagot there now rode, with the gold chain of his rein softly ringing, a dark-violet knight with the gloomiest, never smiling face. His chin rested on his chest, he did not look at the moon, he was not interested in the earth, he was flying alongside Woland, thinking some thoughts of his own.

"Why has he changed so?" Margarita asked Woland quietly to the whistling of the wind.

"That knight once made an unfortunate joke," replied Woland, turning his face with the gently burning eye towards Margarita, "his play on words, thought up while he talked about light and darkness, was not an entirely successful one. And after that the knight has been obliged to joke a little more, and for a little longer than he had supposed. But this is a night when accounts are totted up. That knight has settled his account and closed it!"

The night had also ripped off Behemoth's fluffy tail, had torn the fur off him and sent its tufts flying over the marshes. He who had been the cat that amused the Prince of Darkness proved now to be a slim young man, a demonic page, the best jester that had ever existed in the world. Now he too had fallen quiet and was flying soundlessly with his young face upturned to the light that was pouring from the moon.

To one side of them all flew Azazello, the steel of his armour gleaming. The moon had changed his face too. The absurd, ugly fang had vanished without a trace, and the blindness in one eye had proved fake. Both of Azazello's eyes were the same, empty and black, and his face was white and cold. Now Azazello flew in his genuine guise, as the demon of the waterless desert, the killer-demon.

Margarita could not see herself, but she could see very well how the Master had changed. His hair was now white in the moonlight and was gathered at the back into a plait which flew in the wind. When the wind blew the cloak away from the Master's legs, Margarita could see on his jackboots the little stars of spurs, now dying down, now lighting up. Like the young demon, the Master flew without taking his eyes off the moon, but he was smiling at it as though it were very familiar and loved, and, after the habit acquired in room No. 118, muttering something to himself.

And finally, Woland also flew in his genuine aspect. Margarita could not have said what his horse's rein was made of, and thought it possible that it was chains of moonlight, and the horse itself was just a mass of gloom, and the horse's mane was a thundercloud, while the rider's spurs were the white specks of stars.

Thus in silence they flew for a long time until down below the terrain itself started to change. Melancholy forests were lost in the earthly gloom and carried away with them the dull blades of rivers too. Boulders appeared down below and began gleaming, while between them came the blackness of chasms which the light of the moon did not penetrate.

Woland reined in his horse on a rocky, joyless, flat summit, and then the riders moved off at walking pace, listening to the way their horses crushed the flints and stones with their shoes. Bright green moonlight flooded the platform, and in this deserted place Margarita soon made out an armchair, and in it the white figure of a seated man. It is possible that this seated man was deaf or too deep in thought. He did not hear the shuddering of the rocky earth under the weight of the horses, and without disturbing him, the riders approached him.

The moon was a great help to Margarita, shining better than the very best electric lamp, and Margarita could see that the seated man, whose eyes seemed blind, was giving his hands an occasional brief rub and had those same unseeing eyes fastened on the disc of the moon. Now Margarita could already see that beside the heavy stone armchair, on which the moon was making sparks of some kind glitter, lay a dark, huge, sharp-eared dog, which was gazing anxiously, just like its master, at the moon. At the seated man's feet there lay the pottery fragments of a broken jug, and there stretched a never-drying, red-black puddle.

The riders stopped their horses.

"Your novel has been read," began Woland, turning to the Master, "and only one thing said – that it is, unfortunately, unfinished. So then, I wanted to show you your hero. For some two thousand years he has been sitting on this platform and sleeping, but when the full moon comes, as you can see, he is tortured by insomnia. It torments not only him, but his faithful guard too, the dog. If it is true that cowardice is the gravest sin, then the dog is probably not guilty of it. Thunderstorms were the only thing the courageous dog feared. But still, the one who loves should share the lot of the one who is loved."

"What's he saying?" asked Margarita, and her perfectly calm face was covered by a cloud of compassion.

"He is saying," Woland's voice rang out, "one and the same thing. He is saying that even in the moonlight he has no peace and that he has a bad job. That's what he always says when he's not asleep, and when he's asleep, he sees one and the same thing – a path of moonlight, and he wants to set off along it and talk with the prisoner Ha-Nozri, because, as he claims, he didn't finish saying something then, long ago, on the fourteenth day of the spring month of Nisan. But, alas, for some reason he is unable to step out onto that path, and nobody comes to him. What can he do then? He has to talk to himself. However, some sort of variety is required, and to his speech about the moon he not infrequently adds that more than anything in the world he hates his immortality and unparalleled fame. He claims he would willingly exchange his lot with the ragged tramp Levi Matthew."

"Twelve thousand moons for one moon once, isn't that too much?" asked Margarita.

"Is the episode with Frieda repeating itself?" said Woland. "But, Margarita, don't trouble yourself here. All will be right, the world is built on that basis."

"Let him go!" Margarita suddenly gave a piercing cry as she had once cried when she was a witch, and this cry made a rock break away in the mountains and fly over the ledges into the abyss, its roar deafening the mountains. But Margarita could not say whether this was the roar of the fall or the roar of Satanic laughter. Whatever the case, casting looks at Margarita, Woland laughed and said:

"You shouldn't shout in the mountains, he's used to landslips anyway, and that won't alarm him. There's no need for you to intercede for him, Margarita, because the one with whom he so sought to talk has already interceded for him." Here Woland again turned to the Master and said: "Well then, you can now complete your novel with one phrase!"

It was as if the Master had already been waiting for this while standing motionless and looking at the seated Procurator. He cupped his hands into a megaphone and shouted so that the echo set off jumping over the unpeopled and unwooded mountains.

"You're free! Free! He awaits you!"

The mountains turned the Master's voice into thunder, and that same thunder destroyed them. The accursed cliff walls fell. There remained only the platform with the stone armchair. Above the black abyss into which the walls had sunk a boundless city was lit up, with glittering idols reigning over it, set above a garden filled with the luxuriant growth of many thousands of these moons. Straight to this garden stretched the Procurator's long-awaited path of moonlight, and the first to rush to run down it was the sharp-eared dog. The man in the white cloak with the blood-red lining rose from the armchair and shouted something in a hoarse, cracked voice. It was impossible to make out whether he was crying or laughing or what he was shouting. It could just be seen that following his faithful guard, he too started running headlong down the path of moonlight.

"Am I to go that way after him?" asked the Master anxiously, touching the reins.

"No," replied Woland, "why ever chase after what is already finished?"

"So that way, then?" the Master asked, and he turned and pointed back to where, hidden to their rear, there was the recently abandoned city with the gingerbread towers of the convent and the sun smashed to smithereens in its glass.

"No as well," replied Woland, and his voice condensed and began to flow above the cliffs. "Romantic Master! The one that the hero invented by you and just released by you yourself so thirsts to see, he has read your novel." Here Woland turned to Margarita: "Margarita Nikolayevna! It is impossible not to believe that you tried to devise the very best future for the Master, but truly, what I am offering you, and what Yeshua requested for you too, for you, is even better. Leave the two of them alone," said Woland, leaning from his saddle towards the saddle of the Master and pointing in the wake of the departed Procurator, "we'll keep out of their way. And perhaps they'll come to some agreement," and here Woland waved a hand in the direction of Yershalaim and it was extinguished.

"And there too," Woland pointed to the rear, "what are you to do in the little basement?" At that point the broken sun in the glass went out. "Why?" continued Woland, convincingly and gently. "O thrice romantic Master, don't you want to walk in the daytime with your girl beneath cheerful trees coming into blossom, and to listen in the evening to the music of Schubert?* Won't it be pleasant for you to write by candlelight with a goose quill? Don't you want, like Faust, to sit over a retort in the hope that you'll succeed in fashioning a new homunculus? That way, that way! A house and an old servant already await you there, the candles are already lit, but soon they'll go out, because you'll meet the dawn at once. Down that path, Master, down that one! Farewell! It's time for me to go."

"Farewell!" Margarita and the Master answered Woland in a single cry. Then black Woland, without picking out any path, flung himself into a chasm, and his suite went crashing down noisily in his wake. There were no more cliffs, nor platform, nor path of moonlight, nor Yershalaim around. The black horses had disappeared too. The Master and Margarita saw the promised dawn. It was starting right away, immediately after the midnight moon. The Master walked with his girl in the brilliance of the first rays of morning across a stony, mossy little bridge. They crossed it. The stream was left behind the faithful lovers, and they walked along a sandy path.

"Listen to the soundlessness," said Margarita to the Master, and the sand hissed beneath her bare feet, "listen and enjoy what you weren't given in life – quiet. Look, there up ahead is your eternal home, with which you've been rewarded. I can already see the Venetian window and the climbing vine, it reaches right up to the roof. There is your home, there is your eternal home. I know that in the evening those you love will come to you, those who interest you and will not trouble you. They'll play for you, they'll sing for you, you'll see what light there is in the room when the candles are lit. You'll fall asleep wearing your soiled and eternal nightcap, you'll fall asleep with a smile on your lips. Sleep will fortify you, and you'll reason wisely. And now you won't be able to drive me away. I shall be the one guarding your sleep."

Thus spoke Margarita, walking with the Master in the direction of their eternal home, and it seemed to the Master that Margarita's words were flowing in just the same way as the stream that was left behind had flowed and whispered, and the Master's memory, his uneasy memory, covered in pinpricks, began to fade away. Someone was releasing the Master to freedom, as he himself had just released the hero he had created. That hero had gone off into the abyss, had gone off irretrievably, forgiven in the night preceding Sunday, the son of the astrologer-king, the cruel fifth Procurator of Judaea, the horseman Pontius Pilate.

Epilogue

B UT ALL THE SAME, what happened next in Moscow after Woland left
the capital at sunset on the Saturday evening, vanishing along with
his suite from the Sparrow Hills?

It does not even have to be said that over the course of a long time
throughout the whole capital there was the heavy rumble of the
most improbable rumours, which very quickly spread to distant and
remote parts of the provinces too. It is nauseating even to repeat those
rumours.

The writer of these truthful lines himself personally heard in a train,
when heading for Theodosia, a story of how two thousand people in
Moscow had left a theatre stark naked, in the literal sense of the word,
and in that state had made their various ways home in taxicabs.

The whisper "unclean spirits" was heard in queues standing at dairies,
in trams, shops, apartments, kitchens, trains, both suburban and long-
distance, at stations and railway halts, at dachas and on beaches.

The most developed and cultured people, it stands to reason, took
no part in these tales of unclean spirits visiting the capital, and even
mocked them and tried to get the tellers to see reason. But a fact
nonetheless remains, as they say, a fact, and brushing it aside without
explanation is just not possible: someone had visited the capital. The
embers that remained of Griboyedov alone, and much else besides,
confirmed it too eloquently.

Cultured people took the point of view of the investigating team: a
gang of hypnotists and ventriloquists with a magnificent command of
their art had been at work.

Measures for their capture, both in Moscow and beyond its borders
too, were, of course, taken immediately and energetically, but, most
unfortunately, brought no results. The one calling himself Woland
had vanished with all his associates, and neither did he return again

391

to Moscow, nor appear anywhere at all, and nor did he reveal himself in any way. It is perfectly natural that there arose the assumption that he had fled abroad, but nowhere did he show any sign of himself there either.

The investigation of his case lasted a long time. After all, one way or another this was a monstrous case! Without even mentioning the four buildings that had been burnt down and the hundreds of people that had been driven mad, people had been killed too. This can be said for certain of two: of Berlioz, and of that ill-fated official of the Bureau for Acquainting Foreigners with the Sights of Moscow, the former Baron Maigel. They had, after all, been killed. The charred bones of the latter were discovered in apartment No. 50 on Sadovaya after the fire had been extinguished. Yes, there had been victims, and those victims demanded an investigation.

But there were other victims too, after Woland had already left the capital, and those victims were, sad though it might be, black cats.

About a hundred of these peaceable animals, devoted to man and useful to him, were shot or else destroyed by other methods in various parts of the country. Fifteen or so cats, sometimes in an extremely mutilated state, were delivered to police stations in various towns. In Armavir, for example, one of these entirely innocent beasts was led into a police station by some citizen with its front paws tied together.

The citizen had captured this cat at the moment when the animal, with a thievish look (what can you do about tomcats having such a look? It's not because they're depraved, but because they're afraid that one of the creatures stronger than they are – dogs and people – might do them some harm or injury. Both the one and the other are very easy to do, but there's no honour in it at all, I can assure you. No, none at all!), yes, so, with a thievish look the cat was for some reason about to charge into some burdock.

Falling upon the cat and ripping the tie from his own neck to tie him up, the citizen muttered venomously and threateningly:

"Aha! So now you've come to see us in Armavir, Mr Hypnotist? Well, we're not frightened of you here. And stop pretending to be dumb. We can already tell what sort of a goose you are!"

The citizen led the cat to the police station, dragging the poor beast by the front paws, bound with the green tie, and using little kicks to get the cat to be sure to walk on its hind legs.

"Just you stop," shouted the citizen, accompanied by whistling little boys, "stop playing the fool! It won't work! Be good enough to walk like everyone else does!"

The black cat only rolled its martyr's eyes. Denied by nature the gift of speech, it could not justify itself in any way. The poor beast is indebted for its salvation first of all to the police, and apart from that, to its mistress, a venerable old widow. As soon as the cat was delivered to the station, they satisfied themselves that there was the strongest possible smell of spirits coming from the citizen, in consequence of which they immediately found his testimony doubtful. And in the meantime the old woman, who had learnt from neighbours that her cat had been run in, hurried down to the station and arrived in time. She gave the cat the most complimentary references, explained that she had known it for five years, ever since it had been a kitten, vouched for it as for herself, demonstrated that it had not been observed doing anything wrong and had never been to Moscow. Just as it had been born in Armavir, so had it grown up and learnt to catch mice there.

The cat was untied and returned to the owner, having drunk, it's true, from a cup of woe, and learnt from practical experience what error and slander are.

Apart from the cats, some insignificant unpleasantness befell certain people. Several arrests took place. Among others, detained for a short time in Leningrad were Citizens Wolman and Wolper; in Saratov, Kiev and Kharkov three Wolodins; in Kazan, Woloch; and in Penza, and why is utterly unknown, a Doctor of Chemical Sciences, Vetchinkevich. True, he was of enormous height and with a very dark complexion and hair.

Caught in various places apart from that were nine Korovins, four Korovkins and two Karavayevs.

A certain citizen was removed, bound, from the Sevastopol train at the station of Belgorod. This citizen had taken it into his head to amuse his fellow passengers with some card tricks.

In Yaroslavl, just at lunchtime, a citizen appeared in a restaurant carrying a Primus which he had just got back from the menders. As soon as they saw him in the cloakroom the two doormen abandoned their posts and ran, and out of the restaurant after them ran all the customers and staff. While this was happening, in an incomprehensible manner the cashier lost all the takings.

There was a lot more besides, you couldn't remember everything. Minds were in great ferment.

Over and over again, credit has to be given to the investigation team. Everything was done not only to catch the criminals, but also to explain everything they had got up to. And it was all explained, and those explanations cannot but be deemed both sensible and irrefutable.

Representatives of the investigation team and experienced psychiatrists established that the members of the criminal gang, or, perhaps, one of them (suspicion for this fell principally on Korovyev), were hypnotists of unprecedented power, able to show themselves not where they actually were, but in imaginary, displaced positions. Apart from that, they could readily suggest to those who encountered them that certain things or people were to be found where they actually were not, and, on the contrary, could remove from a field of vision those things or people which really were in that field of vision.

In the light of such explanations absolutely everything is understandable, and even the thing that worried citizens the most, the seemingly totally inexplicable invulnerability of the cat when being fired at in apartment No. 50 in the attempts to take him into custody.

Naturally, there had been no cat on the chandelier, and nobody had even thought of firing back; shots had been fired at an empty space, while Korovyev, who had suggested that the cat was making mischief on the chandelier, could have readily been behind the backs of those shooting, acting up and enjoying his enormous, but criminally employed capability for suggestion. It was he, of course, who had set the apartment alight after spilling out the petrol.

Styopa Likhodeyev, of course, had not flown off to any Yalta (such a trick was beyond the power even of Korovyev) and had not sent any telegrams from there. After he had fainted in the jeweller's widow's apartment, frightened by Korovyev's trick of showing him the cat with a pickled mushroom on a fork, he had lain there until Korovyev, making fun of him, had rammed a felt hat onto him and sent him to the Moscow aerodrome, suggesting beforehand to the representatives of the CID meeting him that Styopa was climbing out of an aeroplane that had flown in from Sevastopol.

True, the Yalta CID affirmed that it had received the barefooted Styopa and sent telegrams regarding Styopa to Moscow, but not a single copy of those telegrams was discovered in any files, from which was drawn the sad but utterly indestructible conclusion that the band of hypnotists had the ability to hypnotize at a huge distance, and, moreover, not only individuals, but also whole groups of them. Under these conditions the criminals could drive people with the most stable psychological make-up out of their minds.

So why bother even mentioning such trifles as a pack of cards in a stranger's pocket in the stalls, or women's dresses that disappeared, or a miaowing beret and other things of the same kind! Such tricks can be played by any professional hypnotist of average power on any stage, including the straightforward trick with the ripping off of the compère's head. A speaking cat is downright trivial too. In order to present people with such a cat, it is enough to know the first basics of ventriloquy, and no one is likely to have doubted that Korovyev's art went significantly further than those basics.

No, this isn't a matter of packs of cards at all, and not of forged letters in Nikanor Ivanovich's briefcase. That's all trifles! It was he, Korovyev, that drove Berlioz under the tram to certain death. It was he that drove the poor poet Ivan Bezdomny out of his mind, he that made him dream and see in his torturous dreams ancient Yershalaim, and sun-scorched, waterless Bald Mountain with three hanged men on poles. It was he and his gang that made Margarita Nikolayevna and her maid, the beautiful Natasha, vanish from Moscow.* Incidentally, the investigation worked on that business with particular attention. It demanded to be cleared up whether these women had been abducted by the gang of murderers and arsonists, or had they fled along with the criminal grouping willingly? On the basis of the absurd and muddled testimony of Nikolai Ivanovich, and taking into account Margarita Nikolayevna's strange and mad note left for her husband, a note in which she writes that she is leaving to be a witch, and considering the fact that Natasha had vanished, leaving all her personal items of clothing where they were – the investigation came to the conclusion that both the mistress and the maid had been hypnotized, like many others, and in that state abducted by the band. There also arose the probably perfectly correct idea that the criminals had been attracted by the beauty of both women.

But what remained quite unclear for the investigating team was the motive that had made the gang abduct the madman calling himself the Master from the psychiatric clinic.* This they were unable to establish, just as they were also unable to get hold of the surname of the abducted patient. And so he was lost for ever under the lifeless alias: "No. 118 from block 1".

And so almost everything was explained and the investigation came to an end, as everything in general comes to an end.

Several years passed, and citizens began to forget both Woland, and Korovyev and the rest. Many changes took place in the lives of those who had suffered because of Woland and his associates, and no matter how minor and insignificant those changes, they ought to be noted all the same.

George Bengalsky, for example, having spent three months in the clinic, got well and came out, but was forced to leave his job at The Variety, and at the very busiest time, when the public was swarming for tickets – memories of the black magic and its exposure proved to be very long-lived. Bengalsky gave up The Variety because he realized that appearing every evening in front of two thousand people, inevitably being recognized and endlessly subjected to gibing questions about what he preferred: with a head or without? – was too excruciating.

Yes, and besides, the compère had lost a significant dose of his cheerfulness, something which is so essential in his profession. He was left with the unpleasant, distressing habit of falling into a state of alarm every spring at full moon, suddenly grabbing himself by the neck, looking around in fright and crying. These fits would pass, but all the same, given them, it was not possible to do his previous work, and the compère went into retirement and began living on his savings, which, according to his modest calculations, ought to suffice him for fifteen years.

He left and never again met with Varenukha, who won universal popularity and love with his unbelievable, even among theatre managers, responsiveness and politeness. Complimentary ticket seekers, for example, never called him anything other than their father and benefactor. Whatever time anybody phoned The Variety, in the receiver would always be heard a soft, but sad voice: "Hello," and to the request to ask Varenukha to come to the phone the same voice would hurriedly reply: "I'm at your service." But on the other hand, how Ivan Savelyevich did suffer for his politeness too!

Styopa Likhodeyev no longer has to talk with The Variety on the telephone. Immediately after leaving the clinic, in which Styopa spent eight days, he was transferred to Rostov, where he was appointed to the position of manager of a large grocery store. There are rumours that he has completely stopped drinking port and drinks only vodka infused with currant buds, which has made him much healthier. They say he has become taciturn and started avoiding women.

Stepan Bogdanovich's removal from The Variety did not bring Rimsky the joy of which he had dreamt so greedily over the course of several years. After the clinic and Kislovodsk, the ever so, ever so old Financial Director with his shaking head handed in his resignation from The Variety. It is interesting that this resignation was brought to The Variety by Rimsky's spouse. Even in the daytime Grigory Danilovich himself could not find the strength within him to be inside that building where he had seen the cracked pane of glass in the window, flooded in moonlight, and the long arm reaching through towards the lower catch.

Having left The Variety, the Financial Director joined the children's puppet theatre in Zamoskvorechye. In this theatre he no longer had occasion to clash over matters of acoustics with the most venerable Arkady Apollonovich Sempleyarov. In two ticks the latter had been transferred to Bryansk and appointed manager of a mushroom preparation point. Muscovites now eat pickled saffron milk-caps and marinated boletuses, can't praise them enough, and are extremely glad of this transfer.

It's a thing of the past, so it can be said that Arkady Apollonovich had not got on too well with the acoustics business, and however much he had tried to improve them, they had remained just as they had been.

To the ranks of those who broke with the theatre, besides Arkady Apollonovich, should be added Nikanor Ivanovich Bosoi too, although he was not even linked in any way with theatres, except by his love of free tickets. Not only does Nikanor Ivanovich not go to any theatre either for money or for free, he even changes countenance at any theatrical conversation. Not to a lesser, but rather to a greater degree has he come to hate, besides the theatre, the poet Pushkin and the talented artiste Savva Potapovich Kurolesov. The latter to such a degree that last year, when he saw in a newspaper a black-bordered announcement that, at the very height of his career, Savva Potapovich had suffered a stroke, Nikanor Ivanovich turned so crimson that he himself almost set off in Savva Petrovich's wake, and roared: "Serves him right!" Moreover, that same evening, Nikanor Ivanovich, who was plunged by the death of the popular artiste into a mass of painful memories, alone, with only the full moon illuminating Sadovaya for company, got terribly drunk. And with every glass the accursed chain of hateful figures before him lengthened, and in that chain were Sergei Gerardovich Dunchil, and the beautiful Ida Gerkulanovna, and that red-haired owner of the fighting geese, and the candid Nikolai Kanavkin.

Well, and what happened to them? For pity's sake! Precisely nothing happened to them, and nothing can happen to them, for they never existed in reality, as the likeable artiste and compère did not exist, and as the theatre itself, and the old skinflint, Porokhovnikov's auntie, who left foreign currency to rot in the cellar, and, of course, the gold trumpets and the insolent cooks did not exist. All that was only dreamt by Nikanor Ivanovich under the influence of that rascal Korovyev. The only living person that flew into that dream was actually Savva Potapovich, the artiste, and he got mixed up in it only because he had engraved himself in Nikanor Ivanovich's memory thanks to his frequent radio performances. *He* existed, but the rest didn't.

So perhaps Aloizy Mogarych didn't exist either? Oh no! Not only did he exist, he does even now, and, to be precise, in the post that Rimsky gave up, that is, in the post of Financial Director of The Variety.

Coming to his senses in a train somewhere outside Vyatka approximately twenty-four hours after his call on Woland, Aloizy found that, leaving Moscow for some reason in a disturbed state of mind, he had forgotten to put on his trousers, but had, on the other hand, incomprehensibly for him, stolen the house owner's register of tenants, which he did not need at all. Paying a colossal sum of money to the carriage attendant, Aloizy acquired an old and soiled pair of trousers from him, and he turned back from Vyatka. But the privately owned little house was, alas, no longer to be found. The ramshackle clutter had been completely wiped out by fire. But Aloizy was an extremely enterprising man. Two weeks later he was already living in a splendid room on Bryusovsky Lane, and after a few months was already sitting in Rimsky's office. And as Rimsky had suffered previously because of Styopa, so now Varenukha went through torment because of Aloizy. Ivan Savelyevich dreams of only one thing, that this Aloizy should be removed from The Variety to somewhere out of his sight, because, as Varenukha sometimes whispers in intimate company, never in his life has he apparently met such a bastard as that Aloizy, and he apparently expects anything you can name from that Aloizy.

However, perhaps the manager is biased. Aloizy has not been seen to have done any dirty work, nor indeed any work at all, if you don't count, of course, the appointment of someone else to the job of the barman, Sokov. Andrei Fokich himself died of liver cancer in the First Moscow University Clinic some nine months after Woland's appearance in Moscow...

Yes, a few years passed, and the events truthfully described in this book dragged on and died away in the memory. But not for everyone, not for everyone!

Every year, as soon as the festive spring full moon arrives, towards evening there appears under the lime trees at Patriarch's Ponds a man of thirty or thirty plus. A rather ginger-haired, green-eyed, modestly dressed man. He is a member of the Institute of History and Philosophy, Professor Ivan Nikolayevich Ponyrev.

Arriving under the limes, he always sits down on that same bench on which he sat that evening when Berlioz, long forgotten by all, saw the moon breaking up into pieces for the last time in his life. Now whole, white at the beginning of the evening and later gold, with a dark little horse-cum-dragon, it floats above the former poet, Ivan Nikolayevich, and at the same time stays in the same place in its eminence.

Everything is known to Ivan Nikolayevich, he knows and understands everything. He knows that in his youth he became the victim of criminal hypnotists, afterwards underwent treatment and recovered. But he also knows that there is something he cannot control. He cannot control this spring full moon. As soon as it begins to approach, as soon as the luminary which once hung above the two five-branched candlesticks begins to grow and fill with gold, Ivan Nikolayevich becomes uneasy, he frets, loses his appetite and sleep, and waits for the moon to mature. And when the full moon arrives, nothing can keep Ivan Nikolayevich at home. Towards evening he goes out and walks to Patriarch's Ponds.

Sitting on the bench, Ivan Nikolayevich already talks openly to himself, smokes, squints now at the moon, now at the turnstile he remembers so well.

Ivan Nikolayevich spends an hour or two like this. Then he moves off from his place and, always by one and the same route, via Spiridonovka, with empty, unseeing eyes he goes to the side streets of the Arbat.

He passes by the oil shop, turns where the crooked old gas lamp post is, and steals up to the railings, behind which he sees a splendid, but as yet undressed garden, and in it – tinged by the moon on the side where the skylight with the triple-casement window juts out, and dark on the other one – a Gothic detached house.

The Professor does not know what draws him to the railings or who lives in this house, but he knows he does not have to struggle with himself during the full moon. Besides that, he knows that in the garden behind the railings he will inevitably see one and the same thing.

Sitting on a bench he sees an elderly and solid man with a little beard, wearing a pince-nez and with slightly piggish facial features. Ivan Nikolayevich always finds this resident of the house in one and the same dreamy pose, with his gaze turned towards the moon. Ivan Nikolayevich knows that, after feasting his eyes upon the moon, the seated man will be sure to transfer his eyes to the skylight windows and fasten his gaze on them, as though expecting them to fly open at any minute and something extraordinary to appear on the window sill.

All that follows, Ivan Nikolayevich knows by heart. At this point he must be sure to take cover a little further back behind the railings, for now the seated man will begin restlessly turning his head round and round, trying to catch something in the air with his roaming eyes and smiling ecstatically, and then he will suddenly clasp his hands together in a kind of delicious anguish, and will then both simply and quite loudly mutter:

"Venus! Venus!… Oh what a fool I am!"

"Gods, gods!" Ivan Nikolayevich will start to whisper, hiding behind the railings and not taking his burning eyes off the mysterious stranger. "There's another victim of the moon… Yes, that's another victim, like me."

And the seated man will continue his speeches:

"Oh what a fool I am! Why didn't I fly away with her? What was I afraid of, old ass that I am! Got myself a document! Oh dear, put up with it now, you old cretin!"

Thus he will continue until a window bangs in the dark part of the house, something whitish appears in it, and an unpleasant female voice rings out:

"Nikolai Ivanovich, where are you? What are these fantasies? Do you want to catch malaria? Come and drink your tea!"

Here, of course, the seated man will come to and answer in a lying voice:

"Air, I wanted to get a breath of air, my darling! The air's really very good!"

And here he will rise from the bench, stealthily shake his fist at the closing window and trudge off into the house.

"He's lying, lying! O gods, how he's lying!" mutters Ivan Nikolayevich, moving off from the railings. "It isn't the air that draws him into the garden at all, he sees something at this spring full moon, on the moon and in the garden, up on high. Ah, I'd pay dearly to get to the heart of his secret, to know what Venus it was he lost and now fruitlessly gropes for with his hands in the air, trying to catch her."

And the Professor returns home, by now quite unwell. His wife pretends not to notice his condition and hurries him into bed. But she herself does not go to bed, and sits by the lamp with a book and looks at the sleeping man with bitter eyes. She knows Ivan Nikolayevich will wake up at dawn with an agonizing cry, will start sobbing and tossing about, and that is why in front of her on the tablecloth beneath the lamp lies a syringe in some spirit, prepared in advance, and an ampoule of liquid the colour of strong tea.

The poor woman, bound to a man with a serious illness, is now free and can go to sleep without any misgivings. After the injection Ivan Nikolayevich will sleep till morning with a happy face and dream dreams unknown to her, but somehow sublime and happy.

The scholar is woken up and driven to that piteous cry on the night of the full moon by one and the same thing. He sees an unnatural, noseless executioner, who, with a little jump and a sort of hoot, stabs a spear into the heart of Gestas, who is tied to a pole and has lost his reason. But it is not so much the executioner that is terrifying as the unnatural lighting in the dream, resulting from some sort of cloud which seethes and falls upon the earth, as happens only during natural disasters.

After the injection everything in front of the sleeping man changes. From the bed to the window stretches a broad path of moonlight, and a man in a white cloak with a blood-red lining climbs up onto this path and begins walking towards the moon. Beside him walks a young man wearing a ragged chiton and with a disfigured face. As they walk, they talk about something heatedly, arguing, trying to come to an agreement about something.

"Gods, gods!" says the man in the cloak, turning his haughty face to his companion. "What a vulgar execution! But tell me, please," here his face turns from a haughty to an imploring one, "it didn't take place, did it? I beseech you, tell me it didn't?"

"Well, of course it didn't," his companion replies in a hoarse voice, "you imagined it."

"And can you swear to that?" the man wearing the cloak asks ingratiatingly.

"I swear it!" his companion replies, and for some reason his eyes are smiling.

"I need nothing more!" the man wearing the cloak cries out in a cracked voice, and climbs still higher towards the moon, drawing his companion on. Behind them walks a calm and majestic, gigantic sharp-eared dog.

Then the track of moonlight boils up, out of it starts gushing a river of moonlight, which spills out in all directions. The moon dominates and plays, the moon dances and misbehaves. Then in the torrent a woman of inordinate beauty takes shape and leads out by the hand towards Ivan a man with a growth of stubbly beard who gazes around in fright. Ivan Nikolayevich recognizes him immediately. It is that No. 118, his nocturnal guest, and Ivan Nikolayevich stretches his arms out to him in his sleep and asks greedily:

"So that was how it ended then?"

"That was how it ended, my disciple," No. 118 replies, and the woman comes up to Ivan and says:

"Of course that was how. Everything ended and everything is ending... And I shall kiss you on the forehead, and everything will be as it should be for you."

She bends towards Ivan and kisses him on the forehead, and Ivan strains towards her and peers into her eyes, but she steps back and goes away together with her companion towards the moon...

Then the moon becomes frenetic, it rains torrents of light straight down on Ivan, it sprays light out in all directions, a flood of moonlight begins in the room, the light is rocking, rising higher, submerging the bed. Then it is that Ivan Nikolayevich sleeps with a happy face.

In the morning he wakes up taciturn, but perfectly calm and well. His pricked memory quietens down, and until the next full moon the Professor will be troubled by no one: neither the noseless murderer of Gestas, nor the cruel fifth Procurator of Judaea, the horseman Pontius Pilate.

Note on the Text

The text used for this translation, approved by the Bulgakov estate, is found in M.A. Bulgakov, *Izbrannye proizvedeniia* v 3-kh tomakh (Moskva: 'Natasha', 'Literatura', 'Algoritm', 1996), reproduced in Mikhail Bulgakov, *Izbrannye proizvedeniia* v 2-kh tomakh (Moskva: RIPOL Klassik, 2004).

Notes

p. 1, *so who are you... Faust*: The quotation is from the 'Faust's study' scene from part 1 of the drama *Faust* (1808–32) by J.W. von Goethe (1749–1832), lines 1334–36.

p. 5, *MASSOLIT*: The organization is an invention of Bulgakov's.

p. 5, *Bezdomny*: The poet's pseudonym, reminiscent of those of Maxim Gorky ("bitter"), Demyan Bedny ("poor") and others, means "homeless".

p. 5, *Narzan*: Sparkling mineral water.

p. 7, *Philo of Alexandria*: A philosopher and religious thinker (*c*.25 BC –50 AD).

p. 7, *Josephus Flavius*: Roman historian (37 AD–after 100).

p. 7, *the celebrated Annales of Tacitus*: The chronicle *Annales* by Gaius Cornelius Tacitus (*c*.55–*c*.120) deals with Roman history of the years 14–68.

p. 8, *Osiris... and earth*: The Egyptian god of death, life and fertility.

p. 8, *Tammuz*: The Mesopotamian god of fertility.

p. 8, *Marduk*: The most important god in the Babylonian pantheon.

p. 8, *Huitzilopochtli... Aztecs in Mexico*: The Aztec sun and war god.

p. 11, *Immanuel's idea... also unconvincing*: A reference to the philosopher Immanuel Kant (1724–1804), his analyses of the traditional arguments for the existence of God and his own attempt at a new one.

p. 11, *Schiller*: German poet and dramatist Friedrich von Schiller (1759–1805).

p. 11, *Strauss*: German theologian David Friedrich Strauss (1808–74). In his major work, *The Life of Jesus*, he made the pioneering step of taking a historical approach to Christ's existence.

p. 11, *Solovki*: The popular name for the prison camp established at the Solovetsky Monastery on an island in the White Sea.

p. 16, *Gerbert of Aurillac*: Otherwise known as Pope Sylvester II (938–1003).

p. 17, *Nisan*: The Jewish month which lasts for twenty days at the end of March and the beginning of April, with the seven days of the Feast of the Passover beginning on the 14th.

p. 17, *Herod the Great*: Herod (74–4 BC) was king of Judaea from 40 BC until his death.

p. 17, *Pontius Pilate*: Pilate was Procurator of Judaea from 26 to 36 AD.

p. 17, *Yershalaim*: An alternative transliteration for "Jerusalem" from the Hebrew.

p. 20, *Hegemon*: "Leader" (Greek).

p. 20, *Yeshua*: "The Lord is salvation" (Aramaic).

p. 20, *Ha-Nozri*: "From Nazareth" (Aramaic).

p. 26, *Dismas… Gestas… Bar-rabban*: Dismas and Gestas are the apocryphal names given to the two thieves crucified alongside Jesus. Bar-rabban is a lesser-known variant of the name Barabbas.

p. 26, *Battle of Idistavizo*: The battle was fought between the Romans and German tribes on the right bank of the Weser in 16 AD.

p. 28, *Lit the lamps*: Jewish law apparently required that two candles were lit to establish that hidden witnesses were able to see the accused properly.

p. 29, *Emperor Tiberius*: Tiberius Claudius Nero (42 BC–37 AD), second Emperor of Rome from 14 AD.

p. 29, *caligae*: The Latin term for the boots worn by Roman soldiers.

p. 31, *Bald Mountain*: Known in the Gospels as Golgotha.

p. 31, *ala*: A division of allied horseman providing flanking cover for a legion in battle, from the Latin word for "wing".

p. 35, *horseman of the Golden Lance*: This refers to an equestrian order of the Roman nobility, below only the Senate in its importance. By Pilate's time, many members of the order filled administrative posts.

p. 51, *wedding candles*: A traditional part of the Orthodox marriage ceremony, during which they are held by the bride and groom.

p. 52, *tolstovka*: A traditional Russian shirt.

p. 53, *the opera Eugene Onegin*: Tchaikovsky (1840–93) wrote this opera, first performed in 1879, which was based on the novel in verse *Eugene Onegin* (1825–32) by Alexander Pushkin (1799–1837).

p. 53, *Tatyana*: Tatyana Larina, the heroine of *Eugene Onegin*.

p. 54, *The house was called... Griboyedova*: A reference to the writer Alexander Sergeyevich Griboyedov (1795–1829), a playwright and poet whom Bulgakov was known to admire.

p. 54, *The Misfortune of Wit*: Also translated as "Woe from Wit" and "The Woes of Wit", this verse satire, first published in 1825, was Griboyedov's masterpiece.

p. 54, *Perelygino*: The area outside Moscow where there was a concentration of dachas for writers in Soviet times is called Peredelkino.

p. 58, *Basedow's disease*: A thyroid disorder also known as Graves's disease.

p. 59, *Hallelujah*: The foxtrot by Vincent Youmans (1898–1946) was published in Leningrad in 1928.

p. 61, *we're alive, you know*: An allusion to the response of colleagues to the death of Ivan Ilyich in the 1887 story of that name by L.N. Tolstoy (1828–1910).

p. 68, *the composer*: Hector Berlioz (1803–69), among whose works are several that are thematically connected with *The Master and Margarita*, notably *The Damnation of Faust* (1846).

p. 72, *metal man on a pedestal*: The monument to Alexander Pushkin by A.M. Opekushin (1838–1923), officially unveiled in 1880.

p. 73, *Stormy darkness*: The opening words of Pushkin's poem of 1825 'A Winter's Evening'.

p. 73, *White Guard... immortality*: Pushkin died following a duel in January 1837 with Georges d'Anthès (1812–95), whose social position as the adopted son of an ambassador made him the pre-revolutionary equivalent of an anti-Bolshevik White Guard.

p. 73, *Abrau*: Abrau Durso is a North Caucasian sparkling wine.

p. 75, *pokoi*: This refers to the letter that in Russian script looks like this: П. *Pokoi* can also mean "peace, quiet".

p. 77, *pyramidon*: A pain-reliever like aspirin.

p. 79, *Woland*: Bulgakov may have taken this name from a demon's name (Voland) in *Faust* by J.W. von Goethe.

p. 81, *On the door handle... wax seal on a string*: This usually meant that someone had been arrested and their possessions had been sealed for further investigation.

p. 84, *Messire*: "Sir" (French).

p. 99, *Eins, zwei, drei*: "One, two, three" (German).

p. 100, *speculating in foreign currency*: Speculating in foreign currency was illegal under Soviet law.

p. 105, *A False Dmitry*: Grigory Otrepyev became the figurehead for the opposition to the rule of Boris Godunov in 1604, when he claimed to be Dmitry, a son of Ivan the Terrible believed to have died in 1591. He was hailed as tsar after Godunov's death in 1605, but was deposed and killed the following year.

p. 106, *the cliffs, my refuge*: A line from 'Aufenthalt' by Schubert (1797–1828), from his *Schwanengesang* cycle – the words were written by the poet Ludwig Rellstab (1799–1860).

p. 124, *Avec plaisir*: "With pleasure" (French).

p. 130, *Oui, madame*: "Yes, madam" (French).

p. 131, *Louisa*: Louisa Miller is the heroine of *Intrigue and Love* (1783) by Friedrich von Schiller (1759–1805).

p. 132, *His Royal Majesty… The cutest girls in town*: A reworking of lines from the vaudeville *Lev Gurych Sinichkin, or The Provincial Debutante* (1839) by D.T. Lensky (1805–60).

p. 136, *Faust*: The opera of 1859 by Charles Gounod (1818–93).

p. 145, *Old Believer*: "Old Believers" was the name given to those who separated from the Russian Orthodox Church after the schism of the seventeenth century.

p. 155, *Ai-Danil*: A Crimean table wine named after its place of origin near Yalta.

p. 164, *La Fontaine fables*: The great collection of verse fables by Jean de la Fontaine (1621–95) appeared in 1668.

p. 167, *the Miserly Knight… Pushkin*: One of Pushkin's four *Little Tragedies*, composed in 1830.

p. 169, *Einem*: The best-known firm of Russian confectioners, which became Red October after the Revolution.

p. 170, *Great piles… to me*: From an aria in Tchaikovsky's opera *The Queen of Spades* (1890), based on the story by Pushkin of 1834.

p. 193, *sacred Baikal*: The song 'Glorious Sea, Sacred Baikal' is a popular song about the experience of prisoners in Siberia, based on an original poem 'Thoughts of a Runaway on Baikal' (1848) by D.P. Davydov.

p. 193, *Barguzin*: The name of a particularly strong wind that blows on Lake Baikal.

p. 194, *Shilka and Nerchinsk*: Two place names with which the third verse of the song 'Glorious Sea, Sacred Baikal' begins.

p. 195, *Lermontov*: The poet, playwright and novelist Mikhail Yuryevich Lermontov (1814–41).

p. 198, *the monument to Prince Vladimir*: The monument to Vladimir I (St Vladimir, *c*.956–1015) by V.I. Demut-Malinovsky (1779–1846) and Baron P.K. Klodt (1805–67), unveiled in 1853.

p. 202, *Passport*: A passport was required to live, travel and receive an inheritance, among other things.

p. 203, *Everything... in the Oblonskys' house*: The second sentence of Tolstoy's *Anna Karenina* (1875–77).

p. 211, *Newton's binomial theorem*: A complex mathematical formula invented by Sir Isaac Newton (1642–1727) to calculate the expansion of powers of sums.

p. 217, *Sister of Mercy*: The Sisters of Mercy is an order of Catholic women which was founded in 1831.

p. 227, *Lovelace*: Lovelace is a character in *Clarissa* (1748) by Samuel Richardson (1689–1761), and is a notorious womanizer.

p. 251, *Claudine*: Claudine, Countess of Tournon, (1520–91) was a lady-in-waiting to Marguerite de Valois (see next note).

p. 251, *Queen Margot*: Marguerite de Valois (1553–1615), Queen of Navarre and first wife of Henri IV of France, often referred to as "la reine Margot".

p. 251, *bloody wedding of his friend Guessard in Paris*: The marriage of Marguerite de Valois and Henri IV was marked by the St Bartholomew's Day massacre of Huguenots in Paris in 1572; François Guessard (1814–82) was the publisher of Marguerite's correspondence (1842).

p. 260, *Gans*: "Goose" (German).

p. 261, *Sextus Empiricus*: A Greek physician and philosopher of the second and possibly third century AD.

p. 261, *Martianus Capella*: A fifth-century writer and philosopher.

p. 261, *donna*: "Madam" (Italian).

p. 263, *maître*: "Master" (French).

p. 268, *Vieuxtemps*: Henri Vieuxtemps (1820–81), Belgian composer and violinist.

p. 268, *Johan Strauss*: Presumably "the younger" (1825–99), the Austrian composer of hundreds of waltzes, who eclipsed his father (1804–49), the founder of the Viennese waltz tradition.

p. 270, *Monsieur Jacques*: Jacques Cœur (*c*.1400–56), French financier and merchant, accused of poisoning Agnès Sorel, mistress of Charles VII of France.

p. 271, *Count Robert... his wife*: Robert Dudley, Earl of Leicester (1532–88), favourite of Elizabeth I, suspected of involvement in the suspicious death of his first wife.

p. 271, *Tofana*: Teofania di Adamo (1653–1719) the alleged inventor of the poison *aqua tofana*.

p. 272, *Spanish boot*: An instrument of torture.

p. 273, *nothing to feed the child with*: This is the story of a Swiss seamstress, Frieda Keller, as described by the psychologist August Forel (1848–1931).

p. 274, *over their inheritance*: Marie-Madeleine-Marguerite d'Aubray, Marquise de Brinvilliers (1630–76).

p. 274, *Minkina*: Nastasya Fyodorovna Minkina, mistress of Alexander I's all-powerful minister, Count Arakcheyev, was murdered by domestic servants in 1825.

p. 274, *Emperor Rudolf*: Rudolf II (1552–1612), Habsburg Emperor of Germany.

p. 275, *Gaius Caesar Caligula*: Caligula (12–41) was the third Emperor of Rome.

p. 275, *Messalina*: Valeria Messalina (d.48 AD), wife of the Emperor Claudius.

p. 275, *Malyuta Skuratov*: Grigory Skuratov-Belsky (d.1573), nicknamed Malyuta, was the right-hand man of Ivan the Terrible (1530–84).

p. 276, *office with poison*: The one-time People's Commissar for Internal Affairs, G.G. Yagoda (1891–1938), and his secretary, P.P. Bulanov, were accused in their show trial of this crime against Yagoda's successor, N.I. Yezhov (1895–1940).

p. 279, *accordance with his beliefs*: See Matthew 9:29: "According to your faith be it unto you."

p. 281, *noblesse oblige*: "Rank imposes obligations" (French).

p. 295, *Bruderschaft*: "Brotherhood" (German).

p. 301, *a door banged... Annushka... her head against the wall*: This is an example of inconsistency on Bulgakov's part: on page 295, we are told that Mogarych is thrown through the window of Woland's bedroom. Bulgakov never properly revised the second part of *The*

Master and Margarita, so inconsistencies like this remain in the text.

p. 309, *Falernum*: A Roman white wine.

p. 309, *Cecubum*: A Roman red wine.

p. 310, *Feast of the Twelve Gods*: The twelve senior gods and goddesses of Roman mythology.

p. 310, *lares*: This originally meant "good spirits of the earth", but later came to mean "spirits of ancestors and guardians of human habitations" (Latin).

p. 313, *Afranius*: One Afranius Burrus carried out police duties as Praetorian Prefect of Rome, dying in 62 AD.

p. 326, *I, a foundling... the beautiful Pila*: Pilate's genealogy here is taken from medieval legend.

p. 328, *Valerius Gratus's time*: Valerius Gratus was Pilate's predecessor as Procurator of Judaea in the years 15–25 AD.

p. 335, *pure river of the water of life... crystal*: See Revelation 22:1: "And he showed me a pure river of water of life, clear as crystal, proceeding out of the throne of God and of the Lamb."

p. 338, *a large asphalt-covered square*: Moscow's secret police headquarters looks out on Lubyanskaya Square, hence its popular name, the Lubyanka.

p. 346, *starka*: A kind of Lithuanian or Polish vodka.

p. 353, *Torgsin*: The name is an abbreviation for "trade with foreigners".

p. 354, *the story of the renowned Caliph Haroun-al-Rashid*: The fifth Abbasid Caliph of Baghdad (763–809) was immortalized in *The Arabian Nights*.

p. 357, *bitter... at an old-time wedding*: It is the custom for the guests celebrating a Russian wedding to shout "bitter" to encourage the bride and groom to kiss and make life sweet.

p. 359, *Don Quixote*: The novel (1605–15) by Miguel de Cervantes Saavedra (1547–1616).

p. 359, *Faust*: A reference to the play *Faust* by J.W. von Goethe.

p. 359, *Dead Souls*: The uncompleted intended trilogy (first part published in 1842) by N.V. Gogol (1809–52).

p. 359, *Melpomene, Polyhymnia and Thalia*: The Greek Muses of Tragedy, Hymns and Comedy respectively.

p. 359, *The Government Inspector*: The comedy (1836) by Gogol.

p. 359, *Eugene Onegin*: The novel in verse by Pushkin.

p. 361, *Panayev*: There had been two Panayevs in Russian literature: Vladimir Ivanovich (1792–1859), a poet known for his idylls, and Ivan Ivanovich (1812–1862), a writer of prose fiction and a noted journalist.

p. 361, *Skabichevsky*: A.M. Skabichevsky (1838–1910), the critic, literary historian and publicist.

p. 365, *one of the most beautiful buildings... before*: The Pashkov House, built by V.I. Bazhenov (1737–99) in 1784–86.

p. 368, *Salut*: "Greetings" (French).

p. 368, *Timiryazev*: The monument by S.D. Merkurov to the natural scientist K.A. Timiryazev (1843–1920), standing since the early 1920s on Tverskoy Boulevard.

p. 370, *It's Time! It's Time!*: An allusion to a Pushkin poem of 1834: "It's time, my friend, it's time! My heart is seeking peace now".

p. 378, *you think... how can you be dead?*: An allusion to the proposition of René Descartes (1596–1650): "I think, therefore I am."

p. 389, *Schubert*: Franz Schubert (1797–1828), the famous composer.

p. 395 *Margarita Nikolayevna and... Natasha, vanish from Moscow*: Obviously there is a significant discrepancy between this and the last scene of chapter 30 – no doubt Bulgakov would have amended the mistake if he had had time to revise the complete text.

p. 395 *abduct the... Master from the psychiatric clinic*: Obviously there is another discrepancy between this and the last scene of chapter 30.

Extra Material

on

Mikhail Bulgakov's

The Master and Margarita

Mikhail Bulgakov's Life

Mikhail Afanasyevich Bulgakov was born in Kiev – then in the Russian Empire, now the capital of independent Ukraine – on 15th May 1891. He was the eldest of seven children – four sisters and three brothers – and, although born in Ukraine, his family were Russians, and were all members of the educated classes – mainly from the medical, teaching and ecclesiastical professions. His grandfathers were both Russian Orthodox priests, while his father lectured at Kiev Theological Academy. Although a believer, he was never fanatical, and he encouraged his children to read as widely as they wished, and to make up their own minds on everything. His mother was a teacher and several of his uncles were doctors. *Birth, Family Background and Education*

In 1906 his father became ill with sclerosis of the kidneys. The Theological Academy immediately awarded him a full pension, even though he had not completed the full term of service, and allowed him to retire on health grounds. However, he died almost immediately afterwards.

Every member of the Bulgakov family played a musical instrument, and Mikhail became a competent pianist. There was an excellent repertory company and opera house in Kiev, which he visited regularly. He was already starting to write plays which were performed by the family in their drawing room. He was a conservative and a monarchist in his school days, but never belonged to any of the extreme right-wing organizations of the time. Like many of his contemporaries, he favoured the idea of a constitutional monarchy as against Russian Tsarist autocracy.

A few years after her first husband's death, Mikhail's mother married an uncompromising atheist. She gave the children supplementary lessons in her spare time from her own teaching job and, as soon as they reached adolescence, she encouraged them to take on younger pupils to increase the family's meagre income. Mikhail's first job, undertaken when he was still at school, was as a part-time guard and ticket inspector on the local railway, and he continued such part-time employment when he entered medical school in Kiev in 1911.

He failed the exams at the end of his first year, but passed the resits a few months later. However, he then had to repeat his entire second year; this lack of dedication to his studies was possibly due to the fact that he was already beginning to write articles for various student journals and to direct student theatricals. Furthermore, he was at this time courting Tatyana Lappa, whom he married in 1913. She came from the distant Saratov region, but had relatives in Kiev, through whom she became acquainted with Bulgakov. He had already begun by this time to write short stories and plays. Because of these distractions, Bulgakov took seven years to complete what was normally a five-year course, but he finally graduated as a doctor in 1916 with distinction.

War   In 1914 the First World War had broken out, and Bulgakov enlisted immediately after graduation as a Red Cross volunteer, working in military hospitals at the front, which involved carrying out operations. In March 1916 he was called up to the army, but was in the end sent to work in a major Kiev hospital to replace experienced doctors who had been mobilized earlier. His wife, having done a basic nursing course by this time, frequently worked alongside her husband.

In March 1917 the Tsar abdicated, and the Russian monarchy collapsed. Two forces then began to contend for power – the Bolsheviks and the Ukrainian Nationalists. Although not completely in control of Ukraine, the latter declared independence from the former Tsarist Empire in February 1918, and concluded a separate peace deal with Germany. The Germans engineered a coup, placed their own supporters at the helm in Ukraine and supported this puppet regime against the Bolsheviks, the now deposed Nationalists and various other splinter groups fighting for their own causes. The Government set up its own German-supported army, the White Guard, which provided the background for Bulgakov's novel of the same name. The Bolsheviks ("The Reds"), the White Guard ("The Whites") and the Ukrainian Nationalists regularly took and retook the country and Kiev from each other: there were eighteen changes of government between the beginning of 1918 and late 1919.

Early in this period Bulgakov had been transferred to medical service in the countryside around the remote town of Vyazma, which provided him with material for his series of short stories *A Young Doctor's Notebook*. Possibly to blunt the distress caused to him by the suffering he witnessed there, and to cure fevers he caught from the peasants he was tending, he dosed himself heavily on his own drugs, and rapidly became addicted to morphine. When his own supplies had run out, he sent his wife to numerous pharmacies to pick up new stocks for imaginary patients. When she finally refused to acquiesce in this any further, he became abusive and violent, and even threatened her with a gun. No more mention is made at any later date of his addiction, so it is uncertain whether he obtained professional help for the problem or weaned himself off his drug habit by his own will-power.

He returned to Kiev in February 1918 and set up in private practice. Some of the early stories written in this period show that he was wrestling with problems of direction and conscience: a doctor could be pressed into service by whichever faction was in power at that moment; after witnessing murders, torture and pogroms, Bulgakov was overwhelmed with horror at the contemporary situation. He was press-ganged mainly by the right-wing Whites, who were notoriously anti-Semitic and carried out most of the pogroms.

Perhaps as a result of the suffering he had seen during his *Turning to Literature* enforced military service, he suffered a "spiritual crisis" – as an acquaintance of his termed it – in February 1920, when he gave up medicine at the age of twenty-nine to devote himself to literature. But things were changing in the literary world: Bulgakov's style and motifs were not in tune with the new proletarian values which the Communists, in the areas where they had been victorious, were already beginning to inculcate. The poet Anna Akhmatova talked of his "magnificent contempt" for their ethos, in which everything had to be subordinated to the creation of a new, optimistic mentality which believed that science, medicine and Communism would lead to a paradise on earth for all, with humanity reaching its utmost point of development.

He continued to be pressed into service against his will. Although not an ardent right-winger, he had more sympathy for the Whites than for the Reds, and when the former, who had forced him into service at the time, suffered a huge defeat at the hands of the Communists, evidence suggests that Bulgakov would rather have retreated with the right-wing faction, and maybe even emigrated, than have to work for the victorious Communists. However, he was prevented from doing this as just at this time he became seriously ill with typhus, and so remained behind when the Whites fled. Incidentally, both his brothers had fled abroad, and were by this time living in Paris.

From 1920 to 1921 Bulgakov briefly worked in a hospital in the Caucasus, where he had been deployed by the Whites, who finally retreated from there in 1922. Bulgakov, living in the town of Vladikavkaz, produced a series of journalistic sketches, later collected and published as *Notes on Shirt Cuffs*, detailing his own experiences at the time, and later in Moscow. He avowedly took as his model classic writers such as Molière, Gogol and particularly Pushkin, and his writings at this time attracted criticism from anti-White critics, because of what was seen as his old-fashioned style and material, which was still that of the cultured European intellectuals of an earlier age, rather than being in keeping with the fresh aspirations of the new progressive proletarian era inaugurated by the Communists. The authorities championed literature and works of art which depicted the life of the masses and assisted in the development of the new Communist ethos. At the time, this tendency was still only on the level of advice and encouragement from the Government, rather than being a categorical demand. It only began to crystallize around the mid-1920s into an obligatory uncompromising line, ultimately leading to the repression, under Stalin, of any kind of even mildly dissident work, and to an increasingly oppressive state surveillance.

In fact, although never a supporter of Bolshevism as such, Bulgakov's articles of the early 1920s display not approval of the Red rule, but simply relief that at last there seemed to be stable government in Russia, which had re-established law and order and was gradually rebuilding the country's infrastructure. However, this relief at the new stability did not prevent him producing stories satirizing the new social order; for instance, around this time he published an experimental satirical novella entitled *Crimson Island*, purporting to be a novella by "Comrade Jules Verne" translated from the French.

It portrayed the Whites as stereotypical monsters and was written in the coarse, cliché-ridden agitprop style of the time – a blatant lampoon of the genre.

But by 1921, when he was approaching the age of thirty, Bulgakov was becoming worried that he still had no solid body of work behind him. Life had always been a struggle for him and his wife Tatyana, but he had now begun to receive some money from his writing and to mix in Russian artistic circles. After his medical service in Vladikavkaz he moved to Moscow, where he earned a precarious living over the next few years, contributing sketches to newspapers and magazines, and lecturing on literature. In January 1924 he met the sophisticated, multilingual Lyubov Belozerskaya, who was the wife of a journalist. In comparison with her, Tatyana seemed provincial and uncultured. They started a relationship, divorced their respective partners, and were entered in the local registers as married in late spring 1924, though the exact date of their marriage is unclear.

Between 1925 and 1926 Bulgakov produced three anthologies of his stories, the major one of which received the overall title *Diaboliad*. This collection received reasonably favourable reviews. One compared his stories in *Diaboliad* to those of Gogol, and this was in fact the only major volume of his fiction to be published in the USSR during his lifetime. According to a typist he employed at this time, he would dictate to her for two or three hours every day, from notebooks and loose sheets of paper, though not apparently from any completely composed manuscript.

But in a review in the newspaper *Izvestiya* of *Diaboliad* and some of Bulgakov's other writings in September 1925, the Marxist writer and critic Lev Averbakh, who was to become head of RAPP (the Russian Association of Proletarian Writers) had already declared that the stories contained only one theme: the uselessness and chaos arising from the Communists' attempts to create a new society. The critic then warned that, although Soviet satire was permissible and indeed requisite for the purposes of stimulating the restructuring of society, totally destructive lampoons such as Bulgakov's were irrelevant, and even inimical to the new ethos.

The Government's newly established body for overseeing literature subsequently ordered *Diaboliad* to be withdrawn, although it allowed a reissue in early 1926. By April 1925,

419

Bulgakov was reading his long story *A Dog's Heart* at literary gatherings, but finding it very difficult to get this work, or anything else, published. In May 1926, Bulgakov's flat was searched by agents of OGPU, the precursor of the KGB. The typescript of *A Dog's Heart* and Bulgakov's most recent diaries were confiscated; the story was only published in full in Russian in 1968 (in Germany), and in the USSR only in 1987, in a literary journal. In 1926 Bulgakov had written a stage adaptation of the story, but again it was only produced for the first time in June 1987, after which it became extremely popular throughout the USSR.

The White Guard   Between 1922 and 1924 Bulgakov was engaged in writing his first novel, ultimately to be known as *The White Guard*. The publishing history of this volume – which was originally planned to be the first part of a trilogy portraying the whole sweep of the Russian Revolution and Civil War – is extremely complex, and there were several different redactions. The whole project was very important to him, and was written at a period of great material hardship. By 1925 he was reading large sections at literary gatherings. Most of the chapters were published as they were produced, in literary magazines, with the exception of the ending, which was banned by the censors; pirated editions, with concocted endings, were published abroad. The novel appeared finally, substantially rewritten and complete, in 1929 in Paris, in a version approved by the author. Contrary to all other Soviet publications of this period, which saw the events of these years from the point of view of the victorious Bolsheviks, Bulgakov described that time from the perspective of one of the enemy factions, portraying them not as vile and sadistic monsters, as was now the custom, but as ordinary human beings with their own problems, fears and ideals.

It had a mixed reception; one review found it inferior to his short stories, while another compared it to the novelistic debut of Dostoevsky. It made almost no stir, and it's interesting to note that, in spite of the fact that the atmosphere was becoming more and more repressive as to the kind of artistic works which would be permitted, the party newspaper *Pravda* in 1927 could write neutrally of its "interesting point of view from a White-Guard perspective".

First Plays   Representatives of the Moscow Arts Theatre (MAT) had heard Bulgakov reading extracts from his novel-in-progress at literary events, realized its dramatic potential, and asked him to adapt the novel for the stage. The possibility had dawned on him even before this, and it seems he was making drafts for such a play from early 1925. This play – now known as *The Days of the Turbins* – had an extremely complicated history. At rehearsals, Bulgakov was interrogated by OGPU. MAT forwarded the original final version to Anatoly Lunacharsky, the People's Commissar for Education, to verify whether it was sufficiently innocuous politically for them to be able to stage it. He wrote back declaring it was rubbish from an artistic point of view, but as far as subject matter went there was no problem. The theatre seems to have agreed with him as to the literary merit of the piece, since they encouraged the author to embark on an extensive revision, which would ultimately produce a radically different version.

During rehearsals as late as August 1926, representatives of OGPU and the censors were coming to the theatre to hold lengthy negotiations with the author and director, and to suggest alterations. The play was finally passed for performance, but only at MAT – no productions were to be permitted anywhere else. It was only allowed to be staged elsewhere, oddly enough, from 1933 onwards, when the party line was being enforced more and more rigorously and Stalin's reign was becoming increasingly repressive. Rumour had it that Stalin himself had quite enjoyed the play when he saw it at MAT in 1929, regarded its contents as innocuous, and had himself authorized its wider performances.

It was ultimately premiered on 26th October 1926, and achieved great acclaim, becoming known as "the second Seagull", as the first performance of Chekhov's *Seagull* at MAT in 1898 had inaugurated the theatre's financial and artistic success after a long period of mediocrity and falling popularity. This was a turning point in the fortunes of MAT, which had been coming under fire for only performing the classics and not adopting styles of acting and subject matter more in keeping with modern times and themes. The play was directed by one of the original founders of MAT, Konstantin Stanislavsky, and he authorized a thousand-rouble advance for the playwright, which alleviated somewhat the severe financial constraints he had been living under.

The play received mixed reviews, depending almost entirely on the journal or reviewer's political views. One critic objected to its "idealization of the Bolsheviks' enemies", while another vilified its "petit-bourgeois vulgarity". Others accused it of using means of expression dating from the era of classic theatre which had now been replaced in contemporary plays by styles – often crudely propagandistic – which were more in tune with the Soviet proletarian ethos. The piece was extremely popular, however, and in spite of the fact that it was only on in one theatre, Bulgakov could live reasonably well on his share of the royalties.

At this time another Moscow theatre, the Vakhtangov, also requested a play from the author, so Bulgakov gave them *Zoyka's Apartment*, which had probably been written in late 1925. It was premiered on 28th October, just two days after *The Days of the Turbins*. The theatre's representatives suggested a few textual (not political) changes, and Bulgakov first reacted with some irritation, then acknowledged he had been overworked and under stress, due to the strain of the negotiations with OGPU and the censors over *The Days of the Turbins*.

Various other changes had to be made before the censors were satisfied, but the play was allowed to go on tour throughout the Soviet Union. It is rather surprising that it was permitted, because, in line with party doctrine, social and sexual mores were beginning to become more and more puritanical, and the play brought out into the open the seamier side of life which still existed in the workers' paradise. Zoyka's apartment is in fact a high-class brothel, and the Moscow papers had recently reported the discovery in the city of various such establishments, as well as drug dens. The acting and production received rave reviews, but the subject matter was condemned by some reviewers as philistine and shallow, and the appearance of scantily clad actresses on stage was excoriated as being immoral.

The play was extremely successful, both in Moscow and on tour, and brought the author further substantial royalties. Bulgakov was at this time photographed wearing a monocle and looking extremely dandified; those close to him claimed that the monocle was worn for genuine medical reasons, but this photograph attracted personal criticism in the press: he was accused of living in the past and being reactionary.

Perhaps to counteract this out-of-touch image, Bulgakov published a number of sketches in various journals between

1925 and 1927 giving his reminiscences of medical practice in the remote countryside. When finally collected and published posthumously, they were given the title *A Young Doctor's Notebook*. Although they were written principally to alleviate his financial straits, the writer may also have been trying to demonstrate that, in spite of all the criticism, he was a useful member of society with his medical knowledge.

Bulgakov's next major work was the play *Escape* (also translated as *Flight*), which, according to dates on some of the manuscript pages, was written and revised between 1926 and 1928. The script was thoroughly rewritten in 1932 and only performed in the USSR in 1957. The play was banned at the rehearsal stage in 1929 as being not sufficiently "revolutionary", though Bulgakov claimed in bafflement that he had in fact been trying to write a piece that was more akin to "agitprop" than anything he'd previously written. *Censorship*

Escape is set in the Crimea during the struggle between the Whites and Reds in the Civil War, and portrays the Whites as stereotypical villains involved in prostitution, corruption and terror. At first it seems perplexing that the piece should have been banned, since it seems so in tune with the spirit of the times, but given Bulgakov's well-known old-fashioned and anti-Red stance, the play may well have been viewed as in fact a satire on the crude agitprop pieces of the time.

The year 1929 was cataclysmic both for Bulgakov and for other Soviet writers: by order of RAPP (Russian Association of Proletarian Writers) *Escape*, *The Days of the Turbins* and *Zoyka's Apartment* had their productions suspended. Although, with the exception of *Zoyka*, they were then granted temporary runs, at least until the end of that season, their long-term future remained uncertain.

Bulgakov had apparently started drafting his masterpiece *The Master and Margarita* as early as 1928. The novel had gone through at least six revisions by the time of the writer's death in 1940. With the tightening of the party line, there was an increase in militant, politically approved atheism, and one of the novel's major themes is a retelling of Christ's final days, and his victory in defeat – possibly a response to the atheism of Bulgakov's time. He submitted one chapter, under a pseudonym, to the magazine *Nedra* in May 1929, which described satirically the intrigues among the official literary bodies of the time, such as RAPP and others. This

423

chapter was rejected. Yevgeny Zamyatin, another writer in disfavour at the time, who finally emigrated permanently, stated privately that the Soviet Government was adopting the worst excesses of old Spanish Catholicism, seeing heresies where there were none.

In July of that year Bulgakov wrote a letter to Stalin and other leading politicians and writers in good standing with the authorities, asking to be allowed to leave the USSR with his wife; he stated in this letter that it appeared he would never be allowed to be published or performed again in his own country. His next play, *Molière*, was about problems faced by the French playwright in the period of the autocratic monarch Louis XIV; the parallels between the times of Molière and the Soviet writer are blatant. It was read in January 1930 to the Artistic Board of MAT, who reported that, although it had "no relevance to contemporary questions", they had now admitted a couple of modern propaganda plays to their repertoire, and so they thought the authorities might stretch a point and permit Bulgakov's play. But in March he was told that the Government artistic authorities had not passed the piece. MAT now demanded the return of the thousand-rouble advance they had allowed Bulgakov for *Escape*, also now banned; furthermore the writer was plagued by demands for unpaid income tax relating to the previous year. None of his works were now in production.

Help from Stalin   On Good Friday Bulgakov received a telephone call from Stalin himself promising a favourable response to his letter to the authorities, either to be allowed to emigrate, or at least to be permitted to take up gainful employment in a theatre if he so wished. Stalin even promised a personal meeting with the writer. Neither meeting nor response ever materialized, but Bulgakov was shortly afterwards appointed Assistant Director at MAT, and Consultant to the Theatre of Working Youth, probably as a result of some strings being pulled in high places. Although unsatisfactory, these officially sanctioned positions provided the writer with some income and measure of protection against the torrent of arbitrary arrests now sweeping through the country.

Yelena Shilovskaya   Although there was now some stability in Bulgakov's professional life, there was to be another major turn in his love life. In February 1929 he had met at a friend's house in Moscow a woman called Yelena Shilovskaya; she was married with two children, highly cultured, and was personal secretary at MAT to the world-famous theatre director Vladimir Nemirovich-Danchenko. They fell in love, but then did not see each other again for around eighteen months. When they did meet again, they found they were still drawn to each other, divorced their partners, and married in October 1932. She remained his wife till his death, and afterwards became the keeper of his archives and worked tirelessly to have his works published.

Over the next few years Bulgakov wrote at least twice more to Stalin asking to be allowed to emigrate. But permission was not forthcoming, and so Bulgakov would never travel outside the USSR. He always felt deprived because of this and sensed something had been lacking in his education. At this time, because of his experience in writing such letters, and because of his apparent "pull" in high places, other intellectuals such as Stanislavsky and Anna Akhmatova were asking for his help in writing similar letters.

While working at MAT, Bulgakov's enthusiasm quickly waned and he felt creatively stifled as his adaptations for the stage of such classic Russian novels as Gogol's *Dead Souls* were altered extensively either for political or artistic reasons. However, despite these changes, he also provided screenplays for mooted films of both *Dead Souls* and Gogol's play *The Government Inspector*. Once again, neither ever came to fruition. There were further projects at this time for other major theatres, both in Moscow and Leningrad, such as an adaptation of Tolstoy's novel *War and Peace* for the stage. This too never came to anything. In May 1932 he wrote: "In nine days' time I shall be celebrating my forty-first birthday... And so towards the conclusion of my literary career I've been forced to write adaptations. A brilliant finale, don't you think?" He wrote numerous other plays and adaptations between then and the end of his life, but no new works were ever produced on stage.

Things appeared to be looking up at one point, because in October 1931 *Molière* had been passed by the censors for production and was accepted by the Bolshoi Drama Theatre in Leningrad. Moreover, in 1932, MAT had made a routine request to be allowed to restage certain works, and to their surprise were permitted to put *Zoyka's Apartment* and *The Days of the Turbins* back into their schedules. This initially seemed to herald a new thaw, a new liberalism, and these

425

prospects were enhanced by the dissolution of such bodies as RAPP, and the formation of the Soviet Writers' Union. Writers hitherto regarded with suspicion were published.

However, although *Molière* was now in production at the Leningrad theatre, the theatre authorities withdrew it suddenly, terrified by the vituperative attacks of a revolutionary and hard-line Communist playwright, Vsevolod Vishnevsky, whose works celebrated the heroic deeds of the Soviet armed forces and working people and who would place a gun on the table when reading a play aloud.

Bulgakov was then commissioned to write a biography of Molière for the popular market, and the typescript was submitted to the authorities in March 1933. However, it was once again rejected, because Bulgakov, never one to compromise, had adopted an unorthodox means of telling his story, having a flamboyant narrator within the story laying out the known details of Molière's life, but also commenting on them and on the times in which he lived; parallels with modern Soviet times were not hard to find. The censor who rejected Bulgakov's work suggested the project should only be undertaken by a "serious Soviet historian". It was finally published only in 1962, and was one of the writer's first works to be issued posthumously. It is now regarded as a major work, both in content and style.

Acting   In December 1934 Bulgakov made his acting debut for MAT as the judge in an adaptation of Dickens's *Pickwick Papers*, and the performance was universally described as hilarious and brilliant. However, though he obviously had great acting ability, he found the stress and the commitment of performing night after night a distraction from his career as a creative writer. He was still attempting to write plays and other works – such as *Ivan Vasilyevich*, set in the time of Ivan the Terrible – which were rejected by the authorities.

At about this time, Bulgakov proposed a play on the life of Alexander Pushkin, and both Shostakovich and Prokofiev expressed an interest in turning the play into an opera. But then Shostakovich's opera *Lady Macbeth of Mtsensk* was slaughtered in the press for being ideologically and artistically unsound, and Bulgakov's play, which had not even gone into production, was banned in January 1936.

Molière, in a revised form, was passed for performance in late 1935, and premiered by MAT in February 1936.

However, it was promptly savaged by the newspaper *Pravda* for its "falsity", and MAT immediately withdrew it from the repertoire. Bulgakov, bitterly resentful at the theatre's abject capitulation, resigned later in the year, and swiftly joined the famous Moscow Bolshoi Opera Theatre as librettist and adviser. In November 1936, in just a few hours he churned out *Black Snow* (later to be called *A Theatrical Novel*), a short satire on the recent events at MAT.

In mid-1937 he began intensive work on yet another redac- *Play on Stalin* tion of *The Master and Margarita*, which was finally typed out by June 1938. Soon afterwards, he started work on a play about Stalin, *Batum*. The dictator, although in the main disapproving of the tendency of Bulgakov's works, still found them interesting, and had always extended a certain amount of protection to him. Bulgakov had started work in 1936 on a history of the USSR for schools and, although the project remained fragmentary, he had gathered a tremendous amount of material on Stalin for the project, which he proposed to incorporate in his play. It is odd that this ruthless dictator and Bulgakov – who was certainly not a supporter of the regime and whose patrician views seemed to date from a previous era – should have been locked in such a relationship of mutual fascination.

Although MAT told him that the play on Stalin would do both him and the theatre good in official eyes, Bulgakov, still contemptuous of the theatre, demanded that they provide him with a new flat where he could work without interruption from noise. MAT complied with this condition. He submitted the manuscript in July 1939, but it was turned down, apparently by the dictator himself.

Bulgakov was devastated by this rejection, and almost im- *Illness and Death* mediately began to suffer a massive deterioration in health. His eyesight became worse and worse, he developed appalling headaches, he grew extremely sensitive to light and often could not leave his flat for days on end. All this was the first manifestation of the sclerosis of the kidneys which finally killed him, as it had killed his father. When he could, he continued revising *The Master and Margarita*, but only managed to finish correcting the first part. He became totally bedridden, his weight fell to under fifty kilograms, and he finally died on 10th March 1940. The next morning a call came through from Stalin's office – though not from the leader

427

himself – asking whether it was true the writer was dead. On receiving the answer, the caller hung up with no comment. Bulgakov had had no new work published or performed for some time, yet the Soviet Writers' Union, full of many of the people who had pilloried him so mercilessly over the years, honoured him respectfully. He was buried in the Novodevichy Cemetery, in the section for artistic figures, near Chekhov and Gogol. Ultimately, a large stone which had lain on Gogol's grave, but had been replaced by a memorial bust, was placed on Bulgakov's grave, where it still lies.

Posthumous Publications and Reputation After the Second World War ended in 1945, the country had other priorities than the publication of hitherto banned authors, but Bulgakov's wife campaigned fearlessly for his rehabilitation, and in 1957 *The Days of the Turbins* and his play on the end of Pushkin's life were published, and a larger selection of his plays appeared in 1962. A heavily cut version of *The Master and Margarita* appeared in a specialist literary journal throughout 1966–67, and the full uncensored text in 1973. Subsequently – especially post-Glasnost – more and more works of Bulgakov's were published in uncensored redactions, and at last Western publishers could see the originals of what they had frequently published before in corrupt smuggled variants. Bulgakov's third wife maintained his archive, and both she and his second wife gave public lectures on him, wrote memoirs of him and campaigned for publication of his works. Bulgakov has now achieved cult status in Russia, and almost all of his works have been published in uncensored editions, with unbiased editorial commentary and annotation.

Mikhail Bulgakov's Works

It is difficult to give an overall survey of Bulgakov's works, which, counting short stories and adaptations, approach a total of almost one hundred. Many of these works exist in several versions, as the author revised them constantly to make them more acceptable to the authorities. This meant that published versions – including translations brought out abroad – were frequently not based on what the author might have considered the "definitive" version. In fact to talk of "definitive versions" with reference to Bulgakov's works may be misleading. Furthermore, no new works of his were published after 1927, and they only began to be issued sporadically, frequently in censored versions, from 1962 onwards. Complete and uncut editions of many of the works have begun to appear only from the mid-1990s. Therefore the section below will contain only the most prominent works in all genres.

Despite the wide variety of settings of his novels – Russia, *Themes* the Caucasus, Ukraine, Jerusalem in New Testament times and the Paris of Louis XIV – the underlying themes of Bulgakov's works remain remarkably constant throughout his career. Although these works contain a huge number of characters, most of them conform to certain archetypes and patterns of behaviour.

Stylistically, Bulgakov was influenced by early-nineteenth-century classic Russian writers such as Gogol and Pushkin, and he espoused the values of late-nineteenth-century liberal democracy and culture, underpinned by Christian teachings. Although Bulgakov came from an ecclesiastical background, he was never in fact a conventional believer, but, like many agnostic or atheistic Russian nineteenth-century intellectuals and artists, he respected the role that the basic teachings of religion had played in forming Russian and European culture – although they, and Bulgakov, had no liking for the way religions upheld obscurantism and authority.

Some works portray the struggle of the outsider against society, such as the play and narrative based on the life of Molière, or the novel *The Master and Margarita*, in which the outsider persecuted by society and the state is Yeshua, i.e. Jesus. Other works give prominent roles to doctors and scientists, and demonstrate what happens if science is misused and is subjected to Government interference. Those works portraying historical reality, such as *The White Guard*, show the Whites – who were normally depicted in Communist literature as evil reactionaries – to be ordinary human beings with their own concerns and ideals. Most of all, Bulgakov's work is pervaded by a biting satire on life as he saw it around him in the USSR, especially in the artistic world, and there is frequently a "magical realist" element – as in *The Master and Margarita* – in which contemporary reality and fantasy are intermingled, or which show the influence of Western science fiction (Bulgakov admired the works of H.G. Wells enormously).

429

The White Guard   Bulgakov's major works are written in a variety of forms, including novels, plays and short stories. His first novel, *The White Guard*, was written between 1922 and 1924, but it received numerous substantial revisions later. It was originally conceived as the first volume of a trilogy portraying the entire sweep of the post-revolutionary Civil War from a number of different points of view. Although this first and only volume was criticized for showing events from the viewpoint of the Whites, the third volume would apparently have given the perspective of the Communists. Many chapters of the novel were published separately in literary journals as they appeared. The ending – the dreams presaging disaster for the country – never appeared, because the journal it was due to be printed in, *Rossiya*, was shut down by official order, precisely because it was publishing such material as Bulgakov's. Different pirate versions, with radically variant texts and concocted endings, appeared abroad. The novel only appeared complete in Russian, having been proofread by the author, in 1929 in Paris, where there was a substantial émigré population from the Tsarist Empire/USSR.

The major part of the story takes place during the forty-seven days in which the Ukrainian Nationalists, under their leader Petlyura, held power in Kiev. The novel ends in February 1919, when Petlyura was overthrown by the Bolsheviks. The major protagonists are the Turbins, a family reminiscent of Bulgakov's own, with a similar address, who also work in the medical profession: many elements of the novel are in fact autobiographical. At the beginning of the novel, we are still in the world of old Russia, with artistic and elegant furniture dating from the Tsarist era, and a piano, books and high-quality pictures on the walls. But the atmosphere is one of fear about the future, and apprehension at the world collapsing. The Turbins' warm flat, in which the closely knit family can take refuge from the events outside, is progressively encroached on by reality. Nikolka Turbin, the younger son, is still at high school and in the cadet corps; he has a vague feeling that he should be fighting on the side of the Whites – that is, the forces who were against both the Nationalists and Communists. However, when a self-sacrificing White soldier dies in the street in Nikolka's arms, he realizes for the first time that war is vile. Near the conclusion of the novel there is a family gathering at the flat, but everything has changed since the beginning of the book: relationships have been severed, and there is no longer any confidence in the future. As the Ukrainian Nationalists flee, they brutally murder a Jew near the Turbins' flat, demonstrating that liberal tolerant values have disintegrated. The novel ends with a series of sinister apocalyptic dreams – indeed the novel contains imagery throughout from the Biblical Apocalypse. These dreams mainly presage catastrophe for the family and society, although the novel ends with the very short dream of a child, which does seem to prefigure some sort of peace in the distant future.

The Life of Monsieur de Molière is sometimes classed not as a novel but as a biography. However, the treatment is distinctive enough to enable the work to be ranked as semi-fictionalized. Bulgakov's interpretative view of the French writer's life, rather than a purely historical perspective, is very similar to that in his play on the same theme. The book was written in 1932, but was banned for the same reasons which were to cause problems later for the play. Molière's life is narrated in the novel by an intermediary, a flamboyant figure who often digresses, and frequently comments on the political intrigues of the French author's time. The censors may have felt that the description of the French writer's relationship to an autocrat might have borne too many similarities to Bulgakov's relationship to Stalin. The book was only finally published in the USSR in 1962, and is now regarded as a major work.

The Life of Monsieur de Molière

Although he had written fragmentary pieces about the theatre before, Bulgakov only really settled down to produce a longer work on the theme – a short, vicious satire on events in the Soviet theatre – in November 1936, after what he saw as MAT's abject capitulation in the face of attacks by Communists on *Molière*. *A Theatrical Novel* was only published for the first time in the Soviet Union in 1969. There is a short introduction, purporting to be by an author who has found a manuscript written by a theatrical personage who has committed suicide (the reason for Bulgakov's original title, *Notes of the Deceased*; other mooted titles were *Black Snow* and *White Snow*). Not only does Bulgakov take a swipe at censorship and the abject and pusillanimous authorities of the theatre world, but he also deals savagely with the reputations of such people as the theatre director Stanislavsky,

A Theatrical Novel

431

who, despite his fame abroad, is depicted – in a thinly veiled portrait – as a tyrannical figure who crushes the individuality and flair of writers and actors in the plays which he is directing. The manuscript ends inconclusively, with the dead writer still proclaiming his wonder at the nature of theatre itself, despite its intrigues and frustrations; the original author who has found the manuscript does not reappear, and it's uncertain whether the point is that the theatrical figure left his memoirs uncompleted, or whether in fact Bulgakov failed to finish his original project.

The Master and Margarita *The Master and Margarita* is generally regarded as Bulgakov's masterpiece. He worked on it from 1928 to 1940, and it exists in at least six different variants, ranging from the fragmentary to the large-scale narrative which he was working on at the onset of the illness from which he died. Even the first redaction contains many of the final elements, although the Devil is the only narrator of the story of Pilate and Jesus – the insertion of the Master and Margarita came at a later stage. In 1929 the provisional title was *The Engineer's Hoof* (the word "engineer" had become part of the vocabulary of the Soviet demonology of the times, since in May and June 1928 a large group of mining engineers had been tried for anti-revolutionary activities, and they were equated in the press to the Devil who was trying to undermine the new Soviet society). The last variant written before the author's death was completed around mid-1938, and Bulgakov began proofreading and revising it, making numerous corrections and sorting out loose ends. In his sick state, he managed to revise only the first part of the novel, and there are still a certain number of moot points remaining later on. The novel was first published in a severely cut version in 1966–67, in a specialist Russian literary journal, while the complete text was published only in 1973. At one stage, Bulgakov apparently intended to allow Stalin to be the first reader of *The Master and Margarita*, and to present him with a personal copy.

The multi-layered narrative switches backwards and forwards between Jerusalem in the time of Christ and contemporary Moscow. The Devil – who assumes the name Woland – visits Moscow with his entourage, which includes a large talking black cat and a naked witch, and they cause havoc with their displays of magic; however, the epigraph to the novel from Goethe's *Faust* implies that although Woland is the force that works evil, that force will always in the end conduce to good (perhaps an attempt to explain why, if there is a loving God, there is evil in the world) as part of a divine plan.

In the scenes set in modern times, the narrative indirectly evokes the atmosphere of a dictatorship. This is paralleled in the Pilate narrative by the figure of Caesar, who, although he is mentioned, never appears.

The atheists of modern Moscow who, following the contemporary party line, snigger at Christ's miracles and deny his existence, are forced to create explanations for what they see the Devil doing in front of them in their own city.

There are numerous references to literature, and also to music – there are three characters with the names of composers, Berlioz, Stravinsky and Rimsky-Korsakov. Berlioz the composer wrote an oratorio on the theme of Faust, who is in love with the self-sacrificing Margarita; immediately we are drawn towards the idea that the persecuted writer known as the Master, who also has a devoted lover called Margarita, is a modern manifestation of Faust. Bulgakov carried out immense research on studies of ancient Jerusalem and theology, particularly Christology. The novel demands several readings, such are the depths of interconnected details and implications.

The book opens with two mediocre writers living in Moscow, Berlioz and Ivan Bezdomny ["Homeless"] – they are members of The Griboyedov House. This institution is a satire on major Russian literary clubs and artistic bodies of the time, with their mediocre, hypocritical, time-serving authors and artists of all genres. Many of the portraits of the members of this club are recognizable figures of the time.

Berlioz and Ivan bump into the Devil at Patriarch's Ponds – the Devil assumes the role of a professor of black magic, and tells them a story based on the biblical episode of Pilate's questioning of Jesus. He then accurately predicts the exact circumstances of Berlioz's death, which happens very soon afterwards. Ivan witnesses this, and tries to chase after the Devil and his entourage, suspecting them of conspiracy. However, he is unable to catch them, and becomes manic, ending up in a psychiatric hospital. While there, he meets a character known only as "the Master", who had once written a book about Pontius Pilate – it received such savage treatment from the critics that this caused his breakdown.

While Ivan and the Master are stuck in the psychiatric hospital, the Devil and his associates cause chaos in Moscow. They establish themselves in the apartment vacated by the late Berlioz, and put on a black-magic show in which they distribute money and women's clothing, which later vanish, creating riotous scenes among the populace.

We are then introduced to the character of Margarita, the Master's former lover, who still pines for him. The couple became separated when he was arrested; after his release, he ended up being admitted into hospital, but she doesn't know that this happened, and from her perspective, he vanished with no explanation at all. The Devil sends one of his associates to her, who suggests to her the prospect that she may be reunited with her lover if she acts as the host for one night at Satan's ball. Apparently this is a Satanic tradition – she is chosen for the role because the hostess must have the name Margarita. She agrees to this.

After Margarita has endured the ball, she is reunited with her lover. The Pilate narrative is resolved, and Moscow returns to something like normality, although the events of the novel continue to haunt Ivan Bezdomny.

Days of the Turbins Apart from novels, another important area for Bulgakov to channel his creative energy into was plays. *The Days of the Turbins* was the first of his works to be staged: it was commissioned by the Moscow Arts Theatre in early 1925, although it seems Bulgakov had already thought of the possibility of a stage adaptation of *The White Guard*, since acquaintances report him making drafts for such a project slightly earlier. It had an extremely complex history, which involved numerous rewritings after constant negotiations between the writer, theatre, secret police and censors. Bulgakov did not want to leave any elements of the novel out, but on his reading the initial manuscript at the Moscow Arts Theatre it was found to be far too long, and so he cut out a few of the minor characters and pruned the dream sequences in the novel. However, the background is still the same – the Civil War in Kiev after the Bolshevik Revolution. The family are broadly moderate Tsarists in their views, and therefore are anti-Communist but, being ethnically Russian, have no sympathy with the Ukrainian Nationalists either, and so end up fighting for the White Guards. Their flat at the beginning is almost Chekhovian in its warmth, cosiness and air of old-world culture, but by the end one brother has been killed in the fighting and, as the sounds of the 'Internationale' offstage announce the victory of the Communists, a feeling of apprehension grips the family as their world seems to be collapsing round them. The final lines of the play communicate these misgivings (Nikolka: "Gentlemen, this evening is a great prologue to a new historical play." / Studzinsky: "For some a prologue – for others an epilogue."). The final sentence may be taken as representing Bulgakov's fear about the effect the Communist takeover might have on the rest of his own career.

The Soviet playwright Viktor Nekrasov, who was in favour of the Revolution, commented that the play was an excellent recreation of that time in Kiev, where he had also been participating in the historic events on the Bolshevik side – the atmosphere was all very familiar, Nekrasov confirmed, and one couldn't help extending sympathy to such characters as the Turbins, even if they were on the other side: they were simply individuals caught up in historical events.

At around the time of the writing of *The Days of the Turbins*, another Moscow theatre, the Vakhtangov, requested a play from Bulgakov, so he provided them with *Zoyka's Apartment*, which had been first drafted in late 1925. Various alterations had to be made before the censors were satisfied. At least four different texts of *Zoyka* exist, the final revision completed as late as 1935; this last is now regarded as the authoritative text, and is that generally translated for Western editions. *Zoyka's Apartment*

The setting is a Moscow apartment run by Zoyka; it operates as a women's dress shop and haute-couturier during the day, and becomes a brothel after closing time. At the time the play was written, various brothels and drug dens had been unearthed by the police in the capital, some run by Chinese nationals. Bulgakov's play contains therefore not only easily recognizable political and social types who turn up for a session with the scantily clad ladies, but also stereotypical Chinese drug dealers and addicts. Zoyka is however treated with moral neutrality by the author: she operates as the madam of the brothel in order to raise money as fast as possible so that she can emigrate abroad with her husband, an impoverished former aristocrat, who is also a drug addict. In the final act the ladies and clients dance to decadent Western popular music, a fight breaks out and a man is murdered. The play ends with the establishment being raided by "unknown strangers", who are presumably government inspectors and the police. At this point the final curtain comes down, so we never find out the ultimate fate of the characters.

The Crimson Island   In 1924 Bulgakov had written a rather unsubtle short story, *The Crimson Island*, which was a parody of the crude agitprop style of much of the literature of the time, with its stereotypical heroic and noble Communists, and evil reactionaries and foreigners trying to undermine the new Communist state, all written in the language of the person in the street – often as imagined by educated people who had no direct knowledge of this working-class language. In 1927 he adapted this parody for the stage. The play bears the subtitle: *The Dress Rehearsal of a Play by Citizen Jules Verne in Gennady Panfilovich's theatre, with music, a volcanic eruption and English sailors: in four acts, with a prologue and an epilogue*. The play was much more successful than the story. He offered it to the Kamerny ["Chamber"] Theatre, in Moscow, which specialized in mannered and elegant productions, still in the style of the late 1890s; it was passed for performance and premiered in December 1928, and was a success, though some of the more left-wing of the audience and critics found it hard to swallow. However, the critic Novitsky wrote that it was an "interesting and witty parody, satirizing what crushes artistic creativity and cultivates slavish and absurd dramatic characters, removing the individuality from actors and writers and creating idols, lickspittles and panegyrists". The director of the play, Alexander Tairov, claimed that the work was meant to be self-criticism of the falsity and crudeness of some revolutionary work. Most reviews found it amusing and harmless, and it attracted good audiences. However, there were just a few vitriolic reviews; Stalin himself commented that the production of such a play underlined how reactionary the Kamerny Theatre still was. The work was subsequently banned by the censor in March 1929.

The Crimson Island takes the form of a play within a play: the prologue and epilogue take place in the theatre where the play is to be rehearsed and performed; the playwright – who, although Russian, has taken the pen name Jules Verne – is progressive and sensitive, but his original work is increasingly censored and altered out of all recognition. The rest of the acts show the rewritten play, which has now become a crude agitprop piece. The play within *Crimson Island* takes place on a sparsely populated desert island run by a white king and ruling class, with black underlings. There is a volcano rumbling in the background, which occasionally erupts. The wicked foreigners are represented by the English Lord and Lady Aberaven, who sail in on a yacht crewed by English sailors who march on singing 'It's a Long Way to Tipperary'. During the play the island's underlings stage a revolution and try unsuccessfully to urge the English sailors to rebel against the evil Lord and Lady. However, they do not succeed, and the wicked aristocrats sail away unharmed, leaving the revolutionaries in control of the island.

Bulgakov's play *Escape* (also translated as *Flight*), drafted between 1926 and 1928, and completely rewritten in 1932, is set in the Crimea during the conflicts between the Whites and Reds in the Civil War after the Revolution. *Escape*

The Whites – who include a general who has murdered people in cold blood – emigrate to Constantinople, but find they are not accepted by the locals, and their living conditions are appalling. One of the women has to support them all by resorting to prostitution. The murderous White general nurses his colleagues during an outbreak of typhus, and feels he has expiated some of his guilt for the crimes he has committed against humanity. He and a few of his colleagues decide to return to the USSR, since even life under Communism cannot be as bad as in Turkey. However, the censors objected that these people were coming back for negative reasons – simply to get away from where they were – and not because they had genuinely come to believe in the Revolution, or had the welfare of the working people at heart.

Molière was one of Bulgakov's favourite writers, and some aspects of his writing seemed relevant to Soviet reality – for example the character of the fawning, scheming, hypocritical anti-hero of *Tartuffe*. Bulgakov's next play, *Molière*, was about problems faced by the French playwright during the reign of the autocratic monarch Louis XIV. It was written between October and December 1929 and, as seen above, submitted in January 1930 to the Artistic Board of MAT. Bulgakov told them that he had not written an overtly political piece, but one about a writer hounded by a cabal of critics in connivance with the absolute monarch. Unfortunately, despite MAT's optimism, the authorities did not permit a production. In this piece the French writer at one stage, like Bulgakov, intends *Molière*

437

to leave the country permanently. Late in the play, the King realizes that Molière's brilliance would be a further ornament to his resplendent court, and extends him his protection; however, then this official attitude changes, Molière is once again an outcast, and he dies on stage, while acting in one of his own plays, a broken man. The play's original title was *The Cabal of Hypocrites*, but it was probably decided that this was too contentious.

Bliss and Ivan Vasilievich   A version of the play *Bliss* appears to have been drafted in 1929, but was destroyed and thoroughly rewritten between then and 1934. Bulgakov managed to interest both the Leningrad Music Hall Theatre and Moscow Satire Theatre in the idea, but they both said it would be impossible to stage because of the political climate of the time, and told him to rewrite it; accordingly he transferred the original plot to the time of Tsar Ivan the Terrible in the sixteenth century, and the new play, entitled *Ivan Vasilyevich*, was completed by late 1935.

The basic premise behind both plays is the same: an inventor builds a time machine (as mentioned above, Bulgakov was a great admirer of H.G. Wells) and travels to a very different period of history: present-day society is contrasted starkly with the world he has travelled to. However, in *Bliss*, the contrasted world is far in the future, while in *Ivan Vasilyevich* it is almost four hundred years in the past. In *Bliss* the inventor accidentally takes a petty criminal and a typically idiotic building manager from his own time to the Moscow of 2222: it is a utopian society, with no police and no denunciations to the authorities. He finally returns to his own time with the criminal and the building manager, but also with somebody from the future who is fed up with the bland and boring conformity of such a paradise (Bulgakov was always sceptical of the idea of any utopia, not just the Communist one).

Ivan Vasilyevich is set in the Moscow of the tyrannical Tsar, and therefore the contrast between a paradise and present reality is not the major theme. In fact, contemporary Russian society is almost presented favourably in contrast with the distant past. However, when the inventor and his crew – including a character from Ivan's time who has been transported to the present accidentally – arrive back in modern Moscow, they are all promptly arrested and the play finishes, emphasizing that, although modern times are an improvement on the distant past, the problems of that remote period still exist in contemporary reality. For all the differences in period and emphasis, most of the characters of the two plays are the same, and have very similar speeches.

Even this watered-down version of the original theme was rejected by the theatres it was offered to, who thought that it would still be unperformable. It was only premiered in the Soviet Union in 1966. Bulgakov tried neutering the theme even further, most notably by tacking on an ending in which the inventor wakes up in his Moscow flat with the music of Rimsky-Korsakov's popular opera *The Maid of Pskov* (set in Ivan the Terrible's time) wafting in from offstage, presumably meant to be from a radio in another room. The inventor gives the impression that the events of the play in Ivan's time have all been a dream brought on by the music. But all this rewriting was to no avail, and the play was never accepted by any theatre during Bulgakov's lifetime.

In January 1931 Bulgakov signed a contract with the Lenin- *Adam and Eve* grad Red Theatre to write a play about a "future world"; he also offered it, in case of rejection, to the Vakhtangov Theatre, which had premiered *Zoyka's Apartment*. However, it was banned even before rehearsals by a visiting official from the censor's department, because it showed a cataclysmic world war in which Leningrad was destroyed. Bulgakov had seen the horror of war, including gas attacks, in his medical service, and the underlying idea of *Adam and Eve* appears to be that all war is wrong, even when waged by Communists and patriots.

The play opens just before a world war breaks out; a poison gas is released which kills almost everybody on all sides. A scientist from the Communist camp develops an antidote, and wishes it to be available to everybody, but a patriot and a party official want it only to be distributed to people from their homeland. The Adam of the title is a cardboard caricature of a well-meaning but misguided Communist; his wife, Eve, is much less of a caricature, and is in love with the scientist who has invented the antidote. After the carnage, a world government is set up, which is neither left- nor right-wing. The scientist and Eve try to escape together, apparently to set up civilization again as the new Adam and Eve, but the sinister last line addressed to them both is: "Go, the Secretary General wants to see you." The Secretary General of the Communist Party in Russia at the time was of course Stalin, and the message may well be that even such an apparently apolitical government as that now ruling the world, which is supposed to rebuild the human race almost from nothing, is still being headed by a dictatorial character, and that the proposed regeneration of humanity has gone wrong once again from the outset and will never succeed.

The Last Days   In October 1934 Bulgakov decided to write a play about Pushkin, the great Russian poet, to be ready for the centenary of his death in 1937. He revised the original manuscript several times, but submitted it finally to the censors in late 1935. It was passed for performance, and might have been produced, but just at this time Bulgakov was in such disfavour that MAT themselves backtracked on the project.

Bulgakov, as usual, took an unusual slant on the theme: Pushkin was never to appear on stage during the piece, unless one counts the appearance at the end, in the distance, of his body being carried across stage after he has been killed in a duel. Bulgakov believed that even a great actor could not embody the full magnificence of Pushkin's achievement, the beauty of his language and his towering presence in Russian literature, let alone any of the second-rate hams who might vulgarize his image in provincial theatres. He embarked on the project at first with a Pushkin scholar, Vikenty Veresayev. However, Veresayev wanted everything written strictly in accordance with historical fact, whereas Bulgakov viewed the project dramatically. He introduced a few fictitious minor characters, and invented speeches between other characters where there is no record of what was actually said. Many events in Pushkin's life remain unclear, including who precisely engineered the duel between the army officer d'Anthès and the dangerously liberal thinker Pushkin, which resulted in the writer's death: the army, the Tsar or others? Bulgakov, while studying all the sources assiduously, put his own gloss and interpretation on these unresolved issues. In the end, Veresayev withdrew from the project in protest. The play was viewed with disfavour by critics and censors, because it implied that it may well have been the autocratic Tsar Nicholas I who was behind the events leading up to the duel, and comparison with another autocrat of modern times who also concocted plots against dissidents would inevitably have arisen in people's minds.

The Last Days was first performed in war-torn Moscow in April 1943, by MAT, since the Government was at the time striving to build up Russian morale and national consciousness in the face of enemy attack and invasion, and this play devoted to a Russian literary giant was ideal, in spite of its unorthodox perspective on events.

Commissioned by MAT in 1938, *Batum* was projected as ◦*Batum* a play about Joseph Stalin, mainly concerning his early life in the Caucasus, which was to be ready for his sixtieth birthday on 21st December 1939. Its first title was *Pastyr* ["The Shepherd"], in reference to Stalin's early training in a seminary for the priesthood, and to his later role as leader of his national "flock". However, although most of Bulgakov's acquaintances were full of praise for the play, and it passed the censors with no objections, it was finally rejected by the dictator himself.

Divided into four acts, the play covers the period 1898–1904, following Stalin's expulsion from the Tiflis (modern Tbilisi) Seminary, where he had been training to be an Orthodox priest, because of his anti-government activity. He is then shown in the Caucasian town of Batum organizing strikes and leading huge marches of workers to demand the release of imprisoned workers, following which he is arrested and exiled to Siberia. Stalin escapes after a month and in the last two scenes resumes the revolutionary activity which finally led to the Bolshevik Revolution under Lenin. Modern scholars have expressed scepticism as to the prominent role that Soviet biographers of Stalin's time ascribed to his period in Batum and later, and Bulgakov's play, although not disapproving of the autocrat, is objective, and far from the tone of the prevailing hagiography.

Varying explanations have been proposed as to why Stalin rejected the play. Although this was probably because it portrayed the dictator as an ordinary human being, the theory has been advanced that one of the reasons Stalin was fascinated by Bulgakov's works was precisely that the writer refused to knuckle under to the prevailing ethos, and Stalin possibly wrongly interpreted the writer's play about him as an attempt to curry favour, in the manner of all the mediocrities around him.

One Western commentator termed the writing of this play a "shameful act" on Bulgakov's part; however, the author was now beginning to show signs of severe ill health, and was perhaps understandably starting at last to feel worn down both mentally and physically by his lack of success and the constant struggle to try to make any headway in his literary career, or even to earn a crust of bread. Whatever the reasons behind the final rejection of *Batum*, Bulgakov was profoundly depressed by it, and it may have hastened his death from the hereditary sclerosis of the kidneys which he suffered from.

Bulgakov also wrote numerous short stories and novellas, the most significant of which include 'Diaboliad', 'The Fatal Eggs' and 'A Dog's Heart'.

Diaboliad   'Diaboliad' was first published in the journal *Nedra* in 1924, and then reappeared as the lead story of a collection of stories under the same name in July 1925; this was in fact the last major volume brought out by the author during his lifetime in Russia, although he continued to have stories and articles published in journals for some years. In theme and treatment the story has reminiscences of Dostoevsky and Gogol.

The "hero" of the tale, a minor ordering clerk at a match factory in Moscow, misreads his boss's name – Kalsoner – as *kalsony*, i.e. "underwear". In confusion he puts through an order for underwear and is sacked. It should be mentioned here that both he and the boss have doubles, and the clerk spends the rest of the story trying to track down his boss through an increasingly nightmarish bureaucratic labyrinth, continually confusing him with his double; at the same time he is constantly having to account for misdemeanours carried out by his own double, who has a totally different personality from him, and is a raffish philanderer. The clerk is robbed of his documents and identity papers, and can no longer prove who he is – the implication being that his double is now the real him, and that he doesn't exist any longer. Finally, the petty clerk, caught up in a Kafkaesque world of bureaucracy and false appearances, goes mad and throws himself off the roof of a well-known Moscow high-rise block.

The Fatal Eggs   'The Fatal Eggs' was first published in the journal *Nedra* in early 1925, then reissued as the second story in the collection *Diaboliad*, which appeared in July 1925. The title in Russian contains a number of untranslatable puns. The major one is that a main character is named "Rokk", and the word "rok" means "fate" in Russian, so "fatal" could also mean "belonging to Rokk". Also, "eggs" is the Russian equivalent of "balls", i.e. testicles, and there is also an overtone of the "roc", i.e. the giant mythical bird in the *Thousand and One Nights*. The theme of the story is reminiscent of *The Island of Doctor Moreau* by H.G. Wells. However, Bulgakov's tale also satirizes the belief of the time, held by both scientists and journalists, that science would solve all human problems, as society moved towards utopia. Bulgakov was suspicious of such ideals and always doubted the possibility of human perfection.

In the story, a professor of zoology discovers accidentally that a certain ray will increase enormously the size of any organism or egg exposed to it – by accelerating the rate of cell multiplication – although it also increases the aggressive tendencies of any creatures contaminated in this manner. At the time, chicken plague is raging throughout Russia, all of the birds have died, and so there is a shortage of eggs. The political activist Rokk wants to get hold of the ray to irradiate eggs brought from abroad, to replenish rapidly the nation's devastated stock of poultry. The professor is reluctant, but a telephone call is received from "someone in authority" ordering him to surrender the ray. When the foreign eggs arrive at the collective farm, they look unusually large, but they are irradiated just the same. Soon Rokk's wife is devoured by an enormous snake, and the country is plagued by giant reptiles and ostriches which wreak havoc. It turns out that a batch of reptile eggs was accidentally substituted for the hens' eggs. Chaos and destruction ensue, creating a sense of panic, during which the professor is murdered. The army is mobilized unsuccessfully, but – like the providential extermination of the invaders by germs in Wells's *The War of the Worlds* – the reptiles are all wiped out by an unexpected hard summer frost. The evil ray is destroyed in a fire.

'A Dog's Heart' was begun in January 1925 and finished the following month. Bulgakov offered it to the journal *Nedra*, who told him it was unpublishable in the prevailing political climate; it was never issued during Bulgakov's lifetime. Its themes are reminiscent of *The Island of Doctor Moreau*, *Dr Jekyll and Mr Hyde* and *Frankenstein*. *A Dog's Heart*

In the tale, a doctor, Preobrazhensky ["Transfigurative", or "Transformational"] by name, transplants the pituitary glands and testicles from the corpse of a moronic petty criminal and thug into a dog (Sharik). The dog gradually takes on human form, and turns out to be a hybrid of a dog's psyche and a criminal human being. The dog's natural affectionate nature has been swamped by the viciousness of the human, who has in

443

his turn acquired the animal appetites and instincts of the dog. The monster chooses the name Polygraf ["printing works"], and this may well have been a contemptuous reference to the numerous printing presses in Moscow churning out idiotic propaganda, appealing to the lowest common denominator in terms of intelligence and gullibility. The new creature gains employment, in keeping with his animal nature, as a cat exterminator. He is indoctrinated with party ideology by a manipulative official, and denounces numerous acquaintances to the authorities as being ideologically unsound, including his creator, the doctor. Although regarded with suspicion and warned as to his future behaviour, the doctor escapes further punishment. The hybrid creature disappears, and the dog Sharik reappears; there is a suggestion that the operation has been reversed by the doctor and his faithful assistant, and the human part of his personality has returned to its original form – a corpse – while the canine characteristics have also reassumed their natural form. Although the doctor is devastated at the evil results of his experiment, and vows to renounce all such researches in future, he appears in the last paragraph already to be delving into body parts again. The implication is that he will never be able to refrain from inventing, and the whole sorry disaster will be repeated ad infinitum. Again, as with *The Fatal Eggs*, the writer was voicing his suspicion of science and medicine's interference with nature, and his scepticism as to the possibility of utopias.

Notes on Shirt Cuffs   From 1920 to 1921, Bulgakov worked in a hospital in the Caucasus, where he produced a series of sketches detailing his experiences there. The principal theme is the development of a writer amid scenes of chaos and disruption. An offer was made to publish an anthology of the sketches in Paris in 1924, but the project never came to fruition.

A Young Doctor's   *A Young Doctor's Notebook* was drafted in 1919, then pub-
Notebook   lished mainly in medical journals between 1925–27. It is different in nature from Bulgakov's most famous works, being a first-person account of his experiences of treating peasants in his country practice, surrounded by ignorance and poverty, in a style reminiscent of another doctor and writer, Chekhov. Bulgakov learns by experience that often in this milieu what he has learnt in medical books and at medical school can seem useless, as he delivers babies, treats syphilitics and carries out amputations. The work is often published with *Morphine*, which

describes the experience of a doctor addicted to morphine. This is autobiographical: it recalls Bulgakov's own period in medical service in Vyazma, in 1918, where, to alleviate his distress at the suffering he was seeing, he dosed himself heavily on his own drugs and temporarily became addicted to morphine.

Adaptations

Bulgakov's masterpiece has been adapted many times for the stage and screen, with a wide variety of approaches to a text which makes very particular demands on anyone making the attempt. Several notable versions are discussed below.

In 2002, a German-language adaptation premiered at the *Stage Adaptations* Wiener Festwochen in Vienna. Directed by Frank Castorf, it made much use of video-shot footage, which was effectively deployed to bring out the unreal/surreal atmosphere of the novel.

In 2004, an adaptation by David Rudkin and directed by John Hoggarth was put on by the National Youth Theatre at the Lyric Hammersmith in London. Running at around three hours, some reviewers considered it overlong. There was also criticism made of changes made to the text to enhance contemporary relevance, though there was praise for the special effects.

In 2004, Edward Kemp's adaptation, directed by Steven Pimlott, was staged at the Chichester Festival Theatre. The production was notable for changing the Master from a novelist into a playwright – making the Yeshua narrative a play within a play – and also altering the chronology into a linear narrative.

In 1971, the Polish director Andrzej Wajda made the film *Screen Adaptations* *Pilate and Others*, based solely on the biblical part of the book.

In 1972, a joint Italian-Yugoslavian production of *The Master and Margarita* was released, directed by Aleksandar Petrovic. It was based loosely on the book – one of the major differences is that the Master in the film is given the name of Nikolai Afanasyevich Maksudov: throughout the book he remains anonymous.

In 1989, another Polish director, Maciej Wojtyszko, made a TV mini-series.

In 1991, *Incident in Judea* was released: directed by Paul Bryers, this covers only the Yeshua narrative.

In 1994, Yuri Kara directed an adaptation involving a number of famous actors, with a score supplied by a prestigious Russian composer. However, it has never been officially released: there were wrangles between Yuri Kara and the film's producers, who were unhappy with his work, and in addition, the grandson of Bulgakov's third wife stepped into the dispute, claiming the rights on his grandfather's literary inheritance, and forbidding the film's release. However, there have been DVDs circulating of it since early 2006.

In 2005, a TV miniseries adaptation was aired, directed by Vladimir Bortko, who had previously adapted *Heart of a Dog* and *The Idiot* by Dostoevsky. It received a mixed reception from the critics, some questioning the casting decisions. Bortko took great pains to stay as faithful to the original as possible, and his adaptation is considered by many to be the closest to the book.

Select Bibliography

Standard Edition:
Bulgakov produced numerous different and amended versions of his most famous work, and as it was never published during his lifetime, no definitive text of the novel as he finally envisaged it exists. There is therefore no standard Russian edition of *The Master and Margarita*, and there are various, usually minor discrepancies to be found in the many Russian editions now available.

Biographies:
Drawicz, Andrzey, *The Master and the Devil*, tr. Kevin Windle (New York, NY: Edwin Mellen Press, 2001)
Haber, Edythe C., *Mikhail Bulgakov: The Early Years* (Cambridge, MS: Harvard University Press, 1998)
Milne, Lesley, *Mikhail Bulgakov: A Critical Biography* (Cambridge: Cambridge University Press, 1990)
Proffer, Ellendea, *Bulgakov: Life and Work* (Ann Arbor, MI: Ardis, 1984)
Proffer, Ellendea, *A Pictorial Biography of Mikhail Bulgakov* (Ann Arbor, MI: Ardis, 1984)
Wright, A. Colin, *Mikhail Bulgakov: Life and Interpretation* (Toronto, ON: University of Toronto Press, 1978)

Letters, Memoirs:
Belozerskaya-Bulgakova, Lyubov, *My Life with Mikhail Bulgakov*, tr. Margareta Thompson (Ann Arbor, MI: Ardis, 1983)
Curtis, J.A.E., *Manuscripts Don't Burn: Mikhail Bulgakov: A Life in Letters and Diaries* (London: Bloomsbury, 1991)
Vozdvizhensky, Vyacheslav, ed., *Mikhail Bulgakov and his Times – Memoirs, Letters*, tr. Liv Tudge (Moscow: Progress Publishers, 1990)

On the Web:
www.masterandmargarita.eu
cr.middlebury.edu/public/russian/Bulgakov/public_html

Appendix

Letter and Diary Extracts

Letter – 31st Dec 1917 – To his sister Nadezhda from Vyazma, the remote town where he had been sent on medical service during the Civil War:

"I have been fondly reading authors from the past... and I've been revelling in scenes from bygone eras. Ah, why was I so late in being born! Why wasn't I born a hundred years ago?"

Letter – 1st Feb 1921 – To his cousin Konstantin from Vladikavkaz:

"I'm writing a novel...* but as usual it's my misfortune that I'm pursuing individual creativity just when what seems to be called for nowadays in literature is something totally different..."

[*There is no evidence as to what this novel was; opinion is that it was not an early draft of *The White Guard*.]

From Bulgakov's diary – 9th Feb 1922 – when he was living in Moscow:

"This is the blackest period of my life. My wife and I are starving. I have had to accept a little flour, vegetable oil and some potatoes from my uncle. I have run all over Moscow, but there are no jobs. My felt boots have fallen apart."

From Bulgakov's Diary – 26th October 1923 – On hearing that Diaboliad *had been accepted for publication by the magazine* Nedra:

"It's an idiotic story, not fit for anything... I bitterly regret that I abandoned medicine and condemned myself to an uncertain existence... But God is my witness that my love of literature was the only reason for it.

Literature is a difficult business at present. For me, with my opinions... it's difficult to get published and just to live... we are a barbaric and unhappy people..."

Autobiographical note to a friend – 1926 (exact date uncertain):

"I need to listen to music... it's very conducive to creative work... I am very fond of Wagner... My favourite writer is Gogol."

Letter – July 1929 (precise date uncertain) – to Stalin, other senior Soviet politicians, and the writer Maxim Gorky, who was in good standing with the authorities:

"This year ten years will have passed since I began to pursue a literary career in the USSR... at the beginning of this [theatrical] season all my plays have finished up by being banned."

[Bulgakov then says at length that all his written works have now been banned – new works are not permitted to be published, and works which had been published before are now vetoed for reprinting.]

"As my works have come out, Soviet critics have paid me more and more attention, although not one of my works, whether fiction or drama [*sic*], has ever received an approving review anywhere. On the contrary, the more my fame in the USSR and abroad has grown, the more savage the press reviews have become, until in the end they have simply turned into frenzies of vituperation.

"All of my works have received grotesque and unfavourable reviews, and my name has been slandered...

"At the end of this tenth year, my strength has been broken. Since I no longer have the strength to survive, since I am persecuted and know that that it is impossible that I should ever be published or staged in the USSR again, and since I am close to suffering a nervous breakdown, [I am requesting you and the Soviet government] TO EXPEL ME FROM THE USSR TOGETHER WITH MY WIFE... [Last part in caps in original]

Letter – 28th March 1930 – A very long letter, to the Soviet Government, asking once again whether he could either be expelled, or at least be permitted to find gainful employment in the theatrical world:

"…when I carried out an analysis of my albums of press cuttings, I discovered that there had been 301 references to me in the Soviet press during my ten years in the field of literature. Of these, three were complimentary, 298 were hostile and abusive."

[Bulgakov continues at length that, among other abuse, he has been accused of suffering from "dog-like senility", of being a "literary scavenger who pokes around in rubbish tips", that he is one of the "nouveau bourgeois breed, spraying vitriolic and impotent spittle over the working class and its communist ideals" – and also that critics have said that "Anyone who writes satire in the USSR is questioning the Soviet system…" He then continues]:

"At present I have been annihilated."

Letter – 22nd-29th July 1931 – to Vikenty Veresayev:

"There are two theories going round Moscow. According to the first… I am under the closest, most unremitting surveillance, and therefore my every line, thought, phrase and step is being weighed up… There is another theory. It has almost practically no advocates – but I at least am one of them.

According to this [latter] theory – there's absolutely nothing there! No enemies, no crucible, no surveillance, no desire for praise – nothing. No one is interested, no one needs it…

I am being destroyed by nervous exhaustion…. I have nothing good to look forward to now… I have become anxious and fearful, I keep expecting disasters, and I have become superstitious."

Letter – 11th July 1934 – To Vikenty Veresayev:

"By the beginning of this spring I had become seriously ill. I began to suffer from insomnia and debility, and finally, the most awful thing I have ever suffered in my life, a fear of solitude, or to be more precise a fear of being left on my own. It's so repugnant, that I would prefer to have my leg cut off!

"And so, of course, it's been doctors, sodium bromide, and all the rest of it... I was afraid of the streets, couldn't write, found people either exhausting or frightening, I couldn't bear to see the newspapers, and had to walk with either [my wife or her younger son] holding my arm – it would have been ghastly on my own."

From the diary of Yelena Sergeyevna Bulgakova [his third wife] – 11th Feb 1936 – on the first performances of Molière *at MAT*:

"I think there were twenty-one curtain calls at the end, [but] today, in the journal *Soviet Art* [*Sovyetskoye Iskusstvo*], there was an article about *Molière*... dripping with malice."

From Yelena's diary – 16th May 1937:

"M.[ikhail] is in a terrible state. He's once again become scared of walking the streets on his own..."

From Yelena's diary – 15th August 1939 – the day after Bulgakov's play had been rejected, apparently by Stalin himself:

"Misha [i.e. Bulgakov] is in a terrible state. Early this morning he was incapable of going out anywhere. He spent the day in the darkened flat, he can't bear the light."

From Yelena's diary – 17th Aug 1939 – regarding the rejection of Batum. *Mikhail and others have now heard that the reasons were that*:

"It was unacceptable to turn a figure such as Stalin into a fictional character, and it was unacceptable to place him in invented situations, and put invented words into his mouth. The play was not to be staged or published. The second thing was that at the top they considered that Bulgakov had submitted the play out of a wish to rebuild bridges and to improve people's opinion of him."

Yelena's diary – 27th Aug 1939:

"Misha feels crushed. He says that he has been totally knocked off his feet. It's never been like this before."

Letter – 28th Dec 1939 – from Bulgakov to a childhood friend, Alexandr [sic] Gdeshinsky:

"So here I am, back from the sanatorium. And how am I? To tell you frankly and in secret, I am consumed by the thought that I have come back to die. I can clearly perceive within me a struggle between the manifestations of life and death."

Yelena's diary – 15th Jan 1940:

"Misha is correcting the novel [*The Master and Margarita*] as much as his strength will allow, and I am copying it out..."

Yelena's diary – 10th March 1940:

16.39
Misha has died.

Letter – 5th Jan 1961 – Yelena wrote to Bulgakov's brother Nikolai that when she and Mikhail had first met each other in 1932, he had told her:

"'Just bear in mind that I will die a very painful death; give me your word that you won't hand me over to a hospital and that I will die in your arms.'"

[Bulgakov then prophesied he would die in 1939 – in fact it was early 1940. Yelena continues, saying to Nikolai that during the last few hours]:

"His legs ceased to obey him. My place was on a cushion on the floor next to his bed. He held my hand all the time, right up until the last seconds." [The day before he died]: "...Misha was only semi-conscious… [the previous day] he'd been suffering dreadfully, his whole body was in pain."

[On the day of his death, she continues, she left the room very briefly, and her eldest son came running out]:

"'Mum, he's groping for you with his hand.' I ran back and took his hand. Misha began to breathe faster and faster, then suddenly opened his eyes very wide and drew a deep breath. There was amazement in his eyes, they were filled with an unusual light. And he died… this was at 16.39…"

The Opening Pages of
The Master and Margarita in Russian

1

Никогда не разговаривайте с неизвестными

В час жаркого весеннего заката, в Москве на Патриарших прудах появились двое граждан. Первый из них – приблизительно сороколетний одетый в серенькую летнюю пару,– был маленького роста, упитан, лыс, свою приличную шляпу пирожком нес в руке, а аккуратно выбритое лицо его украшали сверхъестественных размеров очки в черной роговой оправе. Второй – плечистый, рыжеватый, вихрастый молодой человек в заломленной на затылок клетчатой кепке – был в ковбойке, жеваных белых брюках и в черных тапочках.

Первый был не кто иной, как Михаил Александрович Берлиоз, редактор толстого художественного журнала и председатель правления одной из крупнейших московских литературных ассоциаций, сокращенно именуемой МАССОЛИТ, и редактор толстого художественного журнала, а молодой спутник его – поэт Иван Николаевич Понырев, пишущий под псевдонимом Бездомный.

Попав в тень чуть зеленеющих лип, писатели первым долгом бросились к пестро раскрашенной будочке с надписью «Пиво и воды».

Да, следует отметить первую странность этого страшного майского вечера. Не только у будочки, но и во всей аллее, параллельной Малой Бронной улице, не оказалось ни одного человека. В тот час, когда уж, кажется, и сил не было дышать, когда солнце, раскалив Москву, в сухом тумане валилось куда-то за Садовое кольцо,– никто не пришел под липы, никто не сел на скамейку, пуста была аллея.

– Дайте нарзану,– попросил Берлиоз.

– Нарзану нету,– ответила женщина в будочке и почему-то обиделась.

– Пиво есть? – сиплым голосом осведомился Бездомный.

– Пиво привезут к вечеру,– ответила женщина.

– А что есть? – спросил Берлиоз.

– Абрикосовая, только теплая,– сказала женщина.

– Ну, давайте, давайте, давайте!..

Абрикосовая дала обильную желтую пену, и в воздухе запахло парикмахерской. Напившись, литераторы немедленно начали икать, расплатились и уселись на скамейке лицом к пруду и спиной к Бронной.

Тут приключилась вторая странность, касающаяся одного Берлиоза. Он внезапно перестал икать, сердце его стукнуло и на мгновенье куда-то провалилось, потом вернулось, но с тупой иглой, засевшей в нем. Кроме того, Берлиоза охватил необоснованный, но столь сильный страх, что ему захотелось тотчас же бежать с Патриарших без оглядки.

Берлиоз тоскливо оглянулся, не понимая, что его напугало. Он побледнел, вытер лоб платком, подумал: «Что это со мной? Этого никогда не было… сердце шалит… я переутомился… Пожалуй, пора бросить все к черту и в Кисловодск…»

И тут знойный воздух сгустился перед ним, и соткался из этого воздуха прозрачный гражданин престранного вида. На маленькой головке жокейский картузик, клетчатый кургузый воздушный же пиджачок… Гражданин ростом в сажень, но в плечах узок, худ неимоверно, и физиономия, прошу заметить, глумливая.

Жизнь Берлиоза складывалась так, что к необыкновенным явлениям он не привык. Еще более побледнев, он вытаращил глаза и в смятении подумал: «Этого не может быть!..»

Но это, увы, было, и длинный, сквозь которого видно, гражданин, не касаясь земли, качался перед ним и влево и вправо.

Тут ужас до того овладел Берлиозом, что он закрыл глаза. А когда он их открыл, увидел, что все кончилось, марево растворилось, клетчатый исчез, а заодно и тупая игла выскочила из сердца.

– Фу ты черт! – воскликнул редактор. – Ты знаешь, Иван, у меня сейчас едва удар от жары не сделался! Даже что-то вроде галлюцинации было…– он попытался усмехнуться, но в глазах его еще прыгала тревога, и руки дрожали. Однако постепенно он успокоился, обмахнулся платком и, произнеся довольно бодро: «Ну-с, итак…» – повел речь, прерванную питьем абрикосовой.

Речь эта, как впоследствии узнали, шла об Иисусе Христе. Дело в том, что редактор заказал поэту для очередной книжки журнала большую антирелигиозную поэму. Эту поэму Иван Николаевич сочинил, и в очень короткий срок, но, к сожалению, ею редактора нисколько не удовлетворил. Очертил Бездомный главное действующее лицо своей поэмы, то есть Иисуса, очень черными красками, и тем не менее всю поэму приходилось, по мнению редактора, писать заново. И вот теперь редактор читал поэту нечто вроде лекции об Иисусе, с тем чтобы подчеркнуть основную ошибку поэта.

Трудно сказать, что именно подвело Ивана Николаевича – изобразительная ли сила его таланта, или полное незнакомство с вопросом, по которому он писал,– но Иисус у него получился ну совершенно живой, некогда существующий Иисус, только правда, снабженный всеми отрицательными чертами Иисус.

Берлиоз же хотел доказать поэту, что главное не в том, каков был Иисус, плох ли, хорош ли, а в том, что Иисуса-то этого, как личности, вовсе не существовало на свете и что все рассказы о нем – простые выдумки, самый обыкновенный миф.

Надо заметить, что редактор был человеком начитанным и очень умело указывал в своей речи на древних историков, например, на знаменитого Филона Александрийского, на блестяще образованного Иосифа Флавия, никогда ни словом не упоминавших о существовании Иисуса. Обнаруживая солидную эрудицию, Михаил Александрович сообщил поэту, между прочим, и о том, что то место в пятнадцатой книге, в главе 44-й знаменитых Тацитовых «Анналов», где говорится о казни Иисуса,– есть не что иное, как позднейшая поддельная вставка.

Поэт, для которого все, сообщаемое редактором, являлось новостью, внимательно слушал Михаила Александровича, уставив на него свои бойкие зеленые глаза, и лишь изредка икал, шепотом ругая абрикосовую воду.

– Нет ни одной восточной религии,– говорил Берлиоз,– в которой, как правило, непорочная дева не произвела бы на свет бога. И христиане, не выдумав ничего нового, точно так же создали своего Иисуса, которого на самом деле никогда не было в живых. Вот на это-то и нужно сделать главный упор...

Высокий тенор Берлиоза разносился в пустынной аллее, и по мере того, как Михаил Александрович забирался в дебри, в которые может забираться, не рискуя свернуть себе шею, лишь очень образованный человек,– поэт узнавал все больше и больше интересного и полезного и про египетского Озириса, благостного бога и сына Неба и Земли, и про финикийского бога Фаммуза, и про Мардука, и даже про менее известного грозного бога Вицлипуцли, которого весьма почитали некогда ацтеки в Мексике.

И вот как раз в то время, когда Михаил Александрович рассказывал поэту о том, как ацтеки лепили из теста фигурку Вицлипуцли, в аллее показался первый человек.

Впоследствии, когда, откровенно говоря, было уже поздно, разные учреждения представили свои сводки с описанием этого человека. Сличение их не может не вызвать изумления. Так, в первой из них сказано, что человек этот был маленького роста, зубы имел золотые и хромал на правую ногу. Во второй – что человек был росту громадного, коронки имел платиновые, хромал на левую ногу. Третья лаконически сообщает, что особых примет у человека не было.

Приходится признать, что ни одна из этих сводок никуда не годится.

Раньше всего: ни на какую ногу описываемый не хромал, и росту был не маленького и не громадного, а просто высокого. Что касается зубов, то с левой стороны у него были платиновые коронки, а с правой – золотые. Он был в дорогом сером костюме, в заграничных, в цвет костюма, туфлях. Серый берет он лихо заломил на ухо, под мышкой нес трость с черным набалдашником в виде головы пуделя. По виду – лет сорока с лишним. Рот какой-то кривой. Выбрит гладко. Брюнет. Правый глаз черный, левый почему-то зеленый. Брови черные, но одна выше другой. Словом – иностранец.

Пройдя мимо скамьи, на которой помещались редактор и поэт, иностранец покосился на них, остановился и вдруг уселся на соседней скамейке, в двух шагах от приятелей.

«Немец» – подумал Берлиоз.

«Англичанин…– подумал Бездомный.– Ишь, и не жарко ему в перчатках».

А иностранец окинул взглядом высокие дома, квадратом окаймлявшие пруд, причем заметно стало, что видит это место он впервые и что оно его заинтересовало.

Он остановил свой взор на верхних этажах, ослепительно отражающих в стеклах изломанное и навсегда уходящее от Михаила Александровича солнце, затем перевел его вниз, где стекла начали предвечерне темнеть, чему-то снисходительно усмехнулся, прищурился, руки положил на набалдашник, а подбородок на руки.

– Ты, Иван,– говорил Берлиоз,– очень хорошо и сатирически изобразил, например, рождение Иисуса, сына Божия, но соль-то в том, что еще до Иисуса родился еще ряд сынов Божиих, как, скажем, финикийский Адонис, фригийский Аттис, персидский Митра. Коротко же говоря, ни один из них не рождался и никого не было, в том числе и Иисуса, и необходимо, чтобы ты, вместо рождения или, предположим, прихода волхвов, изобразил бы нелепые слухи об этом приходе. А то выходит по твоему рассказу, что он действительно родился!..

Acknowledgements

The Publisher wishes to thank Brian Reeve for writing the apparatus and Andrew Nurnberg and Jenny Savill of Andrew Nurnberg Associates for their support during the preparation of this volume.

ALMA CLASSICS

ALMA CLASSICS aims to publish mainstream and lesser-known European classics in an innovative and striking way, while employing the highest editorial and production standards. By way of a unique approach the range offers much more, both visually and textually, than readers have come to expect from contemporary classics publishing.

~~

To order any of our titles and for up-to-date information about our current and forthcoming publications, please visit our website on:

www.almaclassics.com